*****T H A N K Y O U······

This is a "Author's Edition" of "The Songbird / Volume Two."
This "unedited" version of the story is complete just as Beverly
intended it to be read.

Only a limited number will be printed for family and friends. "The
Songbird / Volume Two" is the second of a five volume series. This
should make this a treasured keepsake for those friends who have
continued to support our efforts to bring recognition to a truly gifted
writing talent. Your help is so very essential to "The Songbird"
success.

Beverly Louise Oliver-Farrell was never given the opportunity to
show her incredible writing and storytelling gift to the world. She
represents all of those with exceptional talent who are bypassed in
life simply because the every-day existence of life's struggles never
affords that opportunity to be recognized and showcased. Beverly
talks about this "Conveyor Belt" of responsibility in "The
Songbird".*(Page 4 / Volume 1)* To all gifted talents out there who never
get the opportunity to jump off. This is for you.

The original manuscript was handwritten in twelve five-subject
notebooks over an twelve year period. I just couldn't allow such
talent to be lost in a box in the attic.

Thank you so very, very, very much for supporting "The Songbird."

Brian B. Farrell

2/10/2014

Brian B. Farrell

The Songbird

Volume Two

By

Beverly Louise Oliver-Farrell

***** A C K N O W L E D G E M E N T S *****

Getting "The Songbird" Published would never have happened had it not been for the efforts of some very special people. They make up "The Songbird" team. It took me two weeks to type the first twenty-nine pages into the computer. I hit the wrong button and lost it all. I realized then that I couldn't do this myself. I'll be eternally grateful for each of their contributions.

A "Very Special Thank You" to "The Songbird" Editorial team.

Brian J. Farrell
Benjamin G. Farrell
Amber Massie
Karalee Shawcroft
Lisa Cramer
Kimberly Niven

*****

I have had fantastic support from some very learned technical people. The patience they have shown in dealing with such a computer klutz as me and keeping my equipment running and meeting the needs of "The Songbird" project. Your efforts are greatly appreciated by all of us.

A "Very Special Thank You" To "The Songbird" Technical team

Benn Farrell at Dockrat Entertainment (Website)
Lee Sanchez at PC & Mac Repairs (Computers)
Bill & Sharon Price at Laserpro II (Printers)
Jean-Claude Picard at Microcrafts (Lamination)
Amber Massie (Cover Design /Volume Two)
Jon Best (Graphic Designer/Cover Assembly)
Wishing Well Glass Blowers (Unicorns)

***** A C K N O W L E D G E M E N T S *****

Every Wednesday night I go to an "Independent/Assisted Living" facility and read and share "The Songbird" with a group of "Very Special" people who have become my close friends.

I don't think they will ever fully understand how much they have taught me and caused me to grow. I thank them so very much for their support and encouragement.

A "Very Special Thank You" to "The Songbird Book Club"
at "Viewpointe"

Virginia Rabun	Harriet Spangenberg
Ruth Goetzman	Genevieve Campbell
Jean James	Margaret Stevenson
Herva Simpson	Vonceil Kisor
Chet Derezinski	Jo-Ann Clayton
Bertha Lang	Eleanor Wright
Vernon Peckham	Beverly Osburn
Phyllis Mueller	Elizabeth Nichols
Gladys Mercier	

*****

A "Very Special Thank you" to members of the Viewpointe Staff for their valuable assistance in gathering our group together each Wednesday night.

Judine Carkner   Natalie Mutch   Patty Wright

*****

One person deserves "Special Recognition." His encouragement and living example has shown me that "you never give up your dreams."

A "Very Special Thank You" to my "Best Friend"

Robert Louis Tyler

***** S Y N O P S I S *****

"The Songbird" is a love story about a young woman named Jeneil who believed in fairy tales, a prince charming, and happy endings. She goes on a quest to find herself before the "conveyor belt" of responsibility forces her to accept a lesser existence. In her quest for superlative, she almost destroys herself and the lives of some of those people around her.

Jeneil, a white girl from Nebraska, finds her Prince Charming in Peter, a Chinese gang kid from the streets of New York's Chinatown, who is in his last year as a residence in a New England hospital where they meet. "The Songbird" is their story. Add Steve, Peter's best friend, whose life began as a baby left on the doorsteps of an upper New York state orphanage, to the mix and life will never be the same for this triad of friends
.

It is a story of love, communication, murder, mystery, danger, betrayal, suspense, honesty and dignity, personal achievements, and a look at life which covers the trials of human relationships. It is steeped in a reality that will cause everyone who reads "The Songbird" to identify with their own life experiences. There are physical relations, but are done with taste and an intricate part of the story.

COMMENT: *The complete story of the "The Songbird" is a five volume series. Beverly Louise Oliver-Farrell has laid out "The Songbird" from beginning to end, stacking one incident on top of another like a set of logo blocks, carefully interlocking the past, present, and future together in a not-so-perfect world. Beverly leaves clues and dangles unanswered questions throughout "The Songbird", but is very successful in tying it all together and being able to keep the end of the story a secret until the closing pages.*

I love you, Baby

I'm going to miss you

F O R E W A R D *****

When I embarked on "The Songbird" project to try to bring recognition to the writing and story-telling skills of my wife Beverly, I was told on more than one occasion that it was a nice gesture that I was doing to give her a legacy to be remembered by. Such comments couldn't be further from the truth. The truth is that I was in "awe" of her talent. Listening to the readings and sharing her ability for the twelve years she spent writing "The Songbird" told me I was witnessing something very special. It was that "talent" I couldn't ignore and to see it end up in a box, stored in some attic and eventually lost, was unacceptable.

Beverly writes about such talent in the story of "John Stanton Milesoft" A sub-character in "The Songbird". He is introduced in "The Songbird/Volume Three" in an event that has tragic results. Jeneil, the main character reflects on the incident some months later as part of her Thanksgiving preparation.

I offer this to you that you may have a sample of some of her writing that somehow seems to fit my reasoning for doing what I'm trying to do.

*****

"This is a tough Thanksgiving" She sniffed. It was traditional in my family to spend some time on Thanksgiving Day reviewing the year and seeing what needed mending or changing. It was an exercise in gratitude. I have a beaut this year, in John Stanton Milesoft."

Steve slipped onto the bed beside her. "Why are you even allowing yourself to remember him, Honey? That's a nightmare that's best buried." He kissed her shoulder and rubbed her arm gently, remembering the horror of the scene at Wonderland.

"I owed him, Steve. Some of that night at Wonderland was my fault. I set him up. I let him believe that I wanted him to stay even allowing whatever fantasy he may have fostered in his mind and then I ran out on him, leaving him feeling like a joke probably." Tears ran down her cheek. "The night destroyed him."

"He destroyed himself." Steve corrected.

"But I was the catalyst. I know it was a matter of survival, but between us, it's left a bitter taste in my mouth. He was a gifted misfit. The brilliance of a star that never understood how to shine." She shook her head. "That was his only real problem, he

didn't know how to belong here. He probably spent some strange years trying to make sense of the whole process called life."

I promised him that professionals would listen to his music, He found in me an audience for his greatness. I'm going to hire a detective to locate his family. Maybe in death he can provide what he probably struggled to offer in life but couldn't quite cope with his share of the burden of existence. At least I'll have set the record straight between John Stanton Milesoft and me and I can pay my debt to him by keeping my promise."

He Watched her. "Do you set all your relationships to rest like that?"

She nodded. "It must sound pious, but it's really a matter of conscience and gratitude. My family thought both were important. One without the other wouldn't work and both were connected to self-esteem."

*****

Beverly's life circumstance never afforded her a opportunity to shine. "The Songbird" is a brilliant piece of writing and storytelling. She gave up her God-given gift for me. She shouldn't have and in that sense, I failed her. Being her husband allowed me to see her "Gift" first hand. I want to share with all the "Gift" Beverly was never given the opportunity to give. The story of John Stanton Milesoft best describes my reasons for wanting to publish "The Songbird".

Brian B. Farrell

The Songbird

One

Lying in the darkness Peter thought about Jeneil's idea of them missing each other in life. He touched his stomach and his network of scars. If that was true then they were worth it. He turned onto his side and was soon asleep.

Peter woke up and turned over. Reaching out for Jeneil, he lifted his head, surprised that she wasn't next to him. He looked at the clock. "Six," he said, "I have an hour to get to work." Standing up and tying his robe, he walked to the living room. Jeneil was sitting on the sofa with a drawing board on her lap and a notebook on top of the drawing board.

"Jeneil," he said, going to her, "you haven't been to bed at all, have you?"

"No," she said, lost in thought, "but I'm fine. I feel great." He sat next to her and she kissed him gently. Her eyes sparkled and her cheeks were flushed.

"You look beautiful," he said, "incredibly beautiful."

"I'm cosmic," she corrected.

"Great and I overslept. I can't do a damn thing about it."

She laughed. "It's okay. I'm at a universal level anyway; I'd be totally useless right now."

"Have you been drawing all night?" he asked, reaching for the notebook. She slapped her hands down on it to keep him from taking it, surprising both of them.

"I'm sorry. No, I haven't been drawing, I've been writing. It's a journal kind of thing. You know, like a diary. I'm sorry, but I don't want to show that much of myself to anybody. If I ever leave it lying around, promise me that you won't read it."

"I promise," he said, still surprised.

She kissed him again. "You get showered. I'll get breakfast."

"Aren't you tired?"

"Not yet, maybe in an hour," and she went to the kitchen. Looking at the notebook, Peter shook his head then went to shower.

Coming from the bedroom, he sat in the kitchen. "I don't think I have time for breakfast."

"A power shake and cornbread," she said, handing him a glass and a plate. "Eat standing up. Your juice is there," and she nodded toward a glass, and wrapped some cookies and added them to a brown bag, folding the top. "Lunch is ready."

"Are you going to try to sleep?"

"Yes, I'll dance, shower then relax. Don't worry about me; I have a firm grasp on what's happening." She hugged his arm. "I'm all right, blue sky on top, green grass on bottom."

He smiled and kissed her. "I've got to go. Please get some rest."

She nodded. "You will remember to get home for the Elm's party, won't you?"

"The art thing?"

"You promised when I got Mike Phillip's invitation in the mail," she reminded him.

He laughed. "Lost my head that day but now you'll see what you're living with, baby. Wait till you see me at an art party. You'll have my bags packed for me by midnight." He shook his head and left. Jeneil smiled and went to change into leotards.

*****

Peter returned the medical chart to the rack and signed out. "I'm leaving," he said to the head nurse, who nodded. Heading for the locker room, he looked at his watch. "I'll just make it," he said, hurrying to undo the lock.

"Hey, Pete. This first shift isn't bad at all, I almost feel like a normal part of society. I've got a date with Rita," and Steve whistled, stopping at Peter's locker.

"Rita. Where's Debbie?"

"Met a weightlifter. She'll be back. She has to get him out of her system. Where are you off to with your free night?"

"A party," Peter answered.

Steve turned in surprise. "A party? But I thought you and Sunshine were a secret?"

"These are people she knows," Peter explained.

"Her friends know about the two of you, but yours don't?"

Peter was at a loss for words. He hadn't seen it that way.

An intern yelled into the locker room. "Is Doctor Bradley here?"

"Yeah, right here," Steve answered.

"ICU is looking for you," the intern yelled.

"Must be the Morris case." Steve put his lab coat back on. "Well, you and Sunshine have fun tonight at her friends' party," Steve said quietly and left.

Peter wondered if the tone in Steve's voice had anything to do with his not having met Sunshine. Peter didn't like the inconsistency now that he'd been made aware of it. He left the locker room on edge.

*****

Jeneil came from the bedroom as Peter walked in. "You kept your promise." She smiled. "I made a quick dinner for you."

"Won't the party have food?" he asked, following her to the kitchen.

"This is more of a private viewing and cocktail thing," she said, taking a cheeseburger and French fries from the warming oven.

"A cheeseburger and French fries? Are you trying to bribe me or something?"

"It's my thank you for going to the party with me."

"I hope you say that when we get home, too." He laughed. "I have a suit, but I haven't worn it for a while. I don't know how it fits."

She smiled and kissed his shoulder. "You don't need a suit. Your good jeans are on the bed, and I bought a nice shirt for you. If you don't like it, you can wear one of your others."

"An art party in jeans? This might not be too bad."

Peter stood before the mirror. The black shirt was definitely modern, but he could deal with it.

"Well," Jeneil said, "you can change it if you want to."

"No, it's not bad but don't you think I look too tough in it?"

"Tough?" She stepped back to look at him. "Bad to the bone maybe, but that's your field, isn't it?" She chuckled and apologized. "That was bad. I didn't get the pants that went with it then you'd look tough. With your jeans, you get a mixed style. It makes you an individual."

He laughed. "Well then, let's get to your party."

Peter slid behind the wheel. "You look terrific," he said, starting the car, "but I don't think we match. You look expensive and feminine, and I look like I mug people."

Jeneil laughed. "Forget our looks, Peter. You look fine. I'm wearing what I felt like wearing. I'm still cosmic and feeling slightly disconnected."

"You look beautiful," he said, noticing the glint to her eyes and her coloring. "Cosmic makes you look healthy."

Peter pulled into the Elm's Art Gallery parking area. He opened the door for Jeneil and they walked to the gallery entrance.

"Hi, Jeneil," the girl at the desk said, smiling.

"Hi, Sue. This is Peter Chang. Sue keeps order here," Jeneil explained to Peter. "Are we somewhere in a polite middle time wise, I hope?"

"Sure are, everybody's been gathering in the main area."

"Thanks." Jeneil took Peter's hand and walked across the small lobby. She stopped at a section where there were photographs on display. "Oh, I didn't know he was into photographs, too."

"Who?" Peter asked.

Jeneil looked at him. "Peter, do you know the name of the artist this party is for?"

"No," he answered.

"Oh, I thought you did. I've talked about him. Come on, we'll look at the write ups on him so you'll be familiar with him." They picked up some printed material and Peter leafed through it while Jeneil looked at photographs. Taking his arm, they walked into the main room. Peter felt better about how he was dressed. Styles went from bizarre to conservative but everybody looked comfortable.

"I could have worn a suit," he whispered to her.

"Did you want to?" she whispered back.

"No." He smiled.

She grinned. "He's done sculpting, too. Let's go look at them then we'll look at his canvas work. I bought two for the office," she mentioned as they squeezed past people, heading for a section roped off from the general party. "Gosh he's bold," she commented, looking at a bronze piece. "And I love his texture. I wonder what he's like in person."

Peter looked at the pieces and wondered what a man who worked in art for a living would be like. He felt like he didn't belong there. He couldn't tell the difference between texture and boldness, much less have thoughts about them. He watched Jeneil. She was gently touching one of the pieces and he could tell that she liked it. Opening the catalog he was holding, he looked it up and checked the price; $150. "Whew!" he whistled to himself. Turning to Jeneil, he saw her lovingly touching the other pieces. She was completely absorbed in the work. He smiled to himself then noticed a man about his own age watching Jeneil and smiling, too. Checking the photograph in the catalog, Peter realized the man enjoying watching Jeneil absorb the work was the artist, Robert Danzieg.

"Jeneil," Peter heard a man call. A balding man with curly hair walked toward her. "Jeneil, I want to introduce you to Robert Danzieg." The man took the artist by the elbow and brought him to Jeneil.

"Hi." Jeneil extended her hand. "I've been looking at your sculptures. I thought you had only paintings. It surprised me to see photographs, too. I really like the one of the construction site. You caught some bold shadows in that." Jeneil looked at the balding man. "I think you and I will talk about that one, Mike."

"Why does the construction site interest you?" Danzieg asked, never taking his eyes off Jeneil. Peter didn't like the way Danzieg was absorbing her.

"Because I like the feeling I got from it. The workers were creating a sculpture of their own, but I love the bold shadows and angles you captured. It created a composition of an everyday happening and turned it into art. It reminded me to open my eyes." Danzieg smiled broadly, still riveted to her. Peter could tell Danzieg liked her answer.

"Robert, this is Jeneil Alden-Connors. She bought two of your canvasses," Mike said.

"Well, I'm really pleased to meet the woman who's paying my next month's rent." Danzieg smiled again. Jeneil laughed then looked around.

"Peter," she called.

Peter could feel a tightness in his throat as he walked over to them. He was aware that Robert Danzieg was sizing him up, and Peter knew he was sizing him up because Peter had done it himself. The feelings from the streets of New York returned for a second and he felt himself walk taller and tighter. Whenever an opposing gang member had been around he'd do that to psych himself up and to psych out the other gang. It was the damn clothes, he thought to himself. Jeneil took his hand. Robert Danzieg noticed and looked from Peter to Jeneil. Peter noticed.

"Peter," Jeneil smiled, "this is Mike Phillips, owner of the gallery, and Robert Danzieg, owner of the artwork." Peter felt Danzieg watching and again his New York street cool surfaced as he extended his hand to both of them. "This is Peter Chang. He's into sculpting too of sorts."

Peter looked at her, shocked at the lie. She almost blew his cool. Danzieg caught the look. Jeneil squeezed Peter's arm.

"I like to tease Peter," she said, laughing. "He's really an orthopedic surgeon." Looking at Peter, she grinned. "If Robert Danzieg can find art on a construction site, he'll see sculpting in what you do."

Mike Phillips laughed and Peter noticed Danzieg smile broadly at Jeneil. Peter deliberately put his arm around her shoulder. He noticed Danzieg look from one to the other and Peter wished Jeneil was Mrs. Peter Chang. They passed pleasantries and Mike excused himself, taking Robert to meet someone else.

"Let's look at the paintings," Jeneil said. "Were you finished here?"

"Yes," Peter answered, and in his thoughts added, about ten minutes ago if I'm reading Robert Danzieg right. He followed Jeneil, barely conscious of the artwork. Whenever he looked around Robert Danzieg would be looking their way so Peter stopped looking.

"Jeneil Alden-Connors, Sociology 212." Peter turned to see a guy walking up to them. "I remembered after I dropped you off."

Jeneil smiled. "That's right, it was Sociology 212. You're good. Peter, this is Franklin Pierce," Jeneil said, looking straight into Peter's eyes and pleading for peace; Peter caught it.

"Franklin. Peter Chang." Franklin extended his hand to him. Peter didn't like him at all, but extended his hand, too. "Well, our hard working resident. It's good to see that you get some time off to enjoy the finer things in life."

"Every once in a while we take a break," Peter said dryly. "Jeneil mentioned that you took her to dinner after the concert." Peter felt Jeneil squeeze his arm. He had mentioned it deliberately to let Franklin Pierce know that while he may leave Jeneil alone, he knew what was going on.

Franklin smiled. "Yes, I enjoyed it myself, too."

Arrogant son-of-a-bitch, Peter thought to himself. He had never said she enjoyed it.

"Jeneil, we haven't seen you at anymore concerts," Franklin said, looking at Peter.

Peter hated the guy. He was a son-of-a-bitch, Jeneil, he thought. She saw what was good in the guy, but Peter wouldn't turn his back on him.

Jeneil nodded. "Peter's work schedule had given him Sunday afternoons off but not long enough to fit in a concert."

"That's too bad," Franklin said, looking at Peter again.

Peter's jaw tightened. Did this jerk think it was deliberate to keep him away from Jencil? Peter wished they were on the streets of New York. One well placed jab to the center of Franklin's stomach would be great right now.

Peter heard Jeneil add, "Well, I'm not missing Rossini."

Franklin smiled. "Have you found his tape yet?"

"No, after two stores I stopped."

"Let me try for you. I'll bring it to the concert. Which piece was it?" Franklin asked.

"Sonata No. 5. I'd appreciate that," she added. "Thank you."

Franklin made a note in his notebook and put it in his jacket pocket. Peter wished he had worn a suit; he felt street level dressed like he was. Franklin had a tie. Robert Danzieg didn't, but he wore a jacket.

Franklin Pierce walked away and Peter felt like spitting on the ground, a habit the Dragons had when they encountered an opposing gang member and had words with him. As they'd walk away, they'd spit to show contempt.

Jeneil squeezed Peter's arm. "I love you," she said, forming a kiss with her lips. "You handled that like a gentleman."

"Dealing with him doesn't deserve a pretend kiss. I earned the real thing behind that potted plant."

Mike Phillips came up to her. "Jeneil, can you take some time to stop in my office before you leave.

"All right," Jeneil accepted. "Is there something special?"

"Robert Danzieg wants to talk to you," Mike explained. Peter tensed.

"To me?" Jeneil was surprised.

"And I do, too. I have an opening here if you're interested, but stop by my office and we'll talk about the photograph."

"Fine," she said matter of factly.

"Meet Robert in my office in twenty minutes," Mike said, and walked on to another group.

"Well, things are getting to foot stomping, aren't they?" Peter asked. Jeneil looked at him, wondering about his mood as Robert Danzieg joined them.

Robert smiled. "Jeneil, I just saw the paintings you chose. Why those two?" Jeneil never got a chance to answer as they were joined by a third man who was short and pudgy with pale shiny skin.

"Mr. Danzieg, your work is tremendous. I find it very moving," the man commented with a strained smile.

"Well, thank you," Robert answered politely.

The short man looked at Peter and Jeneil. "And I find you two a fascinating couple. I saw you holding hands. You don't match. You look like a lady from the Victorian era," he said to Jeneil, "and you look like…."

"An orthopedic surgeon," Jeneil interrupted. Peter noticed Robert Danzieg's grin.

"Oh my gosh, you're a doctor?" The man stepped back slightly.

"A resident," Peter added. "Why?"

"Were you around patients today?" The man winced.

"I was on duty at the hospital, why?"

The man tried to smile. "All those diseases. Are you possibly carrying anything?"

Robert Danzieg looked shocked. "He's a bone surgeon."

The man paled. "Oh my goodness, you cut into human flesh. That's too gross," and he shivered. Peter was getting annoyed when he heard Jeneil speak in an accent he'd never heard her use before.

"Hey, Pete," she said, pretending to chew gum. "Can I use my brass knuckles on dis here creep, huh? I think he's insultin' yous doctors and it's makin' me real mad. Real mad. One punch to da nose and he's your next knife victim, huh. Whadya say, Pete?" The man looked aghast at her. Peter stared at her in shock and Robert Danzieg put his head back and laughed loudly, turning heads.

The man laughed limply, looking at Robert Danzieg. "Oh, I get it. That was a joke. That's funny," he said, backing away.

Robert Danzieg laughed louder. "I love it."

Mike Phillips came over. "Robert, the Downing Group is here."

"Okay," Robert answered, calming down. "I'll see you later," he said to Peter and Jeneil as he walked away, still quietly laughing.

"Where the hell did you learn that accent?" Peter asked, grinning.

Jeneil shrugged and put her arms around his waist. "Forget the potted plant and the raw vegetable who was here," she said, and she kissed him.

"I'm free now Jeneil if you are," Mike Phillips said.

"Sure. I'll be back soon." She smiled at Peter. "Do you want to come, too?"

"No," Peter answered. "That cushioned bench looks comfortable. I'll wait there."

Peter sat thumbing through a catalog when Robert Danzieg sat down. Peter looked at him.

"Where's Jeneil?" Robert asked.

"In the office with Mike Phillips." Peter wondered why Danzieg was buddying up to him.

"I'd like to talk to you," Danzieg started.

Well he was direct, Peter thought. He nodded. "Okay. Go ahead."

"I want to paint Jeneil," Robert said, getting straight to the point. "Do you have a problem with that?"

"Why Jeneil?"

"There's a quality in her I'd like to try to capture. I don't do portraits. It might not even look like her. I'm not sure where it would go."

"What quality is it?"

"I wish I could tell you, but I don't know."

"Then how can you paint it?"

Robert Danzieg grinned. "Peter, if she was mine I'd guard her, too, but I'm more interested in the painting. To investigate, I'd test colors around her, get to know her, see what material looks good near her." Peter was silent. "Why don't I answer the question that's between us? No, she won't be nude and I promise that the painting won't be nude. I see her in vibrant color, not flesh tone. Some women are nudes, good nudes, class nudes, but Jeneil has something about her." Danzieg shrugged. "I don't know, something unfinished."

Peter looked at him. "Why are you asking me?"

"Because you and Jeneil are tight, I can see that. If she agrees and you don't, it affects her and the project wouldn't work. She's got to come free of conflict so I decided to explain it to you first." Peter decided to trust him and hoped he wasn't wrong. This guy was a new breed to him. Inside, he hoped Jeneil would say no.

"It's ok with me," Peter heard himself say.

Danzieg studied Peter then smiled. "Thanks," he said, standing up.

Peter smiled to himself as Danzieg walked away. He knew she wouldn't be nude. He lived with her and she didn't sit around nude in front of him. Peter smiled. "There is something nice about being in love with a lady," he said to himself. "It feels like trust," and he smiled again and shook his head. Not even King Arthur had to fight off this many men, just one; Lancelot. Jeneil would have driven him crazy in Camelot.

Peter stood up and walked around. He felt changes in the air, strange changes. The crowd was thinning. Peter looked at some paintings and noticed the signature on one, *Robert L. Danzieg*. If the L stood for Lancelot, the deal got cancelled. Peter chuckled and went back to the bench. He saw Mike Phillips mingling. Turning his head, he saw Jeneil and Danzieg walking down the corridor together. Danzieg was talking to her and she was listening without emotion. Peter couldn't tell if she had said yes. She smiled when she saw him. He smiled, too.

"I'll call you," Peter heard Robert Danzieg say as they approached. "It was nice meeting you, Peter." Danzieg extended his hand and Peter shook it.

"It's been interesting," Peter commented. "By the way, what's does the L in your name stand for?"

"Ludlow," Danzieg answered. "Why?"

Peter shrugged. "No reason. I just wondered."

Peter put his arm around Jeneil as they walked to the car. "The air feels good," Jeneil said. "We're into summer through and through."

Peter kissed her lightly before holding the door for her. He drove from the lot wondering what she had decided. He couldn't resist any longer. "Jeneil, do I get to hear your answer to Phillips and Danzieg?"

"I haven't answered them, but I don't think it will be yes to either one."

"Not even the job in the gallery?"

"What's wrong with my hospital job? Everyone is so critical of me working there."

"It's just the gallery seems more along your interests and capabilities."

"Sometimes I think you hear but don't listen. I don't want a job that interests me; I want a job that protects me from being swallowed up by the corporation. The hospital clerk's job does that. It doesn't ask anything more of me than to keep records in order. I'd have to apply myself to the gallery job and it would distract me from my goal of finding the pieces. I don't need another interest."

"What about Danzieg?" he asked, interested.

She looked at him. "Did you really say it would be all right with you if I posed for him?"

"Yes."

"My goodness, you are getting sophisticated."

"Well, he told me not nude." She laughed and kissed his shoulder. "What's so funny?" Peter asked.

"You're a simple man, Peter the Great," and she laughed again. "You protect me from exposing my body before him, but it's not easy for me to expose my soul either. In fact, coming to a choice, it might be easier to expose my body to a stranger."

"What?" he asked, stopping for a light.

"Peter, he's a sensitive man. I don't want him knowing me that well even objectivity. I can't share myself that easily. I don't like being photographed so posing for an artist would be really tough. No, I can't. I don't even know what quality he sees in me, although I do think it's interesting he calls me unfinished." Peter smiled and relaxed. "If you're not very tired, could we go to the ocean? I'd like to face the wind."

*****

They drove home in silence. The fact they could be quiet together was a calming feeling for Peter. He tried to remember what Jeneil's father had said about the chaff being blown away because it was so light and the kernel of wheat landing solidly on the ground. She had said it was the same with people facing the wind; if they could face the truth and deal with it, they could land solidly on the ground.

Peter unlocked the apartment door and let Jeneil walk in first. She barely knew he was there. She changed behind the dressing screen and walked to the living room. Hearing the music, he realized she was dancing. Remembering her words, 'soul takes time,' he sat in bed and waited. When the music ended, the lights went out and she walked in, still wrapped in thought. He wasn't sure about this mood; this wasn't cosmic. As she changed behind the dressing screen, he thought how provocative it was knowing she was taking her clothes off behind the screen. He could never understand her thoughts on nudity. She wasn't able to walk around nude, but once in bed she was fine, then it didn't matter if she was covered at all. He liked her craziness, it made her Jeneil.

The phone rang. Jeneil came from behind the screen tying her robe. "Hi, Robert," she said, answering the phone, surprised. "Yes, I have decided. No, I don't think I will. Thank you anyway. A lot of reasons that would make sense to only me. There's nothing to discuss." She was silent and Peter turned to look at her. Danzieg wasn't taking no for an answer. "Robert, really, I have given it some thought. All right. Okay, I'll think about it one more day." Peter watched her. She hung up and he moved in. Taking her hand gently, he pulled her to bed. He took her hair pins out and let her hair fall. Undoing her robe, he slipped it off her shoulders and kissed them gently. She responded passionately and he relaxed inside. She couldn't fake making love; things were all right between them. He kissed her passionately. He meant everything he was doing.

"Are you all right?" he asked as he settled in beside her.

"Just great," and she cuddled to him. He smiled, putting his arm around her and rubbing her back gently. They lay together quietly.

"Danzieg won't back off, huh?"

She shook her head. "You know, I couldn't understand the boldness of his artwork, he seems so understated in person, but the boldness is surfacing."

"I can see to it that he backs off."

"No, it's fine. I can handle it. By tomorrow his other projects will fill his mind and I'll be old what's-her-name who bought two paintings and a photograph." Peter squeezed her hand gently and hoped that she was right.

"Honey, I have to ask you something. Since my grandfather and Hollis know about us, can I tell Steve?" She looked at him. "Jeneil, of everybody, he's the least threat to us."

"Is he?" she asked. "He hates secrets. Look at his determination with The James Gang. He had the whole hospital buzzing about it. One slip up there and we're ruined. He scares me, Peter. I wish I knew why."

"He's my best friend, honey. It's getting awkward."

"I'm sorry, you're right, Peter. Tell him if you have to, but please make him understand the need for secrecy."

Two

Tony was scheduled for surgery again, this time for his left arm. The surgery was going to be extensive and he was getting tired of being in the hospital. Jeneil visited and brought some fudge

Steve and Peter stopped by. Noticing the fudge, Steve took a piece. "Hey Pete, this is good fudge, too. Who made it, Tony? Your mother?"

"No," Tony said uncomfortably, "Jeneil did."

"Who?" Steve asked. "Oh, the girl from Records. Pete's girlfriend makes great fudge, too."

Tony looked at Peter. Peter put his head down. The game felt silly to him and he decided he needed to find the right time to tell Steve.

Arriving home early, Peter found Jeneil writing. "Hi, honey," he said, bending down to kiss her. She closed the notebook quickly. "Wow, what are you putting in that thing? You're truly getting touchy about it."

"My very innermost feelings. It isn't easy being that open and seeing it before you."

Peter smiled. "Just remember, any complaints about us come to me, not the notebook, okay?" He walked into the bedroom. "Jeneil," he called, "where'd the flowers come from?"

"Robert Danzieg," she answered.

Peter came out with the vase and put them on the table before her. "Not in the bedroom."

"Why?"

"Because every damn night the guy calls just as we get into bed. I don't need a visual reminder that's he's a pain in the ass." He turned and walked back to the bedroom.

Jeneil watched him walk away then raised an eyebrow looking at the flowers. "Peter, he's called twice," she said under her breath.

When they sat down to dinner later that evening, Peter noticed the flowers. Standing up, he took them to the kitchen. Jeneil watched as he returned. "We're running out of room for the flowers," she said, laughing.

"Try the bowl in the bathroom and flush them," he snapped.

"That does it," she said, standing up. "They're a beautiful summer bouquet and I can't stand your attitude any longer." She went to the kitchen and returned, carrying the flowers out of the apartment. He heard her go upstairs to Adrienne's. She returned empty handed and sat down. "Now," she said, picking up her fork, "why don't we talk about why you don't like Robert Danzieg?"

He looked at her. "I thought you were going to handle him?"

"I am."

"Well, he's still calling."

"Peter, he's called twice."

"That's not enough."

"Why are you angry at him?"

"I'm angry at you."

"Me?"

"You said you'd handle him. Now do it."

"Are there any other orders for me?" she asked sarcastically.

"No, prove that you can handle that and we'll go for something tougher."

"I don't like your attitude."

"I don't care," he said, not looking at her. She picked up her plate and went to the kitchen. Peter sat back and threw his napkin on the table. He rubbed his forehead. "You jerk," he said out loud to himself, "you're playing right into his hands," and he went to look for her, finding her in the bedroom as she was dialing the phone.

"Hi, Robert, this is Jeneil. I've thought about your offer more carefully. When do you want to begin?"

Peter closed his eyes. "Nice going, Peter. You just handed him three aces. Shit," he said to himself and walked out. The bastard was too persistent. He sat on the sofa feeling surprised and disappointed. It wasn't like Jeneil to be spiteful.

She sat down next to him, smiling. "Well, I handled it," she said, gloating. "I told him I would sit starting tomorrow night. He's going to find out why I said no. I'm not an easy subject." She put her arms around Peter's neck and kissed his cheek.

Peter shook his head. She thought she'd pleased him. He smiled and put his arms around her. "You're crazy, Jeneil. No one else in the world thinks like you."

"What happened to eccentric?"

"You passed go, baby. It's history."

"I'm not sure I understand, but I love you anyway." She kissed his neck.

"How can you be so brilliant and then do such strange things?" He shook his head.

"Does that mean you love me, too?"

He chuckled. "I must for all I put up with."

She kissed him warmly, snuggling to him. "And at least he won't call tonight when we're going to bed."

"Shut up, you're making it worse," he said, laughing.

She giggled. "You don't like my cure?"

He squeezed her. "I love you. Can you remember that?"

"Well, gosh," she mocked, talking like an airhead. "Peter, is that the tougher problem you said you'd give me if I handled Robert Danzieg?"

"You're looking to get your ass slapped woman."

"Ooo, Peter's getting macho. Do more Peter. More."

"I'll give you more," he said, tickling her.

"No," she screamed, "not tickling."

He kissed her. "I lost my cool over Danzieg for awhile. I'll be okay now. I thought you were been spiteful."

She smiled. "Thank you, Peter"

"Is it difficult being perfect?"

"Are we starting a new argument?" she asked simply.

"No, it just seems to me that I apologize a lot more than you do around here. I think relationships are easier for you."

"I'm sorry, Peter. I'm really sorry."

"Why?" he asked curiously.

"I'm really sorry that you're wrong more than I am." She tried not to laugh, but couldn't help herself.

"You're cute," he said, "and funny, too, very funny." She kissed him and he pulled her closer.

*****

Steve and Peter sat at the computer reviewing Tony's case. Steve stood up and paced as Peter stretched. "Damn it," Steve said. "I hate getting so close and not reaching success."

"This time," Peter reminded him, "this time." Tony's operation had mixed reviews. It had gone well, but not all of the nerve damage had been reversed. It was now a wait and see situation.

"I can't stand seeing the guy like this," Steve said. "His morale is too low. I wish he'd turn it around."

Peter turned off the computer. "He's dealing with reality, Steve. He hoped he'd walk out of here after surgery, but he can't use crutches because of his left arm. He's facing a wheelchair. That's hard to take."

"And he'll stay in it, too, if he doesn't get himself back into gear. He's not responding to anybody, Pete. Did you see the therapist's reports?" Steve asked, still pacing.

Peter nodded. "Making the patient partnerships in medicine work is really tough. I've used all my pep talks and I'm out of new approaches."

"Me, too," Steve agreed, "and he knows attitude is essential." Steve ran his fingers through his hair. "I wish something would happen in his life to pick him up. I'd settle for a winning lottery ticket, anything to bring him up so we can reach him. His case isn't hopeless."

Jeneil went by the nurse's station to drop off reports on her way to see Tony. When she saw Peter and Steve at the computer, she stopped and watched, touched by Steve's struggle. Peter had told her they were agonizing over it and that had drawn her to Steve, which surprised her. He had never inspired compassion in her, but Tony liked him, he had told her that. At that moment, she was impressed with Steve as a doctor, almost as much as she was with Peter. Walking to the door, she hesitated, then opened it and stood there. Peter and Steve turned around. She hesitated nervously. "I just wanted to tell the two of you that I think you're great doctors. I'm impressed with the way you're dealing with Tony."

Peter was behind Steve. He smiled at her, knowing she was there for Steve since she had already told him that at home. He knew it wasn't easy for her and he loved her for it.

Steve stared at her in open and total surprise. "Thank you," Steve managed to get out.

"Okay," she said, blushing, then shrugged and opened the door. "Thank you." She backed out quickly and walked away.

Steve turned to Peter. "That was the girl from Records, wasn't it? I didn't hallucinate, did I?" Peter smiled; Jeneil had gotten to Steve. "Will wonders never cease." Steve shook his head and opened the folder to find the therapist's report then looked at the door where Jeneil had been standing. "And I thought blush was makeup that women used. She uses the real thing." He looked at Peter, smiling. "She looked sort of cute standing there all self-conscious and blushing, didn't she? That surprised me." Picking up the therapist's report, Steve sighed. "Tony, Tony, Tony, low self-worth and feelings of uselessness, we don't have a pill for that." They sat reviewing the reports for awhile. "Let's go see him," Steve suggested. "Maybe the two of us can reach him. These reports have hope in them. Let's tell him that."

As they reached Tony's room, Steve opened the door and stopped short. Peter dropped his stethoscope then bent down to pick it up. His stomach tightened sharply. He straightened back up and fought his dizziness. He couldn't believe they had just seen Jeneil kissing Tony just like Jack had kissed her at The Watering Hole. Anger began to rise in him and he struggled to remember that he was a doctor. Jeneil looked stunned while Tony looked shocked and embarrassed.

"I'd better go," Jeneil stammered. She turned and took Tony's hand. "It's okay, Tony. I'll be back." She smiled and touched his face gently. Peter could feel a pulse in his ears. He was furious and they avoided looking at each other as she left.

Steve chuckled. "Well, look at the medicine you're taking when my back is turned."

Peter tightened his hands into fists in his coat pockets. His head was throbbing and he was seething with anger. "I've forgotten something," Peter said, struggling to gain control of his anger. He walked to the door and Steve turned in surprise. "I'll be back later."

"Peter…Dr. Chang," Tony called. "I need to talk to you."

"I'll be back, Tony," Peter said.

"No, now please. It's important. I'm worried," Tony pleaded.

Steve looked from one to the other. "I have a patient to see," Peter said. "I'll be back later, Tony." The door closed. Peter hoped he could deal with this. He was so angry at Jeneil right now he couldn't think straight.

After giving himself time to calm down, Peter went back to check on Tony's medical condition.

"Peter, sit down," Tony said.

Peter hesitated. "Tony, I don't want to talk about what happened earlier right now."

"You got to listen to me, Peter. It wasn't her fault. It wasn't. It just happened. She came here to tell me that she needs me in her office. She offered me an apartment in the building so I can get to work on my own, even in a wheelchair. I'm not sure I can explain it. She was just being Jeneil. She sat here on the bed holding my hand. I never expected a job and here she was telling me that she's been hoping frantically that I'd get well enough to work even part time. Then she gives me a long list of my abilities and where she needs them in the corporation. And she wasn't just saying it, Peter. I could tell that she meant it. It wasn't pity. She really needs me. I've always liked her a lot. I got too close. She kissed my cheek and hugged me then everything rushed at me at once. Mostly the feeling that I was human, alive, and a man somebody needed. I kissed her, Peter, and it got out of hand. I'm sorry. Blame me. It wasn't her. She resisted. She really did, but I'm here all bandaged up, she couldn't belt me, could she? Peter, please believe me. I couldn't stand it if you blamed her."

Peter stared at the floor. He could picture that happening and his stomach began to relax. "Tony thanks for explaining that to me. I would have sorted through it, I think, but you've spared me some bad times."

"What about Jeneil?" Tony asked. "Are you okay about her?"

Peter nodded. "I know what you mean about getting too close. I've been there."

"Thanks Peter, you don't know how much better I feel. You're a lucky guy. She's something else."

"I know she is," Peter said, standing as a nurse came in. "I'll stop by later."

"Thanks a lot," Tony said. Peter heard the sincerity behind it.

Peter walked down the corridor. He was a lucky guy. She really was something else. Didn't anybody see his good points? He was smiling while all these guys surrounded his woman. Was he the only one who struggled with that? Jeneil, Jeneil. The price he paid for loving her, he thought, shaking his head.

Steve caught up to him. "What is it, Pete?"

"What's what?"

"Tony. What's he worried about, impotence? Stress can cause temporary problems, but boy kissing her like that will cure anything."

Peter smiled. "He was worried about a few things, but you're right, she was good medicine for him. Things are happening in his life right now. I think there will be a change for the better in this case."

"Oh great," Steve said. "I'm glad he opened up to one of us anyway, but that girl throws the fastest curveballs. She stands before us and blushes then goes to him with powerful cures, makes him feel like a man. Now and then I'm wrong about a woman. She might be one of those few." Steve smiled and hit Peter's arm, winking.

Peter smiled to himself. Soon he had to tell Steve exactly how wrong.

*****

Peter was asked to work a double. He wished he hadn't been. He needed to talk to Jeneil about Tony, but she was going to be at Danzieg's tonight. Shit, he thought, where the hell was the simple girl and the simple life he had had before? They had changes all around them now. He dialed but there was no answer. "Danzieg's," he sighed, walking back to the floor. "I don't know about him, honey. I just don't know."

Peter left as soon as his shift ended, anxious to get home. Jeneil was sitting on the sofa when he walked in. "I'm glad you waited up for me," he said, sitting next to her. "I called to tell you that I was working a double but you'd left already."

Tears rolled down her cheeks. "I thought you were staying at the dorm again and I wouldn't blame you if you had."

"Tony explained it all to me," he said, holding her. "Come on, let's go to bed." He lay on his pillow wondering how things had gone at Danzieg's while she changed behind the dressing screen. He turned as she walked toward the bed. She was wearing one of his favorite nightgowns.

She snuggled to him. "I love you. Thanks for understanding everything."

"You haven't told me what happened at Danzieg's."

"Everything I expected to happen. I'm not a good subject. I don't open up easily."

"What happened?"

"Well, I was upset about us and Tony, and not hearing from you, and he sensed something was wrong. He's very sensitive, which I found unnerving. He held colors of fabrics near me. He didn't like the lighting and I sat on a cushion while he fussed with colors in the background. Then he had me lean up against the background in poses. I know it wasn't a portrait, but I don't understand how he ever saw me in some of those poses. They weren't me."

"What was wrong with them?"

"They were too provocative," she said, and Peter's stomach tensed.

"Provocative?"

"Maybe more sensuous," she corrected. "Then he nailed markers where my hands were supposed to be." She was silent for a minute. "He was frustrated, I could tell that. I could feel myself resisting all of it, and he yelled at me to relax. Then he took my hairpins out to loosen my hair, and he kept running his fingers through it to style it. That unnerved me. Nobody's done that to me except you. I didn't like it. He yelled at me again and I cried. He kicked the background over and stretched out on the floor to rest, and told me I was a different person from the one he'd met on Saturday." Peter smiled and his stomach completely relaxed. "I came home very upset."

"Has he given up?" Peter asked, smiling in the darkness.

"No, he wants me there Saturday morning."

"Are you going?" he asked, surprised.

"I'm not sure, partly because it was such a fiasco and partly because I felt for him in his frustration. I used to watch my mother struggle with her work. But mostly I'm curious about why the whole thing unnerved and upset me. I'd like to understand why I'm resisting all of it. I know I don't open up easily, but I was rebelliously resistant."

He held her, kissing her temple and cheeks with deep feeling. "Jeneil," he said, "I want to make love to you right now." She looked at him surprised then nodded.

Afterwards, Peter lay awake holding her. He felt comforted, lying there, holding her as she slept. She was his. She belonged to him. The vibrations he was getting about Danzieg were strong, too strong. The way Danzieg looked at Jeneil kept passing through his mind. Was Danzieg a professional or a man? Remembering how Jeneil had gotten caught up in Tony's moment made Peter doubt her ability to deal with Danzieg. But what could he do? Jeneil stirred, turning over and leaving his arms. He had to let her go and be there for her. "Jeneil, baby, where's this change going?" he asked, staring at the ceiling. Civilization, he thought, she believed in civilization. At least on the uncivilized streets there had been clear cut rules. Everybody was clear about the rules and street life worked if you knew them. He didn't understand these rules. There didn't seem to be any. He turned over and tried to sleep.

*****

Peter eased up on worrying about Danzieg as he watched Jeneil. She seemed her old self. Tony was improving rapidly and that excited her. She and the journal spent a lot of time together. He was impressed with her Wall of China. She was studying Chinese civilization and listing what she learned on the wall heading to the bedroom. He found himself checking it every day for new information. She was keeping busy and everything seemed fine between them. Peter liked having life normal again and he relaxed. Saturday at Danzieg's didn't worry him anymore.

*****

Jeneil climbed the stairs to the second floor and knocked. Robert Danzieg opened the door holding a piece of toast and a coffee mug. Jeneil stepped in and looked him over. "You're not dressed," she commented, noticing his bare feet and missing shirt.

"Enough to be decent." He grinned. "You look great at six-thirty in the morning. We may have something here this time. How are you feeling today? Resolve the fight with Peter?"

"We didn't fight," she insisted.

"Call it what you want," he smiled, "but take a message to Peter. Friday night sex has to be great, is that clear? I want you radiating on Saturday mornings."

Jeneil was annoyed at his intrusion into her personal life. He was too bold. She liked it in his work, not in his personality. "Does my sitting for you mean that you have license to make bawdy remarks about my personal life?"

Robert looked at her surprised then grinned. "Well, I'll be damned. You really are Victorian. I thought it was just an act."

"That's quaint. Actually I'm more Elizabethan and you think showing people respect is quaint?"

He bit into his piece of toast and smiled. "Is this real with you?"

"What?" she asked, fighting annoyance.

"The humanity trip?"

"Is there another trip in life?"

"Well I'll be." He smiled again then sat down next to her.

"Jeneil," he said in a whisper, "do you experience orgasm?"

"Do you paint it?" she rebutted quickly. "Mr. Danzieg, let's stay in the lines of art. On second thought, let's not," she said, standing up. "My first instinct was right. This won't work. I'm leaving." She headed for the door.

"Jeneil, come back here. Why do you give up so easily?"

She turned quickly. "I don't but you're not the person I met Saturday either. I liked him better."

"Jeneil, if you leave, I'll have to get my Dobermans after you."

"I'll risk Dobermans, Homo sapien wolves are another breed of animal altogether."

"Homo sapien wolves?" He laughed. "You really aren't from this century, are you?" he asked, walking over to her.

"Neither is sophistry. It dates back to early Greece, but you seem comfortable with it. Don't manipulate me, Robert Danzieg."

"Lady, you need manipulating. Do you know where babies come from?"

"I love your work Mr. Danzieg. Good luck with your career." She opened the door and headed out. He ran into the hall after her.

"Jeneil, come back. Let's start again," he offered, holding her by the shoulders.

"No," she insisted. "It won't work. It won't."

"I'm sorry, I apologize. I had no idea you were so straight. Who the hell did I meet Saturday?"

"I was straight Saturday. I don't know what you mean. What did I do Saturday that made you think you could talk to me like this?"

"I don't know. I guess I'm reacting. I want to take your hair down and experience the real you."

"But I don't do that easily. I barely know you. You can't ask that of me," she insisted. He studied her face then gently kissed her forehead. "And no touching," she added plainly.

"I have a new respect for Peter." Danzieg smiled slyly.

"I live with Peter. You paint me. There's a vast difference in those roles."

"It's a deal. I show respect and no touching. Please come back."

She paused, struggling with thought then sighed. "We can try again. I have strong doubts, but we'll try again."

Returning to the studio, she put her purse and jacket down. The background had been fixed and there were vibrant shades of gold, red, orange, and rust.

"Why do you have me in these colors?"

"You mix with them," Danzieg said. "You interact with them. Electricity happens. I have a dress for you. It's behind the screen."

Jeneil went to the corner and looked around. "Gosh, it's so airy," she said to herself, examining the garment.

"And Jeneil," Robert called, "nothing underneath." She raised her eyebrows, feeling her resistance begin again.

"It'll be fine," she told herself, "you'll be covered." She undressed and slipped into the rust colored silk dress. Ignore him, she thought, pretend you're home where you hang around like this. She stepped from behind the screen and went to pose. Sitting on the cushion, she folded her arms. Danzieg walked to her and knelt down before her. Under the strong light of day, her eyes matched her dress.

"Wow!" he said, holding her chin in his hand. "Look at what I found. Loosen up, Jeneil. Stop trying to hide from me." She looked at him. "I've got to paint it. I need to look at it." He unfolded her arms. "Come on," he said gently, "I'm going to paint you, not make love to you."

Sitting back in the cushion, she relaxed and let her mind wander. Danzieg went to his easel. Jeneil watched as he studied the canvass. Mixing some colors, he began to work. She liked the way he became totally absorbed. He forgot she was there and she relaxed even more, feeling like background.

Later he sat down on the floor and stretched out. "Do you want a break, Jeneil? You must be tight by now, too."

"I am," she said, standing up and moving her head around on her shoulders. She jumped as she felt him massage her neck.

"You're a great artist's model. Some of them yak away until your ears hurt. You haven't spoken for hours. Where'd you go?"

"I mind travel."

He smiled. "You have great skin."

She moved away from him and walked to the canvas. "How's the job beginning?"

"It's not," he said. "I'm struggling with it. I'm feeling resistance."

"From me?"

"All of it," he answered, stretching. "I can't recreate what I saw at the gallery." Jeneil sensed his frustration again.

"I'm sorry," she said, feeling for him. "I'm trying to relax."

"I know you are. I'm hungry. Let's have lunch."

Jeneil changed into a terry cloth robe that was hanging behind the screen. She walked to the far wall where a collection of photographs was displayed. She became lost in one of a rainy day.

"You like rainy days, too?" he asked, coming up behind her.

"Why did you take that one?"

"That's an early one. I was in a rainy mood."

"I can feel the sadness in it." Her eyes became moist.

"Do you find rainy days sad?"

"Not all of them, especially a quick moving rainstorm on a hot day. You can smell the wet pavement and feel the rain renewing the earth, cooling it, cleaning it."

"What do you do, Jeneil?"

"Do?"

"Work?"

"Not much," she answered, evading the question.

"Is every question about you too personal?" he asked, smiling.

"No, but jobs and ethnic backgrounds are traps, I think, little pitfalls that trip people so they form images without looking deeper at each other. We put little Plexiglas walls up around us so we see all around and we think we're part of a group, but we don't touch so we don't feel relationships are fulfilling and that they fall short of their purpose." He studied her with growing interest. "See what your rainy day composition started," she laughed lightly.

He smiled. "I'm hungry, let's eat."

"I brought a lunch," Jeneil said, going to her purse then sat at the counter in the small kitchen. He sat down with a candy bar and a soft drink. "That's your lunch?" she asked, horrified.

"Oh no! You don't give lectures, do you?"

"Well, you must eat other things, too. Your teeth are in great shape." He looked at her and she opened her brown bag, embarrassed she'd said that.

"Oh my gosh, you blush." He laughed, standing up. "Come over here. I've never seen a blush." He pulled her to the window, looking closely at her face.

"I've learned something from this experience already." She moved her head from side to side.

"What?"

"I have a new compassion for lab animals."

"I'm sorry." He laughed again and hugged her gently. "What are you eating?"

"Green grapes and cheese."

"Continental are we?"

"No," she said, sitting down, "diet conscious." She broke off some grapes to share with him.

"How long have you and Peter been together?"

"A little over two months. Why?"

"You seem so settled for so short a time. Are you planning marriage?" She nodded. "When?" She shrugged. "Are you into Mime?" She laughed and suddenly swallowed a grape whole then coughed. "You have beautiful hair. How long has it taken you to get it to this length?"

"Since I was eleven years old."

"Where are you from?"

"Nebraska. What about you?"

"California."

"What brought you here?"

"Art school and I stayed on. And you?"

"College."

"Are my paintings in your apartment?"

"An office," she answered.

"How come you're buying paintings for an office? Are you a decorator?" She shook her head, not adding an explanation. "Am I being too personal again?"

"Yes," she said quietly.

"You're different. Questions about your feelings are okay, but questions about your work are too personal. I like your directness, and I like you, Jeneil."

"I like you, too. You're more like the artist I met at the gallery."

He smiled. "And I wish you'd turn into the girl I met there."

"I'm sorry. I don't know what you mean. I'm just me."

"No, there was another dimension, but not to worry, we'll find it. Ready for the cushion again?"

"I'll change and be right there," she said, standing up.

Three

Jeneil heard Peter call for her. "I'm in the laundry room, Peter," she answered.

Peter walked in. "What the hell is this glop?" he asked, standing at the tub she was working over.

She smiled. "I'm making paper."

He sighed. "Oh good, I thought for a second it might be dinner. Jeneil, why are you making paper?"

"I thought it might be fun. Did you know that the Chinese made paper? It was one of the many technical achievements of the Han dynasty. Then I remembered seeing instructions on making paper in a craft book, so I decided to try."

"What's it made of?" he asked, wrinkling his nose.

"You can use anything, flowers, lettuce, cabbage, coffee grounds, even cornflakes. I'm using grass. The Chinese used hemp."

"Grass?" He raised his eyebrows.

"Grass that grows tall and dry by the roadside. Of course, this isn't the authentic Chinese method. I used a blender to mix it."

"Jeneil, no more power shakes for me," and he grinned.

She chuckled. "I have a blender just for crafts."

Peter smiled as he watched her put the glop in a frame. She turned on a small electric heater and cleaned up at the sink.

"The things you find fun in," he said. She kissed him as she walked past.

Lighting the candles for dinner, she then ran to the bedroom and returned wearing a long light yellow dress that Peter liked. "Do my snaps please," she asked, turning her back to him. He liked doing snaps and zippers. He couldn't understand why, he just loved doing it. He smiled and kissed her neck gently.

"What's for dinner?"

"Chinese chicken."

"Oh, not Chinese food, and I came home starved."

"Good, there's a lot." She left for the kitchen.

"Swell," he said, sitting down.

She returned with a wok. Serving from the side table, she placed the dish in front of him and sat down.

"Oh, this doesn't look too bad."

"Not one bean sprout or bamboo shoot." She smiled.

"And it's Chinese?"

"An authentic Chinese chef might argue the point, but what do we care. My warlord is happy with it." She touched his arm and he smiled. "I love you."

"This is nice," he said. "All of it, the table, the candles, you in that dress. I'm calming down."

"Twenty-first century life; you were healing the sick and diseased an hour ago and I was making paper, now we want our bodies and minds to relax and to be romantic. How do you spell stress?" She sipped her water.

He smiled. "How did it go at Danzieg's?"

"It didn't. No, maybe that's not quite right," she corrected herself. "It started off badly. The work is nowhere, but we got to know each other better." Peter looked at her. "He became the person he was at the gallery, simple and understated. He's really very nice."

"Why is the work nowhere?"

"It's fighting him or he's fighting it. I'm not sure which. And he keeps insisting I'm different. I'm beginning to share his frustration. I don't know what he's talking about, but he fixed the background."

"When do you go back?"

"Tomorrow morning. I'll be in Nebraska next weekend so he wants me there to make up for it. Do you know that he actually has candy bars and soft drinks for lunch and toast and coffee for breakfast? No wonder he gets hyper. I've got to straighten that out."

Peter looked at her. "How?"

"Do you want dessert now?" she asked, standing up and going to the kitchen.

Peter rubbed his forehead. "Jeneil, how are you going to straighten out his eating habits?"

She returned with dessert and sat down. "By packing some lunch for him when I pack mine."

"Won't he mind you rearranging his life?"

"I doubt it." She laughed. "He really needs a woman." Peter put his fork down and stared at her. "I didn't say that right. His home and his life need's a woman's touch. Is that reverse chauvinism? Did that sound like reverse chauvinism to you?" She laughed.

"Why are you taking on the job?" he asked, concerned.

"I'm not," she answered. "I'm only bringing him lunch."

"You got along with him then."

"Yes, I did. I'm surprised, but we did get along. Are you finished?"

"What?" he asked absently.

"Are you finished with your dessert?"

"Yes," he answered quietly as she went to the kitchen. Peter sat wondering if he should worry about her and Danzieg.

"Peter, will you clear the table?" she called.

After clearing the table, Peter sat on the sofa. Jeneil put some music on.

"Come and dance with me."

"I don't dance."

"What?" she asked surprised. "You don't know how to dance or you don't like to dance?"

"Both."

"Have you ever tried?"

"No."

"Then how do you know that you don't like it?"

"Because it looks stupid."

She laughed and sat next to him. "Hey, you get hold of a girl. You like that, don't you?"

"Funny." He smiled. "Very funny."

"Please dance with me," she said, kissing his shoulder.

"Jeneil, I'd feel dumb. I'm just getting used to candles at dinner. Don't push. Chang can only handle so much civilization at one time."

She chuckled. "Didn't you go to school dances?"

"Jeneil, I don't think our school had dances. The police probably couldn't afford that many cops for riot duty."

"What about when you moved here?"

He laughed. "I was too busy making up what I missed from not going to school there."

She kissed him. "You are a wonder."

"That's me." He smiled. "The Chinese miracle kid."

Jeneil smiled, noticing he called himself Chinese. She looked around. "Where's the newspaper? We can watch TV in bed."

"Now that sounds like fun."

Reaching across for the paper, she opened to the listings. "There's a murder mystery on in fifteen minutes. How does that sound?"

"Great," he said, standing up and taking her hand. "One thing I like about you, you know how to show a guy a good time."

"Funny Chang, very funny." She stood up and he put his arms around her and kissed her. She smiled. "You've got the holding part right. Now if I can get you to move your feet, we'll call it dancing."

"You don't quit, do you?" He grinned.

"But that's what you like about me, right?"

"You're right, beautiful. You are right." They walked to the bedroom, turning off lamps on their way.

*****

Jeneil arrived as Robert Danzieg was taking the background apart. "What happened?" she asked, surprised.

"It isn't working," he said sullenly.

"Shall I go home?"

"No. Why?"

"You won't be ready for me, will you?"

"Can you stay?" he asked quietly.

"I was planning on this as my morning. I have nothing else waiting."

"Then put on the dress and stay. Maybe it'll help to see you in it. At the gallery, I was sure it would be easy. It was all to the surface on you."

"What was?" She was curious.

"That certain something."

"I'm feeling guilty about this."

"No, don't. Let's not add to the other things we have to sweep aside. Relax for awhile."

Jeneil changed and wandered around his bookcase. She thumbed through his music. "Would music distract you?"

"No," he answered, moving a ladder. He was sweating hard. The background was high and he moved the ladder several times to get everything just right.

She put on a Rossini tape, pulled out a book on introducing art, and stretched out on her stomach across a brown divan that was in front of the bookcase. Crossing her feet at her ankles, she swayed her legs gently, completely absorbed in the book. The silence broke her concentration. She looked up. Robert was standing on the ladder watching her. "Is something wrong?"

"No," he said, smiling and continued on the backdrop. She stood up, turned the tape and went back to her book. He walked over to her a while later. "Would you like a cold drink?" he asked. She looked up. He was covered in sweat.

"Yes," she said, a bit taken back. He disappeared, later returning, handing a tall glass to her. She sipped it. "Oh, cranberry juice, thank you."

He had changed to cut off jeans and he wore nothing else. Sitting on the floor, he rested his head on the divan. Jeneil moved back. She could smell the shampoo he had used and he seemed more relaxed from his shower.

"Jeneil, you surprise me."

"I do?"

"Yes, I really thought you were uptight about your body. You're not. You're very comfortable with it, but you don't share it easily. You hide it in your street clothes and you aren't too comfortable with me looking at it."

"But I warned you about that."

He turned his head and smiled. "So you did. You said you aren't an easy subject. You also said that you don't open up easily." He sipped a soft drink. "What were you frightened by, the children's book, *The Emperor's New Clothes*?"

"What?"

"I'm teasing." He laughed.

She smiled. "You seem like a Californian. You're completely comfortable with your body barely covered. No pun or insult intended."

He smiled. "You have a great body. Why aren't you comfortable showing it?"

"It's another pitfall, a trap. We stop at physical and cheat ourselves of the soul. We spend millions making our bodies beautiful and our souls starve and decay, I think. My father told me to look for the man who looks past the facades."

"Lucky Peter, he was smart enough to solve the riddle, and you are an enigma."

"No, I'm a simple person."

He laughed. "Maybe once a person finds his way through the maze of complexities and opposites you are."

She pinched his arm. "Hey, I may be lying on the couch, but I didn't ask for an analysis."

He chuckled. "You're also funny."

"Robert, I don't know what you saw at the gallery and I'm wondering if it was a reflection?"

"No, Jeneil, it was there. I'll find it."

"How?"

He turned to face her. Looking into her eyes, he whispered, "By getting to your soul." He smiled and gently touched her arm.

"Do you know how to do that? To get to a person's soul?"

"It has something to do with your eyes, right?"

"I asked you first." She laughed. "And there are some civilizations that have believed that the spirit of a person enters and leaves through the soft spot at the top of the skull."

"Are spirit and soul the same?"

"I don't know," she giggled, "but you can't find it if you can't define it."

He grinned. "You're also bright and witty." He kissed her hand quickly and stood up.

The rest of the morning was spent putting the backdrop together. He stood at the bottom of the ladder looking it over. Jeneil watched. He shook his head and ran his fingers through his hair. Turning, he put his arms through a rung and rested his head. Jeneil sensed his feeling of failure.

"I'm sorry, Robert. Maybe you should put the project aside."

"No," he answered quietly. "I'm doing some paintings for the Downing Building next. I need this to work. I need it as a bridge for the other project."

"You mean to settle something in yourself?" she asked and he nodded. "Would you like to stop for lunch now?"

"Yeah, why not. A whole mornings work and it still looks artificial." He shook his head.

Jeneil went to change into the robe then went to the kitchen. Taking out the small cooler she'd brought, she unpacked lunch. She cleared off the small kitchen table and set it. Filling the sink with soapy water, she washed the glasses that were accumulating. Quickly straightening up, she then went to find Robert. He was clearing the debris from the recycled backdrop. Seeing Jeneil reminded him of lunch.

She shook her head. He forgets to eat, she thought. She walked back to the kitchen and waited.

"What's all this?" he asked, looking around, smiling. "You are all girl." He put his arms around her and held her close. She was in total surprise and very uncomfortable. She hadn't been against a man's bare chest like this before except for Peter's. "Thanks for caring," he said, touching her cheek gently. "It's nice having you around. You're quiet, you keep yourself entertained, and you're soft and cuddly."

"Aw shucks, it ain't nothin' any cat couldn't do."

He laughed. "And you make me laugh." He looked at her and shook his head closely. "We'd better have lunch," he said, going to the table. "Now, this is a sandwich. Where did the milk come from? I don't buy any, it goes bad before I use it all and I hate black coffee, too."

"Try buying heavy cream and add water. Keep it in a glass jar so it stays colder. It'll last longer than milk."

"Really?"

She nodded. "It doesn't spoil as fast and you'll use less of it in your coffee."

"Girls, you can't beat them for making a place feel homey. I feel better," he said, finishing his milk. "I didn't know I was so hungry. Now if only work could come together."

"Peter...I mean Robert, why don't we go out for some fresh air. Take your camera."

"That's a good idea. I'll take some shots of you. It'll give me some exposure to your features. Yeah, let's do it." He stood up and left the room.

"Shots of me, oh great." She shook her head. "Big mouth."

*****

Peter walked to the phone booth. Taking the same coins from his pocket, he waited for the tone and dialed. "No answer." He looked at his watch. "Four-thirty" He had been trying for over an hour. The vibrations deep inside of him signaled Danzieg. He hung up the receiver.

*****

Jeneil and Robert walked up the stairs together. "Well, that was painless, wasn't it?"

She laughed. "Once I forced myself to forget that you had a camera, it became painless."

Putting his camera down quickly, he pulled off his shirt, kicked off his shoes, and went to the canvas wearing just cutoffs. "Get changed, Jeneil. I think my muse is awake."

She changed quickly and took her place on the cushions. The work began and Robert lost himself amongst the paints. Jeneil watched and smiled then let her mind travel. She heard her name being called and was surprised that so much time had passed.

"Jeneil." Robert smiled. "You can break if you want to. I'm concentrating on the background shading now."

"How's it coming?"

"There's progress. At least the background is cooperating"

"I'm still wrong?"

He looked at her and smiled. "Don't worry. Once my muse starts to work, a breakthrough follows. Find a spot and relax." She went back to the divan and the book. A buzzer sounded. Robert jumped then slammed down his brush. "Shit. I put the signal up. Who the hell can that be?" He left the room. Jeneil returned her thoughts back to the book. She heard noises and looked up.

"Peter!" she said, sitting up.

"I tried to call you," Peter said apologetically, "then I saw your car so I came up." He felt uncomfortable. It shocked him to see her dressed in what she would wear to bed and he had trouble dealing with Robert so bare, but Jeneil was a total mind twist, and she seemed comfortable in it. She seemed comfortable there.

"It's okay, Peter." Robert smiled. "I've kept her longer than expected. We've just had a breakthrough and I was making the most of it."

Jeneil put her arms around Peter. "Why were you calling?"

"My shift has been extended. There's no phone here, I couldn't call."

"Oh, okay." She hugged him. "I'm glad you stopped in."

"What does your shift extended mean?" Robert asked.

"I'll be working late," Peter answered, noticing Robert's strong shoulder and chest muscles. He was awfully muscular for someone who painted.

"Then is it all right if Jeneil stays longer? I'll take her to eat when we're through."

Peter shrugged. "That's up to Jeneil."

"Maybe I should stay," she said. Peter looked at her. "The background is working, but I'm not, and there's no sense in having dinner out. I have dinner in the slow cooker at home, but I'm not a fancy cook," she said to Robert. Peter noticed an easiness between them. They were comfortable with each other. The vibrations started again.

"Why aren't you working?" Peter asked Jeneil. She shrugged.

"It's me," Robert said. "I probably haven't stretched enough yet. I'll get there."

"Is this where you sit?" Peter asked, going to the cushion.

"Yes," Jeneil answered, getting into position. Peter's heart pounded. Robert had almost recreated the way Jeneil had looked on the balcony in Vermont.

"What do you think?" Robert asked.

"It's not Jeneil that's not working; it's what's around her. She gets lost in it. She should blend into it, become a part of it."

Robert looked at him, surprised by Peter's clear opinion. "What makes you say that?"

"I've seen her like this."

"You have? Where?" Robert asked, becoming very curious.

"When she stands in front of a sunset."

"A sunset?" Robert smiled. "A sunset. Peter, I think you just helped me discover my muse. I knew there was something missing."

"What's missing is cosmic," Peter added without thinking. Jeneil looked at him, shocked by his comment.

"What's cosmic?" Robert asked. Peter looked at Jeneil.

"It's difficult to explain," she said, obviously unnerved. Peter noticed that she pulled her arms closer to her and held her hand near her throat.

She was withdrawing, Peter thought. He had exposed too much of her. He felt bad.

"Whoa," Robert said, going to her and gently holding her arms. "Don't go back to square one on me, Jeneil. What's the matter?"

"Nothing," she said quietly. "I think I'm getting tired."

"Oh." Robert sighed. "I thought you were withdrawing." Peter was surprised at Robert's sensitivity to her moods.

It was time for him to leave and he knew it. "I've got to get back to the hospital," Peter said, going toward the door.

"Peter Chang," Robert said, standing up, "thank you for stopping by. Thank you very much," and he went back to the canvas. Peter smiled at Jeneil and headed toward the door again.

"Peter!" Jeneil called and ran to him. She put her arms around his waist and held on tight. He could feel her shaking slightly.

"What's wrong baby?"

"I don't know," she said, "just hold me."

"I love you," he whispered, holding her and kissing her gently.

"Thank you," she answered quietly. "I think I'm okay now. Thank you." She pulled away and touched his face. He left feeling concerned about her.

Sitting in his car, Peter rested his back. "This guy is physical," he said half aloud, remembering Robert's physique. "And no scars." He closed his eyes. "Chang, I'm beginning to regret having buried you. This is beyond Peter. He's soft. He's too far from the streets. He doesn't breathe survival like you do. He just handed Danzieg the fourth ace. Now it's him and her and cosmic. And I gave it to him. I put her right in his hands." The vibrations were pulsating through Peter's chest. He rubbed his forehead, sighed, and drove away.

*****

"Jeneil," Robert hugged her, "I want to see you in front of a sunset. Can you survive that long?"

"Where will we go for a sunset?"

"Here at my west window."

"That'll be fine with me." She returned to the divan and the book.

Later, Robert knelt beside Jeneil. "Sunset time," he said, touching her arm gently.

Going to the west window with him, Jeneil could see the colors of the sky burning into the room, painting a glow on the walls. The window was immense and framed the sunset perfectly. She smiled approvingly. "Magnificent." She held her hand out to the sun then, remembering Robert was there, she put it down again. Positioning a bench in front of the window, he put the cushion on it.

"Sit," he said. He sat on the floor studying her. The colors from the sunset surrounded them, enveloped them, and drew them into the magnificence of nature. Jeneil wanted to see the sunset and experience it, but she stayed sitting with her back to the window.

Robert smiled and shook his head. "This is it. Peter was right. Incredible." He moved closer to Jeneil, watching the light change on her skin. He touched her face and ran his fingers through her hair. He looked deeply into her eyes. "You are beautiful," he said, as if he had just discovered that fact. The vibrant colors that filled the room faded into quieter tones and subtle shadows. The sunset was in its afterglow. Robert stood up and took her hand. "Face the afterglow." Jeneil turned and Robert stood at her side. "The sun knows you, Jeneil. It welcomes you into the sunset." Kneeling beside her, he touched her cheek gently, kissed it softly and stood up. He held his hand to her. She took it and stood up. "Can I have you at sunsets this week?" he asked, smiling. "I want to become more familiar with it and you together."

"Possibly Monday and Tuesday, the rest of the week has claimed me."

"I'll take that. Now, let's concentrate on dinner."

Jeneil was surprised that the pot roast wasn't ruined. She had left everything prepared so she and Peter could just sit and have dinner. Robert sat in Peter's chair. They talked easily about different things. Having mentioned making paper, Robert was interested in seeing it. After clearing the table together, they headed to the laundry room.

"Explain this wall to me," he said, stopping.

"That's my Great Wall of China. I'm studying the Chinese. I guess I don't need to explain why," she said, not adding more.

"This is great PR stuff. You look like your trying to impress someone." She smiled and they continued to the laundry room.

Peter unlocked the front door. He was surprised no one was around. He'd noticed Danzieg's car out front. He could hear muffled voices. He looked at the bedroom. The door was closed. He closed the front door harder than expected and headed that way. Stopping at the laundry room, he realized they were in there. He rubbed his forehead. "Get real, Chang," he lectured himself then knocked.

Jeneil opened the door, surprised. "Hi, honey. I'm showing Robert the paper I made."

"I like it," Robert said. "Can you get me instructions for this?"

"I'll have them photocopied for you."

"Peter, dinner is still warm. Are you hungry?"

"Starved," Peter answered.

She kissed him. "Robert and I will have dessert with you after you have dinner. This is great timing."

"Peter, thanks for the lead on the sunset. The whole project turned around after that."

They all sat around the table. Robert and Jeneil became involved in a discussion of making paints from scratch like artists did long ago. Peter listened and actually enjoyed their conversation. He felt better now that he'd eaten. Even Robert didn't seem so threatening, especially with more clothes on. They brought their coffee to the living room and Jeneil put on a tape. Handing Peter his piece of pie, she pulled the hassock near his chair. Sitting down, she leaned against Peter's legs. He noticed that and loved her for it. She could have sat on the empty sofa. He noticed that Robert watched, too. Peter smiled to himself thinking thing were fine.

Robert and Jeneil continued to discuss different artists and movements in the art world while Peter ate his pie.

"What's going on in your plants?" Robert asked, noticing the figurines.

"It's a hobby of mine. I collect them." She didn't mention Camelot or the quest. Peter noticed.

"There seems to be a whole story going on in there. Well, I'm going to leave," Robert said, standing. "Jeneil, you are very patient and a good cook. Thank you. I'll see you tomorrow."

"I enjoyed having you here." Jeneil smiled.

Robert kissed her cheek. "Peter, don't get up. Your hours are as bad as mine. Relax."

"Thanks," Peter said, and stayed sitting. Jeneil closed the door and returned to Peter.

"Got room for a woman on your lap?" she asked.

"Always, beautiful." He smiled at her. She sat on his lap and snuggled up against him. He put his arm around her. "Are you feeling better now? You had me worried earlier. I could feel you shaking."

"It was strange," she explained. "I suddenly felt very vulnerable. I was so glad you were there." He smiled and kissed her gently. She responded, letting him know that she wanted him.

"Honey, is everything going alright at Danzieg's?"

"Yes. Why? The work is moving slowly, but it's moving."

"I mean between the two of you. He's there half naked and you look too good for other men to see you. Then when you held on to me, I began thinking about it and wondered. Danzieg is staying on his side of the paint brush, right?"

Jeneil smiled. "I love Chang's protection."

"Baby, it's not only Chang. You and Danzieg are working under some strange conditions. Anything could happen."

"He's fine, Peter. He's very nice and he's very sensitive. I feel comfortable with him." She kissed him again. "I'm getting ready for bed." She smiled and got up.

Peter sat thinking. "I'd feel better if his woman was somewhere to be seen. He's been with mine since six-thirty this morning. It's almost ten-thirty now. Where's his?" He got up and turned off the light, heading to bed.

Four

Peter was concerned. There was nothing concrete on which to base his feelings, but the vibrations stayed, especially after Jeneil got home from Danzieg's on Monday. The change was slight, but it was there. She was quiet and her mind wasn't always with them, but Peter had nothing but vibrations to go by.

He sat in the apartment then he paced. He wished his shift had been extended. The spare time on his hands was torture. Jeneil was at Danzieg's; Steve had a date. He called his grandfather. Parking the car out of the driveway in case someone came home, he went to the greenhouse. His grandfather offered him a cold drink then sat across from him, studying him closely.

"How do you happen to be free tonight?" the grandfather asked.

Peter shrugged. "It happens now and then."

"Where's Jeneil?"

"She's visiting a friend."

"Why didn't you visit, too?" The old man continued to study Peter.

"I don't have time to visit with all her friends. She could do with fewer friends though." Peter swallowed his drink hard.

"But that's the way of the songbird."

Peter looked at his grandfather. "Why do you call her a songbird?"

"She loves people. She pleases people. She wants happiness in life and sings a cheerful song. You were attracted to it, why not others?"

"If songbirds are rare, how can you keep them from other people?"

"Why do you want to? Would a songbird be happy with no one to sing to? When I bought my first songbird, I chose the one making the most music. When I got it home, it was silent. I thought it was sick until one day I chirped at it and it sang and flew around the cage. It was silent again until the next time I chirped. I felt sorry for the bird. This poor bird had to wait until I had time for it, so I bought the second songbird. There was more chirping, but not much. I began to wonder if they didn't like the small cage. I decided to train them to fly free. Now they fly free and sing all the time."

"But it's not the same with people," Peter argued.

"Why not?"

"You can't train people like songbirds."

"Why not? My songbirds weren't unhappy in their cages; they just needed a larger world. I made sure they knew how to come home and that they wanted to."

"How?" Peter asked.

"I was consistent. I was always there and they could count on me. They learned to trust me."

"Aren't you afraid they'll get hurt?"

"I protect as much as I can. I watch; I'm aware. The doors are closed and the cat never comes in, but the birds know they can come home when a storm is coming or when it begins to get dark. They come for my protection. They're bright. And Peter, I can call them and they'll come. They only come to me. If I come home late, my songbirds are in their cages waiting. I've found them to be very loyal."

Peter shook his head. "Birds, not people, Grandfather."

"Peter, how can you teach trust if you don't understand and feel trust? How do you suppose I know that Jeneil is a songbird if I hadn't seen at least one?"

Peter looked up at him. "Grandmother?"

His grandfather smiled. "Songbird's require a lot of care, a lot of watching over, but their song is worth it, and because they're loyal, you have to make sure you want the responsibility or the songbird could be hurt. You can't gain their trust and then not be there for them. They are delicate and sensitive, and people are very attracted to them."

The greenhouse door opened. "Peter, I thought that was your car out front."

"Hi, Mom."

"Come and have tea and visit."

"I can't stay too much longer though."

"Why are you leaving so early?" she asked as he walked out

"I want to check on a songbird," he said softly. His grandfather smiled.

*****

Peter was glad he'd visited his grandfather. "I must be getting older," Peter laughed to himself, "I'm beginning to understand him." He had seen Jeneil's car in the lot and was looking forward to seeing her. She was at her desk writing when he walked in. She closed the notebook as he knelt beside her and kissed her shoulder. "Hi." He smiled. "My grandfather said to say hello."

"Oh, I would have gone to visit him, you didn't tell me you were going there."

"Just as well, the mother got in early."

Jeneil frowned. "Peter, why can't you say my mother instead of the mother? You depersonalize your relationship with her when you say 'the.' You need to work at personalizing your relationship with her."

"Hey, it's only a word."

Jeneil sighed and shook her head. "No, it's an indication of an attitude. How is your grandfather?"

"He's fine. I like visiting him when it's not a greenhouse talk." He kissed her hand. "How did the painting go?"

Jeneil smiled. "Robert is pleased. That's progress. Peter, he is so incredibly sensitive. His understanding is unique, I think." Peter felt a twinge in his stomach. "He was telling me about himself. He had to resist following his family into their business in order to be an artist. His family was furious. His father was anyway and things got really ugly between them. They didn't speak for years, but he kept working at it and last year his dad hired him to do some artwork for the corporate offices. I could see the pleasure in his face when he said that. Isn't that sad? To this day he makes sure he works out with weights to keep a muscular build. That's his dad's level of man. It's so sad in one sense, but he's probably healthier for doing it since he tends to neglect his health. He's cerebral, and I mean very cerebral. He's on another level of thought from everyday life." Peter watched as a glow developed in her cheeks. "It is so beautiful communicating with someone at that level." She was silent then smiling she looked at Peter and kissed him with a promise of passion. "I'm thirsty. I think I'll have some grapefruit juice. Do you want anything?" she asked as she walked to the kitchen.

"No," Peter answered quietly, still kneeling near the desk. He stood up slowly. He didn't like what he was seeing. Was Robert getting to her, he wondered. He sat on the sofa.

Jeneil came from the bedroom. "Are you coming to bed?"

"Yes," he answered, looking at her as she walked back to the bedroom. Peter could feel anger deep inside of him. "He turns her on and then she comes home to me." He remembered the rule from the Dragons; you smile at him, you're his. Peter got up and went to the bedroom reluctantly. "Tell me about songbirds and loyalty, Grandfather." He got into bed and faced away from her.

She snuggled to him and kissed his shoulder. "I love you, Peter." He could feel her body next to his and the thought to get out of bed kept creeping into his mind. Chang was insulted. Peter was struggling for control.

He'd put four aces in Danzieg's hand already. Did he want to put her in his bed that easily? Peter turned quickly to face Jeneil, startling her. He kissed her powerfully, leaving her surprised and breathless. "Whose woman are you?"

"Yours," she said softly, still surprised by his show of power.

"Say it so you can hear it, baby."

"What?" she asked puzzled. Peter looked down at her. She was startled and confused.

He kissed her cheek gently and touched her face. "Jeneil, I love you. I really love you." He loved her softness. He wanted her. He kissed her passionately and listened as Chang screamed inside his head; if Danzieg messes with her, I'll tear his heart out!

She cuddled to him after he'd loved her. "What turned Chang loose tonight?"

"He missed you." Peter smiled and kissed her gently.

"Ooo, then I can't wait to see him Sunday night when I get back from Nebraska." She cuddled closer. Peter smiled and hugged her.

"Honey, be careful with Danzieg," he said seriously. "Sensitive, cerebral or anything else, he's still a man. He's human."

"No, Peter. We're platonic. Our souls communicate. It isn't sexual," she reassured him. He sighed and tried to ignore the vibrations inside of him.

*****

Except for Jeneil's spells of quietness, life was normal. She wasn't seeing Danzieg until her return from Nebraska. Peter relaxed and joined Steve on Friday after work for dinner and a tour of foreign car dealerships. Steve had a thing for sports cars and always joked that expensive fast cars and fast woman were meant for him. A sports car was one of the first things Steve planned to treat himself to when he started into private practice, until then he said he'd have to get along with only fast women. Peter enjoyed the break.

Peter worried Sunday afternoon with the rainstorm that moved in. He always worried when she flew chartered. Every time a clap of thunder would break, it would pass through his nervous system. Arriving home at six-thirty, he was relieved to see Jeneil's car. He breathed deeply and smiled then ran all the stairs to the apartment. Bolting into the apartment, he looked for her then heard the shower running. Opening the bathroom door he called, "Jeneil, I'm home. Talk to me, I want to hear your voice."

"Hi, honey. I'll be right out." He smiled and closed the door then went to sit on the bed. Hearing the bathroom door open, he stood up. He met her as she walked into the bedroom and put his arms around her.

"Oh, you feel good. You smell good. I love you, beautiful."

She smiled. "Did you miss me like crazy?"

"Now what do you think?" He kissed her and she clung to him. "Jeneil, that storm was driving me crazy."

"It scared me witless." The telephone rang. "Uncle Hollis, I'll bet. He checked the weather report and wanted me to stay over." She answered the phone. "Hi, Uncle Hollis. No, I'm fine. We plowed right through it. That's a lot of hours to worry. Relax now, I'm safe. Okay, I'll be in touch after I've done the paperwork, and I love you for worrying about me. Thank you." She hung up and put her arms around Peter again. The telephone rang again. "What's happening?" She smiled. "Robert?" she answered, surprised. "No, considering the storm the flight wasn't bad. Well that's nice of you. Yes, I'll be at your place tomorrow for sunset. Okay, before sunset. I can't Tuesday, I'm meeting my lawyer. Uh, just a small legal paper, it's nothing. Well, I guess after I meet him. You've done the backdrop again? Well, I don't know, Peter just got home. I'll have to discuss...a week earlier. Do you think we'll get to finish this? Okay then, I'll see how much time I can put aside. Your soul misses me?" She laughed. Peter stiffened. "I'll be there tomorrow and we'll settle the other days. Fine, I'll see you then." She hung up and turned to Peter. "If the phone rings again, let's pretend I'm not home." She kissed him and passion quickly surfaced between them.

She kissed his arm several times after renewing their love together. "Mmm, I love it when Chang misses me." She smiled and smoothed Peter's hair then snuggled into his arms.

"Danzieg is speeding up the project?"

"Yes, his next project has been moved up a week. I don't know if he'll finish. I'm still not fitting in. My quality is still missing."

"Will you cosmic there?" Peter asked quietly.

"I don't think so. I'm comfortable with him, but cosmic is very personal to me. Do you really think that's the missing ingredient?" Peter shrugged, but he hoped not. "If it is, can you believe the man's sensitivity to have picked up on that at a party? He's incredible. He thrives on intense. It makes him come alive. You can feel it in him during the sunsets."

Peter looked at her. "Jeneil, get out of this whole thing."

"What? I can't now. Look at the work he's done. Oh Peter, is that fair to him?"

"Who cares?"

"Oh Peter, he's put himself into this. I feel guilty enough not fitting in. If I cancelled, I'd really feel bad. What is it, too much time?"

"No, I'm concerned about sunsets and intense."

She kissed him and smiled. "You think everybody sees me like you do."

"In that dress you wear, he does."

"Peter!"

"His soul misses you. What a bunch of bull…."

"Don't do this. Don't ruin my homecoming."

"Then tell him to paint faster or I'll kick his muse's ass and wake it up," he said gruffly, and she began to laugh. "You find this funny?"

"No, the thought of Chang doing that to his muse is."

He smiled and hugged her. "I'm glad you're home, baby."

"Oh Peter, I love your simplicity." She kissed him.

*****

Jeneil was scheduled to spend every night at sunset with Danzieg. Peter watched and except for quiet moments when she'd withdraw, she was herself. Peter stayed around the hospital longer on the nights she was at Danzieg's. It kept his mind occupied and the vibrations muffled. ER got busy; a bar fight had broken out over a woman. Peter worked on one of the men involved. Peter hadn't thought of him as a man, he seemed like a kid. The man was very agitated and his speech was very animated. Peter noticed the nurses raising their eyebrows and shaking their heads in disapproval. Both men required stitches. With legitimate accidents and emergencies to handle, brawls and fights over women were low on the ladder of status. Peter watched the staff giving looks to each other. He felt for the guy. Steve came in to assist as Peter was finishing.

The man continued his tirade. "That sucker. Teach him to mess with my woman," he said as he sat up and Peter finished.

"Stepped onto your turf, huh?" Peter smiled. He thought the man had a lot of dignity. Someone got too close to his woman and he stepped in. Somehow at the moment that sounded heroic to him.

"Yeah, the sucka got shit bold with me right there."

"What did you do?" Peter asked, smiling. The staff was surprised he was talking to the patient.

"Muscled him good, the son-of-a-bitch, and I had enough juice for more too if they didn't stop me. Do you blame me?"

"Me?" Peter laughed. "Well, back on the streets, I'd do what you did. I'd want to kick his ass all over hell." The staff turned away laughing at Peter's street level approach. "But since I'm off the streets now, I'd think about it first. Getting myself locked up would leave him an open field with her, and I think I'm smarter than he is. I'm not handing her over to him so easy." The man looked at Peter; Peter smiled. "I'd hope I wouldn't get mad. I'd get even."

The man smiled. "You're alright, Doc. You've been there. You got a woman who gets to you where you live. You understand. Don't get mad, get even." He chuckled. "Yeah, like I should slash all four of those great new tires he just put on. He'd have to work so much overtime to replace them, he might as well become a priest for all the women he'd have time for."

Peter smiled. "Sounds like community service to me." The staff broke out into laughter. Steve smiled as he watched Peter.

"Oh Doc, thanks. I like you," the man said. "You know what life's about." He stood up.

Peter laughed. "Sure do. And if you mess up my great work on your face, I'll add a few lumps myself the next time you're in here."

The man laughed. "It's a deal." He extended his hand to Peter.

Peter shook it. "Good luck out there."

The man winked. "And you and your woman, too."

Steve came over. "What got into you?"

Peter looked at him and shrugged. "Every now and then my street blood surfaces."

Steve laughed. "Got time for coffee?"

"Boy, I could use some," Peter accepted. They sat in the doctor's lounge relaxing before signing out.

"Sunshine's been busy, hasn't she? You've had a lot of time on your hands."

Peter smiled. "How are things with you and Debbie?"

"Balanced. I'm sharing her with the weightlifter right now."

Peter looked at him. "And that doesn't bother you?"

"Not really," Steve answered. "Why?"

"That's a very sophisticated attitude. I sometimes wonder if I'll ever get used to being civilized."

Steve laughed. "You see life too simply, Pete. Mess with my woman and I'll mess with your face doesn't work anymore, not since the braless lesbians told women they belonged to themselves." Steve laughed. "I'm kidding, Pete, but in a way, I'm not. We've got to accept the fact that if our women are out in the world, some guy is watching her ass when she walks and guessing the rest of her dimensions. It's the price they paid for being set free. There's nothing we can do about it. Besides, you're one of the lucky ones. Sunshine is committed to you. You can sleep nights. Its guys like me who have to worry where our next meal will come from who have it tough," Steve teased.

*****

Jeneil wasn't in when Peter got home. He didn't like it. "Sunset was over an hour ago," he said, taking the dinner container to the kitchen and washing it along with some glasses. He heard the door open.

"Peter, I'm home," Jeneil called. He didn't answer. She came to the kitchen. "Hi," she said, kissing his cheek then going to the bedroom to put her purse away.

That's it, he thought, hi, not even sorry I'm late. "I hate civilized," he said to himself, drying his hands. He walked to the bedroom. She was writing in her notebook. Leaning against the door, he watched her. She was glowing and completely absorbed in what she was writing. She never even looked up. He wanted to take the notebook and throw it against the wall. "Jeneil, aren't you late?"

"I guess…I'm sorry about that…," she began.

"No, you're not," he shouted. "No, you're not at all. You come marching in here, say hi and go to the notebook. Don't sell me this sorry business. I'm not buying it. It's just more civilized noise."

She stared at him. "Peter, I didn't say when I'd be home, did I?"

"Jeneil, sunset was over an hour ago. What the hell is he painting by? Street lights?"

"We got to talking." Peter turned quickly and left the room. "Peter…," she said, following him.

"Drop it, Jeneil. You won't be able to explain it to me, I promise you that. Go back to your notebook."

"I'm really sorry, Peter. I'm not handling all this very well. Things are changing for me," she said, smiling.

"No kidding. Tell me about it," he said sarcastically.

She stopped smiling. "No," she said. "No, I don't think I will."

Peter stayed sitting on the sofa and Jeneil stayed in the bedroom. Beginning to cool off, he got up and went back to the bedroom. She was lying across the bed writing in the notebook. He sighed. She was a different Jeneil. She lacked conscience. She was self-absorbed.

Entering the room, he stopped near the bed. "Jeneil, I don't want you to go back to Danzieg's."

"I can't do that," she said quietly, never looking up.

"Why not?"

"I just can't."

"You can't or you don't want to."

She closed the notebook and sat up. "Fine, I don't want to. No. Make trouble from that. Is that what you want to hear?" she snapped.

"I want to hear what you're really feeling, not polite words."

"No, Peter, you're looking for trouble. You're looking for something to be jealous about. You have this idea that all men are out for only one thing. You worry that I'm such an airhead, I can be seduced by any man who decides that I meet his primal needs."

"Oh, now you tell me primal needs don't exist."

"The argument isn't about primal."

"Tell me Tony didn't happen."

"There it is." She stood up. "There it is."

"Yes, there it is, Jeneil. It happened, didn't it? You didn't handle that. You didn't even see it coming. Tell me not to worry."

"Peter, it isn't like that with Robert and me."

"Bullshit, Jeneil. He's half naked and you're not much better off. You're in the glow of the sunset and he gets intense. Tell me that's not volatile and I'll call it bullshit again," Peter said hotly.

Jeneil paced. "Peter, when a woman comes to you for help at work, is she in danger from you?"

"No."

"Then why can't you give Robert the same benefit of the doubt."

"Get real, sweetheart. When a woman comes into the hospital she's usually sick and just wants to feel better, and doctors are there trying to figure out how. Your situation is not the same. You're both healthy and putting yourselves in the middle of magic land. Really, it's too much fiction."

She looked at him. "Peter, what are you worried about? That he'll try something or that I'll give in?" He looked at her, stymied by the question. She raised her eyebrows. "Well, no answer? Maybe the issue here is really about trust." She walked past him and out of the room.

His grandfather's words came to his mind. How can you teach trust if you don't understand it or feel it? "No," he said, sitting on the bed, "it's not that simple." He remembered the sparrow who hopped near Jeneil and the way the bird's parents were trying to warn it. "It's not about trust, Grandfather, it's about protection. The cat's in the greenhouse, I can feel it. I knew Jeneil wouldn't hurt the sparrow. I don't know that Danzieg won't hurt the songbird." He walked out of the bedroom. Jeneil was standing near the cassette player. She pushed the play button, undoing her hair and letting it fall loosely, and she sighed.

"Jeneil." She didn't turn around or answer. "Remember that day in the park a sparrow got close to you and the birds in the trees were really making noise. That's what my noise is all about."

She turned around slowly. "Well then the issue is still trust, isn't it? You don't trust my judgment in this. Peter, I can't hide from every situation that you see danger in. Can I? Robert, without knowing it, is supplying some pieces for me, important pieces. His struggle seems similar to mine. I need Robert right now. It isn't physical and it's far from primal. I'm sure of that much. Primal has strong indications. I understand that you worry about me and I understand that you want to protect me, but I'm a woman, your woman, not your daughter. I'm going to change for bed."

Peter stood in the living room. He shook his head. His grandfather was wrong about training people like songbirds. Birds had better instincts. He shook his head again. "Primal has strong indications," he repeated her words. Try telling that to rape victims who came into the hospital, women on dates who thought they had the situation controlled. Tell it to the experienced hooker who missed the primal indications of a John off center from coke. They had more experience than her and they missed the strong primal indications. He rubbed the back of his neck then his forehead. What was it Chang? What were the vibrations? Was that what he was worried about? Was he protecting her or was he remembering that they started out as friends, too. Good friends who got closer. Who was he trying to protect, him or her?

The subject hung between them like a grey mist, each not seeing the other clearly. Peter tried to ignore the vibrations but their life was made off-center from it. Situations that normally wouldn't have touched them became awkward and irritated. Each tried to keep peace and the effort only caused more tension between them. Peter was beginning to wear down from it. He wondered if it might be wiser to move back to the dorm before real damage was done. Each time he thought about doing that he reminded himself that it would only put her into Danzieg's hands even more. He stayed, feeling more and more like an intruder.

Five

Steve and Peter got on the elevator together. Peter felt tired. It wasn't even lunch time and he was exhausted. He leaned up against the back of the elevator and closed his eyes. Steve studied him. "Is everything okay?" he asked. Peter nodded. Three interns and a resident got on the next floor.

"She's a real sweetheart, that one. I'd mess up my reports deliberately if I could be sure she'd be the one to help me," one of the interns said. "I keep trying to ask her out, but every time I'm near her, she's all business."

"Who?" Steve asked, curious.

"The girl in Records." Peter's eyes opened, his jaw tightened. Why not, he thought; join the crowd, line up.

The resident smiled. "Her name is Jeneil. Fits her, doesn't it? She's different, but don't waste your time asking her out."

"Why?" the intern asked.

"I did last week. She's got someone in her life and it's serious," the resident explained.

"Oh shit, is that what she said?" the intern asked, sounding disappointed. "I was hoping that was just crazy gossip. She's really nice."

The resident nodded. "I didn't even mind being rejected. Geez, her eyes nearly melted my stethoscope. I wonder what she's like under all that quiet refinement. Mmm, makes my blood pressure rise."

Peter's jaw hurt from clenching it. This all began to drain on a guy, he thought. What the hell was this? Where were these guys before he showed up? What did she do that made guys get like this?

The elevator stopped, the door opened and everyone fidgeted, looking at each other and grinning as Jeneil got on with a man in a suit jacket and designer blue jeans. Peter guessed him to be close to his own age, maybe a little older.

"Thanks for your patience in digging these reports out," the man said to Jeneil.

"It wasn't too difficult," she answered.

"We usually don't handle accident cases in our law office, but this is a friend of the family."

"You work in your family's law office?" she asked, making conversation.

"Yes, we're all lawyers. No one has been anything else for generations."

She smiled. "Like some families are in the restaurant or laundry business for generations, I guess."

The man laughed. "I guess so. That's an odd analogy and I find it odd that you work here."

"Oh really," she said, not wanting anymore conversation.

"You don't add up to a clerk, you know." He smiled at her.

"You've been a lawyer too long. You're super suspicious." She smiled benignly.

"Oh no? Look at you, a linen suit, a real leather purse the size of a continent, and my guess is perfume, French at a hundred dollars a sniff."

"I get my cousin's hand-me-downs."

"Sure you do," he grinned and spoke in French. Jeneil turned her head quickly staring at him, shocked by his words.

Steve watched with growing interest. Something was being revealed here. Who was this woman? She did know the finer things.

Peter was annoyed; he could spot a pickup, especially on his woman.

The lawyer smiled. "Ah, the lady knows French, too."

"Remember that you said lady," Jeneil said icily.

"Do I get an answer to my question?" the lawyer persisted.

Steve smiled and wondered. She had a quick wit. The thought triggered a memory from somewhere about someone.

Jeneil looked at the lawyer. She said something in Gallic, smiling sweetly.

"What language was that?" the lawyer asked, laughing.

"It was Gallic," she said in an Irish dialect. "I just said that my dear old dad came from Dublin and he told me that if a man ever asked me that question, he was no gentleman and I was to kick him in the shin, which is a definite no."

Steve kept wondering. She seemed so familiar all of a sudden. Did he know her from somewhere? Was that why she didn't like him? The doctors on the elevator laughed lightly, except Peter.

The lawyer raised his eyebrows. "How come you didn't kick my shin?" He smiled, staring into her eyes sexily.

Jeneil smiled. "Oh, but my father was a simple man, you see," she explained, continuing in the Irish dialect. "He never thought a gentleman lawyer would ever say that to a lady, and he didn't know that in America, if I kicked your shin, you'd probably sue me for assault and battery. Can I have you arrested for asking your question?"

The lawyer laughed. "That's a highly involved legal question. You'll need a lawyer." The elevator doors opened. "What are you doing tonight?" he asked as they stepped off the elevator. All the doctors followed, smiling and watching the two walk toward the records department.

Peter stopped and Steve stopped, too. "What's wrong?" Steve asked.

"I need to fix my shoe," Peter said. "I'll catch up with you."

Steve walked away then turned around to see Peter watching Jeneil as she stood near the entrance to Records with the lawyer. Her back was almost completely toward Peter. He leaned against a beam. Steve watched Peter with deep interest. He could tell Peter was annoyed and he studied Peter as Peter watched Jeneil. What was he doing? He thought Peter had to fix his shoe. Why was she so familiar all of a sudden? He'd seen her before and she sounded familiar, that's it. That quiet awareness.

The lawyer reached into his pocket and handed Jeneil a business card. She took it. He touched her face lightly with his hand and smiled, chucking her chin gently. He smiled and winked. Steve could see the anger on Peter's face. "Holy Shit, Pete, what are you so angry about?" Steve asked, watching. The guy wasn't hurting her. Man, Peter was always defending that girl. What was with him? She could handle herself. She was quick and she always had an answer. She reminded Steve of Sunshine. The thought made Steve stand up straight. He remembered the call about the medical card during the poker game. "That's it, that's it," he said. "That's crazy."

The lawyer walked away. Jeneil turned, tore up the business card and tossed it in the trash. She looked up, surprised to see that Peter was standing there, watching her. Peter smiled at her. Steve watched them look at each other. Jeneil smiled, blew a kiss to him, and walked into Records.

Steve stood near a beam in total shock. The girl in Records was Sunshine! No, it couldn't be. He watched as Peter walked toward him. He'd seen that look on Peter's face for weeks now every time he dealt with Sunshine. It was her, but that was impossible. She wasn't Chinese. She wasn't even Asian. She couldn't have him getting up at five-thirty in the morning. That was impossible. She wasn't his type. But Peter lived with her. Then where the hell did Tony fit in? And the whole James Gang? What was she running, a commune? He had to be wrong. Watching as Peter caught up to him, he looked at Peter. He wasn't wrong.

"What's the matter?" Peter asked, seeing Steve's expression.

"Uh, nothing, I need to eat lunch I think. I'm imagining things, I hope." They walked to the cafeteria together. Steve didn't speak. He was afraid to ask Peter about the girl.

"What a creep that guy was," Peter said. "She never did anything to encourage that. She should've told him to go to hell."

"You're always defending her, Pete. Any reason?" Peter looked at Steve quickly.

"Yes, she's a nice kid and I like her." Peter was uncomfortable. He knew he should tell Steve. Now was the time.

Steve was afraid of what his gut was telling him. He was afraid to ask Peter if she was Sunshine. He didn't want her to be Sunshine. She wasn't what he had imagined. He had to be wrong.

"You're awfully quiet," Peter said.

Steve looked at him. He felt hurt. The girl was under his nose all along. He began to understand why it was a secret.

Peter studied Steve as he handed his coffee to him. "Steve, listen…."

"Hey guys, got room for another here?" Dan Monetti sat down.

He had to tell him soon, Peter thought, wondering if Steve had seen what happened at the elevators.

*****

Peter noticed Steve was different every time they saw each other after that. Steve would say very little when they were together and Peter felt sure that he knew. Late in the afternoon, they got on the elevator together. "Steve, I want to tell you something. I've been meaning to for a while." Steve looked at him. Peter noticed a difference in him, something in his eyes. The elevator doors opened and they were surprised to see Jeneil standing there. She stepped on and stood near the door, clutching her purse to her.

"Been to see Tony, Jeneil?" Steve asked. Peter caught something in his tone. Jeneil turned and nodded, then turned again. "How is he today, Jeneil?" Steve asked. Peter didn't like the way Steve said her name.

"He's doing fine, but then you know that, don't you?" Jeneil sensed hostility in Steve's voice and it puzzled her.

"Jeneil, I hear that you have someone in your life and it's serious. Is that true?"

Peter looked at him. Jeneil turned around cautiously. "Yes," she said quietly.

"Someone I know? Let me guess, it's not an intern. Gosh, they're all disappointed. Is it someone in The James Gang? The one called Jack likes you a lot." Jeneil was stunned;

Peter could see it. Steve didn't stop. "And gosh, there's the rest of the group. That's quite a crowd."

"Steve!" Peter said, almost choking.

"Then, of course, there's Tony." Steve looked at Peter. "She's been a ray of sunshine in his life."

"Steve!" Peter said strongly.

"Wait, listen. No, Pete, I don't think it's any of those guys." Steve looked at Jeneil where she stood immobilized. "No, Jeneil likes secrets. I know one other person full of secrets, so it must be Peter. Am I right, Jeneil? Oh, my guess is right, isn't it, and now you don't have any more secrets. Will someone explain to me why you two are keeping your relationship quiet? What's the big deal? Why does it need to be a big secret? That's a little stupid, isn't it?"

"So people with the IQ of a cabbage and think they're too, too funny, would feel free to trash what we have, like they do in their own lives," Jeneil spit out. The doors opened and she got off quickly, not looking back.

"Am I bleeding at the neck?" Steve asked. Peter stared at him, smoldering. "I could have sworn she severed my jugular."

"I'd like to sever your head you son-of-a-bitch. Shit, Steve, why the hell did you do that?"

"I know why it was a secret from me. She's not crazy about some of your friends, Pete."

"Damn it. That's not the whole of it, believe me. She's come a long way and you just set her back. You were insulting, and I don't appreciate it at all. I'd like to take a swing at you for some of it. You know better about her."

"Don't sweat it, Pete. She couldn't stand me before anyway."

"Steve, Barbara Prescott is a friend of hers."

Steve looked at him, surprised. "Oh shit."

"Yeah and she sang a different song about you to Jeneil."

"Oh shit, I'm sorry. You're lucky she didn't dump you when she found out we were friends."

"I wish you'd told me that you knew instead of pulling that. You're not funny, man," Peter said angrily. "Not funny at all."

"You're right, I was insulting. I guess I was feeling like you guys had made a fool of me, but that didn't give me the right to do what I just did. I don't know what it is with her and me. There are sparks when we're near each other, and she's been sending me dinners.

Shit, I messed it up with her again. I can't believe she's Sunshine. Peter, she's not even Asian."

"So I've noticed."

"This is the same girl, right? Tiel's and up at five-thirty to see her?" Peter smiled and nodded. Steve shook his head. "I can't believe it. I just can't believe it, you and the choir girl. I can't believe it, man; the dinners, the change in you. And she handles you! She keeps up with you! I can't believe that especially."

"You're wrong about her." Peter smiled.

"The leather jacket. You've been talking about children. Man, I didn't think she even knew where they came from. And all the while, she's got the Chinese Stud falling off a mountain. Incredible. I've never been this wrong. She still doesn't look like your type, Pete."

"She's my type, Steve. She's my type," Peter said quietly.

"Well, son-of-a-bitch." Steve shook his head in disbelief. "Can you apologize to her for me? Will it even help? I really don't want her mad at me. I don't understand what happens between her and me, I don't."

"She'll think you're the greatest if you'll just keep us a secret around here."

"I really don't want Sunshine mad at me. Hell Pete, I expected your girl and me to be friends. Jeneil and I can't even stand to be on the same planet together." Steve paused then laughed. "I do love one thing about her; she wanders around here totally confusing the gossip line." Steve laughed again. "She's something else. She must be in love with you. Jeneil is Sunshine. Whew, I need a tranquilizer. I'm sorry, Pete. I was mad at you for not telling me and that sounds the most ridiculous, doesn't it?"

"I've been meaning to for a while."

*****

Peter went to the phone booth when he knew Jeneil would be home. He was concerned. With the Danzieg situation tearing at him, he wondered what this would do to the strain between them. "Hi," he said when Jeneil answered. "I'll be working until seven. I figured you'd be at Danzieg's when I got home. I wanted to get to you about Steve."

"Thanks, but he got to me just fine on his own."

"He was hurt. He felt that we'd made a fool of him."

"He did that on his own. Don't blame me."

"It's my fault partly. I should have told him long before this really. I can understand his feelings. He's sorry about what he said about all the guys. Actually, I made him sorry. It made me want to hit him and I've never felt like that before. We've always been good friends, always." Jeneil could sense the strain this was putting on Peter; he was between her and Steve. "I wanted to hit that creep lawyer, too. I think King Arthur was lucky he had only Lancelot to worry about."

"I'm not Guinevere, Peter. You've learned diplomacy from Steve, too. That's insulting. You're creating the worry for yourself."

"Jeneil, I don't want to fight, that isn't why I called. I hate the way things have been between us lately. I can't believe me in this. When Chang was in the uncivilized streets, he never fought over a woman, never." Jeneil smiled as she listened silently. "I promise I won't say another word about Danzieg. Chang is new at this civilization business and the rules don't come clear to him. His women have had to be his and his only."

"Peter, get this clear to Chang, I'm not anyone else's but I can't live on a leash. Not now especially. I'm finding pieces, Peter, and it feels terrific. I can't give it up, not for anybody."

"Baby, I love you," he said, "and not on a leash, believe me."

"I love you, too, Peter. I really do. I'll be home right after sunset tonight. I promise."

"For me?" he asked, smiling hopefully.

"No, for us."

"That's even better."

"I'll see you later then, Peter. I'm glad you called, really. Chang has impressed me yet again. I'll see you later." Peter replaced the receiver, rested his head on his hand then went back on duty.

*****

Jeneil arrived earlier at Robert Danzieg's than he did. She sat in her car reviewing items to be done during the week. Robert drove up and parked in his spot. Walking up to her car, he knocked on the window, scaring her.

"Does living in a warehouse rattle your nerves?" she asked as they walked into the building together.

"Not at all. Why?"

"You don't have any neighbors. The building is so huge, it has a hollow sound."

"Jeneil, Jeneil, when will you learn to come out of the great mass of humanity and allow your own muse to work?"

"But I like people," she answered.

"So do I, but not surrounding me. You're right into them up to your elbows. When will you allow yourself to expand?"

"I hadn't realized I was so narrow."

"You're not mentally, but your life is. Open up and experience the world."

"I don't experience too easily. I'm more of an observer, a spectator. And the world needs an audience, too. Doesn't it? That's how I experience things, I observe them." Robert unlocked the door to his living quarters, and Jeneil put her purse and jacket on a chair.

"I'm talking about tasting life and unleashing that force within you."

"I'm tasting life and experiencing it at my own speed. Being overpowered unnerves me. It makes me feel too consumed."

Robert shook his head and smiled. "How do I wake you up?"

"I'm awake, Robert. Why do you keep insisting that I'm not?"

"Because I sense it, Jeneil. I can sense a strong pulse from somewhere inside of you, like distant jungle drums."

"Jungle drums?" Jeneil laughed. "Robert, I think what you see in me is a reflection. You are the jungle drums type."

"I am and that's why I hear it in you."

"Bongos maybe," she laughed again, "but not jungle drums. Do you want me to change now?"

"Why not? I can't get you to change any other way." Jeneil returned wearing a smock that matched the silk dress. Robert looked up from the canvas. "What's this new addition to your outfit?"

"Just a top for when you're not painting me."

"Did Peter design it?" he asked. Jeneil looked at him. "Uh-oh, is Peter raging?"

"No, Peter doesn't rage."

"But Peter is the 'Me Tarzan, you Jane' type."

"Which means?" Jeneil asked, challenging Robert.

"You're his woman." Robert graveled his voice.

"I've chosen to be his woman. He didn't use force." She grinned. "Stop trying to cover him in chauvinism, Robert."

Robert smiled. "Loyalty looks pretty good on you. What did he say? Cover up that body, woman, it's mine." He graveled his voice again, teasing her.

Jeneil gave him a look of warning. "I find Peter's approach to life very refreshing. He has the ability to put aside the trappings and get to the essential."

"Ooo, that sounds sexy," Robert teased. She gave him another look and thumbed through a magazine. "Is he your first?"

She looked up quickly. "I thought we had settled the rule about questions like that."

"Jeneil, loosen up. What's the big deal? People talk about their sex lives, it's mentally healthy."

"Humanity lacks reverence. We trample things too easily. Everything becomes too commonplace."

"You're sexually inhibited."

"Sticks and stones," she answered in a little girl voice.

He laughed. "Jeneil, just tell me. Do you enjoy sex?"

"Robert, you once said I was Victorian. Men didn't ask ladies a question like that in those days."

"Jeneil, this is the eighties."

"The eighties," she mocked, "the high tech age of advancement, everything at the speed of sound. We're losing our humanity. In the Victorian era, a real man would have had the intelligence and sensitivity to use his intuition. He could deal with the mystique of the covered body."

"And he ended up marrying a refrigerated lady," Robert commented, smiling.

"A lesser man maybe," Jeneil answered. "Besides, I don't think there are any refrigerated ladies. They just haven't met a real man."

"Ooo Jeneil, you go for the…," she looked at him warningly, "…throat. Peter's your first. I can tell. When will you try your second?"

"I don't even understand that question," she said, scowling deliberately.

"You're certainly not going to stop at one are you?" Robert asked, surprised. "Jeneil, expand and grow. Don't you listen to what I say to you?"

"Robert, when our souls communicate, I really understand you, but there are times when your earthly quality takes hold and we lose each other completely."

Robert put down his brush and walked over to her, putting his arms around her. "You're so cute. How do I wake you up?" He kissed her cheek and hugged her. The bell at the outer door rang and Robert left to answer it.

Jeneil shook her head. She was back to being cute again. Robert wanted to wake her up and Peter hoped she'd never wake up. She must project some strange image of a dream state or semi-consciousness. She laughed at the thought.

Robert returned with another man. "Have a seat Dennis. I'll get some drinks. Jeneil and I were having a discussion about sex," Robert said, smiling at her. "Jeneil, this is Dennis Blair, director of the Summer Stock Playhouse. Jeneil is sitting for me, Dennis. A lite beer for you?"

"Fine," Dennis answered.

"Wine for you, Jeneil?"

"Fruit juice or water, thanks."

"Jeneil's a teetotaler," Robert teased.

"Jeneil's allergic," she answered.

"Really, what would happen?" Robert asked.

"Hives and itchy skin."

"Sound like something you'd want to paint, Robert?" Dennis asked. "I'd get the girl her fruit juice if I were you." Dennis winked at Jeneil.

"One grapefruit juice it is," Robert said, disappearing..

"You don't look like a model," Dennis commented casually.

"Should I be offended?" Jeneil asked.

"No, I shouldn't do that. I didn't mean…too much type casting." Dennis laughed, shaking his head.

"Actually, I'm not a model," she answered, smiling. "I'm sitting for this one painting."

"Well, have you signed her up yet, Dennis? She needs the experience of the stage," Robert said, returning.

"Why?" Dennis asked.

"She's bottled up. She needs to project herself into other personalities and situations."

Jeneil shook her head. "Robert, before I sat for you, I was happy and well adjusted. Now I'm developing insecurities."

"Actually," Dennis continued, "I'm here to recruit people. I hoped I could persuade Robert to come and oversee the art on our new production. My art person broke his leg water skiing, and vacations have eaten into my community volunteers. So if you have time and can move a paintbrush, I'd really welcome your help, Jeneil."

"Put her on stage," Robert interrupted jokingly. Jeneil ignored him.

"If Robert ever finishes with me, I'll have some time. I never thought about helping out. I've always sat in the audience."

"She's a born observer, Dennis," Robert teased. Jeneil made a face at him. "Hey, it's sunset time, Miss Turtle. Let's go study you in your natural habitat. Come on, Dennis, come watch the butterfly emerge."

"Well, which is she, a turtle or a butterfly?" Dennis asked.

"She's both, an exasperating combination. She hides and struggles to be free," Robert chuckled as they walked to the west window. "Here my beauty." Robert took down Jeneil's hair, fluffing it in spots. Dennis stayed to one side, watching. "Look at that, Dennis. Look at that. Now off with the top, Jeneil." Robert reached to undo the tie to her smock as she held it to her.

"No, I'm not sitting right now, only when I'm sitting."

"I may kill Peter," Robert said. "Sweetheart, I need to see the colors of the sunset reflect off your dress and your skin."

"Oh," Jeneil said, and undid the tie.

"Stand in place, Jeneil. Face the sunset," Robert ordered, taking the smock from her. "Behold my sun goddess, Dennis." Jeneil folded her arms. "Jeneil," Robert sighed, "forget we're here. Walk into the sun. Unfold those arms, please."

Jeneil tried to concentrate on the sun. "Shouldn't sun goddesses have blonde or red hair?"

"No, my sun goddess doesn't disappear into the sun; she makes love to it and still keeps her identity while on fire from it." Jeneil looked at him, surprised. "Isn't this another person altogether?" Robert asked Dennis

"You're right," Dennis agreed, "she emerges."

"Now radiate that missing jolt, Jeneil," Robert said.

"What jolt?" Jeneil asked.

"Take the last step and give yourself to the sun."

"You've lost me, Robert."

"What the hell did Peter call it? He saw something missing too, but he named it." Robert paced and studied.

"Paint around it," Jeneil replied.

"Sassy little brat tonight," Robert held her chin in his hands and smiled, "but a beautiful brat. Jungle drums, Jeneil."

"Boy, Robert, you've jumped into this with full speed," Dennis observed.

"It's alive, Dennis. She's intense, but she locks it up."

"Then paint me surrealistically," Jeneil suggested.

Dennis laughed. "You've got a smart model."

Robert studied her. "Jeneil, you might have something there. I haven't done much along that line. It would be an experience."

"Good, does that mean practice and study are finished and the work will begin?"

Robert grinned. "You'd make a terrible muse, Jeneil. They motivate by life and gentleness, inspiring great performances. I've never met a sassy muse."

"Its past sunset Robert, would you mind if I leave?" Jeneil asked in an apologetic tone.

"Does Peter have you punching a time clock?"

Jeneil slipped her smock on. "Was anything accomplished here tonight Robert?"

"Does he want a report card, too?"

"I'm asking Robert. Me. I don't think I'm the model for you. I'm just not working out."

"I'm holding the brush, Jeneil. I'll decide." Robert and Dennis followed her to the center room.

"Well, how can we help Mr. Blair at the playhouse if we're spending all our time at the window?"

"Jeneil, please call me Dennis. Your youth has made me feel ancient at 31 as it is. Don't make me feel carbon dated by calling me Mr. Blair and I'll push Robert here to finish if I can have your help at the playhouse."

"Now that's a deal." She extended her hand to him. Jeneil changed quickly. Picking up her jacket and purse, she went to Robert. "When shall I be here again?"

"Are you going to cooperate next time?"

"You're blaming me?" she teased.

He smiled. "Yes. Ask Peter what was missing and I'll see you Thursday."

"Goodnight then," Jeneil said as she left.

"She's different," Dennis commented when he was sure she had gone.

"She is," Robert agreed, "and she grows on you the more you have her around."

"Is that why you're dragging your feet on the project?"

"No," Robert answered. "I keep hoping she'll come in here with the quality I saw in her once. It's locked inside of her and she knows it. I'm certain of it. She doesn't trust me yet, I guess. She'll give just so much to me and no more."

"Uh-oh, Robert. It sounds like you're accepting the challenge of the job and the woman, too."

Robert smiled. "You want her for your kid sister until you get too close and you hear the jungle drums then realize she's no kid and your sister never made you feel that good."

"Are those her drums or yours?" Dennis laughed.

"Oh, they're hers. I knew she was one hell of a sexy woman."

"How did you know that?"

"You should see the guy she lives with, he hovers over her like a prehistoric man. He's found something in her that makes him watch for thieves."

"She lives with a man?" Dennis asked, surprised. "I've really done too much type casting."

Robert nodded. "And she's devoted to him, the lucky bastard."

*****

Jeneil smiled as Peter drove in the lot. She waited for him. "You worked later than you expected to," she said as he walked over to her.

"Emergency surgery," he said, stopping near here. He noticed the smock. "Why did you bring the dress home?"

"I didn't, it's a smock I wear to cover up when Robert's not painting me."

Peter looked at her surprised and then he smiled. She moved closer to him and kissed him warmly. He responded gently, wanting to hold her tight.

"Let's get upstairs," he said, pulling away. She nodded and slipped her arm into his.

Six

Peter walked into the doctor's lounge from the parking area whistling.

Steve watched him. "It's five-thirty man. You sound like it's your day off. People will get suspicious," he teased.

Peter smiled. "I don't even care about that today."

"She wasn't upset about me knowing then?"

"I was planning on telling you. She expected it, just not the way you handled it, but she'll deal with it. She's quite a person when you get to know her."

"So I hear from all the interns and half the residents," Steve said. Peter shot him a warning look. "I didn't mean anything by that," Steve insisted then sighed. "I hope our friendship can survive her. I wish I didn't know about her." Changing his attitude, he smiled. "She's been sending out strong female vibes around here since being with you."

Peter shook his head. "It's not the guys here I worry about."

Steve looked at him. "Trouble?"

"I don't know." Peter smiled. "It's okay with us again."

"What, another guy?"

"Yeah, and what bothers me the most is that he's on her level."

"She has doubts about you two?"

"No, I don't know. She's hard to read lately, but I don't think so. She claims not anyway. Things are just different between us."

Steve sipped his coffee. "Well, if she's purring for you again then blow the sucker out of the water."

"Life isn't that simple with us. With her. She has a lot of friends who are men."

Steve laughed. "Yeah, but I've never had anyone cuddling and purring for me. That whole James Gang would get me rattled, especially Tony and Jack. I've seen Jack talking to her in the hallway. I'd watch him."

"At the moment he's not my worry. There's one in particular I'd like to spread all over the street."

Steve laughed. "Well, the Dragon Kid is walking in civilized. Tough country road, huh?"

Peter gave a half smile. "The rules are different. I wouldn't even call the game civilized. At least on the streets I knew where the hell the shit was. Nobody wasted time jivin' you or themselves. This was the rule. You knew it. I knew it. Break it and you paid, clean and simple. In the civilized world it seems all jive and head games, and that's uncivilized to me. Jeneil is always saying that great civilizations had order and order means rules, doesn't it?"

Steve stared at him. "You talk about civilization and cultural stuff. You talk about children. Man, where's the Pete I knew? He talked about fast women, medicine, and a good beer."

Peter laughed. "He met a lady and fell off the side of the mountain."

Steve laughed, too. "And she's right for you?"

"Like breathing," Peter said seriously.

Steve shook his head. "It still strangles me when I think about it and hearing her name shakes me. She's not the Sunshine I pictured."

Peter smiled and finished his coffee. "That's because you haven't gotten close enough to her yet."

"That's something you shouldn't count on, Pete. She and I will always have a distance between us. A miracle between us would be peace." Steve smiled and they headed for the OR.

*****

Jeneil looked up from her book when she heard the crash to see Robert staring at the easel that lay sprawled on the floor. The painting had slid across the room. Walking to it, he picked it up, held it by one end and put his foot through it.

"What are you doing!?" Jeneil all but screamed, going over to him. "Look what you've done!" she said, staring at the torn canvas in shock. His sullenness was beginning to wear on her. "Robert, what's the matter with you lately? You've just ruined hours of work. I'm finished with this project."

Jeneil left the room to change. She returned carrying her things. Robert sat on the divan with a beer, studying the mutilated painting lying on the floor in front of him.

"Robert, I'm sorry but I've reached my limit. This was the final blow. I won't be back," she informed him quietly.

"It's just as well," he said, not looking up. "You've never cooperated."

"How can you say that?" she asked, almost shrilling.

"It isn't here, Jeneil. You have never given it to me and you know what I'm talking about. That's the exasperating part." He pushed at the painting with his foot sending it sliding across the floor. Jeneil watched. He ran his fingers through his hair, tousling it. Jeneil's heart turned over. She knelt down in front of him.

"It is really that important?" she asked quietly.

He lifted his head and looked at her. "You mean you're at least willing to admit that you know what's missing?"

She nodded. "I think so."

"Then what the hell is the holdout for?" he asked sharply.

"It's too personal for one thing, and if it is what I think, then I don't understand how you could paint it. I can't sustain that for a sitting."

"What Jeneil? Sustain what?" he pleaded.

She closed her eyes. "Cosmic." Her answer was barely audible.

"What's that?"

"It's something I do. Simplified, it's like meditation but more deep and intense."

"Why couldn't you sustain it?" he asked curiously.

"The atmosphere is wrong to begin with, and the intensity is so great, the energy release would make it impossible for me to sit still."

"I've got to see this. That's what Peter said was missing, too. I remember it now."

"Robert, I can't. It's too, too personal. I couldn't."

"But Peter saw it," he argued.

"That was a special moment and it was very brief."

"Then how the hell could I pick up on it at the gallery?"

"You saw me shortly after an intense experience," she explained. "I still find it hard to believe that you even noticed it."

"Jeneil, it throbbed like a pulse. I saw it. I felt it. It was muffled, but I thought that was just your reserve."

"That's incredible," she answered.

"How did you achieve it? Drugs?"

"No, nothing like that, it's completely natural."

"Then how?"

"I connect to the elements surrounding me."

He looked at her blankly. "I don't get it. What elements and how do you connect to them?"

"I connect cosmically, Robert."

"To what?" he asked then raised his eyebrows understandingly. "To the sunset, Jeneil, you connect to the sun." He took her hands in his. "I knew it. I knew there was naturalness between you and the sunset. Jeneil, I want to see this. Please for all the reasons we've talked about in the past."

"Robert, I can't. How about painting me a day after a cosmic experience, like you saw me at the gallery."

"No, Jeneil. I was hoping to intensify what I saw at the gallery. I don't want it muffled."

"No, Robert, you're asking me to share the center of my being, the me that belongs to only me and no one else."

He put his hands gently on her neck. "Please Jeneil, I've seen this cosmic thing whispered in you. I've been trying to get it on canvas. It won't happen unless I hear the full volume. Please." He pulled her to him and held her. "I feel it, sweetheart. I feel it. I know it's sacred to you and I'll treat it that way. I promise." He kissed her temples gently. She felt the warmth of his arms, his closeness and intensity. She wanted to trust him.

Pulling away gently, she took his hand. "Let me think about it. It wouldn't be easy for me; I'd have to work up to it."

He smiled and gave her a lingering, gentle kiss. "That must be the jungle drums I hear. It's cosmic."

She smiled. "Robert, you project your own intensity and give me the credit. It's you, not me."

Studying her face, he smiled. "I've never thought of humility as being a fascinating and attractive quality. You wear that well, too."

She shook her head. "Robert, its truth, not humility. You insist on seeing more in me than there is."

He held her chin gently and smiled. "You're incredibly beautiful and I find you fascinating."

"Enough," she said, standing up. "Or I'll lose this humility you so generously see in me." He laughed as she opened the door. "I'll call you soon."

He nodded. "Very soon, please." She smiled and left.

*****

Peter noticed the quietness in her. It was different from the quietness when she wrote in her notebook. Her mind was hardly ever with them. He picked up a textbook and stretched out on the sofa. Jeneil came into the room so quietly it distracted him. She wandered in slowly and absentmindedly, her arms folded. She was too quiet, he thought as he watched her from over the book, pretending to read. Taking her small cassette player and a tape, she tossed a pillow to the floor and sat amongst the potted trees and figurines. She turned the music on. It was classical, soft and smooth. Sitting with her back against the wall, she closed her eyes. Sitting amongst the potted trees was something new to him, but a lot of what she did lately was new and different. He felt that she barely knew he was around. She had barely spoken at dinner and he sensed that she hadn't listened to what he had said. This was new since the last sitting at Danzieg's. Getting up quietly, he walked over to her and knelt on the floor near her. "Honey," he said softly. She opened her eyes quickly, startled by his voice.

"What?" she asked from what seemed like a great distance.

"What's wrong?" he asked, taking her hand.

"You surprised me. I didn't know you'd come over here."

"No, I mean, why are you sitting here like this?"

"I need to get in touch with myself, my feelings."

"Do you want to talk?" Peter noticed she withdrew her hand from his. He was really becoming concerned.

"Peter, I need some space right now," she said, not looking at him.

"How much space, baby? Should I go back to the dorm?"

"No."

"Then what?"

"Just leave me alone," she said without emotion.

He stood up and returned to the sofa. He didn't like this. Resting back, he picked up his book but the words were a blur. He was rattled. This wasn't cosmic, it was frightening. Her silence had him concerned. She stayed with her eyes closed listening to the music. Peter watched. The tape ended and she opened her eyes and rubbed her temples. She stood up and walked to the bedroom as quietly as she had entered the room. He sat there a while thinking then got up and walked to the bedroom. He got there in time to hear the telephone conversation end.

"I'll see you tomorrow, Robert. Yes, we'll go ahead with it."

Peter stood near the door as the shockwaves passed through him. She didn't need space from Robert? The question flashed like neon through his brain, but that's where it stayed as she passed by him with her robe over her arm.

"I'm going to bed. This week has been a drain on me. The extra meetings at the office have taken their toll. I'll be glad when Tony is finally well enough to be released and working there," she said, and continued past him.

Peter stayed standing by the door with his hands in his pockets. He had no thoughts and his feelings were mixed. He was still standing there when Jeneil returned. She stopped by him long enough to kiss his cheek and say good night. As she pulled back the covers to the bed, Peter wanted to remind her of their agreement that when another guy's kisses felt better to her, she was to tell him straight and fast, but the words scrambled up through his chest and stuck in his throat, choking him. He just swallowed hard as she got under the covers and turned off the lamp. He left, closing the door behind him.

Sitting on the sofa, Peter tried to sift through the thoughts passing through his mind. His thoughts were in opposition to each other making a clear decision impossible. As he rested his head back, he made one clear decision and that was to get things out in the open with Jeneil. If she was struggling between him and Robert, he intended to know for sure. After quieting his mind, he drifted off to sleep. Awaking an hour later, he got up, turned off the lights and stretched out on the sofa where he spent the rest of the night.

Jeneil jostled him awake at five. "Peter, you've spent the night on the sofa. Don't you have early surgery with Dr. Maxwell?" He laid there trying to collect his thoughts. "Peter, are you awake?"

"Yes, I'm awake. What time is it?"

"It's five."

He sat up. "Thanks for waking me," he said, standing up. He was tired. His body felt as if it was tied in knots.

She touched his face gently. "You're going to have a very long day. You look exhausted." Kissing him gently, she went to the kitchen. He watched her walk away, surprised by her tenderness toward him.

What the hell was happening, his mind asked of him.

She had breakfast prepared and lunch packed when he walked into the kitchen. She was almost her old self. Finishing breakfast quickly, he turned to leave. She touched his arm and asked him to hold her. Shocked, he readily put his arms around her, pulled her close to him and held her tightly.

"Jeneil, what's happening?"

"I've got to step beyond myself," she answered. "It isn't easy for me."

"I don't understand."

"Just hold me, Peter." She kissed him. It was her old kiss, warm and gentle. She pulled away. "You'd better go to work."

"I don't want to," and he pulled her closer and kissed her again.

She pulled herself away and smiled. "Go to work."

He shook his head. "You're never boring, honey," he said, going to the door thinking blue sky on top, green grass on the bottom."

*****

Jeneil was right. Peter had a difficult time. Emergencies were no problem, but the slow periods were the most difficult. He sat in the medical room behind the nurse's station with his head resting against the wall. Steve joined him and sat on a table.

"You look rough."

"I'm tired," Peter answered, keeping his eyes closed. "And I have the beginning of a headache."

Grace Barber, an LPN, walked in quickly trying to cover a sneeze. "I think I'm catching a cold. I have a sinus headache."

"Thanks for sharing the germs with us," Steve said.

"Well, I don't want to get them all over the desk." She returned to the station.

Steve looked up. "Hey Pete, here comes something that'll make you feel better."

Peter opened his eyes. "What?"

Steve nodded toward the nurse's station. Jeneil had arrived at the desk to deliver some material. Peter liked her in the black and yellow outfit she was wearing. She and Grace were talking. Peter watched as Jeneil walked behind the desk. Grace extended her hands to Jeneil who held each hand with her thumb and index finger.

"What the hell is she doing?" Steve asked, standing up to get a better look.

Peter stood up. "I don't know." They both watched. Shortly they heard Grace tell Jeneil that she could feel it working.

"That's unbelievable!" Grace smiled.

Peter and Steve walked over to them. Two other nurses joined them along with three interns.

"What are you two doing?" one nurse asked.

Grace smiled. "Jeneil is curing my headache using acupressure and its working, can you believe it?"

"By pinching her hands?" an intern asked.

"That's the pressure point controlling that part of the body," Jeneil answered. "But Grace has two problems, the headache and the swollen membranes." Jeneil released Grace's hands.

Grace moved her head. "I really feel better. Where did you learn that?"

"I'm interested in homeopathy," Jeneil answered. "Would you like to learn the points for your sinuses?"

"Sure," Grace said. "Show me."

Steve was standing near Peter. "You two must have some interesting times together," he whispered. Peter nudged him with his arm. Jeneil showed Grace some pressure points on her face and two on her hands.

"Let me try one I'm not sure would do much," and Jeneil stepped behind Grace, felt her spine near her shoulders and pressed using her knuckle.

"That did something, Jeneil. I felt that go through me."

"Then you're developing congestion in the bronchial area. You're probably going to get a cough with the cold," Jeneil commented.

"My throat does feel ticklish," Grace answered. "That's amazing." The doctors and nurses looked at each other.

Jeneil smiled. "How experimental do you feel? Would you like to try a natural remedy?"

"Yes," Grace said enthusiastically. Jeneil wrote something on a piece of paper and held it out for Grace. Steve reached for it, grabbing the paper. Jeneil held on tight, preventing him from taking it.

"What's in it?" Steve asked.

"Different things, but the main ingredient is the right thumb of an unbelieving neurosurgeon. Are you volunteering?" Everyone laughed. Peter watched the two of them.

Steve chuckled. "I'm not an unbeliever, just curious." Jeneil let him take the paper. "Do you really think mashed raw garlic, lemon juice, and honey will do anything?"

"That's what's wrong with you. You're so used to seeing people after an illness is chronic. This is for prevention. If it does nothing else, at least the garlic will keep people away from her and she won't be infectious." The nurses chuckled as Jeneil snapped the paper away from Steve and handed it to Grace.

Steve grinned mischievously. "Jeneil, Dr. Chang here has a headache. Can you cure it for him?" Steve stared at her challengingly.

"I know I can." Jeneil grinned and opened her purse. Taking out a small plastic bottle, she handed it to Steve.

"These are headache tablets," he said, taking the bottle.

"Yes, he should take two and see his doctor if it persists." Everyone laughed.

Steve looked at Jeneil, amused. "You're quick."

"I just see the advantages of both types of medicine," she answered. Steve grinned and tossed the bottle to Peter.

Dr. Sprague walked over to the group. "What's happening here?"

Steve looked at Jeneil and smiled. "Jeneil here just cured Grace's cold using acupressure."

"Acupressure?" Dr. Sprague asked, going to Jeneil. "Where have you learned acupressure?"

"It's a hobby of mine."

Dr. Sprague smiled. "That's very interesting. Do you know herbs?"

"Some of them."

"Acupressure is Chinese, isn't it?"

"Yes," Jeneil answered. Everyone looked at Peter.

"Don't look at me," Peter said. "I'm holding a bottle of headache tablets, remember. I don't know anything about acupressure."

"Don't get so defensive, Chang," Dr. Sprague laughed. "We wouldn't revoke your medical license if you did." Everyone laughed.

"I've got to get back to work," Jeneil said, picking up her things.

"We all do," Dr. Sprague said. He walked away with Jeneil, talking to her about herbs and acupressure. Peter walked into the medical room to take the tablets. He watched Steve staring after Jeneil and Dr. Sprague. Steve shook his head and went back to sit with Peter.

"Man, you've struck gold with her. She's got Dr. Sprague eating out of her hand. You should see him. He really is interested. She's going to be a great doctor's wife. You can really move in your career with a woman like that. I guess she is a smart move." Steve stood up and watched Jeneil with Dr. Sprague. Steve smiled as Jeneil got on the elevator smiling and Dr. Sprague walked away laughing. "Shit, she's good with him. Who would have thought the choir girl was a tiger underneath. She completely fooled me. How did you discover it?"

"Steve, we were friends. I didn't think career or wife or anything. It just happened."

"Then what a stroke of luck, and she's a firebrand, too. She didn't even back down from me. I like that. She's alive, isn't she?"

Peter smiled. "You just got a little closer, Steve."

Steve looked at him and laughed. "Geez, I'll be talking like the interns soon. Good thing they don't make you nervous."

Peter stood up and gathered the medical charts. "Just the one I mentioned."

"The one who's on her level?" Steve asked. Peter nodded. "You must be on her level. She's with you."

"Not like this guy. He's got it all, art, family background, style. All of it."

"Yeah, but you've got her," Steve reminded him.

"Will she wake up?"

"How long have you been together?"

"A couple of months."

"Man, mine lasted six months, and if I had lived with her, probably two weeks. Man, Jeneil's different."

"Don't I get any credit?" Peter smiled.

"Yes, you appreciate her." Steve laughed. "Come on, let's break for lunch and then tackle the reports."

"I'll meet you in the cafeteria. I want to return the headache tablets," Peter answered, grinning.

Steve smiled. "That's a bad habit, getting dessert before your meal." He held the door for Peter. "Tell her I'm impressed with her acupressure."

Peter knew Jeneil was covering the records department while everyone was at lunch. She didn't mind eating alone. He opened the door.

"What are you doing here?" she asked, surprised. Peter held up the bottle of headache tablets and leaned on the counter.

"Where did you learn acupressure?" He grinned and kissed her cheek.

"Peter, what if someone walks in!"

"Who cares?" he said, kissing her again. "Let's tell the whole damn world."

"Did I give you the wrong medicine?" She laughed. "Those are aspirin right?"

"Get my reports from Wednesday," he said, walking behind the counter, going to the corner near the filing area which was secluded from the door. Jeneil did, looking confused. She held out the file to him. He took her wrist. Putting the folder aside, he put his arms around her and kissed her passionately.

"Peter!" she said, pulling away. "You are feeling reckless."

He smiled. "I love you. I came here to tell you that."

She smiled. "I love you, too."

"What's going down tonight? I'm not working too late."

"I'm sitting until just after sunset."

"How is it going?"

"It's not. I think we're at cure or kill. We'll know tonight."

"Will you come home right after sunset?"

She put her arms around him. "Yes," she said, "Jetline Express." She kissed him, he held her closer, and he kissed her again.

She pulled away, breathless. "Get out of here right now. You have a nerve kissing me like that. You're taking unfair advantage of me."

He walked away smiling. "Fifteen minutes after sunset do you hear, or I'll go there and drag you out."

"Neanderthal." She smiled.

"Don't mess with New York street kids unless you can take it." He smiled, opened the door and left. She smiled and shook her head.

Seven

Robert smiled as Jeneil joined him in the center room. "Jeneil, I can't thank you enough. I know this isn't easy for you. That's what makes it special. You're doing it for me."

"I am, Robert, and don't thank me yet. I may not be able to concentrate intensely enough. This really is very personal."

"I love you for this," he said, hugging her. "Come on, I've prepared."

"Prepared what?" she asked, puzzled.

"Atmosphere. Let's let our souls visit for awhile," he said, taking her by the hand. He opened a small room near the sunset window. It had a thick green rug and a thick green cushioned wicker swing on a thick rope hanging from the middle of the ceiling. The walls were painted with life's greenery. Exotic plants and trees bent and overlapped each other in a realistic jungle atmosphere. Real plants sat in baskets and pots along the walls in groupings. Several sky windows were implanted in the ceiling giving a clear view of portions of the sky. Jeneil took it all in, turning in awe.

"This is some fantastic room. Why did you make it?"

"I take many exotic trips here. That swing and I have logged many miles." She looked at him and smiled understandingly. "Come on, try the swing," he said, taking her hand. He held the swing still for her as she sat down.

"It's oversized," she said, feeling it. "I feel small. It surrounds me. Is that deliberate?"

"Do your senses ever go off duty? Yes, the swing is designed to make me feel like a kid. We had one on our porch when I was growing up. I spent a lot of hours sketching and dreaming in its roominess. So I had an oversized one made to accommodate an oversized child."

She laughed lightly. "I like that, what a great idea."

"Don't go away," he said, walking to the corner of the room. Jeneil took off her shoes, dropping them on the rug. Moving to the back of the swing, she snuggled into the cushion. The swing was set into motion by her movements. Robert returned carrying tall glasses of cranberry juice. "Hey, don't leave without me." He backed into the swing to stop it.

She laughed. "This will hold the two of us, right?"

He looked at her and grinned. "I can personally guarantee it." She held the glasses while he climbed on and backed against the cushions.

"This is really great," she said, leaning back. "Do you spend much time here?"

"I have since trying to paint you."

"Oh now don't try to make me feel guilty."

"No guilt, just a statement of fact," he answered, and watched as Jeneil tossed her hair off her shoulder. "Your color looks good amongst the green cushions. Like the earth amongst the foliage."

"Or an insect on a leaf," she added. He grinned. "How high have you swung in this?"

"Not very," he answered, "it's a soothing swing, not a record setter."

"Yes, it feels peaceful. I had an oversized swing as a child, but it was a board on a rope from a tree. A friend of mine and I would swing on it together and get ourselves really high then jump off together at its highest point."

"Were you a tomboy?"

"I still am." She smiled.

"That's impossible, you hold yourself too well to be a tomboy."

"It's the truth," she insisted.

"How did you get into cosmic?"

She looked at him, editing the full story in her mind. "I was at a point in my life when I felt isolated from my surroundings, like the photograph of your rainy day, very grey. I enjoyed walking on the beach at night, especially around the time of a full moon. The energies of the elements seemed very intense. Then one time I felt the energy from all of them pass through me for just an instant, but it was so exhilarating that I worked hard to recapture it."

"You have more control now? You can do this at will?"

"Yes, in a sense, but I don't have great control. There's a greater force out there. It's more like standing on the brink of the universe, feeling its pulse and joining hands with it."

"That's amazing. I can feel that description."

"Can you?" she asked, surprised. "Your sensitivity totally impresses me."

"It made my life tough growing up."

"Did you feel everything deeply and intensely until you thought you'd go mad?"

"For years I thought I was. How did you know that?" He stared at her.

"I go through that, too," she answered, "but I've learned to deal with it better than when I was younger."

"Me, too, as I get older and I understand myself better," Robert said. She nodded, understanding and agreeing.

"Did your peer group understand you?" she asked curiously.

"Are you kidding? They almost had me convinced that I was a freak. Most of them thought I was gay, including my father, I think. He was so glad when I brought a girl home that he even let us sleep together in the house." He laughed lightly as he remembered it.

Jeneil smiled sympathetically. "I can't seem to make sense from childhoods. We live through those years trying to fit in the groups ourselves, being tossed against rocks like small boats because we lack the understanding of ourselves and what's around us."

"I don't think everyone does, Jeneil. There are kids at the prom who really have a grasp on the moment, but there are some of us who don't grasp the music being played."

"We live in the cracks," she said quietly.

"The cracks?"

She nodded. "We jump onto the cracks of the sidewalk. We play the music in the cracks on the keyboard. We hear the noise going on in two squares of the sidewalk because we're in the cracks. It gets easier to sort out the different noises as we get older."

He leaned back. "That's exactly right. Those were well chosen words. That's really how it is. Your sensitivity impresses me too, Jeneil." He took her hand. "Wow, your hand is freezing cold."

She laughed. "Tall glasses filled with ice tend to do that."

Robert looked up at the sky windows. "It's getting close to sunset. Let's get to my west window and see what evolves from this cosmic sensitivity of yours." Robert stopped the movement of the swing and Jeneil stepped off.

"Robert, I've enjoyed the swing. It was a soothing trip."

"I knew you'd like it. You and I are alike in many ways."

"I've noticed that, too."

The room with the sunset window was beginning to be ablaze in color. "It's like walking into hell after the cool green of the jungle room." Robert laughed.

"We're a little bit early," Jeneil said, going to the window.

"I wanted to be sure everything was the way you needed it to be."

"I've never tried being cosmic indoors. This will be something new."

"What happens if the weather is bad?"

"Meditation puts me on the right path, but nothing like cosmic."

"Then stand in position and rehearse. Where do you want me to be?"

"We don't have a choice. I face the sunset and you'll have to face me, won't you? How can you see if this is what you wanted if you aren't watching? That's the different part. I've never had an audience."

"What about Peter?"

"Peter wasn't an audience, he became part of it."

"Is that right? Can I be?"

"I doubt it, Robert. Besides won't you need your objectivity in this?"

"Yes, I suppose so. I'm just so damned curious about all this."

Jeneil smiled. "I hope this works out for you."

"It will. Whatever happens, I know it will. I want it to. Come on. Let's begin."

Jeneil faced the west window. Studying the colors before her, she could tell this was premature. It wasn't full sunset. She closed her eyes to gather mental notes and feelings.

Robert stayed to one side, but close by with his arms folded. He watched Jeneil and smiled. Jeneil shook her head and opened her eyes. "Don't quit so fast," Robert pleaded.

"It won't work," Jeneil sighed. "The wind is missing. I had never noticed how vital the wind was in this."

"Shit," Robert said, putting his hands to his waist. "Is air movement really so necessary? Air movement? Jeneil, how about a fan?"

"Robert, I'll try it for you, but I have to tell you that this is all feeling artificial as it is. I miss the expanse of the sky. The window is a shield between me and the sun. And the wind; the wind made it all come together and blend. I especially miss the wind."

"Are you saying to forget it?"

"No," Jeneil answered. "I'm prepared to follow this through, but I can't promise the usual intensity. I feel like I can rely on past experiences to recapture the moment, but what result I'll get is the question."

"I'll take whatever we get. Let me get you a fan."

Jeneil removed the smock hoping to feel free. She studied the sunrise. A portion of the sun was peering above the horizon. Squinting, she followed the colors to the perimeter of the fireball. She could feel the energy stir from deep inside. Holding her hands at the perimeter colors, she slowly brought her hands together, barely touching but covering the sun itself. Jeneil let her mind take control. *I am a being of life,* her mind whispered.

Robert walked slowly to her, watching with deep interest. Jeneil opened her eyes and put her hands down. He held her chin. "How intense do you get when it's natural?"

"Why?"

"Your coloring is great." He kissed her cheek gently. Setting up the fan, he turned it on. "What speed?"

"I don't know. I've only used the wind. I couldn't regulate it."

Robert smirked. "I asked for that." He pushed a button.

Jeneil could feel the breeze. "Is that high speed?"

"Yes, I thought it might compensate for not being surrounded by it. Is it too much?"

"I guess not." Jeneil closed her eyes and put her head back, letting the breeze whip at her hair. It didn't behave like the wind. The only similarity was the gentleness of it smoothing over her skin and pushing at her body. She concentrated harder, noticing how much she relied on the wind to achieve cosmic. Once she began to concentrate, she was surprised she could forget Robert by degrees. The experiment was an education for her as she compared it to the real experience. Without the true elements surrounding her, she was able to see what part she contributed. Realizing sunset must be full she partially opened her eyes and studied it. It was in full phase. Concentrating, she held her hand to the front of her as she touched the sun.

Robert walked quietly around her, studying her from different angles. Jeneil stayed touching the sun. As he came almost to her side, he caught the angle where she looked connected to the sun. He stopped. He could tell that she was in deep concentration. He could see that the surroundings were artificial and he wished now that he had tried to get to a natural environment.

If this was the result of artificial, what must natural be, he thought. Every angle was a whole new dimension with its own value. He felt energy pass through him. She was incredible, he thought, to have achieved this level of sensitivity.

Jeneil could feel energy pulsing, bringing warmth, but the sense of harmony and peace was missing. The encompassing intensity wasn't part of it. The warmth was there comforting her, filling her, radiating through her. She opened her eyes and dropped her arms to her sides. She felt separated from what was around her, but not disconnected. It felt like she was two individuals, one on a positive piece of film and one negative, one acting and one as a shadow.

Robert walked over to her and touched her face. The afterglow was working its magic. She interacted with the colors and her warmth surprised him. Robert lacked words. She radiated life; he felt it. She smiled at him as he studied her face. "Jeneil, you are so incredibly beautiful," he said, and putting his arms gently around her, he held her to him, feeling the warmth pass through him. He kissed her cheek. It felt like warm velvet.

Jeneil liked the comfort of his arms as she waited for the feeling of separateness to pass. She let him hold her. She felt his lips move to her neck and his arms around her felt tighter. Something felt wrong to her, but what? She was in slow motion inside. Robert's hold on her, it felt familiar, but what? She struggled to remember. Her shadow self was beginning to join her acting self. It was trying to scream, but why? In slow motion, the memory of a hold like that returned. Chang! The name dragged slowly through her; the night she had deliberately seduced him. Her shadow self panicked. Her acting self began to react slowly as her shadow self desperately screamed something. She felt Robert's kisses on her neck more clearly and she heard primal echo through her. She no longer felt separated, just off center. Her mind tried to deal with what was happening.

"Robert, you're holding me too tight. I can hardly breathe." She tried to put her hands between them, but his grip was incredibly strong. "Robert, please." She struggled to free herself. He kissed her passionately. She desperately tried to recall what to do from her self-defense class and what she'd read about rape prevention. Rape! The word froze in her mind, frightening her and causing the feeling of panic to grow. No! It couldn't be, not Robert, her mind reasoned. His body was so close to hers, she could sense the seriousness of the situation. She wanted to reason with him. When will he stop kissing me, her mind screamed. She wrenched free of his kiss, turning her head. "Robert, don't do this, please don't. I'm sorry, I should have realized." She spoke and gasped for air at the same time.

"Jeneil, stop struggling. Wait a minute."

"Robert, let go of me!" she screamed. He loosened his hold on her and reached for her wrists. She seized that fraction of a second with the agility, skill, and desperation of a cornered animal. She was away from him! That surprised her. She turned and ran from the room leaving him standing there. Running down the short corridor, she entered the center room and headed for the dressing screen for her clothes. She could hardly think, her heart was beating furiously and she felt like she was all movement and not getting anywhere. She was shaking and had a feeling of vulnerability. She felt exposed and endangered, and at that moment she realized that she was behind the dressing screen, and from fear, had stopped to change her clothes. She shook violently. Get control her mind ordered. Get the dress back on and get out of here. She struggled with her shaking hands but couldn't make out the top from the bottom. And then she felt all her vital signs stop functioning. She felt every nerve tingle throughout her body as Robert stepped behind the dressing screen.

"Jeneil," he said quietly, walking toward her. She watched, unable to think then realizing she was naked, she held the silk dress in front of her and backed away.

"Robert. No." Tears filled her eyes and she felt herself begin to shake, her cheeks wet with tears. "Robert, it won't be seduction, it will be rape." She heard the words and wondered who had said them, not recognizing her own voice. He put his hands on her shoulders.

"Jeneil, why did you panic? You spoiled it. I wouldn't have hurt you." He kissed her forehead lightly. "Look at you. You're a wreck." He held her gently. "You're shaking so badly that you can't think straight. Good grief. I'm not an animal; I just wanted to make love to you." She closed her eyes in relief as she recognized the sincerity and gentleness in his voice. She felt weak and faint. "I'm sorry, sweetheart. I came on too strong. Calm down."

She pulled away. "You wouldn't let go."

"I don't want to now," he said, touching her face gently. "I want to make love to you."

"But I belong to Peter."

"I know that, so what?"

"So what?" she repeated in disbelief.

He looked at her, surprised. "He really is your first relationship, isn't he? Jeneil, honey, grow up. You and I wouldn't affect you and Peter." She stared at him, not believing what she heard. "Your cosmic energy is beautifully intense. I didn't think we should waste that. Do you realize how incredible we would have been together at that moment? Get dressed," he said, kissing her cheek. "You've at least stopped shaking. I'll take a cold shower. We'll talk." He walked away.

Jeneil stared at the edge of the screen where he disappeared. Looking around then down at herself, covered only by the flimsy silk dress held against her, the whole scene felt ugly and she hated being part of it. She began to cry, overwhelmed by the mixture of emotions flooding her mind. Dressing quickly, she ran from the building to her car. She pulled into the parking area of her building and snapped off the car lights. Tears still streamed down her cheeks and a violent anger welled up inside of her that answered a need but frightened her, too. She didn't recognize herself, and she didn't like that feeling. After struggling with the lock on the entrance door, she stepped inside and closed it hard, making sure it was secure. She stopped to breathe, beginning to feel safe now that she was around familiar surroundings. Hurrying upstairs, she unlocked the door, opened it and slammed it behind her as she headed toward the bedroom.

Peter looked up when he heard the key. He had waited for her. He was looking forward to being with her since their encounter at noon. He stood up, shocked by her entrance and her appearance. She never wore her hair just loosely hanging down, and her clothes looked thrown together on her. Something was wrong. He followed her to the bedroom. She tossed her things on the bed and pulled open the closet looking for her robe. Peter reached to her. "Jeneil, what's wrong?"

"Nothing," she snapped.

As she turned to walk past him, feeling drained from his chest as he saw her face. He went to her, reaching for her arm.

"Leave me alone," she warned, moving away. "I'm very angry right now. Just leave me alone." This was serious, he could tell that. His stomach knotted as a guess began to develop inside of him. He put his hands on her shoulders, but she pushed at him. "Get away from me. Get out of my life!"

He was immobilized from shock for an instant as she ran from the room. Following her, he could hear the shower running. He could hear her crying.

"Jeneil," he called through the door. "What's happening? You've got to talk to me. Unlock the door." There was no answer. "Jeneil, now! Right now, damn it!" Oh no, he thought to himself, as his guess became a word in his mind. The telephone rang. He ignored it. It kept ringing. He sighed and went to answer it in the living room. It was Robert. Peter braced himself.

"Is Jeneil there?" Robert asked.

"Robert, what happened?" Peter asked, surprised that his voice sounded calmer than he felt.

"Didn't she tell you?"

"She just got in. She's in the shower. I don't need her to tell me something happened I can see it. Now what the hell happened, Robert?" Peter was shaking inside. Robert was silent. "Robert, this is the last time I'm asking on the phone. The next time I ask, it will be at your place." Chang was surfacing. Peter struggled to stay calm.

"Nothing happened. She overreacted."

"Shit!" Peter shouted. "She's no airhead. She doesn't overreact to nothing. Now what is it?"

"Peter, I swear she overreacted. She scared the hell out of me."

Peter was torn. Was this guy lying? He sounded sincere and genuinely concerned about Jeneil. "You put a move on her, didn't you?"

"Peter, listen to me, something almost happened. Okay, I even wanted it to happen. But nothing could have accounted for her reaction to it. She freaked out and I didn't set her up. The whole thing just evolved. It wasn't planned."

"Robert, right now I'm so freaking mad I want to wring blood from your pores. She's a wreck, you son-of-a-bitch."

"Shit man, I know that. I didn't want her to leave. I wanted to talk it out with her. I'm sitting here confused about the whole thing."

"Man, so help me, if you're shittin' me about all this I'll be by and twice as furious. That's a promise."

"Peter, I swear it's the truth. I am so damned impressed with her right now."

"Why?" Peter asked, surprised by the statement.

"For a lot of reasons, but all I keep picturing is her looking at me and saying, 'but I belong to Peter.'" Peter choked up. "How the hell do you get her to do that? What do you use, some ancient Chinese sex technique?"

Peter couldn't believe the question or the timing. "Robert, I want to check on Jeneil."

"Sure. Have her call me when she settles down, and when this has passed, I want to uncork a bottle with you and have a long talk about women."

Peter looked at the receiver in disbelief. Chang had a phrase he desperately wanted to use, but Peter answered, "I'll tell her you called," and he hung up. He ran his fingers through his hair. "Jeneil, baby, I'll never understand civilized. The son-of-a-bitch puts a make on my woman and then wants me to come over and tell him what he's doing wrong. An artist. Mr. Sensitivity, shit." He shook his head.

The bathroom door opened and Jeneil walked into the bedroom. Peter watched then went to her. She was standing near a bureau brushing her hair. "Robert just called." She stopped brushing for a moment then began brushing again. "You got into some trouble, huh?" She began brushing faster as tears rolled down her cheeks. He took her wrist gently and removed the brush, setting it on the bureau. Putting his arms around her, he pulled her to him. She resisted then moved closer to him, putting her arms around him and sobbing into his chest. He held her, letting her cry. At that moment Chang wanted to kill Robert. She stopped crying after awhile, but stayed holding onto him. "Let's sit down," he said, gently taking her to the bed. She sat down and pulled herself together. He sat next to her. "Honey, what happened?"

She was silent for a minute. "My feelings aren't sorted out yet. I don't want to talk about it."

"Jeneil, I need to know what happened. Not your feelings, the facts." Chang wasn't settled. She looked at him then down at the tie from her robe that she twisted around her finger. "Did you sit for him?" Peter questioned. She nodded. "In the dress?" She gave another nod. "He didn't stay on his side of the brush, huh?"

"It was my fault," she said as tears rolled down her cheeks. Peter was surprised. Robert hadn't said that.

"How?"

"I decided to share cosmic with him."

Peter closed his eyes. "In the brown dress at sunset? Oh, Jeneil." He sighed.

She looked at him. "Being indoors, everything felt different. I forgot Robert was there."

"What did he do?"

"He kissed me, but he was holding me so tightly and he wouldn't let go of me when I asked him to, then I panicked I guess. I thought he was going to rape me. My mind wasn't clear from the cosmic thing."

"He said you overreacted "

"Did he really?" Her tone was sarcastic. "Well, I'm not used to men coming behind my dressing screen while I'm changing. I felt threatened," she said angrily.

Peter looked up, shocked. "What? He was behind the dressing screen with you naked?"

"I didn't know he wasn't going to rape me. He was heading for serious business. I knew that much before he asked me. He even admitted that. It was hard to read and I couldn't remember anything from my self-defense class. The cosmic thing got in my way. He came behind the screen and I can't believe I stopped to change. I couldn't get the dress on and he was there." Peter was stunned as the picture unfolded in his mind. Peter stared and reminded himself to breathe. Jeneil began to shake and her tears began again. "I was so scared," she sobbed.

Peter held her. He realized that the guy had seen Jeneil experiencing a cosmic experience at sunset. That was powerful in itself. Then to walk in on her naked and still not rape her left him feeling overwhelmed. He didn't believe it. His throat was tight. "Honey...what did he...did anything happen?"

"Yes, I began shaking and crying. I heard myself tell him that he'd have to rape me because it wouldn't be seduction."

Peter was stunned. "What did he do?"

"He told me he wasn't going to rape me. He sounded sincere and I began to gain control." She heaved a sigh as she stopped to breathe. "You were right. You were right." She began to cry again and he could see why she was behaving like this. In a sense, she had been violated. He had never seen her changing behind the dressing screen. It was Jeneil's way. There were areas to Jeneil's life that were only Jeneil's. She was a private person and she had been thrust into exposure. He held her wishing he could have spared her that. She cried more softly. Peter's stomach tensed when he thought of how close she had come to serious trouble. He held her closer as if to shield her from anything else.

"Baby, you've got to learn to see these things coming at you," he said, kissing her temple.

"Why do men make everything physical? Cosmic isn't physical."

"People are human, honey. That's our level. When you walk amongst us, you look like us so we'll treat you the way of our level. It isn't meant to be insulting. We don't know you're different. You look like us." He heard Chang scream, why are you defending the son-of-a-bitch?

She smiled at him, wiping away tears. "Did you understand the music at the prom, too?"

He wrinkled his brow. "What do you mean?"

"You seem to understand what's around us."

He smiled. "You expect people to be nice. I expect them to be human. It's your ivory tower, that's all."

"You mean that I see man as noble and you see him with his failings."

"That's another way to say it." He kissed her forehead and hugged her. "What am I going to do with you? You're like a kid living amongst adults. You take their hand and trust them."

"You're the second person within three hours to tell me to grow up, and for different reasons." She stood up, wiping a stray tear.

"Are you okay? Are you still angry?"

"I'm feeling many things." She paced.

Peter went to her. "Honey, I'm not defending the son-of-a-bitch, but if you think about the situation, it could have been a lot more serious. A lot more." He shook his head and held her. "It scares me to think about it." She let him hold her, enjoying the security she felt in his arms.

"Peter, I didn't mean it when I said to get out of my life. I was so angry and it seemed that every time I turned around a man was grabbing at me. I like having you hold me. I'm glad you were here. Sometimes things rush at me." Peter smiled and he squeezed her. They sat together, talking if they had words, but mostly he held her until it was time for bed.

Eight

The alarm rang. Peter lifted his head groggily. He had slept but he wasn't rested. Saturday. He turned over to look at Jeneil. She was gone. He wondered. By the time they had gone to bed the night before, she had become quiet and withdrawn. He sat up. Their lives had been jumbled ever since Danzieg came into it. He wanted life settled again. Was it ever settled, he wondered. Yes, when they first began their relationship she was by his side constantly and they had been inseparable. Since Danzieg, he wasn't sure when to approach her or how. He missed her. He missed being with her. He remembered her words, 'why do men make everything physical?' His desire at the moment added up to physical to him. He missed her attention; he missed her body. That was physical all right, he thought, and all his way. Danzieg should try living with her and sleeping next to her and not touching her when she went cosmic. Hey, the street kid just out classed Mr. Sensitivity. He smiled, impressed with himself. Match that for sensitivity. He grinned, getting up, feeling proud of himself.

Jeneil was sitting under the potted trees writing in her notebook. While he showered and dressed, Jeneil got breakfast for him and made his lunch. It amazed him that she continued to be perfunctory about the details of life even when her mind was elsewhere, like today. He grinned, wondering about the possibility of teaching her perfunctory sex. Right now he wondered why some men complained about it then thinking twice, he smiled. What? And give up his sensitivity trophy. Nah, eat your heart out Danzieg. The street kid beat Danzieg at the sensitivity game. He wondered if he'd blown Danzieg out of the water.

"Are you okay?"

She nodded. "I'm just feeling a little at odds about myself and everything around me."

He touched her face. "I wish I could stay home with you."

"I really need to be alone," she replied quietly. "The path to me is a bit staggered right now. I've got to straighten out a few things in my mind."

"I'll check with you later, honey." He kissed her cheek, wanting to stay longer.

"Thank you for understanding, Peter."

He smiled. "I love you, and I'm learning what that phrase means." She looked at him and tears filled her eyes. "Oh, come on." He smiled. "I can take you meditating under the trees as a memory, but not tears." She smiled, and he kissed her lips lightly again.

At work, Peter thought about her often. He tried to call her several times but there was no answer. Coming back from the telephone booth for the fourth try, Steve came over to him.

"What's on? You look concerned." The girl from Accounting walked past them. Steve turned to watch her walk away, smiling. "Oh, yes indeed. I've got to see how she looks against the upholstery of my car."

Peter shook his head. "She's a person damn it."

Steve turned quickly. "Whoa. What's yours feeding you at breakfast, liberation food?"

"Stop and take a look at it all. They're people, not just asses or chests."

"What the hell's with you?"

Peter shook his head, calming down. "It's just that they belong to somebody, even to themselves, damn it."

"Pete, when a woman dresses like that one was dressed, she wants attention. What's the matter with you? You know that."

Peter sighed. "Ignore me, I'll be okay."

"No, something's wrong. You're wearing a path to the phones today and you never jump on soapboxes." Steve watched his face. "Is the shark circling closer to your property?"

"He put a make on her."

Steve looked sober. "Oh shit, what now? Change partners?"

"No, he scared her pretty good."

Steve looked puzzled. "From a make? What did he use, a whip and chains?"

"She wasn't expecting it," Peter explained. Steve looked again, puzzled. "She's different, Steve. She doesn't see it coming."

"She's new at this then. I wasn't wrong about her, was I?"

"She's not into the games."

"Is that why you keep calling her? Is she okay?" Steve asked, concerned.

"I can't get an answer. I'm a little worried."

"Go check on her then. I'll cover for you."

Peter thought for a minute. "Maybe I will, thanks Steve."

Peter heard the music as he unlocked the apartment door. It was classical, but loud and angry. Jeneil sat under the trees. "Honey," he said, going to her and turning the music down. "What's all this? Are you back to being angry at Robert?" He could tell that she had been crying.

"This has nothing to do with Robert. It has to do with me."

"Gee, baby, this is a heavy mood. You've got to lighten up. You're letting things get too serious. I've been calling you."

"I'm sorry. The phone has been ringing every few minutes. I don't want to answer it." The telephone rang. "See."

"I'll answer it."

"No," she insisted, "please go back to work."

"Not with you like this."

"Peter, please, I'll deal with it."

"Withdrawing isn't dealing with it."

"It is for me now, please go to work."

"Jeneil, honey, I'm worried. Why don't we go to a crisis center?"

"Peter, I don't need a crisis center. I wasn't raped. It wasn't even close. I know that much now. Please go back to work. I really don't need the extra pressure."

He studied her. "Honey, I'm going to trust you. Please don't let me down."

"I'm fine," she insisted.

"No, you're not. I've never seen you like this."

"This is normal for me. This is how I dealt with things before you lived here."

"But I'm here now. Let me help."

"Then go back to work so I can finish Jeneil, or at least this installment of her."

He kissed her lips then her temple and cheek. "Call me if you need to."

"Peter, I've gotten through this before. I will now."

"What is it? What are you going through?"

"Too much noise. Everything is rushing at me. I need to sift through things. You hear clear drum beats. I don't. Please go to work, I don't need more noise."

He shook his head and sighed. "Okay, but remember, I love you," and he went back to work reluctantly.

Steve met him. "Is she okay?"

"She's not answering the telephone. I wish I could have stayed with her. She's low right now."

Steve grinned. "You hover over her you know."

"She needs it. She doesn't see speeding trains."

"She handled herself alright here."

"She gets too close to people. Once she trusts a person, she's in trouble. I kept telling her this guy had to be watched. We even fought about it."

Steve smiled, watching Peter. "Poor Peter, love isn't easy. When's your day off?"

"Not until Tuesday," Peter answered. "Why?"

"Stanton's got tomorrow off. He owes me for covering his ass one day and for teaching him what he missed in class. I'll collect on it then I'll switch with you."

"How will that go down with Sprague?"

Steve smiled. "I filled in for him on a minor surgery case."

Peter laughed. "You've got this game working covered your way, don't you?"

"I keep telling you, Pete; you hand out markers then you collect on them."

"Well, give me more than one marker for tomorrow. I can't repay you for it."

"What? A New York blood brother. No way. We take care of our own, man. You know that. It still tickles me that you protect her like she'll break and yet she stands up to me like she's a trained guerilla fighter."

"Get closer, Steve. Get closer."

"Sure, sure, so you keep saying. I really think love is blind." Steve laughed. "I'll catch Stanton and get this worked out."

"Thanks again," Peter said sincerely. Steve grinned and walked away.

*****

Peter was anxious to get home. As seven approached, a call came in from the paramedics. Peter was asked to stay on and big names were called in for an emergency surgery, a serious accident involving two cars. Five people were involved and three were in critical condition. The staff geared up for the chaos that would surround them shortly. Maxwell was called in and Peter was scrubbing in with him. The sound of sirens got louder and everyone was ready. Peter entered the OR and the team prepared for Maxwell's arrival. Someone mentioned that Maxwell was going over the material from ER. The patient was brought in. It was a nine year old boy. Maxwell entered and everyone got down to business.

Peter left the operating room drained. The young boy was in trouble. The surgery was brilliant; the rest was up to the boy and fate. As Peter walked through the corridor, he saw Dr. Maxwell talking to a man; the boy's father. Dr. Fisher joined them. The man turned pale and sat down. His wife hadn't survived. Peter watched the heart drain out of the man, and he felt for him as the man cried openly. Maxwell asked Peter to stay and monitor recovery for him. Sitting in the doctor's lounge with coffee, the image of the man kept passing through Peter's mind. He went to the phone and called Jeneil. There was no answer. He wanted to talk to her, to know she was okay. After staying the required time and conferring with Dr. Maxwell, he left.

*****

Everything was dark as Peter drove up. She was asleep. He was disappointed; he wanted to see her, to hold her. The image of that man was stuck in his memory. He was exhausted. Turning on the overhead light, he noticed a note on the small table. He picked it up. *Peter, I couldn't stand the telephone ringing so often. I needed quiet. Will stay at the motel. Be back tomorrow. Jeneil.* He sat down, disappointed. He couldn't remember the name of the motel she owned. Crumbling the paper, he put his head against the wall and sighed. The telephone rang. It was Robert.

"I've been calling Jeneil for hours. Is she there?"

"No," Peter answered. "She's away and won't be back until tomorrow."

"She never returned my call."

"Well, I guess she didn't want to," Peter said through clenched teeth.

Robert was silent. "I'm not surprised." He hung up.

Peter got into bed. He hated the apartment without her. Her blue robe was at the foot of the bed. Pulling it to him, he smelled it. The smell of her perfume filled him. He missed her. The man's tragedy had left him with a need to cling to her. It seemed like years since they had been together. He closed his eyes. He awoke in the middle of the dream about Ki and Reid; most of the time he remembered it vividly when he woke up. Jeneil had done that for him. It was five. He was used to waking for early surgery. Getting up, he poured some juice and leaned against the counter. Maybe the telephone book. No good. They didn't have a phone book for the southern end of the area. Or did they? He finished his drink and went to the computer. Punching different keys, he found that he couldn't gain access. Adrienne would know, but he'd have to wait until she got up. Most everything had been moved to the office, but a small filing cabinet was still in the corner. He pulled the drawer. It was unlocked. He thumbed through the file folders. Twin Pines Motel. Smiling, he opened it. Route 105, Warnell.

"Thank you very much," he said, closing the drawer. He quickly showered and changed. He always found early Sunday morning driving pleasant. The weather promised to be beautiful. Turning on the radio, he settled in for the forty-five minute drive. As he pulled into the parking lot, he scanned it for Jeneil's car. It wasn't there. He went to the office. The smell of freshly brewed coffee met him. A man with a warm smile came from the back room.

"Morning," he said. "Want a room?"

"No, I'm looking for Jeneil." The man's smile disappeared and he looked Peter over.

"Is she expecting you?"

Then she was there, Peter thought. "I hope so."

"I'll dial her room." The man hung up. "There's no answer." A dark haired woman came from the living quarters. "Has Jeneil left?" the man asked.

"No, she went to the...."

"It's alright," the man interrupted her. "She'll be back sometime today, I guess. Sorry, I can't help you."

Peter smiled. "Thanks anyway," he said, and left. Another good friend of hers. He smiled. He liked the way the man protected her. She went to the...beach. Peter smiled and turned his car east. He pulled into the parking lot of the beach where he and Jeneil had run into each other. Thinking about that day made him miss her all the more and he realized how much he loved her. Her car wasn't there. He looked up at the house on the bluff in the distance. Children were playing in the yard which surprised him. He felt like that was his house. He drove away smiling. "Chang, you are getting possessive; first Jeneil then a house."

Jeneil must be at the rocky beach near the marsh. Turning off the main road, he drove in for a half mile then noticed her car. His heart flipped. Parking next to her car, he got out. The gulls were screeching over head and the breeze caught his shirt. Walking a short distance, he stepped onto a bed of various sized rocks and headed for the grassy ledge. Half way there, he caught sight of her sitting, facing the ocean. He saw her turn her head then stand up quickly. Stepping off the ledge, she came toward him.

"Peter? Why aren't you at work?"

"I have the day off," he answered, studying her. She seemed pulled together.

"I thought Tuesday was your day off."

"It got changed. Do you mind that I came here? I'll be quiet."

She smiled. He wanted to kiss here but he just smiled, too. They lay down on the blanket together. She turned to him. "Did you have breakfast?"

"Honey, I didn't come here to be looked after."

"You didn't have breakfast." She sat up and put a basket between them.

He sat up. "What's this?"

"The Beecham's packed some food for me. She makes great muffins." Jeneil poured coffee and set a muffin on a napkin for him.

"I don't want to eat your food."

"They gave me a lot. Besides, you can buy me a cheeseburger for lunch."

"You're feeling better, aren't you?" He smiled, studying her face.

She nodded. "I need to live through those moments. I worried you. That's why you're here." He finished his coffee.

"I came here to be quiet with you. Even I need quiet from time to time." They lay back on the blanket facing the sky.

"I had a chance to face the wind."

"Is everything okay?" he asked, glad that he was there.

"Yes, I shouldn't have shared cosmic. Robert misunderstood. It was foolish of me to have expected him to understand. You're right about people being human. I have the greater fault, I should have known better. A lot of things I have neglected lately. I've tapped into something new and I let everything else fall apart. I really appreciate your support and understanding."

Electricity passed through his chest and he smiled to himself. The street kid won. Chang blew him out of the water. He felt good.

She turned and faced him, and smiled. "You really are something special." He stayed quiet, listening and loving her words. "You understood cosmic more than Robert did. That time on the balcony, you knew what to do. You knew it wasn't physical." Peter listened, pleased that she had noticed that. "All these days that we've been out of sorts with each other, you've never complained that you've been neglected, and you have been. I've neglected our love. I slip into cerebral too easily. You sleep next to me and accept it. Peter Chang, I think you understand love better than I do. I need to improve." She moved closer to him. "I've noticed a lot of things."

Peter smiled through the lump in his throat, not looking at her. "Don't make me out to be a hero. If you keep talking like that and get any closer, I'm going to lose my four star rating and we'll be back to wondering why everything is physical."

She smiled. "I have a new question. Why is being physical okay with you, but no one else?" She kissed his shoulder gently. "I love you."

"Honey, you're all I want. You keep telling the Robert Danziegs of life that you belong to me."

"I do belong to you, Peter."

He kissed her. "Jeneil, I've missed you."

"What happened at work?" He was surprised by her question. "I can tell that something has upset you."

"There was an accident, a man lost his wife. I just needed to be with you, that's all." She smiled and kissed him. He held onto her to erase the image of the man at the hospital. He kissed her neck; she felt great to him. "Jeneil, let's go back to the motel. I'm going to destroy my four star rating for celibacy and sensitivity."

She smiled. "Oh good."

*****

Peter parked his car and went to help Jeneil with her luggage. Taking the keys, he unlocked the trunk. Carrying the weekender in one hand, he put his other arm around her shoulder. She hugged him. "I love you. I'm glad you came to find me. I needed this afternoon with you, away from all that's familiar. It set things right between us again."

He smiled and kissed her. "That's why things are physical." Closing the front door behind them, Peter stopped to kiss her. Adrienne came down the stairs carrying a bouquet of flowers.

"Hey, you two are acting like newlyweds. How romantic! A snuggling weekend." She smiled and handed Jeneil the flowers. "These were delivered to you. That was some delivery man. After he left, I recognized him from a newspaper article on his artwork. You never told me that you knew Robert Danzieg. And how come he sends you flowers and delivers them himself?"

"We worked together on an art project," Jeneil answered. "I guess this is his thank you." Peter's arm tightened around her.

"Hey, I'm going for milk. Do you want anything?" Adrienne asked.

"Oh yes," Jeneil answered. "I took the weekend off. I probably need bread and milk. I'm not sure anymore."

"Ooo, you guys know how to live right, lock life away and hold onto each other." Jeneil smiled. "Be right back," Adrienne said, opening the door. Peter and Jeneil walked upstairs holding each other.

"The guy doesn't know how to quit," Peter said. "He was the one calling you yesterday."

"I think I'm ready for him now."

Peter unlocked the door. "I'll put your things in the bedroom." He kissed her and smiled. "Welcome back."

"Thank you. This seems nice after my lost weekend." Jeneil opened the note resting in the bouquet.

Peter returned. "A note, too. Now what?"

"Nothing really. He asks forgiveness. He apologized for not fully understanding cosmic. Another apology for his lack of sensitivity, and he asks me to call. That's it."

"I'll get a match and we'll burn it." Peter grinned. Jeneil laughed and put her arms around his neck.

"You've been so incredible about all this. What would you say if I continued to sit for him?"

"Honey, you're kidding?" Peter was surprised.

"Does that destroy you?"

"Why would you do that?"

"To face what I ran from. To finish what I started."

Peter shook his head. "You, Mother Teresa, and Joan of Arc, is this a race for the greatest woman in life?"

Jeneil chuckled. "Does that mean you're okay with it?"

"So help me, the next time I'll turn Chang loose. I'll never understand civilized. You people are weird."

"Good," she said, snuggling closer to him. "Neanderthal is definitely your element anyway. You proved that today." She kissed him.

"Are you complaining?" He smiled.

"Are you serious? Irish was just getting started when you quit." She grinned.

Peter laughed. "Oh? Prove that to me, beautiful. Talk is so cheap." She kissed him. The telephone rang.

"Robert, I got your flowers and note. Yes, I think we need to talk. Tomorrow is good for me. We'll talk about that tomorrow. Okay?" She hung up.

"Talk about what tomorrow?" Peter asked.

"Painting me cosmic again."

Peter shook his head. "Geez, the guy must be made of solid brass. Honey, get real. No fiction on this, okay?"

"Come on, Peter. Jeneil grew a bit more over the weekend. I can handle it."

"Oh shit, here we go again."

Jeneil held him around the waist. "I figured out a way to achieve a cosmic look without the cosmic experience."

"How?" he asked, disbelieving.

"A sip of wine so I can border on an allergic reaction. I'll radiate so much he'll paint by the glow."

Peter smiled and held her. "You're beautiful."

She snuggled to him. "Now tell me how much you love me because of my brilliant mind."

"Mmm and the body it's wrapped in." He kissed her neck as the door buzzer sounded.

"When is Tony moving in?" Adrienne asked, returning with milk and bread.

"Probably in another two weeks. I'll need to send the furniture from the model apartment to his this week, and I'll need to check with the therapist about training him in his new surroundings."

"That's why I asked. I'll get that done for you."

"Thank you, Adrienne. I sleep well because of you. I hope you know that."

Adrienne smiled. "Well, I'll leave you two with your bread and milk. You look hungry." She grinned and left.

"Are you hungry?" Jeneil asked Peter.

"Starved," he answered, pulling her to him.

"Oh, I love Neanderthals." She smiled. "They have insatiable appetites."

Nine

Peter met Steve and they went to lunch. "She sent a lunch for you," Peter said, handing Steve a bag. Steve looked at him. "Thank you for yesterday."

"I saw her earlier. I'll take the lunch." Steve laughed. "She looked great."

"We both needed yesterday."

Steve smiled. "It's okay. Name one of your sons after me and we'll call it even."

The man from Saturday's accident walked past them. "I wish his son would improve," Peter remarked.

"The little guy looks bad," Steve commented sadly. "Everybody's doing extra, hoping to change his condition."

There was a steady stream of hospital staff checking on the boy all week. Peter stayed a few minutes extra and mentally pleaded with the boy to pull out of it. He was so young; he never really had a chance at life. Peter lectured himself for letting his objectivity slip. It wasn't good to get too involved personally. It happened but it never turned out well. At least his home life had improved. Jeneil was in a buzz about something. Robert and she had worked things out and a mutual admiration was again in effect between them, and she and the notebook had regular sessions together. None of it mattered to Peter. He was impressed that she kept everything juggled. She seemed to have a pattern of falling back and recovering stronger than before. He smiled to himself; and they were great together. He couldn't ask for more. If life stayed just as it was now, it would suit him just fine. Almost fine, marriage and children would make it perfect. He smiled again. They were close to it.

Everyone was rooting for the boy. Each passing day gave them hope. Peter caught a glance at the father; he looked rough. The funeral for his wife was held. The man's grief touched Peter deeply. Something about the man's pain over the loss of his wife stayed with Peter. Friday morning, Peter stopped in to see the boy on his way back to the lab. "Any sign of a change?" he asked the nurse.

She shook her head. "He's stable, that's it and his father could use some good news for a change."

Peter agreed. Standing by the bed, he touched the small arm. Come on Magwai, get it together, he thought. The boy seemed lost in the hospital bed, so helpless. Peter thought he felt a twitch. Letting go of the arm, he took his stethoscope and held it to the little boy's chest. Standing back, Peter looked at him then at the monitor. There was a change! Come on kid, come on! A little stronger! Peter was getting excited. He went to the nurse's desk. "Have Dr. Fisher paged. The kid seems to be responding. He wanted in on it."

The nurse stood up quickly. "You're kidding! That's great!" She dialed the telephone.

Peter went back to the bed. He saw the small thumb twitch. "Good boy, keep going." The monitor noise sounded like beautiful music to Peter as the readings got stronger.

Dr. Fisher rushed in. "Chang, thanks for calling. Look at that," he said, smiling at the monitor.

Dr. Maxwell followed shortly after Dr. Fisher. "Is it time for champagne?"

"The very best," Dr. Fisher said as the boy opened his eyes. Peter felt the excitement of success pass through his whole body. Dr. Sprague and Steve came in. The boy looked bewildered. "Get his father," Dr. Fisher told the nurse.

"Mommy?" the boy whispered weakly. Peter's throat tightened realizing what the young boy still had to face physically and emotionally. He stepped back slowly and left the room. Steve followed.

"This one got to you, didn't it?" Steve asked.

"Yeah, it did. You try hard not to let it, but sometimes they do."

"I know. The kick in the gut can be tough. I'm glad this one turned out well."

Peter smiled. "At least we'll all breathe again."

The news went through the medical staff quickly and there was a steady stream of people walking past the boy's room to make sure the news was true. Peter was at the desk when the boy's father rushed past. Peter smiled to himself. He loved medicine, and at times like this nothing could equal the feeling of pure joy in one's work. Peter was checking a medical log when he heard the code blue. The unmistakable onslaught of activity through the hall brought him to his feet. Visitors turned in surprise as the staff rushed to the emergency. Peter followed and stopped for a second. The young boy's room. The father paced in an anxious, steady movement in the corridor. Peter slipped into the room. Dr. Fisher was anxiously working on the boy. Peter watched the monitor as the sickening sound of the steady beep pierced the air without interruption. Dr. Fisher's shoulders slumped and he shook his head. Someone disconnected the monitor. Dr. Fisher went to the corner of the room alone. The staff stood in silence mourning for the life they weren't able to save. Peter felt sick. The air felt heavy as the feeling of death filled the room. Peter walked out quickly, avoiding looking at the boy's father. Going to the desk, he signed out. "I'm gone."

Steve looked at him. "Oh no," he said, "I'm sorry, Pete. Can I help?"

Peter shook his head. "I'm going home." Steve patted his shoulder. Peter walked away.

*****

A feeling of discouragement began on the drive home. By the time he arrived, he had a feeling of hopelessness. The struggle with life made no sense when he saw the grief and suffering of the boy's father. To have hope handed to him and removed so cruelly seemed beyond any justice. "What was it all for anyway?" Peter asked himself as he climbed the stairs slowly and unlocked the door.

Jeneil went to him. "Peter, you're early. What's wrong?"

"Nothing," he said abruptly. Looking around, he wondered why there were green and white streamers decorating the ceiling and gathered at the center by a ball of flowers. Groups of balloons hung here and there. A table at one end of the room was covered with a cloth. On that was set a punch bowl and a tray of pastries. "What's happening here?" Peter asked, bewildered.

"It was a surprise. You came home too early. I'm not ready."

"Honey, really, this isn't the right time for a party, and people and all this."

"What's wrong?" she asked, concerned.

"I just need some quiet."

"I understand," she said, and went to the kitchen.

Peter looked around. He couldn't believe the work she'd put into this. "Honey, are people coming here tonight?"

"Only two," she answered quietly.

It must be important to her for two people to rate all this work, he thought. He was tired and he wondered who they were and if it might be better to leave instead of spoiling the whole evening for her and her friends. He watched her bring a plate to the small table. Her hair was hanging loosely and she was in her robe.

"I made a light dinner for you. I've eaten already," she said as he sat down.

"Honey, whose coming?"

She sat across from him. "Just us."

"You've done all this for us? Why?"

"It was a surprise. It seems sort of silly now."

"But what was it?"

"Nothing," she answered, looking embarrassed.

"I want to know. It must have been important. You put a lot of work into it."

"Well, I remembered that you had never been to a prom, and I haven't been to one either. My mother died a few months before my high school prom so I didn't feel like going. My father insisted that I should go and have some fun. Billy and I went, but I couldn't take it so we left and just hung around until it was time to go home. I was a zero in college. I never went to any of the dances. This was just my way of changing history. I thought it would be nice to go to a prom with you."

He smiled at her. "You get crazier every day."

She smiled. "We can have the punch and desserts, and have a quiet evening for you. Something must have happened. What was it?"

He shook his head. "No, let's go to your prom."

She looked at him. "You don't have to be nice. I can understand wanting to be quiet. I don't mind."

He stood up. "Give me a couple of minutes to shower and get rid of the hospital."

"But Peter."

He kissed her cheek. "Come on, get dressed," he said, walking away then turning around, he asked, "Did you rent a tux for me?"

"No," she laughed. "That's what's nice about personal proms; you can wear jeans if you want to."

"Not bad," he said, walking away.

Jeneil was still dressing when Peter finished. He sat at the small table waiting. He looked at the decorations again. A prom, he thought, sometimes she did resemble an airhead. He couldn't believe the work she had put into it. It must have been what she was buzzing about all week. He shook his head. That girl was some kind of crazy and was definitely getting worse. He thought about her parent's dying. They didn't get to see what they had only begun in her. He thought of the man at the hospital again. He hadn't even had a chance to see what he'd created begin to develop, and even his chance for more children with his wife. It didn't make sense. You push yourself making plans and for what, they get aced right out from under you. Even Jeneil had her high school prom ruined for her because fate had lousy timing. He looked at the work she'd put into the night. What was she working so hard at figuring out life for? Fate didn't give a damn.

The bedroom door opened. Jeneil walked out fixing the dark blue velvet sash around the waist of a light blue gown. Peter stood up stunned by the way she looked. She smiled. "I made this for my high school prom."

"Honey, you look terrific."

"Thank you," she said. "You're really sweet to go along with this." She turned off the bright overhead lights and the room was bathed in dimmer, softer light from two small lamps. She put her arms around him. "We wouldn't have looked at each other twice in high school, but this is what's nice about rewriting history. We can, once we have our eyes open, enjoy a prom with someone we'd really like to go to a real prom with."

"Hold on to me tight," he said, hugging her, hoping her fire for life would warm him.

"What's wrong, Peter?"

"Don't people hug at proms?" he asked, kissing her cheek.

"This is our prom, we design and create it."

"What else does your prom have?"

"Music." She smiled and went to the stereo to start the tape. Music began with a strong saxophone carrying the melody. Looking up at the ball of flowers, he stretched his arm and pulled out a daisy, handing it to her. She smiled and settled it in her hair.

"Why did you do all this?"

"I told you, because I wanted to go to a prom with you."

"But you worked your fingers off for what, an hour or two of pleasure. Is it all worth it?"

She looked at him. "That sounds like a philosophical question. Yes, it's worth it to me because with the work and effort I created a memory. A good memory, I hope, and nothing can take that memory away. It can't be destroyed by anything. I lived it, I breathed it. I was a part of it for even a short time. I will have left a memory in the history being written by us, about us. I cared enough about us and life to create it. We aren't handed guarantees, only days and time to fill. We choose how to fill them and the memories and knowledge we leave will live in those who have shared it with us. That's worth the work." She paused. "After tonight we will both have gone to a prom. And this is a special prom; I designed it for just you because I wanted to tell you something in a special way." He looked at her as she took his hand. "You'll have to dance with me for the message."

"Dance?"

She grinned. "Trust me, you can dance." She put her hand on his shoulder and he put his arm around her. She kissed him gently. "The music is the key to the message, Peter. It was chosen very carefully so you'll have to forget that you're dancing and listen to the lyrics."

He looked at her. "You are strange."

"I know but that's why I can enjoy a private prom, and understand the music and grasp the moment. I've decided to accept being strange as normal and the nicest part is that I can go to this prom with a guy who accepts my strangeness. I didn't have to spend hours on the phone finding out what other people would wear so I could fit in. I didn't worry that I wouldn't be asked. This is my special prom. I did it my way to coin a phrase." She grinned.

Peter smiled. "When you're discovered, I wonder if I'll lose my license for not getting you some help."

She chuckled. "Eccentric doctor, eccentric. You have one more song to practice your dancing then the message music begins." He smiled and shook his head. "And you're a better dancer than you think." The song ended and there was a pause.

"Now what?"

"A glass of punch." They stood at the table as Jeneil filled two glasses. "Isn't this a nice group tonight? They don't make any noise. They don't smile and pretend that they're having fun. They don't laugh too loudly to convince those around them that they understand and enjoy the moment. They don't pop off and react to each other like ping pong balls. Groups like this make me feel comfortable." Peter grinned and drank his punch. There was a tone signal from the tape. "Uh-oh, our music message is ready." She took his hand and walked to the center of the room. He held her. "No talking is allowed. You can only listen."

"I can handle that," he said. "That's easy."

She looked into his eyes. "Is it?"

The music began and Peter was ready to listen, fascinated by her scheming. A heavy saxophone started then a female singer began to sing. *"I say, I'd go through fire and I'll go through fire as he wants it, so it shall be. Crazy he calls me, sure I'm crazy. Crazy in love, you see."* The singer stopped and the saxophone played.

Peter looked at Jeneil. "Jen…" She covered his mouth with her fingers to remind him not to speak. He kissed her hand.

The singer interrupted. *"I'll say I'll care forever and I mean forever, if I have to hold up the sky. Crazy, he calls me, sure I'm crazy. Crazy in love am I."* The music ended. There was a brief pause. Peter put his lips to her temple and held her closer. Jeneil looked at him, smiled, and put her face near his again.

A different tempo began. It sounded like country western to Peter and the words filled him. *"May I have this dance for the rest of my life?"* He choked up, putting both of his arms around her tightly.

"Jeneil…," his voice almost gave out.

She held him. "I'm sorry about the young boy dying," Jeneil whispered.

Peter released her slightly. "How did you guess?"

"Your question about why go through all the work."

Peter swallowed hard as his emotions rushed at him. His chest hurt and his throat had a lump in it.

"Peter, I saw the man in the elevator. I listened to him talk to a nurse about loving his wife. He'll be okay. He's made of the right stuff. He knows that their lives will be wasted if he wastes his. There's no explanation and no blame for it. Like any other disaster, you pick up and keep walking. We're all fragile and alone, but we have each other as a people. You see all the tragedies. Many families live out normal, uneventful lives watching generations grow. I can't explain who and why, but there is a balance. There is. I love you, Peter. I belong to you. I know that with everything in me. I want us to get married and have children, as many children as we can manage together and we'll watch them grow up and marry. They'll bring us their children. I want that, Peter. I can't imagine myself married to anyone else."

Peter swallowed past the lump, cleared his throat, and breathed deeply. "I needed this, Jeneil. I needed all of this. You've been magic for me since I met you." He kissed her. Her lips felt warm and soft. She felt alive to him. "Jeneil, I love you for all of this craziness." He kissed her again. He could feel the fire and passion in her kiss. Clinging to her, he felt the warmth of her passion fill and renew him. "Are we allowed to leave the prom?"

"Why? Do you want to visit the hay barn?"

Peter smiled and lightly kissed her lips.

Jeneil lay with her head resting on Peter's chest, enjoying being with him and close to him. He smiled at her, continuing to twist a strand of her long dark hair around his hand. She had made alive feel good to him. He looked at her hardly believing that she was real.

"Mrs. Peter Chang, I love you so much. I don't recognize myself right now."

She smiled. "Mrs. Peter Chang. That sounds so right." The telephone interrupted. Peter reached for it and handed it to her. "Dennis Blair. Yes, of course I remember you," she said, and Peter wondered who Dennis Blair was. "Don't apologize. How can I help you? Did Robert give you a schedule? Then you know more about my schedule than I do right now." She laughed lightly. "Tomorrow morning is fine. It's only things that I can schedule. No really, I'd like to help out. I really would. I'll be there. You're welcome." She handed the receiver to Peter to hang up.

"Who's Dennis Blair?"

"Director of the Summer Stock Playhouse," she answered, stretching out beside him and snuggling against him. "He needs some volunteers for his next production."

"Robert gave him your number?" Peter asked, annoyed.

"I met Dennis at Robert's place and I offered to help."

"When?"

"Saturday morning."

"Honey, aren't you spreading yourself too thin?"

"I love your concern, but both Robert and the Summer Playhouse are short term projects. A few weeks I would guess, and I'm really curious about being backstage. I feel like having dessert now." She sat up. "I'll be right back."

Peter watched her walk away. He wondered what Dennis Blair would drag into their lives. Didn't she have more than a usual quota of men? Women outnumbered men yet there didn't seem to be a shortage of them in her life.

Jeneil returned and kissed his lips lightly then put a miniature cheesecake into his mouth. "When did you find time to make all of these?"

She chuckled. "Peter, you must be confusing me with a former girlfriend. I make brownies, gingerbread or carrot cake, remember. Fancy pastries will never be something I'll achieve. I bought these in the French bakery at the mall."

He took her hand. "I'm not confusing you with anybody. I never dated anybody who could cook. I don't think so anyway. I never asked. I never cared."

"See why living together is important."

He smirked. "Trust me I wouldn't care if you couldn't cook."

She kissed his cheek. "Sure, sure, this from a guy who loves Sunday dinners."

"I never cared for Sunday dinners until you," he defended.

Putting her head next to his, she touched his shoulder gently. "Right now, I have a very strong desire to be Mrs. Peter Chang." She smiled, putting her arms round his neck. "There's something else I'd like."

"Oh, that last one about being Mrs. Peter Chang will be tough to beat, honey, but try anyway. Name it; it's yours," he said, "anything."

"It's about having children."

"What about them?" He looked at her with curiosity.

"I want us to plan when we'll have them."

"That should be easy. Everybody should."

"No, you don't understand. I want us to decide that we're ready for a child, prepare ourselves physically and emotionally, then plan a special night when we conceive a child so we'll know that we created a life together at that moment. I want that moment to be sacred." Her words echoed to the center of him. He stayed looking at her. It surprised him that he was choking up.

"I've never thought about the details of having children." He took her hand and kissed it. "You're more ready for marriage than I am. You're more ready for life. You have a reverence and a respect for the whole idea and purpose." He kissed her hand again. "I just want you to be Mrs. Peter Chang. I'll catch up, honey. I promise you that." He kissed her lips, trying to let her know how much deep emotion and respect he felt for her. There were moments when he could feel his love for her increase. This was one of those times. It left him without words. He looked at her. "I love you, Jeneil, and that doesn't cover what I'm feeling right now," he whispered, kissing her cheek gently.

"That reached you where you live, didn't it?" she asked softly. He nodded, resting his lips near her neck and enjoying her warmth. "Good, we're going to be great together when were married, Peter. I can feel it."

"I think so, too, songbird," he whispered.

"Songbird?" she asked questioningly.

He looked at her. "My grandfather is right. You are a songbird." He kissed her. She responded. Each was surprised by the passion that resulted.

Ten

Jeneil was up before Peter in the morning. As he walked through the kitchen door, she kissed him. "I love you, Peter the Great," she said, handing him some juice.

"Well you're a bundle of energy this morning," he said, yawning.

"I'm excited about the Summer Stock. I hope it's everything I imagine."

"What're you imagining?"

"Hard work, camaraderie, a united effort."

"What are you helping out with?" he asked, noticing the faded jeans she was wearing.

"Painting scenery, but I'll do anything, even costumes or sweeping floors if I have to, but probably painting. Robert is Art Director and he's painting, too."

Peter's spine stiffened. "Robert's involved, too? I didn't know that. One thing about you civilized people, you don't hold a grudge. It's business as usual."

She smiled. "Here, I made you and Steve those sandwiches you guys like. Put it all together after you heat the container in the microwave."

He kissed her cheek. "Thanks honey, Steve loves those sandwiches. Have fun at the playhouse," he said, walking to the door.

*****

Jeneil arrived at the playhouse early. Dennis arrived shortly after. "Wow, a person who arrives early. I don't know if I can deal with that," he teased, smiling. He unlocked the side door which led to a long corridor. "Wander around while I get some work together in the office. Get a feel for the place. The others will straggle in soon. The cabaret ran late last night; the hours are killing the cast. That's why volunteers are so important to us."

Jeneil walked into a large room filled with racks of clothes lined up in sections. Walking into the next room, she found a large table littered with old paper coffee cups, partially eaten sandwiches, and ashtrays filled with old cigarette butts. On another table were a coffee maker and several cans of coffee.

"Ugh," she said, smelling the mixture of odors and stale air. Going to the window, she unlocked the metal latch and lifted the dirty-paned panel as far as it would go. Cool morning air rushed in and Jeneil breathed deeply. Noticing a large waste barrel in the corner, she pulled it to the table and began cleaning it of debris. A double sink in the corner was full of sponges and soiled clothes. She grimaced, but took a sponge, rinsed it under warm water, and wiped the table clean. Next, she attacked the area with the coffee maker. Carrying it to the sink, she emptied it of old coffee and cleaned the metal container, setting it back on the clean table. Noticing instructions for making coffee taped to the wall, she followed the directions and soon had a fresh pot brewing. Scanning the room, she saw a closet and looked into its darkness. She caught sight of a broom handle behind some boxes of rags and wrapped paper cups. Rescuing it from its hostage position, she quickly swept the floor.

Dennis appeared at the door. "I smell coffee," he said, stepping inside the room. "Jeneil, what have you done? I think you've located our lunchroom. It's been missing for a while now. Look at this place! Boy, the group will love you. And coffee, too." He smiled, pouring himself a cup.

Robert Danzieg walked in. "Coffee? I really smell coffee? I thought that machine was a replica. I've never seen it make coffee." He laughed.

"Jeneil is a self starter, Robert." Dennis smiled.

Robert put his arm around Jeneil. "Told you that we needed her here, Dennis."

"Well, next time I'll make toast too, and really impress everyone," Jeneil said.

"Bagels, cream cheese, and oranges, Jeneil," Dennis corrected. "That's the popular food here."

"All right, I can remember that," she answered.

"She's not a go-fer, Dennis. She's mine. Remember that," Robert interrupted between sips of coffee

"Okay, okay. She's yours," Dennis surrendered. "Just so we get the scenery done."

"Can we start now?" Jeneil asked.

Robert smiled at her and squeezed her shoulder. "I love your fire, Jeneil."

"Where do I start? Shall I take inventory of any tools and buckets of paint we have around?" she asked. Robert looked at Dennis, and they both smiled.

"I love her already. Jeneil, we lost control of what's around. If you could do that while Robert and I catch up on scene changes that would keep expenses down." Dennis poured another cup of coffee. "Robert, my blood pressure has just fallen several points, I love her."

"Gosh, you guys are easy to impress." Jeneil laughed. "I'll get started now. When the season began, was there a spot for all the inventory?"

"Move over Robert, I feel a hug coming on. Jeneil, I love the way your mind works. Yes, the room at the end of the corridor, the one with ladders and staging in it. It looks like a garage." He kissed Jeneil's cheek. "Welcome to the madness. Robert, excuse me, I'm going to my office to cry joyful tears. Meet me there." He left pretending to wipe away tears.

Jeneil laughed. "They really are shorthanded here, aren't they?"

"Sadly so," Robert said, "and sometimes the volunteers they attract want to be part-time actors and actresses who don't grasp the elbow work end of the production. Thanks for coming in. I feel calmer knowing I have you on my art staff."

"You're welcome," she said, "now let me get to that room and see what we have here."

"I'll meet with Dennis then join you there."

Jeneil surveyed the room. Observing the clutter, she decided what was lacking was management. With everyone working on everything, order had been lost. Taking a notebook from her purse, she started toward the storage shelves. She surprised herself by having an understanding of what was happening there. The whole situation seemed to fall quickly into place in her mind. Realizing that she'd have to plow through debris again, she searched for barrels, making a note of the need to keep trash barrels near the work areas. She pulled a corrugated box from a heap of boards and labeled it trash with a black marker then turned toward the debris and launched her attack. Robert walked in as she was listing needed items in her notebook.

"Jeneil, you don't waste any time." He looked around and grinned as she climbed down the stepladder. It amused him to see her in a carpenter's apron. "You got spunk kid. I like your style."

Jeff walked in. "Jeneil! I didn't know that you were here. I heard that we had a new volunteer with great promise." He hugged her.

Robert was surprised. "You know each other?"

"She's my landlady and a good friend." Jeff laughed and kissed her cheek. Looking at Robert, he shrugged. "I'm assigned to you today until noon, and then I go into rehearsal."

"Oh great! You're one more than I thought I'd get. The staging for the largest pieces of backdrop should have the joints reinforced. It's labeled 'PC105.' Here's a sketch of it in stages," he said, handing Jeff a sheet of paper. "It might be good to tack that to the wall and label it 'Do Not Remove.'"

"Okay," Jeff answered, and walked away to begin work.

Jeneil smiled. "You're organized, Robert. This should go well."

"Landlady, huh? You're full of surprises."

"Robert, really, I make sure water runs but not through the roof. How surprising can a landlady be?"

He laughed. "I don't know about you, mystery lady."

"I noticed several hammers. Does that mean there's a crew?"

"I'm afraid not," Robert answered, opening his folder. "I have a list of cast members who are assigned to me at odd hours during the day. That's it."

"Is there a list of volunteers somewhere?"

"Yeah, I think I saw one in here." He thumbed through some papers. "Here it is."

"Let me call them," Jeneil suggested, "and try to organize some help."

Robert smiled. "Be my guest. It could help."

"Maybe being Saturday morning, I can catch a few at home." She headed to the office. Knocking on Dennis's door, she asked to use the phone. "Will it disturb you?"

"No, go ahead." Dennis watched her as she dialed and spoke to volunteers. He liked her way with people. By the end of the list, he was impressed with her sense of organization and her ability to enlist people.

"Dennis, what do you think of announcing the need for help?"

"I wish we could, but we would get an influx of people suffering from summer boredom and not really committed. We need to be careful about who we take on."

"Then how about everybody in the cast and crew recruiting at least one person, they'll be prescreened that way."

"That's an idea. I'll get a memo out. I like that. I do," he said, closing a file drawer.

"I hope it works." Jeneil smiled. "I'd better get back to Robert," and she left. Dennis stared at the door after she'd gone, then smiled, raising his eyebrows.

During lunch break, Dennis went to find Robert and found him sitting on some corrugated boxes having lunch with Jeneil and Jeff. He laughed. "Well, I was going to invite you to lunch but you seem to be well looked after."

"Join us," Jeneil offered.

"Are you the caterer?" Dennis asked, sitting down.

Robert teased. "Jeneil has a compulsion to make the world healthy."

"I'm going to ignore that, Robert," Jeneil said.

"Well, it beats a greasy burger." Dennis smiled, biting into a sandwich.

Jeff stood up. "I've got some lines to study. Thanks for lunch, Jeneil."

"Wait Jeff, I'll go with you. I've got a phone call to make. You can show me where the payphone is. I'll be back in fifteen minutes, Robert." They walked away talking.

"Something developing there?" Dennis asked, watching.

"Are you serious?" Robert laughed, watching Jeneil.

"Robert, you're drooling." Dennis grinned. "What she does to jeans is unreal," he said, shaking his head. "You're very open about your attraction to her, Robert."

"It's deliberate," Robert answered, putting a grape in his mouth.

"Aren't you afraid of Mr. Muscle?" Dennis laughed.

"No, it's her stinking loyalty to him that makes me crazy. But let him screw up just once and I'll be right there."

Dennis looked at him. "I've never seen you so predatory."

"I know, and at times I hate myself for it, until she gets within two feet of me again then my conscience dies."

"She's a nice kid," Dennis commented.

"Dennis, that's no kid. That's a woman in solid capital letters man, pure woman."

Dennis grinned. "I don't know how long you can have her exclusively."

"What?" Robert asked, surprised. "Why?"

"I heard her on the telephone. She's got some abilities I can use."

"Nice kid, huh?" Robert teased.

"Robert, believe me, look at the age difference. She's got a professional cool to her. What does she do for a living?"

"Who the hell knows? She's Jeff's landlady. That's all I know, except for Peter."

"Mr. Muscle?" Dennis laughed.

"An orthopedic surgeon. Can you see her wasted on the likes of a doctor?" Robert shook his head.

"Why do you say that?

"The girl throbs with art and sensitivity, Dennis. What can a science man know about a woman of her caliber? It's a damn shame."

"Boy, Robert, you're not only getting predatory, you're getting narrow-minded, too. What's the girl doing to you?"

"Nothing, that's what makes me mad." Robert and Dennis both laughed.

By two, volunteers were arriving asking for Jeneil. Robert and Dennis walked into the scenery room. "Jeneil," Robert smiled, "I don't know what the hell you told them, but we're getting all kinds of help."

"The problem is management, I think," Jeneil said. "You people need someone to be liaison with volunteers. Most of the comments I got were, 'We never knew what to do.'"

Dennis looked thoughtfully. "Really? Can you keep an eye on it and get back to me?"

"I can do that." She smiled. "Would you feel okay about each of the volunteers bringing in a recruit, if details were explained to them?"

Dennis smiled broadly. "Don't get too comfortable in scenery. I think there's a place for you in another area here." He hugged her. "Thank you for coming in."

Robert groaned. "Dennis, you promised."

Jeneil smiled. "I'm enjoying this. I really am."

"See," Robert remarked, "she likes it right here."

"Let me see what can be worked out." Dennis sighed and walked away.

Robert smiled and put his arm around her.

Toward late afternoon, Dennis watched as Jeneil talked to two volunteers, an elderly couple, who were leaving. They liked her, Dennis could see that. As they left, he joined her. "Jeneil, the day has been a success because of you."

"Dennis that couple shouldn't be in here. They did inventory for me today and they're good at detail, but they're physically limited in the painting and constructing. Do you think we could find a place for them in costumes and props? I know they'd be an asset there. They're really enthusiastic. I'd hate to see their enthusiasm lost."

"I don't see why not, that would free two others for here if necessary."

"Great." She made a note on her list. "I have commitments for hours this week for all the volunteers who were here. I'll call them the night before to thank them for helping as a reminder."

Dennis shook his head and smiled. "You're good, Jeneil, really good."

"I like order Dennis and so do the other volunteers."

"Order? I'm not sure we know how to spell that around here."

Robert joined them. "Dennis, I'd like Jeneil to take a copy of the script home. She seems to have an understanding of staging. It would be good to have two minds working on the details."

"Now where did you pick up staging knowledge?" Dennis asked.

"I love theatre. I'm your audience," Jeneil answered.

"How much can we pile on her, Robert? She's still sitting for you."

Jeneil sighed. "Actually you'd be doing me a favor. Peter has been on a special medical case these past few weeks so his hours have been regular, but I'm afraid now that the case had been discharged he'll be on an alternating schedule again. When that happens then we'll have only weekends together. This project would fill my weeknights, so give me a script."

Robert looked at Dennis and smiled broadly, raising his eyebrows in delight. "Give her a script, Dennis. Go get the woman a script," he insisted.

Dennis frowned. "Are you sure, Jeneil?"

"The script is no problem, Dennis. I can fit that into odd hours. Sometimes I do have other commitments that take up my time at night, but I'll work that out."

Dennis cleaned a smudge of dirt from her cheek. "Promise me that you'll let me know when it starts to be too much."

She smiled. "I promise."

"Then I'll get you a script," Dennis said, looking at Robert, who could hardly contain his excitement.

*****

Jeneil arrived home tired but excited. Putting the material from the playhouse on the small kitchen table, she headed for the shower. Peter unlocked the apartment door and heard the water running. Opening the bathroom door, he called, "Honey, I'm home. Tell me you love me."

"I love you." Jeneil laughed.

"Thanks," Peter answered and closed the door. Going to the kitchen, he sat down at the table. He picked up the material from the playhouse. A business sized envelope fell to the floor. Picking it up, he read the note on the front. *Sweetheart, these are my notes on staging. Great to have you working so closely with me. Let's get together soon and go over this. Love RD.* Peter's jaw tightened. Jeneil walked in wrapped in her blue robe with a towel around her wet hair, the scent of her perfume floating on the air. "What's this?" Peter asked.

Taking the envelope, Jeneil read the note. "Robert and I are working on staging together for the scenery. These are his notes."

"No, what's with sweetheart and love RD?"

"Oh gosh, you know Robert. He puts his arm around shoulders and kisses cheeks. He doesn't mean anything by it." She went to the bedroom.

Peter's mind answered like hell he didn't, he knew exactly what he was doing. Had Robert hoped he'd find the envelope? Peter grinned. He'd bet Robert was just waiting for him to mess up once with her. Danzieg, you've got a lot of street kid in you. Robert couldn't stand it that Jeneil was his. Peter chuckled, and went to the bedroom. Jeneil was at the bureau combing out her hair. Peter lay on the bed and watched her. "You look tired, baby."

"I am. There was lots of climbing up and down ladders, but I loved it. Dinner won't take long."

He smiled and got up. Standing behind her, he kissed her neck. "Let's go to dinner."

"Ooo, where?" She smiled, pinning the last strand of hair up.

"That small relaxed place near the ocean"

"That far away? I got a video and planned to relax together tonight."

He turned her around. "We could walk on the beach near the cove and then spend the night at Twin Pines."

She looked at him then grinned. "Do I hear the distant rumble of a schedule change? Tony was released on Thursday. They've switched you, haven't they? You rascal, you're trying to ploy me with romance to soften the blow. What shift is it next week?"

He looked at her. "The second shift for the next month."

"A month!" She couldn't hide her shock. "Peter a month? But why?"

"There are a couple of conventions coming up. We'll lose doctors to that. Vacation schedules are still in effect. Steve and I were asked to cover it."

"Stinker, when were you going to tell me?" She slipped her arm around his waist. "When does it begin?"

"Tomorrow."

"Ooo, you slithering sneak. This will cost you a baked stuffed shrimp dinner."

"Well, I'm willing to go for more than that." He grinned, pulling her closer to him.

"For starters, my love, for starters," and she snuggled against him. "I'll pack quickly, you sneak."

The telephone rang while Jeneil was packing. Peter answered. "Robert Danzieg, how the hell are you these days?" He chuckled. "Yes, she's here. She's packing. I'm taking her away from the dull routine of life for a short while, so don't keep her too long. Okay? I'm anxious for us to get away alone. Hold on." Peter grinned, enjoying having put the screws to Robert, and he put the receiver down. Good Chang, go right for the throat. He'd bet Robert was still stunned. He called Jeneil, hung up when she answered, and then went to the bedroom.

"I can't Robert. I won't be back until late tomorrow afternoon, but I'll have all the time in the world at night. Peter's been switched to second shift as I expected." Peter straightened up at that thought and went to her. Putting his hands at her side, he kissed her neck and tickled her. She screeched. "Peter! I'm sorry, Robert," she said, embarrassed. Peter bit her neck. "Peter!" she said, wriggling away.

He took the receiver from her. "Robert, we've got to go. Call her tomorrow night, okay? Right now she belongs to me," and he hung up.

"Peter, that was rude. What's gotten into you?" she asked, shocked.

"No, it wasn't rude." He held her by the waist. "He's a guy; he knows exactly what's happening," and he held her close. Eat your heart out, Danzieg, he smiled to himself, and then he kissed her. "Whose woman are you, baby?"

"Yours, you maniac."

"Then let's get away from here right know." He hugged her and lifted her off the floor.

*****

Peter started on the second shift smiling at how well the day had gone. Steve walked in, quickly getting into his lab coat. "Well, here we are, back at it again, Pete. So much for the Glory Boys. Here's your shovel, find the shit, and what the hell are you looking so pleased about?" Steve asked angrily.

"It's been a great day." Peter shrugged.

"Shit, you're high and I'm getting pimples."

"She sent you a pot roast dinner," Peter added.

"Yeah, well what I need is her clone with her mouth sutured so we won't fight."

Peter laughed. "You're determined to be miserable. I'll catch you later."

"Reformed drunk," Steve shouted at him, laughing. "I hate this shift," he added to the nurse at the desk.

"Why fight it," the nurse said, shrugging. She smiled and walked away.

"What is this? Was there a sale on happy pills somewhere?"

By the end of his shift, Peter's good mood had worn off as he realized the strain the new hours would put on his relationship with Jeneil. The apartment was quiet and dimly lit when he arrived home. Jeneil was asleep. Getting into bed and lying in the darkness, he missed having time to talk to her. She was therapeutic. He could talk to her about anything; Ki, Reed, the dream. Thinking about the first time they'd been together, he smiled. Then he remembered her fear of the changes that would affect them. He smiled again, pleased that their relationship had survived a few bumps. "I guess we'll survive this, too," he said as he stretched and closed his eyes.

Peter woke up as Jeneil was changing her purses. "Hey beautiful," he said, causing her to jump in surprise.

"Oh, I woke you. I'm sorry."

"Do you have time for a kiss?" he asked. She smiled, coming to his side of the bed and sitting down. He held her close as she kissed him. "I miss you already."

"I miss you, too," she said. "Robert stopped by last night. We went over the script together and Franklin Pierce called. The orchestra is doing Rossini this coming Sunday. I'd like to go to that."

He touched her arm. "I'd like to take you."

She smiled. "I'd like that, too. Would you mind if I went anyway?"

"That's the agreement."

"Thank you." She kissed him again. "I've got to get to work. Everything is in the fridge for you and Steve." She gathered her things, blew him a kiss from the doorway and left. Peter turned on his side and held her pillow against him. He sighed, thinking about all the men who surrounded her. Her pillow felt cool to him as he fell asleep.

Eleven

Peter couldn't believe almost a week had passed by already. His work schedule had been difficult; he had been called in for emergency surgery, and shift extensions were common and expected. He and Jeneil hadn't even seen each other. He never heard her leave and she never heard him come in. Plus, she was so busy at the playhouse. Putting his dinner in the microwave, he decided to call her but there was no answer. He wondered where she was. He shook his head thinking about their schedules. Next weekend was the Nebraska trip. Well at least they got to see each other tomorrow morning. Peter smiled at the thought.

Steve walked in. "Did you heat mine, too?"

"Yes."

"Oh good, I'm starved," Steve said as he stretched. "She's really too much sending me dinners, but I really appreciate it."

Peter put the heated containers on the table. "How come you're revved up lately? These hours don't seem to be affecting you at all."

Steve looked at him then around the room cautiously. "Pete, there's a nurse's aide on the third shift who's unbelievable. She's got the whole thing down to a fine art. You're out of there before you realize that you walked in. She's worth every dime she charges."

Peter stared at him. "Where the hell do you find the bed?"

Steve looked shocked. "Oh come on, Pete. Have you really gotten that civilized? Didn't you ever do without? Pete, you are living a sheltered life since you fell in love." Steve laughed. "Man, you've lost it all. She's one of the shrewdest pros I've ever seen. Haven't you noticed all the single guys on the second and third are smiling? I swear the hospital looks the other way. She's decreased the tension around here. Only you married guys are suffering."

"Physical is a strong force," Peter said, thinking out loud.

"What does that mean?"

"Nothing, Jeneil just wonders why everything becomes physical."

Steve laughed. "Hasn't she seen herself in a full length mirror?" He looked up quickly. "I'm sorry, Pete. I shouldn't have said that. She's yours."

Peter laughed and shrugged. "I know she's turning heads."

"That she is man. You've made the flower blossom, and the bees are attracted. Is everything okay with you two? Why, is she complaining about physical?"

Peter smiled. "We're fine. She doesn't like swarming bees."

"You're lucky."

"I am," Peter answered, missing her, "I really am."

The night was riddled with emergencies and Peter ended up working a double. As he opened the front door to the apartment building, Jeneil was coming down the stairs, dressed in jeans. Her arms were full. Seeing Peter, she put down everything on the stairs and hugged him. "I'd guessed that you'd worked a double. It's good seeing you awake." She kissed him.

"Honey, its seven. Where are you going?"

"To the playhouse, I have a volunteer crew coming in at eight. People get discouraged when they arrive and stand around."

"But we only have Saturdays and Sundays together."

"Well I planned on being back at one. Get some sleep. We'll have lunch together here." She smiled.

"But I'm due in at two, baby."

"But you've worked a double! They can't do that," she snapped.

He was surprised by her outburst. "It's getting to you already?"

She closed her eyes. "It's not a routine yet. Give me some time to get used to it. I'm spoiled, too."

"I haven't minded cerebral. I guess I'd better get used to it." He held her.

"Robert wants me to sit tomorrow morning."

"No," Peter said emphatically. "No, Jeneil. He knows we only have weekends. What's he pulling?"

"He's not pulling anything, Peter. We've both been knee-deep in the playhouse. But you're right, Sunday is ours. He's taking me to dinner and the production at the playhouse tonight. Okay?" Peter didn't like it and Jeneil noticed. "I won't go."

"No, go with him. He sees you more than I do. That's hard to take."

"That's not his fault," Jeneil defended Robert.

"It's not mine either," Peter defended himself.

"I know that. Why are we looking for blame here?"

"I don't know. I'm just tired. You'd better get to your volunteer crew," he said quietly.

She smiled. "Let's make tomorrow special, Sunday dinner and us."

"Promise?" He smiled.

"Promise." She kissed him. Picking up her things, she kissed his cheek and left. Peter sat on the stairs. Adrienne came down, watching him.

"Counting stair treads?" she joked, sitting next to him. He smiled tiredly. "I heard about your month on the second shift. Jeneil just left for the playhouse, huh?" He nodded. Adrienne sighed. "She loves it, Peter. It's all she talks about. I don't know how she's managing the schedule she keeps. At this point, I think she'd give up the corporation for the playhouse. She's on fire over it."

Peter looked up at her. He knew it, too. "Thanks Adrienne."

Adrienne laughed. "In her eyes, Dennis Blair walks on water."

That surprised Peter. "We haven't talked. We haven't seen each other. I don't know any details."

"She's different, Peter. She's alive over this and fiercely defensive. Ask Hollis. Ride it out, hun. Just lay low. What you two have is very good. Give her some space."

"With my hours that's all I can give her."

"Look at it as a lucky break then, Peter. At least you'll be too busy to notice that she's not around. I've got to go," she said, patting his arm. "You'd better get some sleep, you look beat." She stood up.

"You're right," he said, standing. "Thanks for the advice."

"You're welcome. Actually I'm jumping into this for Jeneil. She's a sister to me. This playhouse thing is good for her. I can see that, but you're good for her, too. I don't want her to lose it. I want her to have both of you."

Peter climbed into bed. The sheets felt cool and his body let him know how much lying down was appreciated. He fell asleep.

The sound of his telephone ringing startled him awake. He answered groggily.

"Peter, are you still sleeping?"

"Jeneil? Yes, I was." He looked at his watch. "Honey, its one-fifteen, where are you?"

"I'm still down here at the playhouse. Things ran late. I'll never make it back in time for lunch. I'm glad I followed my instincts and got your meals ready. Be sure you eat. You'll need to be careful with the hours you're keeping." He was disappointed, but he stayed silent. "Peter, are you awake? Did you hear me?"

"I'm awake," he answered. "Thanks for the food and for calling. I would have overslept." He was getting annoyed.

"I'd better let you get ready. Don't fall asleep again."

"I won't."

"I'll see you later then, bye." He waited for her to hang up then placed the receiver back hard. Snapping the covers back, he went to shower. Stepping into the tepid water, he turned the hot water off. Cold water slashed at him. He was getting used to cold showers.

*****

The shift was busy because they were shorthanded. Peter wouldn't let himself think about Jeneil and Robert at dinner and the theatre. He was already in a dark mood and was afraid of the anger that may ensue. Steve sat across from him during dinner break. "Oh Pete, go visit Lucy on the second shift. You look bad."

"I'm going to the exercise room," Peter said, cleaning up.

"Jeneil won't have to know about Lucy."

"Steve, it isn't about sex. Okay?" he snapped.

"Okay," Steve answered, backing off.

Peter apologized. "I'm having trouble dealing with civilized right now."

Steve looked at him. "Do you want to explain that?"

"No." Peter was paged to ICU. "So much for the exercise room." He left, slamming the door.

Peter's shift was extended. It didn't surprise him. The ER was strange, full of odd cases and odd circumstances. He ran from the ICU to the ER most of the night. By midnight, the ER was full. Everyone worked at a panicked pace to handle the workload. A drug overdose patient was brought in on a stretcher, bleeding badly from a head wound and was out cold. The paramedics and two police officers were furious with him. Because of hallucinations, he had wildly attacked anyone who had tried to help him. An intern dressed the patient's head wound and left the patient alone as other cases demanded attention while the paramedics administered first aid to each other and the officers, one of whom had a laceration. No one noticed the patient regain consciousness and sit up until a nurse screamed as he jumped off the gurney and shoved her to one side, placing himself in a corner of the ER. Wild eyed and frantic, he reached into his boot and slipped out a six inch knife.

"Holy shit," one officer said. "That guy has an arsenal on him. You should see what I took off him and he's still got more."

"Shoot the bastard," the other officer snapped as he held a bandage to his cut arm. "I'm sick of protecting scum from themselves."

A paramedic tried to reason with the patient. In a glassy-eyed frenzy, he lunged at the paramedic. Everyone backed away. No one could get near him.

Peter finished working on his case then walked out to see what the fuss was about. Steve walked off the elevator as Peter stepped into the main area.

"What's this?" Steve asked.

"I'm not sure, I just got here." They moved to the front and understood all too well.

"Oh shit," Steve cried. "What's he on?"

"We don't know. We were treating his head wound," the paramedic answered as a crowd began to form.

Peter yelled to security. "Get these people out of here, except for ER cases, and call the cops. These two need more help than we can give. Divert any emergencies to Central General until this is cleared up."

With the crowd gathering, the patient was becoming more agitated. Picking up filing brackets from the desk, he threw them into the crowd, sending people scattering, screaming from fright.

"They never listen." Steve shook his head. "They always want to watch the action."

"Tighten security around us, damn it," Peter yelled. The patient went wild, picking things up and throwing them into the crowd. The sound of screaming and glass breaking filled the air as the patient tossed bottles from shelves. "He's over the edge," Peter said to Steve.

Sirens could be heard in the distance. The patient was pulling at everything around him. Peter's stored anger rose to the surface as the crowd pushed against them from behind and the patient lunged at them from the front. Taking a large metal tray as a shield, he inched toward the patient, ducking the flying debris. The patient stopped his frantic tossing as he spotted Peter getting closer. Peter stopped, watching the man with the caution of a loaded gun. Keeping his eyes on the man, he called behind him, "Get everybody back. I'll try to get him out of the corner so we can surround him." The crowd eased back, spellbound. Moving carefully across the cluttered floor, Peter inched himself closer. The man watched blinking, trying to focus on what was happening.

"We won't have too many seconds to handle this. Everyone get into position," Peter ordered. Steve organized the group of staff around him. Peter edged closer, his mouth dry. He tried to remember what Ki had taught him about focusing on what he wanted to happen. Clearing debris from his path with his foot, he inched closer. In his peripheral vision, he could see broken pieces of bottle scattered on the floor. Shit, he thought, where the hell was he supposed to land this guy?

Peter zeroed in on the man mentally, watching closely, hoping to notice the slightest indication of a lunge. It was close; Peter could feel the tension building. Peter breathed deeply as he knew the next second could be it. The man screamed and came at Peter with the force of a stampede. Peter turned as best he could to put the man's back to the waiting police and staff. The man pushed against Peter, sending him against the wall. Stunned, Peter punched at the man, sending him back only about a half foot. The man came at him again and Peter felt the unmistakable pain of a sharp blade against his flesh. Knowing this was his only chance Peter pushed at the man again and in that instant hit him in the stomach with the metal tray as hard as he could. The impact of the collision sent the man sprawling across the floor toward the waiting police, ricocheting Peter back over the desk into the chair behind it. Peter felt his head go numb and blackness circled for an instant. His leg was in pain. His arm felt wet. Steve was at his side, moving quickly, checking him out.

"Man, you're one tough guy when you get mad. That was crazy. You know that, don't you?"

Peter concentrated on breathing. Everything hurt. "How deep is the cut?"

"Maybe a stitch or two. I'd beat you up right now if you didn't look so pathetic. What if that had been a tendon. Goodbye surgeon. Shit man."

"I could work on the SWAT team." Peter laughed.

Steve shook his head angrily then laughed, too. "Come on, I'll get you to a booth and check you out properly."

*****

Jeneil opened her eyes and stared into the darkness. A cold chill passed through her. Turning on the lamp, she looked at the clock. Another double? The hospital usually didn't do those two nights in a row. She felt uneasy. Picking up the telephone, she began to dial the hospital. She put the receiver back and paced. The feeling of uneasiness wouldn't pass. She went to the kitchen and poured a glass of milk. The telephone rang. Her heart skipped a beat. Going to the bedroom, she stared at Peter's telephone as it rang. Why were they calling here if he was there? She approached the ringing phone. Lifting the receiver, she answered softly.

"Jeneil?" The voice sounded familiar, but she couldn't place it. "It's Steve Bradley. Is Pete there?"

"He's on duty, isn't he?" she asked, puzzled. Steve was silent. The uneasiness in her turned to fear. There was something in Steve's voice. "What happened?"

"He should be home soon. Have him call me at the hospital."

"No, something has happened. What is it Steve?" There was a pause. "Steve, please."

"Pete was in a scuffle here in the ER. He's banged up. I wish that I had driven him home, that's all."

Jeneil's heart stopped. "Why didn't you call me, Steve? I would have gone to the hospital for him." Her voice was shaky.

"He insisted he was all right. My timing is bad, he's probably almost home now."

Jeneil heard the key in the door. "He's here now, Steve. Hold on." She put the receiver down and rushed to the bedroom door. Peter limped in. She noticed his bandaged arm.

"Steve's on the phone." She managed to get her words together.

Peter grimaced as he sat on the bed. "I made it," he said into the receiver. "The pain killer is starting to work now. If I hadn't fallen over the desk, I'd be fine now." He chuckled. "Thanks for your concern. I'll be okay. Yeah, tomorrow." He hung up.

Jeneil sat next to him. "Still haven't lost your taste for street fights, huh?"

He started to laugh. "Ooo, don't make jokes."

"Oh, Peter." She leaned against him. "Who did you scuffle with?"

"A drug victim," Peter replied. Jeneil sighed. "Honey, it was a strange set of circumstances. It won't happen again in my lifetime."

"And your arm?"

"I got cut."

"How?" Peter was silent. "How, Peter?" she asked again.

"He had a knife. Baby, the whole thing was unusual."

"Can I get you anything?" She stood up quickly, trying to stay calm.

"Something to drink. I'm really thirsty."

Jeneil's hand shook as she poured apple juice into a glass. She took a deep breath so she wouldn't cry. It didn't work. Handing the glass to him, she then reached for a tissue.

"Come on," he said, taking her hand, "don't get worked up. I was surrounded by help. Most of the damage happened when I landed on a metal chair." His telephone rang. He picked up the receiver. "Dr. Sprague. No, I'm not hurt badly. I know it wasn't procedure but the situation didn't fit the textbook. He just kept destroying the place. Believe me, I'm not a hero. Well, I wouldn't mind that at all. Yeah thanks, bye."

"What did your bravery get you? A lecture?" She shook her head.

"Honey, they're concerned. It got me tomorrow off. I've got to lie down."

Jeneil undid his shoes and removed them as he laid back. She got into bed and faced him. "I'll sleep on the sofa."

"No, don't go, stay next to me. The pain is easing up. You lying there makes it perfect. How did your evening go?"

"Uneventful compared to yours."

"Robert behaved himself?" Peter asked openly.

She looked at him. "Robert and I settled that weeks ago. In fact, one of the actresses has been sending vibrations his way."

"Is he listening?"

"I don't know." She laughed. "Should I ask him?"

He smiled. "And what about Dennis Blair?"

"I don't know anything about Dennis Blair's personal life. I like him a lot. He's easy to talk to, knowledgeable about a lot of things, and an all around nice guy. He's professional at work and sincerely interested in people. He thinks I have talent I haven't tapped into yet, and he and I are becoming very good friends."

"And how old is this specimen of near perfection."

"Somewhere in his early thirties. Now don't start imagining anything. We're good friends. We like each other, we trust each other. I really like him."

"Uh-huh, and isn't this how you and Robert started out?"

"Now that's enough, Peter. Robert and I are good friends, too. Considering the fiasco we went through, we are very close. I still trust him."

He tried move closer to her. "Ouch. Damn it, the first time in a week we're both awake and in bed together and I can't move."

"What do you want?"

"Don't be naïve. I'll settle for a kiss." She smiled, leaned over him and kissed him warmly. "Ooo, you're feeling good, baby. We'd better stop."

Jeneil snuggled next to him. They lay together silently for awhile and Peter fell asleep. Jeneil smiled, kissed his shoulder lightly and fell asleep shortly after.

Twelve

The pain in Peter's arm woke him as he turned over. He opened his eyes and looked for Jeneil. She was gone. He sighed. He laid there wondering what to do. He was stiff and sore. He needed a painkiller. It was nine. He had slept well. The bedroom door opened slowly. Jeneil peaked in. "Oh, you're awake." She smiled and walked in. "How are you feeling?"

"Pain."

"I'll get some water." She returned with a glass. "Where are your pills?"

"In my pocket," he answered, reaching for a small envelope. Jeneil handled it for him. He lay back.

"When that takes effect, maybe you should change into your robe so you can relax."

"Yeah, I will. How long have you been up?"

"Since seven. We should bathe your arm, shouldn't we?" She felt his head. "You're slightly feverish." She left and returned with a glass of juice and some white tablets.

"What's this?"

"Vitamin C. You don't have a choice. Take them," she insisted.

"Jeneil, really."

"Humor me, medicine man. Take all eight of them."

He did. "I don't believe this."

"Oh quiet." She kissed him gently. "When you're in my hospital, you go by my rules. Let's bathe your arm." Mixing peroxide in a plastic basin of hot water, Jeneil put it on the counter. She undid the bandages on Peter's arm. The cut was red and swollen. "Stitches? It required stitches?" She looked at him and sighed. "Put your arm in the solution." Jeneil left Peter soaking his arm. She returned with a bowl of muddy green water and a strainer. Drying his arm, she emptied the basin and rinsed it. Filling it again with the green water she poured through the strainer, she added hot water. "Okay, now you can soak in this."

"What is it?"

"Herbs," she replied. He looked at her. She pointed to the basin. He put his arm in it, shaking his head.

"Ouch! It's burning. What's in it?"

"I told you, herbs. Keep your arm in it."

"This is worse than the peroxide"

"Soak until the water is cool. Is it biting deep inside the cut?"

"Yes," he said, wincing.

"Oh good, we got to you in time. I'll be right back." She returned with his robe and pajamas. She turned on the shower then toweled his arm dry. "Your shower will rinse off the residue."

"Are you coming in with me?" He grinned.

"Your painkiller is working, isn't it?" She smiled and he kissed her cheek.

Jeneil had the kitchen buzzing when Peter stepped through the door. "What are you up to?" She handed him a glass of water and eight more tablets. "Oh come on, I just had eight."

"That was an hour ago."

"Jeneil, enough of this."

"Take them now!" she said adamantly.

"Gee, I'm glad you didn't go into nursing." He swallowed the eight tablets.

"Now go lie down."

"I don't want to. I'm okay."

"No, you're not. You're not in pain so you think you're fine."

"Then lie down with me. We can talk."

She checked the oven and adjusted the heat. "Okay, let's lie down." She settled him into bed and fixed the covers.

"You do love to fuss." He smiled. "Lay down damn it."

"Ooo, you can't stand not being in charge." She grinned as she slipped onto her side of the bed.

"I know," he said. "I'm frustrated. I want to make love to you but I know my arm and leg can't handle it." She nestled near him and kissed his shoulder, running her hand gently across his chest. She kissed his neck and pressed against him. "And you're not helping the situation doing that."

"Sure I am," she whispered. "I can handle this."

He looked at her. "What?"

She smiled then kissed him. "I've learned a few things being with you." She kissed him again passionately as he held her close to him.

"You're serious!" he said, surprised and breathless from her kiss.

"Of course, what do you think you have here, a child?"

He smiled. "You are beautiful." She kissed him more passionately. He let her handle the situation. "Lay in my right arm, honey. I want to hold you." He kissed her several times. "You're incredible, you know that?"

"Some things are instinctive." She grinned.

"You are one hell of a woman. You're an odd mixture of woman and child." He kissed her warmly. "You've impressed me." He smiled, and Jeneil smiled, enjoying his lavish words for her.

Jeneil spent the rest of the morning fussing over him. From breakfast in bed to vitamin C every hour, she had overwhelmed him completely. He smiled to himself thinking about her. Something smelled good. He couldn't believe he was getting hungry again. She brought in his tray.

"I'm starved," he said, looking at his plate. "I love your Sunday dinners."

The telephone rang. "Hi, Franklin. Did you really?" She smiled. "Where? Well, I never thought to look there. I won't be able to go to the concert. Is there somewhere I can meet you during the week to get the cassette?"

Peter touched her arm. "Go," he mouthed to her. She shook her head no. He interrupted. "Honey, I'll take you."

"Peter, I can't."

"I'm going to work tomorrow. I can go to a quiet concert today. I insist."

"Franklin, I will be there. Yes, that's fine. I don't know, Peter," she said, hanging up.

"I do. We're going." He finished eating his squash. "I'm feeling a lot better and I only had one pain pill. I'm really improved. Get yourself ready."

She kissed him. "I love you," she said, taking his tray.

His telephone rang. "Hey Pete, your voice sounds strong."

"Steve, I feel fine. Jeneil has pampered me all day. I'm rested. I'll be in tomorrow."

"Oh good, this place is crazy right now. She'll have to take me as a patient if I'm alone another day. Are you sure you can deal with it so soon?"

"Well I'll know by tonight. We're going to a concert."

"A concert! Pete, are you shittin' me?"

Peter laughed. "So help me it's true. I'll know how well I can handle being up and around after that."

Steve laughed. "A concert, my roommate. Boy, what's she doing to you? I'll call you later then." Steve hung up, laughing.

Peter got up to get ready. He was a bit stiff, but he could deal with it. Jeneil insisted on driving to the concert. Franklin Pierce came up to them as they walked in.

"Jeneil, you look beautiful." He kissed her cheek. Reaching into his pocket, he pulled out the Rossini cassette.

"Franklin, you're great," she said, taking it. "Thank you so much."

"So Peter, another day off. Good to see you here," Franklin said. Peter smiled.

"Is this a private party or is anybody invited?" Robert Danzieg asked, walking up to the group.

"Hey, Robert Danzieg." Franklin smiled and extended his hand.

"Franklin, how are you? Hi, sweetheart." Robert kissed Jeneil's lips lightly. Peter felt tension in his spine.

"You didn't tell me that you were coming today when we talked about it," Jeneil said, surprised.

Peter looked at Robert. Transparent as hell, Robert, he thought to himself.

Robert smiled. "Peter, good to see you."

Peter's mind answered, I'll just bet it is. Peter smiled. "Now and then I'm free."

Jeneil took Peter's arm. "If you people don't mind, I'd like to get Peter to a seat. He has the day off to recuperate from a scuffle in the emergency room. I don't want him to overdo it."

"I'm fine, honey." Peter put his arm around her.

"I heard that on the news. That was more than a scuffle. I heard the guy almost destroyed the place. I didn't realize that was you involved." Franklin shook Peter's hand. "That was an awfully brave thing you did."

"Believe me, I didn't do it alone."

"He's being modest. He has stitches and bruises to show for his efforts." Jeneil smiled at Peter.

Peter squeezed her shoulder and noticed Robert watching. Peter looked at Robert. "But it got me a day of pampering at home."

Robert forced a smile. "That should ease the pain."

"Come on, Peter. Let's get you seated." Jeneil took him by the hand.

"Here, let me help find a seat," Robert said and joined them. Robert found three seats and Jeneil sat between them. "Do you like Rossini, Peter?"

"I'm the Rossini fan, Robert," Jeneil intervened. "Peter is sensitive enough to my needs to put aside his pain and suffering to be here with me."

"Jeneil, that almost makes me sound like a candidate for the Medal of Honor," Peter said, embarrassed.

Jeneil laughed. "Well, I'm impressed." She squeezed his hand and looked at him lovingly. His heart surged as he watched Robert taking it all in. "Actually, Peter has a better appreciation for classical than he did a month ago," she grinned at him, "but we share an interest in rock." Peter noticed Jeneil wasn't letting anybody snob the conversation. He loved that about her.

"Do you two have a lot in common?" Robert asked. Peter wondered if Robert was looking to make trouble.

"Do people take inventory? I don't know how to answer that." Jeneil laughed. Peter noticed how her absolute innocence always sabotaged a smart mouth.

The orchestra warmed up, people settled into their seats, and the concert began. Peter watched Robert make comments into Jeneil's ear from time to time, sitting as near to her as propriety would allow without being obvious.

He was a pro, Peter thought, and he wondered if the attraction was Jeneil herself or the fact that Robert couldn't get her, and Peter was determined that Robert wouldn't have her since he couldn't be sure. Peter looked down at her hand in his; her beautiful long, graceful fingers and beautiful soft white skin. He squeezed her hand. She turned her head and smiled at him, returning the gentle squeeze. He loved her. She was his and he loved that, too. "Mine," he said to himself, "not the art pro's to her left. Mine." He smiled and enjoyed the concert.

When intermission began, two women came over to Robert, one obvious about her interest in him. Peter noticed they both looked Jeneil over carefully. Peter chuckled to himself deciding that the streets of New York were basic training for life amongst the intellectual and civilized.

"Robert, please come and meet Matthew, convince him our building is gauche because of those awful lithographs."

"But that's not fair, there are some very good lithos," Robert argued.

"Oh please," one of the women pleaded while the younger one smiled enticingly. Robert turned to Jeneil. "Excuse me." Jeneil nodded. The women smiled broadly at Jeneil after Peter made sure they saw him holding her hand. He hoped they'd tie and gag Robert to wherever they'd taken him.

"Are you feeling okay?" Jeneil asked.

"I'm fine really."

"Would you like something to drink?"

He shook his head. She looked around. "I smuggled some fudge in," she whispered, opening her purse.

Peter smiled. "Great." He took a piece.

"How are you enjoying Rossini?"

"This music isn't as stiff as some you've played."

"I like that about him, too."

Peter couldn't believe he had just expressed an opinion about classical music. He smiled realizing that he'd say it only to Jeneil. She had accepted his comment as intelligent enough to agree with him. She was clearly not an intellectual snob. She was one hundred percent real. He smiled thinking of Steve's words, 'Boy, what she's doing to you?'

Franklin stopped by. He smiled at Jeneil. "How are we doing with your boy Rossini?"

"I'm carried away." She grinned.

"I told them that a real aficionado would be here."

"That's bad, Franklin. You're lucky Robert showed up." She laughed. Peter couldn't grasp Franklin's humor, but at least he wasn't as pushy as Robert. "Did you notice if Bennett's had his other works?"

"Not many," Franklin said.

"Gosh, Robert has quite a few. I wonder where he got them."

"Got what?" Robert asked, coming up to them.

Shit, Peter thought to himself.

"Your Rossini cassettes."

"New York, why?"

"I can't find too many here," Jeneil said.

"Is that right? I'll shop for you the next time I'm there. You can borrow mine any time."

"All right, Franklin," Jeneil smiled, "we've made a connection."

Robert looked her over as he smiled. The attraction was real, Peter could see it. He sighed.

"I'll check in Boston this week," Franklin offered, not to be outdone. The orchestra returned and Franklin excused himself. The concert resumed and Peter began to feel more comfortable.

The audience stood, applauding their approval. The orchestra took their bows. The conductor showed up for his attention. The house lights were turned on and a smiling audience filed out slowly. "Why don't we wait until everyone leaves then you won't have to stand on your leg so long?" Jeneil suggested.

Someone from the crowd called Robert's name and several people waved to him. He went over to them as they moved along. Good, Peter thought, and he relaxed. Workmen began cleaning up. "Ready?" Peter asked.

"Yep," she answered, "it ain't sitting polite, is it?" she drawled. He laughed, enjoying her low-key attitude. He loved her simplicity; nothing turned her head.

"Nothing spoils you, does it?"

"What do you mean?"

"Nothing," he said smiling, not wanting to lose the moment with her. He stepped into the aisle. She followed taking his hand and they walked slowly to the lobby. Franklin came over to them.

Jeneil smiled. "I'm impressed, Franklin. I think I'll subscribe."

"How nice." Franklin smiled.

Peter noticed Robert in a corner with a group of people and there was a lot of laughing. One woman had her arm around Robert's waist. He didn't lack for female attention, Peter thought. Why the hell was he zeroed in on mine?

"I'll put you on our mailing list, Jeneil," Franklin said.

"Oh good, here's my address." She wrote it on Franklin's list. Peter noticed Robert walking toward them and he wished he and Jeneil had left.

"Where are you off to now? Tiel's with the other concert crowd?" Robert asked.

Franklin laughed. "Some of us can only afford The Grainery, Robert."

"Don't apologize, Franklin. What's at The Grainery won't give you gout," Jeneil commented.

"And where are you going?" Franklin and Robert both asked.

"Well me, I'm a country girl. I'm goin' home to git my man here some vittles leftover from his Sunday dinner," she drawled. Peter smiled, Franklin laughed, and Robert grinned, enjoying her humor.

"Sounds like you've got the best deal, Peter." Franklin laughed.

"Believe it, Franklin." Robert grinned. "This country girl's vittles won't be chitins and grit."

"Oh, you've had her vittles, have you?" Franklin asked.

"I'll bet its meat, potatoes, and gravy biscuits. Like down home, right shuga?" Robert chucked her chin gently.

"Am I that predictable?" She laughed.

Franklin stopped. "You mean a real Sunday dinner?"

"You've got it," Robert said.

"Oh Peter, you lucky man," Franklin groaned.

"Why Franklin?" Jeneil asked.

"I've been away from home for so long, I can barely remember a real Sunday dinner."

She looked at Franklin and Peter could see the look of compassion on her face. He held his breath. "Then come home with us and share ours."

Shit, Peter thought, just what he needed, someone drooling over her food and her.

"Jeneil, I'd really like that."

"You have my address. Come by when you finish here."

"Well don't I even get a doggy bag?" Robert laughed.

"Are you free?" Jeneil asked, surprised.

"I sure am."

"Then come on over, too."

"I'll be there." Robert kissed her. "Thanks sweetheart."

Peter gritted his teeth. Super shit, the king drooler himself.

Jeneil looked at Peter. "Let's get you home, love." He smiled and put his arm around her shoulder.

"I'll be by shortly," Robert said.

"Me, too," Franklin added.

"Fine." Jeneil smiled and walked out with Peter.

*****

"Peter, the bath for your arm is ready," Jeneil called. Peter came to the bathroom door.

"Honey, you have people coming for dinner. Don't worry about me."

"Peter, everything is warming. Its leftovers, remember. Boy, am I glad I always cook extra to freeze. I at least have enough. This party sort of mushroomed. Let's do your arm." Peter soaked in the herbal solution while Jeneil brought more vitamin C. "I'm cutting back the dosage."

He smiled. "Good, I think I could spit oranges if I tried hard enough."

"Tease all you want, but that cut is getting better already." Peter just grinned disbelievingly. "Ooo, your head is so thick." She laughed then kissed his cheek, putting her arms around his neck. "Thank you for taking me to the concert."

Jeneil went to change while Peter bandaged his arm. "Can you do my snap?" she asked as she walked in. She had put on one of her long African dresses that he liked her in it. He kissed her neck as the front doorbell rang.

"Are you ready?"

"I hope they are. They'll find my food ordinary, but I never promised more."

He smiled. "I'll get the door. Your mom's cooking really rattled you, huh?"

"Oh, she was exceptional, Peter. She really was."

"But your dinners warm the soul. Don't worry about it." He kissed her cheek and went to answer the door. Jeneil checked the food then went to the living room. Franklin walked in smiling. Peter followed.

"Jeneil, this is so you," Franklin said, looking around.

"What do you mean?"

"You've chosen to live in a restored house. You've given it back its dignity, and look at this, it's warm and interesting and alive. Thank you for a Sunday dinner, it smells great." He kissed her cheek and hugged her. "This is really nice." He went to her African wall grouping. Jeneil stared at him in surprise.

"Men like soul, honey," Peter whispered, smiling. The doorbell rang again. Peter went to get it. Robert walked in as Jeneil was bringing the food to the serving hutch.

"I got some wine for dinner and some sparkling burgundy for later," Robert said. "You look great in that."

Franklin frowned. "Thanks Robert, I feel like a piker. I've come empty handed."

Jeneil smiled. "No, Franklin, you've brought all those great stories about the composers. I love them. You've got to tell us about Tchaikovsky's absentminded habit of nibbling the corners of paper." Franklin smiled. Peter loved her sensitivity. Robert noticed and absorbed her with his look "Well, I'll get the wine glasses and chill the burgundy."

Dinner went better than Peter expected. Both men were really after a home cooked meal. Franklin ate and ate. Except for Robert drinking Jeneil in with his eyes from over the edge of his wine glass, nothing rattled Peter. The conversation was easy and light and Franklin had a lot of amusing stories about the composers. Peter was surprised that he enjoyed it all.

Jeneil served coffee in the living room and assigned Franklin to put the music on. Robert stretched out on one of the soft chairs. Peter wondered when Robert had unbuttoned his shirt that far down. The guy knew he had a great chest, but Peter consoled himself, remembering Robert would go home and Jeneil would get under the covers with him. Peter smiled to himself.

Jeneil fussed over Peter. She would feel his forehead from time to time and stroke his hair, even while Robert had her engrossed in conversation. Robert noticed, and Peter loved it and her. Franklin mentioned that he played the flute and that he had his in the car. Jeneil begged him to get it and perform. She really enjoyed these people and they knew it. It gave the group a closeness that Peter hadn't seen very often. Franklin played a diversity of pieces and even Peter enjoyed it. Jeneil discovered that Robert played guitar, but he didn't have one in his car. She had one in a closet and brought it out along with bongos, and soon Robert and Franklin were playing duets.

Jeneil brought out the sparkling burgundy and set up dessert buffet style. Peter recognized the pastries from the prom she had frozen, and she had fudge, cheese and crackers, and fruit. Everything was easy and she was having the most fun. She really was a great audience, even joining in on one arrangement with the bongos. Peter enjoyed watching her enjoyment.

The door buzzer rang. Adrienne and Charlie stopped by with a big bowl of strawberries. Charlie's brother was a trucker and had brought some in a haul. Jeneil invited them to stay. She hulled the strawberries, melted some chocolate and added that to the dessert table. The group was mixing well and Jeneil surprised Peter by bringing out a tambourine and Adrienne joined in the music. They were into a heavy rhythm with Franklin improvising the melody. It sounded pretty good. Charlie sat next to Peter and they talked easily.

"You didn't learn to play anything?" Peter asked.

"Yeah, football in high school. How about you?"

"Hooky," Peter answered, and they both laughed.

Charlie looked at his glass of wine. "I don't know about you man, but this gay juice does nothing for me. I've got some beer I can bring down. Are you brave enough to slum with me?"

"Sure, we'll drink it from glasses to show them our good taste," Peter said. Charlie laughed, enjoying it all. The telephone rang. Peter got it.

"Hey, Pete."

"Steve, how's it going?"

"Not as well as it is there, man. What's going on?"

"We ran into Jeneil's friends at the concert. They came home for dinner and it's turned into a party."

"She sure looks after her friends," Steve said. Peter wondered if there was a hidden message. "Yours too, I guess," Steve added. "She's always sending me dinner." Peter wondered if that was a subtle reminder that he'd never been invited over.

"Is the hospital still busy?" Peter changed the subject limply.

"Not like last night. Are you coping any better, Pete?"

"I'm fine. I'll rest all day tomorrow and I'll be ready for work by three."

"Great," Steve answered. "Well, I'll let you get back to your party."

"Okay, Steve, I'll see you tomorrow."

Jeneil withdrew from the group. "Who was that, honey?"

"Steve," Peter answered quietly.

"Everything okay?"

"Yeah, Jeneil could we have Steve…."

"Come on, Jeneil. We're going to try a Latin beat," Robert interrupted, taking her arm, pulling her.

"What did you say, Peter?" she asked, moving away.

"Later," Peter said. She blew him a kiss and rejoined the group. The party quieted down as everyone nibbled desserts and Robert played guitar, conversation flowing easily.

*****

Peter was lying in bed when Jeneil came in. After running a brush through her hair a few times, she snuggled next to him. "That was fun," she said, yawning. "Not our usual quiet Sunday dinners, but fun."

"Your highbrows are fun when they really get down."

"We're not highbrows," she defended. He looked at her. "Well, maybe Robert, and I guess Franklin, but they are really nice guys. How do you feel now?" she asked, touching his forehead.

"Tighter than the whole day."

"You're warm. You're in pain, aren't you?"

"A little."

"Why don't you take a pain pill and at least sleep well."

He thought for a minute. "Okay."

"I could take tomorrow off and look after you," she offered, returning with water so he could take his pill.

He smiled. "I love your fussing, but I'm going in tomorrow so why don't you go to work."

"We'll see in the morning." She kissed him. "I love you a lot."

"This is the best part of the whole day, except for this morning." He laughed and she kissed his shoulder. They fell asleep snuggled together.

Jeneil's alarm clock sounded. She stretched and Peter slipped his arm around her waist. "Hi, beautiful." He kissed her shoulder and back.

"Ooo, you're feeling better." Jeneil smiled. "I can tell."

"Can I talk you into giving up yoga this morning?" He bit her earlobe gently.

"Only for another type of exercise." She stretched, enjoying his touch.

"That's a deal." He kissed her neck and ear.

"I'll handle it."

"No, you won't. I will."

She turned over and faced him. "But I thought I did well."

"You did, but you're my woman, beautiful, and I'm back in charge."

"Ooo Peter, you are a chauvinist."

"Damn right, sexy. You can have all the freedom you want out there. In this room, you're mine."

She looked at him. "Well, are we going to talk about the rules or do we get to play the game?" She grinned. He smiled then kissed her passionately.

Thirteen

Jeneil ran to catch the elevator so she wouldn't be late for work. Steve held the door for her." "Thank you," she said. "I'm running late today."

"How is he this morning?"

"He's just fine. He'll be in later."

Steve grinned noticing the glow to her skin, the flushed cheeks and the glint in her eyes. She looked great. Understanding his grin and his stare, she blushed a bright red and fidgeted. The door opened to her floor and she rushed to get off, bumping into two nurses. "Excuse me. I'm sorry," she said, rushing past them.

"What did you do, Steve, make a pass at her? She's bright red."

"Too much sun, I guess," he said, shrugging.

"Sure." They looked at him, shaking their heads disapprovingly. "You're bad, Bradley. The girl's studying to be a nun. She's not your speed." The nurses got off on the next floor.

Steve put his head back and laughed. "A nun! Jeneil, I love it."

Everybody at the hospital was talking about Peter and the drug victim. Jeneil was surprised at some of the details she heard; they were frightening. At three, she stopped at the nurse's station to leave some memos and reports. The nurses were talking about it as Peter walked in.

"Here he is!" one intern said.

A nurse went up to Peter and put her arms around him, hugging him. "Peter Chang, you are one brave man." Peter looked completely surprised. Jeneil watched as the nurse kept her arm around his waist as others talked to him. Another nurse went over and put her arm around his. The interns gathered around, asking questions. Jeneil stepped into the records room to leave some discs and gather some reports. Her hands were shaking.

Steve backed in smiling as he watched the fuss being made over Peter. He turned and saw Jeneil. "Hero for the day."

"I guess," she snapped and walked past him quickly, going to an office then to the elevator. Steve watched her leave.

"Now, what did I do?" he asked under his breath.

Jeneil hit the elevator button. She sighed. What was she doing, she lectured herself. It was only natural. He was a hero of sorts. A stupid unintentional hero, but they didn't have to maul him. She got on the elevator. Three nurses got on, one of whom had been holding Peter around the waist and another had been holding his arm. They ignored her as they talked and giggled to each other.

"Isn't he something else?" the first one asked.

"He's so understated about it all," the third nurse said. "And did you feel the guy's body! He's as solid as a rock. I couldn't take my hands off him." She fanned herself jokingly. Jeneil's hand hurt from clutching her pile of memo envelopes.

"Well forget it, he only dates Chinese." The second one laughed.

"Yeah, well from the feel of that guy's chest, it's worth an eye operation and a black dye job for my hair." The others giggled. Jeneil could feel her ears getting red and hot. "I can just imagine why they call him the Chinese Stud."

Jeneil felt her legs go weak. She wondered if the air thinned or whether she stopped breathing.

"Is he the one?" the second nurse asked.

"Lucy on second shift said she's dying to get the one they call the Chinese Stud."

Jeneil could hear her heartbeat.

"Well, personally, I think he's got somebody looking after his needs; somebody pretty good at it, too. He looks awfully good lately. I'd love to get hold of her memoirs and her techniques, lucky girl. Do you think he shares with Bradley?"

Jeneil choked, her throat was so dry.

"Why would he?"

"They're close, and I hear Bradley is into kinky."

"Can you imagine one woman with the both of them? She must be some woman."

"I'd like to see what nature gave her to have attracted both of them."

Jeneil felt moisture develop on her forehead. She wanted to scream for them to get out of her air. She felt sick. The doors opened and they stepped off. Jeneil held her head. "Oh, thank heaven," she said, and concentrated on breathing. The doors opened on the next floor and she stepped off quickly, looking around for a water fountain. Finding one, she sipped, rinsing her mouth and swallowing. She wet her fingers and patted the back of her neck. A janitor walked by.

"Are you all right, Miss? You look sick."

"Allergies."

"To what?"

"Pollution and filth."

"Well, take it easy. You look rough."

"Thank you." She smiled weakly. "I'm okay." Taking another drink, she swallowed then breathed deeply. She took her memos and walked to the nurse's desk. They were talking about Peter. She left quickly, hoping the memos were where they needed to be. After stopping at two more floors, her body was getting back to normal but she was angry. She hated gossip. She hated filthy gossip even more. She was angry at Peter for being friends with Steve and being called the Chinese Stud, but most of all she hated being dragged into it; Peter Chang's woman, the Chinese Stud. Getting on the elevator, she headed for the basement catacombs for some records. The door opened. Steve and Peter stood there. They both smiled. She stepped off the elevator. The halls were deserted.

"Hi," Peter said quietly.

"Well, Tonto and Kimo Sabe," she said, and kept walking. Peter was stunned for a second.

"Hey!" he yelled after her. She kept walking.

"What's wrong?" Steve asked, surprised by Peter's outburst.

"She just called us stupid and know nothing." Peter went after her and grabbed her arm, turning her around.

Steve joined them. "Peter, ease off."

"Apologize for that right now," Peter demanded.

"Oh, I'm sorry," she said sarcastically. "I guess you expected hero-worship. Try Lucy on the second shift, she's just waiting for the Chinese Stud. Join him there, Steve. I'm sure she'll handle his kinky friend, too. You might even split the fee."

"Jeneil!" Peter was shocked. She wrenched her arm free and walked away quickly.

Peter was speechless. Steve shook his head and called to her. "Jeneil, its gossip, it isn't even true."

Jeneil ran down the corridor away from them.

"What isn't true?" Peter asked, surprised.

"Word's around that Lucy's waiting especially for you."

"Oh shit." Peter sighed. "Why? How?"

"Who the hell knows?" Steve said. "Go after her, Pete. I'll cover for you. She's obviously heard it."

Peter sighed. He didn't like this at all. "Shit," he said angrily, "she hates gossip. It makes her paranoid." He walked quickly to the records storage room. "Jeneil." He knocked. The door was locked. He shook the door. "Jeneil!" he shouted.

She opened it quickly. "Why don't you yell louder? Yell it through the hospital, Peter, then they'll know who the woman is whose meeting your needs and being shared with your kinky friend, Steve."

"What?" he asked, stepping inside and closing the door.

"That's what I heard in the elevator today. Are you really called the Chinese Stud?" she asked, glaring at him.

"Yes," he answered. "Jeneil, this is crazy. It was a nickname in New York.

"Well, this isn't New York and they're still calling you that. Why?"

"Lin Chi spread it around. How the hell it got here, I don't know. It's gossip. I've never even talked to Lucy."

"Well, I'll bet your filthy, kinky friend has. If you lie down with dogs, you get fleas, Peter."

"That's enough, Jeneil. That's more than enough. Steve's been a good friend. The best friend I've had around here. Watch it."

"Why don't I listen to my instincts?" She paced. "The minute I heard you were friends I should have run the other way. I don't want fleas, Peter. I was on the elevator and three nurses were snickering about your woman and wondering if you shared her with Steve. I felt dirty, Peter, very, very dirty."

"Jeneil, its gossip, they don't even know about you. You know this screwy place for gossip."

"I can't take him, Peter. We're dragged into gossip because of your friendship with him."

"He didn't start the gossip, Jeneil. Leave him alone. I can't take Robert and Franklin, but they were at our place for dinner yesterday."

"You can't compare them to Steve," she defended.

"Bullshit," he snapped at her. "I'll bet Danzieg lays around more than Steve does. You just don't want to see it."

"Well, at least I don't have to hear about the graphic details every other day. Steve is common gossip around here."

"Shit, Jeneil. He'd be dead by now if it was all true. Wake up."

"Tell me he doesn't go to Lucy or Rita. Tell me it's just gossip."

"Jeneil, this isn't the time, this isn't the place. I'm not even sure what the hell this is all about."

"It's about fleas, Peter."

"No, Jeneil, I think it's about loyalty." He sighed and ran his fingers through his hair. "Well, now what? Where do we go from this?"

"I don't know, but you're right, this isn't the time or place." She picked up her packet, locked the storage drawer and walked to the door. She waited for Peter, who was leaning against a storage cabinet. He straightened up slowly and walked to the door. Turning off the lights, she closed the door behind her. They walked to the elevator together in silence. They stepped on to the elevator and Peter pressed the buttons for them. He turned and leaned toward her for a kiss. She turned her head away. He straightened up. The door opened and he got off without looking back. He knew this was a huge split in their relationship. He walked into the ER.

"It didn't work?" Steve asked. He could tell by the look on Peter's face that there was a problem. Peter shook his head. "I don't believe it. You stand up stronger after the problems you've both faced and gossip can knock you two over? It doesn't make any sense." Peter just looked at Steve. "There's more to it, isn't there?"

"Let's put it aside," Peter said, sighing.

"I want to check your arm," Steve said, stepping into a cubicle. Peter sat down and Steve removed the bandage. "Wow, this thing is healing fast. There's only a trace of infection and swelling. What have you used on it?" Peter chuckled and shook his head. "What?" Steve grinned.

"A herb bath and vitamin C." Peter smiled.

Steve laughed. "Sunshine's homeopathy? She's good, Pete. This looks great."

"It feels great, too. I'm using the arm already without a problem."

"Yeah, I know. I saw her in an elevator this morning, she looked radiantly beautiful. Shit, Pete. What can be worth giving that up?"

"It's her, Steve. She's got to deal with it. I can't change any of it. Man I would if I could, but it's her decision."

"Well, you're pretty cool about it."

"Not inside, believe me. I'm standing on thin ice and I hear it cracking. I'm preparing for the cold plunge."

Steve bandaged Peter's arm and sat down, sighing. "Just when I began to believe in rainbows. Damn it!"

*****

Jeneil sat on the sofa, not bothering to put her things away. There was an emptiness inside of her. It had no name. "Be positive," she said, "do something, standup, participate." She didn't like the emptiness; she didn't want to face it. Going to the kitchen, she filled the watering can and walked to the plants. Kneeling down, she looked at Arthur and Guinevere. "Well, look at this old twist in my Camelot," she said to them. "My king is angry at me because I don't like Lancelot. We can't win, Guinevere. It doesn't work if we like Lancelot and it doesn't work if we don't like Lancelot. Maybe Camelot's the problem. Nothing is perfect. Is that it? We have to accept the flaws so there is no Camelot. No superlative? No good, gooder, goodest? If that's true," she sighed, "that's a big yuck. No unicorn? No magic? What a bummer. I don't want it then." She watered the plants and stopped at the gnomes. Picking up the glass unicorn, tears rolled down her cheeks. "Jeneil, why don't you visit the ocean and face the wind?" The telephone rang, interrupting her thought. She stared at it. It kept ringing.

"Dennis," she answered, breathing easily. "No, I won't be there. There's no volunteer group tonight and Robert has to appear at some banquet. To help you? Do what? I don't know, Dennis, that's not my area of expertise. I'd get a pro if I were you. Yes, I know the feeling of being up against a wall. I've read the script, but with staging in mind. No, I haven't had dinner. No, let me take you to dinner, my treat. Please, I insist. I need to do something that makes me feel liberated. You'd do me the favor. I'll drive down there. Dennis, thanks for calling. I'm already feeling better. Oh nothing, just a day off. Give me twenty minutes and I'll be on my way. I'll pick you up at the theatre. Dennis, are you married? Oh, divorced. Nothing really, I just wanted to be sure your wife would understand, that's all. I'll see you shortly."

Jeneil hurried around getting ready. Grabbing her copy of the script, she left. The telephone rang. Peter let it ring several times. He wondered where she was then he hung up.

Jeneil dropped Dennis off. The drive home tired her. It had been an exhausting day. The telephone was ringing as she walked in. She hesitated then lifted the receiver. "Peter. How have you held up? Is your leg hurting?" Peter could tell the concern was forced. The fire was missing.

"I've been calling you all night."

"I met with Dennis," she said, not allowing more.

"We have to talk, Jeneil."

"I'm not ready to. I'm still angry. I haven't had a chance to think about my feelings. Have you?"

"I think you're the one with the problem."

"That's an easy out, just blame me." Her throat tightened as she held back tears.

"I'm not blaming you. I only meant that you have to deal with things I can't change."

"You can change them, Peter," she insisted emotionally.

"I can't change the gossip, Jeneil. I can't change being called the Chinese Stud."

"I'm tired, Peter"

"Do you want some space?"

"Yes, I guess so."

"Then I'll stay at the dorms."

She sighed. "That's your answer for everything."

"I don't know what to do."

"Suit yourself."

"I'd like to suit you, but what do you want?"

"I don't know, but I know that people don't separate every time there's a flare up in the relationship. That's not healthy."

"Neither is fighting with each other."

"We're not fighting, we're trying to communicate."

Peter sighed. "We can't even agree on whether we're fighting or not. Jeneil, what do I do?"

"About what?"

"How do I make it right?" he clarified.

"Get out of the gossip and away from Steve."

"Damn it, Jeneil, that's not fair. It isn't his fault."

"Yes, it is. He's a complete yuck. This morning in the elevator, he was studying me for signs of a sex life."

"Jeneil, that's shit. Okay, he's shrewd; he can pick up on things. He told me you looked radiant."

"Oh, terrific, now you two discuss me. Will I get a grade or a written report from one of you?"

"Jeneil, you're way out of line. You're not even being reasonable. I'm getting upset. I'd better stay at the dorms."

"If you do, Peter, you probably won't be back."

"Is that an ultimatum?"

"No, it's my opinion."

He sighed. "I just feel that if we step back for even a day or two, we'll get a better focus on this."

"I think that would be true if we were both going to be alone, but you'd be with Steve and he's the problem."

"He isn't, Jeneil. He isn't. I'm tired of saying it."

"Peter, is what we have love?"

"It is for me."

"Then we shouldn't separate, we should stay and work it out. That's what people in love do."

"Okay, I'll be home tonight. I've got to get back on duty."

"Yes, I know. There's no time to talk, no time to think, no time for anything."

"I give up. Is there a safe subject for us?" he asked, discouraged.

"Peter, stay at the dorms. I give up, too. I've had it." She put the receiver back, hanging up. She sat on the sofa and cried.

"Oh, songbird," Peter said, putting the receiver back. "What the hell is the answer?"

Steve watched Peter leave the telephone booth and go to the medical room to view an x-ray. "Did you get her?" Steve asked. Peter nodded. "Well?"

"I'm your roommate again."

"Oh shit," Steve said. "I mean...you know what I mean. I'm going home. I worked a double so it's been a long day." Steve turned to leave. Turning around again, "Pete, don't come back to the dorms. You can't work it out from there. Go home. Some night you'll turn over, she'll turn over, and everything will take care of itself. But not if you're not there, man."

Peter shook his head. Jeneil, the guy agrees with you and you pick on him.

*****

The evening was becoming a quiet one. It was nearing the end of the shift and Peter was ready to leave. His body ached. He pushed himself to get through the last two hours. Going to the doctor's lounge, he bought some coffee and sat down. He hated the empty feeling inside of him. He couldn't change any of it. She hated gossip. He was starting to think she was afraid of it. Another scar. He shook his head. She must feel exposed and threatened by it. Words from his grandfather returned to him, 'the songbirds come for my protection.' He sighed. He had an intelligent songbird; she kept telling him the problem, but he forgot to listen. He kept leaving the cage open at the wrong times. He stood up and returned to the floor. After finishing the last of his paperwork and shift change, he left.

Parking his car in the lot of the apartment building, Peter sat wondering what to do after he went up. It was time for bed; he would go to bed and sleep. That's what he'd do, let the songbird know he was there for her. He smiled.

Peter could hear the typewriter clacking in the computer room when he entered the apartment. He knocked. The clacking stopped suddenly. He opened the door. Jeneil sighed with relief when she saw him.

"I didn't expect you here," she said. "You scared me."

"I'm sorry." He went to her, but she didn't open to him. He kissed her temple. "I'll let you get back to work."

"Peter, what about your arm? I'll get the herbs together."

"And the vitamin C," he added. She looked at him then smiled.

When Peter opened his eyes in the morning, the apartment was quiet. It was six. He was surprised. No dancing? No yoga?

There was a note on the small table.

Peter. Breakfast with Dennis. Left two jars of herbal solution. One in the a.m. and one before work. Vitamin C on top of jar. Meals are in the fridge. Jeneil.

Peter shook his head. It was hard to believe that he was there for her and she didn't need him. She'd have less work if he wasn't there. Who was Dennis Blair to her that she'd give up dancing and yoga? Was she even resting? He hadn't heard her come to bed.

Peter went to class at one then to work. Steve met him in the locker room. "I was glad to see your bed empty this morning. Things worked out, huh? Sunshine is glowing today. I saw her at the desk." Peter was surprised. He walked out quickly and looked around for her. Steve followed. "What is it, Pete?"

"I haven't seen her at all today," Peter replied sharply.

"Oh."

"How the hell is she glowing? I don't think she's even sleeping."

"Do you two really live together?"

"Steve, I don't know. Life used to be simple. Lately we need a traffic controller and secretaries to get our schedules worked out."

Steve stared at Peter then asked, "Who is he, some insurance agent?"

"My guess is Dennis Blair."

"What's he into?"

"Her other life," Peter replied. Steve looked at him and said nothing.

*****

Peter couldn't get an answer when he called. His shift had been extended, and she was asleep when he got home and gone when he woke up. It seemed he was only at the apartment to pick up his food and clean clothes. They never saw each other. The whole week went that way. Peter was feeling foolish by Friday. He got to work at lunchtime and walked to the records department. He'd had it. Things had to be settled before she went to Nebraska for the weekend. He walked in, surprising Jeneil. She was helping an intern with some reports. Peter sat down. As time passed, he went to the counter, scribbled a note and left it there. He left before the others returned from lunch and headed to the record storage room in the catacombs to meet her as he had said in the note. He paced then heard light footsteps on the concrete floor. He went to the corner. It was her. She unlocked the room and they both walked in.

"What's wrong?"

He stared at her in disbelief. "What's wrong? Jeneil our life is. Look at us! We have to sneak down here to talk to each other. We live together and I haven't seen you all week. I can't take this anymore." He paced.

"What can we do about it? Your schedule is controlling our lives right now."

"My schedule? I can't even get you by telephone anymore. Your schedule isn't helping any. We've lost control of all of it. I don't know you. I don't know your life anymore. You're leaving for the weekend and you haven't even tried to contact me. I get notes on a table. If this is what I wanted for a life, I'd live with my mother. She'd leave my food and do my laundry, too."

"What do you want me to do?" Jeneil's voice began to crack and tears filled her eyes.

"Put as much effort into seeing me as you do with Dennis Blair. Have breakfast with me."

"But you're always asleep from working so late."

"Jeneil, what's happening to us? We're beginning another fight and we haven't settled the last one. We're not important to each other anymore."

"That's not true. I get your food, I look after you, and I do your laundry because I care about you."

"It's one sided, baby. What do I do for you?"

"What do you want me to do, Peter? I don't know what to do about our schedules."

"Quit the hospital."

"And do what? Sit and wait until you're not working so we can make love to each other."

"Boy, you're really into cerebral."

"It's how I survive, Peter. If I quit the hospital, I'd be in the corporation and we'd still have the same problem. I work days and you work nights. Besides, it's only two more weeks isn't it and then you'll alternate your shifts." She sighed. "We didn't want our relationship to be only physical."

"We don't even have the weekend, Jeneil. This is hopeless."

"What would happen if we were married, Peter?" He looked at her. "Would you divorce me?"

"Jeneil, you're wrong. You said we don't have time to be physical. I could have made love to you right here, right now. I'd settle for our relationship being only physical."

"You don't mean that."

"Yes, I do. A physical relationship is better than nothing. It's a lot better than feeling like your pet."

"My pet!"

"That's right. I'm all curled up on the bed asleep and you leave my food and go to work." The idea was so silly it was funny and Jeneil began to laugh as she pictured it. Watching her, Peter began to laugh. He went to her and put his arms around her. She held onto him. "Jeneil, I'm sorry about the gossip. I don't want to be a part of the gossip, but I can't stop it."

"I know Steve is your best friend. My friends are important to me, too. I love you, Peter. I know that. I don't care if you were the Chinese Stud." He kissed her gently and she kissed him back. He had missed her and he kissed her passionately. "Peter," she turned her head to breathe, "this is getting out of hand."

"Good." He kept kissing her neck and face.

"We'd better stop," she said, pushing at him.

"No," he answered. "I want to make love to you."

"We can't in here!" she replied, totally surprised.

"Sure we can. I'll teach you."

"What? Something from Lucy?"

He quickly let go of her. "Goodbye, Jeneil." He walked away.

"Peter! Wait, I'm sorry," she called, going to him. "I didn't mean that she taught you personally. I meant that she's been teaching people…it doesn't matter what I meant. I'm not Lucy, Peter."

"Hell, I know that. I don't want you to be, but Jeneil, what's wrong with fast sex sometimes? My favorite is in bed all night with you, but baby, look at us. Look at our schedule. I'm sorry, but I feel physical about you. I haven't seen you. I need to touch you. I need to be with you. My way, not Lucy's."

"I'd rather you wake me up in the middle of the night when you get home then."

"Fine, you've got it. There, another argument settled. We're on a roll, sweetheart. Come on, you'll have just enough time to eat your lunch," he said, taking her hand to leave.

"No." She grinned, pulling her hand away. "How fast is fast sex? What do I do?" She made sure the door was locked, turned off the lights then kissed him passionately.

Later, Peter was in the medical room when Jeneil stopped by the nurse's desk. He watched her, totally spellbound. She had him in awe for having pleased him like she had.

"Pete, keep looking at her like that and everyone will know about you two." Steve chuckled. "She's radiant again."

Peter smiled. "I know."

"You didn't tell me that things were settled."

"It was recent."

"She wasn't radiant before lunch. Was it as recent as here in the hospital?" Peter didn't answer. Steve chuckled. "I love it. You two are great."

Fourteen

Jeneil returned from Nebraska. Peter had someone cover for him at the hospital and he slipped home. He ran up the stairs grinning and unlocked the door, holding the flowers behind his back. He was shocked to find Jeneil sitting at the table having dinner with a man. Jeneil stood up, surprised.

"Peter!" She went to him and hugged him. Peter felt awkward. He handed her the flowers, embarrassed that he had them. Jeneil was shocked. "Thank you," she stammered, and kissed his lips lightly. "Come meet Dennis Blair."

"I'm sorry," Dennis apologized, standing up, "Jeneil thought you'd be working. I'll leave so you two can have some time together."

Peter looked him over, feeling less awkward. "No, I have to get back to work. I just wanted to say hello to her."

Jeneil was pleased. "Dennis and I are going over the script. Did you have dinner?"

He smiled. "As long as your freezer lasts, I'm fine. I'll be getting back to work. Nice to meet you, Dennis."

"Yes, I'm glad to have met you, Peter."

Jeneil stepped outside the door with him. "Peter, I'm so pleased with my flowers."

"I missed you."

"Me, too," she answered. He kissed her warmly and she clung to him. "Wake me when you get home."

He smiled. "Count on it."

Jeneil went back inside, smiling. "Give me a minute to put these flowers in water and we'll get back to work."

"He seems like a nice guy," Dennis commented when she returned.

Jeneil sat down. "Dennis, he's the greatest. He really is. I don't think anyone else could put up with me and my life."

Dennis smiled. "That's important to a relationship. My wife couldn't after awhile."

"I'm beginning to wonder if anybody's life schedule is kind to a relationship."

Dennis leaned back. "I wonder what's the magic ingredient that will make one relationship last and another fail. It can't be love alone. All relationships presumably start out with love, yet some work and others don't."

"Millions are spent trying to figure that one out."

Dennis laughed. "Well, let's tackle scene five. It's not as complex a problem as lasting love."

*****

Schedules didn't change. If anything, they got worse. Jeneil worked with Dennis at a frantic pace, even taking two days off to help him. Peter was getting nervous about their relationship. He had never seen Jeneil so dedicated to helping anyone as much as she was to helping Dennis. She was totally absorbed in the project. Many nights, Peter couldn't wake her without feeling guilty because she was so exhausted, and many nights she went to bed after he did because she stayed up working on the script.

They were back to not seeing each other by the beginning of the fourth week in the month's second shift schedule. Peter tried to ignore the annoyance growing inside of him, but a strong resentment was building towards Jeneil's relationship with Dennis. Peter sat reviewing his thoughts before getting out of bed. He could tell another confrontation was coming, as much as he hated it, but he resented having to remind her to pay attention to him. He was tired from his own schedule and he knew his tolerance level was low. He'd worked a double Saturday and was called in for a surgery Sunday, ruining their weekend together. That more than anything kept him cool. His schedule ruined the weekend, not her. He snapped back the covers, stood up and stretched. He could tell it was going to be a mean Monday; his attitude was rotten. Finding a note on the table telling him that she'd gone to breakfast with Dennis, he exploded. He crushed the paper and threw it against the wall. "Take a day off for me, damn it!"

His telephone rang. "Go to hell," he shouted, but being well trained, he went to answer, figuring it was the hospital.

"Hi, Peter."

"Who is this?" he pretended, having recognized Jeneil's voice.

"What! It's me, Jeneil."

"Jeneil who?" he asked sarcastically.

"Ooo, subtle, very subtle. Wrong side of the bed this morning?"

"Cute, Jeneil, I'm hysterical," he said, not cheering up.

"This is the same Jeneil who made the weekend available for a certain doctor whose schedule messed things up. Are you ready to put down your sword?"

"Okay, I'm wounded. How come I'm getting a call?"

"Have lunch with me."

He sighed. "I'm not very hungry and I'm lousy company right now."

"You don't understand. That's wasn't a question, it was an order. It's important, Peter."

"Okay, where?"

"1217 Chaucer Street."

"Give me the name of the restaurant."

"It's a small place near the hospital. It'll be easier to look for the address."

"Okay, I'll be there."

Jeneil laughed. "Gosh, Jeneil, it was nice of you to call and ask me to lunch. I really appreciate that. Thank you," she said teasingly.

He chuckled. "I told you, I'm lousy company right now."

"All the more reason to meet me."

He shook his head. "Okay, at twelve-thirty."

"Make it twelve forty-five."

"But you only have a half hour."

"Be there Chang! You got that?" she shouted, then laughed.

He smiled. "Okay, twelve forty-five. We'd better have soup. There won't be time to chew."

"I'm going back to work now. I've enjoyed talking to you, too. Goodbye," she sang, being deliberately cheerful.

He hung up and laughed. "Frustratingly sexy broad." He went to shower.

Peter found Chaucer Street easily. Driving down the street slowly he checked the numbers and stopped. Odd, 1217 wasn't a restaurant, it was a...motel. He backed the car up quickly. Her car was there. He turned in. She had to be kidding. He got out and walked to her car. He noticed a card with a red heart on it matching the keys to her apartment attached to a door in front of her car. "Frustratingly sexy broads are sure fun," he said, going to the door and knocking. The door opened. She stood there smiling, dressed in his favorite nightgown.

"Welcome to Happy Heart Fast Room Service, Doc. We aim to please, quickly." She winked.

He laughed, putting his arms around her. "You crazy kid."

"Listen; don't waste time with sentiments of gratitude, I've only got an hour for lunch. I told them I had a doctor's appointment. That's not a lie, is it?" He laughed and kissed her. "You have to admit this is a lot nicer than the records storage room, right? Come on, Doctor, let's get this appointment started." She pulled him by the arm.

The lunch hour with her made him smile throughout the week. He loved the way she'd plan schemes and surprise him. It was part of her fire and he loved her for caring. It also made him realize that his concern about Dennis was unfounded. He was grateful for the rejuvenation in their relationship. She loved him and he knew it.

*****

The end of Peter's second shift arrived and he felt relieved. He knew he'd be working second shift alternately, but at least he could deal with that. His life with Jeneil was important to him and the second shift added too much stress. He smiled to himself realizing that he was committed to a life with her, happily committed. Jeneil was still deeply involved with the playhouse and while having her gone all evening sometimes irritated him, they at least went to bed together. There was time for talking and being together. He visited his family, or he and Steve bummed around. He felt married. That surprised him and he loved the feeling of having life settled. He wondered if that was part of love and why hell-raising wasn't appealing anymore. He did know that he cared more about her than anyone or anything else in his life, even medicine, which was a very close second. At times that frightened him, but as his grandfather explained, that was part of the songbird and it was that kind of commitment that made the responsibility easier. It made sense to Peter, but he wondered when he'd start being responsible for her. She was so independent and giving. His grandfather just smiled when Peter told him that. Someday it'll be clear, Peter, he had said.

There was another change he was enjoying; he and his grandfather were closer since Jeneil. Peter appreciated being with him and talking to him, and since being on first shift he could take Jeneil with him to visit his grandfather. Peter was looking forward to being married so he could just visit and not scheme. There was no possible way they could figure to tell his mother. Anything they discussed never seemed right. His grandfather felt Peter's regular visits would let his mother see the change in him and hopefully she'd appreciate Jeneil just as his grandfather had, but Peter had his doubts. He felt more comfortable with the thought of quietly marrying Jeneil and bringing her to meet the family. Whichever way it developed, Peter was certain it wouldn't be smooth. It never was between him and his mother.

The second shift wasn't even difficult. Though he and Jeneil didn't see each other often, there was an attitude of patience between them as they accepted the different hours. The only concern in his life at the moment seemed to be for Steve. A young man was admitted to the hospital, a victim of an industrial accident. His wife was four months pregnant with their first child. As one of the doctors assigned to the case, Peter watched as Steve became increasingly more personally involved. Peter was concerned as he saw Steve's objectivity slip. Steve admitted that the guy's situation touched him deeply, although for no clear reason. Some cases were like that; they got into your gut and settled there. It was difficult to not be compassionate. The guy was left legally blind from the accident, only a beginning of all that was wrong. Steve put in extra hours on the case beyond being reasonable and that concerned Peter, too. He felt that Steve was wiping out his energy reserve; he was getting too close to the edge. Dr. Sprague had warned Steve, but the case seemed to be the flame and Steve was the moth. Peter watched and waited, hoping for the best, but chances seemed slim. Even the young man's wife seemed more objective than Steve, who seemed to be trying to single handedly turn the case around.

Friday's second shift was surprisingly quiet and Peter's hours hadn't been extended. After quickly showering, he ran to the parking garage to his car and left. He and Jeneil hadn't had a Friday night together in a long time, and they hadn't been together for almost a week. He parked in the apartment's lot surprised that her car was gone. He sat in his car for a few minutes and got out as the midnight news began. He was disappointed. Jeneil drove in as he walked to the door. Jumping off the front steps, he ran across the parking lot to her car. "You scared me, baby. I thought our schedules got crossed again." He held the door open and locked it as she got out.

"A Friday night!" She smiled, hugging him. "We haven't had a Friday night in ages."

"Come on, beautiful," he said, grabbing her hand. "There's a better place to talk."

"Wait, my notes are on the back seat."

"Okay," he said, getting them for her. "Now, come on." They ran to the door and up the stairs. He tossed her purse and briefcase onto a chair and hugged her, lifting her off the floor and spinning her.

"Tell me that you're free tomorrow morning and everything will be perfect." He laughed, but she didn't answer. "What a volunteer group?" She nodded. "Aw, baby."

She smiled. "I know what to do. I'll send the assignment list in with Jeff. Robert can supervise and I'll go in at ten-thirty or eleven."

He hugged her. "I love you. Give me that list and I'll tack it to Jeff's door right now." When Peter returned, Jeneil was changing. He got his robe and changed for bed.

"I'll make some fruit drinks," she said, heading for the kitchen.

He took her wrists. "No, no fruit drinks, nothing, just us. Please." He kissed her. She moved closer to him, enjoying the feeling of being in his arms and kissing him. Peter lulled her closer as he got beside her. "Stay right here all night." He smiled and kissed her. "I don't want this feeling of closeness to end." She smiled and snuggled against him. "Has sex gotten more exciting or has it been so long that my memory is failing?" he asked, kissing her forehead.

"It's been so long since we've had time to slow down for lovemaking," she whispered softly.

"Honey, when is the project at the playhouse over?"

"The hours should be more realistic, but I'm staying to the end of the season, I think. Robert has me scheduled for two more sittings and then that's over."

"How does it look?"

She laughed. "Dramatic, intense, and sensual. He painted me surrealistically. It doesn't look like me, thank heavens, but I like it. It's different. His boldness is in there. I kept telling him that he was projecting his quality onto me. His interpretation is turbulent. He claims that's what he saw. Do I look turbulent to you?"

"He saw you surrounded by turbulence?" Peter asked. Jeneil nodded. "He wasn't seeing cosmic, he was painting your schedule."

Jeneil laughed. "Let's go to the gallery and see it. You won't believe the cataclysm surrounding me and at the center, I'm blending with the sun, stretching to resist the turbulence."

"How come you're staying on at the playhouse?"

"I love it, Peter. I love the work that Dennis and I have done. I can't wait until the play opens. I haven't seen rehearsals on it yet, but Dennis is excited. The script had to be adapted to eliminate some characters and adapt it to our smaller facilities."

"Won't the author be upset?"

"Peter! Dennis is the author. That was his deal. The last part of the season, he could put an original piece of work into production. He is so incredibly talented, but the end of the season brings with it problems of budget shortages and a host of nuances, but he doesn't care. He's alive right now. You should see him. There's a fundraising ball at Linden Court Mansion. I got an invitation. Would you mind if I go? I thought I could ask Franklin to take me."

"Franklin? Why Franklin?"

"I think Franklin would get a kick out of the lavish evening."

"Jeneil, did my name ever occur to you?"

"Would you really go and dance in a tux? And of course your name occurred to me, until I read the letter. The names of the committee members were listed on the stationary. Dr. Sprague's, Dr. Maxwell's, and Dr. Fisher's wives are on the committee."

"Oh," Peter answered understandingly. He didn't say anything else.

"I don't have to go at all," she said, smiling.

"No, honey, go to the ball."

"What is it then?"

"If we were married, we wouldn't have to sneak around. I could take you to the ball. Jeneil, I want us out in the open."

"Please, Peter. I couldn't take it at the hospital. The corporation is growing so fast that I probably won't be there much longer anyway. I don't want to look for another job and I'm over-qualified for the type of job I'd look for. The hospital only took me because I have library and computer skills and I don't care about the money. Why is this being brought up?"

"Honey, I want to get married. I'm ready for marriage. I feel married."

"You do?" She was surprised. "Without soul?"

"Soul? Another superlative? I fell in love; that qualified me for marriage. I don't need soul."

"I thought we had agreed to wait for me?"

"Are you having trouble with love in this relationship?"

"No, of course not, we were going to wait for me to get Jeneil together though, remember?"

"Ooo, this is maddening," he groaned.

"Please don't make me feel bad, Peter. Let's not ruin what we just shared here."

He smiled at her and shook his head. "Okay, but baby, please, soon?"

"Yes." She smiled. He kissed her and she responded passionately.

"Don't try to bribe me." He laughed.

"What's going on at work? Has there been a change in that industrial accident case?"

"Only very slight, and I'm worried about Steve."

"Why?"

"He's gotten too close to it."

"It's amazing to me that doctors can keep their feelings away from a case. People really become a leg operation or a bypass?"

"Honey, it's for the protection of both the patient and the doctor."

"Gosh, you're like mechanics."

"The separation is necessary."

"Then the passion, the superlative is in the case and the struggle to restore health." She smiled. "You are passionate about your work."

"If you want to see passion, check Steve out on this case."

Jeneil lay in Peter's arms silently. He ran his hand along her arm and shoulder absentmindedly. His hand stopped moving and she knew he'd fallen asleep. She loved him. She loved being with him, near him. Soon she was asleep.

Fifteen

Jeneil heard that the young man Peter had talked about had gotten worse. She stopped at the nurse's desk and leafed through the papers she had to drop off. She noticed Steve in the medical room. He was sitting on a table pouring over some papers, totally wrapped up in reading. He sighed; she sensed his concern. He rubbed the back of his neck and head, and sat up to straighten his shoulders. He looked up and saw her watching him. She turned her head quickly. There had been an awful awkwardness between them since the day of her outburst, and there were days when her conscience bothered her and she'd think about apologizing. When it got to that point and her courage was strong, she'd come upon him with a nurse biting his ear or he'd be making some off color remark to someone. She gave the apology up as a lost cause, but she did hate the awkwardness. For Peter's sake, she had been trying to be at least tolerant toward Steve. Her outburst had set her and Steve further back and Jeneil reminded herself that nothing good ever came from losing her temper. What was it about him that immobilized her, she wondered as she walked to the elevators.

On Saturday Peter called Jeneil. The young man was critical and Peter was concerned for Steve so was going to stay with him to make sure he rested. Peter said he felt Steve needed to get away from the hospital for awhile and was going to be sure that he did. Jeneil took the time to thoroughly clean the apartment then began cooking and baking. Time moved along quickly and she was surprised that it was nine o'clock at night. Peter called again at eleven. The case was serious and he wanted to stay on with Steve. Jeneil understood and admired his loyalty and concern. Friday had been good for them so she went to bed. Jeneil's alarm went off the next morning and the phone rang as she was stretching. She jumped at the sound.

"Peter, you must be exhausted."

"Honey, I am and tense as hell."

"How's it going?"

"The patient died in the middle of the night."

"Oh, I'm sorry," she said sadly.

"I'm worried about Steve. He's down. This case was tough on him."

"I understand. You're going to stay on with him then? You'll be at the dorms?"

"Jeneil, we were at the dorms yesterday. He was like a caged animal there. He drove me crazy."

"Then where are you going?"

There was a silence. "Jeneil, I'd like to bring him home. Dr. Sprague gave both of us the day off. I think one of your dinners might help. He needs new surroundings and fussing over." Jeneil was silent as she twisted her hair around her finger. "Okay, forget it," Peter said, noticing her hesitation.

"Peter…I…Steve and I…." She pinched her lower lip then sat up straight. "Peter, if Steve wants to come home with you then bring him."

"I'm bringing him home, Jeneil. He won't have a choice. You're sure about this?"

"If you can get him to come here then go ahead." She replaced the receiver and sighed then jumped out of bed to get ready. Peter had sounded determined to have his way in this decision. She ran to the shower. Shampooing quickly and rinsing, she then wrapped her hair in a towel. She rushed back to the bedroom to comb out the long wet strands. "Mother, how did you ever survive having people thrown at you last minute? This is terrible! I'll die if they walk in on me like this." She dried and fluff brushed her hair then went to change. She had her doubts that Steve would even come.

"Jeneil!" Peter called. "We're here."

Jeneil was behind the dressing screen. We're here? Steve had actually come home with Peter? He must be handcuffed. "I'm dressing, Peter. Give me a minute." She reached into the closet for something to wear.

The house smelled of furniture polish and baking, and Peter noticed how everything was in order. He wondered what she had made. He noticed Steve looking around. "I never told you we lived in a state park," Peter said, chuckling, pointing to the trees.

Steve smiled. "With those elves and fairies on the door, I half expected Mother Goose."

Peter laughed. "Camelot is Jeneil's statement that life will be her way – perfect."

"If she manages that, I want the formula," Steve said quietly.

"Maybe we should sit down," Peter suggested.

Jeneil walked from the bedroom, trying to get her slip-on sandal on right. Peter could tell she was nervous as she fumbled with it. Her hair was hanging loosely and she had on the long electric blue dress with short puffy sleeves. Finally managing her shoe, she stood up. Her hair fell in cascades over her shoulders and over her left eye. She pushed it back and went to Peter.

"Hi," she said, kissing him lightly. She smelled of shampoo and perfume. She had the storybook princess look that Peter liked. "Hi, Steve," she said nervously. Peter turned and wanted to laugh when he saw Steve stare at her completely shocked. Steve had never seen Jeneil with her hair down. The look was really a transformation.

"Hi, Jeneil," Steve said, barely audible. Peter enjoyed seeing Steve speechless. He was usually in command, especially around women. It was good to see him knocked off center.

"You look done in, Peter," Jeneil commented.

"I am. I've got to crash. I'm going to bed."

Jeneil's heart stopped. Oh my gosh, please don't leave me here with him, she pleaded in her mind.

"What about you?" Peter asked Steve.

"I don't know if I'll sleep, but I do need to lie down."

"I'll get you some juice," she said, breathing again, and went to the kitchen. "Here," she said, returning, handing each of them a glass, "I'll straighten out the bed for you."

Jeneil disappeared again, and Peter noticed the awkwardness between her and Steve. He hoped this day would work out. Jeneil was finishing straightening the pillows as they walked into the bedroom.

"All set." She smiled uncomfortably. "I'll just get my brush and hairpins and leave." She quickly grabbed the items from the bureau. As she passed Peter, she kissed him quickly and left, closing the door.

Steve looked around. "Peter Chang, is this really where you live? I don't believe it." Peter could see Steve was impressed by the room. "She's not real is she? That's not the same girl from the hospital."

Peter smiled as he unbuttoned his shirt. "It takes a while but then you begin to fit in here." He chuckled. "It shocked me, too."

"She's really beautiful, Peter. Why does she keep it hidden?"

"She's very shy, Steve. She doesn't like attention drawn to her."

"Why?"

"A long story but she likes to float in and out of life. It answers her need for freedom. She likes to observe."

Steve shook his head. "She's different."

"That she is," Peter agreed, laughing.

"And you deal with it," Steve said, surprised, pulling up the covers. "It's hard to believe that you sleep together, she looks like a virgin."

Peter smiled. "She has different looks and different moods, different feelings. She's different."

"Well, you won't get bored." Steve grinned.

"That's for sure." Peter laughed.

"These pillows...."

"She makes them."

"The bed smells like her," Steve said, obviously surprised.

Peter laughed again. "I said that to her once and she said, 'I sleep here, who should it smell like?'" They both chuckled. Peter yawned and turned over. "I've got to sleep. I'm exhausted."

Steve could faintly hear the classical music she was playing. The apartment had a calming effect and he actually liked all the plants. They added life and right now he needed to feel life. The colors felt cool. He thought about Jeneil. She was a total surprise. He really had her figured very differently. Lying there in the coolness, he felt himself relax. He liked the order he felt there. He even enjoyed the smell of furniture polish that lingered and her perfumed scent on the bed. It wasn't hospital and he liked that. Even the dorms would begin to smell like the hospital sometimes but here was health and life; he could feel it and he calmed down inside and soon closed his eyes.

Jeneil went to the kitchen. She couldn't believe how unnerved she was with Steve there. Steve Bradley in her bed. Good grief, what the hospital could make of that sentence. Her stomach tightened and she could feel guilt surfacing. She needed to get a handle on this so she busied herself with the food preparation.

*****

Peter opened his eyes. He turned. Steve was lying on his back staring at the ceiling. "Did you sleep at all?" Peter asked, yawning.

"Yeah, I can't believe it, but I just woke up, too."

"Do you think we'll ever sleep eight hours straight someday?" Peter asked, sitting up. "I think I smell food." He went to the closet and put on his robe.

"What is this?" Steve teased. "With a dragon on the pocket no less."

"She made it for me."

"What's that for?" Steve asked, nodding at the dressing screen.

"She changes there and her sewing is there, too."

"She changes behind a screen?" Steve asked, surprised. Peter just looked at him and nodded. "You two do not sleep together."

Peter smiled. "Well, don't wait for a video as proof." Steve chuckled. "What's it going to be? Eat first or shower."

"I don't know."

"Come on, let's eat first."

Steve did up the last button on his shirt and tucked it in.

Jeneil heard them moving around. She went to the kitchen and put the eggs and biscuits in the microwave, and turned on the coffee pot. She was pouring juice when she heard them come out of the bedroom.

"I don't think I'll stay, Pete," Steve said.

"Yes, you are," Peter insisted.

"I really don't feel...I feel like an intruder." Jeneil heard it. She knew he meant he didn't feel comfortable. She wasn't surprised. The handle for the situation surfaced in her mind. She walked out of the kitchen.

"Steve, I would really like you to stay." Peter and Steve looked surprised, and Peter heard her sincerity. "Breakfast is ready," she said, twisting the towel she was holding around her fingers as she walked toward them. "Steve, it's important to me. You're Peter's friend and I'd like you to feel comfortable and welcomed here. You and I haven't seemed to understand each other easily, and I owe you an apology that I've tried only half-heartedly to deliver. I'm sorry about my outburst at the hospital and for my rudeness. I would really like you to stay. I mean that. I need to get to know you the way Peter does. I have a suggestion. Why don't we put aside the other Steve and Jeneil and begin here and now? You'll get to know the Jeneil who lives here and I'll get to know the Steve who has been such a good friend to Peter." Steve was speechless. Peter was completely thrown and totally impressed. "Is it a deal?" Steve nodded, still speechless as Jeneil extended her hand. "And you'll stay?" He nodded again, taking her hand. "Oh, good," she said, and hugged him briefly. The microwave buzzer sounded. "I hope you two are hungry, I made a lot." She went back to the kitchen. Steve looked at Peter, still surprised.

Peter grinned. "You find that she comes at you sometimes from right angles." He hit Steve's arm. "Come on, let's get ready for breakfast."

Steve noticed the china, cloth napkins, and placemats, and was overwhelmed by Jeneil and her style.

After eating, Steve sat back and sighed. "I'm stuffed. I've never had eggs with everything in them like that before. They're good." Peter poured himself more coffee and sat down. "I can see why Peter has gained weight. Your dinners have gotten us through some tough shifts. I didn't think girls liked to cook anymore."

"I don't but I like to eat so I learned to cook. I freeze everything, ask Peter." She slipped her hand into Peter's. "I spent yesterday cooking and baking, so you visited on the right day. What are we doing today?" Jeneil asked Peter.

Peter shrugged. "I haven't thought past a Sunday dinner day."

Jeneil looked at Steve. "Well, Steve, you've had the worst week so you get to choose. What do you like to do when you're not at the hospital? Uh, how about your second favorite thing?" she asked. Peter leaned back and laughed.

Steve smiled, embarrassed. "Some of that's gossip, too," he said, defensively. Jeneil smiled and Peter chuckled, enjoying Steve's embarrassment.

"I know he likes to visit sports car showrooms," Peter said.

Steve laughed. "Except most of the ones here are tired of me wearing out the upholstery and not buying."

"Then let's cross the state line. Highway 83 has a row of dealerships. Have you been there?"

"No, I haven't," Steve said, brightening.

Jeneil stood up and gathered her dishes. "Then that's what we'll do." Peter stood up and helped her. Steve noticed and raised his eyebrows then stood up and helped her, too. Jeneil put the roast in the oven and set the timer. Steve and Peter were sitting in the living room talking when she returned. She had changed into slacks and a long shirt with a belt around her waist. Slipping on some brightly colored bracelets, she picked up a light wool shawl and threw it over her shoulder. She looked up; both Peter and Steve were watching her.

"What's wrong? Not what you wear for visiting car dealers?"

"You look so different from the hospital," Steve responded.

"That girl is my clone."

They laughed. Peter put his arm around her shoulder and kissed her cheek. "You look great."

They decided to take Jeneil's car because it had air conditioning and they all piled into the front seat with Peter driving. Jeneil was surprised how comfortable she felt with Steve once she had apologized and made up her mind to get to know Peter's friend. He really could talk about a lot of different subjects. The biggest and most pleasant surprise was finding him to be much less arrogant than his hospital personality. Hearing him and Peter talk, she realized how very close they really were and Steve was beside himself having several new showrooms to wander through.

Peter walked back to the car with his arm around Jeneil. "Honey, you've done it. Your magic worked. Steve is still fighting it, I can tell, but he's enjoying himself. That makes it easier. You're terrific," he said, holding the car door open for her.

She smiled. "Whatever makes you adore me is worth it." Peter kissed her lightly.

"I think I'm in love," Steve said, getting in and closing the door. "That white SX7 has my name on it. I heard it call to me."

Jeneil laughed. "You are an addict."

"He lives for private practice and the sports cars it will buy," Peter said.

"Damn right," Steve said. "That's my reward for sleepless nights and bloodshot eyes." Peter and Jeneil both laughed.

"Could we stop at the foreign car dealership on the way back?" Jeneil asked.

"What, you've caught the virus, too?" Peter laughed.

"I need to check on something."

Steve and Peter wandered around the showroom while Jeneil talked to a salesman.

"Does Jeneil own a Bentley?" Steve asked Peter.

"No. Why?"

"I heard her ask about transporting one."

"Not that I know of." Peter shrugged. "But Jeneil does things sometimes that make sense to only her."

"She's really nice, Pete. Does she come from money?"

"She looks like it." Peter laughed. "She'll tell you her parents were just plain folks, but they weren't. She has an unusual background, but she really is a regular person. Just like us." Jeneil walked over to them. "Honey, what are you doing with the Bentley?"

"I'm bringing it in from Loma. I thought I'd use it as a rental car for weddings and special occasions with a driver provided." Peter's mouth dropped open in shock as she continued toward her car.

Steve laughed as Jeneil walked away. "Just a regular person like us, huh, Pete? What're you doing with your Bentley? I'm taking mine to the opera," he roared as he walked toward the car, too. Peter ran to catch Jeneil.

"Jeneil, where the hell did you get a Bentley? You're teasing, aren't you? This is a 'gotcha,' isn't it?" Steve continued to laugh at Peter's reaction.

"No, I have four cars," she said, "one from my parents and three from Mandra."

"Bentleys?" Peter asked in shock. Steve stopped laughing.

"No, I have one Bentley, one whale called a Coupe Deville, a car like the one in the movie *Christine,* and a small English roadster. That was my dad's car."

Steve choked. "A 1958 Plymouth Fury?"

"Yes," she said. Steve gave a long whistle.

Peter stared at her. "I didn't know that."

"It's really no fun driving them, Peter. You're always worried about scratches and dents or having them stolen. It isn't worth having them on the road." Steve laughed again. "I've thought about putting the Bentley to work for a while now and letting word out among collectors about the others. They might be used in films. I haven't checked on the legalities and headaches yet." She got into the car.

Peter and Steve looked at each other. "She's full of surprises," Peter said.

"She's more of a regular person than I am, Peter. Those cars would turn my head pretty good." He laughed as they both got into the car.

"Can we stop at the park on our way home? My schedule has been so tight I haven't had time to enjoy the outdoors. Is there anywhere else you'd like to stop, Steve? This is your day."

"No, I'm quite happy having sat in an SX7 and sitting next to someone who owns a Bentley."

Jeneil chuckled. "You have a dry sense of humor. What's wrong, Peter?" she asked as Peter stared out the windshield.

"I just found out that my girl owns a Bentley."

Steve laughed. "You two are real fun."

They pulled over to the sidewalk at the park and got out. The park was crowded, but more so at the zoo and concession areas than where they were.

"Where to, honey?" Peter asked.

"I don't know, let's just walk and enjoy the air and sky."

"Okay," Peter said. She took his hand. Steve noticed and grinned.

Peter and Steve talked hospital. Jeneil watched life in the park and breathed it in. They walked past an ice cream vendor then past a little girl crying. Jeneil looked back. The little girl had dropped her ice cream and a dog was eating it. The little girl stood near it crying. Jeneil let go of Peter's hand and stopped.

"Jeneil?"

"I'll be right back," she answered. They followed her back to the vendor. "That little girl has lost her ice cream," she said to the vendor.

"Yeah, I know. Whaddaya want from me?"

"Why don't you replace her ice cream?"

"Because she doesn't have any more money," the vendor said sarcastically.

"How much is an ice cream?"

"Fifty cents," the vendor replied. "Why, you wanna pay?"

"What's your name?" Jeneil asked, and Peter and Steve looked at each other.

"Why?" the vendor asked, surprised.

Jeneil stared into his eyes. "Because I plan to be an organ donor and I want to have your name listed so I can make sure you don't receive anything from me if you ever need it. I couldn't stand the thought of my cornea giving sight to someone who could watch a child cry over a fifty cent ice cream and not help." She took out her wallet. "Give her another ice cream. Here's a dollar. I'd like to buy one for you, too, and I hope the money burns a hole in your heart and sours the taste of the ice cream for you. I'm going home today and make a voodoo doll in your likeness. Your features are burned in my memory." She glared at him then smiled. "Have a nice day." She rejoined Peter and Steve, taking Peter's hand again.

The little girl took the ice cream from the vendor. "Thank you, mister. You're a nice man." She smiled and walked away. The vendor looked guiltily at Jeneil.

"Merry Christmas." Jeneil smiled to him and walked away.

"Jeneil, the things you get into," Peter lectured. "Why didn't you just quietly buy her some ice cream?"

"What? And have him think I was just another do-gooder. I want him to sweat over that money. You'd think I had asked him to feed Ethiopia alone. What a scrooge." She shook her head.

Steve tried to keep from laughing but burst out, "I love it," and laughed heartily.

Peter smiled. "Boy, Jeneil, even your revenge is creative."

She sighed. "I'd make a lousy Christian, even the lions would spit me out." Peter and Steve both laughed. Peter hugged her.

They walked a short distance before Jeneil looked across the street and pointed. "Look at that bluff," she said. "Come on." She ran across the street and they followed. "Who wants to run it with me?"

Steve looked amused. "Are you real? That's almost straight up."

"No, it isn't, there's more of an incline there than Hadley's Bluff and Billy and I used to run it."

"I pass," Steve said, "that's too much like exercise."

She looked at Peter. "Don't look at me. I do knee surgery on damaged runners, I know better." He laughed.

"Oh, I have to run it! I have to. Hold my things for me, please." She handed her purse to Peter and ran back to the sidewalk.

"Is she up to this?" Steve asked. "She doesn't look very athletic."

"You're looking at a girl who gets up at five-thirty every day to dance and do yoga."

"Oh, civilized exercise," Steve smiled, "but that thing is almost straight up."

"She usually knows her limit."

Jeneil ran across the short plain then up the bluff, struggling at the top. Grabbing the grass, she brought herself to the top. She turned and waved her arms over her head to them then, in a deliberate spiral pretending to faint, she dropped to the ground to rest.

"See." Peter smiled.

Steve smiled, too. "Gutsy kid, but how does she get down?"

"She's cool, Steve. She'll do it."

"Bet a six pack?" Steve challenged.

"You're on," Peter accepted. Jeneil stood up and walked across the top of the bluff.

"Where's she going?" Steve asked as he watched.

"There's probably an elevator there," Peter said jokingly.

Jeneil stopped, faced back the way she had just walked and stepped off the ledge, starting down the face of the bluff diagonally, taking short quick steps to hold back her momentum until she reached the bottom.

"Well I'll be. Who knew her ancestors were mountain goats." Steve chuckled.

Peter laughed. "Make that Miller Lite." Steve shook his head, still surprised.

Jeneil stopped near them, breathing hard. "I wish you guys had reminded me that the last time I did that I was thirteen. My body is reminding me of that now and look at my hair. Once I start falling apart I have to begin all over again. Does everybody vote for home?" They nodded. "Good. Can we take a bus to the car? I'm dead."

Peter smiled. "Stay here and rest. I'll go and get it."

"No, I'll see this through." She put her arm around Peter's waist. "Just hold on to me, please." Peter smiled and hugged her. Steve watched them and smiled.

The aroma of the roast cooking was beginning to drift when they arrived home. "Oh, dinner smells ready. I'll change fast," and she disappeared.

"Change again?" Steve asked.

"She doesn't like to relax in jeans; it makes her feel tied up like a mummy." Peter grinned.

Steve smiled. "She's cute." Peter nodded and smiled. "You two are good together."

They divided the two Sunday newspapers and sat down. Jeneil called them to dinner. She was back into the electric blue dress and had redone her hair. Dinner was what Peter hoped it would be. The candles, the conversation, it all went well. He was impressed with Jeneil more for pulling it off. She had come through for him.

"Let's go get comfortable with coffee," Jeneil said, standing up from the table.

They all spent some time quietly reading as music played softly. Steve looked up at them. They were both involved in their reading. This all felt good to him and he was glad he had come over. Jeneil looked up and smiled at him then returned to her book. He returned to reading his paper thinking wonders never ceased. The two of them were in the same room and they were being pleasant to each other.

Jeneil brought out dessert and more coffee, setting it on the small serving table in the living room. Putting a cushion on the floor, she sat next to Peter, leaning against him as he ate his dessert. "You two have been a good cure for me," Steve said, watching them. Peter noticed a slight tone of embarrassment in his voice. Peter smiled to himself, remembering his first few encounters with Jeneil and how sentiments and good manners he wasn't aware he had surfaced whenever he was around her. He saw that same reaction in Steve now. She never advertised the fact, but the brain instinctively knew the lady had class.

Jeneil smiled at Steve. "I'm really glad that you stayed."

He grinned. "Am I a different Steve than the one at the hospital?"

Peter coughed and cleared his throat. "Uh, Steve, maybe you shouldn't ask."

"Why not?" Steve laughed. "I'm curious to see if her experiment worked. Jeneil, am I different?" She nodded. "How?"

"Aw, come on Steve," Peter warned, and Jeneil looked at him.

"Don't look at him. I asked the question." Steve laughed.

"You don't seem so arrogant," she answered quietly.

Steve smiled broadly, almost laughing. "And you seem less stiff to me. I like the Jeneil who lives in Camelot."

Jeneil laughed. "Stiff, huh? I can see how you'd think that."

"Don't push your luck, you two," Peter interrupted.

Jeneil kissed Peter's cheek. "What's wrong, honey? Are you feeling like Jimmy Carter with Sadat and Begin?"

He nodded and smiled. "There's a similarity, there's a similarity." Jeneil and Steve laughed.

Steve put his coffee cup on the tray. "I've got to get going, but I'm really glad I came over today. I enjoyed the whole day." They all stood up and Peter walked Steve to the front door while Jeneil took the tray to the sink.

Peter walked into the kitchen as she was rinsing the dessert dishes. "Put down the dishes, baby. Your man wants a kiss." She smiled and dried her hands quickly then slipped her arms around his neck.

"I'm ready," and she grinned. He held her close, kissing her passionately. "Ooo, I'll give you carrot cake more often if this is what it does to you," she said, a little breathless as he kissed her face several times.

"You were terrific to Steve, honey. Thank you."

"I meant what I said, Peter. I really intend to get to know him better. I intend to like him." He smiled and pulled her closer, holding her tight.

"You are something else all together. Marry me now," he said, kissing her neck.

"Marry you?" She laughed. "How did we get to that subject?"

"Because I want all this to be real."

"It is real." She chuckled.

"I mean permanent. Mine. No ours. Us baby, you and me. Are the dishes done? Do you want some help?"

She shook her head. "No, everything is finished."

"Oh good." He smiled.

"Why?" She grinned. "Are you going to tell me a bedtime story?" He smiled and kissed her lips warmly, pulling her against him.

Sixteen

At the hospital, Peter continued to watch Steve. Sunday hadn't been a total cure for him and he was still dealing with the after effects of the case. Peter joined him in the doctor's lounge.

"You look rough," Peter said, studying Steve's face.

"I feel a cold starting," Steve answered, leaning back in the chair and rubbing his sinuses.

"What are you taking?"

Steve laughed. "Do you have a cure for a cold?"

Peter grinned. "Yes, dinner with us."

"Again, I was there Sunday."

"So what, you once asked if you'd get dinner invitations. Now you complain?"

"Have you asked her?"

"No, she's not home yet, but I'm sure it'll be okay."

"Maybe you should ask first."

"No," Peter insisted, "it'll be okay. Trust me. You can leave early if you have someone to visit tonight."

"Not feeling like this."

"You let yourself run out of everything on this one, man," Peter reminded him.

"I know, but I couldn't see it at the time."

"Let's close up shop and leave then," Peter said, standing up.

Steve sighed. "Might as well for all the good I'm accomplishing here."

"Jeneil?" Peter called as he opened the apartment door. He looked around. "She's not home yet."

"Then I'm leaving," Steve said. "If she's late, she won't like another mouth to feed."

"Stay put. Sit down and rest."

"I don't know, Pete. Women get touchy about these things, don't they?" The door opened and Jeneil walked in.

"Peter?" She called to the bedroom as she closed the door. She had on her grey suit and carried her briefcase. Peter answered from the living room. Jeneil turned quickly in surprise.

"Playing tycoon?" Peter asked, going to her. She smiled, putting down her briefcase. Steve was surprised by this image, too.

"Hi, Steve." She kissed Peter's cheek then looked at Steve again. She walked over to him. "You're getting sick."

"It's just a cold," Steve answered, looking her over in surprise. "What are you dressed for?"

"Life, and you're heading for more than a cold."

"I'm finding out that you have more than a few of those 'lives.'"

She looked at Peter. "You should have him stay for dinner. He needs help."

Peter smiled broadly at Steve as he put her arm around Jeneil. "I told you."

"Don't thank me yet," she said, taking off her suit jacket. "Now that you've been admitted to Alden-Connors General things may not be so pleasant." Steve looked at Peter, puzzled.

Peter grinned at him and kissed Jeneil's cheek. "Thanks honey."

Steve noticed her pink blouse, that her pearls were real, and that her earrings matched. This girl was a puzzle to him.

"Please sit down," she said, indicating the sofa, then went to the kitchen.

"Pete, I think the girl comes from money more than you think," Steve said in a confidential tone.

"She doesn't need to work at the hospital," Peter offered.

"She always did seem to be out of place in that job." Steve shook his head. "Why is she?"

Jeneil returned with a glass of cloudy water. "Try this," she said, holding the glass to Steve. She went to one of the potted plants and snipped off a bunch of green stems from one. "I'll just wash these. Apple juice for you, Peter?"

"Fine," Peter answered.

Steve tasted the drink. It was warm and sour. "Yuck!" he said, wrinkling his nose.

Jeneil returned in time to see it. She handed Peter his juice. Handing Steve the green sprigs on a plate, she smiled. "You should really finish both the drink and the parsley."

Steve looked at her. "You're using homeopathy on a physician?"

She grinned slyly. "Nervy, aren't I?"

"Quite," he said, grinning.

"Then prove me wrong." She smiled, still holding out the plate of parsley to him.

"And what will this do?" he asked, amused.

"Nothing unless you eat it. Once you eat it, it'll cleanse your insides and fill you with vitamins." He looked at her. She could tell a smart remark was coming. "Don't say it," she warned, smiling. "This is my hospital, Bradley, not yours."

"Bossy, aren't you? You'd make a good chief of staff," and he laughed as he reached for the plate. Jeneil noticed the cut on his wrist.

"What's this?"

"Just a cut."

"It's not healing well."

"I know, it's one of those minor things that you don't fuss over when it happens, but it's in a spot that's always disturbed so it's a little out of hand."

Jeneil shook her head. "You and Peter, you could be twins if it weren't for genetics. Stubborn clear to the marrow," she said, walking away.

"Is she always like this?" Steve asked Peter.

Peter smiled. "Only when she likes you and she's made up her mind to like you."

"She doesn't miss a trick," Steve said, grinning. "She would've made a great doctor."

"No, I wouldn't. My conscience wouldn't let me prescribe acrylic pills," Jeneil teased, returning. She had on an apron and was bringing the hassock to Steve with her foot while she held a small basin of water and a brush. "Soak your wrist and use the brush to reopen the cut once it's softened."

"What?"

"Not completely," she clarified. "Don't bleed. We'll need to undo the damage that's been done. You've run down. You're susceptible to anything right now."

Steve looked at her. Tell me about it, he thought to himself. He liked her softness and caring. It felt good, especially since he felt sick. He put his hand into the solution.

"Now wasn't that painless?" she chided him. "Finish your parsley." He looked at Peter and raised his eyebrows.

Peter laughed. "She warned you."

"I'll get dinner going," and she disappeared again.

"She's good at fussing," Peter added.

"Yes, she is," Steve said, "and it feels good." He brushed the cut gently and winced. Jeneil returned wearing a long dress in earth tones.

"The bath must be cold by know," she said, handing him a glass of water and eight tablets. He looked up and was shocked by her change of outfit.

"I like costumes," Jeneil explained. "It's a self indulgent weakness. That and...," she stopped. "I'll take this," and she walked away with the basin.

"And what?" Steve asked Peter after she'd left.

Peter grinned. "Nightgowns."

Steve smiled. "Now that's a real waste of time and money on that body." Peter turned his head and looked at Steve. "Well, who the hell wouldn't notice?" Steve said defensively.

Peter smiled. "Look man, I've already got a third of the states' population to worry about and that's until the other two-thirds meet her. I don't need you in the lineup."

Steve laughed, put the eight tablets in his mouth absentmindedly and drank the water to swallow them. "What the hell did I just take?" he asked, sitting up and tapping his chest.

"Probably vitamin C."

"Damn, I've swallowed more oddities since coming here."

Jeneil folded her arms and stared at him, having overheard his complaint.

"He's just hungry for real food," Peter defended him.

"Dinner is ready," Jeneil announced.

"So soon?" Peter asked. "What did you make?"

"Warmed lasagna in the microwave and a tossed salad."

Peter hugged her. "Sounds good."

"And tell your friend that if complains anymore, I'll put it in a blender and he'll wear it as a poultice."

"Ooo, a real Amazon," Steve teased, then smiled at her warmly. "Thanks for mothering me."

Jeneil smiled. "You're welcome, sonny."

Steve noticed the nice touches; the large candle on a wooden base, the glass globe in the center of the table, the background music. He really liked her style and he was happy for Peter having found her. It touched memories from his past.

"There's some wine in the cupboard and some beer in the fridge. Where did that come from anyway?" she asked Peter. He and Steve exchanged glances.

"I won it," Peter said, not elaborating.

"What do you want with dinner guys?"

"Beer," Peter said.

"Wine," Steve answered. "Pete, wine goes with dinner."

"Well, get the change in you." Peter laughed.

"Don't ruin her dinner," Steve said.

Jeneil looked at Steve, surprised. She smiled. "That's very nice of you, Steve, but Tony Pingareo's mother is one of the most gracious hostesses I've ever met. Her dinners are an experience. She lets it happen. Wine, beer, Perrier, even soft drinks turn up on her table at the same time, along with the love, the comfort, and the feeling of being welcomed. I've decided that my dinners would be wonderful if I equaled that. So to each his own is my rule."

"Way to go, Jeneil," Peter said, squeezing her hand.

"And what are you having?" Steve asked out of curiosity.

"Milk." She stood up to get the beer and wine.

"Milk?" Steve mouthed to Peter, grimacing.

"She's allergic to wine and liquor."

"Probably why she was a virgin so long, they couldn't get her drunk." Peter looked at Steve. "I'm sorry, Pete, that slipped out. It's that damn refined air about her, it makes you want to ravage her."

Peter covered his face with his hand. "Oh shit," he laughed, "already with the White Stallion."

"I'm teasing." Steve laughed.

"I doubt it." Peter shook his head.

"I am," Steve insisted.

"You are what?" Jeneil asked, returning with drinks. Peter and Steve looked at each other. "Okay, private joke," she said, sitting down.

Steve looked at Peter and grinned then raised his eyebrows. He was feeling reckless. "Actually, I told Peter that your air of refinement makes a guy want to ravage you." Peter held his breath, not believing that Steve had set her up like that.

"I have an air of refinement?" she asked, surprised. Peter and Steve burst into laughter, not believing that she had completely ignored the ravaged part. "The third person on a private joke never quite gets it do they." They leaned back and laughed harder. Jeneil shook her head as she watched their hysterical comedy.

"Oh, she's not real," Steve said, laughing quietly.

Peter got up and kissed her cheek. Again he was amazed at how her natural innocence could disarm someone. "I love you, baby," he said, squeezing the back of her neck and leaning down to kiss her hair.

She smiled at him. "I'm going to believe that you two are not laughing at me."

Peter smiled. "We're not, honey, believe it," and he squeezed her hand.

"No, Jeneil, the jokes on me." Steve touched her arm gently then quickly took his hand away, embarrassed by his forwardness toward her and the jolt he received from her unexpectedly soft skin.

She looked at Peter then Steve. "Okay." Excusing herself, she went to the kitchen and returned with eight more tablets.

"What? More?" Steve asked, surprised. "The others haven't even dissolved yet."

"Trust me," she replied, holding the tablets for him to take. He shook his head and took them.

"Peter, maybe you should supplement with C if this is passing through the hospital." She went to him and felt his forehead. He took her hand away and held it.

"Honey, I'm not your son."

"Oh gosh, I've embarrassed my man. I'm sorry." She grinned at him. "I guess my approach was all wrong, huh? I should have slithered over to you," and she slithered sexily behind him, "and then I should have run my hands slowly across your shoulders to your neck, pulling your head back gently and kissing your forehead to see if you were feverish." She kissed his forehead lightly. "Was that better?" She laughed, teasing him. He smiled, took her wrist, pulling her around, forcing her to sit down on his lap.

"Will you please behave yourself?" He grinned, holding her.

"You didn't like that, either?" She laughed, kissing his cheek.

Steve smiled. "Gee, Pete, I think it beats the hell out of a thermometer." He was impressed with her openness and her display of affection. He hadn't expected her to be like that. She was full of unexpected surprises, including her sense of humor. He liked her. He really liked her.

"Well, if you guys will help me clear this up, I'll go to work and you two can discuss surgical techniques." She kissed Peter as she got off his lap. Taking her place setting, she went to the kitchen. Steve and Peter stood up and gathered dishes.

"Where is she going to work?"

Peter grinned. "Jeneil, Steve wants to know where you're going to work."

Jeneil returned, picking up the bread basket. "Right here in the apartment."

"Doing what?" Steve asked. Jeneil looked at Peter then shrugged.

"I have a small business," she answered, picking up the wine bottle and leaving for the kitchen. Steve looked surprised.

Peter laughed. "She's good at understating." Steve and Peter brought their dishes to the kitchen as Jeneil was filling the sink with soapy water.

Steve couldn't resist. "Jeneil, using more than one word and one sentence, tell me what your business is."

"It's a small company that invests in other businesses. That's it. I can't make it into another sentence." She rinsed out the glasses and soaked the silverware.

Steve looked at Peter, puzzled. Peter grinned and asked, "Are you working for the corporation or the Mandra Foundation tonight?"

"The foundation," she said, rinsing dinner plates.

"The Mandra Foundation," Steve said. "I've heard that name before, but where?"

Peter laughed. "Please Jeneil, let me tell him."

"Tell me what?" Steve was very curious. Peter looked at Jeneil.

She sighed. "But it stays here with the three of us. Is that clear?"

"What?" Steve asked again.

"The Mandra Foundation sounds familiar to you because of Tony and The James Gang."

"Oh, that's right." Steve looked at Jeneil. "You're connected with the Mandra Foundation?"

Peter laughed. "She is the Mandra Foundation."

Jeneil turned quickly. "I am not!" she insisted seriously. "I'm only on the board."

Steve stared at her. "On the board of a foundation? How is The James Gang connected to a company that provides college funds? I could never figure that one out."

Peter grinned. "They're not. They're owned by the Alden-Connors Corporation and she is the Alden-Connors Corporation. Deny that," Peter said to Jeneil.

"This all stays right here. I hope everyone remembers that," she cautioned.

"She owns The James Gang?" Steve asked, completely shocked. Peter nodded. Steve looked at Jeneil. "Were you the one that started the mafia rumor?" he asked, beginning to make sense of everything. She looked at him sheepishly and nodded. Steve laughed. "I knew that was a smoke screen. I thought somebody was waging war on me."

"It wasn't personal," she explained. "I didn't even know it was you who was snooping."

Steve shook his head in disbelief then smiled broadly. "You have a diabolical mind. I'm totally impressed."

"Don't be," she insisted. "It was self-preservation, not a keen mind."

Steve hit Peter's arm. "And you buddy, letting me make an ass of myself trying to find out who was behind it all. You're some kind of loyal."

Peter smiled. "I'm sorry, Steve, but I had to choose sides. I didn't want to make her mad, she has a vicious temper."

Jeneil looked at him, shocked. "You beast," she said, throwing a glop of soap suds at him, hitting him on the chin and neck.

"See what I mean," Peter said, getting behind her and holding her arms in the water while he wiped the suds on her neck. He took a hand towel and dried himself. Jeneil reached for the hand towel, too. Peter put it behind him. "Not until you apologize."

"You started it," she insisted.

"Apologize," he repeated. Steve watched, enjoying the lighthearted struggle. Jeneil put her hands back into the dishwater then lifting them, wiped them on the front of Peter's shirt.

"Punishment for a smart mouth," she replied defiantly. Steve chuckled.

"Oh, we're talking punishment here, are we?" Peter said, putting the towel down and rolling up his sleeves.

"Don't you dare, Chang?" She backed away. "We're even now. Don't cheat." Steve smiled, enjoying her spunk.

"We're not even, not by my rules," Peter replied. "You haven't apologized."

"And I won't. You started it," she answered faintly.

"Fine, then you take the punishment," Peter said, then looked at Steve. "Jeneil has a thing about water. She just loves to get people wet so as a community service I keep trying to break her of that bad habit." Peter moved to the sink and wet his hands in the dishwater. Jeneil quickly grabbed the hand towel. Steve laughed at her quickness. Peter grabbed her around the waist, wetting her dress with one hand and her face with the other.

"You brat," she screamed, "you barbaric beast."

"Apologize," Peter insisted, still holding her as she struggled.

"No, it was your fault, not mine." Peter scooped up some water and dropped it on her shoulder, wetting the front of her dress. "That's not fair! You cheater," she said, struggling to get at the dishwater herself. Holding onto the sink, she managed to get her hand on a plastic cup full of dishwater. Lifting it out, she aimed it behind her and brought it past her shoulder, hitting Peter and getting herself wet, too.

"Ooo, you bitch." Letting her go, he went to reach into the water but she kept getting in front of him. Grabbing her around the waist again, he tickled her.

"No tickling!" she screamed. "No tickling!"

"Apologize."

"No."

"Then it's tickling."

"No, no, I apologize," she said, out of breath. He turned her around to face him. They were both wet and breathless. Jeneil's hair was slipping out of its pins and wisps of hair fell across her face. Peter's hair fell across his forehead.

"Say it sincerely," he ordered. She fired a look at him, warning him not to push. "Sincerely," he insisted.

She sighed. "I sincerely apologize because you cheat." She grinned.

"Close enough." Peter kissed her lips lightly. Steve put his head back and laughed, leaning against the refrigerator.

Jeneil looked at herself and sighed again. "Now I have to change."

"You started the water fight." Peter laughed.

"Your right, I did." She smiled. Picking up the towel, she dried his face then hers. She turned to put the towel back and reached into the pan, getting a palm full of suds. Keeping it by her side, she went to change and smeared it on Steve's face as she walked by. "That's for acting so mature and dignified while we weren't." She laughed and walked quickly to the bedroom. Peter laughed, handing Steve a towel.

Steve smiled. "Well, now I know why you came home looking like you did sometimes," he said, drying his face. "The girl is total wildfire."

Peter laughed. "She's too much. She's the greatest tension reliever and I don't mean sex. She's so gentle, she's a tranquilizer."

"Gentle?" Steve chuckled. "If you say so, she's a complete puzzle to me. She's on the board of a foundation, owns her own company, and works at the hospital as a clerk."

Peter smiled and began washing dishes. "Steve, the hospital job is important to her. She wants to be anonymous there. That's why she overreacts to getting near her."

Steve chuckled. "That's funny because gossip touches everybody at the hospital, even her. I've heard that she's studying to be a nun, that's she's a lesbian, and that she's been kept by a man with money."

Peter shook his head. "That place is incredible."

Steve laughed. "And all the while, she's right under their noses, keeping the Chinese Stud happy. She's beautiful. She just blissfully goes about her life."

Peter rinsed a dinner plate. "No, Steve, she takes life seriously. Sometimes too seriously, I think. She's sensitive, intensely sensitive at times. That's why I hover over her. There are times when I think she's not prepared for the real world at all. She lives and thrives at a higher level than the rest of us. We can never come up to her level." He rinsed a handful of silverware.

"What are you talking about? Look at the two of you, you're great together. She's not a snob at all. What a total relief that must be. I had to watch everything I did wondering if Marcia would be offended."

"I find I'm doing it with Jeneil, like having wine with dinner. In Jeneil, you've got someone who'll be able to entertain the stuffed shirts in the career game and allow you to relax and be your kind of man with her."

"Boy, you're lucky, Pete. She's rare. At least I haven't seen too many like her."

"When you're really close to her, Steve, you can see how fragile she is. She loves people too easily. They're a weakness with her. She has a compulsion to feel love for everybody. I'm beginning to think that's why so many guys respond to her. They come at her at their level and her mind is on another planet in another galaxy, and then she wonders why everything is physical. She doesn't see it until she's into it past her elbows. And yet, anything less just wouldn't be Jeneil. I don't know what the answer is for her. I just hope she'll keep coming across guys who don't want to see her hurt because she really is fragile when it comes to her personal life."

"You are way over your head about her, off the mountain and into oblivion. Get married soon, Pete," Steve said seriously. "Don't let the world find out about her until she's yours." Peter looked up at him as he put a serving dish in the draining rack.

Jeneil walked in. "Why are you standing in here? Go get comfortable. I'll make some iced coffee and then I've got to tend to business."

Peter stopped as they walked past her into the living room. "I love you, Jeneil."

"I know and I love you, too." She kissed him warmly. "Go keep your friend company." She touched his cheek lovingly. He took her hand and kissed her fingertips.

"Thanks for looking after him," Peter whispered. Jeneil nodded and smiled. She disappeared into the computer room while Peter and Steve spent the evening talking.

Later that night, Peter knocked on the door. The typing stopped. "Come on in," Jeneil called.

Peter stuck his head in. "Got time to talk?"

"Sure, where's Steve?" she asked, getting up and stretching.

"He just left. You were great tonight."

"You're so glad that Steve and I don't argue that everything I do seems terrific."

"No, you fussed over him. That wasn't something I expected." He hugged her. "He didn't either. He's not used to it."

"Now I doubt that. You two are very close," she said, smiling. "I think of you as brothers."

Peter smiled. "He said to thank you for dinner. He wants to take us out to dinner someday."

"No, this isn't to be repaid. He's your family. Maybe when you're both in private practice we'll go to dinner with him and his wife."

"Steve, married, that I can't handle, but I couldn't imagine Peter Chang begging a girl to marry him either and look at me."

"Begging?" She seemed hurt by the remark.

"It's just a phrase, honey. Ignore it."

She sighed. "I'm beginning to believe that Steve really has been maligned by gossip. He's been here twice this week. That disproves some stories I've heard about him and his needs."

Peter smiled and kissed her. "Almost done in here?"

"About another half hour I think."

"Okay, I'll read in bed and wait for you."

"Oh good." She kissed him. He closed the door and Jeneil returned to her typewriting.

Boy, how we can misjudge someone, she thought. She'd always tried to be so careful about being prejudiced and yet that's what she was toward Steve. She had believed every story she'd heard about him, she thought as she massaged her neck gently, but to balance the guilt, he had behaved deliberately to make the gossip seem believable. He still had a reckless streak. She shivered.

*****

Steve caught sight of Peter as he headed for the west wing and ran to catch up. "Pete, you won't believe it. My cold symptoms are gone and the cut is healed. She's good. She is good."

Peter smiled. "She sent you a dinner and some white tablets." Steve smiled and shook his head. "I like the fussing she does," Peter said. "I always have. I think it was what attracted me first. She cares. She'd mother the world if she could."

"I like her, Pete, and I was dead wrong about her."

Peter smiled broadly, enjoying Steve's admission. "I was waiting for the day when you'd eat your words about her." Peter pushed the elevator button. "Well, this is the day. You two are adjusting to each other faster than I expected."

"Man, what's not to like about her," Steve said, holding the door open for Peter and following him on.

"She'll be in Nebraska for the weekend so if you have any free time let me know."

"Sounds good. I wonder if we should start playing golf. After this year, I go into private practice then the routine begins."

Peter shook his head. "I can't imagine what it will be like to have work come to me normally."

"Normally." Steve laughed. "Dr. Sprague is giving me pep talks about settling down and being normal. Find a decent girl, he says, and get a real life. He makes normal sound like being buried alive."

Peter smiled. "It's not as boring as I expected it to be."

Steve raised his eyebrows. "You aren't calling her normal, are you?"

"Maybe not, but our life is, and I like it."

Steve laughed lightly. "Huh, your normal would be fun. Dr. Sprague's tone sounded like no sex. Hell, I don't want to get old. Most especially, I don't want to walk around like the living dead. I sometimes wonder what Debbie's reaction would be if I took her to a Sprague party. What's wrong with marrying a Debbie?"

"Marry her then."

"Maybe I will."

"Do you love her?"

"Pete, I honestly don't think I can feel love. I loved Marcia and nobody since."

"Steve Bradley, a one woman man?"

"No, just smart enough not to get chewed up and spit out twice. I'd marry for sex or my career, that's it." They stepped off the elevator and headed to the lab.

Peter was asked to work a double. With Jeneil leaving the next night for Nebraska and facing the second shift the following week, he wished he didn't have to. He had hoped for a quiet evening before the second shift's tension began the next week, but it wasn't meant to be. He worked the double.

Seventeen

Peter heard the alarm go off. He wondered where the night had gone. Forcing himself awake, he opened his eyes. He could tell that it was still very early. He looked at the clock. "Four forty-five?" He turned over to look at Jeneil. She was resting on one elbow smiling. "Honey, what's going on?"

She smoothed his hair back gently. "Oh, I thought we could say a proper goodbye to each other this morning. After all, next week's the killer schedule."

"That's a great idea. I almost woke you up last night but you were sleeping so peacefully."

"Well, you're nicer than I am. I didn't care; I woke you up this morning."

"Good." He grinned, and smoothed his hand along her arm. "The weekends that you're away seem a month long." She moved closer to him and snuggled sensuously. "Mmm, you feel great." He held her, enjoying her closeness. "I'm crazy about you, baby." He kissed her neck. He enjoyed her when she was in the mood to be seductive. He let her work her spell on him until he couldn't stand not having her any longer then he took over.

"Now that will be a very pleasant memory." He held her in his arms, still a little breathless. She felt warm and soft to him.

"Peter Chang, I love you. I'm glad I belong to you." She clung to him. He loved that about her. "Peter, I'm taking next week off from the hospital. I'm asking for a weeks' vacation without pay."

He was surprised. "Will they do that?"

"I think so."

"Why, honey?"

"Dennis needs help. The play opens in another two weeks. I'd like to be there for him to help bring things together, to be a support for him."

That surprised Peter, too. He kissed her forehead tenderly. He was concerned that Dennis could get her to do that. "I've never known you to do that so it must be important to you."

"It's important to Dennis. I'm excited and I'd like to see everything work out for him."

"You two are working close. Does his wife mind?" he probed without conscience.

"He's divorced."

"No woman either?"

"You mean living with him? No."

Peter closed his eyes. Vibrations began. "You must love the theatre. It's gotten into your blood and given you a fever for it."

She laughed lightly. "It has, but I think its Dennis more than the theatre. He's so talented. I want this for him. I've enjoyed the work a lot. It's all been wonderful."

Peter wondered how things between her and Dennis had gotten this far without him noticing. His concern had been with Robert and he had missed this completely. He lay in bed thinking about it while she showered and got ready for work. He watched her pinning up her hair. She had a great body. She was letting the world see more of her beauty, and she seemed more comfortable with and confident about herself. Turning, she noticed him watching.

"Uh-oh, you're wide awake." She frowned. "You were supposed to go back to sleep."

"I won't be awake for long," he assured her.

She left the bedroom and returned with a glass of juice for him. She smiled and kissed his cheek. "Miss me like crazy."

He nodded. "I do already."

"And you try to rest this weekend."

"I will." He touched her cheek gently. She kissed him then gathered her purse and left for work. The apartment was quiet without her. He hated the empty feeling when she was gone. Turning over, he closed his eyes. Dennis Blair. The name trickled through his mind. Maybe it was time he checked things out. He was starting to see a pattern to her relationships and it was easier for him to handle if he saw things first hand. He had decided to never ignore vibrations. Robert Danzieg had taught him that. Early next week, he thought, but now, on his day off and Jeneil away, he was going to sleep and enjoy the feeling of her warmth that lingered with him.

*****

Peter was glad to fill the weekend hours. He and his grandfather went to dinner and spent the evening talking. His grandfather was surprised to hear that Jeneil was so involved with business, and was very pleased at the progress the two were making and that their lives seemed settled. He liked the man his grandson had become and enjoyed their time together.

Steve had called and asked if Peter would take one of a double shift for him. Steve wanted to spend the night and most of the day with Debbie, and Peter was glad for the chance to repay Steve for some favors and to keep busy. Both shifts were full speed and he got home exhausted Saturday night, sleeping until it was almost time to go to work the next day. He woke up remembering that Jeneil would be home in a few hours. He smiled and got ready for work. During his shift, he watched the clock from four-thirty on. He called her and relaxed when she answered.

"I just wanted to know that you're safe," he said.

"I am and I missed you like crazy."

"Did you get the week off?"

"Yes, no problem at all. I'm glad."

"Can you wait up for me then?" he asked boldly.

"I was planning to."

He relaxed even more and smiled. "I'll be home by eleven-thirty. Boy, I'm glad you're back."

"Missed me like crazy, too?" she asked with a slight laugh.

"And then some. I've got to get back on duty. I'll see you tonight." He replaced the receiver and walked back to the floor smiling.

He realized how much he had missed her when he got home. He couldn't have her close enough to him and he couldn't get enough of her.

"Chang missed me, too, didn't he?" She grinned, breathlessly lying against him, enjoying the strength of his arms around her. She was surprised at his passion even after making love.

"Yes, I did, honey. My grandfather said to say hello. He thought it was very like you to be doing work for the foundation."

"That's two visits I've missed now. Can we have him here?"

The thought took him by surprise. "Hey, that's not a bad idea. I'd like him to see your Great Wall of China. That'll impress him, and I see you've added new information. The Han Dynasty was really something."

Jeneil thought to herself, Peter Chang, now you've gotten into it. She hugged him. "Any nightmares this weekend?"

"Yes, and the dreams are beginning to change."

"How?" she asked, concerned.

"I break loose from the tubes and bindings and start after Rees."

"And then what?"

"I woke up in a sweat. My rage woke me up. I felt the hatred all through me, like it was my blood." She felt him tense up and she snuggled closer to him, kissing him gently. He looked at her and smiled. "I'm glad you're home."

"Me, too." She smiled. "Me, too." She wondered about the dream.

Jeneil made breakfast. Doing dishes together, their few light kisses became more passionate and they went back to bed. She kissed him as he laid back to rest. "I hate to leave you," she said, tracing his chin with her finger, but I've got to get to the theatre."

"What would you do if I asked you to stay?"

"Beg you to let me go." She smiled.

He laughed and held her close. "Go then."

She smiled and kissed him. "I love the freedom you allow me. I love you for that." She kissed him again then went to shower.

He wondered if there should be any concern about Dennis. But look at us together, he thought. He wasn't even worried about Robert today. He felt a vibration and he thought about it for a moment. Maybe he would check just to see how Dennis was handling Jeneil's devotion. It must be flattering.

Jeneil kissed him. "That was some daydream. You were oceans away." She smiled.

He pulled her onto the bed and kissed her passionately. "Remember, you're my woman."

She laughed. "How can I forget after a kiss like that?"

He hit her bottom. "Now get to the theatre." He grinned. She smiled and kissed him.

"I wish I was staying, you're crazy right now. This could be a fun day."

"Out of here by the count of five or I get to chain you to the bed," he joked. At the door, she stopped and blew a kiss to him, smiled, then left. He smiled and stretched. "One of the sexiest girls I've ever met. Change that," he laughed, "she's the only really sexy girl I've ever met. Steve's right, I'm off the mountain and into oblivion about her."

*****

Jeneil began spending her days and evenings at the theatre, coming home only at night to sleep. Wednesday morning Peter watched as she flitted about getting ready to leave. Sitting down on the edge of the bed, she put her arms around his neck. "This schedule is madness." She sighed.

"Having fun?" he asked, smiling.

She nodded. "Yes, I am. A lot of fun, but I'm glad we've had at least mornings together." She kissed him. "I've got to leave. I love you." She kissed him again. Peter watched her pick up her purse, several large envelopes, and a notebook. He got up and showered after she left.

He found his way to the playhouse, arriving at eleven-thirty. He hoped to take Jeneil to lunch. What he really hoped was to see Dennis with her. It was all part of his hovering routine for a songbird. He locked his car and went to the side door of the playhouse. It was unlocked. Opening it, he stepped inside. He heard voices but couldn't see anyone. A woman in a flowing dress and stage makeup appeared in the corridor.

"Need some help?" she asked, noticing his lost look.

"I'm looking for Jeneil."

The woman looked him over closely, carefully smiling the whole while. "Well, look at what's she's getting to volunteer. She is good." Peter smiled. "Dennis. She's always with Dennis…or Robert, or Jeff, or David. Try the double doors on the right. They're at rehearsal, I think."

"Thanks."

"Sure. Glad to have you here." She grinned meaningfully. Peter walked away, raising his eyebrows. Opening one door slowly, he looked in. Except for lights on the stage, the room was dark. He stopped just inside the door and stayed in the shadows. He heard Dennis's voice.

"Lisa, you're supposed to be deliberating about having an extramarital affair. Sweetie, you look like you're agonizing over a bad breakfast."

"The line is too stiff," the actress answered.

Dennis raised his hands in frustration. "Why does everybody want to rewrite the script?" Peter watched as Dennis turned around. Someone was talking to him from a chair. Dennis turned back to face the stage. "Lisa, Jeneil is more patient than I am. She wants to know what you'd say."

The actress shrugged. "I don't know what words, but why is this woman deliberating about an affair, doesn't that kind of thing just happen?"

Dennis sighed. "Lisa, my love, your youth takes my breath away."

Jeneil stood up. "Lisa, the woman's husband means something to her. She's a sensitive, intelligent woman. It wouldn't be easy for her to ignore those feelings and the problems the affair would create. Their marriage needs defining, but it isn't over. She's lonely and in transition about herself and her life." Dennis smiled. He went over to Jeneil and put his head on her shoulder.

He was too close, Peter thought.

The actress shrugged again. "Okay, I can deal with that."

Dennis released his hold on Jeneil, but kept an arm around her shoulder. "Start the scene over again so Lisa will have time to deal with the new definition off stage." Peter heard groaning. "Come on, come on, the rest of you aren't so polished that you can feel smug," Dennis called. An actor positioned himself on stage and the scene opened again. The actress walked on stage and got into the part. Peter watched as Dennis squeezed Jeneil when the actress got past the part she had stumbled over before. The scene ended and Dennis kissed Jeneil's cheek.

Here we go again, Peter thought. Every time these guys began with a little friendly physical, things got carried away.

"Okay, everyone," Dennis called to the group, "let's do lunch." The cast quickly disappeared. Standing before Jeneil, Dennis stretched his arms then his body.

Peter grinned. Son-of-a-bitch. He was showing off for her. She had done it again. It was hormone and heartbeat time again. He continued to watch. Jeneil picked up her purse and took out her script. Thumbing through it, she stopped and pointed to a page.

Peter smiled. "Not impressed with muscle flexing, are you, baby?" Jeneil appeared to be saying something to Dennis about the script then she pointed to the stage. Dennis listened then smiled. Casually resting his wrists on Jeneil's shoulders, he continued to stretch and talk to her. Jeneil removed his arms gently as part of a turn then hugged her large leather purse in front of her with both arms.

Peter smiled broadly from the shadows. "Atta girl, baby, good strong body language, tell the son-of-a-bitch no." He was proud of her. Steve was right, she could handle herself. Jeneil looked up to talk to Dennis and caught sight of Peter.

"Peter?" she called, surprised. "Is that you?" Peter stepped forward into the brighter light then walked to them. "Is something wrong?" she asked, shocked that he was at the theatre.

"No, I thought I'd surprise you and 'do' lunch." Peter used Dennis's phrase hoping Dennis would know how long he'd been there. Dennis looked down at the floor. Jeneil smiled broadly. Peter could tell she was pleased.

"I'd like that." She kissed his lips lightly.

He smiled to himself. Songbirds did make terrific women.

"Just give me time to freshen up and find a volunteer to eat the lunch I packed this morning."

"What is it?" Dennis asked.

"A cold cooked vegetable salad on lettuce. I brought dressing separately."

"I'll pass. That's not enough, I'm starved." Peter held his breath, wondering if Jeneil would invite Dennis to eat with them. "Peggy's dieting," Dennis added. "She tries to skip lunch then is starved by two."

"Then let me check with her. I'll be back soon, Peter." Jeneil walked quickly to the doors.

"How are you, Peter?" Dennis asked. "Tough schedule for you this week?"

"Not too bad. How's the play going?"

"We open in two weeks. There are times I would like to cancel it. I really appreciate having Jeneil here."

"Yeah, I noticed," Peter answered without emotion.

Dennis looked at him and grinned. "Robert told me that you hover over her. She's in her element here, Peter. Let's not get into snarling over her. She belongs here. She's a natural around all of this. Don't pull her out of here for what you think you saw."

Peter grinned. "My eyesight's fine, Dennis, I know what I saw. She trusts the world, I don't."

Dennis smiled. "You must be a good surgeon. I didn't even feel any pain on that cut. Never kid a man of science, huh?"

"I don't like games."

Dennis nodded casually. "Oh and isn't the surprise lunch a game? You're snooping, Peter, and you know it. You're hovering over her. Are you afraid of something?"

"No, just curious about you," Peter replied, still without emotion.

"Satisfied now?"

"I'm not surprised. She's special. Hero worship is intoxicating to the hero."

"You won't pull her then?"

Peter shook his head. "She makes her own decisions. I don't own her."

"You're that sure of yourself?" Dennis smiled.

"No. I want Jeneil to be sure, that's all."

Dennis was silent for a second. "How can she be sure without choices?"

Peter felt the ball fall into Dennis's court. "You're good at word games, Dennis."

"Words are my scalpel, Peter. I'm in my element here."

"Which means?" Peter asked dryly.

"This is my operating room."

Peter chuckled. "So I've noticed, but she didn't."

Dennis studied Peter carefully. "How sure do you want to be? I haven't gotten near serious."

"Oh, you're past the mark, Dennis, if you think I'm going to give you permission to make a pass at her. That civilized I'm not. You're on your own."

"You're serious," Dennis remarked, surprised.

Peter folded his arms. "Hey, you're heading that way, aren't you? She'll handle it."

Dennis studied Peter's face. "I like your style, Peter. You've got guts, but I play the game for keeps. I'm not a kid just starting out, I've been through a marriage. Jeneil's unspoiled. Aren't you afraid she'll become confused?"

"Dennis, she's unspoiled, not stupid. Very few things confuse her."

Dennis nodded and grinned. "You're a good poker player."

Peter shook his head. "Oh no, I'm not playing this game with you. Now really Dennis, did anyone ever promise you that life would be easy?"

Dennis gave a hearty laugh. "You're a surprise, Peter, and so is she. I can see why there's an attraction." Peter smiled at Jeneil as she walked toward them.

"All set," she said, taking Peter's arm.

"Dennis, I'll bring back tonight's dinner for us."

"Thanks, Jeneil. I'm glad you're here, especially this week."

"What are friends for?" Jeneil answered. Peter smiled broadly at Dennis, the meaning of which didn't go unnoticed by Dennis.

"I've enjoyed talking to you, Peter. It was interesting."

"Same here," Peter answered. Jeneil and Peter walked away holding hands.

"What did you two talk about?" she asked.

"A poker game, I think," Peter answered. Jeneil looked at him, puzzled. The girl in the flowing dress was walking toward them in the corridor. Noticing the two of them holding hands, she stopped abruptly.

"Aw Jeneil, I thought he was a volunteer. It's not fair to tease people like that."

Jeneil laughed warmly. "Sorry, Sylvia, this one qualifies, but I saw him first. You'll have to fight me for him."

"What does he do for a living?"

"He's a doctor, Sylvia," Jeneil replied teasingly.

"Oh, Jeneil, I thought you were a nice person. You're enjoying this, I can see it."

Jeneil laughed. "See you in an hour."

"An hour," Sylvia gasped. "See that, you're too young for him then. I wouldn't even come back."

Jeneil laughed, enjoying the joke. "I'll keep looking for you. He's out there, I know he is."

"All five S's, Jeneil, all 5."

"What five S's," Peter asked as they stepped outside.

Jeneil grinned. "She wants a man who is straight, sincere, sensitive, strong, and sexy."

Peter held the car door open. "Well, well, and you said that I qualify?"

"Ooo, you do, my love, you do." She kissed him. He got behind the steering wheel.

"Would you really fight for me?" he asked, touching her face lovingly.

"Like a crazed she creature." Jeneil smiled. Peter smiled then they kissed warmly.

Eighteen

The hospital seemed quiet when Peter went on duty. Taking his cup of coffee, he sat in the medical room reviewing reports. They held his interest when Steve walked in and sat without speaking. After a few minutes, Peter looked up. "Something's wrong. You haven't made any noise. You and Debbie having trouble?"

"Pete, Debbie and I don't fight and we're good in bed. I'm really wondering if I should ask her to marry me."

Peter stared at him. "Do you want to get married?"

"I think I was spared all those human feelings, but left to myself I would probably never get married. Facing Sprague's lectures about settling down and a real life, I have to think about it."

"I don't know, Steve. That's a big commitment to make if you're not in love."

"But that's my point. Debbie and I get along fine. Neither one of us is into emotional ties."

"Then how will a marriage work? Will you continue to share her with weightlifters after you're married?"

Steve stared at him and raised his eyebrows. "I don't know. I just assumed she'd settle for me. Actually I was hoping I could bring Debbie to meet you and Sunshine. I'd like to see what changes might happen between us if we're around people who are committed to each other."

Peter smiled. "What do you have in mind?"

Steve grinned. "One of Sunshine's dinners, nothing very fancy, Debbie wouldn't quite make it to that, but I'd like her to see Sunshine's touches. Debbie doesn't nest." He stopped then sighed. "Oh boy, I'm not sure Debbie and Sunshine would get along. Debbie can be very opinionated."

Peter laughed. "This doesn't seem easy for you."

"It isn't, Pete, and I know Sprague. He's serious. He's guided me all the way. I've always understood clearly when he has grabbed me by the back of the neck to get my attention. His lectures are aimed at a good career more than finding a soul mate. He's serious."

Peter was annoyed. "Will you have to get Sprague's approval of Debbie, too?" he asked, deliberately sarcastic.

Steve laughed. "Shit, she'll never make it the way she is, but I'd like to see how much change is in Debbie. How much would she conform if she was committed to me and my cause?" Steve leaned forward and sighed. "Oh, I don't know, that doesn't sound fair. I wish I could find a computer somewhere that would match up a wife for me."

"This is really tough, isn't it?"

Steve shook his head. "It is for me. I don't belong married. Boy, I envy you not having to face all this."

Peter smiled. "I'll talk to Jeneil about meeting Debbie."

"Ah, let it go," Steve answered, pacing. "It all seems so phony and planned. I've got to get to the lab. Do you have first dinner break?" Peter nodded. "Then I'll meet you in the cafeteria"

"No, the doctor's lounge. She sent dinner for us."

"Oh great, I could use that right now. Do you think we could both marry her?" Steve smiled. "Hey, what a great idea. Polygamy."

Peter laughed. "I thought in polygamy, the man had more than one wife, not the woman having more husbands."

"More than one wife." Steve grimaced. "Oh geez, I'm having enough trouble finding one wife. No, I like my idea better. Feminists would complain about equality in polygamy I'm sure then we could both have Sunshine."

Peter smiled understandingly. "Steve, keep that up and I'll believe the gossip about you being kinky."

Steve laughed. "Hey, speaking of kinky, you should hear about the weekend I had with Charlotte. Joe Bartoli was telling me about it." Steve laughed and shook his head. "I don't even know who Charlotte is."

"You know, Steve, you might have caused yourself some damage by kicking at the gossip line like you have. Maybe Dr. Sprague wouldn't be at you now if the gossip hype wasn't as bad as it is. It's getting pretty weird."

"Pete, I started one rumor about being the White Stallion as a joke. The rest of it grew on its own."

Peter smiled. "Well, Rita and Lucy keep the White Stallion story going."

Steve laughed. "Hey, I had the Chinese Stud for a roommate. I took notes." They both laughed. "See you at break." Steve said, still laughing as he left.

Peter was glad to see Steve more cheerful. The idea of getting married as a career move was real to Steve and that surprised Peter. For as long as he had known Steve, he never had a problem where women were concerned. Seeing him with his confidence so shaken was a real surprise. Peter thought about Jeneil and smiled. How had he gotten so lucky? The rest of the shift was quiet. By eleven-fifteen, Peter left. Jeneil was sitting up in bed writing in her notebook when Peter got home.

"Hi." She smiled. "Slow night?"

"Yes, for a change." Getting into bad, he kissed her shoulder. "What's happening at the playhouse?" He decided he needed to be more interested in everything since talking to Dennis, and he wanted to keep up from now on. It all reminded him of being with the Dragons; you always kept an ear on what the other gangs were doing. Even a minor change could mean something. He had decided he was going to listen intently to everything Jeneil said about Dennis and what he was up to.

"Oh, the theatre? It's the usual." Jeneil turned off the lamp and slipped down under the covers. Peter was surprised at her lack of fire. She was usually full of excitement. He felt a vibration. He put his arms around her. She cuddled to him and he relaxed a bit.

"Are you tired?"

"No, why?"

"Just wondered," Peter dodged.

"It's really curious." She smiled. "I put in long hours, but I don't wear out. I enjoy being at the playhouse." He kissed her forehead gently.

"Jeneil, would you consider having Steve and his girlfriend to dinner some night?"

"He has a girlfriend?"

"Debbie."

"Then Rita and Lucy are just gossip, too?"

"No."

Jeneil looked up quickly. "Oh no, he doesn't cheat on Debbie, does he?"

"No, they have a different style of relationship."

She was puzzled. "Something you can describe?"

Peter chuckled. "Nothing x-rated, honey, they just have other people in their lives besides each other, that's all."

"Physically, too?"

"Yes."

Jeneil still looked puzzled. "Then why did you call her Steve's girlfriend?"

"Because he's thinking about a serious relationship with her and he wants her to meet us. He's thinking about marriage."

"Does she work at the hospital?"

"You know better than that. No, Debbie works at a health spa."

"Oh really, what does she do?"

"I don't know. Does it matter?"

"No, of course not, I'm just curious. Steve Bradley's serious about someone. Imagine that." Jeneil chuckled.

Peter smiled. "I'm anxious to meet her, too. It'll be interesting to see the woman who might be Mrs. Steve Bradley."

"I guess so. That is one wedding I'm going to be sure to attend. Mrs. Steve Bradley. Wow!"

There was silence between them again. Peter rubbed her back gently and kissed her cheek several times. He was starting to get concerned that she wasn't snuggling the way she usually did.

"Peter," Jeneil said, breaking the silence. "How can a woman tell when a guy is coming on to her?"

The question hit Peter in the center of his chest with a thud. The bastard hadn't wasted any time. He sighed to himself. "Why?"

"I'm just wondering."

"That's an odd thing to wonder about, isn't it?"

"Is it? Then forget I asked," she replied quietly. He wished he had watched his words.

Damn it, he lectured himself. Don't corner her, let her talk. "Honey, I would think the safest thing for a woman to do is to assume the man is coming on to her even if the signals aren't clear, then she can decide what she wants."

She sighed. "It's so awkward. You can't say anything because you might be wrong. Yet, if you ignore the signals, you wonder if that will encourage the guy. It's a delicate situation. It must be infuriating to be part of a sexual harassment situation."

"Why are you concerning yourself about all of this?"

She was silent then answered, "No reason."

He was disappointed that she didn't open up to him. "That isn't like you. What's this all about? Who's coming on to you?"

She looked at him. "I'm not sure about...."

"Who?" he interrupted, hoping to get Dennis out in the open.

"You're getting upset," she said. "This was stupid of me. It isn't the sort of thing to discuss with your man, is it?"

"Honey, I'm not upset. I think you're terrific. Other men probably do, too." He held her closer. "Who is it, baby."

"David Gibson."

"Who?" Peter asked in total surprise. "Who the hell is David Gibson?" he asked sharply.

"See, you're upset."

"No, no, I'm not," he assured her, kissing her lips lightly. "I'm just shocked. I've never heard his name before."

"He's in charge of staging, props, and sound effects at the playhouse. He's a cinematography major at the university doing graduate work."

"What's he doing to make you wonder?"

"He looks at me the way you did sometimes before we became serious. Well now, wait a minute, you weren't coming on to me then. You see, I am wrong. This isn't fair to David."

"That's all, just looks?"

"No, he'll touch my face now and then, but all he's ever said is, 'Jeneil, you're so gentle.' He kissed my cheek once. None of this proves anything. I'm sorry, there's nothing to all of it. I'm so anxious to avoid another Robert situation that I'm too cautious. I'll never get relationships worked out right. Poor David, this is so unfair to him."

Peter kissed her forehead. "Jeneil, you were getting to me before we were serious. I think you should assume he's coming on to you."

"And then what, Peter? How can I prevent it?"

Peter smiled and kissed her lips lightly. He suddenly saw the situation from her side. "I guess you'll just have to wait until he makes a move that's more aggressive and clear."

"Oh gosh," she said quietly.

"Honey, believe me, he won't be hurt if you don't make him feel like a creep. Most guys know the odds are fifty-fifty for a turn down." She snuggled closer to Peter and he realized that she was looking for protection; she didn't like these situations in her life.

"Well, I talk about you to him hoping that he'll realize I'm committed."

"What has that done?"

"Not much from what I can see."

"Then it sounds like he might be just getting some kicks." Jeneil looked at him and wrinkled her eyebrows, puzzled. "Well, if he knows he can't have you," Peter hesitated, wondering how to describe the situation, "then he must find you gentle. Your skin is soft. You smell good. You're a girl. It reminds him that he's a man. That can feel good. That's all," and then Peter laughed. "Why the hell am I defending these guys?" He shook his head. "Being around civilized people can make a guy do strange things. No more playhouse for you!" he said sharply as a joke. "I'm going to keep you locked in this apartment. Do you hear me? It's over for you." He smiled and kissed her. "No more freedom, woman. This body stays chained to this bed. I'll leave you food and water." He kissed her neck and held her close.

"I'm glad I asked you about that," and she laughed, feeling lighter. "That's not a bad thing. Men and women making each other feel like men and women. It sounds so natural."

"Well, now wait a minute. We can't have the whole world turned on to each other."

"Why not?" she asked, smiling. "Make love, not war." She laughed.

"Oh nice," he whispered, smoothing his lips lightly over her ear and caressing her. He felt her body respond and he kissed her lips. She moved closer to him. He looked at her and moved her hair off her shoulder. "I can feel sorry for those guys, baby. I know what you're like, they can only imagine it." He kissed her lips passionately.

*****

Peter ran into Steve in an elevator. "Do you have first break tonight?"

"Yeah, why?"

"Dinner in the doctor's lounge?"

"Sounds good. What did she send?"

Peter shrugged. "I don't know." The elevator stopped, the door opened, and Peter headed onto the floor.

Steve got off the elevator on the administration floor and headed to Dr. Sprague's office. He used to enjoy meeting with him, but since the marriage lectures began, Steve dreaded being summoned to Sprague's office. The receptionist smiled enticingly at him. Steve gave her a weary smile. He was getting tired of the whole White Stallion joke, the White Stallion image. He felt dirty from it. There was so much gossip being spread about him lately that whenever a woman smiled at him, he assumed she had heard some rumor. He was beginning to feel like a freak. He avoided looking at the receptionist who was passing glances his way. Dr. Fisher walked out of Dr. Sprague's office. He nodded to Steve and left.

"Dr. Bradley," Dr. Sprague sighed, "come on in." Steve felt trouble in his gut. He gripped the pen he was carrying tightly as he closed the office door. "Sit down, Steve." Dr.

Sprague motioned to the brown leather chair across from his desk. "I'm going to have your initials carved in that chair, Bradley. You and I are meeting together quite a lot lately."

"Seems that way to me too, Sir," Steve said calmly. "What am I up against this time?"

Dr. Sprague watched him closely. "I thought I was quite explicit in our last meeting about cleaning up your act."

"I don't remember you telling me to clean up my act."

"Bradley, I told you to get your life together."

"You suggested that I get married. I'm looking," Steve defended.

"So I hear." Dr. Sprague leaned forward, looking annoyed. "Tell me about Charlotte."

"Charlotte?" Steve asked, surprised. "I don't know Charlotte."

"That isn't what I heard." Dr. Sprague glared at him.

"Dr. Sprague, really, I was as shocked to hear about me and Charlotte as you seem to be."

"Come on, Bradley."

"It's the truth." Steve stood up. "I swear it."

"Steve, that gossip was downright filthy."

"Dr. Sprague, I mean it, I don't even know who Charlotte is."

Dr. Sprague motioned him to sit. He felt his stomach knot as he sat back down.

"How would that get started then?"

Steve lowered his head. "My guess is that it got started as a joke."

"A joke?" Dr. Sprague sat up rigidly. "A joke? Do you know that Charlotte Spencer handed in her notice?"

Steve looked at him, totally shocked. "She quit? Sir, I don't even know her. Why is she quitting?"

Dr. Sprague glared at him. "Because she's getting propositioned and mauled every time she turns around as a result of that filthy gossip."

"Well, didn't she tell you that it wasn't true?"

"No, she didn't." Steve's heart felt like a solid mass of concrete in his chest. "You mean she claims it's true?"

Dr. Sprague shook his head. "No, she won't talk about it. We thought she was protecting you."

"And that means I'm guilty?" Steve asked, trying to stay calm.

"You're telling the truth," Dr. Sprague said, studying Steve's face. "You've been in here enough over the years for me to know you as well as one of my sons." Dr. Sprague stood up and sighed, walking to a window. "This hospital has always been lousy with gossip. I guess we're not isolated, no hospital is." He exhaled loudly and sat down again. "Steve, I've got to give it to you with both barrels. As a doctor, you'd be a great addition to our office, but my colleagues are afraid of you personally." Steve looked at Dr. Sprague as he felt a knife slip into his stomach. "We've watched you from the time you came here. Your exceptional good looks have always concerned us, but we waited to see what would come of them. You turn women's heads, Steve. That in itself we can handle, but the legend that has sprung up around you can't be ignored."

"Dr. Sprague, it's mostly gossip."

"Maybe so Steve, but you fed it or at least fanned the flame."

"What's the bottom line?"

Dr. Sprague stared into his eyes. "Steve, I have to tell you that this is the bottom line, that it's a guarantee."

"What is it?" Steve asked, feeling a surge of heat go through him and braced for the worse. He knew it would be final.

"Conditional probation to the end of your residency."

Steve sat back in his chair, glad he at least had probation. "What conditions?" he asked through a very dry throat.

"My colleagues seem to feel that you know how to manipulate the gossip. They want you to get the gossip stopped. The fun is over."

"How?" Steve asked in disbelief. "I'd like that, too."

"You're on your own Steve, but I will tell you that we're looking for a thorough end to prove that you sincerely want to be part of the medical profession and our group in particular. My advice is that you don't so much as whisper anything off color into the ear of any woman within a twelve-mile radius of the hospital. When you leave here, you act like you're preparing to join a monastery. This is a deep blow for me too, Steve. I've watched you progress like a son, but my colleagues are right, you've become untouchable. I'm counting on your dogged determination to turn this around. If you think about it, you'll understand their concern, too."

Steve nodded. "I do. I'm just at a loss about how to change it. I mean how do I stop stories like Charlotte from starting?"

"Other than getting married next week and shaping up around here, I don't know. I've never faced your unique problem of being a lady-killer. To be honest, I'm glad I haven't. It seems like a nuisance to me. Can you even find a real relationship?"

Steve rubbed his forehead. He felt flushed. "Dr. Sprague, I'd use a computer to find me a wife if I could. Believe me, you find the girl, I'd become a model husband."

Dr. Sprague smiled understandingly. "Actually, there is one girl I've thought about, but your reputation has probably ruined your chances with her."

"Who's that?" Steve asked, very curious.

"The young woman in the medical records department."

Steve wanted to laugh. "Uh, she's taken from what I hear."

"More gossip, Steve. You know when we hear gossip so varied about one person we can tell it's only ignorant and idle gossip. I've talked to her personally from time to time. I don't know why she's in the job she's in, but she does it so well that we don't care. She's intelligent and really quite beautiful if you take the time to look at her. My advice is to develop a taste for her type of woman, Steve. She'd be there for you more than the Ritas' and Lucys'. Maybe life with her would be tamer, but you'd get more mileage from it. Now get back to work. We do understand each other on this, don't we?"

"Yes, sir," Steve answered, standing up and extending his hand. "Thank you, Dr. Sprague. I have a feeling that my conditional probation is largely supported by only you."

Dr. Sprague smiled and shook Steve's hand. "Get it together then I can go back and smile with delight when it's over."

Steve smiled. "You've got it, signed in blood." The receptionist gave him a sensuous smile as he left the office. He shot her an icy look, leaving her surprised. "Women, no wonder men turn gay." He looked at his watch. "Five-thirty, good, I can use some dinner and a friend."

Peter was heating their dinner when Steve walked into the doctor's lounge. He looked up as Steve walked in. "Something's wrong," Peter said, sitting down.

"Life is shitty right now," Steve said, sighing.

"What happened?"

"My joining Sprague's team after my residency has been put on hold."

"Holy Shit! How come?" Peter was shocked.

"My deadly good looks and lousy reputation," Steve tried to joke, but Peter could see he was very upset. "I've been put on probation. They want me to turn the gossip around so men won't be afraid to leave their wives and daughters with me. And Charlotte, I don't know who the hell she is but I'm going to find out real soon. She's got some explaining to do."

"Charlotte?" Peter asked. "Charlotte Spencer?"

"I don't know. Is she the one I spent the weekend with?"

"So I hear."

"Well, I've got to talk to her. She's not denying the gossip and she quit. That dumps that shit on me, too."

"What?" Peter asked. "This is getting way out of hand."

"Hmm, isn't it though? Nothing like trying to wash shit off yourself for a bunch of men who don't want you on their team. Will I ever get the smell off?"

"What a mess," Peter commented and sighed. The microwave buzzer sounded and he brought back their dinners.

"Pot roast," Steve said, smiling. He looked at Peter and laughed. "By the way, Dr. Sprague found a girl he'd like to see me marry."

Peter looked at him, shocked. "Aw, come on man. You're shittin' me now, right?"

"No, I'm not."

"Are you going to take that, too?" Peter asked, not believing what he was hearing.

"I like his choice."

"You know her? Who is it?"

Steve grinned. "Jeneil."

Peter choked. "He said that? Jeneil? Really?"

"Ideal choice for a doctor's wife. Home life might be a little tame, but so what. Man, I'll take her kind of tame." Steve smiled and laughed.

Peter smiled. "Well, you have something in common with her. You've both been done in by gossip."

Steve looked up. "What? Her, too?"

Peter nodded. "When she was a kid. Small town, small church, small minds. She defended the minister's son and the gossip turned it around so that she was having sex with him. It caused a big fuss and left her paranoid. It also left her with names for little boys to call and a telephone number to change. So she never dated. She's still trying to catch up on what she missed learning as a teenager."

Steve shook his head. "That explains her innocence. I'll never laugh at gossip again as long as I live. How did you two get together in this relationship anyhow?"

"Jeneil claims it's our scars."

Steve smiled. "And you?"

"I don't analyze it, I just enjoy it."

Steve laughed. "My kind of living. Well, I better be good to Debbie. Sprague said Rita and Lucy are off limits, and any other women around here except Jeneil." He laughed. "Sorry Pete, but he is the head of Surgery. Maybe he can find one for you, too."

Peter smiled. "Speaking of Debbie, there's a play opening a week from Friday. Jeneil wondered if you and Debbie would like to come to dinner then the theatre?"

"You told her!"

"Only that you're getting serious and want us to meet her."

"The theatre. Well, let's see what Debbie will do with that evening. She and Jeneil are different types of women, Pete. I really should warn you."

"Jeneil's pretty good with people."

"I'll check with Debbie then." Steve sighed. "I don't know how I'm going to get through this. I feel like separating myself from everything and everyone here to let the gossip die down then I get so mad I want to yell."

"Concentrate on being a good doctor and let your friends help get you through the rest."

"Like you? Dinner and talking. You two are good friends."

"No, we're family Steve, but you have other friends here, too. We'll all help." Peter was amazed. He had never seen Steve so in need of anything and so vulnerable before; he'd been hit hard.

Steve appreciated Peter's friendship. "Well, I better go and stir up my gossip hounds. I want to know why Charlotte would rather quit than tell the truth." He stood up. "Thank Sunshine for dinner."

*****

Steve was a changed person. Peter watched as a nurse sauntered over to Steve as he was doing medical charts. "Hey, Steve." She pressed her body against his arm. Peter wondered if they got some cheap kick from it or if they were trying to turn Steve on.

Steve picked up the chart and turned away. "Hi, Sharon," he answered and walked into the medical room. The nurse looked insulted and Peter felt for Steve. The story about Charlotte was bizarre and Steve was getting a lot of attention. He worked hard to ignore all of it, especially the women rubbing up against him.

Steve was worn out and feeling low by the end of the shift. Peter walked out with him. "Want a roommate for tonight?"

"No." Steve smiled.

"Then how about bunking on our sofa tonight? It makes up into a bed."

"Thanks Pete, but my conscience and I need to be alone. I can't believe the number of women rubbing up against me. What was I doing? I'm lucky to be on probation."

"Oh man, what did Sprague do; a lobotomy on you? Come on Steve, the White Stallion wasn't all bad. There's a place and even a need for his kind of joking with all the tension around him."

"Well, the title's up for grabs." Steve smiled. "I've got to be a good boy and I intend to be the best behaved doctor who ever swung a stethoscope."

Peter watched him. "Well, I think you're moving too fast. People are already noticing. They think you're being rude."

"Good then the women will hate me. The faster, the better." He got into his car, waved to Peter and drove off. Peter sighed.

When Peter got home, he slipped under the covers and yawned. He was tired, too. Worrying about Steve had worn him down. Steve was being too drastic and offending people. Damn the whole situation anyway. He sighed.

Jeneil poked her head into the room. "Want a pineapple drink?"

"Sure," Peter answered, and Jeneil disappeared. Returning with two glasses, she put them on the night table and got into bed. She handed one to Peter and he drank it slowly.

Jeneil noticed his silence. "Honey, I know there's no reason to do handstands over a pineapple drink, but could you smile and say thank you," she teased.

He looked at her and smiled. "I'm sorry, I was thinking about something."

"Can I think about it, too?"

"Steve's in trouble," Peter said, sighing.

"Trouble? How?" she asked, surprised.

"The gossip at the hospital caught up with him. He was scheduled to join Dr. Sprague's group after his residency but they're putting him on probation. He's got to become Mr. Clean in his personal life or he's out. The story about Charlotte Spencer was more than they could take and it isn't even true." Peter shook his head.

"Yikes, the fleas are killing the dog."

"Aw, come on Jeneil, the guy's down. Do you have to kick him?" he asked angrily.

"Peter, I'm observing, not picking on him. I know the story about Charlotte isn't true."

"How?"

"Because the weekend that was supposed to be happening he was with you most of the time and with us on Sunday. Remember? That was the weekend his patient died."

Peter's mind grasped the memory. "That's right!" he said, sitting up. "That's right." He kissed her shoulder. "Thank you."

"Will that help anything?"

"Not unless push comes to shove, but it's something to keep in mind. He was at the hospital most of the time. He signed in on their records. Ooo, baby, I love your brain and the way it soaks up details." He kissed her cheek.

"What can he do about the gossip?"

Peter shrugged. "They want him to undo all of it and the image he's created. They feel he allowed it to happen."

Jeneil shook her head. "Here's a spoon, now go empty the desert of all the sand." Peter stared at her. "I'm not picking on him. Emptying the desert would be easier than what he's facing. How does he plan to undo the gossip?"

"I don't know." Peter sighed. "He's really low. He's watching every move he makes. Can you believe that he's grateful for probation? He can't believe the number of women coming on to him. He's grateful for a chance to prove himself."

Jeneil grinned. "Hmm, a true repentance, conscience and all."

"Your sympathy sounds strange. I thought you'd understand having been through this yourself."

"Peter, I feel for him, I really do. I don't know why Dr. Sprague would even ask him to undo the gossip. That's impossible, isn't it?"

Peter put his glass down. "They feel his effort to change it will prove how much he wants a position with their group, but Steve's being too drastic. He barely talks to the women and they're becoming offended. I can see it myself. This isn't over for him yet. I can feel it."

"Gosh, that's too bad. Nothing turned my gossip around. By the time everyone got through adding their own spice to the story, it sounded like a new story and it started making rounds on the gossip line again. Until Mandra stepped in, I thought I was destined to have different versions of the story follow me to my grave. I owe her for that." Jeneil became silent, thinking about her own gossip.

Peter sighed again. "It'll be a shame if this costs him his career. He's a hell of a surgeon. I feel so helpless and there's nothing I can do about it."

"It can't cost him his career, can it?"

"Why not? It's widely known that he's Sprague's protégé. Everyone expects him to join that group. If they don't take him, don't you think other doctors who are considering bringing him into their practices will ask why? And don't you think they'll find out about the gossip? This is bad."

"You mean he'd have to become a doctor in a tree house somewhere in the backwoods of an underdeveloped nation."

Peter started to laugh. "You have the craziest brain."

"You just said you loved by brain. Stabilize it, Dr. Chang," and she laughed.

Peter kissed her forehead as she snuggled against him. He didn't like the atmosphere at the hospital. Steve was getting tense and the nurses were becoming so annoyed with him they were finding ways to get even. Peter felt really sorry for him. When you crossed a nurse you faced a strong army that could make life a living hell, and that's just what they were doing to Steve. Peter had tried to explain to Steve that breaking off so drastically had the nurses thinking he was snubbing them, but Steve couldn't see it. He was so anxious to stop the gossip that he'd decided to live through the hell. How long could they keep it up? They'd lose their taste for blood eventually, wouldn't they? He was glad it was Saturday and he looked forward to the shift change just to get away from the nurses on the second. He was having trouble watching the small ways they were sabotaging Steve.

"Gosh I'm afraid to go back to work Monday," Jeneil said. "It sounds like a nightmare."

"I hear the nurses on the first shift are just waiting for him." Peter sighed.

"Why doesn't he tell them about his probation so they'll understand?"

"Are you kidding? He'd never wash that off himself. It would pass through all the hospitals in the state like a virus. Shit, I only hope that Sprague sees what Steve's living through. The guy has to watch his ass every time he turns around. Those bitches are deliberately making him miserable. This could go the other way for him; the brass could decide that he's become too ineffective on the team. Shit, I can't stand this."

Jeneil silently snuggled to him and soon fell asleep. Peter held her closely as he continued to stare into the darkness.

Nineteen

Jeneil returned to work on Monday. Delivering material to the fifth floor, she saw Steve in the medical room. He looked tired and thin. She had noticed the nurse's wouldn't talk to him, actually avoiding him like he was contagious. What a change from the way they used to fuss and faun over him. It wasn't overly obvious but it was there and very real. She felt a deep compassion for him. Steve looked up and saw her watching him. She smiled warmly. He smiled and winked at her. She went to the elevators and got on with two nurses.

"If he thinks the first shift nurses are different he can stick it in his stethoscope," one nurse said.

"Why are we angry at him?" the other asked.

"Who knows? He struts in one day and treats the second shift nurses like they have typhoid. A real behavior switch. We'll show him that doctors need nurses."

Jeneil closed her eyes. They had no idea what the war was about. Things had gotten so warped. She wanted to cry and she breathed deeply, hoping to calm herself. She turned around to face them. "Are you talking about Dr. Bradley?"

"Yes. Why?"

"I know why his behavior has changed," Jeneil offered, shaking nervously inside.

"You do?"

"Yes, and it's really too bad. He's not one of my favorite people but fair is fair I think. He fell for the granddaughter of my neighbor, a really nice girl. I couldn't believe she'd even look twice at a woman chaser like Steve Bradley. I almost said something to the grandmother to protect the girl." Jeneil paused as the nurses listened with interest. "Well, the girl knows someone here at the hospital apparently and they told her the story about Charlotte." The nurse's looked at each other and stepped closer to Jeneil. "The girl was crushed when she heard. The family is very moral. She told him not to call her anymore but I guess she's giving him one more chance because the grandmother told me the girl issued Dr. Bradley an ultimatum. If she hears so much as a whisper about his name connected to another woman they're finished for good. He's afraid to fool with anybody anymore. He doesn't know who the spy is so he keeps to himself. He must be really crazy about her, don't you think? The grandmother said that he's asked her to marry him."

The nurses' eyes opened wide. "Steve Bradley!"

"Isn't that a shock though?" Jeneil grinned. "Like I said, he's never been a favorite of mine, but I feel sorry for him because the weekend he was supposed to be with Charlotte, I personally saw him at my neighbor's house helping his girl work in the yard. They sat on the front steps and ate lunch together. I couldn't believe my eyes. Dr. Bradley that tame? It couldn't be I thought. But it was him."

"Are you positive?" one nurse asked.

"Does he drive a burgundy Lynx, MW942 license plate?"

"Yes, he does!" both nurses answered simultaneously.

"Then that's him all right. I don't know how his name became involved with Charlotte, but I know that story isn't true. I saw him myself with his girl. I think it's a shame that he's paying for that gossip when it's a lie. And have you seen him? He looks so tired and thin. I think he's really in love this time. It can't be easy for him to be working all his hours wondering when someone will pass on untrue gossip to his girl. She won't accept the ring until he proves himself." Jeneil shook her head. "I feel bad for him. He got a bad deal. That Charlotte story was filthy and the poor guy is innocent."

The nurses looked at each other as the doors to the elevator opened and Jeneil went to get off. "Thanks for that information," one nurse said to her.

Jeneil turned and held the elevator door open. "Sure, like I said, he's not one of my favorites but fair is fair and I don't know how to help him. You know how it is once gossip starts around here, there's nothing you can do about it. Poor Dr. Bradley. Thanks for listening anyway. I just get so upset when I hear the Charlotte story because I know it isn't true and he's paying for it. That's a shame, don't you think?"

"It sure is," one nurse said. "Thanks again."

"Sure," Jeneil answered, and let the doors close. She grinned and sighed. "Let's hope for the best from that," and she turned to deliver her materials.

Peter and Steve returned from afternoon rounds together. They walked to the nurse's station where several nurses stood together talking, stopping as Peter and Steve approached. Walking into the medical room, Steve laughed. "I'm diseased, Pete. You'd better find a new friend. Look at them. Something's up," he said, watching the nurse's whisper and look their way.

Peter nodded, looking at the group of nurses. "Something is up, Steve. This whispering is for real."

The telephone rang. Peter answered. "It's for you, Dr. Sprague's secretary."

"Oh shit," Steve said softly. "Dr. Bradley here." He listened. "I'll be right down." He put the receiver back and leaned on the phone with his eyes closed.

"What?" Peter asked.

Steve took a deep breath. "Sprague wants me," he said quietly. "I don't think I can take anymore."

"Want some coffee before you go?"

Steve shook his head. "I can't risk it. It won't stay down if there's more trouble. If there is more trouble, this is probably it for me."

"You can't be sure it's trouble."

"Oh no? Check the whispering. That's new. Something's going on. I'd better go see Sprague. You can have my stethoscope if I don't come back." Steve sighed.

"Yeah, well they can have mine too if you don't come back."

As Steve left, Peter watched as the nurses whispered to one another as they watched Steve walk to the elevators. "Bitches," he mumbled.

Steve walked into the office and the receptionist coldly told him to go right in. Steve knocked on the oak door, wishing he didn't have to. Dr. Sprague looked serious when he opened the door. "Come in Steve, sit down."

Steve sat stiffly. The look on Dr. Sprague's face was intense as he sat down and sighed. He rubbed his face with one hand as if he was tired. "Bradley, you lead a charmed life. You have the luck of the Irish."

Steve stared at him, wondering what he was talking about.

"If anyone had told me that you would pull out of what the nurses have been doing to you, I wouldn't have placed a nickel on that bet."

"You know about that then?" Steve asked quietly.

"Of course I know about it. Do you think I'm here to keep dust off this chair? It's been tough, hasn't it?"

"Yes."

"Have an appreciation for nurses now?"

"I thought that's how I got into this trouble in the first place," Steve said, and Dr. Sprague leaned back in his chair and laughed. "What do you mean pulled out of it?" Steve asked, confused.

Dr. Sprague looked at him. "You don't know?"

"Know what?" Steve asked, even more confused.

"This hospital has had quite a day today. It seems that a battalion of nurses confronted

Charlotte Spencer with proof of your innocence. Charlotte was in here for an hour confessing to having made up the story. Not the story the way it got retold but she started it."

"Why?" Steve asked, totally surprised.

Dr. Sprague shrugged. "Between her sobs I'm not sure I have the whole thing straight but she was trying to get the attention of a guy in Maintenance. Apparently being linked to you is very chic. Good way to pick up dates and so on and so on. The story got out of hand, but one thing confuses me, she kept apologizing for causing trouble between you and your girlfriend. She said the girl wouldn't marry you unless you straightened out. What's she talking about?"

Steve's mouth opened in shock. "I don't know," he said, not believing what he was hearing.

Dr. Sprague chuckled. "You are a lucky son-of-a-bitch. Do you want to know who was here when Charlotte's conscience caught up to her? Doctors Turner and Young."

Steve looked at him and grinned, recognizing the names of Dr. Sprague's senior partners.

"I don't have to tell you that hearing her confession firsthand went a long way in clearing your name, but the probation still holds. You're to keep it straight, understand?"

Steve nodded. "By choice, Dr. Sprague. I've reviewed my image and it stinks. Where does Charlotte work? I'd like to thank her for coming to see you."

"In the engineering office," Dr. Sprague answered. "I'm sorry about this, Steve. I like the Bradley I've seen around here lately." He smiled and laughed lightly. "There's not as much for administrators to talk about over coffee since you're so quiet but I like that. I'm proud of you, Steve."

"I told you that the promise was signed in blood."

Dr. Sprague smiled. "Good, now maybe the Chinese Stud will share his secrets with you. He must be doing some horsing around somewhere because his life is straight and it looks like he's on a steady diet of it. Take notes, Bradley. We were there once, too. We don't mind it happening, we just don't want headlines and videos of it."

"I'll remember that."

Steve felt lighter as he left the office. He had to get to a phone to call Charlotte. Who the hell were the nurses, he wondered, and what happened? After talking to an apologetic Charlotte, Steve rode the elevator, impatient to get back to Peter. He saw him in the medical room as the doors opened.

"Hi, Steve," the nurses said as he walked by

"Hi," he answered quietly, surprised they were talking to him. Closing the door to the medical room, he turned to Peter. "You're not going to believe all this."

"I heard and you're right, I don't. Charlotte confessed and you're getting married!" Peter laughed. "Where the hell is that from?"

"Who knows? Charlotte said Jane Sloan was one of the nurses who confronted her. She's on a break. When she comes back, I'll ask her about the story."

"Shit Steve, don't kill it. The nurses are rallying around you and this is just the cover story you need. I'd almost believe you started it because of the timing and the type of story. It was too perfect to cover your behavior change without telling the truth."

"But who did start it if I didn't and neither did you?"

"I don't know," Peter laughed, "but let the story work its magic."

"Damn right," Steve said, smiling. He nodded toward the desk as Jane Sloan returned from break. "Oh good, let's go find out where this came from. I'm curious as hell."

"Me, too," Peter said, "that story's brilliant," and they walked out of the medical room together and over to the nurse.

"Jane," Steve began sincerely, "I found out about you going to Charlotte today. I can't thank you enough."

Jane smiled and patted his hand. "It's okay Steve, fair is fair. That was a dirty deal to get stuck with. The nurses are sorry we didn't know the whole story. You should've told us."

Steve smiled. "Jane, who did tell you?"

"The neighbor of your girlfriend's grandmother."

"Who?" Steve asked.

Jane chuckled. "You know she's really the one to thank. If she hadn't told us the story you'd still be sitting in the chicken coop up to your elbows in it." She laughed. "Go thank her."

"Who?" Steve asked again.

"The girl in Medical Records."

Peter stood up straight and rigid from shock. Steve thought he felt his jaw hit his chest. "Oh, her," Steve managed to say.

Jane gave Steve a sympathetic smile. "I hope things work out for you. We can't believe the roving Steve Bradley has actually asked a girl to marry him. That's so terrific. What's her name?"

Steve was stumped. "Uh, didn't my girl's grandmother's neighbor tell you?"

"No, she only knows the grandmother. Boy was she fired up. She was upset about all of this. I've never heard her talk so much."

Peter and Steve exchanged a quick glance. "Yes, I'll have to thank her."

They walked back to the medical room and closed the door.

"I can't believe it was Jeneil!" Peter tried not to laugh.

"That girl is something else." Steve smiled and picked up the phone.

"What are you going to do?"

"Thank her."

"But Steve, you could blow her cover."

"Hi, Mrs. Sousa, is that girl who works in your office there? You know the one with the long hair. She was going to photocopy something for me. Thanks." He handed the telephone to Peter. "Ask her to meet us in the catacombs."

"Hi," Peter answered when he heard Jeneil's voice.

"How can I help you?" Jeneil asked, shocked at hearing Peter's voice.

"Can you meet me in the records storage room?"

"I'm leaving at four. I'll do that before I go to my car."

"Great. I love you."

"Thank you," Jeneil said, continuing in a professional tone. "I'll stop by before I leave."

Peter replaced the receiver. "She's leaving in ten minutes."

Steve smiled. "We should have known. After the mafia story, this must have been a piece of cake for her."

Peter shook his head in disbelief. "She never once said anything. She just listened to me talking about it."

"The girl is brilliant." Steve laughed thinking about how her story had changed so much of his trouble in so short a period of time. He felt gratitude deep in his chest.

"She really is brilliant," Peter agreed, "and full of surprises. If I hugged her right now I'd probably crush her to pieces."

Steve grinned mischievously. "You know Pete, Dr. Sprague asked me to find out if you'll share your life's secrets with me. He said he can tell you're on a steady diet of it from somewhere. He likes your secrecy." Steve shook his head. "I don't know, Pete. He keeps sending me to Jeneil."

Peter smirked. "Yeah, well my secrets I'll share with you. Jeneil's not a secret anymore."

"Ooo, good dodge, good dodge." Steve laughed. "Oh man, I'm so impressed with her. Totally overwhelmed."

"Me, too." Peter smiled. "Lets' go talk to this brilliant mind."

Peter knocked lightly when they got to the records storage room. Jeneil opened the door.

"Hi, honey," she said, and was surprised to see Steve. "Oh gosh, is there bigger trouble?" she asked, putting her arms around Peter's waist.

Peter smiled and hugged her. "Not anymore," he said, kissing her forehead.

Steve laughed. "Thanks to my girl's grandmother's neighbor."

Jeneil looked surprised. "Oh, it's out already. I'm sorry. I thought I'd have a chance to tell you before it spread. The story must have shocked you."

Steve smiled. "It worked out fine; not knowing made me look and sound totally innocent. Do you know what you caused with that story?"

Jeneil stared at him. "Oh please, Peter said no more trouble right?"

"Right." Steve smiled. "But with that story you managed to bring peace between the nurses and me, you got Charlotte to confess to starting the gossip, and I'm a lot less dirty as far as Sprague and his partners are concerned. I don't know how to thank you." He smiled broadly. "I don't have words for what I feel." Jeneil looked at Peter dumbfounded. He nodded. "I was in deep sh…uh, trouble."

"It's true, baby."

Jeneil went to Steve and hugged him, startling him. "Oh, that's great news." She then went to Peter and clung to him with her arms around his waist.

"I want to thank you, too. Steve's right, there aren't enough words," Peter said, hugging her more tightly.

She sighed. "I happened into the right place at the right time," she said, enjoying Peter's arms around her.

"With the right story," Steve added.

"I'm not sure. The problem's been on my mind for days watching you worry. Then two nurses on the elevator were talking about it and I saw how hopeless the truth would be. The story rolled off my tongue surprising even me."

Peter and Steve laughed, amused by her shocked innocence. "Well, I've got to get back on duty, but I wanted to thank you in person. I owe you big for this," Steve said sincerely.

"No, you don't, Steve. I think I repaid a debt I owed to someone who helped me out of some gossip once."

Steve smiled, completely impressed with her. He hadn't realized how beautiful her eyes were. "I'd better get back," he said, going to the door. "Jeneil, thank you isn't enough, believe me."

"I'm glad it worked out, and take care of yourself. You look tired."

After Steve had left, Peter kissed Jeneil warmly then hugged her. "I love you so much right now. I'm glad I get to come home to you tonight."

She smiled, loving the warmth of his words. Peter kissed her lightly, not daring to start anything more at the moment.

"I'm out at seven tonight," he said, heading to the door.

"Okay, I'll hold dinner."

"Is there enough for Steve if he wants to come home with me?"

She smiled and nodded. He stopped and watched her for a minute then smiled and left.

*****

Peter enjoyed watching the nurses on the second shift apologize to Steve and he loved Jeneil more with every apology. Steve still kept to himself, but everyone now understood why. By the end of the week Steve's name wasn't even a whisper. Everyone was trying to help him by making sure his name wasn't linked with gossip in any way since no one knew who the spy was.

Steve bought two cups of coffee and looked for Peter, finding him in the medical room on fifth. Steve handed Peter a cup and they stood viewing an x-ray. "A spy," Steve laughed, "that's too clever. It stopped the gossip so fast you could hear the brakes squeal in the administration offices."

Peter chuckled. "I can't believe the number of problems she cleared up with that one story."

Morgan Rand stopped at the door. "Hey Bradley, full truth now, you started that story about a girlfriend, didn't you?"

"Full truth Rand, no I didn't. Why would I do that?" Steve asked mockingly.

"Maybe you're worried that Sprague's team wouldn't want the fair-haired boy tracking mud into their offices."

Steve grimaced with annoyance. "Stick to scalpels and sutures, you'd make a lousy reporter," he answered, trying to sound nonchalant.

Morgan Rand studied Steve for a few seconds. "I don't trust it Bradley, it's made you too clean too fast. I think it's too lucky."

"Oh, I almost care what you think, Rand," Steve replied. "Go practice faking medicine. You're getting good at it."

"I don't trust it, Bradley." Morgan Rand walked away.

Steve sighed with relief. "That guy's too smart for his own good. He's uncanny and he's been on my ass since medical school. I'll be glad to be rid of him after my residency."

Peter chuckled. "Don't count on it. I heard he's expecting Dr. Turner to bring him into Sprague's office. There's a family connection."

"Oh shit." Steve sighed. "Imagine spending the rest of my life working with Morgan P. Rand. Hand me a scalpel."

Dr. Sprague walked in holding a cup of coffee, closing the door behind him. "Steve, I've got to ask. Between you, me, and the other half of the dynamic duo here," he nodded at Peter, "did you plant that story?"

Steve shook his head. "No, I didn't," he insisted. "I was as shocked to hear it as you were."

"I thought that," Dr. Sprague said, nodding.

Steve held his breath. "Why? Are Turner and Young accusing me of having started it?"

"No. Besides we all think it's damn clever if you did," Dr. Sprague admitted, smiling. "Do you know who did start it?"

"Just between the three of us?" Steve asked. Dr. Sprague nodded. "Yes, I do."

Dr. Sprague grinned. "Want to say who?"

"No way," Steve answered quickly. "I'm not risking my lucky charm."

Dr. Sprague studied the two of them and smiled, "Well, if you ever change your mind, let me know. We can use that kind of talent in PR. Reminds me of that mafia story that was going around here a while ago." He looked at Peter, who was facing the x-ray. "And what's new with you, Chang?"

"Not much, Dr. Sprague," Peter answered, not turning. Peter felt things were getting too tight.

Dr. Sprague grinned. "I hear that you're not seen around the dorms these days."

Peter shrugged. "I keep busy."

Dr. Sprague smiled as he enjoyed the game. "You've gained some weight, haven't you?"

"A little," Peter replied, and sipped his coffee.

"Well, it must be more than food. I hear you and Steve keep the microwave busy with some great meals, but Steve's a mess. So what's your secret?"

"Maybe a change in my metabolism?" Peter grinned, suddenly realizing the game.

Dr. Sprague laughed. "Yeah, sure. My instincts tell me you're both sharing the same PR talent, and that's got to be more than talent. It's got to be a gift to be able to clean up the images of the Chinese Stud and the White Stallion both." He smiled. "But I like it. I like it very much and I hope it continues."

Peter sighed heavily after Dr. Sprague left. "Oh man, if Jeneil even knew he was so close in figuring her out, she'd quit," and he let out a low whistle.

"Don't kid yourself. My guess is he already knows."

"What?" Peter choked. "How?"

"Same way we found out and he's guessing the rest."

"Oh shit."

Steve smiled. "Relax. He likes us. His microscope doesn't settle on just anybody. We won't have to worry about him. You heard him, he likes it. And would he burst his jugular if he knew we've become so civilized that we're going to dinner and the theatre tonight."

Peter smiled. "Songbird."

Steve looked at him. "Songbird? Is that what you call her?"

"No, my grandfather does."

Steve was shocked. "He knows?"

"He's met her. He likes her a lot."

"Wow, things are falling into place for the two of you."

"They are Steve and it feels terrific."

Twenty

Peter rushed home and ran up the stairs. He was later then he had planned to be. Jeneil was setting the table and she looked up as he walked in. "Thank goodness! I was getting worried." She smiled. "I imagined myself freezing dinner and going to the play alone."

"Sorry, honey, scaffolding broke on a job site."

"Ooo, very serious?" she asked, concerned.

"No, luckily just bruises and bumps. One man with slight chest pains is being admitted."

Jeneil went to the kitchen. Peter followed. "Peter, I'm worried. Dr. Sprague is acting very strange."

Peter straightened his back. "How?"

"I got on an elevator that he was on and he smiled at me very strangely. Then he mentioned that there was an opening in the PR office. He wondered if I might be interested."

Peter rubbed his forehead, thinking Steve had been right. "Are you worried?"

"Yes, I think he knows that Steve's cover story came from me," and she sighed.

Peter held her. "Don't worry about Dr. Sprague, honey. He loves the story and he's behind Steve. He won't mess up anything."

"I hope not," and she sighed again.

"Trust me." He kissed her cheek.

"I'll just quit. That's all, quit."

He kissed her. "Don't worry about it, honey. It'll be okay. I'll get changed."

Peter was putting on his tie when Jeneil walked into the bedroom. She smiled noticing how nice he looked. "Do you like the blazer?" she asked, hugging him from behind and kissing his back.

Peter shook his head and grinned. "You're impossible. I've never had so many clothes. I'm beginning to feel like one of your dolls."

She chuckled and faced him, looking at the tie. "I love shopping for you." She kissed him then went to the dressing screen.

"Honey," Peter said, "would you mind if Steve was here a lot? He's already feeling the squeeze. All the things he used to do he's had to give up. Debbie's the only girl left." He heard Jeneil giggle. "That didn't sound like sympathy to me."

"Sorry. Is the conveyor belt getting to him?"

"Yes, it is. The dorms are a great pit stop, but you don't feel human if you spend too much time there."

"I don't mind, Peter. I'll dust around him."

Peter smiled. "You're great you know."

Jeneil stepped from behind the screen wearing a long dress in a red print. "Do my snap, please," and she held her hair to one side.

Peter kissed the back of her neck gently. She smelled so good to him. Slipping his arms around her, he caressed her.

"Peter," she whispered, "they're due here in ten minutes. I'll never be that fast. I find you too sexy."

He chuckled and squeezed her then did the snap. "Ooo, that kind of talk keeps a man coming home at nights."

"Thank you," she said, going to the bureau to fix her hair.

"What can I do to help?"

"Nothing right now really. You can take care of pouring the wine when they get here. The white one."

"Are we trying to impress tonight?"

"No, I didn't have time to get fancy. Poached chicken isn't fancy, it's easy."

Peter smiled. He knew her. The meal might be easy but she would make it look fancy.

"Since Debbie's working in a health spa, I assumed she's into healthy dieting so I planned a meal around that."

Peter grinned and shook his head. "You're something else."

"I'm anxious to meet her," Jeneil said, finishing her makeup, and putting on earrings and bracelets. Peter watched, realizing it was her attention to detail that added the stylish touch about her, the same with her cooking.

"You look great," he said, smiling.

"Thanks, but I'll change before the play. I'm too sloppy. That's why my hostess dresses are all in prints, they hide what I drop and spill."

Peter laughed. "Don't you ever show off?"

"Bad habit, it causes illusions and I end up missing the real people around me." The front doorbell rang. "This is it. If you'll get the door, I'll make a final check on dinner."

Jeneil walked from the kitchen as Steve and Debbie walked into the apartment. Steve stared at Jeneil, looking her over. Peter fidgeted, glancing at Debbie. Jeneil looked at them, waiting to be introduced. She went to Debbie, who was eyeing her carefully. "Hi, Debbie, I'm Jeneil," she said, smiling, wondering why neither of the men had introduced her.

"Hi," Debbie replied, "I didn't know we were supposed to wear long dresses."

Jeneil laughed lightly. "This is my apron. Besides anything goes, you wear what you want to. Come in and sit down. We have time to relax."

Debbie stepped into the living room and looked around. Jeneil didn't understand Peter and Steve's behavior. Steve looked at the ceiling and shook his head. Peter bit his lower lip. Jeneil tossed a look at them as Debbie looked around the apartment. Noticing Jeneil watching him, Steve stared uncomfortably at the floor and Peter looked at Debbie then to Jeneil, raising his eyebrows. Jeneil looked at Debbie. She wore a red chiffon dress that not only plunged at the neckline but committed suicide, clearly exposing the contours of her breasts. Her stockings were black and had embroidered designs on them. Her eyebrows revealed she wasn't a natural blonde, and she wore several gold necklaces that nestled inside her cleavage.

"Debbie, would you be more comfortable sitting?" Jeneil asked, smiling warmly at her dinner guest.

"Sure," Debbie replied, taking a seat on the sofa. "Boy, you are into collecting stuff; books, art things, plants."

"And I regret it every time I dust. Peter, why don't you get the wine?"

"Right," Peter said, going to the kitchen.

"Debbie, would you rather have tonic water?" Jeneil asked.

"Wine is okay," Debbie answered.

Jeneil looked at Steve. "You look very nice in a suit, Steve."

Debbie giggled. "We're always in the pool or in bed. I almost didn't recognize him dressed up."

Steve rubbed the back of his neck and fidgeted at Debbie's remark.

Jeneil smiled. "He's the casual type too then? I always feel sorry for Peter when he's dressed up. I know he'd rather be in jeans. And those surgical outfits look even more comfortable than street clothes. Well if you'll excuse me a minute, I'll help Peter."

Going to the kitchen, Jeneil took a small tray of cheese and crackers from the refrigerator. Peter looked at her. "Want to cancel going to the play?"

"Why?" Jeneil asked, surprised. "I can't. Dennis is expecting me to be there and we have special seats." She glared at him. "You promised me you wouldn't complain. Now you keep that promise. Bring the wine. I'm having tonic water."

Peter was surprised. Imagine that, he thought, Debbie didn't bother her. He chuckled.

Steve was glancing over Jeneil's books when she returned. "Jeneil, these books by Neil Connors…."

"My father," Jeneil answered.

Steve stared at her, surprised. "Then you're named for him."

She nodded. "I'm named for both my parents. My mother's name was Jennifer."

"How about that," Debbie said, "an original name."

Jeneil smiled. "Yes and my last name was a killer to handle in school. It took me almost the whole morning in kindergarten to write it."

Steve laughed.

"What's your last name?" Debbie asked.

"Alden-Connors, hyphenated."

Debbie giggled. "Wow. I wonder if people realize what they're doing to their kids when they combine both of their names." Peter returned with the wine as Jeneil held the tray of cheese and crackers to Debbie. "No thanks, too many fats and carbohydrates." Steve closed his eyes and shook his head. Peter nearly spilled the wine he was pouring. He looked at Steve and frowned.

Jeneil smiled. "I thought you might have a special diet when I heard you worked at a health spa. Which diet are you on?"

"My own," Debbie said, taking a glass of wine from Peter.

"Really?" Jeneil asked, sitting on the hassock with a piece of cheese on a napkin. "How did you develop it? I really believe that every person's body is as biologically individual as the personality is psychologically."

"I think so, too." Debbie smiled. "I don't go too far from my scale. I eliminate something I'm eating if I gain weight."

"Gosh, that sounds really uncomplicated," Jeneil said. "I'm in a rut; I keep trying to survive on the four food groups."

Debbie laughed. "That's really old fashioned."

Peter and Steve looked at each other, sharing their annoyance with Debbie.

"Come on, Debbie," Steve said, "you can eat a package of cookies by yourself at one sitting. I've seen it."

Jeneil looked at Steve, surprised by his rudeness. "I binge, too." Jeneil smiled, hoping to soften the blow of Steve's remark. "And my scale reminds me of it. Can't get too much past that monster, can we?" Debbie laughed. Steve and Peter looked at each other and smiled, loving Jeneil's sensitivity. Jeneil glanced at her watch. "I'd better get dinner served so we won't have to rush."

"I'd help you," Debbie said, "but I know I'd be in the way. The kitchen's not my place. I'll stay and cheer up the guys."

"That's fine," Jeneil answered, standing up. "I just have to serve it. Everything's done. Excuse me."

"Well Debbie, read any good headlines lately?" Steve asked, smiling. Peter chuckled as Jeneil turned in shock at Steve's put down then continued to the kitchen.

Jeneil put the warm meal into dishes then, taking the dinner to the buffet, opened the drawer for matches. Blowing out the match after lighting the candles, she went to the living room. "Dinner is ready. You can bring your wine if you'd like."

Peter stood up and kissed her cheek. Steve smiled as he watched Peter's gentleness with her. Jeneil served the meal from a side table as they settled themselves.

"This looks great, honey." Peter smiled. "I thought you said it wasn't fancy. You always put extra work into your meals."

Jeneil was puzzled by Peter's lavish praise. "Peter, it's only poached chicken with herbs and sliced mushrooms."

"Jeneil's a terrific cook," Steve said, cutting into his dinner.

Jeneil looked at Steve, noticing the obvious compliment. Debbie stared at the serving dish. "This is gravy, it's fattening," she said, pouting.

"It's thickened with arrowroot, Debbie," Jeneil explained.

"Ugh, what's that?" Debbie covered her mouth in disgust.

Peter was annoyed. "Jeneil's into health food, Debbie. It won't hurt you and I'm sure it's low in calories. Why do you think Jeneil looks the way she does?"

Jeneil looked at Peter, wondering why he was annoyed. "That's right, Debbie," Steve said. "Maybe your mood swings are from bad nutrition. Ooo, this is good chicken, Jeneil. Mmm, I love good food," he added.

Jeneil stared at Steve and wrinkled her eyebrows. "Debbie, scrape the gravy off if you want to, I won't be offended."

"Taste it first," Steve interrupted. "Don't be so narrow."

Jeneil took a deep breath as the insults started to get to her. "Debbie, which health spa do you work in?"

"The Fitness Chain, I'm at the one on Oakland Road," Debbie answered, not eating. Jeneil noticed and wondered what to do, feeling that the insults were most of the problem.

"Debbie, would you like something else?" Jeneil asked. "I can microwave a piece of fish in no time."

Debbie looked at her with a scowl. "No thanks."

Steve stared angrily at Debbie. "Eat the vegetables, Debbie. They're cooked crisp. It's healthier for you. Jeneil, this is terrific."

"Sure is," Peter agreed.

Jeneil looked from Peter to Steve, worried things felt tense. "What do you do at the health spa, Debbie?"

Debbie scowled at Jeneil. "Are you always so damned polite?" she snapped.

"Back off," Peter said strongly.

"Peter!" Jeneil said, shocked at his openly rude remark.

Steve glared at Debbie. "That's right, Debbie, back off. She's innocent," he said sharply.

Jeneil looked at Steve and was speechless. She couldn't believe his treatment of Debbie.

Debbie glared at Steve. "Oh and can't we all tell that she's innocent just by looking at her! Don't think I'm missing what's happening here, Bradley. You think you're so smart."

Jeneil was in shock. She stood up. "That's it folks. I've had enough. I don't like to pull rank, but I've invested more in this evening than anyone else here. I've planned, I've shopped, I've cooked, and I expected to enjoy it. That's not happening so when I sit down I want an explanation." She sat. "Now we'll start with Debbie since she's the one most upset."

Debbie looked stunned. "This is really going over your head, isn't it?" she snarled.

"So far, but I'm not stupid so explain it to me," Jeneil answered. Peter and Steve chuckled, grateful that Jeneil had put Debbie in her place. "Quiet the two of you," Jeneil snapped.

Debbie grinned looking at them both, pleased by Jeneil's defense. "You don't realize that these two clowns are waving you in front of me as a good example?"

"Why?" Jeneil asked, surprised.

Debbie was surprised, too. "Aw, come on now. Here you are Miss America and Betty Crocker all properly wrapped in good manners. I was supposed to get the message and take notes." She glared at Steve.

Jeneil was puzzled. "Debbie, that can't be true. If you really knew me, you'd know that I'm not Betty Crocker or Miss America."

Debbie sat back and threw up her hands. "Holy shit! She's humble, too. Can I win here at all?" She stood up. "I'm leaving."

Jeneil was stunned. "No, you're not. You can't!" Jeneil stood up and went to her. "I mean I've never had anyone leave one of my dinners offended. I would like you to stay. Please. We can turn this around if we talk it out."

Debbie smiled. "I thought you were faking. You're not. But I think you'd better fix up Steve with one of your girlfriends. He's looking for a doctor's wife obviously." Debbie turned to Steve. "I told you from the beginning Bradley, aprons are not in my closet. I like men. I enjoy men. I'm not a one-man woman. I hate the kitchen."

Jeneil was deeply touched by Debbie's honesty. "Debbie, you're here tonight because Steve wanted us to meet you. He's getting serious about you. Don't be insulted by that."

Debbie was surprised. She looked at Steve. "Well that explains why you wanted me to take notes. But damn it, I'd pop my buttons if I tried to be like her."

Jeneil laughed, liking the phrase. "That's exactly how I feel sometimes, like I've popped my buttons." Peter and Steve laughed too, loving Jeneil's warmth and acceptance of Debbie. Jeneil put her arm around Debbie's shoulder. "Debbie, you're wrong. You're exactly what I thought you'd be."

"What the hell does that mean?" Debbie frowned.

Jeneil squeezed her shoulder. "You are a female Steve Bradley. You could be related you're so alike. You're perfect for him. I'm not his type. Why would he want you to copy me? Until recently he and I were always at war."

Steve watched Jeneil, realizing how untrue that was now. Jeneil looked at Steve. "Come on Steve, I can't apologize for you."

Steve smiled at Jeneil then glared at Debbie. "Sit down," Steve said sharply. "I was getting on your case but you were being a pain in the ass. Eat, damn it. You're the one faking it, not her."

Jeneil folded her arms angrily. "What a nice sentimental apology."

Peter stood up quickly and put his arm around Jeneil's shoulder. "Stay out of it now, baby. They know each other better than we do. Come on, sit down." Jeneil went to her seat.

Steve pointed to Debbie's chair. "Park it, Debbie. I apologize for my half of it." Jeneil shook her head and covered her face with her hands.

Debbie sat down. "I'm sorry, Jeneil," she said sincerely.

Jeneil smiled sympathetically at her. "It's okay, Debbie. We got off to a bad start."

Debbie looked embarrassed. "I was being a bitch. You're so perfect you were making me mad."

Jeneil smiled. "Get to know me. I'm not perfect, believe me. Ask Peter. And if he agrees, he'll wear his chicken to the play." They all laughed.

Debbie picked up her fork. "Dinner smelled really great. I kept wishing I'd shut up and eat."

Jeneil smiled wearily, relieved the tension had eased. "There's no time to reheat it all so we'll have to eat it cold."

"That's okay," Debbie said, "sometimes I eat a thawed out diet dinner without heating it. I hate the kitchen so much."

"How come?" Jeneil asked.

"I don't know. There are things to do, fun to have, people to meet."

"Isn't that interesting, it's compulsive," Jeneil commented sincerely. "I think it's amazing you can handle that. I need order in my life, and fun too, and I'm always trying to balance them. It leaves me feeling scattered. Then who does your housework, maid services?"

Debbie laughed. "No, my girlfriends and I have a cleaning co-op. We get together and have tequila then put on music real loud and we each take a room and clean it while dancing to the music. Then we go to the next apartment and have more tequila and do the same thing."

Jeneil laughed. "How many of you are in the co-op?"

"Just three. We can't handle more tequilas than that."

Loving Debbie's straightforwardness, Jeneil sat back and laughed into her napkin then caught her breath. "Now that's funny."

Debbie smiled. "Well at least you think so," she said, looking at Steve and Peter, who were watching Jeneil and smiling, fascinated by how genuine she was.

"Do you go to the theatre a lot?" Debbie asked Jeneil, who brought in dessert.

Peter chuckled. "Are you kidding? She's been all but living there while working on this play."

Steve was surprised. "I didn't know you worked on it."

"What did you do?" Debbie asked.

"Helped the volunteer workers mostly," Jeneil answered.

"Jeneil, what about you and Dennis rewriting it," Peter corrected her.

"Who's Dennis?" Steve asked.

"The director and writer of this play. She helped him rewrite it," Peter explained.

"Peter, that's really more than it was. I helped him adapt it to a smaller cast and stage. It's a great play and it's all Dennis's work."

"Humble is easy for you, isn't it?" Debbie asked, smiling.

"It isn't humility, Debbie. It's the truth."

Peter and Steve grinned at each other as Debbie seemed to warm up to Jeneil. Jeneil sipped some water. "And we'd better get to the theatre or we'll miss some of the play. Let's leave all this and just go. This is Dennis's first work performed on stage and I don't want to miss a line of it." Jeneil stood up. "I have to make a quick change. I'll be right back."

Jeneil returned carrying her pearls. "Make a deal, Peter. I'll help you with your blazer if you do my clasp."

Peter smiled and took the pearls. Steve watched, smiling as she held the blazer for Peter.

"You two look married," Debbie commented.

Steve laughed. "They should, he lives here."

Debbie's mouth dropped open. "Really? She looks like a vir...," she stopped herself.

"I look like a what?" Jeneil asked. Steve coughed uncomfortably to distract Jeneil from the question.

"We'd better leave, baby." Peter took her hand quickly.

"Jeneil, I like you. You're real," Debbie said, smiling.

"Thanks, Debbie. I like you too for the same reason." Peter and Steve looked at each other and raised their eyebrows in surprise.

*****

The crowd gathered as they arrived at the theatre. Debbie was turning heads; she didn't notice as she and Jeneil talked about movie stars, diets, and exercise books. "I can't believe this," Steve said to Peter as they walked behind the girls, "Debbie missing all the drooling men. She thrives on it."

As they made their way to the box office, Jeff walked past them through the lobby. "Hey, Jeneil," he called. Jeff was turning women's heads and Debbie's eyes opened wide as she took in his wonderfully good looks. Jeff hugged Jeneil and kissed her cheek. "You look super." The usherette came over for their tickets. "They're in the director's box. I've got to get backstage. I'll tell Dennis you're here, Jeneil." Jeff kissed Jeneil's cheek again then walked off.

"That one caught Debbie's eye," Steve whispered to Peter, and Peter smiled.

The usherette held a flashlight as they walked up a small flight of stairs.

"The director's box, wow!" Debbie gushed. "That sounds special. She's a real surprise, isn't she?" she whispered to Steve. Steve smiled, also impressed.

As they followed the usherette, Jeneil noticed Franklin Pierce in the crowd. Excusing herself, she went over to him. Peter watched as they talked to one another before both returning to the group so Jeneil could introduce everyone. "Debbie Potter, Steve Bradley, this is Franklin Pierce." Franklin shook their hands. "Come and sit with us Franklin, there's room."

"Are you sure?" He smiled. "I really wouldn't mind. I'm so far in the back everyone has a closer seat. Where are you sitting?"

"In the director's box," Debbie said, smiling.

Franklin looked at Jeneil. "Well excuse me, invitations to formal dances at mansions, seats in the director's box. You are full of surprises."

"Simple explanations for it all," Jeneil said, laughing.

The lights dimmed signaling to be seated. Franklin put his arm around Jeneil and began walking with her then stopped. "I'm sorry, Peter," he said, stepping aside. Jeneil took Peter's hand as they walked up to the director's box.

Steve watched as Franklin took her other hand and Debbie smiled. "Betty Crocker has an interesting life," she whispered.

During the play, Jeneil could tell it had an effect on the audience without seeing them; she squeezed Peter's hand excitedly. Peter smiled and put his arm around her. As the final curtain came down, the audience stood as it continued its applause. After several curtain calls, the curtain rose and a bouquet of roses was handed to the female star. The cast stepped back and began applauding, calling for someone in the wings. Dennis walked on stage with his sweater sleeves pushed up to his elbows and his collar opened at his throat. His hair was tousled. The audience gave him a standing ovation. Peter looked at Jeneil. Tears rolled down her cheeks as she applauded. Dennis nodded a few times at the audience then turned to the director's box and bowed at the waist. Then, standing up straight, he blew a kiss to Jeneil. She laughed and wiped her tears. The audience strained to see who the kiss was for but couldn't see. Peter rubbed his forehead as Steve watched. The curtains closed and the applause quieted. Jeneil sat down and dried her eyes with a handkerchief.

"It was great, sweetheart. He's got a winner," Franklin said, sitting next to her, rubbing her back. He kissed her temple. Jeneil nodded and cried again. Franklin brushed her cheek tenderly with his hand. Peter noticed that Franklin had gotten bolder since having taken Jeneil to the ball at the mansion. Steve watched Franklin then looked at Peter, who was standing with his hands in his pockets. The curtains to the box parted and Robert Danzieg stepped inside.

"Hi, Peter," he said, nodded to Steve and Debbie, then went to Jeneil, who had stood up. He hugged her, holding her to him.

Steve leaned near Peter's ear. "What the hell is this?"

Robert held Jeneil's face in his hands and kissed her lips lightly. "You're terrific. He's beside himself back there."

Jeneil smiled. "It had magic in it. I could feel it."

Robert smiled and hugged her again. "I'm going back stage again. Want to come?"

"No, I brought guests."

"See you later then." He kissed her lips again and left.

Franklin smiled. "I've got to be going. Thanks for letting me share the excitement. It was electric." He kissed her lightly. "Next concert. Okay?"

"Yes." She smiled. Franklin kissed her again and left. "Wasn't this evening something?"

"To say the least," Debbie said, totally surprised by all Jeneil's men.

Jeff stopped in. "Jeneil, are you coming backstage?"

"No thanks, Jeff."

"You should you know. This is yours, too."

Jeneil smiled. "Tell him I said congratulations and that I'll call him later."

Jeff smiled. "He'll be disappointed."

"Ooo, that guy is so massive," Debbie swooned as Jeff left.

"If he comes by once more, I'm going to hit him. She's flexed her pectoral muscles so much she's added an inch," Steve whispered to Peter.

"He's gay," Peter whispered in response.

Steve smiled broadly. "I love the theatre. I think I'll bring her here from now on."

Peter chuckled as they stepped into the corridor and took a few steps toward the lobby.

"Hey," a voice called from behind them. They all turned around. Dennis stood with one hand on his hip, holding a white rose with baby's breath in the other. It was tied with a white satin bow. Robert and Jeff stood behind him. "Where do you think you're going?" Dennis smiled at Jeneil.

Jeneil ran to Dennis, surprising Peter. She put her arms around his neck and hugged him. Dennis held her tightly, closing his eyes, and then lifted her off the floor.

"She's coming backstage," Dennis said, holding her in his arms. "You're all welcome to come. She belongs there." He turned and walked off with her. Jeff and Robert followed. Jeneil motioned to them to come along.

"Gee, let's go, it sounds like fun." Debbie smiled excitedly.

"Forget it, Debbie. Jeff's married. His wife's name is Bruce," Steve informed her, grinning.

"Aw, I guess I'll go and fix my makeup," she said, disappointed, then turned and left.

"Go get Jeneil," Steve said, watching Peter as he rubbed his forehead.

"No, they're right. She does belong there."

"Then be with her. Forget us."

Peter shook his head. "No, this is hers alone."

"Is the great Peter Chang from New York handing over his woman without a struggle? What would the Dragons say?"

"New streets, new rules."

"Wow, you are cool about it."

Peter grinned. "Oh, am I? When she comes back she'd better be all giddy and excited and attached to me like my jacket. If she isn't, I'm going to have a hell of a lot of fun kicking a few asses back there starting with the great white shark who carried her off in his arms. You can tell he's in show business. He can't just walk off with her; he has to sweep her off her feet like King Kong. And the white rose and the kiss from the stage." Peter sighed. "He has killer instincts. Can any woman resist all that?"

"Aren't you sure?" Steve asked.

"I want her to be sure. She's so inexperienced it scares me. I want her with me with no doubts."

"This is it for you, isn't it? I mean station wagons, babies, and diapers, the whole scene."

Peter nodded. "I don't have any doubts."

Steve smiled. "That's great, Pete. I wish I had it in me to feel that kind of commitment."

"Steve, I think it's the girl that makes the difference. I never felt this before Jeneil."

Steve sighed. "I don't know about this man-woman syndrome, Pete. You worry that Jeneil is settled because she's too inexperienced, I worry that Debbie can't settle because she's too experienced. What's the answer?"

"The formula." Peter smiled.

"What formula?"

"Jeneil's dad left her with a formula so she'd know which man was right for her."

"You're joking, aren't you?"

Peter shook his head. "Do you think I've lasted this long with her because I'm smart about women? She clings to her father's formula. I laughed about that damn thing, but it's what keeps me calm when the sharks circle. My reasoning begins with the formula."

"Man and they do circle her, don't they? What's the formula?"

"Wait for your heart, mind, and body to agree on someone."

"There's a problem in it," Steve said.

"What's that?" Peter asked.

"A person needs to think, feel, and care in order to do that. No one works that hard at relationships anymore."

Peter smiled. "Jeneil does."

*****

Peter paced as they waited for Jeneil and Debbie. Debbie returned and groaned. "She's not back yet? Well, I say let's go to the party. We were invited," she pouted.

They heard laughter and talking. Turning around, they could see a group of people coming from left of the stage. Jeneil stood between Robert and Dennis. One had his arm around her shoulder. The other had one arm around her waist.

"Do they let her breathe?" Steve mumbled to Peter.

Peter watched as Jeneil moved away from them and turned, obviously saying goodbye. They each kissed her. As she walked away, one person in the group counted to three and the group in unison yelled, "Goodbye, Dana!"

Jeneil laughed and turned around. "I can't hear you," she sang back to them. The group laughed. Peter and Steve watched, fascinated.

Jeneil joined them smiling and glowing. She put her arms around Peter's waist and hugged him tightly. "It was crazy back there," she laughed. "I feel giddy. The electricity is high voltage." She kissed Peter's cheek and squeezed him, snuggling to him.

Peter glanced at Steve. Steve smiled broadly and winked, recognizing the behavior Peter had expected from her.

Jeneil looked at all three. "Why didn't you come to the party?"

"See," Debbie said. "Doctors! What deadheads!"

Steve grinned at her. "Aw, you're still sulking because of Jeff."

"Oh, shut up," Debbie said angrily.

Steve laughed. "Ooo, I'd better take this one home. She needs cheering up." Debbie grinned, and Peter and Jeneil smiled. Peter kissed Jeneil's cheek.

"Why did they call you Dana, Jeneil?" Debbie asked.

Jeneil shook her head. "They were talking about a play and someone mentioned that I'd be right for the part of Dana."

"Are you going to do it?"

"Debbie, you really don't know me at all. There's no way I could get on a stage and act. No, I'm audience or backstage."

Peter smiled to himself. She was still the songbird.

*****

Peter and Jeneil cleared up the remains of dinner together. "What a fantastic night." Jeneil smiled as they walked to the bedroom, putting the white rose and baby's breath in a vase on the bureau. "I'm so pleased for Dennis. It's only a small playhouse and summer stock, but he opened a few doors. He's been offered a job with the Repertory Company as one of the assistant directors, and Dean Conklin was there tonight and asked him if he'd consider being an advisor on their drama department committee. That could mean more of Dennis's work will be performed. Oh, he deserves it," she said excitedly. "The theatre is adding his name and photos to the ad campaigns for the play. That's terrific exposure. And the critics gave every indication that they were pleased. They looked like they were enjoying it whenever I glanced at them." She smiled, reliving the night in her mind.

Peter watched her as he undid his shirt.

She looked at herself in the full-length mirror. "I don't know, Peter. I think I'm too blah."

"Blah?" He smiled, taking off his shirt.

"Yes, blah. I need redoing. A makeover. I need style. Look at Debbie. She boldly lets people know she's a woman."

Peter shook his head and laughed. "Jeneil, she didn't say it, her dress did by exposing her body and proving she's female."

"But she has the courage to let the dress make the statement, 'I like men, I enjoy men.' That's bold. That's style."

"You don't like and enjoy men?"

She thought a minute. "Well, yes, but I don't say it with boldness and style."

Peter smiled and walked over to her. "You have style, honey. Believe me you have your own style."

"I do?" she asked, looking at him in the mirror as he stood behind her.

He grinned. "Sure you do. Men get close to you and they think, 'she's soft, I think she's a woman. She smells good, she must be a woman. She's gentle, I'm almost certain she's a woman.' By that time they're so close to the fire that it's too late for the moth to turn back." He undid the clasp of her pearls and took them off. Undoing the snap on her dress, he kissed her back and neck gently. He turned her around to face him. "You see, men who know real women know the flame is worth looking for because it's fiery and passionate. That's real style, baby. That's a woman." He kissed her warmly and she responded to him, bringing him to passion.

Afterwards she lay beside him, smoothing her fingers across his jaw line. "I love your features, they're so even." She gave his cheek a lingering kiss. "You are one hell of a stylish and bold woman." He sighed; she chuckled.

"Oh really? Those aren't even your words."

"But it sounds classier than you're one hell of a sexy broad." He hugged her. "You saved dinner. I'm impressed with what you did for Debbie."

"Are you kidding? I did that for Steve. He doesn't know women at all! He was going to lose her. He isn't a lady-killer. What an absolute shock! What is his fatal attraction with women?"

"His good looks and...," Peter stopped.

"He can back up the White Stallion legend?" Jeneil added.

Peter nodded and smiled. "I was going to say he's good in bed." He laughed.

"Good grief, do we really sell out that easily. Is a good sex partner so rare that we'd put up with being stepped on like he did to Debbie?"

"Honey, it's their relationship. Let's stay out of it."

"But Peter, if he wants her to marry him, he's certainly not treating her like he's in love with her. Why would she marry him?"

Peter grinned. "Not everyone is a romantic like you."

"Is it romantic to want respect and to be treated decently? I thought that was the basis of human relationships."

"Baby, he's not in love with her."

Jeneil was shocked. "But you said he was getting serious about her."

"He's thinking of marrying her. At least he was. I'm not so sure now."

"Why, what happened?"

"You've taken the pressure off him at the hospital."

"He would marry her for that? That's worse than using her as a sex object! What's wrong with him?" She sighed.

"He fell in love once and got used."

"How did he get used?" Jeneil asked, surprised.

"He was the sex object," Peter answered, surprising himself. "He's not looking for a traditional relationship. He's just looking for a good wife for a doctor."

"Oh my gosh! Then Debbie was right! That's terrible! And there I was in my ignorance trying to convince her that she was wrong. Do I see life clearly at all?"

"Were you that wrong?" Peter challenged. "Wasn't he flattering her? Should she be insulted that he wanted to marry her?"

"If he's not in love with her; yes. Peter, you're not serious, are you?"

"He doesn't even want to get married at all," Peter defended.

"This gets worse with every sentence!" she said, sitting up. "He's a worse rat than I thought he was."

"Jeneil, I can understand him."

"How? Are you doing the same thing?" she snapped.

"Hey," he said sharply. "Want your ass slapped, woman?"

"Don't get macho with me. Answer my question!"

"That's not a question, that's shit," he said angrily. "How the hell can you ask that after the way we just made love? What's wrong with you?"

"I'm sorry," she said quietly, lying back down.

"That's better," he said, kissing her cheek.

"He scares me, Peter, and you tell me that you and he are alike."

"We are. That's how I understand him. If I didn't have you, I could understand marrying for my career."

She sighed. "And we wonder why the divorce rate is high."

"Hey, he'd be a good husband. If he accepted the responsibility, he'd see it through."

"How could he be a good husband if he didn't love her? What if he meets someone he does love after the marriage?"

"Jeneil, you're into romantic fiction again."

"No, I'm not. Why can't he just wait until he falls in love? That's at least honest."

"He claims he's not capable of falling in love. He doesn't want to be chewed up and spit out again."

"How can civilization be maintained with that as rationale? We don't trust each other as people anymore." She sighed again.

Peter kissed her. "Poor Jeneil, the world just doesn't run on romantic love the way you do."

"I couldn't live in a world without love. Isn't that a line from a song?" She tried to laugh lightly as tears rolled down her cheeks.

Peter held her close to him. "Aw, baby. You know I love you. I'm crazy about you. Your world is full of love."

She nodded and wiped her tears. "I know you do. That's how I stay alive. I was crying for Steve."

"Why?" Peter asked, surprised.

"He needs a Camelot. He needs the quest. He needs to feel love. Giving and receiving. He needs to open up so he can feel or he'll miss love."

He kissed her. "Then he's not a rat anymore?"

She shook her head. "What is it about him, Peter? I can't stabilize my feelings about him."

"You're doing fine, baby. You've been great with him. Maybe hanging around with us will be good for him."

"Why?"

"We can be his family and help him to open up."

"Where is his real family?"

"He doesn't have any."

"His parents are gone, too?"

"No, he never knew them. He grew up in an orphanage."

Jeneil's face showed her shock and compassion. Tears streamed down her face. "More scars, Peter," she sobbed softly. "Poor Steve." She quieted and took a deep breath as Peter pulled her to him and held her close. "I think you just helped me stabilize my feelings for him. Let's be his family. That sounds and feels right." Peter kissed her forehead gently and held her.

Twenty-One

The week of second shift was its usual marathon for Peter and Jeneil. They barely saw each other; Jeneil went to the playhouse every night while Peter was kept busy by shift extensions and doubles. He was looking forward to Friday. He needed to relax and was looking forward to being with Jeneil. He hadn't had a chance to hear what was happening at the theatre. They had passed each other yesterday as he came in from working a double and as she was leaving for work. She had seemed quiet to him and the memory of her quietness lingered in the recesses of his mind. She had almost stayed home with him but had decided against it at the last minute. He could tell she was pouring over something. The only times she became indecisive were when she was wading through something in her mind. Peter turned off the engine to his car and walked toward the apartment. He walked up the stairs quickly hoping Jeneil was still awake and was encouraged when he saw the bedroom light was on. He walked in, already beginning to feel relaxed. Jeneil was brushing her hair in front of the mirror.

"Hi, baby. I'm glad you waited up." He kissed her cheek. "Some kids collided at a skating rink, it kept the ER lively." He walked to the closet for his robe. She continued brushing her hair, still in the quiet mood he remembered from yesterday. "Are you okay?" he asked as he tied his robe.

"Yes," she answered softly, still brushing. A vibration passed through his chest. He went to her. Her face was flushed.

"Jeneil, are you sure you're okay?" Putting the brush down, she nodded then turned and walked to the kitchen. He'd let her bring the problem to him. The vibration was stronger but he resisted the urge to follow her. Instead he went to his side of the bed and sat up against the headboard and waited, assessing the situation. She was wearing her fluffy blue robe over her nightgown. That was unusual. Another vibration passed through him. He got up and walked to the kitchen. Jeneil wasn't there. Peter went to the living room. She was sitting on the sofa in the semi-darkness. He paused, rubbed his forehead, then went and sat beside her.

"We'd better talk about it, Jeneil." He resigned to dealing with whatever it was.

She nodded and wound the tie from her robe around her finger.

"Jeneil, talk to me." He studied her profile. The vibration became a steady pounding in his chest. She closed her eyes and cleared her throat slightly.

"Dennis…uhmmm…I…." She drew in a breath and exhaled. Peter's heart stopped at the sound of the name. "Dennis kissed me tonight." She put her hand over her eyes and sighed, obviously struggling with emotion.

"You mean seriously?" He needed to hear all of it.

She nodded. "He's been different lately, but I thought it was like David, just kidding or kicks or whatever you call it. It was more intense than David but then Dennis is more intense."

"Why are you upset?"

"I feel responsible. I didn't watch for it. I didn't expect it again."

Peter tensed. "He's a grown man not a kid. He knows what he's doing. Don't worry about him." He tried hard not to show annoyance. "I'm not worried about him, I'm worried about you."

"I feel like I've betrayed your trust, like I've misused my freedom in our relationship."

"Jeneil put logic and honor aside and get right to basics. What did his kiss do to you?"

She turned her head quickly and stared at him. "Peter, I couldn't even enjoy the kiss feeling that I was betraying you."

"Jeneil, I didn't ask for guilt. What did the kiss do to you?" She stared at him for a second then turned her head away. "Jeneil, are you avoiding the question?" Peter pushed for an answer, his heart beating in his throat.

"No, I'm thinking about the question. You asked about his kiss but you want to know about my feelings for Dennis." Peter felt the pulsing heartbeat in his ears. She twisted the tie of her robe again. "There's definitely something between Dennis and me," she said quietly, "a special attachment for each other."

"Attachment or attraction?" Peter asked, trying to steady his voice.

"A bond," she replied. "Yes, a bond, some kind of connection. If I didn't belong to you, I guess I'd probably get closer to Dennis."

Peter swallowed past the lump in his throat. "Jeneil, listen to me carefully. I don't want you with me if you have any doubts. If there is the slightest feeling for Dennis then you should be free to understand that feeling." Peter was surprised the words were so civilized because he didn't feel civilized. He was struggling to keep Chang from raging.

"I belong to you, Peter," she said, deeply surprised and concerned. "I don't want to belong to anyone else. I don't belong to anyone else. The formula is complete with you."

"Jeneil, talk feelings not formula, please." Peter was nearing panic as Chang struggled to be freed.

Jeneil studied his face. "You don't understand at all. Feelings are what I have for Dennis; friendship, love, and a whole list of surface emotions. With you I have a completeness that goes way past the surface right to the center of me and who I am. I belong to you, Peter. There's no other way to express it. Unless I say I belong with you, I just simply belong to you. I don't want to interrupt what is as natural and as important to me as breathing in order to explore emotions and feeling. I told him that I belong to you. You don't seem to understand that at all. You and I need soul between us."

Peter rested his head against the sofa hoping his heartbeat and breathing would become normal soon. He struggled against Chang who wanted desperately to be free after hearing Jeneil say if she didn't belong to him, she'd probably be closer to Dennis. It had been Dennis all along, not Robert. Chang was furious with Peter for becoming so civilized. Peter's telephone rang. He jumped at the sound then stood up and went to answer it, glad for the interruption. He wasn't handling Chang well and he didn't have any words for Jeneil. He loved her honesty and directness, but at times he was still unnerved by those traits. This was one of those times. Putting the receiver down, he sat on the bed exhausted. The week's schedule and Jeneil had caved him in. He needed desperately to sleep.

Jeneil stood at the bedroom door. "Trouble?"

"It was the hospital. They want me to work first shift tomorrow. They've given me Sunday off in trade. I'd better get some sleep." He stood up and took off his robe. Jeneil went to him, standing near him.

"Peter, I'm sorry. You're upset and I'm sorry I caused it. You look like you feel betrayed."

Peter heard the emotion in her voice; he didn't look at her but he knew she must be crying. He was numb; he couldn't think what to say or do. Exhaustion and Chang's anger had him immobilized. She turned to walk away. He heard the sniffle. He wanted to go to her but he couldn't. He heard her take a tissue from the box on the bureau. She left the room, closing the door behind her. He sighed heavily and sat down, gaining strength in the struggle with Chang. His grandfather's voice pierced his memory, *'Be sure you want the responsibility because the songbird could be damaged if she learned to trust you and you weren't there.'* Peter stood up quickly, put his robe on and went to find Jeneil. Finding her in the kitchen, he stood at the door. Words wouldn't form. She watched him then put her glass of milk down and walked to him. She hesitated then slowly put her arms around him. He put his arms around her and pulled her closer. Holding her, he whispered, "It's late, let's get some sleep." He felt her nod her head gently.

He lay on his back. Jeneil snuggled to him, entwining her arms around his and kissing his shoulder. He loved her, he knew that much. He concentrated on her words, *'I told him that I belong to you.'* In the darkness, he smiled. Turning his head, he kissed her forehead gently. She snuggled closer.

*****

Peter felt tired when the alarm rang. Jeneil was already up. Snapping the covers back, he went to shower. Dressing quickly, he went to find her. She had breakfast ready for him and lunch was packed. The leotards she wore looked good to him; he was glad. He hoped things would be okay between them soon. He was still a little off-center about Dennis, and Chang was struggling with all of it, but Jeneil was his. He had to hold onto that fact. Her hair fell softly over one eye and down her shoulders and back. She looked soft and gentle to him, and he wished he wasn't on the first shift that morning. They needed time together.

"You're going to be late if you don't leave in the next few minutes," she warned.

"I'm leaving right now," he answered, taking the lunch bag.

She studied his face then smiled cautiously, wondering about his feelings. He smiled then leaned toward her for a kiss. She hugged him, surprising him with the sudden display of affection. Putting the lunch on the counter, he held her to him. She felt warm and soft. Pushing her hair back gently with his hand, he kissed her warmly, leaving her breathless. Electricity shot through his chest. He knew they were going to be okay. He squeezed her and kissed her cheek. "A quiet dinner tonight?" he asked. "We need to talk. We seem to have lost touch with each other." She watched his expression then nodded slowly.

*****

Peter caught sight of Steve near an operating room. He looked tired.

"You caught a double today?"

Steve nodded and yawned.

"Time for a break?"

"Sure," Steve said, checking his stethoscope. The doctor's lounge was empty. They sat at a corner table. "You look down."

"So do you," Peter answered.

"The straight life wears thin at times." Steve chuckled.

Peter laughed. "Where's Debbie?"

Steve swallowed some coffee and stifled a laugh. "Jeneil made a great impression on her, she was very inspired. Debbie thinks Jeneil has the right idea, fill your life with men. She has now added a cookie delivery man to the cozy club."

"Along with the weightlifter?" Peter asked, surprised.

Steve nodded. "I tried to explain to her that Jeneil didn't sleep with them."

Peter chuckled. "Do you know how to get a girl to marry you if she's not ready?"

"Insist," Steve answered firmly.

"There are reasons for waiting," Peter replied.

Steve shook his head. "Man, New York is all but gone from you. Why the hell do you settle for all that?"

Peter shook his head disagreeing. "You need to know Jeneil. Those reasons for waiting are important to her. We don't have that kind of relationship. I like it when we blend and harmonize. Pushing doesn't work for us."

Steve finished his coffee and grinned. "Man have you changed. You're heavy into civilized, my friend. Be careful of confusion."

Peter looked steadily at him then down at his coffee cup. Steve seemed to be echoing Chang's rage.

"I've got to get back on duty." Steve tossed his cup into the trash receptacle.

Peter stood up. "Me, too."

Steve pushed the door open with his back. "Smile, Pete. Aren't these the days we'll be looking back on and laughing over?"

"Has that been guaranteed?" Peter chuckled.

Steve laughed. "Don't trust it. Just when you think it's guaranteed, life pushes the button marked 'shit.' That's why you take it now," and they walked back to the floor together, each wrapped in his own thoughts.

*****

Peter drove home slowly, trying to sort out his feelings about Dennis. Chang was in favor of keeping Jeneil in the apartment, possibly forever. Peter had grown enough to know better. There was no way he could insist that she not see Dennis anymore; he was more important to Jeneil than Franklin Pierce and Robert Danzieg combined. Peter was certain of that. His stomach tensed. The only question left was how he would handle it. How he would deal and cope with it. At the base of his insecurity was Jeneil's attraction, or was it attachment as she called it. His heart sank every time he thought of her words.

Turning the ignition off, he sat in his car fighting the low feeling that had followed him home. Songbird, he thought to himself, I don't like sharing you with Dennis, with anybody. Chang can't take it in any way. He sighed and opened the car door.

The apartment smelled faintly of dinner cooking. A feeling of home would always fill him when he arrived and Jeneil was preparing dinner for them. He realized how straight and square that sounded. Steve had been right, he had changed, he thought as he closed the apartment door.

Jeneil came from the bedroom, closing the door behind her. Peter was surprised to see her in the long yellow dress. She knew he liked it and she always wore it when she went out of her way to make dinner and the evening extra special. The dress had some great memories tied to it and a trickle of electricity pierced his chest. The dining room table was set. Cut flowers in a short vase sat on the shelf near the table. A special evening had been planned and the thought warmed him. He noticed her hair was different, very soft looking. She had put herself together like she was expecting a special guest. He liked that, too, and he smiled knowing he was the special guest.

"Hi," she said quietly, standing in front of him.

"Everything looks very nice, especially you."

She gave him a gentle smile. "It's a special evening. We're going to try soul, and I don't mean fish. I mean sensitivity." She lowered her head and turned the bracelet on her wrist a few turns as if searching for words, then looked up at him. "This morning you said that we should talk. I don't want to discuss anything until we've shared the evening. Is that okay with you?" she asked, looking hopeful. He nodded; the less he heard Dennis's name mentioned the better he liked it. She put her arms around him. "Soul takes patience. Can you contribute that tonight?"

He put his arms around her and wrinkled his brow. "You aren't kidding about this soul thing then? It's a planned experiment?"

"No, it's a planned program and I should've given it more attention than I have. Our relationship is behind schedule."

Peter grinned. "Why don't you just let things happen?"

"Superlative doesn't just happen, it's achieved," she defended.

"Still chasing the superlative, are you?"

She looked surprised. "Have you given up the quest?"

He smiled. "I keep forgetting about it. It's a good thing the figurines are together or Peter and his white horse would wander around wondering what they were doing. I told you the two of them needed to be together on the quest." He lightly kissed her lips.

She smiled. "I'll check on dinner."

Peter went to the porcelain figurines. The ogre who had been standing behind them menacingly was now replaced by a witch who was confronting them. Peter smiled and shook his head. The elves had a little world of happiness going on in their pot. A table roughly made from a slice of a tree branch was there along with flowers, fruit, and birds. Jeneil returned and joined Peter near the potted plants. "What happened to the ogre?" he asked, smiling.

"He got tired of raging. Peter and Jeneil passed that test bravely. They endured."

"Has the ogre stopped raging completely?"

"No, he shouts from time to time, but he's not as intense anymore."

"And how is Hollis about us now?"

Jeneil laughed. "Are you deliberately linking the ogre and Hollis together?"

"It's sort of natural." Peter grinned. "You didn't answer my question."

Jeneil shrugged. "Hollis wants me married."

"Not us, just you?"

"He's afraid that eventually the game will be over between us and you'll return to your people leaving me alone." Jeneil put her head down, embarrassed by the remark.

"Return to my people, huh?" Peter asked, noticing the ethnic meaning.

"I know, that's a very dated phrase." She rubbed his back gently.

"Are you sure that isn't what he's hoping will happen?"

"Do you mean because you're Chinese?"

Peter nodded. "Is he afraid I'll come to dinner?"

Jeneil kissed his cheek. "I don't think so. Hollis really isn't a bigot. He genuinely feels that water flows in a natural direction. To him, we've interrupted the natural flow."

Peter looked at her and smiled. "The next time he starts that, remind him about the man-made structures called dams and their contribution to man for opposing the natural flow."

Jeneil snickered. "That's good. That's really good. I reminded him that salmon swim upstream to spawn and that's against the natural flow." She kissed his cheek.

Peter laughed, smiling at her. "You're getting primitive. I think you're too close to Chang."

"Irish was annoyed. Hollis needs to get to know you, that's all."

Peter looked back at the figurines. "And so Camelot will face a wicked witch next. She looks worse than the ogre. At least the ogre was out in the open, she's a sneak. Look at her watching them from the corner of her eye, waiting for a chance to strike. She's silent and sneaky. Good thing it's fiction." Peter chuckled. "I'd almost guess that would be my mother, except my mother isn't silent."

"Now Peter, leave her alone." Jeneil said, then smiled and pinched his earlobe lovingly. The oven timer buzzed and Jeneil stood up. "Dinner's ready."

Peter got up and stretched, wondering if the whole evening would be as great as the beginning. There was an ease between them and he was beginning to relax, but Dennis kept surfacing in his mind. He really needed to feel at ease with her and he was encouraged that they were getting back to normal so quickly. Peter went to the kitchen. "Want some help?"

"If you'll take this to the table," and she handed him a tray with serving dishes of food, "we can begin dinner."

"It smells good," he sniffed, taking the tray to the dining area. Peter sat at the table and waited while Jeneil dimmed the lights. She turned the stereo on to the sound of a soft rhythmic saxophone then sat at the table with him. Peter looked around the room and absorbed what he saw and heard. The candles cast soft shadows on the dining table. "This is high powered stuff."

Jeneil looked steadily at him. "Soul is high powered, only a brave heart can handle it. Would you like to reconsider?"

He returned her stare. "I'll take the challenge."

"Are you sure? I'm talking about soul, not passion. Love, not lust. It's highly charged emotionally and very difficult to maneuver."

He grinned in amusement. It sounded like a malfunction, a gotcha to him. "You can't scare a New York street kid."

"Good." She smiled and lifted her plate, removing a note from underneath. She handed the note to Peter. Puzzled, he took the note and read it.

"Come on, Jeneil, aren't you overdoing this a little? We really can't talk using words; we can only communicate using our eyes and touch? That may be a little too much."

She folded her arms. "We do this right or we don't do it at all. Not strong enough to handle it, street kid?"

He closed his eyes and put his head back. "Geez, the things I get into with you." He shook his head then looked at her. "Okay let's go for it, but this sure looked like fun for a short while."

She laughed. "Starting now, no more words." She smiled, held her fingertips to her lips, kissed them then placed them on his lips.

He watched as she put her napkin on her lap and began to eat her dinner. Peter began, too. After a short silence, he looked at her. "Jeneil," he said, breaking the quiet, "sitting here listening to myself chew and swallow is beginning to feel stupid."

"Then communicate," she replied patiently, trying to be encouraging.

"I can't!" he argued. "Why can't we just have a quiet dinner?"

"Isn't that what you're complaining about?" She chuckled.

"You're funny, but not cute. I like cute and funny."

"Oh Peter, come on. Please give it a chance."

He sighed. "Why the hell I take the aggravation is beyond me. You know, you're getting crazier by degrees."

"No, eccentric, remember green grass on the bottom and blue sky on top. Eccentric, Peter, eccentric."

He shook his head and chuckled. "Okay, let's start again."

"Thank you." She squeezed his arm, pleased by his willingness.

They began eating in silence again. Jeneil glanced at Peter from time to time. Slipping her hand into his, she gave it a gentle squeeze. He avoided looking at her. She could tell he was struggling with embarrassment and she chuckled to herself. She stood up and kissed his temple lightly. Putting her arms around his neck gently, she hugged him. He pressed his head lightly against hers in response. She laughed to herself, loving him for cooperating. She returned to her chair and began to eat again. Resting her chin on her hand, she watched him. He never looked at her. Soon he began to look awkward then in exasperation he sat back in his chair and dropped his napkin onto the table. Jeneil got up quickly and went to him. Stooping beside his chair, she took his hand and touched his face gently. He avoided looking at her. Taking his hand in both of hers, she pressed it to her lips and kissed it lightly. He still didn't look at her. Reaching up, she touched his chin and turned him to face her. He kept his eyes lowered, avoiding hers. She took her hand away, watching him steadily then stood up. She returned to her chair and stared at her clasped fingers resting on her lap. After a few minutes, she looked up at Peter, who was turning his spoon over and over on the place mat. She sighed. "Peter, Dennis and I are very close as far as the theatre is concerned."

He slouched in his seat and rested his ankle on his knee then folded his arms. She recognized his position of belligerence. "I thought we weren't going to discuss anything."

She felt herself becoming tearful. "It came up in soul, Peter," she answered sadly. "I didn't realize that the situation had rested so deeply inside of you. I'm sorry. I wouldn't have planned this night if I had." She sighed again. "You know I want you to understand me, not just tolerate what you don't understand. You've bottled up the issue of Dennis and now it has cramped your soul. Don't put on a civilized veneer for me. It isn't honest."

"I haven't even thought his name," Peter defended weakly.

She watched him steadily, disappointed that he was manufacturing his feelings. "Soul deals in truth, Peter. It's penetrating. You can't even say his name."

Peter fidgeted, her words hitting his conscience hard. He had lied to himself and now to her to cover his first lie.

"Dennis and I have a special bond between us, Peter. It's interesting. We both know it's there. I think he misinterpreted the bond the night he kissed me. He's lonely. I sense that in him. I sense many things about him." Peter rubbed his forehead and she noticed his hurt. She sighed again. "Peter, the part of the formula that's missing with Dennis is the physical. My mind respects his talent and he is incredibly talented. My heart loves him as a human being, his sensitivity, his caring, but his kiss wasn't magic like yours. My mind respects you, Peter. I'm in awe of what you've accomplished in your life, with what you've done with your life. My heart loves Chang. I love his loyalty. I love Peter's sensitivity. I love his strength."

Peter listened carefully. The emotion was too intense for him. She was at a level of communication that immobilized him and it left him speechless. He could only listen and feel her words burn away the anger deep inside of him where he had hidden the lie. Jeneil paused and was silent for a few seconds.

"Peter," she continued, "I love you with everything I'm capable of feeling and thinking. I'm yours totally and completely. No doubts at all. I belong to you. I know that. I want that. You are a superlative in my life. Sometimes I'm frightened by how much of me belongs to you, but I don't want to change that because I'm left with emptiness without you." She paused again. "Right now I think the only way I can really make you understand that is to not go to the theatre again. I won't see Dennis anymore."

Peter caught his breath as her words reached him. He heard the emotion in her voice. Jeneil stood up and left the room. It had taken a lot out of her to say that and he knew it. Her heart was a lot braver than his and she could teach him a lot about commitment. After all, she breathed it. He swallowed hard trying to get rid of the lump in his throat. She had uprooted some very deep emotions within him and he wondered how she could see that in him. Realizing several minutes had passed and she hadn't returned, he stood up. He wanted to hold her. Her words had opened feelings at a level he had never experienced before. He felt awkward within himself. There were no words to match what she had just shared with him, none that seemed right to him anyway.

The bedroom door was closed. He hesitated, wondering what she was feeling right now but he wouldn't find out standing there. He knocked softly. There was no answer. He knocked a little harder. Still no answer. Concerned, rubbing his chest with the palm of his hand, he took a deep breath and opened the door. Stepping inside, he was distracted by the scene before him. The lighting was strange. Jeneil sat on the bed brushing her hair. It seemed to him like she was set into a dream moving in semi-darkness and odd shadows. He looked around the room. The light was coming from candles, dozens of different sized white candles flickering warm dancing light. The room smelled slightly sweet. He looked at the floor. White flower petals were scattered across the rug. He wondered how they had gotten there and if she had torn them in anger. He closed the door and walked slowly to the bed, which was also covered with white flower petals. He watched Jeneil, who was still brushing her hair and not looking at him. She was wearing a dress he had never seen before. It was white, not a bright glaring white, but softer. The sleeves were long with a small trimming of lace or something. He wasn't sure. The neckline was square and outlined in the same type of material as the sleeves. He knelt on one knee before her.

"Jeneil?"

She lifted her eyes and looked at him. "Welcome to the fantasia of soul," she said sadly, looking discouraged.

"Honey, why did you destroy all the flowers and toss them all over the place?" he asked, looking at the sweep of petals. Jeneil wrinkled her brow, bewildered by the question, and then covered her mouth with the tips of her fingers trying not to laugh. She struggled to keep it stifled but couldn't and laughed out rightly until tears rolled down her cheeks. "Jeneil," he said, wondering if she was nearing hysteria. He took her hands. She pulled away, laughing hysterically, curling up on the bed. Flower petals caught in her hair as she wriggled on the bed with laughter. Peter stood up. "Jeneil!" he called firmly, worried.

"Oh Peter!" Jeneil laughed, trying to catch her breath. "This is too funny." She continued to laugh as she rolled onto her back. Peter got on the bed and leaned over her.

"Tell me what's funny, baby," he said, deeply concerned.

"Stop," she laughed, holding onto her stomach.

"Jeneil, honey, talk to me, please."

"Don't," she laughed again. "I'm okay. I'm okay." She wiped the tears from her face and held her stomach, getting herself under control. "Oh, Peter." She sighed and laughed lightly. "Life doesn't like us to write its script." She shook her head as the humor in the situation surfaced again.

"Honey, please make sense," he pleaded.

As she sat up, Peter pushed her hair back and gently began picking the flower petals that had attached themselves. Looking at her hair and the petals that were stuck to the strands, she laughed again, falling back onto the bed. "Don't I look romantic? Without the proper ambiance you look like you're picking out cooties."

"Honey, make sense or I'll sedate you. I swear I will." He lay beside her, rubbing her arm gently. He kissed her cheek and shoulder. She was calming down. Wiping the tears, she smiled at him.

"Peter," she held back a laugh, "I carefully removed the petals from a sinful amount of white roses and just as carefully placed them on the bed and floor. I didn't just toss them everywhere." She laughed and shook her head. "I was trying to create a fantastical atmosphere. The evening got twisted and you thought I had a tantrum in here." She chuckled. "Oh gosh, Peter, never walk in after a play has begun. You'd be totally lost. And then you kept looking at me like I'd lost touch with reality. You looked so funny all concerned and ready to make me your patient. You are so well trained, Dr. Chang." She touched his cheek tenderly, still laughing.

"Well, can you blame me? Look at this room. It has lost touch with reality."

"It was supposed to, Peter. We were supposed to finish experiencing soul in here." She shook her head. "I thought we'd be at a cosmic level by the time we got this far." She gave a laughing sigh.

"Oh shit. I'm sorry, honey. I ruined the whole thing, the dinner and now this. I'm really sorry. This was a lot of work, too," he said, looking around.

"Oh man of science, you do entertain me. You really do." She chuckled, loving his apologetic look.

He smiled and removed more petals from her hair. "I'm lucky that you have a sense of humor. I could be executed for ruining this much preparation."

"Well, I still have a pleasant memory of it." She laughed. "This was one of the funniest things I've ever seen you do." She scooped up a handful of rose petals and threw them at him like confetti, smiling warmly.

He bent down and kissed her. "Honey, I can't match the words you used at the dinner table, I can only say that I love you beyond any words." He kissed her again as she clung to him. "You look so beautiful," he said, kissing her neck. "Why don't we try to salvage this part of the soul experience?"

"Do you mean that?" she asked, touched by his willingness. "You were really struggling with it at dinner."

"Well, your words administered a powerful cure," he said as she smiled and kissed his chin. "Jeneil, I don't want you to stop seeing Dennis or going to the playhouse."

She shook her head, disagreeing. "No, I don't think so."

"I do, honey. It's too important to you. I don't want to ruin that for you."

She hugged him hard. "You really mean that don't you, Peter? I can hear it in your voice." He nodded. "Thank you," her voice cracked, "it's important to me. It's another piece in my life."

"How so?"

"I'm not sure, but I'm comfortable there. I'm alive. Does that make sense?"

"Yes," he answered, smiling. "I feel that with medicine."

She nodded. "Yes, you do. I can hear it in your voice when you talk about it." She hugged him.

"Where's Jeneil going, honey? What's developing?"

"I don't know, Peter. I really don't know. I still can't seem to specialize. I love it all; the staging, the props, the costumes, the people, the whole feeling of it, the feeling of creating something."

"Then you need to stay with it."

She wanted to believe his words. "Are you really sure?"

"Yes." He smiled. "I really loved your energy while you were working to get the play ready."

She lovingly smiled at him. "You're quite a man, Chang."

"Chang, shit. It's all Peter." He laughed. "Chang still wants to keep you chained to this bed."

She laughed and kissed him. She was bordering giddiness having had her freedom restored by him. "I love the way we resolve problems." She smiled at him, smoothing his hair gently.

"We are doing well." He brushed away rose petals. "And you're finding pieces to Jeneil. So do you think we'll be packaging this relationship with wedding rings pretty soon?"

"I would really like that. I would love having Jeneil that resolved."

He kissed her. She responded warmly. "Let's do this the way you planned it. What do I have to do?"

She smiled and hugged him. "You're great, Peter. You really are. Just change for bed."

"Change for bed? You know if we had done this part of soul first, I probably would have gotten a passing grade." He kissed her and got up to change.

Jeneil got up and checked the candles then, inserting a cassette into the slot, she pushed the play button. Pulsating rhythmic music began. Jeneil smiled as Peter returned. "I just need to brush these petals from my hair." She sat on the bed and began brushing.

Peter watched then going to her, he sat beside her. "Let me brush your hair."

Surprised, she handed him the brush. He began brushing the back of her hair in long, even strokes. Jeneil put her head back and closed her eyes. The sensation was erotic. Brushing her hair to one side, he held it there and gently kissed her neck and shoulder. She backed against him, leaning her head to one side. He liked the way she felt to him and it was obvious that she was enjoying him. Electricity filled his chest and pressed through his spine. He continued kissing her neck slowly. The atmosphere of the room was getting to him, the music encircling him. He felt like he moved in time to the rhythm. It felt odd but enjoyable. Wanting to experience more of her, his hands discovered the few buttons on the front of her dress. He undid them, allowing him more freedom. She blended against him indicating the pleasure she was experiencing. Electricity filled him every time she responded to him.

"Jeneil, I love you, honey," he whispered near her ear. She nodded her head and pressed her back against him. "I want the dress off, baby. I want you, and I think I've just ruined soul again," he whispered, smoothing his lips across her cheek.

"It doesn't matter right now," she replied softly, turning to face him. He kissed her while helping to remove the dress. She untied his robe, slipping it off. His body pulsated as he felt her soft skin against his body. He leaned her slowly back onto the bed and kissed her lips passionately. She responded to his kiss and pressed against him. The electricity vibrated through him.

"Jeneil, you're incredible," he whispered breathlessly.

"No, we are when we're in harmony." She kissed his neck. "I love you so much, Peter. I belong to you. I'll always belong to you, remember that." She pressed closer to him. He had to make love to her. He needed to show her how much he loved her. There were no more words for him. The music stayed with him like a light mist and affected his movements, making the experience incredibly pleasurable. He looked at her. She sensed it, too. He could see it. He smiled at her. She smiled and kissed his lips.

"I need you," he said, kissing her shoulder. She responded, giving herself to him completely and openly. He took control of the situation until they achieved a unity that wanted to be fulfilled. He didn't want it to end. She clung to him breathlessly. He felt her begin to respond ultimately. He responded too, giving all that he felt to her.

Lifting his head, he smiled at her. "You're incredible." She touched his face and smiled. He went to move away from her.

She held him. "Please stay. I want the closeness."

He kissed her neck gently. She felt warm and soft. He did feel close to her. "I'm glad you're mine, Songbird," he whispered.

She hugged him. "I am yours, Peter. I mean that."

He kissed her and she responded to it. The evening was proving to be very interesting.

Twenty-Two

The alarm rang. Peter and Jeneil stirred. Peter lifted his head, looking at the clock. Honey, you set the alarm on a day off!" He closed his eyes again.

Jeneil groaned. "Oh, force of habit. I'm sorry." She raised herself onto one elbow, looking around the room. "Oh my goodness."

"What's wrong?" Peter asked, opening his eyes and looking at her.

"The morning after." She sighed. "Half burned candles, hardened wax, the floor filthy with rose petals. How can all this have looked so romantic last night and look like debris this morning?"

Peter chuckled and pulled her to him. "Concentrate on the memory it created."

She smiled. "Ooo, yes indeed."

He kissed her. "That is some memory," he said, twisting a strand of her hair around his finger. "What was that music?"

"Bolero by Ravel. Why, did you enjoy it?"

"Enjoy it? It crawled into my brain and penetrated my nervous system." Jeneil kissed his chest and chuckled. "What's so funny?"

"I've never heard a critique of music using medical terms but that's fine, it only matters that it reached you. That's what music is supposed to do."

"Was that supposed to be seductive?" he asked, wondering about the music. She nodded and smiled. "Well the guy must have had a woman lying next to him when he wrote it because he knew what he was writing about."

Jeneil smiled. "Peter, that's very good. The music was inspired by the story of Scheherazade who kept herself alive by telling the Sultan a story every night for a 1001 nights."

"Yeah, well if the Sultan had listened to the music instead of the words he'd have told her to shut up with the stories and concentrate on other things."

Jeneil laughed. "I love you, man of science."

"Science? Believe me, that didn't inspire science in me." He laughed. "That unleashed Chang."

Jeneil smoothed Peter's hair back. "I know!" She smiled and raised her eyebrows then kissed his chin tenderly.

"Boy, I've got to tell Steve to buy that."

Jeneil laughed. "I don't think Debbie needs gimmicks."

"Honey, that music's not a gimmick, it's...," he searched for the word.

"Primal?" Jeneil suggested.

"Good word." He chuckled. "Besides, Steve isn't with Debbie anymore."

"Uh-oh, what happened?"

"The bedroom was getting crowded."

"Oh, that's too bad. What's he going to do now?"

"He's fasting."

"Steve Bradley?" Jeneil didn't even try to hide her disbelief.

Peter laughed. "Be nice. The poor guy needs our understanding right now."

"I doubt it. I'll bet he's waking up to something soft and cuddly right now."

"No, he isn't. There are no pets allowed in the dorms."

Jeneil laughed. "I'll bet he's not at the dorms."

"I'll take that bet. I'll call him and prove it to you."

"Now that's cute. How would you explain to him that we're discussing his sex life?"

"Let's have him over today, honey. I'm on the first shift next week. We'll have time all week together. He must be needing to get out of the room by now."

She looked at him lovingly, touched by the care he showed for a friend who needed people. "Go ahead Mr. Stubborn, prove it to yourself." She got up and tied her robe. "I want the chance to say I told you so."

Peter shook his head at her and reached for the telephone. Jeneil returned with a broom and dust pan, and began sweeping up rose petals. Peter waited as the phone continued to ring. Someone answered. "Hi, this is Peter Chang. Is Steve Bradley there?" Peter waited again. He covered the mouthpiece. "What will we do? Stay around here with a Sunday dinner thrown in?"

Jeneil sat on the bed to think. "I've got the perfect thing to cheer him up, but he's not in the dorms, you'll see." She began cleaning again.

"Hi, Steve." Peter made a face at Jeneil, who was staring in surprise.

"Hey, Pete. What're you doing up so early? Oh geez, forget I asked that. So why do you need me?"

Peter laughed. "You sound wide awake."

"Hey, man, I've been up for two hours already."

"How come? It's only seven-thirty."

"I've been at the exercise room. All I have left are memories of past Saturday nights and the memories return in my dreams."

Peter laughed; the new life of Steve Bradley was hard to believe. "It gets easier after six months."

"Six months?" Steve groaned.

"What are you doing today?"

"I hear there's a hot poker game starting here after lunch. Why?"

"How would you like to come here?"

"No, you guys don't need me hanging around."

"We insist."

"Come for breakfast," Jeneil called. "The earlier it is, the better, so we can leave."

"Leave for where?" Steve asked, having heard her.

"I don't know. She's aflutter about something you'll enjoy."

"Are you sure about having me along?"

"Positive, so come on over."

"Hey, you two are great. I'm tired of this building."

"I remember that, too. Then we'll see you soon." Peter hung up. "What are you planning?"

"I can't tell you either. It's a surprise for both of you." Jeneil left the room with a bag of debris.

Breakfast was ready by the time Steve arrived. Jeneil packed a lunch, put a roast in the timed oven, then went to change while Steve and Peter read the newspaper and talked. Fixing the collar of her blouse, Jeneil sauntered into the living room.

Steve looked up. "Hey, what are you dressed to the teeth for? I wore jeans. I thought we were going to kick around today."

Peter whistled. "A blouse and slacks are used for kicking around, aren't they?" Jeneil checked her purse for her hair band.

"Yeah sure, but my alligator's missing," Steve said. "Your kick around looks like Palm Beach."

Jeneil was surprised. "How do you know about fashion?"

Steve stood up and grinned. "Hey, we doctors know quality when we see it. Right, Pete?"

Peter smiled and put his arm around Jeneil's waist. "We sure do."

Jeneil looked from one to the other. "Silver tongued demons, the two of you. Help me carry lunch to the car so we can be leaving."

Peter and Steve grinned at each other and followed her to the door. They both liked her easy approach to life. Steve liked her flare for style and it stirred memories deep inside him from a time that seemed so long ago. Now this girl seemed more relaxed to him and that felt warmer to him.

The three got into Jeneil's car. She drove since the destination was a mystery. Watching as they drove toward the fashionable and historic west side of the city, Steve grinned. "Well, now we know why she wore lined white slacks and Gucci's. Are the Dunbars inviting us to a poolside party, Jeneil?"

"They don't have a pool at their townhouse. Their summer home down country does."

"Oh, get how she knows the 'in' people and their living habits."

Jeneil smiled. "You don't miss too much, do you?" She shook her head, looking annoyed. Peter covered his mouth and grinned, amused by Jeneil's values and Steve's lack of them. "All my friends are gossips, and how do you know my slacks are lined?" Steve looked at her and smiled. She scowled at him deliberately. He liked her spunk and her beauty impressed him. She was easy to be with. He was beginning to understand why Peter called her a tranquilizer. Jeneil turned the car into the empty parking lot of a well known art store.

Steve and Peter looked around, confused by where they were stopping. "Honey, what is this? Why are we here?"

"Pete, open your eyes," Steve said, seeing a chance to tease Jeneil. "The Dunbars are having a party. They've invited her and we're here to park cars. Only the Dunbars would use medical residents as parking lot attendants."

"Snob," she mumbled. Steve laughed. "I have to make another stop for the surprise. Wait here for me, please, and face University Street." Peter and Steve got out of the car, and Jeneil drove away.

"This is really strange, Pete. She's slightly off-center, isn't she?"

"Slightly? Get to know her better. I wonder if she's going to leave us here and wait to see how long it takes for us to leave. She loves playing 'gotcha.' She once set me up on the roof of a bank building complete with security guards and guns. Scared the hell out of me."

Steve laughed. "Ooo, a little spitfire."

Peter bent down and tied his shoe. "I hope there really is a surprise. I'd hate to waste my day off standing here as the butt of a joke."

Steve began to wonder. "She'd really do that to us?"

"Possibly, I did ruin a special surprise last night, one that took a lot of work."

Steve chuckled. "Well, it might not be too bad if this is a joke because I'd have a hell of a lot of fun paying her back."

"You and me both."

"At least the weather's good." Steve stretched and yawned. They waited on University Street as instructed. Steve chuckled. "I feel like we're the only two who haven't heard that the parade was cancelled."

Jeneil eased the Bentley she had just exchanged with her car onto Oak Hill and drove slowly to the opposite side of the parking lot where Peter and Steve were waiting. Pulling in, she inched her way toward them. She grinned as she saw them obeying her instructions faithfully. Stopping the car, she leaned on the horn, startling them. They turned quickly, shocked when they recognized her sitting inside the light grey Bentley. "Well, do you want a ride or don't you?" she asked, getting out of the car. Peter and Steve walked to the car slowly. Steve gave a low whistle.

"Holy...look at the lines on this thing," Peter said, stopping to look at the hood.

"Wow, I feel like I should kneel on the ground before it." Steve touched the chrome lightly then wiped it with his shirt sleeve. They walked around the car, taking it all in. "Can I look inside?"

Jeneil smiled and nodded, enjoying their reactions. Peter opened one back door and Steve opened the other. They both got in and studied every inch of the interior, not daring to touch or breathe too hard on it. Jeneil got behind the wheel and turned to face them.

"It arrived two days ago. I'm renting a spot in the Carriage House. This was the only part of the city where the car wouldn't attract attention and the Carriage House has great security. Everyone would stare when we'd drive into Billingsly in it. Parsons would drive and Mandra would say, 'Jeneil, pay attention to how you feel when we drive past people who stare in awe. Take notes on what it does to your heart. Think about that and then we'll talk about it.'"

Jeneil looked from Steve to Peter. They were touching the material on the doors lovingly. Getting out and going to the trunk, she brought back a grey chauffeur's hat and jacket.

Putting them on, along with dark glasses, she got behind the wheel. Starting the engine, she pulled away, surprising Peter and Steve. "Sit back guys. You are being treated to the first ride of my limousine service." She smiled into the mirror. "Any place special? Old girlfriends, people who put you down, old teachers who thought you wouldn't amount to much. How about driving past a new girl you're trying to impress. That last option's not available to you, Peter." Peter and Steve laughed.

"This is incredible." Steve felt the reverence of being near greatness. "Feel the smoothness of the ride. This baby was made to pamper asses. Sorry Jeneil."

"Actually that isn't why Mandra bought this. She had strict plans for her money and cars weren't one of them. She decided to invest her money in one car that wouldn't drastically depreciate in value."

"Well, the woman knew how to live." Steve settled against the seat.

Jeneil glared into the rearview mirror. "Peter, are you tongue tied?"

"Yes, I'm having trouble accepting the fact that I'm riding in a magnificent Bentley and it belongs to my girl."

Steve laughed. "That's a fact I couldn't struggle with for too long. Ooo, this baby is an absolute beauty." He ran his hand across the seat. Peter watched Steve and smiled, enjoying his pleasure and appreciation for a luxury car. Steve noticed students watching as the car passed. "Get the reactions of the college kids we drive by, Pete."

The guys were raising their arms in a united power sign and the girls were waving frantically to get their attention. As they drove further, one tousled haired student in a green army jacket sitting on the back of a park bench made an obscene gesture.

"Humanities major," Steve spat as an insult. Peter and Jeneil laughed. "Lay some money on him, Jeneil, and test his sincerity to the cause of human deprivation," he snarled. "I'll bet he'd head for beer and boobs in the Bahamas."

Peter grinned. "Careful Steve, Jeneil's heart leans toward humanitarians, too."

"But Pete, at least she's straight. She's got her money working for her so she can help people. He parks his ass on a bench and insults people. Hell of a lot of good that does for people in need. His capitalistic old man is probably contributing to more worthy causes than he is."

"How the hell do you know his father is rich?"

"Pete, what were you doing on weekends during this time of year when you were in college?"

Peter thought back. "Steaming my skin off working in a restaurant kitchen."

"There you go, and what's he doing? If he's not working, he's got to have bucks. That university is top quality and expensive."

"We went there."

"Yeah, on scholarships. That's why I hate his type. My college education was paid for by rich capitalistic people like his father who gave a damn about others. I'd see their kids protesting this and that as I'd run from class to work and back again. They're the only ones who had time while the rest of us worked our asses off. They'd sit in the commons and the student union talking to each other about what was wrong with our country politically and socially while they drank imported beer or coffee. They never lacked for something to eat from the snack line. They never put a bag of chips back on the shelf to pay for a new pen they needed or went without lunch to buy a book for a class."

Jeneil looked at Steve in the rearview mirror through her dark glasses. She swallowed past the lump in her throat and felt her eyes moisten.

Steve shook his head in disgust. "I could never figure out how they could be so stupid and be in college."

Jeneil smiled sympathetically. "My father used to say that just because a person made it into college and out four years later didn't necessarily mean that they were intelligent when they arrived or left."

"That is pure truth," Steve agreed as Jeneil turned onto a well-kept, tree-lined street. No one looked at the car as they drove past.

"These people must have money," Peter commented. "They're not impressed with the car."

Steve smiled. "Continentals and Volvos in the driveway? They have enough only to know that it's not chic to stare and drool. They're sneaking peeks after we go by."

Jeneil laughed. "Steve, I'm curious, where did you get your knowledge of money and status symbols?"

"A girl a long time ago," he answered quietly, then added in a drawling tone, "and Morgan P. Rand, resident, and idiot, who was in every class I ever had." Jeneil and Peter laughed as they recognized the mimic of Morgan Rand's rich, tone drone.

Jeneil pulled into a small park and stopped. She got out, went to the trunk, and replaced the chauffeur outfit. Returning, she knelt on the front seat. "Okay, who's driving now?" Peter and Steve looked at each other.

Peter grinned. "This is your fantasy, Steve. You drive."

Steve put his head back. "Oh, Pete, I owe you for that. Thanks." Leaning forward, he put his hands on Jeneil's cheeks. "And you crazy lady, thank you, too." He kissed her quickly, surprising both of them. "I'm sorry," he apologized, sitting back embarrassed and shocked.

"It's okay," Jeneil laughed. "I understand the excitement of a new love. Get behind the wheel, she's all yours."

"Ooo, heaven here I come." Steve got out and moved to the front seat. Peter got in beside Jeneil and put his arm around her shoulder. She snuggled to him. He smiled and kissed her cheek.

Steve caressed the wheel and fondled the buttons on the dashboard. It was obvious to Jeneil and Peter that Steve loved the car. They glanced at each other and smiled. Peter squeezed her shoulder and she leaned into him more closely. They continued watching, completely amused by Steve's love affair with the Bentley.

"Where are we going?" Steve asked, looking up.

"I don't care," Peter answered. "I'm relaxing just being in the car. Or maybe I'm numb."

"How about the ocean?" Jeneil suggested.

"The ocean?" Steve gasped. "And get salty sea air all over my Grey Lady! Girl, that's sacrilege."

Jeneil laughed. "Have you ever seen the expensive cars crossing into Newport?"

"But they don't have the Grey Lady." Steve smiled warmly, smoothing his hand over the dash.

"But they have her sisters and cousins," Jeneil countered.

"Oh, okay, the ocean it is." Steve patted the dashboard. "Don't cry, sweetheart. I'll throw bad Jeneil out of the car before we get there as punishment." Peter laughed. He had never seen Steve's car fetish this out of control.

Jeneil sighed. "Oh good grief, then drive wherever you want."

"Thank you." Steve smiled. "Well, if we go to the country the birds might leave droppings on her. And if we drive in the city she'll be covered with contaminants and pollutants."

"Drive!" Jeneil hit Steve's arm lightly.

"Ooo, the girl gets fiery." Steve grinned. "We'd better go to the ocean and cool her off, Grey Lady."

"Ugh!" Jeneil screamed softly, covering her face with her hands and putting her head back. Peter laughed. Steve smiled and pulled away from the curb.

"Oh, Peter. The balance is great. She handles like she's a feather. What a magnificent creation. You've got to have a turn."

"I can wait. You have a love for expensive cars. I know how to fix the cheaper ones. I still love my car."

Jeneil smiled at Peter.

"Was that car from Jeneil, too?" Steve asked, grinning.

"Who else could maneuver that year car for three hundred dollars?" Peter laughed.

Steve looked at Jeneil. "So you are really a crazy lady."

"Stop calling me a crazy lady. I'm only eccentric."

Steve laughed. "Fine line definition I'll bet."

"Better watch your words before I go from eccentric to ebullient," Jeneil warned.

Steve and Peter laughed. "Pete, what did she just say? And how come you know these fancy words, too?"

"She studies words," Peter answered. "Ebullient is one of her listed words this week. I remember reading the definition. It means demonstrative and boiling over."

Steve smiled at Jeneil. "Fancy tough talk, and how come you work at that hospital job?"

"I'm hiding while I look for Jeneil."

Steve looked at Peter and wrinkled his eyebrows questioningly.

Peter smiled. "It makes sense when you know her well."

"And why aren't you in college, kid?"

"Because I'm old enough to have graduated already."

Steve was surprised by that. "Really? Are you? How old are you?"

"I'm going to be twenty-three in two weeks."

"I thought you were much younger. You look a lot younger. How come you dropped out of college?"

"I wanted to look for Jeneil."

Steve wrinkled his brow again. "More looking for Jeneil? What, is she lost?"

"No, she's underdeveloped."

Steve looked at Peter and grinned, raising his eyebrows in a coded remark about Jeneil's figure.

Jeneil noticed. "Are you two sharing one brain or just that off color thought?" she asked dryly.

"Smart ass," Steve said, grinning.

"Please don't call me smut names. I don't appreciate being trashed."

Steve looked at her and smiled slowly. "You are a brainy little wench with a sassy tongue."

"Real men like it," she replied, and kissed Peter's cheek.

Steve laughed heartily. Peter chuckled and kissed her temple. Steve was quiet then laughed again, enjoying the remark. "You are brainy and sassy, but I won't call you smut names anymore."

"Gracias, hombre."

Peter grinned as he watched them together. Their good natured fun was more than he had expected.

"What part of the ocean do you want to visit?" Steve asked.

"Medfield."

"But that's just rocky cliffs, isn't it?"

"Yes, but there are areas where we can park and stay with the Grey Lady."

"Ooo, yes. Good thinking." Steve took the exit off the highway and headed toward Medfield. There were a few cars parked along the narrow road overlooking the ocean. Picnickers stared as they drove past.

"The car is turning heads." Steve smiled.

"There's a nice grassy area around the bend. It overlooks the ocean, not just the bay area. Let's go there. It's usually unoccupied."

Steve continued on.

"There it is," Jeneil nodded, and Steve pulled off the road and parked the car.

"This is nice," Steve said, taking in the view. Jeneil looked at him and smiled. Peter held the door for her. Jeneil got out and went to unpack the blanket. Spreading it on the grass, she sat down. Peter sprawled next to her as Steve got under the Bentley. "Peter, you should see the workmanship on this car. Qualiteee."

Peter winked at Jeneil. "You've made his day. I can tell. I think I'll see what he's talking about."

Jeneil lay back on the blanket, closing her eyes. The warm sun felt good on her face and the gentle breeze off the ocean timed its arrival in order to cool her. She lay dreamily enjoying the rhythm of the wind.

"Jeneil, can we look under the hood?" Peter called to her.

"Sure," she answered, smiling to herself. She could hear them talking about the quality of the material and the care the car had received.

"Honey, the car has been well looked after. Who's going to look after it here?"

"Charlie is. He's also going to be the driver for awhile. Work gets slow in the winter for him."

"Oh good, he'll be honest and careful with the car."

Peter and Steve returned to the engine. Jeneil grinned, enjoying their interest in the car. Hearing a buzzing, she turned onto her stomach and watched as a bee busily worked on a pink clover blossom. It finished and flitted to another. Picking a small pink petal from the blossom, she put it into her mouth.

"Taste good?" Jeneil looked up quickly as Steve stooped beside her. She smiled, embarrassed he'd seen her behaving like a child. She finished chewing and swallowed. He smiled at her. "Is that lunch?"

"No," and she laughed.

"I think you're more the buttercup type," Steve teased, laughing. Peter walked over to them, wiping his hands. "Careful where you walk, Pete. Jeneil's having lunch. That's her grazing area." Jeneil looked at him and smirked. He picked a whole clover and handed it to her. "Here, have a feast."

"You don't quit, do you?" She chuckled, throwing the clover at him.

He looked at her steadily. "I'm not known to quit."

Peter sat beside her. "Hey, you brought a softball and a bat?"

She nodded. "And a badminton set and basketball. In case we wanted to play."

Steve was completely surprised. He hadn't expected her to be a tomboy since she seemed so stylish. "Do you play softball, Jeneil?"

"I used to with a friend of mine when we were kids."

"Are you any good?"

"So-so."

Steve looked at Peter. "Want to try a game?"

"Sure. Let's try."

"Are you playing in Gucci's, Jeneil?" Steve teased.

"I have running shoes in the car, and I'll play on your head if you don't get off my case," she threatened, standing up.

"Ooo, tough kid. Want her on your team, Pete?" Steve picked up the ball and bat then organized the game. Jeneil noticed it was his way of taking charge. He wasn't arrogant. It seemed more like somebody had to do it, so let's get it done. Peter was more laid back, but resistant if he objected to something. She grinned. Their personalities seemed to complement each other. It was decided by a toss of a coin that Peter would bat, Steve would pitch, and Jeneil would catch and umpire. She took the glove and positioned herself behind Peter.

"Hey, fella, I like your grip," she whispered sexily.

Peter snickered. "Behave yourself, beautiful."

"Hey, I'm just trying to be one of the guys."

"That's impossible for you." He smiled at her.

Steve folded his arms. "Let me know when you two finish with sweet nothings."

"We're ready, Stevie," Jeneil called in a high pitched voice. Peter laughed and put the bat down.

Steve laughed. "Hey, lady, if you wanna play with the guys then show us you've got the right stuff otherwise suit up as a cheerleader."

"You've got it, mouth," she yelled. "Play ball!"

Peter was waiting for a pitch with the count of two balls, two strikes.

"Come on, send this guy to the showers," Jeneil called to Steve.

"Hey!" Peter turned to her. "Where's your loyalty woman?"

She chuckled. "I have to be impartial, honey, but I'll scrub your back for you when you shower." She smiled sweetly.

He laughed. "If I strike out, you'd better get ready to run and fast for telling him to do it."

"Uh-uh, Peter. I think there's a rule about threatening the ump."

"You're tough."

"I love you, too." She made kissing noises.

Steve pitched and Peter hit a fast ground ball to the left that bounced and went past Steve. Peter ran to the one base and back again. Jeneil cheered as Peter ran home. He kissed her after he returned to home plate. "Fair weather friend," he laughed, out of breath.

"Aw Peter, don't be mad. It's not easy playing all the parts." She grinned impishly and hugged him.

Steve came back to the pitcher's mound. "Hey, I hope I hit a homerun, too. I like the way the umpire congratulates players." Jeneil and Peter laughed.

They switched positions. Peter was pitching, Jeneil was batting, and Steve was catcher and umpire. Peter pitched.

"Ball."

"What?" Peter yelled, disputing the call.

"Ball," Jeneil said, laughing. "You heard the umpire."

Peter pitched again. Jeneil hit the ball over Peter's head landing it only a few feet behind him. Peter raced for the ball. Jeneil raced for the plate then turned and ran back as Peter retrieved the ball. He threw it to Steve at home plate just before Jeneil made it. Steve stayed frozen, holding the ball, watching Jeneil run closer.

"Tag her!" Peter shouted. "Tag her or she's safe."

Jeneil touched home plate and overran it. Steve covered his mouth and turned away with his shoulders bobbing up and down from laughing.

Peter went to him. "What the hell happened?"

Steve stopped laughing. "Oh shit, Pete. I didn't know where to tag her." Steve laughed again. "She's all girl. I didn't know where to touch her and I froze. She was coming harder."

Peter laughed, leaning on Steve's shoulder.

"Hey, are you guys letting me win?" Jeneil asked, walking back to them.

They both roared in laughter. "No," Steve answered through a laugh.

"Okay," she said, pulling her blouse from where it was tucked into the waistband of her slacks.

"What are you doing?" Peter asked, calming down.

"I don't want anyone distracted because I'm a girl."

Steve and Peter laughed again. "Too late." Steve shook his head. "You don't miss much, brainy wench."

She smiled, straightening her blouse over her slacks. "There, that'll help," she said, going toward the pitcher's mound.

"I doubt it," Steve whispered. "Maybe a sex change would help." Steve and Peter laughed again.

Jeneil turned around. "I heard that and I'm ignoring it."

"Play ball," Steve called laughingly.

"Come on, mouth," Jeneil called, "pick up the bat. I'm waiting for you. I have a score to settle with you for a lot of things."

Steve chuckled. "Ooo, get this tough lady. I want to see this happen." He picked up the bat. "Let her rip, beautiful." Jeneil threw the ball.

"Strike."

Jeneil smiled. "I love you, Peter."

"Lucky pitch, beautiful. Try it again," Steve called.

Jeneil pitched.

"Ball."

"Told you."

Jeneil paused then pitched. Steve hit the ball, sending it about a foot over Jeneil's head. Jeneil jumped, straining to catch it. The glove flew off her hand and hit the ball, stopping it. She looked up surprised and caught the ball in her hands as it followed the glove to the ground. Steve stood between base and home with his mouth open as Jeneil put one hand on her hip and held the ball up with the other, waving it at Steve. "You're out!" she called, smiling broadly.

Peter applauded. "Great play, baby. Great play."

Jeneil smiled. "Kiss of the leprechaun, me boy," she said in an Irish dialect, "twas the kiss of the old leprechaun."

"I don't believe it!" Steve yelled, returning to home plate.

Jeneil laughed. "Hit the showers loser. We don't do instant replays."

Steve smiled. "You're something else, beautiful. You really are." She curtsied, holding the hem of her blouse as a skirt. Peter and Steve laughed. Steve loved her sense of humor. He watched as she walked to them, tossing the ball up and catching it. Her hair was slipping out of her pins and her blouse was hanging loosely, making her look disheveled. He loved that she always seemed to have fun.

"Shall we do lunch?" She grinned at him.

"I'm starved."

"Me, too," Peter added.

"Lunch it is." She went to the car. "Will you take it over to the blanket?" She took her purse and went to the side of the car.

Peter and Steve sat on the blanket waiting for her. When she joined them, her hair was fixed, her blouse was tucked in, and she was back to sandals. Peter smiled and moved over so she had room next to him. Steve watched, amused that she even did costume changes on picnics. "You don't even resemble the sandlot player anymore."

She smiled and opened the lunch basket. Both men peeked inside. After Peter and Steve finished eating the brownies, Jeneil rested her head on Peter's hip. Steve sighed contently. "Jeneil, you're a great cook."

Steve stretched out on the blanket and put his arms behind his head as a pillow. Jeneil looked up at Peter, surprised by Steve's compliment. He winked.

"Did I say something wrong?" Steve asked.

"No, Jeneil's mother was a gourmet cook and Jeneil never feels that she quite reaches that level."

"I'm not sure what your mother did, but you cook meals that make a person feel good. Mrs. Sprague is always pushing herself by taking cooking courses and all the guy wants is plain food. She's a good cook, too."

"You eat at Dr. Sprague's?" Jeneil asked.

"Sometimes. At holidays mostly. They've been really good to me, and sometimes I eat at Pete's mother's house." Jeneil looked away. The sentiment touched something deep within her. "You get great food there, but Pete and his mother give you indigestion when they start at each other."

Peter laughed. "I guess we do."

"You're getting better though, Pete. You wait until after dessert to explode." Steve and Peter laughed. "Before he learned that trick we'd spend the holiday playing pool in the dorm rec room, eating those stale pastries from the machines. Man, you and your mother are branding irons." Jeneil was surprised to hear Peter's comments supported.

"I told you, baby," Peter said, touching Jeneil's cheek tenderly, having noticed her reaction to the remark.

"What do they argue about?"

Steve turned onto his side. "I don't know. Once she put gravy on something, he made a remark, and she blew up. I always got the feeling that what they argue about isn't what they're annoyed over."

"She starts it," Peter replied, taking a cookie.

"Don't you think that's juvenile?" Jeneil asked, wanting Peter to elaborate in order for her to understand the problem.

"She does start it," Peter insisted. "I try to stay out of her way and she explodes anyway."

"He's right," Steve agreed.

Jeneil looked from one to the other. "That's odd. She seems like a reasonable woman to me."

"You know her?" Steve asked, surprised.

"Only from going to the restaurant."

Peter laughed. "Sure, I always did wish that she'd treat me like the customers."

Steve laughed, too. "Maybe that's it, Pete. They leave tips, you leave dirty laundry."

"Like hell I do. I've been on my own since I could do for myself. I never let her touch anything of mine."

"Couldn't that be some of your problem? Isn't that like rejecting her?"

"But she'll take over your breathing if you let her."

"You say that about me, too." Jeneil laughed and kissed his arm.

"But you're different."

"You mean our relationship is different. I don't have authority over you. She does. I know my limits."

"She thinks she has authority over me," Peter protested.

"She's your mother, she does."

"That's ridiculous," Peter argued.

"That sounds warped to me, too," Steve agreed.

"Then when does a person become their own person?" Peter asked.

"When they achieve peace with the authority figure. I've often thought Peter and his mother were involved in a struggle over authority."

"There shouldn't be a struggle, I'm twenty-five."

"But you yell it instead of telling her. My mom and I used to argue. Whenever I exploded at her, my dad stepped in and made me apologize. He told me that I had a right to outline and define my beliefs, but I didn't have the right to insult or be abusive to my mother or him. He reminded me that they were my parents and that entitled them to respect. He told me that as I grew it would be natural to want to separate from their ways and be my own person, but he said that I couldn't separate from them as people. 'We are bonded together by birth and blood. We can't abuse you, you can't abuse us,' he said, 'so let's learn to talk civilly about all our rights.'"

Steve was impressed. "Man, that's a new twist. I've never heard that before. Even Sprague's sons can be real shitheads at times, and I think the man is the greatest as far as being a parent. Mrs. Sprague, too. Did that really work in your family?"

"I guess that's the key word, work. My dad made it work. Once I understood that I had rights and a place for a fair hearing, yelling wasn't necessary anymore. To this day I always regret losing my temper. If I just wait to cool down, I can usually see another side to whatever has made me angry. I guess that's what my father meant. Whenever I sulked, he'd say, 'Think, Jeneil, think. Use your mind. Life is like a prism, a kaleidoscope. A turn of the glass and the problem will look different to you.' He took a lot of time with me. We talked a lot. It was a revelation to me when my mother pointed out that our words create images in the minds of others. One word means this to you, but the same word might mean something else to another person. Even the way we say it creates an impression. She always said take the time to listen and watch what's around you and those around you. 'Feel the pulse, Jeneil; look for the heart of the issue.'"

Steve had been watching her and listening carefully. "Hey kid, with parents like that how come you're looking for Jeneil? Her identity should have come with your silver spoon."

"I didn't have a silver spoon. Well, yes I did…but…." Peter and Steve laughed. "But not in the sense that you two mean it. We weren't rich. I didn't grow up with luxury."

Steve laughed and looked at Peter. "Maybe every kid in her neighborhood rode around in Bentleys. Maybe they were so common, they were like Toyotas." Peter and Steve laughed again.

"Mandra had money, not me," Jeneil insisted. "She was different. We would ride to Billingsly in the Bentley and eat tuna sandwiches or even peanut butter and jam sandwiches because she thought the prices in the city were outrageous and the quality poor. She had plans for her money. She didn't waste it. She was a lot of fun. She taught me a lot, too."

"Was she your aunt?" Steve asked.

"Not biologically. She and my parents were friends. My dad was foreman of her estate."

Peter laughed. "Oh wait, Steve. You've got to hear this story."

"It's true," Jeneil insisted. "He was."

Peter laughed again. "Yeah right, your dad was a humble immigrant from Dublin and your mom was a homespun simple woman with simple tastes."

"They were. That's true, too," she insisted again.

"Steve, Jeneil was a literature major in college. She deals well with fiction."

"Peter, that story isn't fiction," Jeneil said emphatically.

"Steve, the girl's father was a professor. He wrote history textbooks, and lectured in colleges and private clubs. Her mother was an artist good enough to sell. Both of them were well traveled and well educated people. Mandra owned the town Jeneil grew up in. She's been surrounded by money and luxury all her life, and she's traveled to places we'll never see."

Jeneil sighed. "You're refusing to open your eyes. Those things were what they did, not what they were or who I am. Mandra felt her money belonged to others, too. She felt that she only had it in trust. We all played a game to see how little we could live on and still be comfortable and happy. In fact, I think Mandra's money held her prisoner. The more money she had the more it made a claim on her life. She had to live on a big estate. She had to own a Bentley." Jeneil shuddered at the words, remembering the six year time extension on the claim to Mandra's estate.

"Are you cold?" Peter asked, noticing her shiver.

"No, I'm scared."

"Of what?" Steve asked, surprised.

"Money," Jeneil replied, frowning. Steve looked questioningly at Peter.

Peter rubbed Jeneil's arm soothingly. "Honey, you're finding Jeneil. The corporation won't swallow you whole, you'll control it. Look at the Grey Lady. Mandra left that to you and what did you do with it? You put it to work. You're in control, baby."

Jeneil smiled and kissed his arm realizing he thought she was worried about the corporation and not Mandra's estate. "I hope you're right, Peter, because I don't want money to create limits in my life. I need freedom and mobility. I can't live in a stratum with limitations. I can't."

"Jeneil, poverty is very confining," Steve said. "You'd have more freedom with money. Take it as a fact from someone who knows."

Jeneil studied his features. "Hmm, how curious," she said, "and true, then where is real freedom?"

"When you can choose your stratum and limitations, I guess," Peter answered matter-of-factly.

Jeneil sat up and smiled at him. "Peter, you're waxing philosophical."

He smiled. "Comes from living with a lit major."

Jeneil kissed him. "But I'm still left with a dilemma."

Steve chuckled. "Stop looking under rocks, Jeneil."

"What do you mean?

"Live life, don't study it." He yawned casually

"But in order to live life, we need to think. In order to think, we need to study. Don't we?"

"Eh," Steve said, laying back. "Pete, cut off her helium supply. She's O.D."

Peter laughed. "He's right, honey. Let life come at you. Don't rise above it."

She smiled at him. "You both have such a simple way of looking at things. I can't seem to confine myself that way. Sometimes I wish I could. Life would certainly be less complicated. I wonder if it's your training in the scientific approach to reasoning."

Steve put his arms across his eyes. "Holy shit, does her brain ever take a coffee break?"

"But that's an interesting question, Steve," Jeneil insisted. "Are you two finished because of your simplicity or are you simple because you're finished?"

Steve uncovered his eyes. "Jeneil, if the ninth floor at the hospital finds out about you, I can guarantee that you'll have a lot of time to study confinement." Peter laughed.

Jeneil smiled. "I'm only eccentric. Green grass on the bottom, blue sky on top."

"Unless you're standing on your head," Steve said dryly.

"Don't confuse me," she said, stretching. "I think I'll take a short walk. The lunch basket is full of munchies for you. I'll be back." She got up and walked away.

Steve turned onto his stomach and closed his eyes. "Does she get like that often?" he asked, grinning, having enjoyed her seriousness.

"She's different," Peter said. "The craziest things catch her attention. Sometimes the smallest details become important to her."

"Yeah I know, like wondering what clover tastes like because bees like it. She plays with helium."

Peter laughed. "I know what you mean. She does get spacey, but she has anchors, too," he defended. "She's something else altogether. I don't know where she's headed, but I think she's cute as hell and I love cosmic."

They were silent for a few minutes then Steve laughed. "I think I just solved your problem."

"How?"

"Marry her and get her pregnant. She'll find out the meaning of life nine months later, and the diapers will keep her from reading so much." They laughed together.

"I think we're too simple."

"Simple minded." Steve chuckled. "It comes from working doubles."

"Steve, what's cute about her is that she thinks, she feels, she cares. She's alive, man. She's out there trying to teach the world to spell love. Maybe we shouldn't tell her she's crazy."

Steve nodded. "You're right. She is cute as hell and she's not crazy at all. And she's definitely alive." He sat up. "Where is she?"

Jeneil stood a short distance away looking at the ocean. They both got up and walked toward her. "Where are you going?" she asked.

"To get you."

"Is something wrong?"

Peter put his arm around her. "No, we just missed you."

She looked from one to the other. "What are you two up to?" she asked suspiciously.

"Nothing." Peter kissed her lightly and smiled.

"We were thinking that we might have teased you too much," Steve confessed, fidgeting. The sentiment surprised him and he realized that she was the type who broke down barriers.

"I'm fine. I was too cerebral, so I went for a walk. The wind helps to balance me again."

Steve smiled to himself thinking Peter had been right when he had said she was fragile. "We thought we might have hurt your feelings."

The apology pleased Jeneil. "Thank you for caring about me. That deserves a hug." She slipped her arms around Steve. He tensed, totally overwhelmed by her action. She backed away. "My goodness, you're like Peter used to be. He was afraid to hug, too."

"I, uh, I wasn't expecting it," Steve said self-consciously.

"Hugs are supposed to make you feel good, not scare you."

"I'll improve." He smiled, still feeling self-conscious, realizing that she actually destroyed barriers.

She snuggled to Peter. "It feels good to have people care about me. I love it."

Peter kissed her head and squeezed her. Steve smiled, aware of the ease that Peter had achieved in showing affection and emotion with her. Steve knew that was a major achievement for Peter. Peter trusted her with his emotions and his heart, and Steve was genuinely happy for Peter. He liked her a lot; this brainy, sassy, fragile kid who had taken his locked up, cynical friend and allowed him to care and feel and show it to her. She really was sunshine.

"I'm finding it too humid here," Jeneil said as they walked slowly back to the blanket. "Would anyone mind a quiet Sunday afternoon in an air conditioned apartment doing much of nothing?"

"Sounds good to me," Peter answered.

"Same here," Steve agreed. "Drive back, Pete. You won't believe the Grey Lady's performance."

"Only to the entrance to Ocean Bluff. I'm more curious than fascinated."

Twenty-Three

The apartment felt cool and relaxing. Peter stretched out on the sofa with the newspaper. Steve chose a stuffed chair and a soft hassock. Jeneil watched the two for a second. Bringing two pillows, she handed one to each.

"What's the pillow for?" Peter asked.

"I just thought it would be more comfortable. Take off your shoes." She smiled and went to the kitchen.

After preparing the vegetables for dinner, Jeneil went to the living room. Both Peter and Steve were sleeping soundly.

Jeneil smiled. "Now really guys, what else would two residents want to do on a day off."

Pulling a box from the closet, she sat near the stereo listening to music on her headphones as she mended clothes. Dinner smelled like it was done, but Peter and Steve still slept. She put the dinner aside and returned to mending. Steve turned over then opened his eyes. He sat up quickly. Seeing Peter sleeping, he smiled. "I'm glad I wasn't the only rude one," he said, yawning.

Jeneil smiled. "You were tired, not rude."

"This all feels good," he said, leaning his head back.

She looked up from mending and smiled at him warmly. "I would never have guessed that you enjoyed simple pleasures."

"I like this a lot. What smells so good?"

"A pork roast prepared in my neighbor's, Mrs. Rezendes', special marinade. That's what smells good, not the roast." She put the box of mending aside and picked up some knitting.

"What are you knitting?"

"A sweater for a charity group who fix up old clothes for the needy."

Steve smiled. "Is that what the box of clothes is for?"

Jeneil nodded. "But I think I'll sew a couple of new outfits, too. Mended clothes are after all mended clothes."

"Jeneil, make sure they get to the people you intend them to go to."

She looked up. "They might not?"

Steve shrugged. "One woman used to bring a lot of sweaters she'd knit for Christmas to the house where I grew up. We never got them. A lady in administration used to sell them or she'd give them to her own family as gifts."

Jeneil closed her eyes and sighed then shook her head in disgust. "I'll figure something out. Thank you." She put the knitting aside as tears rolled down her cheeks. Learning about Steve's background apparently had made her very sensitive. Noticing the tears, Steve stood up and went to her.

"Hey, I'm sorry. I didn't mean to upset you," he said, stooping before her. She covered her eyes and waved her hand at him indicating she was alright.

"She feels things deeply," Peter said, having heard the conversation. "I think crying is her release valve. It keeps the pressure gauge steady. It's how she stands intense, I think."

"I cry very easily," Jeneil answered, "too easily." She smiled and wiped the tears. "Don't look so upset," she chuckled at Steve, "my mascara is waterproof." Steve smiled and noticed she had changed into a long dress. He was getting used to her costumes. She stood up. "I'll put dinner together."

Peter went to her and put his arms around her. "You set us up for sleeping you sneak." He held her tightly and she swayed slightly, enjoying being held.

"You two will be easy to shop for at Christmas. I'll give both of you naps Sunday afternoon." She smiled. "Christmas! I can't believe the summer is coming to an end! Labor Day is just around the corner." She kissed Peter's cheek.

Bringing dinner to the table, Jeneil served then sat down. "Steve, when is your residency over?"

"February first, and I can't wait. Jeneil, this roast is really good. And mashed potatoes that don't taste like cardboard, I love it."

She smiled knowing Steve was enjoying the meal. "I like cooking for you guys." She touched Peter's arm. "How come you're on a half year schedule?" she asked Steve.

He shrugged. "I don't do things like other people. I'm lucky Dr. Sprague latched onto me. I would never have gotten this far without him, and Peter helped, too."

"I didn't do anything." Peter laughed.

"Sure you did, and still do."

Peter smiled. "Just returning the favors you've done for me. Honey, Steve is super, super brainy. He's over the IQ chart."

"I am not." Steve laughed. "Don't make me sound like Jeneil. I don't care why bees like clover."

Jeneil looked from one to the other. "I love your friendship. You two are so close. It feels good to just watch it work. It's good to see dedicated doctors in training, too. I'm a little gun shy about doctors."

Steve chuckled. "Well, we are getting bad press. Drugs, alcohol, malpractice suits."

"But you two are really dedicated. Medicine used to be a noble and highly revered profession. It's too bad about the bad publicity."

"The medical profession was powerful, too," Peter added. "Doctors were unchallenged in their word."

"I think the power began to corrupt," Steve said.

Jeneil sighed. "Money and power can do that. Everything has a cycle to it. I admire you both for going into medicine at its decline. The profession needs people who will turn the bad press around. I think my dentist has a great attitude. I once asked him what the silvery stuff was in fillings. I guess I looked surprised when he told me it was lead. He answered my unasked question about health safety and then added, 'I think your generation is great. You don't leave your lives open to question marks. You challenge everything and that's good. It'll make us better doctors who'll be more aware and better skilled in dealing with people. The profession won't be so exclusive. We'll earn the respect that used to be attached to the oath we took as doctors.'"

Steve smiled. "He's right. We're not supposed to cover up when we see someone bungle up a job. That rule used to irritate me when I started in medicine. I used to feel that we're only human, but it didn't take me too long to realize that not only do you step in to prevent a mistake when you see it happening but you also report it. It's what makes you and the other person a better doctor. It's a way of policing ourselves. No group should be above scrutiny."

Jeneil smiled. "Those humanity students may protest, but they are serving a purpose. They're the conscience of society. They're necessary, too."

Steve nodded. "Dr. Sprague calls it the refiner's fire."

"I agree with him," Peter said. "If you can't take the heat then you probably don't belong there at all. And we're all asked to accept these differences and blend them into a creation called civilization." Steve nodded.

Jeneil was quiet then added, "It's difficult in the arts. The vacillation between issues can be unnerving. Seeing both sides and forming a decision or judgment on polar issues is difficult. The humanities can't be as blind as justice in law or as exacting as science in reasoning. The arts deal with the inner man and his struggle with the ebb and flow of life around him. That's why I love literature. It's a journal of civilization's history. You get to see the full mosaic pattern of humanity develop if your studies are broad enough." She sighed.

Steve looked at her. "Jeneil, with that kind of passion and insight maybe you should be teaching."

"That's possible, honey," Peter commented. "I never look twice at history or reading, but you make it interesting."

She shook her head. "Uh-uh, I don't relate well to teenagers and that's the age group that gets introduced to my style of literature and history. Those were my trauma years. The hormonal frenzy makes me crazy and their short-sightedness infuriates me. I don't have the stamina for it. I have trouble with most of my peer group. When I was in college, I related to my professors instead of the students. As I get older it's easier, but not comfortable."

"Except in the arts, Jeneil," Peter said. "Franklin in music, Robert in art, David in cinema…," he paused. "And Dennis."

"It seems to be a pattern, doesn't it?" she mused. "Except I don't play an instrument well. My art doesn't reach mediocre…."

Peter interrupted. "Dennis thinks you belong in theatre."

"But where?" She laughed. "I poke my nose into everything there. I love the whole thing." She sighed. "Sometimes I think my place is in the corporation. There I get to use my interests in the bits and pieces of life by owning different companies. I could buy a theatre and oversee the whole thing then I wouldn't need to specialize." She quieted and watched the flame flicker on the candle.

Steve looked at Peter. They both looked at her. "You're trying really hard to find Jeneil," Steve said sympathetically. "Why don't you just let her evolve?"

"I can live with that," Jeneil said, "but society can't. I like my life right now. I really do. But society wants to know why I work at what is considered a menial job although I have a higher education. Society wants to know why I'm not willingly and enthusiastically running the corporation. Society wants to know why I'm in love but not married." Peter looked at her. Jeneil noticed. "Uncle Hollis, Peter, not you."

"Does Jeneil have any answers for all those 'why' questions?" Steve asked.

"None that society can understand, but I'm comfortable with them. I want Jeneil to evolve uninterrupted and uninfluenced by the demands on her. And even I know that statement sounds adolescent, but I think I'm dealing with arrested development. My life experience was on hold during high school and college. When I quit college, life opened up for me. Society says, Jeneil you're almost twenty-three, get your life together. And Jeneil is screaming I'm not twenty-three in life, I'm only a year old." Peter and Steve looked at each other and smiled. "My life is a chess game. My job at the hospital is a pawn, the foundation is the knight, the corporation a bishop, and they all defend the rook and queen because her secret is that the king is missing and Jeneil's out looking for it before someone calls check."

"That was funny, Jeneil," Peter laughed.

Steve laughed, too. "Kid, you're too brainy. You need to be stupid like the rest of us. Then you could specialize or not give a damn."

"You two aren't stupid. I'm in awe of what you have achieved with what you have been given. I'm very impressed. No, you two aren't stupid at all. It has to be something else. How did you decide to become a doctor, Steve? I'm curious how a boy sitting in an orphanage decides he wants to be a doctor and achieves it. How?"

Steve lowered his head and drew in a breath. "Jeneil, you really don't want to know."

Peter gave a half smile, understanding Steve's reluctance.

"What? Another street gang?" she asked, looking at Peter, hoping for an explanation.

Steve looked up at her then at Peter. He shook his head. "No, well we were on the streets and we were a gang, but not like the Dragons." Steve closed his eyes and put his head back, debating with himself. "Will you promise I get dessert before you throw me out?" Peter laughed at the question.

Jeneil watched Steve steadily. "Gosh, now I'm very curious. You can have two desserts and I won't throw you out."

Steve rubbed the back of his neck, feeling tense. "Well, some of the older kids at the home organized into a group. We didn't have time to get involved in street gangs because we were too busy traveling uptown to the better neighborhoods or shopping areas to pick pockets."

Jeneil stared openly in shock. Steve put his head down to avoid looking at her. "You organized? Who organized you?"

"An adult worker at the home." Jeneil closed her eyes and rested her lips on her fist. "I told you that you didn't want to know." Steve sighed, concerned about how she'd react to the rest of the story.

Jeneil looked up at him. Her voice was tight with emotion. "How did you make the connection from.that to wanting to become a doctor?"

"Jeneil, honestly, it isn't even nice," he said quietly. "I shouldn't have started this."

"Please tell me." She touched the arm he had resting on the table. He took a deep breath and exhaled.

"One day during Christmas season I was assigned to work the Dighton area. I hated that area. You never made decent money there and I wanted a racing bike for Christmas."

Jeneil choked up and bit her lower lip, hoping to avoid crying.

"The weather was cold, the snow was merry, and I was freezing. I had picked twelve pockets and netted only three hundred dollars and a ton of credit cards."

Jeneil's eyes widened. "Only three hundred?" she repeated, amazed.

Steve was getting into the story. Once the confession started, he didn't hold back. "The plastic money wasn't any good to me. Beck was an adult; he could buy things with the cards before the cards got cancelled. But I was planning on skimming some of the cash and turning the rest in. Beck always expected cash. It's how he judged your honesty. He had assigned me to Dighton for skimming off too much cash from my last area. He expected skimming, that was smart, but too much skimming was greedy and he punished you for it."

Jeneil closed her eyes. "Honor amongst thieves," she murmured. Steve looked at her. She was embarrassed. "I'm sorry. It's a phrase from literature. Go on."

"I went into a diner for some coffee to get warm and I sat in a corner booth looking at all the plastic money. The cards were from Dr. Jones, Dr. Smith, Dr. This, Dr. That, and I thought to myself those sons of bitches are deliberately carrying only a little cash because of me. They're smarter than I am. They had membership cards to this club and that place, and I sat there with their plastic money which they would report stolen and cancel. I had a mere twenty-five dollars from each of them, if that for all my efforts. I was stealing from them and stealing from Beck. I had to hide my money and what it bought me from the people at the home or they'd get suspicious. Then I saw clearly that my life was stealing, hiding, and freezing. That's when I realized that the only ones enjoying themselves and laughing at me were those smart-assed doctors in Dighton. Beck couldn't openly show what his crimes were netting him either. How would he explain it? No. The doctors were the smart ones. They'd report the theft and take a tax write-off. It was costing me more to steal than it was for the doctors to lose it. I decided that I was on the wrong side of the street working for the wrong team. That's when I turned my grades around, and my plans, and headed to medicine."

Jeneil smiled. "And you stopped stealing?"

Steve stared at her and smiled, almost laughing at her simplicity. He shook his head. "Jeneil, that wasn't a fairy tale, that's a true story. Believe me, I wasn't noble. There was no way to get out of the gang without big trouble in the home and with the cops. I had been in it since I was five years old."

"What!" Jeneil nearly stood up from the shock. "How could that be? I was still fumbling with crayons at five. How could you pick pockets?"

Peter laughed and Steve shook his head, not believing her innocence. "You're priceless. You really are. At five years old, Beck had me as part of a singing group to attract a crowd. The older kids would work the crowd and the singers would collect the money people tossed."

"When did you get out of that mess?" she asked, almost shaking.

"When I graduated from high school and went away to college. I was no longer a ward of the state. I was legally on my own."

Jeneil stood up quickly. "I'll get dessert."

Steve stared at Peter. "I shouldn't have told her," he said, embarrassed and then he chuckled. "Well, at least I'll get dessert." He shrugged.

Peter slouched in his chair and rested his ankle on one knee. He was concerned. He knew Jeneil was upset and he wondered what would happen next. Jeneil returned with a piece of apple pie for each of them. Steve noticed her hand shaking slightly as she put his before him.

He sighed. "Jeneil…."

"I'm not having dessert," she interrupted. "Excuse me."

They watched her walk to the living room. Steve went to get up but Peter signaled him to sit. Jeneil threw a cushion between the potted plants.

Steve looked at Peter with a puzzled expression. Peter held up his hand signaling Steve to wait. Snapping the cassette player from the shelf, Jeneil grabbed a cassette from the cartridge and sat on the cushion. Leaning against the wall, she closed her eyes. The music began; loud, angry classical music that seemed to rage.

Steve looked at Peter. "Well, I don't need that interpreted for me." He sighed and sat back in his chair, discouraged and wishing he hadn't told her. "I'd better leave."

"Let her work it out," Peter answered. "Let's see what happens."

Neither one ate dessert. They sat and listened to the angry music that filled the room. Steve turned to watch Jeneil. She was crying. "I can't stand it anymore," he said, getting up and walking to her. Peter rubbed his forehead and stood up slowly, hoping for the best. Steve crouched in the small space near the potted plant, getting as close to her as he could. "Jeneil, now I'm really sorry that I told you but please at least stop crying before I leave. I can't stand it."

Steve was surprised with himself. He had never exposed so much of his feelings to a woman. But it was what he felt. It's what he wanted to say.

"Do you really have to leave?" she asked, wiping her tears and taking his hand gently.

"You don't want me to leave?" he asked, completely surprised. Peter was amazed at what he was hearing.

"No, I realize that I must look bizarre to you, but I'm so angry at Beck right now that I think I could strangle that piece of social vermin with my bare hands. I hate him! This music will help me to calm down. Once I deal with my anger over that cancerous blight on civilization, I'll be normal again. I can't tolerate parasitic slime, especially the kind that feeds off children. I'm sorry." She sighed and wiped a stray tear. Peter joined them, sitting on the other side of her, fascinated by what was happening.

Steve squeezed her hand. "Wow, you lit majors get pretty fancy, don't you? I just called him an asshole and son of a bitch." Peter put his head down to stifle a laugh, not wanting to intrude on the moment. Jeneil laughed. Steve smiled. "Don't waste your time on him, beautiful. The anger isn't worth it. Besides, I owe him in a way."

"How do you figure that?" she asked in disbelief.

"He taught me to blend into crowds. I think that helped me at college when I wondered what I was doing there. Being a pickpocket, I developed nimble fingers. I'm great at sutures because of it." Jeneil put her head back and laughed, thoroughly enjoying the humor she found in his attitude. Peter choked up, so impressed with Jeneil for accepting Steve that the word love couldn't cover what he was feeling. The relief in Steve's expression was impossible to describe. She had accepted Steve with a background that he would never have expected her to understand. Something deep within him sighed in relief.

"You are funny, Steve Bradley," Jeneil said. "I can understand how you survived."

Steve studied her, still somewhat overwhelmed that she had taken the story as well as she had. He was touched to the depth of his heart and he was surprised by how much he wanted her to like him. "You're really special, Jeneil. Very, very special." Peter heard the sincerity in Steve's voice and he smiled as he looked from one to the other. The figurines in the potted plant caught Steve's eye. "What's this?"

"That's a village of elves," Jeneil answered.

Looking to another plant, Steve saw the figurines of the man and woman. "Well, I can guess who they are. But who's the witch?"

Jeneil looked at Peter and smiled. Peter took her hand with a gentle squeeze. "This is our Camelot," she answered, hesitating slightly. "The two people are on a quest to find the magical unicorn. The unicorn possesses the power to bring happiness in life. That's protected by gnomes." She pointed to another pot. Steve followed her directing finger and smiled.

"What's the witch doing with them?"

"We don't know yet, she just arrived. She'll be an obstacle to them to see if they can endure the quest."

"And who's the guy raging over there?"

Jeneil smiled slightly. "He's an ogre. He tormented the two for a while but they endured his raging just fine."

Seeing the snarling animal, Steve wrinkled his eyebrows. "That thing looks really vicious."

"Well, it hasn't approached them yet so we don't know how they'll handle that. It does look vicious. It's probably desperate. Most things that are desperate get vicious, even people. But right now the witch is entering their lives. Peter thinks she's sneaky so we'll have to see how they deal with subversion. The hobby started with the male gnome and it's developed into a story that keeps growing."

Steve looked from Peter to Jeneil. Taking her hand, he squeezed it gently. "You're both something else," Steve said sincerely. "You're cute as hell and you've gotten him hooked on helium, too."

Jeneil laughed. "You can't get hooked on helium, it's either in the blood or it isn't, but it's a necessary ingredient for the quest or you can't see the invisible unicorn. The heart won't be light enough otherwise."

"That's new," Peter said, laughing.

"It just got written." Steve watched her with growing fascination. "Why don't you two have your dessert now?" Jeneil suggested.

"Join us?" Steve asked.

Jeneil shook her head. "I need a little longer here." Steve studied her face. "Just for a few loose ends, I promise," she added, noticing his concern.

"Okay," he said, standing up slowly.

Peter leaned toward her and kissed the hand she had resting on her knee. "You're beautiful, kid. I mean that."

"I love you, Peter." She touched his face lovingly. Steve watched and smiled, and noticed the slight ache that passed through his chest.

Peter and Steve returned to the table and their desserts. Jeneil replaced the cassette tape of classical music with Elton John's *Sad Songs*. She folded her arms and paced slowly while listening to it. Then, sitting in a chair, she settled in for the rest of the tape as it played the same song again and again.

Steve looked at Peter with a puzzled expression. "The whole tape is that one song?"

Peter smiled. "Music brings her around. The song cheers her up."

Steve looked over at Jeneil. She was so beautiful.

Peter watched her then smiled. His grandfather was right; she was a songbird, fragile and sensitive.

Twenty-Four

Peter and Steve walked from the OR together.

"You got hit for a double, didn't you?"

"Yeah," Peter answered, stretching his back muscles.

"I can cover for you if you want to leave."

Peter shook his head. "I'd better not. You're liable to be hit tomorrow and it's not smart to work doubles back to back. Are you feeling lost?"

"Cooped up." Steve sighed. "Maybe I should get a motel room for the night just for a change of scenery. Every so often restlessness sets in."

"Meet me in the lounge. I have to let Jeneil know I'm working."

"Okay," Steve answered, heading for the locker room.

Peter dialed. Jeneil answered quickly.

"Hi, honey. What are you planning for tonight?"

Jeneil paused. "Peter, every time you ask that question you've been asked to work a double."

"That's why I'm calling."

"Aha, I thought so."

He hesitated.

"Peter, is something wrong?"

"No, not wrong really, but…."

"What is it?"

"Steve needs a change of scenery."

"Will coming here help?"

"I'm sure it will. Do you mind?"

"Well I'm going to the playhouse until nine, but he can come for dinner and then stay on until I get back. How is that?"

"You're terrific, baby. Honest."

"I know. Isn't it wonderful just to watch me in action?" she asked, jokingly.

Peter laughed. "He offered to cover my double just for something to do, but he could get hit tomorrow."

"I understand, really."

"Can you call and ask him?"

"Ooo, Peter…I…well, alright, I guess. I'll cover the telephone mouthpiece to disguise my voice. What floor?"

"Third, and honey, I love you for this, I really do."

"Oh no you don't, I want the favor repaid my precious love."

Peter was surprised. "Okay. How?"

"You call your grandfather and invite him here for an evening, including dinner."

Peter smiled and shook his head. "Baby, what feeling goes beyond love?"

"Gosh, worship I suppose. Why?"

"Then that covers what I feel for you."

"Ooo, the flattery you're learning is sinful," she teased.

He laughed. "I'll call Grandfather. What night for dinner?"

"How about Friday?"

"I'll get back to you. I love you sweetheart, I do." He meant it with everything he had in him at that moment. He wanted to hold her.

"Okay, Peter. I'll call Steve soon. I'll miss you though."

"Good," he answered, "me, too. Bye, honey." He hung up and dialed again. He recognized his mother's voice. "Mom, is Grandfather home?"

"Yes, he is. How are you, Pete?"

"Doing fine. We're busy at the hospital. Vacations make it tough. I'm working a double tonight."

"That's too bad. Be sure to rest when it's over. You looked so good the last time you were here it would be a shame to ruin that. And stop by soon. I'll get Father."

His mother was obviously in a hurry and he was glad for that. He had been wondering what to talk to her about next.

"Peter," his grandfather answered, "is something wrong?"

"Am I that bad at calling?"

"We don't see you too often. I thought it was decided that coming here would help by seeing the change."

"Grandfather, is my mother right there?"

"Of course not, she and Tom have company. Peter, I'm not senile, just old."

Peter chuckled. "You're not that either and I'm sorry but I'd like to postpone the news there for as long as possible."

"You're being foolish, Peter. Prepare the way as much as you can. Everything will help in the long run."

"I guess I don't believe it will. That's why I avoid dealing with it."

"Peter, doing nothing only leaves everything to chance."

"That sounds fine to me. Chance sounds a long way off."

"I can tell I'm talking to deaf ears. Why did you call me?"

"Well, Jeneil would like you to come to dinner Friday and spend the evening with us." Peter felt pride swell in his chest. It felt great to invite his grandfather to visit. He liked that feeling. It sounded settled.

"Peter that sounds so…normal."

Peter laughed. "I know. I'm surprised, too." He could tell his grandfather was pleased. "Will you come? Jeneil felt bad about missing the other visits with me."

"Peter, she's such a good choice for you. I'm still speechless that you chose her."

"Does that mean you'll come?"

"Of course, I'm honored by your invitation. It was wonderful to be invited by my son when he began his own family, and now to have an invitation from my grandson. Continuity in my family has become important to me. Being patriarch is a custom I wish I had learned to preserve through the years." He paused, and Peter was surprised at how deeply his grandfather felt about his family continuing on. He was glad that Jeneil had invited him.

"Then I'll be by after work at seven on Friday to get you."

"Fine, I'll be ready. I'm looking forward to the evening. Send my thanks." Peter heard the call disconnect and replaced the receiver.

He smiled. "Baby, you keep adding to the list of reasons why I love you so much."

Peter quickly walked to the doctor's lounge. Steve went to answer the telephone as Peter walked in. Steve signaled to him.

"It's Sunshine for you," Steve said, holding out the receiver.

"Sunshine?" Jeneil asked, laughing.

Steve heard her. "It's your code name around here."

She laughed again. "Actually I'm calling you."

"Me?" Steve didn't try to hide his shock.

"Yes, can you come to dinner tonight? I'd hate to waste Peter's since he's working a double. You can watch TV or a video or just relax here while I go to the playhouse for a little while. What do you think?"

"Peter set this up, didn't he?"

"Well, he suggested the invitation but the details are mine. I'd like you to come to dinner and then stay."

"You don't have to do this." He was embarrassed.

"Steve, what's family for?"

The word passed through Steve like electricity.

"Please come, Steve."

Steve looked at Peter questioningly. Peter nodded and smiled. "Okay," Steve answered quietly.

"Good, dinner at six-thirty?"

"That's fine," Steve answered. "And thanks a lot."

"See you then."

"Here's Pete." He handed the receiver over.

"Honey, my grandfather said yes to Friday."

"Oh terrific!" He heard the genuine excitement in her voice.

"You really pleased him with the invitation."

"This is great! I'll make it special, I promise."

Peter smiled. "I'll see you at eleven-thirty."

"I love you, Peter. Things seem to be running so smoothly. I can't believe it. See you at eleven-thirty." He heard the click and hung up, too. Steve had gotten coffee for them and was sitting at a table. Peter sat down.

"You shouldn't have done that, Pete."

"I wanted to." Steve shook his head and looked down at his coffee. Peter could tell that he was touched.

"She's something else," Steve said. "I've never met anyone like her. It's hard to believe that she's real, but she keeps proving it."

"I know. She keeps impressing the hell out of me, too. I am so crazy about her. Sometimes I can barely stand it."

Steve smiled. "That's great. It's great to even watch it. What are you doing for her birthday?"

Peter shrugged. "I checked with her friend, Adrienne. No one has known her long enough to have celebrated a birthday with her. It seems like we're all fairly new to her life. I think she's right, her life did start a year ago."

"Where's her family?"

"They're gone. She's alone except for an appointed uncle who takes the job as seriously as if she was a blood relative."

"Then how will you handle her birthday?"

Finishing his coffee, Peter folded the foam cup. "I think I'll leave it up to her. I'll ask her what she wants."

"Would you mind if I get her a gift? She's been great to me."

Peter smiled. "That's okay with me. I understand. I'd better get back on duty." He stood up. "Now if only the hospital will cooperate so I can celebrate it with her."

*****

Jeneil opened the front door to an embarrassed Steve Bradley.

"Hi, come in," she said, smiling warmly.

He stepped inside awkwardly with his hands in his jean pockets. "I'll have to watch what I say around Peter from now on."

"Why, do I still make you uncomfortable?"

Steve's throat tightened. "No, I didn't mean that."

Jeneil put her hand to her mouth in surprise. "Steve Bradley! You're blushing!"

Steve could feel himself get hotter. He cleared his throat and fidgeted. "Boy, you sure don't waste words."

Jeneil chuckled. "I'm sorry, but it's such a shock to see Mr. Tough blush."

"Mr. Tough, huh?" he questioned, smiling.

She giggled and put her hands on his shoulders. "Listen Elmo, your secret's safe with me.

Nobody but us cousins will ever know."

He laughed. "Who'd believe you?"

"Shucks, if that ain't true. You are one mighty big surprise you know."

"Yeah, well the feeling's mutual," he laughed. "You're a total shock to me."

"Don't feel embarrassed. I'm really glad you're here. Let's have dinner."

Steve followed Jeneil to the kitchen. She noticed that he didn't need any help; he was a natural.

"Where did you get your kitchen training?"

"The home," Steve answered matter-of-factly.

"Your wife will love your kitchen skills."

He grinned. "Why? I can't cook, I can only help."

"That counts, that counts." She handed him a celery stick. He helped bring dinner to the table and held her chair for her. Impressed with his manners, she smiled as she sat down.

Steve proved to be as equally good at dinner conversation as he was at helping in the kitchen and she began to understand why women were attracted to him. He had a polished side to him that she found attractive. Add that to incredible good looks and a body that he displayed comfortably, and the package was definitely far above average. She smiled to herself, wondering how much Peter had learned from Steve. She decided there were similarities but the two men were definitely their own persons. Peter had rougher edges while Steve was almost too studied. With his well-chiseled features, piercing blue eyes and well-styled blonde hair, Jeneil could understand all the fuss over him.

Jeneil realized how her negative opinion of him had blotted out his finer qualities. She decided he must still be uncomfortable with her because he was still presenting a varnished social side to her now. She was disappointed; she thought she had repaired most of the damage between them. If he was going to be family, she had to set things right. She didn't want the veneer; she wanted him to be himself around her, the way he was with Peter. The telephone rang, bringing her from her thoughts.

"Mr. Bowers, how are you? Oh, that's too bad. Has she started on the medication? Good, that should help soon. Well, please don't worry about the playhouse. We can reassign the work. She needs to get well. Your son and his family will be visiting soon. Summer colds can be so exhausting. Sure, you just concentrate on getting her well. No, really, she needs you more than the prop department does right now. You stay with her. If I can help at all be sure to call me. Yes, that's fine. Thank you for calling. Bye."

Jeneil returned to the table and glanced at Steve who was still sitting in his chair, bound by politeness. Hitting his arm gently, she grinned. "Hey man, looks like you're stuck with me. My plans just got crushed. But I'll tell you honestly that your Sunday manners are making me edgy. Are you trying to out-class me? Don't try to impress me; I don't sign your paycheck. But I'll tell ya, anymore of deez Sunday manners of yours an' I'm gonna do opera to relax, is dat clear? You tryin' ta out calls me man?"

Steve, stunned by her words, put his head back and laughed. "Oh geez, was I that bad?" He laughed again, trying to regain his composure.

Jeneil smiled. "No, not at all, but you're dealing with someone who wears costumes and pulls out manners for foundation teas and business meetings. I recognized the veneer. Why are you using them with me?"

"Wow, you go for exposed nerves kid."

"Exposed nerves?" she asked, puzzled. "Does that mean you're touchy around me?"

"Well, I've never had dinner alone with someone whose background is so cultured. I guess I was playing to that." He shook his head, embarrassed.

Jeneil sat back in her chair and folded her arms. "Cultured, huh? Bradley, you're on thin ice right now," she said sharply. "Do you know the definition of cultured?" she asked, pretending to glare at him. "Cultured: one, a state of civilization, a high level of development; two, the growing of bacteria and the product of such culture. Now which is it? Are you calling my parents vermin?"

"You're weird."

She smiled. "That's better. But the word is eccentric: one, a contrivance to transform rotary to linear motion. You were in a strange social conflict with your manners and before our lines of communication could be opened to linear, I had to change that."

Steve laughed. "You're manipulative then."

"Only if you surround it by ethics. You said I was cultured, remember?"

"Brainy, too."

"Takes one to know one," she defended.

He smiled. "Definitely weird."

"Eccentric," she corrected, "two, which means off-center."

"Agreed," he smiled, "definitely off-center."

"Good, I knew you didn't mean three, a queer and erratic person." Jeneil laughed lightly. "Do you play board games?"

He laughed. "Not Scrabble with brainy wenches, that's for sure."

"I'm over twenty-one. A wench is a girl or young woman."

"I wasn't speaking chronologically."

"Ooo, have you ever been hit with a board game by a mental wench?"

He laughed and sat forward. "You win."

"I thought you'd see it my way."

Jeneil stood up and began to clear the table. Steve smiled, shook his head and stood up to help her. The evening went very well after that. Jeneil pulled out the backgammon board and they reviewed the rules, each having become rusty from not playing for a while. The game was full of fumbles, but each enjoyed renewing the skills they had lost. It absorbed both of them and their conversation was easy.

Jeneil yawned. "I like you, Peter's friend. I've decided that you can't be the hospital Steve Bradley."

He smiled. "I like you too, Peter's lady, better than the hospital Jeneil."

"We feel sorry oh gosh we do for that poor girl. She has a tough role."

"Who's we?" Steve asked.

"Irish, Nebraska, and Jeneil; my three selves."

"You're sure about being eccentric?"

"Well, I do avoid being tested."

Peter opened the front door to the apartment. "What are you guys up to?" he asked, closing the door behind him.

"Backgammon," Jeneil replied, then signaled Peter to bend. She kissed his cheek, and he gently squeezed the back of her neck.

"How was the shift?" Steve asked.

"Busy but sane. I was in the ER." Peter sat on the hassock and rubbed his face. "I'm wearing down."

Steve got up. "I didn't realize it was this late. I'd better go."

"Stay over," Peter suggested as a yawn escaped.

"Is that okay?" He looked at Jeneil.

"Fine."

"Aw, come on. Really Steve, take a break from the dorms for a night. That's why I'd go home some nights. It helps to get away."

"Yeah, it does," Steve agreed.

"Then that's settled," Jeneil said, standing up. "Put your car in the lot near Peter's for the night. I'll get your bed ready."

Steve returned to find that his bed had been prepared, complete with pajamas, which had been folded neatly, sitting on the blanket next to a robe. He smiled at Jeneil's little touches. Returning to the living room, Jeneil came from the kitchen with three mugs on a tray. Peter came from the bedroom in his robe and pajamas.

"I made some Ovaltine," she said, setting the tray on a small table near the kitchen. Sitting on a chair, Peter joined her.

"Ovaltine?" Steve laughed. "It sounds so square."

Jeneil looked at him. "For espresso, you go to Italy. For coffee, it's the diner two blocks over. Here and right now, it's Ovaltine. Park it, Bradley," she ordered, pointing to the third chair.

Steve smiled and sat down. "I guess it's okay. It hasn't hurt Pete. He looks great."

*****

Jeneil went about her morning routine while both Peter and Steve showered for work with time left for breakfast. She brought the power shakes and banana bread to the small table with juice, all on one tray.

Steve was impressed. "You're better than McDonalds for speed."

"As long as my microwave, freezer, and blender work, Peter will survive my cooking."

Laughing, Steve finished and stood up to leave. "Jeneil, you're terrific. This has been a good break for me. Thanks a lot. I'll see you two at the hospital."

Peter stood up as Jeneil came from the kitchen. "He forgot his lunch." Jeneil put the bag near Peter's.

Peter smiled and put his arms around her. "I want to say thank you but it isn't enough."

"Then add a kiss to it."

Peter kissed her, holding her close to him. "I love you so much for so many reasons."

She smiled and touched his face lovingly. "Me, too."

He kissed her again then pulled away and cleared his throat. "Oh man, I'd better get to work."

"I'll wait up if you work another double!" She grinned.

"Ooo, sweetheart you even read minds." He smiled, kissed her cheek then left.

Twenty-Five

Jeneil buzzed about all week, clearly excited about having Peter's grandfather coming to visit. Peter smiled at her excitement. "You're going to be exhausted by the time he gets here tonight," Peter said, finishing breakfast. "You've polished, scrubbed, and cooked. Even the wood in the front hallway is polished."

"I hired help for that. But he's special. He's our royalty." She smiled and hugged him.

Peter laughed. "He'd like to hear that. At least his ancestors would, I guess."

"Aren't you excited? I'm hoping this evening will help him accept us. I mean really accept us as a couple. And accept me as part of his family line. That's exciting, Peter."

He held her. "Jeneil, baby, learn to care that it's enough that I accept you, that we accept each other, that we are a family line, ours."

"Oh you," she said, pulling away gently, "you're so negative. Why can't you see that this beginning could affect the future positively? Our future with your family."

Peter smiled and shook his head. "You're like my grandfather. That's just how he talks about minor things."

"There you are. He knows superlative is achieved by small building blocks. You see that, he understands superlative."

He kissed her lips lightly. "I love you, beautiful. I'll pick him up after work and be here by seven-thirty."

She hugged him tightly. He loved her enthusiasm and held her closely.

*****

Peter closed the front door after his grandfather and wondered what was in the package that he had guarded since picking him up. They walked up the stairs together and Peter could tell the old man wasn't missing much. Maybe Jeneil had been right to treat this so special. Peter unlocked the apartment door. He was stunned for a minute. The lighting was low with candles burning in several places and Chinese music played on the stereo. Peter and his grandfather looked around. Peter was overwhelmed.

"Hi," Jeneil said quietly, entering the room behind them. Peter turned to comment on the atmosphere but instead was stunned by Jeneil's outfit. She was wearing a long deep blue dress with red embroidery near the throat. It looked Chinese and she looked terrific. Peter smiled, stunned into silence. He had never seen her as Chinese before. The image touched his heart deeply.

"Jeneil, you look very nice and your home reflects your love," the grandfather said, absorbing every detail.

"Mr. Chang, it's my pleasure to welcome you to our home. Thank you for being gracious and honoring us this way." She hugged him gently.

Peter noticed his grandfather took her hug in stride. He was getting used to the songbird, too.

"No, Jeneil, I can see that I'm the one being honored here tonight. You've gone to a lot of trouble and preparation."

Jeneil held her hand to her throat, seeming to relax, and sighed, "I really didn't know if I was committing a cultural or social blunder here by daring to even presume a Chinese atmosphere, but my interest in Chinese customs and culture is sincere. Since studying China's history, I've developed a deep interest. This is all meant to be complimentary. Thank you for seeing that."

The grandfather smiled; pleased someone so young would care about gentility and not even be Chinese. "I'm definitely not insulted. This is all a great compliment. You've captured the essence of the old ways. I can feel that. And I'm impressed to see that they fit so well into modern surroundings. I'm curious now why my children haven't seen this possibility. They are into early American, colonial or provincial." He smiled. "To them, China is something you put on the table to hold food. No, this is a great compliment." He turned to study the rest of the room, smiling with enjoyment.

Jeneil looked at Peter and gave a look of relief. He put his arm around her, smiling broadly. "Thanks," he whispered. "I can tell he's pleased."

The grandfather turned to Jeneil. "You've studied about Africa, too?" he asked, wondering about a wall grouping.

"No, the collection is from a friend of my parents. She taught me about civilizations. Those are Christmas and birthday gifts from her. I like their artistic values, as well as their cultural meanings."

He smiled warmly at her and then looked at Peter. "I'm amused that life has given my grandson a woman who will teach him so much. He thought school was a place to learn what rival gangs were up to."

Peter shrugged. "Hey, I called it as I saw it."

Jeneil smiled. "Mr. Chang, I saw school as a war zone, too. Anything I've learned about life and people, I've learned from my parents and our friend, Mandra. They taught me how to learn and discover. I only went to school to obey the law. I wasn't happy there."

Peter laughed, pleased by Jeneil's remark. "You see grandfather, I'm amused that life has given me a woman who understands and likes Chang."

"Chang?" the grandfather asked.

"Yes, the one you call 'the boy.'"

The grandfather raised an eyebrow, surprised Jeneil had uncovered that side to Peter. "That's interesting. You told me that he was gone."

Peter looked at Jeneil and grinned. "She won't allow him to stay buried."

"Of course not. You can't be Dr. Peter Chang without him, can you? Besides, I like Chang. He has an honorable spirit."

The grandfather chuckled. "You're right, Jeneil. I often thought that Peter would change his last name to Dragon if he could."

Peter and Jeneil laughed.

The old man held out the package he was carrying to Jeneil. "I understand your note now."

"Oh, thank you!" She smiled, holding back her excitement.

"What note?" Peter asked, confused, looking from one to the other.

Ignoring his question, Jeneil changed the subject. "I'm forgetting to be a hostess here. Let's get comfortable in the living room. What can I bring to drink?"

The grandfather smiled. "A small glass of any juice if you have it."

"I'll be right back," she said, going to the kitchen.

"What note?" Peter repeated.

The old man grinned. "Peter, you're twenty-five. Your patience should be more highly developed by now. It's her evening. Let her present it the way she's planned it."

Jeneil returned with drinks. "Dinner is just about ready so if you'll excuse me, I'll put it together."

Peter watched her leave, still curious about the note. His grandfather watched him. "Still haven't learned about songbirds have you? She's still responsible for you. You're lucky you have such an intelligent songbird. Catch up Peter, catch up."

Peter looked at his grandfather puzzled.

The grandfather smiled. "I'm impressed and surprised she looks so at home around Chinese ways. Even the dress belongs to her."

"She loves costumes. But she does look great in that dress, doesn't she?" He grinned, looking toward the kitchen.

The grandfather watched his grandson then shook his head. "That's not a costume, Peter. It's the result of deep understanding, caring, and love. She has a lot to teach you. Make sure you listen."

Peter stared at his grandfather. "You keep saying that. What do you mean?"

"Learn to listen with all your senses and instincts Peter, like she has. Be more observant. I really admire her family. The girl is a work of genuine art and in an era of pretense and forgeries they have a right to be proud of her."

"You like her a lot, don't you?" Peter asked with a sense of pride.

"I do, Peter, very much."

Peter smiled, enjoying the surge of love he felt for her as it filled his chest.

Jeneil brought a tray with dinner to the dining room. "We can share dinner now. Mr. Chang, my Chinese cooking skills are at a beginner's level. I've also kept the dinner simple because your grandson needs to develop a palate for it."

The grandfather looked at the food. "Jeneil, this is exactly what we ate when I was in China. My family was from the country. The more sophisticated dishes came from the big cities."

"Oh really?"

"Okay Jeneil," Peter laughed, "no more picking on me. Now that we know my chromosomes are those of a simple Chinese peasant, and that I'm proud of it, you can't change them."

Jeneil was completely surprised that Peter called himself Chinese. She looked at the grandfather, who smiled at her and raised his eyebrows. He was used to his grandson resisting Chinese so Peter's words pleased him. He continued to smile as he took his seat.

Dinner went smoothly. Peter liked the food, which surprised him, but it was food he recognized. He listened with amazement at all the information Jeneil uncovered about his grandfather, about the Chinese revolution and the effects it had on his family, and his struggle to fit in here and learn the language. Peter felt guilt rise to the surface as his grandfather explained his reason for working so hard to speak proper English and to learn good manners. He had worked his way from cleaning garbage buckets and floors to the well-mannered, well-polished man who welcomed people into the restaurant. He also told of how he learned to handle rude or drunken customers without losing the quick temper that always had him in trouble as a boy. He had wanted to get the job as maître de in one of the most elite Chinese restaurants in New York because it brought more money. The extra income helped improve conditions for his family and the medical benefits had been a blessing when his wife's health grew worse.

Peter almost choked on his guilt. He had always thought his grandfather's uppity ways were a result of selling out to the white people who owned the restaurant he worked in. He had always thought that his grandfather was a 'white puppet.' Now, viewing his grandfather as an adult, he judged himself as very immature while he was growing up. His lack of understanding of his family and his deliberate separation from them had cheated himself of a lot of what Jeneil had been given by her family. Lately Peter had noticed his grandfather cared deeply about family, but not as forcefully or as clearly as he did now that he took the time to really listen. He truly admired his grandfather.

Peter could tell Jeneil really liked his grandfather. Her attention was glued to his every word, absorbing everything in that special way of hers. He could tell the two had a common understanding, as if they were the two who were related by blood. He sat immersed in his thoughts as Jeneil brought dessert. "Uh-oh, what is it?" he asked, looking at it. "Those round green things look like unripe fruit whose seeds are going bad."

The grandfather sighed. "Oh Peter, my failings with you choke me at times."

Jeneil laughed. "Don't take it personally, Mr. Chang. Peter has improved a lot. At least he's stopped calling what doesn't look good to him garbage." She laughed again. "Peter, it's a steamed cake with a sweet sauce and mandarin orange sections. The green 'things' are sliced kiwi fruit. I promise you that it's fully ripe and not going bad."

The grandfather sighed. "Peter, there's a much more interesting world out there beyond just cornflakes. I thought you would turn into cornflakes." The grandfather shook his head. "Breakfast had to be cornflakes. Don't ever buy crispy rice cereal. Lunch was peanut butter and jelly, and dinner was a cheeseburger."

"I was bad," Peter said quietly, looking embarrassed.

Jeneil squeezed his hand, laughing. "You've improved quite a bit."

The grandfather smiled. "Malien always defended him. She'd say at least he's easy to please. Be grateful he's not like his mother who has to have the exotic, the best, and the most expensive."

Jeneil was surprised to hear that. She hesitated. "Are Peter and his mother very opposite?"

The grandfather thought a minute. "Hmm, now that I think about it, they're more alike than opposite."

"What! Grandfather, I am not like her."

The old man smiled. "Peter, you're as rigid in your ideas as she is in hers. Your tastes are opposite but your stub…rigidness is the same."

"Rigid?" Peter repeated. "She's stubborn. I at least try to listen to reason."

Jeneil touched his arm. "If you can be rigid, why can't she be? Why is she stubborn?"

The grandfather looked at Jeneil with interest. The wisdom in the question pleased him;

she was a peacemaker.

"Humph," Peter said, "you haven't met my mother."

"We're not talking about me," Jeneil argued. "We're talking about you. It's a form of name-calling. You allow you to be rigid, but she's stubborn."

Peter shook his head. "Yeah, well if you asked her she'd say she's rigid and I'm stubborn. She always puts me down. Ask my grandfather."

The grandfather looked at Peter compassionately. Jeneil had never heard Peter say his mother had put him down. He seldom even talked about her.

"How?" Jeneil asked quietly.

The grandfather looked at her. Peter looked up from his dessert, surprised by her question.

"Nothing I ever did was right. She didn't like my friends."

"Who did she want you to be friends with?"

Peter was again surprised by her question. The grandfather looked from one to the other with deep interest. Peter thought again. "Oh I remember now, those weirdoes who used to go to summer camps, the white puppets."

"Why did she want you to hang around with them?"

Peter stopped tapping his spoon on the placemat, looked up at her and grinned. "Hey, you're a lit major not a psychiatrist. Stop practicing without a license." He chuckled.

Jeneil shrugged. "Just curious." She stood up. "I'll get tea. But you have to admit it's an interesting question. Do you think she was worried that you might get hurt in the gang?" Peter stared at her. Jeneil changed her tone. "Did you know there are no Chinese fortune cookies in China? They're American. And the kiwi fruit is called the Chinese gooseberry. I'll go get tea."

Peter looked at his grandfather. "She thinks she's fooling me. She has this desire to spread peace and love amongst people. She doesn't know that she's met her match with my mother and me." He grinned and shook his head.

The grandfather smiled and returned to his dessert. Jeneil was a very skilled songbird with a tremendous capacity for love. Peter needed to grow to equal her. Grow so she'd be his.

Peter finished the last slice of kiwi fruit. "I thought that would be slimy. She's interesting to live with. She gets herself into more things." The grandfather sat back in his chair and smiled. "Grandfather, I'd like you to see her Great Wall of China."

"Great Wall of China? You mean she's made a replica?"

Peter laughed. "No, there's a long wall in the apartment and she's covered it with information about China and its people as she learns about them. It's her learning center.

She calls it her Great Wall of China. I know this is part of her campaign to get me into the culture, but the work she puts into it has impressed me. I've learned a lot about Chinese ways from it. Don't tell her, but I check it often for new material."

The old man was curious. Taking him to the hallway, Peter turned on the track lights. The old man stepped back to take it all in before studying it. "My gosh!" he said. "The work she's put into this is very impressive."

"Right now she's studying the different dynasties, and the effects the history and the economy had on social and moral development and artistic and scientific achievements. The Han Dynasty was apparently outstanding. See the achievements during that period of peace." Peter pointed to one section of the wall.

The grandfather looked closer. "Paper, the seismograph, medical advancements."

Jencil came from the kitchen.

"Jeneil, you've put a lot of work into this," the grandfather commented, smiling at her.

"I love this wall," she said sincerely. "It started out as a way to get Peter to appreciate his heritage, but it has become more to me. There's a pattern here. I can feel it. I want to check on the rest of the world during this time," she said, pointing to the Han Dynasty. "China was into trading and travel, and I'm wondering what the rest of the world was doing. I have my suspicions that if the rest of the world was uncivilized then what the traders brought back was negative and detrimental, which would leave a question of is that the catalyst for the decline in China and the increase of civilization in the rest of the world. There seems to have been a loss in the balance of Yen and Yang."

The grandfather looked surprised. "You know about Yen and Yang?"

"Only the rudiments, Mr. Chang, but that's next. I've uncovered a whole nest of books. There's something very familiar about what I've read. It's magnetized me. I'm drawn to it and I'd like to know why."

"What about your own ethnic background?"

She laughed. "Oh, my dad fed me leprechaun food. He loved Ireland. And my mother didn't have to teach me about her ancestors. History books at school were loaded with information and misinformation about the white English. They are what make America great if you listen to the narrow minded and misguided."

The grandfather was surprised at her cryptic words. "Is that what your father taught you?"

She laughed. "No, my mother, she was English." Peter and his grandfather laughed. "My father taught me about America. He had a passion for the real America with its struggles and foibles and noble ideals. There's no place to equal it he used to say. My mother insisted she was American, and I think she was a real American not descended from anything ethnic or related to the whole world. With what my father, my mother, and Mandra have left me, I'd need to live in the Smithsonian Institute to display it all.

Someday when I'm settled I'll bring it all out of storage. At times, there are pieces of art and collectibles I wish I could hold and look at." She sighed.

"Well, you certainly have gotten into China." The old man smiled with pleasure.

Peter put his arm around Jeneil. "Honey, with your interests, you need to live at the U.N. not the Smithsonian.

She laughed. "Tea is ready. I'll bring it to the living room."

"The girl is obviously intelligent, Peter. What did you say she does at the hospital?" the grandfather asked after Jeneil had left.

Peter looked at him, curious about his reaction. "She's a clerk in the records department."

"That doesn't quite make sense with her interests."

"It all makes sense to her, Grandfather. She's different."

"That she is Peter, and you are very lucky to have discovered her."

"She found me, Grandfather. She rescued me."

The old man looked at his grandson and chuckled. "That's a good word, rescued."

"It's true."

"I know." The grandfather smiled. "The bravest kind of rescue. She's rescuing a man from himself," and he walked to the living room.

Peter followed his grandfather to the sofa, thinking sometimes the old man seemed like her grandfather more than his.

Jeneil carried in a tray with a steaming teapot, cups, and saucers. Placing it on a low table, she sat on the other side of Peter's grandfather. She poured the tea into cups and handed them to the men.

"Peter, I wrote a note to your grandfather and asked him to bring photographs of your family tonight. I'd like to meet them, even if it's only through pictures."

The grandfather looked at her and was reminded of what she had yet to face. He slowly sipped his tea. She really was brave, maybe it was possible. He felt a little sad at the thought of the ugliness that might touch her. He wondered how he could help the situation. It was a thought he'd given a lot of time to and could only see the situation as explosive at the very least. He brought himself back to the moment as Jeneil handed him the package he had brought with him.

Opening the wicker basket, he smiled. "Jeneil, you are an exceptional young woman." She looked at him, surprised. "You give me the gift of a wonderful dinner like those of my childhood and early married years surrounded by an atmosphere that my ancestors would have shed tears over, and now as a crowning touch you ask an old man to talk about his own family and show you old photographs. You're full of magic."

Peter smiled at his grandfather's choice of the word magic.

"Right now I feel curious and excited," she said. "Do you have some of Peter?"

"Yes, a few."

"What?" Peter asked, sitting forward. "How could that be? Let me see them. There better not be any of me in a bathtub when I was too young to know my rights to privacy," he said, reaching for the basket.

Jeneil laughed and hit his wrist. "Wait your turn. Let the magic wicker basket reveal its treasures."

"Boy, it's hard to believe you're going to be twenty-three in a week. You act like a kid sometimes," Peter said teasingly.

"Better than being a spoiled brat like you," she joked.

"Oh, your birthday is soon. What date?" the grandfather asked.

"The twenty-sixth," Jeneil answered. The old man showed some surprise. "Why?"

The old man took a photograph of a young woman and a young man from the basket. "This is a picture of my wife and me," he said, handing it to Jeneil.

Jeneil took it, fascinated and treating it like gold. "Oh, she's beautiful."

"Turn it over," the old man suggested. Turning it over and reading the words, Jeneil looked up surprised and smiled broadly.

"What is it?" Peter asked.

"Your grandmother and I share the same birth date," Jeneil said excitedly.

"Really?" Peter asked, reaching for the photograph. "How about that!" He smiled, looking at it.

The old man brought the photographs out one by one and told stories from time to time about the people, the place or the situation. Peter was completely engrossed in the project. Jeneil smiled as she watched him. She had laughed at the photograph of the furrowed brow little boy with a birthday cake before him determined to be angry about the sentiment being shown toward him, and was touched by the photograph of his mother holding him in her arms as a young baby. Jeneil could see the love the young woman had for the young child. As Jeneil kissed his hand gently, she choked up. Peter had taken that one and studied it.

Peter looked up. "I can't believe that's me and my mother."

"I'd like to know what changed that," Jeneil said softly.

Peter grinned. "I learned to talk."

Jeneil and the grandfather laughed. Turning to see what was next, she gave a short gasp and grabbed a photograph which was partially buried.

"Chang," she whispered. "It's Chang!" she said, staring at a photograph of Peter sitting on some stairs. It was obvious he didn't know he was being photographed. His mind was far away, lost in thought. "What a fantastic photograph!"

The grandfather smiled, noticing the importance the photograph held for her.

"Oh wow! Where did that come from?" Peter asked, totally surprised. "I wouldn't let anyone take my picture past ten years old I think."

The grandfather looked at him. "Your mother took that picture. We had just moved here. You were still healing and faced one more operation. Your mother was so concerned and worried, and I remember her saying that she didn't even have any recent pictures of you. One day she gave that to me and said, 'Hide this from him for me. He'll destroy it if he finds it.' We couldn't get you out of that Dragon jacket. You were angry about moving and spent a lot of your free time doing that, sitting silently and thinking. I guess that's how your mother was able to photograph you. She cared a lot, Peter. She took your accident very hard. She was almost destroyed by Ki's death. She was sick all day after the funeral."

Jeneil watched as Peter stared at his hands. There was a question she wanted desperately to ask. She hesitated, wondering how to word it but something deep inside of her wanted to know if her suspicions were right. "Mr. Chang, why did you move here so quickly after the accident?"

"Jeneil, that street fight and what it did to Peter left us all shaken. My family was here already, but Lien had just gotten a very good job so her plan was to earn enough money to move from that neighborhood. I stayed in New York to be with my daughter and Peter. The neighborhood was changing and real low life was moving in. Most everyone we knew had since moved and Lien knew she was on borrowed time. Peter was nearly on his own anyway, we had very little control over him, but she stayed with her plan until the accident. Lien met Tom when we visited my son here. He was a widower and was very taken with Lien. When she announced they were getting married, we were all stunned as she'd never shown any interest at all in Tom. Without celebrations or parties Tom and Lien were married quickly and quietly. She said she didn't have the heart for a celebration with Peter hospitalized. She stayed in New York until Peter was released a month later then we joined Tom and his children here. Tom is a fine man. I don't think it's every man who would allow his new wife to lie apart from him for a month. I could have stayed with Peter until he was released but Lien wouldn't leave without him. Everything changed so fast. Tom found a place for us while we waited. He drove up to New York the day Peter was released and drove us here right from the hospital. None of us were sure what affect it would have on Peter, but he started doing well with his studies and we hoped he was as ready to leave as we were. He was angry about moving and he didn't get along with Tom's children, but he stayed with his studies. Dr. Davidson kept in touch with Peter, bringing him to New York now and then to visit. We weren't sure Peter would stay in medical school. He never did have much need for rules. Studying on his own was one thing, groups were another. Then he met Steve Bradley and he seemed to be able to reach Peter. Peter still believes he owes Steve the credit for his staying in medicine. And now he's met you. My grandson leads a charmed life lately. Coming here from New York has been great for Peter."

Jeneil smiled warmly.

"How did you two meet?" the old man asked.

Jeneil smiled. "A conveyor belt introduced us."

Peter laughed. "I was always in trouble over my medical reports. Jeneil sat me down and taught me how to avoid that trouble."

"Your good looks are understandable with the family you have. I've loved seeing these photos. Your family is so close. My mind has a hard time thinking of a group this size as a family."

"Don't you have any family?"

"No. Well I have cousins in Ireland, but I've never met them. We never got to Ireland as I got older. They took me there as a little girl, but I'm as old as their children. I remember my dad getting word when his father died and he flew to Dublin."

"Where is your mother from? You said she was American."

"She's from the east. Somewhere in Massachusetts. I've never met her family. I have furniture that my mother inherited from her grandmother but whenever I'd ask, she just said they weren't a close family. That surprises me now since she and my father had such strong opinions about families and getting along. I assume everybody is gone, possibly a cousin here or there. I think that's why I want a large family. I've always been fascinated by sisters and brothers because I didn't have any. And a friend of our family was the last of her line. I have trouble believing that a family can die out like that. I think it's wonderful that you all stay in touch and look after each other. That's warm and human."

The grandfather looked at Peter. Peter fidgeted. The old man smiled. "Well, sometimes the closeness can be too confining." Peter nodded in agreement. "It's good if a family can learn to allow for differences in individuals. My wife and I shocked our families by leaving China but my father always wrote. My wife's mother, too. We never got back. There was never enough money. I keep promising myself to go visit my brothers and sisters, but the money seems so much. My children want to make the trip a collective gift but I don't know, maybe someday. When you consider the cost to fly and the money to cover expenses, it's hard to change old spending habits."

Jeneil smiled. "Are you ever sorry you came here?"

The old man chuckled. "Oh my goodness, that's a question my wife and I chewed over many times. As a country, no. I was so proud the day we became citizens. We had heard about America from a distant cousin who came here. He visited China and told exaggerated stories of easy wealth and easy living. My wife and I were young and adventurous. Life certainly wasn't easy in China. It was hardly easy here, but there was a difference. My wife and I both felt that her health would have failed faster in China. There were people here who resented us coming to this country to live, but there were others who welcomed us. My bosses in the restaurant were like that. They helped us through red tape and laws, helping us to understand our rights and responsibilities. Their parents were immigrants. I'm glad I'm retired though. Their sons had taken over the restaurant and changes were being made. It wasn't easy to watch what was good being destroyed. The next generation just didn't have the pride and honor of their parents."

Jeneil watched him with interest. "That's another question we spend millions to understand, why the decline in tradition from generation to generation?"

"Well, with me, I allowed the struggle for money to interfere with tradition. When I finally sat down to look at it, my children weren't Chinese anymore."

"But your family are good, honest, hard working people."

"Oh yes, I taught that well enough. But they wouldn't understand what you have done here tonight. I think that impresses me the most. You're not Chinese yet you understand. To my grandchildren, I'm an old man who speaks of China because he's getting old and it's time to live in memories. I've neglected tradition, heritage, and my ancestors. To my children the Great Wall of China is in history books of a country far away. To my grandchildren the Great Wall of China is the hutch in their dining rooms. What will it be to their children?" The old man smiled at her and she gently took his hand. "This evening has been wonderful. I've seen a generation reach back to what's good from my ancestors. That gives an old man hope."

Jeneil smiled. "I've never seen it as noble; I just fell in love with your grandson and wanted to understand his heritage."

"What can be nobler than love as a motive?" The old man smiled and patted her hand. "Thank you for the whole evening and the Great Wall of China."

"You're welcome."

Peter watched them, fascinated by their closeness. His grandfather turned. "And now if you'll take me home, I'll add this evening to my book of memories." Peter stood up to get the man's jacket.

"You have a journal?" Jeneil asked.

"Yes, my last tribute to neglected ancestors. I have a book of family records, too. There are names going back for generations. I add to it at each end as my grandchildren marry and have their own children, and as I discover the names of ancestors."

"What an interesting idea. That's a great hobby."

"Oh Jeneil, it's more than a hobby. It's my hope that someone in the future of Changs will see it and ask why I've done it and then take the time to understand an old man's memories, and maybe understand the purpose for learning them." They both stood up as Peter came with his jacket.

"Mr. Chang, I love you." Jeneil smiled.

"Thank you, Jeneil. I love you, too." He smiled in return.

Peter watched, amazed. He had never seen his grandfather get that close to anyone.

Jeneil hugged the grandfather. "I hope you'll come to visit us again."

"I'd like that," the old man said as he walked to the door.

Jeneil watched as the car drove away. She went to the kitchen to wash dishes. Remembering the story of why Peter's family had moved here, she felt more certain her suspicion that Peter's mother got married to get Peter out of New York was right. The woman took on a heroic image in Jeneil's mind. The woman cared deeply about her son, she was sure of that. But what was the barrier? Had they lost their way when she had to leave him in order to make a living? There must be a strong driving force between them because that woman adored that baby. She could see that for herself just from a photograph. Cleaning the counter, she remembered the woman showing such gentle love toward the smiling, happy baby. What a beautiful, loving beginning she had given to Peter's life from an experience that had been so violent and degrading for her. She really liked that woman; she was exceptional. No wonder Peter wasn't ordinary; his grandfather was a sensitive, caring gentleman and his mother was a woman who loved her son deeply. She smiled thinking she'd discovered how Chang's heart got to be so gentle and her heart filled with love for him. She missed him and decided to be waiting for him when he got back.

Peter was out of breath from running up the stairs. The apartment was dark except for the bedroom. He smiled, went to the door, and leaned against the door frame. She waved her fingers sheepishly at him as she sat in bed.

"I've always loved your honesty, baby."

She smiled. "Tonight was so terrific that I missed you after you left. I need to be close to you."

"You read my mind." He smiled, undoing his shirt. He got into bed, facing her. "You're something else. You really are. My grandfather thoroughly enjoyed himself. You touched him with all you did tonight."

"Peter, I loved the whole evening, too. He's such a good man. The night wasn't all me, his stories and caring added to it. Those photos really cemented the magic and the one of Chang really did me in. Your mother really captured him on film. It's incredible!" She snuggled to him.

He kissed her forehead. "Yeah, what a sneak she is."

"Don't call her names. Not tonight anyway," she pleaded. "The woman I saw in those pictures loves her son very much. Let's just remember that tonight." She was silent as Peter held her in his arms. "Peter, I have a very strong feeling your mother got married to get you out of New York and into a stable home."

He looked at her. "I know it can seem that way, but she and Tom have a good marriage. I'm sure it was just a coincidence that she married him while I was in the hospital."

Jeneil smiled. "Well since we can never be sure why don't we just believe that she married to protect you?"

Peter was silent then quietly said, "I don't know that I want to owe her for that."

"Why would you owe her?" Jeneil asked, surprised. "She's not asking to be repaid. No one but your mother even knows for sure."

Peter took her hand. "I'd feel like I owe her."

"Why does that make you uncomfortable?"

Peter sighed. "Honey…," he paused. "I don't know, Jeneil. You have to see us together to understand what I mean. If I feel like I owe her big then I'd lose my footing when she attacks."

"Attacks?" Jeneil asked, again surprised.

"Yeah," Peter said, getting into a train of thought. "As long as I keep my distance she never feels free to muscle in. I know I might be displeasing her, but she can't reach me and she knows it so she never gets to the point of screaming. She's satisfied with jabs. I really don't like arguing with her, but she goes too far sometimes and yelling is the only way to push her off. As long as I'm being reasonable with her, she hammers at me and doesn't let up."

"What does she hammer at you about?"

Peter chuckled. "You're playing psychiatrist again."

"No, I'm not really. I'm very curious. It doesn't make sense that she's so unyielding. Where is she coming from? What's her motive?"

"You heard my grandfather quote my aunt. My mother has to have the best. I don't meet her standard for best." Peter was surprised by that thought; it was new.

"But she loves you. I really believe that."

"You wouldn't think so when she begins picking."

"What does she pick on?"

"Almost anything. I know one thing; Steve meets her standard for best more than I do."

"What?" Jeneil asked, completely surprised.

"It's true. Look at his manners, she'd say. He doesn't even come from a family and he's more polished than you are."

Jeneil's mouth opened in shock. "Oh my goodness."

"What?"

"I didn't count on her being superficial. They're tough to reach." She sighed, quietly thinking. "But there's a piece missing. Your grandfather isn't pretentious and your Aunt Malien certainly doesn't sound that way either."

Peter thought a minute. "You know something, they're not. It's just my mother who pulls out the 'my son, the doctor' routine. I've never noticed that before."

"Then why is she like that?"

"Who knows?"

Jeneil thought for a minute. "What about…," she stopped.

"What about what?"

She hesitated. "The rape," she answered softly.

"And me?" he added. Jeneil didn't answer. "I've always felt like I embarrass her."

"But now we've come full circle. We've come back to the fact that she loves you deeply and she chose to have you. No, we're missing it. Something is getting past us." She kissed him. "You and your mother are a tough puzzle."

He smiled. "Finally admitting defeat?"

"Never say die," she said, smiling. "Somewhere there lays the answer. We'll just keep our eyes open."

He kissed her gently. "How come you accept me? The real me?" She looked at him. The question touched her heart.

"The real you is superlative," she answered, then laughed lightly. "And I'm crazy about your tattoo."

He laughed then stopped as he caught the beauty in her smile. Kissing her warmly, he pulled her closer.

Twenty-Six

"I'll skip breakfast, honey," Peter said as he tied his shoes.

"Then I'll put cornbread in your lunch for coffee break," she said, handing him some juice.

"Listen, what about your birthday? How shall we celebrate it? A party? Private dinner? What?"

Jeneil smiled. "My goodness, my birthday is exciting this year. Adrienne invited me to dinner Friday, Tony asked me to dinner, my lawyer's taking me to lunch, and Bill is flying in Sunday from Asia and wants to take me to dinner."

"Got room for your man on that list?"

Jeneil smiled. "Would you really like to treat me for my birthday?"

"Of course."

"Then take me to Boston to do Christmas shopping. I can never find my way out if I get in or vice versa."

"Christmas shopping?"

"Yes, there are some nice galleries there and I've heard the International Marketplace is fun. I'm eating enough dinners. That would be a nice change."

"Well, Steve's the expert on the area. He was dating a girl in a college up there a few years ago. How about if he comes along then we know we won't get lost? I'll probably have to work Saturday night. He's asked about your birthday anyway. I'm sure he'd like to be part of it."

"That's fine with me as long as I get there. I've always gone by train but that gets me, and I've never been to the marketplace weary."

"Good, I'll work it out." He kissed her cheek. "Now I've got to beat it or get hung."

"I'll get your lunch bag."

*****

Peter joined Steve in the medical room halfway through his shift.

"Boy, this place has run me ragged today," Peter said, sitting down with a stack of reports.

"Me, too." Steve sighed. "You can tell a holiday is coming, the natives get restless. How did dinner with your grandfather go?"

Peter smiled. "That kid outdid herself. My grandfather was overwhelmed. The Great Wall of China all but did him in. He was crazy about her to begin with but last night cinched it." Peter shook his head. "She even picked up a Chinese dress to wear. She puts everything she's got into her plans. She looked so terrific."

"Sounds like the grandson was overwhelmed, too."

"I was and I still am."

Steve leaned against the table. "Wow, what's she done to you? Concerts, parties, art shows. You're even Chinese now. What will she have you into next?" he asked, smiling.

"Boston." Peter laughed. "And you're invited."

"What's going on in Boston?"

"Christmas shopping to celebrate her birthday."

"For anybody else that would be odd, for her it makes sense. Pete, I think I'll pass."

"Oh, no," Peter said, disappointed. "You're doing something else?"

"No, but I feel odd always hanging around."

"You're the only one not grabbing onto this family thing, man. And I'd like you to go with us so we don't end up in New Hampshire. You know the area."

"Yeah, but you guys don't need me butting into your lives all the time."

"Steve, trust me, our life is just fine. We like having you along. After all, come February you won't be hanging with us residents you'll be going for the platinum tongue depressors."

Steve laughed. "I'm counting the hours and minutes, too."

"Any word from Sprague?"

"I'm feeling pretty confident. Sprague's been slapping my back a lot lately. Jeneil's spy story is still working; my name is nowhere to be heard on the gossip line. Sprague's impressed, I can tell."

"There's your reason for going to Boston with us, you can thank her for the story. She's really high about going and there's some market in a suburb she wants to visit, too. We need you with us. I need you with us or I'll have to spend the day reading maps. Have a heart man," Peter argued.

Steve smiled. "Okay. You know she's fun, and she can still have fun doing nothing."

Peter nodded. "Yeah, that caught my eye, too. How about a movie, pizza, and beer tonight?"

"What, no Ovaltine?" Steve laughed.

"It's Saturday night and shift change. This day has me beat. I'd like to break loose and bum around." Peter stretched.

"What about Sunshine?"

"Can't we bring her?"

"She's not a pizza and beer type, is she?"

Peter laughed. "She'll drink ginger ale but she's flexible, Steve, honest. That's one thing I love about the kid. We stayed at this inn once and had a greasy cheeseburger for dinner at a highway diner then a tray of fancy desserts in the room with champagne. Really, she likes life at all levels. She's great like that."

Steve smiled. "I wouldn't mind a movie, and the pizza and beer sound great. I can feel myself relaxing already."

"Good," Peter said, standing up. "I'll get word to her. Why don't you come home with me after work?"

"Are you sure it'll be okay?"

Peter sighed. "How do I get through to you? You're part of Camelot. It's okay with her."

Peter joined Dr. Stevens on rounds then went to the telephone. He was glad he'd caught Jeneil. "Honey, Steve and I would like to go to a movie then out for pizza and beer tonight."

"Oh, okay."

"Want to slum with us?"

"Isn't it boys night out?"

"No, it's shift change and we want to bum out."

"Gosh, I'd like to see what you mean by that. Okay, I'll go."

Peter smiled at her willingness. "Can I bring Steve home with me after work for dinner?"

"Dinner? The pizza isn't going to be dinner?"

"No, at least I didn't think so."

"Then I'm glad you called and explained that. I'll just make sandwiches for dinner if we'll be eating pizza later."

"Make big sandwiches, honey. I'm starved."

"Even with pizza later?"

"Baby, this is bummin' out night. No limits. It's breakin' out."

"Oh," she said, confused. "I guess I haven't grasped what that means. I've never done Miller Time with guys. Okay, see you at seven-thirty?"

"About that," he answered. "See you then."

*****

Jeneil was in the kitchen when they arrived. "Hi." She smiled, poking her head out of the kitchen. "I'm just putting the sandwiches together. Give me two minutes."

Steve stretched. "Ooo, this feels great already. No hospital until tomorrow at four! Mmm, I love bumming out! I'm ready for it."

Jeneil stood at the small dining table with the sandwiches as she listened to Steve. She smiled. "Gosh, you make it sound ritualistic. You have me curious."

Peter chuckled. "You've grasped the idea of bumming out already, honey. These are bummin' out sandwiches," he said, sitting down.

"Roast beef with hot barbecue sauce on a crusty roll is a bumming out sandwich?"

"No, the fact that they're thick and oozy and man handlin' size, that's bumming out."

"Yeah," Steve agreed then noticed Jeneil's plate of neatly sliced roast beef drizzled with barbecue sauce with sliced raw vegetables on the side. "I thought you were joining us in bumming out? That's a civilized plate."

"Oh," she said quietly. "Well, this is my first time bumming out so I'm allowed to bend rules and observe." She smiled, pleased that she defended herself against Steve's tease.

Steve grinned. "Observe? What are you doing, a study in anthropology? Come on now, aren't you an eighties woman? Liberation, equality, keeping up with men? Anything we can do you can do better?"

Jeneil stared him down. "I could probably drink you under the table if I wasn't allergic." She grinned.

Peter laughed and Steve smiled, enjoying her comeback.

"Besides," she continued, "liberationists are realistic. Equality is new to us. We know we're apprentices but we learn fast. You guys are obviously veterans at bumming out. This is my maiden voyage, but I'll hold my own. Just watch me. Don't cut corners on my behalf."

Steve smiled broadly at her. Peter saw a twinkle in his eye as he did and wondered what Steve was up to.

"What movie are we going to see?" Steve asked, finishing his sandwich.

"I hadn't thought about it. I don't even know what's playing."

"Downes campus has a Bergman festival going," Jeneil said.

Peter and Steve stared at her. "For bumming out?" Steve gasped.

Jeneil shrugged. "Sorry, lost my head. Forget I suggested that."

Steve chuckled and winked at Peter. "The rookie's going to be fun. I'll check the paper," he said, getting up and going to the living room.

"Rookie! That's below apprentice!" Jeneil faked insult at the word. "I'll make you eat that insult with your pizza and beer tonight, Mr. Mouth."

Steve laughed. "Sure, sure, talk is cheap woman," he drawled out the last word. "Show me so I'll believe."

"You've got it." Jeneil smiled, drinking her milk.

Peter smiled and squeezed her hand.

"Oh, here's a good movie," Steve said. "It's playing in a small suburb cinema. Night of Vengeance."

"I've never heard of it," Jeneil said. "What is it, a martial arts film?"

Steve smiled. "No, horror, it's perfect for bummin' out."

Peter smiled as he realized Steve intended to put Jeneil through the paces. He had heard people at work talk about the movie.

Steve chuckled. "That's a perfect movie for your initiation into bumming out, Jeneil."

"Fine with me," she said matter-of-factly, and began clearing the table.

Steve looked at Peter and grinned.

"I'll change my shirt and be right back," Peter said.

Jeneil walked into the living room. Picking up two books, she returned them to the bookshelves and straightened a dark metal sculpture. Pulling a book from the shelf below, she browsed through its pages. Steve watched her from over the top of his newspaper. Oh Pete, he thought to himself, I wouldn't allow her out of the apartment in jeans. Even that loose top of her can't hide what she's been given. He raised his eyebrows and shook his head. That wasn't the girl from the records department. He returned to the article he was reading with a sigh.

*****

The cinema wasn't too crowded. The movie had already played in the major cinemas and was making its final run in the suburbs. Taking their seats in the dimly lit theatre, Steve leaned forward to look around Peter. "Hey, Jeneil, if you scream or dig your nails into Pete's arm you don't get your apprenticeship certificate. I'm feeling generous tonight so you can make faces or even turn your head if it starts to get to you."

She grinned. "Don't be generous. We women don't ask for advantages, just an equal opportunity," she said smugly.

Steve sat back and chuckled. "I like her spunk," he whispered to Peter. Peter smiled and put his arm around Jeneil.

The movie proved to be all that Peter had heard about it. It was graphic in terms of violence. He could tell Jeneil was repulsed at times but she sat without screaming in horror like some girls did. Only when blood deliberately splattered the camera lens did she turn away briefly. She was determined to trump Steve in this contest of stamina. Peter smiled as he sat between her and Steve. The two had evolved from an angry struggle as strangers to a struggle of wits as friends. Steve had been right when he said sparks flew between them, but at least they had learned to channel those sparks from contention to harmless fun. While he realized that Steve had toned down quite a bit, Peter gave most of the credit to Jeneil. He knew she had put herself into changing things around with Steve as much as she had put herself into other projects. What pleased him the most was that she had made the effort for him. He smiled despite the brutal murder taking place on screen.

The warm summer air surrounded them as they left the air-conditioned cinema. "I'm glad we have Jeneil's air-conditioned car," Steve groaned. "The night heat is smothering."

"It's hard to believe fall will be here soon," Peter commented.

"We still have Indian Summer to go, Peter. Don't rush it." Jeneil laughed. "I love the days between the blistering summer heat and the icy winter wind. It's my favorite weather. The earth is beautiful, too. After its spring and summer of pregnancy, it finally delivers its harvest."

Steve and Peter looked at her. Steve laughed lightly. "Lit majors are a real kick. You're the only person I've ever heard talk like the earth needed an obstetrician."

Jeneil laughed. "I find some doctors very amusing, too."

Peter held the car door open for her and smiled.

"Where do we go for pizza and beer?" Steve asked. "We can't take Jeneil to The Pits. Too many of the hospital staff go there."

"I don't know. I'm lost," Peter said. "I don't know this end of town."

"I do," Jeneil said. "I went to State."

"Did you?" Steve asked. "Pete, you traitor. A Downes grad with a State coed, stirring up the longstanding rivalry between the colleges."

Jeneil laughed. "Well, I knew what I heard about Downes couldn't be true. I felt sure that at least one Downes grad had to have good taste."

Steve looked at her. "I heard all State coeds were bitches."

Jeneil sent an elbow jab to Steve's ribs.

"Ow! Geez woman," he said, holding his side. "You have bony elbows."

"Now you know the gossip is true." Jeneil smiled.

Steve grinned. "Before you jabbed me, I was about to say I'm glad to see the gossip isn't true."

Jeneil raised an eyebrow at him. "Liar."

He smiled. "Shut up and find us some pizza."

"Okay, you have a choice, Saccio's where everybody goes or Lenny's where the pizza is good."

Peter smiled at her. "Where did you go when you were at State?"

"To Lenny's. I hated crowds. Corner booth near the door. I was shy."

Peter and Steve laughed.

"Why didn't you go to one of the fussy women's colleges near Boston?" Steve asked.

"Isn't that too far to go for pizza?" Jeneil joked, and Peter laughed.

"Yup, she's a State coed all right," Steve said, grabbing her elbow before she could jab him again. "Ha," he smirked before she kicked his shin. "Ouch! Damn it! You are a bitch."

Peter chuckled. "Will you two stop long enough to give me directions to Lenny's?"

Jeneil kissed his shoulder. "It's on the next block. Take a left at the end of this street."

"Humph," Steve groaned. "Some fun, he gets kissed and I get kicked."

Peter and Jeneil laughed.

"Lenny's is just right for bumming out," Steve said as they took their seats in the corner booth near the door in a nostalgic gesture for Jeneil.

"It is," Peter agreed. A woman took their order and left.

Steve smiled. "Jeneil, I'm impressed. You handled that movie really well. Looks like you'll get your certificate."

"Well I'm disappointed in the director. He's done better films than that. It was too graphic and the story line wasn't even bad; he could have leaned on that more. I'd have become psychotic too if I had all that antagonism in my life. I found myself sympathizing with the killer a few times but the sensationalism detracted from the story."

Steve smiled at her just as the waitress brought their order. "Hey, this isn't Lit 202. This is bumming out, lit major. No intelligent comments are allowed. Bumming out is bumming out."

"You mean we can't talk about the movie?" she asked, taking a bite of pizza.

"Sure we can but on a bumming out level."

"What's that?" Jeneil asked, picking off a slice of mushroom and putting it in her mouth.

Steve smiled and winked at Peter. "We can say things like how the mushrooms look like human brain, especially when the killer split the doctor's head open with an ax." Steve picked up a slice of mushroom. "Pete, doesn't that look like human brain?"

Peter smiled and looked at Jeneil out of the corner of his eye. She had picked up her napkin and was holding it against her mouth as she stared at Steve.

"And look at this oozing cheese," he said, pulling it up, "just like tendons when they pull away from bone. And speaking of bone, that fracture of the guy's upper arm when the rotary blade hit it looked real, didn't it? Man, the stuff Hollywood can produce. Crack, snap. Boy, that was almost too real," he said, putting the glop of cheese in his mouth and grinning.

Jeneil pushed the mushroom out of her mouth into the paper napkin, and Peter was having trouble not laughing. She was beginning to look pale as she took a sip of ginger ale.

Steve grinned. "Isn't that odd, I've never noticed how ginger ale looks like bubbly plasma."

Jeneil put her glass down quickly.

"And our beer is the same color as…."

"Don't say it," Jeneil pleaded, choking. "Please don't say it." She put her forehead on Peter's shoulder. "I think I just lost my certificate. I might even lose the bite of pizza I swallowed."

Peter and Steve laughed.

"You're a mean person Steve Bradley, a mean person. And disgusting," Jeneil said, sitting back and sighing.

Steve grinned. "Bummin' out is for the tough, the few, the surgeons." He chuckled and drank his beer.

Looking at Peter, Jeneil took his arm. "I'm glad you're not like that."

Peter laughed and Steve choked on a gulp of beer. "I'm holding back because you're here."

"Oh, that's not fair. This only proves women can't go everywhere. I've inhibited you from bumming out."

Steve smiled. "For a lit major, you were better than I expected."

"Then why did you guys invite me?"

"Because we like you." Peter kissed her temple.

Steve smiled. "Yeah, you're a real kick."

Pulling up to the parking lot at the apartment, Steve yawned, starting a chain reaction. Jeneil struggled not to yawn.

"This has been a fun night," Steve said. "I keep saying thank you and it's beginning to seem weak."

"No, it's not." Jeneil patted his arm. "This was fun."

"Steve, stay over. Are we having a Sunday dinner tomorrow?" Peter asked Jeneil. She nodded. "Then stay Steve. The schedule next week is a killer. Take the break here."

"I can't, Pete," Steve answered. "It's too much."

"You're not imposing if that's why you're hesitating," Jeneil said.

"Are you certain?" Steve asked, looking at her.

"I'm positive. It's no trouble at all."

Steve sighed. "Okay then. I know the second shift is tough and the holiday weekend means extended shifts for sure. The dorm and the hospital will probably be all I'll see for the next two weeks. And I like your place, it's restful and comfortable."

Jeneil smiled. "Good, just get your car off the street so it won't get tagged then come up."

Twenty-Seven

Jeneil turned onto her side and opened her eyes. Nine a.m., she thought, guess that meant no yoga or dancing. She sighed. She felt sluggish from going to bed late and from the smoke in the pizza place the night before. Slipping out of bed, she went to a corner of the room and did some simple yoga positions. Doing a warm up dance routine, she finished with deep breathing. She felt better already. Going to the kitchen quietly, she filled a teacup with warm tap water and lemon juice. When she finished, she went to shower and shampoo her hair. Brushing her hair in front of the bedroom mirror she felt decidedly better.

Peter lifted his head. "Hey sweetheart, how long have you been up and about?"

"Long enough to feel good." She slipped onto the covers next to him.

"You smell good, too," he said, touching her hair gently.

"Are you hung over?"

Peter laughed. "On three small beers? Not hardly."

"Don't you feel contaminated?" she asked, surprised.

He wrinkled his brow. "I feel fine, why?"

She shrugged. "You must have a cast iron constitution."

"Well, I'm going to risk rust. I'll take my shower now."

She chuckled and lay against her pillow after he left. "What's for breakfast?" she asked herself. Her smile turned into a grin. "Wicked, Jeneil, wicked." She giggled. "I love it." Getting up quickly, she changed into a long lounge dress and left the bedroom. Steve was making his bed.

"Good morning."

"Hi, you look all morning fresh and cheerful," Steve commented.

"I feel good," she said, smiling.

He grinned. She was contagious and her cheerfulness was revving him up. "Good, nothing a doctor likes more than to see people who feel good."

"Say Steve, how do you feel about stomping on some different turf today?"

"What do you mean?" he asked, folding the blanket.

"Well, yesterday I bummed out with you. I'd like to see if you can meet the challenge of entertainment of my choice."

"What, a concert?"

"No, nothing stuffy. Very down to earth. Very, just, well…delicate…artistic."

Steve looked at her suspiciously. "I guess I owe you that much."

"Oh good." She giggled and went to the kitchen.

"Shower's free, Steve. You can borrow some clothes from me if you'd like to."

"Sounds good, Pete. What's Jeneil up to?"

Peter shrugged. "I don't know, why?"

"I'm suspicious, that's all."

"Honey, what's up?" Peter asked, walking into the kitchen.

"Nothing," she answered. "We're going out for breakfast."

"Oh, okay. I'll get dressed then." Peter looked at Steve and shrugged.

"It's me then," Steve said. "I'll take a quick shower."

*****

Peter and Steve sat reading the Sunday paper. Jeneil had given them juice and then went to change.

Steve looked up. "Holy shit," he gasped and dropped the newspaper.

Peter looked up and followed Steve's gaze. He stood up fast. "Jeneil, what the hell are you dressed for? I thought we were going to breakfast."

"I'm dressed to go to breakfast."

"Jeneil, that's a costume. And it's…it's."

"Earthy? Ethereal?"

"Ethereal shit. There's no way in hell I'm letting you go into public like that. No way," he said, studying her outfit. The material was thin and a pale celery green. He remembered it from a nightgown. She had called it woven gauze. The material was layered with a lighter shade of green underneath in a scooped top, lower than he'd ever seen her wear in public, and a slightly darker shade of the same material scooping lower still, coming under her breasts and laced together with green ribbon of the same shade. The sleeves were short and puffed, leaving her arms bare. The skirt skimmed her hips and draped at her knees.

Her sandals were so skimpy she was practically barefoot. She had her hair very loosely tied with matching green ribbon. Wisps fell here and there giving her a gentle, windblown look. She looked warm, soft, and innocent. Too soft and innocent, he thought.

"Change," Peter said strongly.

Steve watched, amused. The woman was a total knock out.

"No, this fits in at Elio's. I'm a forest wood fern."

"You're crazy," Peter all but shouted. "Change, Jeneil."

"No," she insisted. "You don't understand. You have to dress for Elio's. It's an experience."

"Fine," Peter answered. "Change and we'll go to the pancake house."

Steve swallowed a laugh, which hurt his chest. She was a total trip, he thought. He covered his mouth with his hand.

"No, Peter. Actually you owe me this breakfast. I bummed out with you last night. Breakfast is my choice. I won't change. If you go to the pancake house, I'll go to Elio's alone. I mean it."

"Not dressed like that you won't."

"What is your gripe? I'm covered, aren't I?"

Peter rubbed his chin. "It's…it's…," he stammered.

Steve wanted desperately to laugh, enjoying Peter's struggle. Try sexy, sensuous, and tempting, he thought to himself, biting his lip to keep from laughing.

Jeneil slipped her arms around Peter. "Oh Peter, come on. Loosen up. You'll see. I'll blend in with the crowd there."

"Jeneil!" He sighed and shook his head. "And what the hell do Steve and I have to wear? Branches from the trees out front as the forest?"

Steve couldn't take anymore. He bellowed a laugh. Peter and Jeneil turned to look at him.

"Thanks for the support man," Peter scowled.

"You guys can wear what you have on," Jeneil answered.

"This sounds weird, Jeneil. Very, very weird. I don't like it."

Steve stood up and joined them. "Pete, I think I understand. This is all aimed at me. She's setting me up today like I set her up last night. Let's do it. Hell, that artsy bunch at this Elio's can't come at us with more than New York ever did, can it? Actually, I'm curious now. Let's go."

Peter looked at him. "You're as crazy as she is."

"Please, Peter," Jeneil pleaded.

"Come on, Pete. There are two of us so why worry."

Peter shook his head. "I'm getting immunized, her disease is spreading." He sighed. "Okay, but you wear a raincoat over that do you hear."

"Agreed!" She gave a squeal of delight and hugged him.

Steve smiled. He wondered what she was up to and was excited to find out. It was definitely a change from the routine he'd been in. She was turning out to be a lot of fun and he liked it.

Peter eased the car out of the lot. "Where the hell is this Elio's? Or should I ask the vice squad. I'll just bet they know."

Jeneil sighed. "Peter, you have to change your attitude. Your scowling will stand out like a neon sign. Please."

"Fine, I'll practice smiling. Now, where is it?"

"Near TAI."

Peter turned his head slowly and looked at her. TAI, the Townsend Art Institute. Robert Danzieg. It smelled of Danzieg's brand of morality. He should have known. He exhaled loudly.

"Peter, drive now," Jeneil insisted. "We're wasting time. We'll miss the morning celebration."

"Oh hell, I didn't know that. Me, miss a morning celebration? Damn, I'll go through red lights now that I know."

Steve turned his head away and laughed silently. He loved this whole thing. The situation was full of life and vibrations. Peter was as funny as hell, and Jeneil sighed in frustration and folded her arms.

"All I know is my attitude was nicer than this during bumming out last night. I'm feeling cheated. You are definitely one-dimensional, Peter. You don't allow for anything new to reach you. I'm not asking for a permanent change, just a willingness to experience some of my things."

"How do you know they wear costumes here?"

"Robert took me to an evening reminiscence at Elio's after working at the playhouse one night. It was entertaining. It's people trying to interpret their feelings for life and sharing it with others. It's interaction or observation; whatever develops within you."

"It sounds harmless enough," Steve commented.

Jeneil looked at Peter. "You've never hassled me before. The concert, the art show. I don't understand why you're being so rigid about this."

"You've never dressed like this for the other things."

"Peter, these people are artists. They experience things dramatically, musically, on film, painting. They dress dramatically sometimes. My costume is mild. It's very conservative compared to the ones I saw when I was there."

Peter smiled at her. "You know you're standing in the middle of eccentric right now on the 'n.' When you get to the final 'c' it's the end of the thread. Make sure there's a knot or the word will unravel and spell something else."

Jeneil chuckled. "I like that, it's clever. You'll like these people. They make you want to think and feel. Elio's is on the street behind TAI. You park behind the building where the Severed Head Boutique sign is."

"This part of town will never change," Steve said. "It's always been offbeat. I can remember when I was in med school. The girls from TAI made me crazy. Man, you couldn't beat them for fun. I had to keep reading my textbook on diseases so I wouldn't be tempted to buy instead of window shop."

Jeneil was shocked. "That's not very nice. Are you saying that TAI girls are diseased?"

Steve smiled. "No. But Jeneil, when one of them swings, believe me it's not like anything else. Their swings are in orbit. Some of my most pleasant memories are TAI girls. Man, they're into another life form entirely. That's the danger. You can't be sure all the life they've been into is from this planet. It got too hectic trying to sort out the ones in orbit from the ones who were in another universe all together. I finally gave up my list of phone numbers at the triad. Dick Bostick and I decided to cremate our lists together when Frank Mosley was prescribed an antibiotic."

Jeneil watched him. "You understand the music at the prom, don't you?"

"What?" Steve smiled.

"Did college make sense to you?"

Steve shrugged. "I guess so. I got through it."

"Interesting," Jeneil mused.

Steve grinned. "Jeneil, sometimes if I close my eyes, you sound TAI. I don't see you in State at all."

Jeneil looked at him. "My gosh, you hear the full orchestra," she said in amazement.

He laughed. "Now that was definitely something you got from a triad, but you don't fit that mold completely."

"I know, because I live in the cracks on the sidewalk."

Steve stared at her. "That makes sense to you, doesn't it?"

"Yes."

Steve shook his head. "Amazing. And my orthopedic friend handles it, double amazing."

"There's the sign, Peter," Jeneil pointed. "Wow, the lot is almost full. Heck, I don't like crowds," she said, disappointed.

Steve poked her gently with his arm. "Aw, come on," he said. "Artsy is artsy, right? Crowd or not we'll be amongst the highly developed consciences in the area, the elite amongst the sensitive people." Steve laughed. "The ones who would starve themselves to protest a poet being imprisoned in Russia, like the Kremlin cared. The bunch at this school made the humanities majors in other schools look like prehistoric animals with their level of sensitivity. You only get two types at TAI, those out hunting with butterfly nets and those who should be caught in them."

Jeneil sighed as Peter laughed. "Oh, you two are impossible. I'm having serious doubts now. This is a Robert and Franklin place. These people are sharing personal creations of poetry, song, and literature, exposing themselves before a group. That isn't easy to do. I can't do it. I don't want the people here insulted by you brutes."

Steve laughed. "Jeneil! What an insensitive attitude you have. I'm the one insulted. Pete, she obviously doesn't realize what a priceless find she has in us. Two, Jeneil, count them, two doctors from Downes. Girl, we doctors know where it's all at. We ooze sensitivity. When the guy who's on a hunger protest decides his body has had enough, who does he go to for advice? His poet friends? No, a doctor. When the TAI freshman pick up strange rashes from orbiting, do they go to their friend who's welding tires and toilet seats into a sculpture? No, he goes to a doctor. Jeneil, we see it all. Sooner or later someone from all walks of life wanders through our doors and we have to relate to them. That's sensitivity."

Jeneil looked at Steve and smiled warmly. "What an astute defense. And your observation is true. Steve, you surprise me at times. I apologize."

Peter smiled, thinking Steve hadn't lost his knack for a fast defense.

Steve nodded. "That's more like it, Jeneil," he said in a sensitive tone. Looking at Peter, he winked. "Come on, Pete. Let's outclass these shitheads." Jeneil covered her face and screamed softly. Peter put his head back and laughed. Steve smiled and opened his car door. "I'm only teasing, Jeneil."

"Wait!" Jeneil said, grabbing Peter's and Steve's arms. "One last bit of preparation. Robert told me that sometimes the presentations get very earthy, but the challenge is to stay above it, to grasp the message without the human appetite interfering with the appreciation. Those were his exact words. Now I'm wondering."

Steve smiled. "Jeneil, you're with doctors. We examine naked women. We can be objective. Boy you don't listen, do you?"

Jeneil looked at him. "Naked people aren't naked here! But earthy is not the same as a sick naked woman." She sighed. "Oh, the pancake house is beginning to sound better to me." Peter laughed.

"Come on, Jeneil. I'm looking forward to showing as much stamina in this as you showed last night for bumming out. That's what's behind breakfast here, isn't it?" She nodded. "Then I accept the challenge." He smiled and got out of the car.

Peter held the door for her, and watched as two girls in jeans and baggy tops walked out of Elio's. "Jeneil, they're not in costume."

"That's odd. No one was dressed like that the night I was here." She sighed. "Well, I'll keep my coat on then."

The entrance door to Elio's was two dark metal doors with a ring knocker on each one. Other than that the building was un-remodeled and looked like the old home it really was. The doors were at ground level and at the back of the house. Steve pushed one of the doors open. There was a small landing then three cement steps leading to another small area hallway. A shirtless young man in leather pants and leather suspenders with silver studs stepped from a small side room.

"Hi," he said, smiling and looking the three over curiously. "I'll take your coat," he said to Jeneil.

"Um…I was thinking of keeping it with me."

The young man smiled. "Are you into dress?"

"Dress?" she questioned.

"Costume."

"Oh yes," she said, fidgeting, "and I have less courage now than when I left home."

The young man smiled warmly. "Don't be shy. You really need Elio's then. This is where the inner you can unleash and float free. Let's see it," he said, reaching for her coat. She hesitated. "Come on, the hair is lovely, very nice. Let's see what your inner self felt like when it left home."

Peter didn't like Jeneil being forced into this but he stayed quiet as she allowed the young man to take her coat. The young man raised his eyebrows. "Ooo, that's very nice," he said, taking her all in. Peter put his hands in his jean pockets to prevent making fists. "What are the bodyguards for, protection from Pan?" The young man laughed lightly. Jeneil smiled and covered her throat with her hand self-consciously. "Wow, you've got the role down perfectly. Even the modest gestures seem natural." He looked at Steve and Peter. "And what happened with you two not in costume? Not as brave as the beauty?"

Steve grinned. "We are in costume, a collective costume. My buddy and I decided that our inner selves felt like coming here as a triad. She's got a more independent inner self."

Jeneil chuckled.

The young man looked at Steve. "Can I guess? Studying the nuclear sciences, right?"

"No, a welder. You know the Fifth Street bridge, well the east section is all my work."

The young man looked surprised. "Are you serious? What a remarkable level you've achieved. Where did you learn about triads?" he asked, very interested.

Steve shrugged. "Hey, you gotta keep up in the world right?" Peter turned away to smile. Jeneil watched, amused.

"Incredible!" the young man said, obviously believing Steve's story. "I love it when people jolt the norm. It's the human spirit in its magnificence. Enjoy your morning here." He shook Steve's hand.

"Thanks." Steve smiled and walked away. Peter and Jeneil followed. Steve looked at them and grinned. "Very gullible, bet he's a TAI freshman."

"Steve!" Jeneil warned as Peter chuckled.

Elio's was a large room with a platform stage in the center. A sign at the room entrance read, '*Part of allowing your inner self to be expressive is choosing your own seat. We only ask that your inner self not interfere with another inner self and its choice of seats. Otherwise float, float. Be free and peaceful.*'

Steve and Peter chuckled. Pushing the swinging doors to the main room open, the three stepped inside. Jeneil spotted an empty table not too far from the entrance. "Let's sit there," she said nervously, just wanting to sit. She felt awkward in her costume. She walked quickly to the table, avoiding looking at anyone. Peter and Steve joined her. She could tell they were trying not to laugh. She glared at them. "Guys," she whispered, "you promised to behave, you promised."

A flautist was performing on stage. Steve leaned over to her. "Jeneil, we're not making fun, we just had no idea you were being literal when you said people here exposed themselves, that's all."

"What do you mean?" she asked, puzzled.

"Look at the couple coming toward our table and the girl on stage."

Jeneil looked casually in Steve's direction. She gave a slight start at the sight of the full bosomed woman wearing a triangle bikini. The man with her was also wearing a brief bikini. The flautist performing was covered only in a single bag of chiffon.

"Robert brought you here, huh?" Peter asked, looking at her with raised eyebrows.

"Peter, I swear when Robert and I were here people were in costumes. Some costumes were odd, but the people were covered," Jeneil said defensively.

A beautiful young waitress came to their table. She was wearing a loose top that was undone to her mid thighs, and nothing else, which was noticeable since the top was thin. Peter and Steve were both stunned into silence by her outfit.

"Are you people just drinking or joining us for breakfast?"

Peter and Steve stayed silent, trying hard not to look at strategic parts of the waitress.

"Makes you want to think and feel doesn't it, Pete," Steve whispered.

Peter grinned. "Jeneil, you didn't understate this place at all."

"Breakfast," Jeneil answered, embarrassed. The waitress thanked her and walked away.

"She didn't take our orders," Peter said.

"We didn't even get menus," Steve added.

"The only choice is whether you're just drinking coffee and juice or having their breakfast," Jeneil explained.

"I'm afraid to ask what the breakfast is," Peter said softly.

"Sweet rolls, bagels and cream cheese, fruit and nuts, with coffee and hot chocolate to drink," Jeneil said soberly. Peter was concerned that he and Steve had not grasped the situation quite as well as others there.

A poet came on next. His outfit was only the leotard of a male ballet dancer's costume. Jeneil sat straight faced and unemotional. Peter glanced at her then at Steve. "She's a natural here. I can't tell if she even notices. I guess she's above it all."

Steve grinned. "The thing's fake," he said, nodding at the poet.

"Think so?" Peter answered.

Steve chuckled. "What? Did you flunk anatomy? Have you ever seen one like that?"

"I can't quite figure him," Peter said. "Is he trying to make these women leave their men?"

Jeneil leaned toward them. "Listen to his poetry. He's answering both of those questions."

They looked at her, surprised she was listening to them, surprised she wasn't mad, and surprised she understood what was happening. There was a brief intermission while breakfast was served. It was a time for mingling and interaction. The waitress smiled at Steve when she returned with their food. "You have a fantastic facial bone structure and features." Peter bit his lip to keep from smiling.

"Really?" Steve said taken back a little.

"Aw, come on," the waitress said. "You honestly mean that's news to you? Does that mean you don't use them to your advantage?"

"I'm a surgeon. My patients are usually sedated and I wear a mask. My looks don't mean anything to them or my associates in the operating room. My skill is more important to them."

"A surgeon?" The waitress was surprised. "What a waste. You should be doing films."

Steve raised an eyebrow. "Films?" He grinned then made a serious face. "Honey, you've got the wrong guy. You need the poet who was just on." Peter laughed as Jeneil watched.

"You mean John?" The waitress laughed.

"He has a sense of humor, doesn't he though?"

"So you're not interested?"

"No thanks." Steve smiled.

"What a shame. But if you change your mind, let me know. I'm a great director. I think you'd be pleased with the result." She smiled at all three. "Enjoy your breakfast." Then, smiling at Jeneil, she said, "Nice outfit honey, keep 'em a guessin'. The word 'maybe' makes a guy crazy. Best gimmick for films, steams up a room in two seconds. You know, anticipation," she sang, and walked away.

"Interesting," Jeneil said. "With her great looks I would have thought she'd be an actress, but a director. Good for her."

Peter and Steve looked at her surprised. "Good for her?" they asked in unison.

"Sure. A female director in porno, she must be pioneering."

Steve smiled. "Jeneil, you are a total mind bend at times."

"Hey, it's not what I'd choose to do but you have to be impressed. With her looks, I wonder if she can even get anyone to take her seriously as a director in that field. Did you hear her? I'm a great director, she said. I say good for her. She probably is good, too."

A dark haired man about their age at the next table turned around to see who had made the remark. Seeing Jeneil, he smiled warmly.

"I'm sorry," Jeneil apologized. "I'll whisper."

He smiled again. "It's all right. My intrusion on you." He turned around to face the two guys he was with. He must have explained Jeneil's remark to them because they looked at her and smiled warmly at her, too.

"Oh dear, get me a muzzle," she said.

"And you have the nerve to lecture us," Peter teased.

"Someone pass the orange to me please." Jeneil shrugged, embarrassed, as they finished sharing the food that had been brought.

"That was more filling than I expected it to be," Steve said, pouring more coffee.

"I'll have more coffee, too," Peter said, moving his cup.

"I'm going to wash my hands, the orange was juicy," Jeneil said, standing up. She walked past the next table going toward the restroom.

Peter noticed the dark haired man move his head slightly to the side to watch her walk away.

"Pete," Steve called. Peter turned his head. "Where were you? I said your name twice."

"Shark," Peter answered, pointing a spoon casually toward the man at the next table.

"Oh yeah?" Steve whispered. "Why worry? He can't try anything with us right here"

"I suppose," Peter said, taking a sip of coffee. He saw Jeneil enter the room again and walk to the side of the door where she stopped to talk to the poet.

Steve chuckled. "I don't believe it."

"Take notice of the shark," Peter whispered.

Steve looked to the table next to them. The man had moved his chair closer to the aisle where Jeneil would be returning. Steve looked at Peter. "Shit bold, man. Better put it on freeze, Pete. She'd have a blow out over a wrestling match in here."

"I'm cool, honest, but I'm sensing something about him. It stays with you from the streets."

"This isn't the streets," Steve replied.

Peter grinned. "I'm finding that the animals are the same. You watch him."

Jeneil walked back, smiling as she opened her purse to put a piece of paper inside. The dark haired man watched her. Jeneil was closing her purse as she reached him. He startled her as he reached out and took her by the wrist. Peter sat up straight and watched. She smiled politely at the man.

"What's he saying?" Steve asked.

"I can't hear," Peter answered, not taking his eyes off Jeneil. "Watch the hand," he whispered to Steve as he noticed the man rubbing her forearm.

"Is he baiting you?"

"I don't think so…oh shit, he's going to put a move on her."

Peter sat on the edge of his seat as he saw the man's hand move to Jeneil's elbow. Jeneil wasn't smiling. She was studying him intently. Peter sat tensed. He gave a short gasp as he saw the hand move from her elbow toward her body. Steve stood up fast. Jeneil's free hand moved quickly. Taking the man's hand in hers, she smiled at him. Then, holding his hand in both of hers, she patted it gently.

"I'm sorry," she said, "I belong to someone. Maybe in another life. Excuse me. My friends are waiting for me." She smiled and nodded a goodbye to his friends, and joined Peter and Steve.

"My loss." The man smiled at her and rejoined his friends.

Steve smiled. "Slick move, sweetheart."

Peter took her arm. "We're outta here, baby. Move it," he said, gently pushing her along in front of him.

Opening his wallet, Peter handed the coat check clerk the ticket and a dollar. Taking her coat, he wrapped it around her quickly and pushed her gently out the door ahead of him to the car. Unlocking the door on the driver's side, he held it open for her and tossed the keys to Steve to unlock his own door. Peter got into the car after Jeneil and slammed the door. He sat in angry silence. Steve got in beside Jeneil and handed the keys to Peter, watching him closely.

Jeneil looked at Peter. "I think you'd better calm down before driving," she said quietly.

"Calm down!" Peter exploded. "I want to hit the son of a bitch, and I warned you about that costume didn't I?"

Jeneil took his arm gently. "Peter, nothing happened."

"You're lucky. Hear me, plain lucky. Why the hell didn't you hit him?"

"Peter, I think he was on something. I'm almost certain that he wasn't all together about what he was doing. Besides, you told me if I turn down an offer not to make the guy feel like a creep and everything should be fine."

"Oh, Jeneil," he rubbed his forehead in exasperation, "I meant the guys who come on to you."

"Well isn't that what he was doing?"

Steve looked at her, surprised.

Peter sighed. "No, Jeneil. That son of a bitch was putting a move on you."

Jeneil put her head back and rubbed her temples. "Oh please, coming on to you, putting a move on you, getting kicks. I can't keep up with all of it."

Steve studied her, totally amazed at her lack of knowledge. He was beginning to understand why Peter hovered.

"Does it even matter?" She sighed. "It's all so stupidly boring. What's the difference?"

Peter looked at her. "Jeneil, baby, there's a difference. Honey, learn it, believe me. Coming on is serious flirting to see where you stand, putting a move on is a physical thing that can lead to trouble, get out fast."

"Primal?" she asked, surprised.

"Primal." Peter nodded.

She looked shocked. "That was primal. My gosh, in a public place!" she said, sitting up straight. "But it isn't really shocking, is it? That atmosphere, flautists in chiffon nothing dresses, waitresses with nothing under what's over, men and women dressed for sunbathing for breakfast, poets with exaggerated leotards. Those people in there are ultra-civilized to behave so well!" she said, pinching her lip. "Or are they?" she wondered. "Are they immune?" she asked, thinking out loud. "Has the mystique of the human body been made so commonplace that it no longer fascinates and excites by itself? Is that why more bizarre thrills are looked for? What a mess. It's the decadence before a great nation falls. Just like China, Greece, and Rome. We don't learn, do we? We don't listen." She sat silently. Peter looked at Steve, covered his eyes and shook his head. Steve looked at her, totally in awe that she was real.

She sighed. "I thought the talent in there was exceptional. The words in that poem were pure truth. I asked him for a copy. I was disappointed that he used a costume as a gimmick, but I'll bet he knew they didn't listen anymore. His costume was to get attention. While we were having breakfast I couldn't help but notice how similar that place was to the horror show last night. The sensational overshadowed the real talent. What is with people? Can't we be around without the sensational and bizarre? Have our senses and instincts become dulled to beauty, simplicity, and truth? It's sad, too. There was an aimlessness about that. There was no celebration. Morning is full of purpose and hope. Morning isn't bawdy." She sighed again. "The evening reminiscence was so different; it was reverent. It wasn't crowded and the performers and audience blended well. It was very moving. I wonder if it was the crowd that changed the atmosphere. Groups can develop a momentum that builds to a strong frenzy, like centrifugal force. Look at the dark ages, Salem's witch hunt." She looked at Peter then at Steve. "I'm sorry guys, I thought we were going for something uplifting but it was only more bumming out without the intimacy, the camaraderie, and the innocence of last night. You two are really great." She kissed Peter's shoulder and held Steve's hand.

Steve watched her, totally fascinated. He had never met anyone that fragile and open to life. Her beauty filled him and he was surprised that he was slightly choked up.

"Let's go home and have our special Sunday celebration because we're special. We're alive. We're humans. We're a triad, right?" She smiled at Steve. Peter kissed her cheek then turned the ignition.

Twenty-Eight

Peter and Steve left their lunch bags in their lockers and changed into lab coats. "I'm scheduled for the ER," Steve said. "That's sure to be fun, everybody trying to kill themselves before Labor Day. What horse are you riding on this carousel?"

"I have fourth floor duty and I'm monitoring three patients in recovery for Dr. Maxwell. After that I think I'm with you in the ER."

"Good, at least I'll have a decent team when the ER goes full moon later. I love it when they give me three interns who've been here a week and one of them is a girl who pounds on her chest screaming, 'I'm as good as you are, woman's lib said so.' I like the kind of female doctor who's the first one with her hand in the shit then looks at you like, 'so help already, we're a team right?'"

Peter smiled. "I've worked with the liberated Dr. Turcell. She's a real pain."

Steve laughed. "On busy nights, I love assigning her to semi-conscious drug victims. She's so frustrated trying to diagnose that she stays out of my hair but drives the lab crazy with tests. Then she's so mad, but won't dare admit she can't be equal in this madness, that she sulks silently."

Peter laughed. "I think I'll remember that."

"When it's slow I spread her around. I sure don't want her turned loose without real training, but it takes so long to chisel through the granite and exchange ideas with her. It's getting noticed though. I think she's riding for a few trips into Dr. Fisher's office. I've reported her to Dr. Sprague." Steve sighed.

"Really?"

"She scares me. I can't trust my team when she's on it, but I'll take her if the rest of the team isn't too green. I don't want her to drop out, just shape up. And if they've given you to the ER then Turcell is there tonight, too. I'm glad I had this weekend with you and Sunshine. Turcell will be easier to take now that I have a real woman to use as a frame of reference."

Peter smiled. "Catch you later."

"Sure." Steve smiled.

*****

Peter headed for the ER. His shift hadn't been too bad so far and he wondered what was happening in there. Two nurses were talking together as he walked in. "What's it like in here?"

"Surprisingly slow," one nurse answered and the other nodded in agreement.

"Is Dr. Bradley here?"

"Yes, in the viewing room."

"Have you noticed anything about him and Dr. Bradley?" one nurse asked the other after Peter had left.

"Like what?"

"They've mellowed out. I was beginning to think the gossip about Dr. Bradley and a girl was faked, but I saw him in the viewing room staring into space with a Mona Lisa smile on his face. He's been bitten all right. Plus, somebody packs him some great lunches. And look at the change in Pete. He always used to scowl, now that's stopped and he's gained weight. I think he's been bitten, too."

"But Dr. Chang brings in food for Dr. Bradley. They use the microwave in the doctor's lounge sometimes."

"Why would Dr. Chang's girl be feeding Dr. Bradley?"

The other shrugged. "They're good friends. Maybe she doesn't mind. Maybe his mother sends the food."

"Can't Dr. Bradley's cook? I heard she's a nice girl, a homebody and all that."

"I don't know but let's drop it. That's all Dr. Bradley needs is to have somebody tell his girl that someone else is sending him lunches. What a mess that would be."

"That's for sure. Boy things were easier when he wasn't attached. You could get all the gossip you wanted about him and Dr. Chang. Now the two of them are shrouded in silence. Hey that's odd, isn't it? The two of them, but they look so good. It's nice to watch them in a way, and if the look on Dr. Bradley's face is true then he's been bitten hard."

"You know, I once heard someone make a comment about them sharing the same woman."

"Oh please, that's impossible. Those two with one woman! She'd have to be a real woman," the nurse exaggerated the words and used hand gestures. "No, Dr. Chang's got one who loves to cook apparently and Dr. Bradley has one who makes him smile when he's all alone." They giggled.

"Hey, you're not the spy are you?"

"No, are you?" They giggled again.

Peter leaned against the table in the viewing room. "You can tell it's slow. The nurses haven't stopped talking and giggling since I got here."

Steve looked at the nurses and smiled. "I'd rather have that type than two alley cats making pouncing noises at each other."

Peter chuckled. "That's true. Speaking of alley cats, did you draw Turcell in here?"

Steve laughed. "Oh yeah, she's assigned. She said she can't stand sitting and doing nothing so she's rearranging the files in the medical room. They've bugged her since she got here all of two weeks ago."

Peter was shocked. "You let her! The head of nursing will explode."

Steve smiled. "Yeah I know, and she's a Turcell type in a white hat. I figure the best way to cure Turcell is to let her ass get kicked by somebody just like her. Maybe it'll turn the granite into clay and we can do something with her. My only problem is I'm not sure which one to inoculate for rabies. I have extra blood on hand, now I just wait for the clash." Peter chuckled. "What time do you plan on leaving for Boston Saturday?"

"Early, that's for sure. Why don't you stay over? It'd save a lot of planning."

Steve smiled. "Geez, the neighbors will start to talk."

Peter laughed. "Jeneil's the landlady."

*****

After their break, Peter and Steve walked back to the ER slowly. "Is it still quiet in here?" Steve asked. A young intern nodded. Steve shrugged at Peter. "They've heard about Turcell. They're going to Cleveland General instead."

The intern choked on his candy bar and laughed. "She's taking inventory in the supply closets and she's going to scrub the shelves in the cubicles next."

"That's it," Steve said, throwing up his hands. "I'm insisting on a urine analysis. She's on something." Peter and the intern laughed.

A nurse handed Peter a message slip. "I'll be at the phone booth if things break loose. My grandfather called." Going to the phone, Peter dialed. He wondered who would answer. "Grandfather, it's me."

"Peter, I'm sorry to call at work but there was no answer at your apartment."

"Jeneil's in New York."

"Oh, will she be home for her birthday?"

"Yes, she'll be back tonight. Why?"

"I have a gift for her. I'm going to Uncle Liam's summer cottage on Tuesday and I won't be back until Saturday night or Sunday, so I wanted to see that she got it."

"That's really nice of you, Grandfather. She'll love that."

"How is she celebrating it?"

"All kinds of ways, a party Friday, lunch then dinner on Saturday, and she went to New York tonight as a gift from a friend in Nebraska. He has a private plane so the trip was easy to arrange."

"Peter, does she come from money? Private plane trips to New York and Nebraska."

Peter thought about how to answer that. "She's surrounded by it. Well actually yes, she has money, Grandfather. She's not wealthy but there's money there."

"I'm surprised. She lives so simply. I wondered about her manners but I never thought of her as being from money. Then why is she a clerk at the hospital?"

"Believe me, Grandfather, only she can do justice in explaining that. It makes sense when she tells it. Her uncle keeps asking the same thing."

"Uncle? I thought she was alone?"

"He's really an appointed guardian and a lawyer her father hired to look after her."

"Peter, her background is much more than I imagined. What does this lawyer think of you?"

Peter was silent. "Not very much, Grandfather."

"What is it, because you're not married?"

"Yes," he answered quietly. The admission hurt and embarrassed him.

The grandfather sighed. "I'm sorry, but it's the price you pay when you step outside what's accepted. It may be her idea to not marry, but you accepted it. Is there a problem about race, too?"

"I don't know for sure. He's afraid I'm not sincere and that I'll leave her to marry someone who is Chinese."

"You two have your struggles, don't you? I can't believe you both get along so well coming from such different backgrounds. It can't be easy dealing with his attitude about you."

"Oh that's easy. He's in Nebraska so our paths never cross. Admitting all this to you isn't easy though. I know you don't approve of my being there with her either."

"Peter, we've never talked about it. You know I don't approve because of our religious beliefs and that's why I'm not lecturing. I know you are conscious of it and that pleases me. But I like what I see, Peter. I hang on to that. You'll be honorable, I know you will. You love her and I see that. I trust you."

"Thank you, Grandfather. I know my name is Chang. I'm proud of that because of her,"

Peter said, surprising himself with the sentiment.

"I know that, too," the grandfather said. "She's a special songbird. I owe her quite a lot, that's why I'd like her to have this gift. Will you come and pick it up?"

"Sure. I wish I knew what to get her."

"But that should be easy," the grandfather answered, surprised.

"Grandfather, with my hours I don't even know where the stores are anymore."

"Then let's go shopping together. I know just the store for you."

"That sounds great." Peter smiled. "Tomorrow morning?"

"Yes."

"Thanks Grandfather, for a lot of things."

The grandfather smiled, thinking she'd taught him to care and so he'd learned to appreciate. He now could say thank you. She truly was a wonderful songbird. "I'll see you tomorrow, Peter."

Peter waited for the line to disconnect before hanging up. He loved his grandfather. How had he missed so much of what he really was? Getting up, Peter headed back to the ER. He and his grandfather had never spoken in detail about his not being married but it had hung between them. He felt relaxed now that they had. He may not have his grandfather's approval, but he had his trust that he would be honorable. It meant a lot to him and it was something he wouldn't forget.

The ER was starting to get busy; a one-car accident with a head injury, a burn case involving an elderly woman, and multiple bruises on a young boy. Peter took the boy's case and was sickened by it. It looked like a case of child abuse but the boy sat in silent defense of his parents. Peter called to find out if the hospital had any records stating the boy had received prior treatment. As he waited for the nurse to pull up the file, he watched the boy. The boy's loyalty to his parents made a feeling of guilt swell within himself. While his own childhood hadn't been strictly ideal, he had never had to face what this young boy was dealing with, and he had offered less loyalty to his family in return.

"There were two other treatment dates within the last four months," the nurse said.

"Thanks, Donna. Get print outs and put a red flag on the file. Make a notation on those dates." He hung up and returned to the boy. "Okay kid, looks like we've got to fix a lot of things up for you."

The boy watched Peter through sad, angry eyes. Peter turned away to reach for bandages wondering what the boy's loyalty was costing him. He sighed. Jeneil was right; did anyone get through childhood unscathed by something? He felt deeply for the boy as he applied the finishing touches on the bandages.

"Let somebody help you and your mother with this problem," Peter said, pointing to the bruises. "You love your mother and she loves you too, but you need help with this so it can stop happening. It can stop if you let somebody help your mother. Can you remember that?" The boy just stared. He took the boy off the gurney and a nurse took him back to his mother. Peter sighed and shook his head. He thought about Jeneil's words, 'Let's plan when we'll have children so we'll know that at that moment we created a new life together.' Two nurses began cleaning up the cubicle while Peter stood there smiling into space as he thought about Jeneil. "Sorry," he said, becoming aware of them, "let me get out of your way," and he left.

"One thing's for sure, Dr. Bradley and Dr. Chang are sharing the same symptoms. That's just how Dr. Bradley looked in the viewing room. I'd call it lovesickness myself." The nurses smiled and finished cleaning.

*****

Peter arrived home to a dark, empty apartment. As it neared midnight, he sat wondering what he could do to find out if there had been an accident or some kind of plane trouble. He sat on the edge of the bed then got up and paced. The sound of the key turning in the lock was beautiful music to him and he breathed deeply as he went to see her.

"Hi." Jeneil smiled warmly and went to him for a hug. He held her to him, enjoying having her safe in his arms. "We had trouble leaving New York. You must have been worried."

"It's okay now," he answered. "Did you have fun?"

"Yes!" she said excitedly, pulling away. "Yes, I did. I can't believe this whole night!"

"You look terrific." He smiled, looking at her black dress. She did look special, more womanly.

"Thank you. I wore my pearls, but Bill gave me a necklace and earrings for my birthday so I changed."

Peter looked at the gold and sparkling clear stones. "Well I'm not going to ask if they're real diamonds," he said, smiling. "People who fly private planes don't buy fakes."

"Oh there are some good fakes," she gushed, "but these are real. He is so changed from Billy Reynolds! When the snag happened in New York, he just took charge. He and his pilot worked out a new route then cleared it with the airport. That's why we're a bit late, but not as late as we would've been if we had waited in line. It's good to see him so strong and in command of his life. He has direction and purpose, and he's happy. That was a nice gift, too. And you won't guess what we did before dinner!" She giggled like a little kid on Christmas morning. "We took in Manhattan and some of the surrounding area in a helicopter! I was so stunned. I can barely believe that happened." She smiled and hugged him, still excited. "What a zany birthday celebration! But I loved it. It was outrageous and I don't know why he spent so much, but I loved it." She giggled again and hugged Peter tighter. "I'm babbling." She breathed deeply as she stepped back. "It's time to land now. I'll get ready for bed then have some Ovaltine or I'll never sleep." She sighed, removing her earrings. "Ooo, that guy is dangerous. He awakens the decadence in me. His taste for luxury and high-living gets heady." She laughed, shaking her head and going to the bedroom.

Peter went to the kitchen and heated some milk for the Ovaltine. Now he could tell Steve he had found what to give a girl who had everything, and it was something neither of them could afford. He smiled at the irony. Boy did she look terrific though! Peter took the mugs of Ovaltine to the bedroom. Jeneil was closing the garment bag where she'd hung her dress.

"Oh, thank you," she said, taking the mug and sipping. He studied her face; she looked beautiful. "I'm going to wash the pollution off my face. I'll be back." She smiled and left the room.

Peter changed for bed and got under the covers. He put his hand on his stomach. The ridges of scar tissue almost pulsated under his palm. He asked her in his mind if her scars were healing. His would never go away and he wondered where their worlds went from there. Jeneil returned with her face scrubbed and her hair undone, hanging freely. He watched her as she brushed it a few times then turned and got into bed. She looked like his Jeneil.

"Everything okay at the hospital?" she asked, kissing his shoulder.

"Yes, why?" he answered, lying on his back, staring at the ceiling.

"Just wondered." She kissed his cheek. "Peter, look at me," she said with gentleness in her voice. He turned his head toward her. "No, don't just look at me. I want you to look at me."

He wrinkled his brow. "I'd ask you to repeat that but it sounded like you said it twice already," and he chuckled.

"Peter, turn and face me then look at me."

He turned onto his side, facing her. She studied his face then studied his eyes deeply.

After a few seconds, he fidgeted. "What are you doing?"

She smiled gently. "Making a path to your soul."

He chuckled. "You flew too high tonight."

She smiled, continuing to look into his eyes. "Peter, I love you so much," she said softly. Her face was serious. She kissed his lips lightly then more warmly. He put his arms around her and returned the kiss. Soul he didn't quite understand but this he could handle. He proved his love his way.

She snuggled into his arms and sighed. "You are terrific."

He noticed that the tone she had used when she had looked into his eyes and told him she loved him was gone. He felt her love now, it was between them strongly at the moment, but he had liked the way she said she loved him before. It was different. He smiled inwardly thinking, a path to my soul, crazy kid. He pulled her closer to him. She smoothed her hand gently over his chest and stomach the way she usually did after they made love. That felt like love to him, too. He kissed her forehead.

Peter's kiss brought her out of deep thought. She kissed his cheek. "You know I told you earlier that I didn't know why Bill spent so much on tonight. That's true but I do know why tonight happened."

Peter looked at her curiously. "Not your birthday?"

She smiled. "Uncle Hollis just told him about us. Bill is beside himself with happiness over it."

"Really? You mean he approves of us?"

Jeneil laughed. "Well he said that he didn't care who the guy was, you're my choice and that's enough for him. Tonight's celebration was for two reasons, my birthday and his release from deep guilt over me."

"Guilt?" Peter asked, surprised.

"There are all kinds of scars, Peter. He's been concerned about my life. Or lack of one as he put it. He's felt very guilty about what happened to him and me in Loma and what the boys used to say about me. He knows why I never dated. That added to the guilt. No one ever believed him when he said it wasn't true. He said that he's watched me over the years and was getting more worried that the damage done had been severe since there was no one in my life. Hollis couldn't believe Bill's excitement over the news. He said that he shook his head, saying I must have a generation gap attitude about this." Jeneil started to laugh.

"What's so funny?"

"Oh Peter," she laughed again, "the gossip about Bill and I is still going on." She laughed harder.

"Are you kidding?"

"No, Bill and I planted some wildflowers at the bottom of Hadley's Bluff. Every summer the flowers have bloomed and multiplied, spreading over the field. We were twelve years old and wanted to make the world beautiful. People think we planted the flowers there because that's where we first made love. Can you believe that?" She laughed. "They think that's why he's trying so hard to buy Hadley's Bluff. We've become a legend now that sexual freedom has come to Loma's younger generation. Loma has the lowest illegitimate birth rate in the county. Bill said all the elderly people boast about Loma's morality, but what they don't know is that all the young girls are wise. They know how not to get pregnant. They probably have the highest rate of sales on birth control. It's become a tradition to begin a relationship in the field of wildflowers like they think we did. He said there are wildflower fields turning up all over Loma." She broke into laughter again. "It's crazy, it's sad, and depending on your perspective, it's also very funny." She laughed until her eyes were moist.

Peter shook his head. "What a town."

She sighed. "Oh gosh, that town will never change. I don't know why Bill stays. He'll never have any privacy there." She was silent as she thought then added sadly, "no, he'll never have any privacy there. That was taken from him when he was a young boy in the hay barn, along with his innocence. And he can't ever get it back. There are all kinds of rapes."

*****

Peter thought about the diamond necklace and earrings Bill had given Jeneil as he drove to his grandfather's. What could he get her that would rise above that? He resented Bill for doing it. To Bill, they were probably small gifts but no one else in Jeneil's life at the moment could match that. Then, thinking a little more, he realized that it wasn't Bill's fault either. It's what he had chosen to give her. The night had been special to him, too. Peter understood that but his uneasiness about finding a gift to equal Bill's was real. He remembered his mother's disappointment whenever she opened one of his gifts. He didn't want Jeneil to be disappointed. Being normal wasn't easy, he thought; shopping, social rules, feeling, caring, doing. He chuckled. Uh-oh, Chang was having a tantrum. Come on, Peter, don't sit and sulk about diamonds, Chang needed help and support. He laughed as he realized she had him split into three people too, and he shook his head.

His grandfather was waiting out front. "It's too bad you weren't here ten minutes earlier. You missed your mother." Peter looked at him blankly. "It would help to say hello."

"Where are we going?" Peter asked, smiling.

"To Beijing," his grandfather answered. "It's a Chinese import store near the west mall."

Peter and his grandfather browsed through the store separately. Peter looked at the price tags and got discouraged.

"Have you seen anything Jeneil would like?" his grandfather asked as he joined him.

"Yes, but not too much that my wallet can afford."

"The area in that corner is reasonable but I can help you out with money if something here is better."

"I don't think so, grandfather. I may not be rich but I can at least be honest. I'm tempted to show off right now to impress her, so that usually means I shouldn't."

His grandfather smiled. "Wise move."

Peter went to the other section of the store. He sighed.

"Peter, you're thinking of you as you look at these things and the price tags. You're worried about how you'll look to her. Turn around, think about Jeneil, then look at everything and choose with her in mind."

"Say, where'd you learn to get so good at shopping for women?" Peter asked, grinning.

His grandfather laughed. "From a songbird, poverty, and three daughters."

Peter laughed. He tried his grandfather's idea and spotted a wooden box with an inlaid wood design on its cover. He didn't know why, but he felt Jeneil would like it. Then, looking farther down the case, he spotted some enameled bracelets. Checking the price tags, he was pleased to find he could afford two. The clerk asked if he wanted it gift-wrapped. "Yes," he answered. "Wait. Can you put the bracelets inside the box and then wrap the box?"

The clerk smiled. "Sure, I'll fill the box with tissue paper so the bracelets won't rattle."

"Thanks." Peter was pleased.

"I think you're getting the idea of this shopping game."

"It's in my ancestral blood. I inherited it from you, Grandfather."

His grandfather smiled broadly, pleased by Peter's remark. He thought about Jeneil. She'd given him a grandson who he had thought might never be this close. "Peter, would you give her my gift when she's alone?"

The request surprised Peter. "Okay, what did you get for her?"

"Something special, it should be private."

Arriving back at the house, Peter's grandfather fixed lunch for them. Peter's mother came in as they finished. "Hi." She smiled, looking at Peter closely. "You still look well even with the busy hospital schedule, and your shirt isn't wrinkled and you use fabric softener."

"How do you know that?"

She laughed. "I do laundry. I recognize the smell. I bought some brownies at the bakery. Want some?"

"Sure."

His grandfather watched.

"I thought you sent your clothes to a laundry?" she asked as Peter drank his iced tea. "How many brownies would you like?"

"Two," he answered, avoiding her previous question.

"Lien," Karen called as she walked in. "Oh, hi, Pete. Who's the girl?"

Peter's heart stopped. "What girl?"

"Now come on, look at you. Somebody's taking care of you."

The brownie stuck in his throat. "Karen, with my schedule at the hospital I don't have time to date. When you get to be my age your metabolism slows down. Besides, my mother gave me orders to eat and sleep."

"And you obeyed her? Boy, have you changed," she teased.

"Karen, go to work," Peter snarled.

"Too bad I was wrong. You're still as bad tempered as ever." She laughed and left the room.

"Buy her a muzzle so she has a shot at marriage," Peter said to his mother.

His mother laughed. "Say, we've seen so little of you and Steve this summer. How is Steve doing? He must be almost finished now."

"February. Can you believe it?"

"What about a girl?"

"What girl? Why does everybody keep asking about a girl?" he answered sharply.

His grandfather held his breath as his mother stiffened. "What are you upset about? I just wondered if Steve was settling down yet. Goodness, forget I asked."

"I'm sorry," Peter answered. "No, he's not settled yet. He's thinking about getting married though."

His mother looked at his grandfather. "This is my son, isn't it? Was that an apology I just heard?"

The grandfather smiled. "Peter's a man, Lien. Enjoy the rewards."

"I guess," she laughed. "I like it very much, a son who apologizes. I'll have to tell Malien that there's hope for Rick."

Peter got up. "I've got to be going. Thanks for lunch and the brownies."

"Keep taking good care of yourself. I worry about you getting run down and working around all those diseases."

He smiled. "I will."

"And will you come for the Labor Day barbecue?"

"I won't have my schedule until Saturday so I can't answer that."

"Okay, I'll call you then."

"Have fun at Uncle Liam's, Grandfather," he said as he headed out the door. "Bye, Mom."

She watched as Peter walked to his car. "He is different, Father. I don't know exactly how. I can't quite figure it out."

"It's a nice change though, Lien. Don't you think?"

"Yes. Yes, it is."

The grandfather smiled and finished his iced tea. "He's grown to be a son we can be proud of. I think you can relax now. He's got his life under control."

Twenty-Nine

Peter's schedule at the hospital took its toll on them. They hadn't seen each other all week. Peter finished some medical reports with that in mind. Looking at his watch, he got up and went to the phone booth. "Hi, honey."

"Uh-oh, did they surprise you with another double?"

"No, I've just been thinking about your birthday."

"Something wrong?"

"No. Well, yes," he said. "It's dumb, but I won't see you alone. I know its Thursday and you work tomorrow but would you wait up for me tonight? I'd like to give you my gift. And my grandfather sent you one, too."

"Oh Peter, that's so romantic. You are a surprise at times, you really are. And your grandfather didn't have to do that. He sent the nicest thank you note about Friday's dinner." Jeneil cleared her throat as she became choked with emotion.

"He wanted to, and I want to have some time alone with you for your birthday. Will you wait up?"

"Yes, that will be my best birthday celebration. I'm excited already."

"Good, I'll be out of here as soon as I can."

"I love you, Peter."

"I love you too, baby."

"I know," she said quietly. "And there's no gift on earth that can match that."

Peter smiled, pleased by her words.

There were several times during the shift when he thought he'd be asked to extend. He even started looking for someone to fill in for him. He sighed with relief as the shift drew to an end and he'd been overlooked. The birthday idea was growing stronger. Her excitement had inspired him and he was sorry that he hadn't gotten a cake somewhere. Walking toward the lab, he noticed an intern getting a snack from the vending machine. He stopped and looked at the selection, smiling. There was a package of two frosted cupcakes in one slot. Inserting the coins, he pulled the knob and the cupcakes slipped into the tray. He looked them over. No mold, they were okay. He put them in the pocket of his lab coat.

The last of the medical reports were filled out. He stretched, signed out and went to shower quickly. Dan Morretti walked in as Peter was putting on his shoes.

"What's wrong, Pete? You look like your wrestling over a problem."

Peter stood up. "Not really, just annoyed with myself that I didn't pick up some birthday candles earlier."

"There's some in a drawer at the nurse's desk. They're always surprising somebody."

Peter thought about it. "No, too many questions."

Dan smiled. "I'll get them for you. How many?"

"Thanks, two would help," Peter answered, surprised.

Dan looked at him. "It's okay. I like the lady with the velvet voice. I owe her for those great treats she sends. You know, I've watched you. I knew you had someone, but there's never any talk about it. I like that. Sometimes the talk around here gets sickening. I've got a sweet deal going too, and I decided to try it your way; tell nobody. It's easier to handle when no one knows. There's less pressure. And I'm glad to see Steve rescued from that mess he was in. Man how can anybody have a real life with a legend following him around. He's lucky he found a girl outside the hospital. Well, I'll get the candles."

"Thanks again," Peter said, somewhat amazed.

"Sure." Dan smiled and left.

*****

Peter drove onto the entrance ramp on the highway. He was really into the birthday mood. Once the idea for the cupcakes began, the candles were added and he wondered about stopping at an all night market for flowers. He couldn't, he thought, it was getting too late. They had to get to bed. Then he remembered a patch of yellow flowers growing by the highway. He had noticed them after Jeneil's story about wildflowers and laughed thinking if anyone had started a sexual relationship on the side of the highway they must have been from TAI. Seeing a cluster of flowers coming up, he pulled into the emergency lane, got out and picked some, leaving two flowers so more would grow. Jeneil had taught him to do that. 'You don't need two to grow more flowers,' she had said, 'I just don't want the last one to be lonely.' He laughed at the thought.

He juggled the flowers and his jacket with the cupcakes in his arms as he unlocked the door. Jeneil came from the bedroom. He hid the cupcakes under his jacket, but the flowers couldn't be missed. She looked surprised then smiled with pleasure.

"Oh boy, a bouquet of roots and sand, dried leaves and red mites." She laughed, looking them over. "I love the flowers," she said seriously, "thank you." She kissed him lightly. "Let me take them to the laundry room and get them civilized."

Peter went to work quickly and before Jeneil returned had the cupcakes on a plate at the small dining table. He brought the gifts and added them to the table. The laundry room door opened and Jeneil came out, admiring the flowers in a clear glass vase. She smiled at him then noticed the table. Placing the flowers as a centerpiece, she put her arms around him.

"This is terrific. It's wonderful. Thank you very much." She clung to him, enjoying the moment. Peter could tell she was sincere about liking it all.

"Hey, let's light the candles," he said, and she pulled away and wiped her tears that had escaped. He noticed and kissed her. "Happy Birthday."

"Thank you," she choked on the words. He lit a match. "Wait," she said, blowing it out. "I need to make my wish and I don't want wax on the frosting." She closed her eyes and he smiled at her silliness. "Okay, I'm ready," she said, opening her eyes again. She blew out the candles and smiled. "Good, I'll get my wish. There aren't too many opportunities in life to make wishes. Birthday candles and first stars at night are about the safest. You can never be sure that a wishbone will split in your favor and I've never found a four-leaf clover; I think they're extinct, probably because people don't believe in the magic of life anymore."

He chuckled. "If you say so."

"Can I have my gifts now? I'm curious to see what you chose for me."

"Honey, it isn't much."

"Much?" she questioned, surprised. "You don't look at the much of a gift. I'm excited to see what's revealed in your choice of gifts."

"Revealed?" he asked, puzzled.

"Yes, the choice of the gift can reflect a lot about the giver and the relationship between those involved."

"Now I'm worried."

"Don't be silly. There's no right or wrong. It's like tea leaves and a crystal ball."

He shook his head and handed her the gift. She took it and quickly unwrapped it. Taking the cover off the cardboard box and pushing back the tissue paper, she raised her eyebrows.

"Ooo, that's beautiful," she said, touching the design lightly with her finger. She removed the wooden box carefully and set it on the table and looked it over carefully, feeling the wood's finish.

"Open it," he said. "There's more inside."

"More?" She took the lid off the box. "Oh, how pretty!" She took the bracelets and looked at them then put them on. "Peter Chang, what a special, special birthday gift."

"You don't have to go overboard. I know they're not diamonds."

"Diamonds?" she replied, surprised. "Peter, there's a beautiful message contained in your gift." She stood up. "I need a hug."

"What message?" he asked, putting his arms around her.

"You mean it wasn't deliberate?"

"Maybe I'm in trouble but no it wasn't. What message?"

"The bracelets are rings symbolic of something unending. You gave me two which is a couple and you put them inside a beautiful treasure box."

He was embarrassed. "I wish it had been deliberate, but my grandfather helped me."

"Oh," she said, disappointed. "Then he chose the gifts."

"No," Peter insisted. "He taught me how. He told me to turn my back and think of you then choose from everything before me."

She smiled at him, the excitement in her eyes returning. "Merlin." She laughed. Peter stared at her. She put her arms around him again. "When I saw that treasure box I knew it was a special gift. And it is, your heart chose it, Peter. That's better than deliberate, that's life's magic. Ooo, I can't wait for soul to work." She hugged him tighter.

He held her and smiled. The magic of life was her romantic way of looking at things that made the magic. He kissed her cheek as he held her close to him.

"This is a great birthday year." She smiled and kissed him.

"Open my grandfather's gift. I'm curious to see what he gave you."

"I am, too." She lifted the package. "At first I thought it might be a book, but it moves inside of the box a bit."

Peter sat across from her as she unwrapped the package. She pushed aside the tissue paper and her face showed total surprise. "Oh my goodness, wow," she said as tears rolled down her cheeks.

Peter got up quickly to see what had touched her so deeply. His grandfather had taken the photograph of him sitting on the stairs and put it in a frame for her. He was a little surprised by her reaction. Even his gift hadn't gotten this many tears. She touched the picture lovingly.

"I had wanted to ask for this photograph, but I didn't want to put pressure on him knowing that photos of you are rare. Now I'm glad that I didn't ask. It means more to me now." She sighed. "I love that man. I really do."

Peter kissed her arm as he knelt beside her. "I wish I had known you wanted it this badly. I would like to have given it to you."

She looked at him and smiled. "I guess you don't see this message either. This photograph wouldn't mean the same thing coming from you as it has from your grandfather. I know he likes me, but I've wondered if he might be accepting me just for the protection of family peace. With this photograph he has given me his grandson. Now I feel that he accepts us together. That we please him as a couple."

Peter held her as tears started down her cheeks. He could see how very fragile she was about his family liking and accepting her.

*****

Peter and Steve walked into an apartment of boxes, wrapping paper, a half eaten birthday cake, and yellow flowers. "I'll get these put away," Jeneil said apologetically. "I just got in a few minutes ago. Would you like some cake? This birthday has been wild."

Peter and Steve smiled at her flurry of activity.

"I'll have some cake," Steve answered.

"Me, too. I'll handle it," Peter offered.

"No, it's traditional that the birthday person cuts the cake and serves it, sharing and increasing the good wishes." She went to the kitchen. Steve went to his duffle bag and got his gift. He put it on the table. She smiled as she returned with the plates. "What, another gift?"

"Steve's." Peter smiled.

"Oh, that's nice of you." She sat down and served the cake then untied the yellow velvet ribbon on the package. "I love gifts," she giggled, "and it's not ticking so I'm safe." Peter and Steve laughed. Opening the cardboard box, she lifted the tissue, peeking carefully. "It's not moving so it won't bite I guess." She looked up at Steve. "What have you done?" She seemed surprised and lifted the silver jewel box out. The lid had a cluster of small flowers embossed in the center. Delicately scrolled silver leaves circled its base and it rested on four small, wide leaf feet. "Oh Steve, it's beautiful. It really is. I'm…I…thank you."

"The card's inside."

She opened the box and raised her eyebrows. A small yellow rose with a shortly snipped stem lay inside with baby's breath and leaves bound by a thin yellow velvet ribbon. She lifted it out carefully and smelled it. Taking the small envelope from the bed of green velvet lining inside, she opened it. The card was handwritten. *Jeneil, the florist said that yellow roses are a symbol of sunshine and friendship. Thank you for both and Happy Birthday.* It was simply signed, *Steve.*

"Thank you, Steve," she said softly. "I'm touched. I really am." She put her hand gently on his. "You never fail to surprise me."

He smiled. "Happy Birthday."

"Thank you." She returned the smile then sighed. "What an incredible birthday I've had. I'm overwhelmed."

Peter watched the two of them. They were really friends, which surprised and pleased him. He smiled, enjoying seeing them together. Jeneil went to the kitchen and returned with a small brandy snifter half filled with water. She placed the rose inside. It tilted to one side and floated happily. She smiled as they watched it then tied the yellow ribbon around the stem of the snifter. "I'll put this on my bureau with my other flowers. I like to see them as I get ready for another day in the world. It's uplifting."

*****

Morning light streamed in past the shades. Jeneil stretched and quickly got out of bed. Boston was facing her and she had been waiting for the day impatiently. Her lists were made and a map was in her purse just in case. She headed to the shower, and breakfast was keeping warm as Peter and Steve slept. She sat behind the dressing screen knitting.

"What are you hiding from?" Peter asked, poking his head around the screen.

"Oh, you're finally awake. I was about to scream from impatience," she said, going to him for a hug.

"Let's get moving then. There's no time for hugging," he said, pushing her away.

"What!" She looked at him. "I'm not that impatient."

He smiled and put his arms around her. "Is there time for a kiss?"

She snuggled to him and kissed him warmly.

"Oh, you're beautiful, beautiful, and beautiful," he said, holding her close. "I'm crazy about you. Marry me right now."

She looked at him. "We're very close to it. Very close."

"Magic words, beautiful." He kissed her again.

*****

"Wow, the traffic congestion has gotten worse here," Steve said as they waited for a light to change.

"I appreciate this, Steve. It was always a strain watching the clock and watching the number of packages I'd carry with me because I could never be sure how crowded the train would be."

Steve smiled at her. "It's okay. But at this rate we'll spend the day sitting in the car."

"Steve, I have an idea. Let's park in the garage of the big hotel near the center. I'll get a room and that way I'll have a place to put my packages as I do my shopping. A single room can't be too much. Besides, I would have had to buy a round trip train ticket anyway. Yes, I like that idea. I'll call it a malfunction."

"A malfunction?" Steve asked.

"Yes, I allow myself to be bizarre from time to time. I call it a malfunction."

"You mean more than usual?"

"You're not getting to me today." She patted his arm. "I'm wrapped in birthday wishes and malfunction excitement. That's my decision. We'll go to the hotel."

Steve looked at her as they waited for another light. Turning away he thought she was cuter than all hell, and he felt his heart turn over.

*****

Jeneil approached them as they sat on cushioned seats in the lobby. "All set," she said. "Here's a key for my husband. I explained the shopping trip to them." Peter smiled and took the key from her. "And I also checked on what's happening in the hotel today. There's a science fiction convention on the third floor. They have movies and other things going on. It sounds like fun. I thought you'd like to check it out while I shop."

"You mean we're not going shopping with you?" Peter asked.

"That's no fun for you," she answered, surprised.

Peter stood up and hugged her. "You are beautiful."

"If the convention doesn't keep you interested then go upstairs and watch TV or sleep. Do whatever you'd like. I'll be back at one and we can meet in the room for lunch. Sound okay?"

"Very okay." Peter smiled.

"Are you sure you don't want company?" Steve asked. "Boston streets are beginning to look like New York."

"I'll be fine," Jeneil replied. "I know my way around and I've even seen some interesting looking shops right here in the hotel. Thank you Steve, but I'll see you both at one." She kissed Peter and left as a group of people walked by in space costumes.

"Hey, they're dressed like the crew from that TV program, Outer Space," Peter said.

Steve laughed. "Follow them to the convention. Imagine a whole group of people like Jeneil. That should be something to see."

Peter and Steve were watching a baseball game on television when Jeneil opened the door to the room and walked in, breathless. "Sorry I'm late, but I passed a deli and decided to pick up some bumming out sandwiches and chips for you two. If you'll call room service and order a pot of coffee and a salad and milk for me, I'll freshen up."

"Oh thanks, baby." Peter sighed. "We were getting really hungry."

They sat finishing their lunches. "Jeneil, why do you do Christmas shopping in August?" Steve asked.

Jeneil shrugged. "Because my calendar is out of whack. I start singing Christmas carols in July and by August I'm ready for shopping. I always have one or two gifts I buy closer to Christmas, but the pace of the season and the crowds depress me. It's a madness that actually hurts my skin and gives me headaches. So during the usual Christmas shopping season I spend my nights going to choir concerts and Christmas plays I wouldn't have time to go to if I was shopping. It's my Christmas present to me. I love Christmas done that way. I end up enjoying the true celebration of the season."

Peter kissed her cheek. "Honey, sometimes the world seems out of step, not you."

Jeneil smiled. "That's really nice to hear. It isn't easy defending my eccentricity to myself sometimes, but it's how I am and as long as I compromise with the normal whenever it demands, and society leaves me to myself, then I'm in balance."

Steve watched her. She had taken her hair down to give it a rest because the city had been crowded and it made her scalp hurt. He loved her outfit. The brown and rust print together with the soft material seemed to blend with her and spell money. The way her eyes changed color shocked him and he loved their softness. There were times she was so damned bossy with her decisions that she reminded him of Turcell, but her approach was different somehow. He didn't mind Jeneil's bossiness at all. It was part of her fire. He grinned as she laid flat on the floor. It was Sava Sana she had said, a yoga resting position.

*****

They put Jeneil's packages in the trunk of the car then got into the car to face the heavy traffic again.

"The gallery is in Cambridge near the Charles."

"Oh good, Pete, and I can stand on the river bank and yell stroke to the Harvard team. I'd like to see if they can be distracted."

"Why don't you come into the gallery with me?" Jeneil asked.

"I'm not dressed like you," Steve replied.

"Well, you'd look strange if you were. They have a name for men who do that." Jeneil laughed.

"Smart mouth." Steve grinned.

"Snob, snob, snob, Steve."

"Yeah but I notice you're dressed money."

"I'm buying," Jeneil explained. "I want merchants to take me seriously."

"More Christmas shopping?" Peter asked.

"Yes, a painting for Marlene, Uncle Hollis's wife. I don't see Robert's work fitting into her life. His boldness would seem out of place. I hope to get sculptures for Uncle Hollis's and Bill's offices there, too. Uncle Hollis isn't bold and Bill has enough boldness in his life already. Actually Bill's office isn't bold at all; it's smooth and passive, almost like a waiting room." She laughed. "His jet seems more like his office. I'm giving Dennis some of Robert's work and I'm giving Robert one of his own pieces. He doesn't have any around his apartment. His work is how he makes his living but I know there's one sculpture he really put himself into that he'd like to have kept."

Steve smiled. "And who said Santa Claus was a myth?"

"A myth?" Jeneil challenged. "He was a real person named Nicolas who actually loved children and did give them gifts. When he died, adults in the village who had received presents from him as children decided to keep up the tradition in his memory. He was sainted for his generous acts after he died. That's where we get St. Nicolas."

"Who told you that?" Peter asked.

"The tooth fairy." Jeneil laughed. "I don't know, I've read it somewhere along the way. I intend to tell my children about St. Nicolas." Steve and Peter laughed. "Laugh all you want, traditions are inspiring and legends are important to civilization. My parents had a rule that at least one Christmas gift had to be handmade. We could give store bought too, but one had to be personally made and given to each person in the family. That was easy for us since we were such a small group. Mandra loved the handmade gifts the most and she got into the habit of giving one, too. I loved the personal essays she'd scroll on parchment and add border designs to. She had an artistic eye and a poetic soul."

Steve laughed. "Jeneil, it's beginning to feel like Christmas. I expect it to snow any minute now."

Peter looked at her. "You had some family, honey." He rubbed her shoulder, thinking about his.

She sighed. "They really were good people."

"Here's your gallery," Steve said, pulling off the street to the curb. They walked into the Brownstone building. A man in a blue business suit came to them.

"Hi, Jeneil, Merry Christmas."

"Thank you, Mr. Jamison."

"We contacted the artist you asked about. He sent some pieces over, and we have a grouping of Sarah's paintings on display in another room."

"Oh, very good." Jeneil smiled. "I love doing business with you. I can always count on having everything ready for me. This is Peter Chang and Steve Bradley. I've been shopping in Boston, and they are my pilot and navigator. I can never execute a successful trip by car on my own."

"I've heard natives of the area say the same thing." The man smiled.

"Do you have any brochures on new artists? I'd like to take them home and study them." She began to walk away then turned. "Are you coming with me?"

"No, we'll wait right there," Peter said, pointing to a bench.

She nodded and walked away. Steve watched her. "She's so comfortable around all this."

"Her mother was an artist. She's waiting for the Nebraska office of Alden-Connors to get to a growth level then plans to begin a foundation that will sponsor artists and promote art in schools and neighborhoods. She said her mother always felt that art and its purpose were too removed from people who were so busy making a living that they didn't have time to understand and study it."

Steve shook his head. "She's not your usual yuppie."

"She's not your usual anything," Peter said. They both sat on the bench wrapped up in their own thoughts.

*****

"We're making good time," Steve said as he approached the exit ramp to the market area.

"How did you find out about this place?" Peter asked.

"Dennis and Robert were talking about it. It's an international type of shopping area. They usually come here when they've tried everywhere else for something and can't find it. Besides being curious to see it, I'm hoping to find something special for Franklin. I'm told there are old curio shops and antique stores mingled amongst the other businesses. Mostly I'm just curious to see the area."

They parked the car in a huge lot at the end of the market center and walked in. A variety of odors mingled in the air.

"I smell coffee beans roasting," Jeneil said. "It reminds me of the gourmet food store in Billingsly where Mandra would buy coffee beans and imported fruit. And there are roasting nuts, bread, and a pungent smell I can't identify."

"Probably coming from a water pipe." Steve chuckled.

"Ah yes, good old hashish." Peter laughed.

"What's hashish?" Jeneil asked.

"It ain't Turkish taffy, sweetheart."

"But you get it from the candy man," Peter added. He and Steve laughed.

"Drugs?" Jeneil asked. "But these are legitimate businesses." Peter and Steve laughed harder.

Steve put his arm around her shoulder. "Where are you from, Mother Goose land?"

She looked at him. "No, I'm just surprised, that's all. I thought you meant that it was being done openly. Oh forget I started explaining, it gets more naive as I try to get out of it."

Steve squeezed her gently. "It's okay, kid. You're refreshing." He looked at her and smiled then he took his arm away and put his hands in his pockets.

Peter put his arm around her waist. "Where to first, honey?"

"The first curio shop I can find that looks like one."

They entered a nondescript store. It smelled musty and old. Its wooden floor boards creaked and there were glass merchandise cases which cordoned off the area where people could walk. An older man came from a back room. His gray hair was tousled and his glasses rested on the end of his nose as he studied them over the rims.

"Something in particular?" he asked.

Jeneil looked around. "I'm looking for something for someone with musical interests. Do you mind browsers?"

Looking her outfit over, he smiled warmly. "Not at all, I'll browse through some drawers back here to see what's around and musical."

Jeneil spotted a case of jewelry and went to look more closely. "Sir, would you mind if I tried some of this jewelry on?"

"Here," the man said, bringing a tray out and putting it on the glass case before her. "These aren't worth much," he added. "I have a tray of better items you can look at."

"Are most of these stones marquisate?"

"Probably."

"I'd love to go hunting for marquisate someday." She smiled. "I'd like to see what a chunk looks like; I've only seen small pieces or chips. I'd like to hunt for that and geodes."

The man smiled at her.

"I like this," Jeneil said, reaching for a ring of silver metal. It was completely filigreed in fine strands of silver. It was scalloped to only a half inch at its widest point and narrowed to a quarter inch at its smallest. Dotted in each of the smaller points was a small marquisate chip that glittered, almost matching the color of the metal. She put it on and held her hand up to look at the ring. "It looks like Guinevere's crown. What am I doing?" she asked herself. "I'm here for Franklin. You'd better put these away."

Jeneil put the ring back and the man returned the tray to the case. Two more customers came in. While the man left to deal with them, Jeneil concentrated on the shelves. She could spend a day just going through touching and holding everything, but nothing seemed to strike her as right for Franklin. She sighed. She didn't have time to visit every store in the area.

"Nothing's reaching you?" the man asked, returning to help her.

"Not really. I've seen a lot I like but nothing for my friend."

"I don't know what you want to spend, but I have a carved ivory page clip in a drawer. I'll get it for you."

Jeneil turned to see where Peter and Steve had gone. They were standing near the door talking.

"How about this?" the man asked, holding an item out to her.

"Yes, yes, this is just right, it's perfect. Thank you," she said, brightening. "I'm sure I can find a box somewhere."

"Oh, allow me. I keep a few boxes for the better things here and there," he said, going to the back room.

"Find something?" Peter asked.

"Yes, a page clip." She showed it to Peter. "It's perfect."

The man brought a small white box with cotton inside.

Jeneil smiled excitedly. "I'm so pleased with it; I think I'll buy the ring, too. I really like it."

The man looked at her. "The one you tried on?"

"Yes."

"I'm sorry, it was just sold."

"Oh no!" Jeneil was disappointed. She sighed. "Well, there's nothing to be done about it. If it's sold, it's sold. That's the name of the game, but I really appreciate you finding this for me."

The man smiled. "I'm glad you understand about the ring."

Jeneil took her package and walked to Peter and Steve. "I'm finished. Do you believe the customers who came in bought the ring I had my eye on."

"There were other rings there," Peter said. "Go look at them."

"No," she said. "The other one stood out to me as being special. It's my own fault. I should have bought it when I had the chance. I'll keep my eyes open. Somewhere there may be another."

"That's too bad," Steve said. "So where to now?"

"Time's getting short," she said. "Would you like to go your own ways and we'll meet again in a half hour or so?"

"I'd like that," Steve said.

"Okay," Peter agreed. "Going to look for another ring?"

"I don't think so. I'd like to look in the India Emporium Store. Those prints are beautiful."

"Shall we meet you there?" Peter asked.

"Yes, that's good. In about a half hour?"

"Fine," Steve said, and they separated.

After browsing through the emporium, Jeneil stepped out of the market and waited in the sunshine. The air felt good even with all its different smells. She was earlier than both Peter and Steve, but the closed air of the market had begun to give her a headache. She watched people on the street going about their business. She jumped as she felt two arms slip around her waist. The arms tightened and Peter kissed her cheek.

"You shouldn't daydream. See how easy I could have kidnapped you."

Jeneil laughed and turned to face him. "Help," she whispered, "I'm being kidnapped by a handsome Chinaman. Ooo, forget the help."

"I love you," he said, smiling and kissing her lightly.

"Me, too."

"Peter Chang! It is you?"

Peter turned. The voice was very familiar. "Lin Chi! What are you doing here?" he asked, smiling.

Lin Chi hugged him. "I couldn't believe it was you! Of all people to see this far from home."

"Lin Chi, you look great. You've been to rehab!"

"Well I was forced to. My kidneys decided they'd had enough and I passed out in a small diner. The owner got me to a hospital and I struggled back to what you see now."

"Well you look really good," Peter said. "I'm glad the rehab took."

"Actually I've had help. The owner of the diner has been a good friend to me. He's here shopping and I decided to wander around on my own. We're together now and it's easier for me to keep it all straight."

Peter hugged her again and held her. "You don't know how glad I am to hear that." He turned to Jeneil. "Honey, this is Lin Chi."

"Hi." Jeneil smiled and held out her hand. Lin Chi took it, studying Jeneil intently.

Peter smiled. "This is Jeneil."

Lin Chi smiled. "I know she's your lady. I could see that as I walked up to you. Peter Chang, you're still shakin' up dust. What does the Queen Mother have to say about the beautiful princess?"

"She doesn't know. I'm a coward."

"You're smart," Lin Chi answered. "Pete, you be smart, too. You look really great yourself. That's too good to let anybody ruin. Come and meet my man, Bo. I've told him about you."

"I'd like to." Peter put his arm around Lin Chi's "Okay with you, baby?"

"Of course," Jeneil said. "I'll wait here for Steve and we'll join you."

"At Spike's on the next block," Lin Chi said.

"I can remember that. You know, Peter has told me about you, too." Jeneil hugged Lin Chi, surprising her. "I'm glad to have met you."

Lin Chi was embarrassed. "She's some lady, Pete."

"I know, Lin Chi. That much I know for certain."

Jeneil smiled. "Go, Peter. Steve will be here soon. I'm sure I'll be fine."

Peter and Lin Chi walked away.

"Pete's not back yet?" Steve asked, joining Jeneil.

"We ran into Lin Chi."

"Oh shit," Steve said. "I'm sorry, Jeneil."

"Peter went to meet the man she lives with."

"You mean she was straight enough to complete a sentence?"

"Yes, she's been to rehab because of kidney trouble."

Steve sighed with relief.

"You worry about him. You're a good friend and you've given up your time for me today. A hug, I need a hug." She put his arms around his waist and he put his arms around her. "You're a nice guy, Steve Bradley. Your secret's out now." She looked up at him and he smiled at her. She kissed his cheek gently. "They're waiting for us at Spike's on the next block."

"Let's go then," he said, putting his arm around her as they crossed the street.

*****

The woman in the store across the street called to her husband. "Tom, come here a minute!" Her husband joined her at the window. "Is that Peter?"

"Of course it is, Lien. Why?"

The woman continued watching at the window in growing shock as the clerk called her husband back.

"Tom, come here quickly," she called to her husband again.

Her husband walked over. "Lien, we'll never get through here if you don't stop…."

"Tom," she interrupted, "tell me who's with Peter."

"Uh-oh," he said quietly.

"Lin Chi, right?" She sighed heavily.

"Lien, don't cause a scene."

"I just wanted a witness, that's all. Go back to your business," and she turned to continue her watch.

*****

Peter and Steve carried Jeneil's packages upstairs. "We made record time today," Peter said, "and we wouldn't have if you hadn't come along Steve."

"Yes, thank you again," Jeneil added. "Come for dinner tomorrow. I'll make all your favorites as a thank you."

"No, I'm always with you two," Steve answered.

"But it's Sunday. Please," Jeneil begged.

"He's coming, honey. I'll make sure of that."

Thirty

Sunday mornings had a different feel at the hospital. Peter wondered why he had never noticed that before Jeneil and her special Sunday routine. There was a quieter tone to everything. The world stopped and it liked being special.

Peter was assigned to the fifth floor. The ER had several cases being admitted and he was transferred until the rush had passed. He saw Steve briefly in the doctor's lounge where they both got coffee.

"I'm looking forward to Sunday dinner," Steve said. "Someone could make a bundle if they opened a restaurant for just Sunday dinner with an atmosphere to match."

"I know what you mean. It's grown on me, too."

Peter was paged. He picked up the phone in the lounge and the operator transferred the call.

"Tom!" Peter said, surprised. "Is something wrong?"

"Can you come over tonight?"

Peter sensed something in his tone. "Tom, if something's wrong don't keep me waiting."

"It's better handled here, Pete."

"My grandfather?" Peter asked, concerned.

"He's okay. He's due back later. When do you get out of work?"

"Probably seven."

"Stop by after that."

"Is my mother okay?"

"She's been better," Tom answered. "Please Pete, right after work?"

"Sure," Peter answered quietly.

"What's wrong?" Steve asked after Peter had hung up the phone.

"Something's wrong. Tom has never called me unless the mother couldn't and my grandfather wasn't available."

"Do you think she's sick?"

"I don't know. I hate it when people do that. Just tell me what it is and be done with it. Well, I'll know after work. Right now I've got a job to do."

"After work? Then I'm not going to your place for dinner."

"That's silly. Jeneil will be there."

"No, Pete. Really, no."

"Hell, I'll go home to dinner and then go over. If it's not urgent enough to tell me now then they can wait."

*****

Jeneil had the table set. The house smelled like Sunday dinner.

Peter smiled as he walked in.

Steve sniffed. "Pot roast."

Jeneil came from the kitchen. Her cheeks were flushed from being near the stove. "I'll put dinner on the table. I know I'm hungry."

After dinner, Peter sat back. "That was good. I wish I didn't have to go out. Relaxing sounds so good right now."

"You're going out?"

"My mother's."

"Oh, I didn't know that."

Peter got up and kissed Jeneil's cheek. "I'll wear another shirt that smells good. She'll be happy." Jeneil looked at him, completely puzzled.

Steve stood up. "I'm leaving, too."

"You're going to his mom's house, too?" Jeneil asked.

Steve laughed. "No."

"Date?"

"No."

"Be mysterious, see if I care." Jeneil shrugged.

"I don't feel right staying."

"That's crazy, man," Peter said, returning and fixing his collar. "Why not?"

"Don't force him, Peter. He doesn't need to babysit for me. So I've been alone all day with no one to talk to. I prepared a dinner expecting some company and I'll be disappointed. It doesn't matter."

"Oh, that gets right to the heart." Steve smiled and Jeneil grinned back at him.

Peter hit his arm gently. "Stay, Steve. I'll bet this is nothing and I'll be back in an hour. Stay." He picked up his jacket and kissed Jeneil. "Keep dessert for me, honey."

"Okay."

Peter closed the door behind him and ran down the stairs.

"Go and relax, I'll do the dishes."

"No, I'll help," Steve offered.

"That isn't necessary."

"I want to," Steve insisted, and he began clearing the table.

They washed dishes together and talked. Steve was surprised they talked easily. No kidding, no teasing, just two people talking. He liked that, too. They went to the living room. Jeneil put on some music and joined him on the sofa with her knitting. He picked up the paper.

"Hey, Pa," she joked, "notice how the house is quiet since the kids is all growed up. Let's chew some gum. The snapping noises will be fun to listen to."

Steve chuckled. "Is that a hint that I'm dull?"

Jeneil laughed. "No, I just realized how comfortable and square this seemed. Like the folks back on the farm."

"That's what I like about Sundays here."

*****

Peter got out of his car and walked to the back door. Opening it, he walked in and saw his mother pacing. She looked upset. Tom was sitting at the table.

"What's up?" Peter asked.

His mother stopped. "Let's wait for your grandfather. He's putting his luggage in his room," she said, not looking at him.

"What's this all about? I thought this was an emergency, and how come you're not at the restaurant?"

His grandfather walked into the kitchen. "What's happening here?"

His mother turned around. "Father, remember how you said that he had grown to be a son we could be proud of, that he had his life under control. Remember? And remember how he told you that he never intended to see Lin Chi again. Well, he's a sneaking liar. I saw him in Sutton yesterday with her."

Peter felt the words hit his stomach with sudden impact. He wondered where. Had she seen Jeneil? His temples began to pulsate. His grandfather looked at him.

"I ran into her there. I wasn't with her," he said, sitting down.

"Stop it," his mother snapped. "Do you think we're fools?"

"I ran into her there. I haven't seen her in months," Peter repeated more strongly.

"You were with her! You had your arm around her! You walked off with her!" she yelled. "Stop lying. When will you ever grow up? You're a doctor. For heaven's sake, why do you hang around with trash! Why can't you stay away from filth? You've always been in the gutter. What's wrong with you?" She began to cry.

"Lien, please," the grandfather said.

"No, Father. He's not lying anymore. He's going to own up to what he's doing with his life. I don't care if he is grown. This grandson of yours has no honor. Do you know that he even got cozy with Steve's girl?"

"What?" Peter looked up quickly. "What are you talking about?"

"Don't deny it. I was standing across the street at a shop window. I saw you go up to her and put your arms around her. You even scared the poor girl."

Peter's heart stopped. She had seen Jeneil.

She began pacing again. "Why can't you learn from Steve? Look at the girl he chose. She's decent, well dressed. She was lovely." Peter looked at her, completely surprised. She shook her head. "And behind Steve's back yet. You have no pride, no honor. He's been a good friend to you. Can't you respect that? Do you have to drag your trash into his life, too? You're lucky he didn't see you pull what you did." She paced and began crying again. "I thought you had finally begun to change your gutter ways."

Peter didn't know what to do or say. He looked at his grandfather, who was totally puzzled.

"Are you making any sense of this?" his grandfather asked him.

His mother turned sharply. "Of course he's making sense of this. Can't you see how guilty he is? We saw him and he can't lie anymore. Are you doing that regularly with Steve's girl? Are you looking to cause deliberate trouble between them? If she ever tells him be sure he won't understand or make sense of it. You embarrass me. Always after girls. Always in trouble with somebody's family for being involved with their daughter. It's disgusting. But to try that on your best friend's girl throws you back into the gutter. Way back," she yelled. "You filthy gutter rat, always amongst garbage!"

"Lien, please," the grandfather said sternly.

"Make him stop seeing Lin Chi. This is her influence. She's filth. Disgusting filth," she cried.

"Mom, you liked the other girl?" Peter asked quietly.

"She's a nice girl, Peter. You can see that about her. You should be happy for Steve, not trying to betray him."

Peter swallowed hard and hoped for the best. "Mom, she's my girl. Her name is Jeneil."

The grandfather sat down and waited in shock.

She looked at him, totally confused. "What are you talking about? The girl is white."

"She's my girl, Mom." He was glad it was out in the open. It suddenly felt good to him.

"That's impossible. She's white. No, she was with Steve. She even kissed him."

Peter looked at her. "Kissed him?"

"Yes, after you left with Lin Chi. She waited for Steve. She put her arms around him and kissed his cheek."

"They're good friends."

"Peter, I know what I saw, and you don't go out with white girls. If this is your way of getting around explaining Lin Chi, it won't work."

"I give up," Peter said, standing up. "We can sit here all night and get nowhere. I ran into Lin Chi. Steve and I drove Jeneil to do some shopping. She's my girl."

She stared blankly. "But Steve…likes her. He cares about her."

"I know that," Peter said. "I told you they're good friends."

She stared at Peter. "How long have you been dating this girl?"

"Since spring."

She sat in silence. "I thought you didn't have time to date. I heard you say that to Karen a few days ago."

"I lied. I didn't want you finding out yet."

"Why?" She eyed him suspiciously.

"Because I didn't know how you would take her not being Chinese. I can't believe you're not angry about that. You've always picked on whites."

She looked at him, studying his face closely. "Are you dating this girl?"

Peter looked at her. "I just told you that she's my girl."

"No, I asked if you're dating this girl."

"She's my girl, Mom," he said, fidgeting.

His mother stood up and walked over to him. "You're not dating her, you liar. You're living with her! That's it! You're living with her!" She was getting emotional again. "That's why we can't get you at the dorms. Of course it is. The clean clothes. You've gained weight. I should have known." She shook her head and walked away. "He leaves Chinese trash and goes to white trash." She threw a towel on the counter.

Peter felt the buzz go through his brain. "Don't you ever call her that again, is that clear?" He fought back his anger.

"No wonder she felt comfortable hugging Lin Chi, they're the same kind."

"Stop it!" Peter exploded. "I told you to watch it and I mean it." He could feel himself shaking inside.

"Peter, please," his grandfather said quietly.

"No. No, Grandfather. She won't do this to Jeneil. She won't. I promise you that."

His mother sat down and shook her head. "And I thought she was a decent girl. I don't care how nicely she dresses, Peter. Clothes can't cover up what she is."

"I'm gone," he said, heading to the door.

"Peter, get back here," his grandfather ordered.

Peter spun around. "No! And how can you let her talk like that. No! You can keep your name."

"Peter!"

Peter slammed the door behind him.

"Go get him, Tom," the grandfather said, and Tom quickly went out the door. "Lien, listen to me."

She sobbed. "He's living with her. He's living with white trash, something else for our people to deal with. It's hopeless."

"Lien, shut up," the grandfather said strongly, and she lifted her head, stunned. "Lien, listen carefully." The old man was shaking. "He's not just angry. When he says he's gone, he means for good. He won't be back. He's asked the girl to marry him."

She covered her mouth. "White trash!"

The grandfather closed his eyes and sighed. "She's not that," he insisted. "She's a wonderful girl."

"She lives with him, Father!"

"It's a different world today. Please, Lien. Trust me. You will lose him completely. He loves her deeply. Look at his life. Look at him. He's happy."

"Of course he's happy. He's always happy when he has a girl."

"He's serious, Lien. You won't see him again."

"It's always this way with us."

"Not this time. The girl is special to him."

"And you know about her?"

"Since your birthday."

She looked shocked. "Then those earrings. He didn't pick them out."

"Oh Lien, it doesn't matter. When he comes back in here, I want you to apologize."

"Me! He's living with her and you want me to apologize! He brings the dishonor and I have to apologize. Are you listening to yourself?"

"Lien, apologize for the sake of peace or lose your son. It's your choice. The girl is a decent girl. Look at what her love has done for him."

"She doesn't love him, Father. I saw her with Steve. I saw them myself. There's something there. I know there is. She won't marry Peter. They always stay with their own kind. Peter's some game to her, probably for kicks."

The grandfather rubbed his forehead. "Lien, I don't know why you draw such a blank when it comes to Peter. I'm going to say it again, if you don't apologize, you'll lose him. If you call the girl names, you'll lose him. He means it. He intends to marry the girl. He's not a boy anymore, he's a man. If you'll give her a chance, you'll see that she's everything you would want for Peter, everything and more. Her name is Jeneil. Call her that."

Tom came back inside. "He won't come in. He said he's too angry to drive right now, but he's not coming back."

The grandfather looked at his daughter seriously. "Apologize, Lien, for the sake of the family," he said quietly. "I'll go talk to him."

The mother began to cry. "I can't apologize," she said to her husband. "I'm telling the truth. No one listens."

"Lien, look at him. The girl has done that for him. Everything that's pleased you about him lately is because of her. Isn't this what you've wanted for him?"

"To marry white trash? Be serious."

"Lien, I've talked to him. Your father's right. You'll lose him."

Peter was leaning against his car when his grandfather went to him and Peter turned his back. "I'm your grandfather, Peter. Don't do that. You turn around and face me."

"Right now I'm angrier at you than I am at her. You weren't even there for Jeneil. I expected that from her, but you stood there and let her call Jeneil those names and Jeneil thinks you're so terrific." Peter choked up. "You're not my grandfather anymore. I'm not a Chang."

The old man felt the words cut deeply. There was no grandfather and grandson in this situation. He understood Peter's hurt. He took the first step and walked around to face him.

"Peter, I was completely shocked by what was happening in there. I had no idea she had seen you and Jeneil. You know the worst thing to do to your mother is to angrily oppose her. It makes the hurt go deeper. I thought we understood that. I kept hoping you'd stay calm and let her work the shock and anger out of her system. We know what Jeneil is. Your mother's words were empty. It was just anger. Getting angry at your mother won't help Jeneil. I've asked your mother to apologize for what she's said." Peter looked at him. "I'd like you to go back inside and settle things. Even Jeneil wants the family. Try to give her that. Your mother never said anything about her being white. That's a total surprise. Cling to that Peter. Let it work for us. Think Peter, if you go back to Jeneil without settling this, what can you tell her? If you try to settle things then think of that message."

Peter looked at his grandfather. He put his hands in his pockets. He sighed then ran his fingers through his hair. "I'll try."

"Thank you, Peter."

"Don't you thank me, I'm doing this for Jeneil," Peter said coldly, heading for the house.

The grandfather felt the anger Peter had for him.

Peter's mother and Tom were surprised to see Peter. Tom smiled. Peter was silent. His grandfather watched, hoping.

"Peter, I'm sorry...," his mother began.

"No," he said strongly. "You're not sorry, you're angry, so don't apologize. You were told to apologize. Let's not be phony." His mother was stunned. "We can spend the rest of the night talking and we'll never agree so let's not pretend. Jeneil doesn't want to cause trouble in the family. She really believes in families. We had hoped everything would work out. She wanted you to like her but I know you can't force that. What I'm asking is that you hold your tongue. No name calling to her face like you did to Lin Chi. If you can't be decent to her when she's around you then I'm asking you to be silent. I've asked her to marry me and she has accepted. We promised each other if the family caused problems for the marriage we would walk away from the family for good. I intend to keep that promise. That's the situation. Can you live with it?"

His mother studied his face. This was a different Peter. She actually admired him and could tell he meant what he was saying. "You don't care what people will say about you two living together?"

"The people we know have accepted us. If you mean the Chinese community, they won't know unless you tell them and no I don't care. If it bothers you then I can stay away. That should make it easier."

"Easier?" His mother began to flare. "Easier to accept the fact that my son chose to give up his family for white tr...."

Peter glared at her. "That's the situation. Can you accept it?"

Tom touched her arm gently. "Yes," she said quietly.

"Okay. That's the treaty. Any violation and it's over."

"What about the Labor Day barbecue? Will you bring her?"

"I'm working so we won't come. Anything you can't handle, tell me, not her." His mother nodded.

"Thank you, Peter," the grandfather said, proud of him. Peter walked out not answering or saying goodbye.

Tom got up and followed Peter out. "Pete, I admire what you just did in there. I saw the girl. She seemed very nice. I'm really glad you're happy. My position will be next to your mother wherever that will be in the future, so I understand what you must do. I hope my son, John, shows your kind of courage someday." Tom extended his hand and Peter shook it. "I'll work for peace, you can count on that."

"Thanks," Peter said, then turned and left.

Driving home, Peter couldn't help but notice the similarities between what had just taken place and negotiating peace treaties with the Dragons. "They were my family, Jeneil. They taught me a lot," he thought out loud.

Jeneil studied Peter's face as he walked in. She watched him hang up his jacket. "Where's Steve?"

"Your telephone rang. It was the hospital. The ER needed help so he went in for you."

Peter smiled. "He's a great friend."

"Yes, he is," she answered, still watching him closely. He sat next to her on the sofa. "What happened at your mother's?"

"I need a kiss." He sighed and held onto her as she kissed him.

"Tell me what happened."

"My mother knows about us."

She pulled away, startled. "How?"

"She saw us in Sutton."

"She knows everything? That you live here?" She caught her breath as he nodded. "Now what?"

He smiled. "Will you marry me?"

She took his arm with her hands. "Oh Peter, don't play games with me. I want to know exactly what happened."

"Oh honey, she isn't happy about it. That's no surprise, is it? But she's accepted it."

"What? You're kidding. She really has?" She put her head back and sighed. "We have your grandfather to thank for this."

"Humph, my grandfather," Peter said under his breath. Jeneil heard the scorn.

"What aren't you telling me?"

"Let's forget it," he said, shaking his head.

"No, we can't. I need to know everything in order to deal with this."

"There's nothing to deal with. She's agreed to shut up."

Jeneil looked at him. "Peter, accepting us and shutting up are two different things. Which is it?"

"Jeneil, I don't know. I don't care. There won't be any screaming, that's all I want."

"Peter, be patient with me. I want to know everything. Who called the meeting?"

"My mother."

"What did she say when she found out we were living together? Did she call me white trash?" Peter stood up and paced. "What did you say when she called me white trash?" Peter continued to pace silently. "You told her to shut up and she didn't so you stomped out. Your grandfather stepped in and brought you two together. He settled things between you. How? He really is a Merlin."

"Oh please, baby. The man has feet of clay," he said sharply, his feeling of betrayal surfacing.

"Why? What did he do?"

"Nothing, not one damn thing, he sat there while she...," he stopped, gaining control of his anger.

"While she called me names besides white trash," she said quietly, standing and facing him. He put his arms around her. "It's alright, Peter. I've been preparing myself for that. Putting myself in her place, I would look like white trash. I'm living with her son and won't marry him yet. It's understandable. That's what I expected. Don't be angry at your grandfather."

"No, baby, we don't talk about him at all. I don't want to hear his name."

"Peter, listen to me. He had the worst position in the whole situation, that of mediator. Do you know how difficult that role is? You can't take sides with anyone so you can keep your place as liaison. If he made her angry that would have been worse for me. I don't want him to defend me; I just want him to keep the line between you and your mother open. He did that, Peter. He did that by being silent." She started to cry. "He defended me the way I would have defended myself. Don't turn from him. He's our only hope." She leaned against him and cried softly.

"Honey, you and my grandfather speak the same language. You sound so much like him." He squeezed her gently. "Now that I'm past my anger, I remember the police captain at our peace meetings didn't take sides. My grandfather thinks you're terrific so it stunned me that he never said a word to help you, but I understand what you've just said. Tom told me he'd try to help smooth the way, too."

"Your stepfather?"

"Yes."

"Well that really is good news. How did your mother tell you that she'll accept us?"

"I told her that I wanted peace, if not that then silence or I'll keep my promise to walk away."

"That's an ultimatum not an agreement." She sighed. "Well, it's a cease fire at least. That can be positive, skimpy but possible."

Peter shook his head. "This isn't what I expected from you at all."

Jeneil smiled. "You and Steve tease me about playing with helium but sometimes looking at things from high above can give you a clearer view of the whole situation. I can take this, Peter. We can create a positive from it. I love your grandfather. Did he know you were angry at him?" Peter didn't answer. Jeneil stepped back. "What? Did you yell at him, too?"

"I turned my back on him and told him he wasn't my grandfather anymore."

Jeneil covered her mouth. Tears filled her eyes. "That must have hurt him deeply. You can't do that. You can't ever walk away from him. He's blood. He's your grandfather. Please call him, Peter. Please."

"Maybe tomorrow," he said quietly.

"No, please," she pleaded. "Don't let him deal with that another minute. Tell him you understand. He doesn't deserve that at all. Oh please!"

He could tell her concern was genuine. "Okay," he said quietly and dialed the phone. "Karen, can I talk to my grandfather?"

"Hey, Pete. What's up?"

"What do you mean?"

"I've heard 'you' whisperings and seen tears for two days around here. Are you in trouble again?"

"No trouble, Karen. Don't eavesdrop. It's not smart."

"It just feels like old times, Pete." She giggled. "I'll get your grandfather."

"Peter?" His grandfather sounded surprised.

Peter hesitated. "Grandfather…I'd like to apologize for the things I said to you. Now that I'm calm, I can understand better."

The old man sighed. "Thank you, Peter. Thank you very much. I know you were defending Jeneil. You were hurt. I hoped you'd eventually see my side, too. I didn't expect it this soon."

"How is my mother now?"

"You know my first thought was it was too bad she had to find out that way, but I think it actually helped. The confusion has thrown her off guard. She's so relieved that you're not with Lin Chi that it's made her more reasonable. But I'm confused about her insistence of something between Steve and Jeneil."

"That's as confused as me and Lin Chi. She's imagining it."

His grandfather smiled. "Probably, I just wish she'd move off that idea. She's getting too upset about it."

Peter sighed. "There's always something with her. She lives on trouble."

"Well, you handled the situation really well, Peter. She said that you surprised her."

Peter smiled. "Songbird, Grandfather."

"Yes, I'm sure and I thank her for your apology, too."

"Hey, I dialed and said the words." They both laughed. "Grandfather, Jeneil and I thank you for everything you're trying to do for us. Your gift meant a lot to her."

"I'm sure it did. Jeneil was right about the gift. She knows it's more than a photograph."

Peter understood. "I'll call you soon."

"Do that, Peter. Be sure to do that."

Peter replaced the receiver. "I don't know why I always resist apologies. You feel good after they're over."

Jeneil smiled and hugged him. "Chang is a terrific guy. He really is. He's misplaced in history, too. I think we're both from the twelfth century."

Peter looked at her. "Jeneil, you're handling this better than I am," and he put his arms around her. "I found out tonight how much I love you." She snuggled to him and smiled. They held each other in silence, feeling protected.

"Peter, I've added to Camelot."

"What did you add?"

Going to the dining room, she returned with two white boxes. She opened one and removed a grey haired figurine in a brown robe. "It's Merlin. Merlin helped King Arthur. He was a wizard full of wisdom and insight." She smiled. "You gave me the idea once when you said that the prince would just wander around without the princess's help. Your grandfather seems to fit in Camelot and he's help and protection for us. So it seemed natural."

"What's in the other box?" Opening it, Peter recognized the blonde figurine from the ceramic store. It was Lancelot. "Steve?"

"Yes, now the prince will have a lot of help on the quest." She headed to the flower pots and placed Lancelot next to Arthur with Merlin facing all three.

"I wish you had gotten the prince from Cinderella instead."

She looked at him. "Why?"

"The story of these three makes me nervous."

Jeneil laughed. "And you tease me about helium. At least I know this is a hobby." She laughed again. "Besides we changed their names, remember."

"Yeah, and you put the ogre in the pot with them and your uncle found out about us. Then you turned the witch loose on them and my mother found out about us."

Jeneil laughed at his words. "Oh Peter, a superstitious doctor, that's funny."

"It's not superstition, it's from the streets. We used to say don't push your luck. Take her out of the pot." Peter smiled, and Jeneil took the witch and placed it with the snarling animal. "That's nice, now you've teamed her up with the worst one of all. The witch doesn't need help; she's trouble enough without that vicious thing as a partner."

"I'm running out of pots." Jeneil laughed. "Besides they have help now, Merlin and Lan...Steve."

"See that, a natural slip."

Jeneil raised one eyebrow at him. "Okay Prince Peter, watch me do my thing." She went to the figure of Lancelot and placed her index finger on its head. "On behalf of the princess, I change your name from Lancelot to Sir Steven, a friend, a true knight in shining honor, who possesses strong loyalty to the prince. There, I broke the curse of the triad. Feel better?"

Peter smiled and put his arms around her. "Do you have the power to do that?"

"Sure do," she said confidently. "The princess is from the land of the leprechauns where the people are favored with magical powers."

"Where's the prince from?" he asked, kissing her cheek.

"Oh he's special," she answered. "He's related to Merlin. They're from the land of the mystics where the answers to life's mysteries are held sacred. And do you know what comes from a union of magic and mysticism?" She dramatized the words.

"What?"

"Beautiful, happy, special children of outstanding powers." She put her arms around his neck and studied his smiling face. "Oh Arthur, my king, canst thou feel the depth of my heart's loyalty to thee. Whilst thou never grasp the magnitude of thy queen's love and devotion?"

"Crazy kid."

She hugged him then kissed him lightly. "Feel like having your dessert now?"

"Yes. It's something with apples in it. I can smell them."

"Apple crisp. I'll be right back."

Peter looked at the ceramic Camelot. Stopping at the figures of Arthur, Guinevere, and Lancelot, he remembered his mother's words about Steve and Jeneil. He shook his head. "Witches can cast evil spells on your mind if you let them. I'm glad she's in another pot. That should hold her for awhile." He smiled and went to help Jeneil.

Peter put the empty plate on the shelf behind him. Jeneil smoothed his hair with her hand lovingly. "What are you thinking about?"

"My mother. She really reached me tonight."

"In what way?"

"I guess I really listened to her complaints for the first time. Either that or I've matured, but everything she was complaining about seemed to stay in my mind." He shrugged. "I don't know, maybe it's my life now by comparison. I realized how much embarrassment I brought to her."

"How?" Jeneil asked, curious.

"She said that I was always in trouble with families about their daughters. Looking back, that's true, but living through it I remember the girls came to me. I never twisted anybody's arm. The fathers yelled because their daughters hung around with me. Then they'd get too serious and I'd break up with them, and fathers would come to my house shaking fists and yelling. Life wasn't easy and not much made sense. Just the Dragons, I understood their rules. Today, when my mother complained about it, I realized how embarrassing it must have been for her. She called it disgusting." He smiled. "Guess I couldn't win. I got involved with Lin Chi and no father to yell. She was a pro and my family still complained and the community talked."

"Peter, you were a rascal, but an honest rascal," Jeneil teased.

"I know now what Steve went through when he was asked to stop the gossip. I feel sort of bad putting her through that. Guess I'll hear it for the rest of my life." He sighed.

"Someday, when the time is right, tell her what you just told me and apologize. Watch for the right moment."

He laughed. "I don't think it will help."

Jeneil smiled. "My father used to say that one of his complaints about religion was that God promised to forgive and forget but when you repent of your wrongdoings the people sitting next to you at church don't. I wonder how he knew that. He never went to church." She laughed. "You and my father seem alike at times." She snuggled into Peter's arms and each drifted into personal thoughts.

*****

Peter was looking over some x-rays when Steve stuck his head in. Peter grinned. "Hey, I owe you another marker for last night. Thanks for doing that."

"It's okay. What was the big deal at the mother's?"

"She saw me with Lin Chi yesterday and added wrong."

"Whoa, you're lucky you didn't show up in the ER as a patient then. How come you're not even bruised? How did you wiggle out of that?"

Thirty-One

Days passed since the encounter with his mother and life was still peaceful. Peter was amazed. Every other earthquake they'd had always had aftershocks. So far all there had been was silence. He took that as a good sign. He could tell Jeneil was rattled. She had become indecisive so he knew something was on her mind. He watched her as he dried dishes, her mind miles away. "Can I take that trip with you?"

"What trip?" she asked, his question bringing her attention back.

"Wherever your mind was," he said, and she smiled half-heartedly. "What is it, honey?"

Jeneil sighed. "Your mother's silence. I can't read it and I can't deal with what I can't read. Has she disowned us?"

Peter laughed. "She's probably still confused. My grandfather said her silence has surprised him, too. He's encouraged."

"It's the middle of September. How confused can she be?"

"Honey, what do you want to happen?"

"I'd like to meet her. Are we such an embarrassment to her that she refuses to acknowledge us? Is that it? Are we being shunned?" She wiped the countertop clean, rinsed the sponge and returned it to its spot under the soap. She heaved a sigh. "Or is she crafty enough to realize that silence would drive me batty?"

"Hey, relax baby, you're beginning to unravel."

"This is your fault," she said, folding her arms in annoyance. "You bullied her into silence." She went to walk past him.

He put his arm out, stopping her. "That's enough, Jeneil. Pull it together." She stood there annoyed. "Trust me, honey. The silence is pleasant. Ask Lin Chi. She got words from my mother. It was brutal. You're not as tough as Lin Chi."

"But we can't settle anything if we don't talk."

"Jeneil, concentrate on me."

She looked at him. "What do you mean?"

"You're marrying me, not my family. I'm reminding you of your promise to me."

She massaged her temples and nodded. "You're right. I guess I'm dealing with an adrenaline surge. All I've ever heard about her is how she screams. I braced myself for that and the silence has left me incomplete. I'm edgy. It's like waiting for the second shoe to drop."

He smiled at her. "You get so intense about things. Relax."

She grinned. "I thought you liked my intensity?"

"Then re-channel this in that direction, too." He kissed her. "I love you, Jeneil. Bring it all back to just the two of us, honey."

"Okay, I'll try," she said, nodding, and slipped into his arms. The front doorbell rang.

"That's Steve. His shift was extended. He's been edgy, too. I asked him to stop over for a short while."

She shrugged. "That's fine."

Peter went to get the door and returned with Steve, who was carrying a white paper bag. Jeneil was sitting in the corner chair sulking. Putting the bag on the small dining table, Steve took off his jacket. "What's wrong with the kid?" he asked loud enough for her to hear.

"I'm having a tantrum," and she sighed.

Steve went over to her. "Not on my time, you don't. Come on, get up girl." He took her hand. "I brought three hot fudge sundaes from Brighton's. Let's get to it before they melt. Best thing for tantrums."

She smiled. "Vanilla ice cream?"

"French vanilla ice cream deluxe. Come on. They're melting."

She got up quickly. "Good, I need that. Maybe I'll put on five pounds and then worry about nothing else except dieting them off again."

"There you go. Now you're in the groove." He pushed her gently to the table. Peter smiled watching them. There was an ease between them now and they were relaxed around each other. That was something he never thought would happen.

Steve and Peter leaned back on their chairs, and Jeneil slowly finished the fudge topping she always left for the last.

"You should have seen the multiple fracture they brought in tonight," Steve said.

"Oh yeah, who took it?"

"Creighton."

"Is that right?" Peter smiled. "Must be his first."

Steve nodded. "And he started to shake when Donnelly told him to scrub."

Peter laughed. "Brings back memories."

"But the kid shaped up. By the time he got to OR, he was steady, like he was born to it. He's going to be okay."

Jeneil got up and returned to the living room while they talked. Peter kept her in view. She paced then took a book from a shelf and put it back. Then she settled on a chair, took her hair down and stretched out across the chair, hanging her head over one arm and her feet over the other. Her hair hung to the floor. She put on some classical music and in a short while was waving her arms in the air like an orchestra conductor, fully engrossed in the music. Peter smiled and Steve turned to see why he was smiling.

"Is something wrong? Why is she pounding the air? It reminds me of the day she sat underneath the potted trees."

"My mother has her rattled by her silence. We haven't heard a thing from her."

"Doesn't the kid know when she's well off?"

"She's a peace freak and into personal communication."

"I wonder if that therapy would work for me. Pound the air, not the walls." Steve chuckled.

"You're feeling the squeeze?"

Steve nodded. "I'm sure it's the pressure of watching my every move at the hospital. Changing a behavior pattern so quickly wasn't easy. Some of the fooling was fun. I miss that. I miss Rita and Lucy. No, I don't." He sighed. "Becoming celibate forces you to study yourself more closely. I don't miss them, I miss sex with them. Not even that really anymore."

"Did I hear that right?" Peter asked, laughing.

Steve smiled. "But now I want what you've got, a relationship. Imagine that from me. I'd begun to live the legend. Someone who cares that I'm here."

Peter smiled and nodded. "I'd like that for you, too. It is good. Ordinary sex can't compare to it. It's more than physical."

Steve nodded. "That's the difference. I've got to find that and I don't know how. Isn't that crazy? Maybe I should go lie on the couches on the ninth floor, get my head checked." He slouched in his chair.

Peter watched him. "I don't know what to tell you. Jeneil and I didn't plan this, it just happened. I wasn't looking for it, but to be completely honest, she's the one who understands relationships. I mean really understands and works at it. I'm learning from her, and for whatever crazy reason, she relates to Chang." He laughed. "She's the only girl who's ever really understood him completely."

"I think that's what I want, that closeness to someone." Steve sighed. "But first things first, I'd better concentrate on getting through my residency. This man-woman thing sounds like a study in itself." He smiled. "But once February second happens, I'm going to date every librarian I can find in this city. Watch me."

Peter laughed. "Librarians?"

Steve nodded. "They must be interested in literature, right? I like lit majors. They're a real kick." Peter laughed, realizing the reference to Jeneil. Steve looked at his watch. "I've got to leave. Thanks for letting me lie on your couch."

Peter smiled. "It's okay; I've worn yours out over the years."

Steve stood and stretched. "I'll go say goodbye to the kid."

Peter followed him to Jeneil's chair. Catching sight of them, she swung her legs to the floor and sat up. "Are you leaving?" Steve nodded. "Is the routine of life getting to you?"

"Sometimes," Steve answered.

"I'm going to Nebraska for the weekend. Why don't you keep Peter company? He hates being here alone. You'd be helping us. I worry about him."

Steve smiled. "I'm doing you the favor, huh?"

Jeneil grinned. "It's a united favor. Isn't that how triads work?"

"That's a great idea," Peter agreed. "I should have thought of it. The atmosphere is better than the dorms for both of us. Plan on that, Steve."

Steve looked from Peter to Jeneil and shook his head. "I'm getting to be a real job for you guys."

Jeneil touched his arm gently. "No, you're not. We love you. People you love aren't jobs."

Steve looked at her steadily. She meant the word love, he could feel that. She really cared.

Jeneil smiled then went to him and put her arms around him in a hug. "We love you, Steve. You belong to us."

Peter looked at her, studying her face. She kissed Steve's cheek and squeezed his arm.

Steve smiled. "Jeneil, you are great medicine. Now I'd better get going." She had touched him deeply with her words, but the sentiment made him uncomfortable.

"Plan on the weekend," Peter said as he walked toward the stairs.

"Yeah, that sounds good," Steve answered as he left.

Peter closed the apartment door. He looked at Jeneil. Her affection toward Steve surprised him. "You really have changed your mind about him."

She nodded. "I really have. He's very different when he lets you get to know him."

"I don't think he's let you. You've crawled into his coat sleeve like you do with everybody," Peter said seriously.

"But he let me," she argued, and then she sighed. "He needs a life; he deserves a life, a happy life. It's due him. When you look at the scales of justice he's due a few warm fuzzies." She put her arms around Peter. "I feel like he belongs to us. Isn't that odd? He really is family. I love him like he's a brother or some close relative. I want to see him happy. What's really odd was my attitude about him before I got to know him well. I rarely resist people the way I did with him. It's a lesson to me; don't prejudge people. I would never have suspected that failing was part of me, but I did judge Steve before I knew him. I'm glad you're his friend. You're more like a brother, and he worries about you, too. That Saturday at the market he was concerned about you with Lin Chi. I could tell that it was a genuine concern. It touched me so much that I kissed him and surprised both of us. Again tonight he touched me deeply. I want him to know he has family. He has us."

Peter listened to her words and held her. "I love you, baby. Man, I love you a lot. Steve's probably going to find a real life that's happy because of being around you."

"Don't do that," she said quietly.

"What?" Peter asked, puzzled.

"Don't nominate me for sainthood. It makes me uncomfortable. Steve will find a real life because he wants one. He's seen ours working and wants what's good in ours. It's not me."

Peter held her closely and something inside of him sighed with relief.

*****

The days continued with only silence from his mother. Peter enjoyed it even more after Jeneil came to accept it and got busy on some project that got her out of bed quite early most mornings. She and Dennis were into something again, too. She seemed conscious of Peter's sensitivity about Dennis and went out of her way to reassure him, often in small ways, of her loyalty. He couldn't say he didn't love the extra attention.

Peter even enjoyed watching as Jeneil and Steve continued to develop a very close friendship. Steve liked her a lot. Peter knew that, it was obvious, but he was comfortable with it since Jeneil's admission of the kiss his mother had mentioned. At the moment, his prime concern was his grandfather's birthday. He knew there would be a party or at least a dinner at his mother's, there always was. It would be a chance for Jeneil to meet the family, but he wondered what his mother would do. Jeneil would handle his mother in her own special way. For now, she kept busy and went on with her life.

Peter smiled as he sat down with some records in the medical room. Jeneil's energy level was high from all the projects she had going on and she seemed happy. He was impressed she was keeping everything in her life balanced. He loved just being around her when her happiness spilled over; she was cosmic often. He smiled again.

"Well, I wish medical reports made all my doctors smile like that." The sound of Dr. Sprague's voice brought Peter from his thoughts. He looked up. Dr. Sprague grinned. "Want to share your secrets for happiness, Chang?"

"A passion for my work," Peter countered, catching his foothold in the tease.

"Passion, huh? Yes, that's my guess, too." He chuckled and walked away.

Steve sat down, chuckling. "You had Jeneil written all over your face. No wonder he noticed. He's getting a real kick out of you. You found the girl in Records and proved his theory true. He loves it when he's right, and he knows about you and Jeneil."

"I know," Peter answered, smiling. "He's a sharp son-of-a-bitch, a real smart ass. Nothing gets past him."

Steve laughed. "He's eyeing me. He can't believe I'm staying so straight. I can't either, but I like being in control of my life. Not having to prove I'm anything but normal and human feels great."

"How the hell did we get on the other track anyway? White Stallion and Chinese Stud?" Peter shook his head.

"That's easy. We're good in bed and we love women. That's tough to hide." Steve laughed at his joke and hit Peter's arm as he stood up.

Peter laughed. "Hey, now there's the Steve I know and recognize."

"Catch you at seven in the parking lot. What movie are we going to?"

Peter shrugged. "Jeneil didn't say but I'm looking forward to it."

"Me, too. It's not exactly bumming out, but it all helps. It's why I'm straight. I'm with you two so much I never have time to feel sorry for myself, but then you guys knew that would happen right?"

"Maybe at the beginning," Peter answered, "but now you're really family."

"Yeah, I know. That's the magic," Steve said, smiling. "I'll be catching you at seven," and he left whistling.

Peter smiled again, watching Steve. "That's Jeneil, too. She knew it's what you needed, Steve. She's working at helping you, too." Peter stopped smiling as his heart filled with love for her. "Songbird, you are pure magic."

*****

Peter signaled to Steve to park in the lot of the apartment building. After locking his car, Steve walked over to Peter.

"What's with all the cars on the street? It's bumper to bumper here."

Peter shrugged. "Beats me. Maybe somebody's having a shower or some kind of party. That's usually what causes it at my mother's place. Our barbecues fill the street."

They were surprised at the voices coming from the apartment as Peter inserted the key in the lock. He pushed the door open and Steve walked in first. Peter looked over his shoulder. Both of them were surprised to see the room filled with people. It was a double surprise to find Jeneil was the only white person amongst a room of black people.

Steve looked at Peter. "What's she got going, a march on Washington?"

Peter looked around and recognized Adrienne and Charlie. Everybody else was a total stranger to him.

"I'm sorry," Jeneil apologized as she came to them, "this isn't going too well so it's running longer than I thought it would. You can watch TV in the bedroom. There's a tray of desserts on the dining table and some coffee. If this doesn't pull together soon, I'll just cancel it and try another time."

"What are you doing?" Steve asked.

"Yeah," Peter seconded.

Jeneil was about to explain when angry voices came from a corner of the living room. She looked at Peter and Steve. "Settle in wherever," and she turned and walked into the living room.

Peter and Steve looked at each other. "I'll get some coffee, but I'm staying. This feels restless to me," Peter said, eyeing the crowd.

"Okay with me," Steve said as they made their way to the dining room.

Jeneil stood in front of the plants and addressed the group that was talking loudly amongst itself, and at times angrily. "People, can I say a few things," she said in a loud but controlled tone.

A man in a corner shouted, "Shut up Negroes, the white liberal wants to educate us." Peter turned quickly. Steve was right behind him.

Charlie stood up. "That's enough, Jake. She's done nothing but try to help us."

Jake laughed. "Help? Look at her." He laughed again, "What is she, a kid just out of college with pipe dreams of inner city peace? She's not even the right color. What would she know?"

"Why do I have to be black to help? My money's as green as yours," Jeneil said quietly, but her remark was heard. Several in the group looked at each other and whisperings went through them until the crowd was quiet.

Charlie continued. "She's been talking to Adrienne and me for weeks now. We thought she was just being the friend that she is, but it's more than that. I can't believe that we've brought our petty disagreements here, too."

"Hey, Charlie," Jake bellowed, "if you want to make speeches, run for Congress. I want to hear white Dorothy talk about the yellow brick road and Oz."

"That's fine with me," Charlie answered, "but remember, we're in her house and we're eating her food."

Jake interrupted. "Oh shit, I forgot that about white liberals. They pass out food but there's always a hook at the end of the line."

Charlie was losing patience. "Jake, so help me."

Jeneil went to Charlie and took his arm. "Thank you, Charlie." She smiled, then turned and smiled at Jake. "Are you interested in my money or not?"

Jake shook his head. "Girl, you ain't got enough or is it the butler's night off?"

"Stop fighting me, Jake. I'm on your side," she said, and then smiled to the crowd. "Jake's right though, I've brought you here and did the social thing because I want you to listen to me. That's my hook. Listen to me."

Jake shook his head and settled back, and Charlie sat down. The crowd watched her.

"We don't have to be from your race to understand why you want to have a youth center in your neighborhood. The tragedy that happened to those three young boys touched everyone. And it's too bad that it cost lives to motivate us."

"Sure," Jake piped up, "that's why white money is saying you have boy's clubs already, why do you need a youth center."

"Some white money, Jake. Some white money," Jeneil corrected.

"Let her talk, Jake," someone said.

"Yeah," another agreed.

"Oh please, wake up people. White money won't do it. We have to. Hear me? Us," Jake snapped. "Shit, that's why we'll always be sitting in white folks' rooms waiting for crumbs. You people won't wake up."

"Shut up, Jake," someone else said.

Jake settled back. "Go ahead, listen. You know at the end of the speech its written that in return for the money we have to be Oreo cookies. Watch for the hook."

"Shut up, man," the crowd answered him.

Jeneil sighed. "I'll be brief. I have access to an organization that can help you." The people in the crowd looked at each other.

Jake sat up. "It's never been that easy, white lady. What's the catch, the hook?"

Jeneil smiled. "Actually Jake, you're quite right about the money having to come from you." The crowd groaned and Jake smiled. "The organization requires that whatever initial money is short, half must be provided by the community."

Jake laughed. "Lady, we've bled every businessman in the area, every church, and every black source out of the neighborhood dry and we still need two thousand dollars."

Jeneil persevered. "This organization requires that for a youth center, the youth must earn some of the money." The group looked at each other. Jeneil continued on, "There is motivational material available to help youth achieve this by giving up a candy bar or recycling cans, bottles or newspaper. They're not allowed to sell anything unless it's their services for a direct donation."

The group didn't sound discouraged; the murmurings were positive.

Jake watched in disbelief. "Come on people, we can't raise one thousand dollars ourselves. How the hell can the kids raise one thousand dollars on their own? Man, you people will buy anything."

"Actually Jake, I'd like to prove my sincerity in this. You can put me down for five hundred dollars." There was a collective gasp.

"Why?" Jake asked cautiously, staring at Jeneil. "That's a lot of money and you don't look like you're swimming in it. Why the hell would you give that much?"

"I told you, Jake, to prove I'm sincere. I believe in what you're trying to do and I'd like to see you reach a point where you can get professional help."

"Professional?" Jake repeated.

"Professional," Jeneil repeated.

Jake stared. "Oh, white girl, you are one slick chick. Talk more plainly. I'm not fooled, and we'll never raise fifteen hundred dollars anyway. At best, our kids can pull in five hundred dollars and that's assuming we can talk them high enough to care that much. Five hundred dollars at best and that's it."

Jeneil stared at him then smiled. "How about if I get you another five hundred dollars?" The group murmured with encouragement.

"What do you want for the thousand dollars?" Jake asked.

Jeneil sighed. "I told you. I want to see you qualify for bigger help. And you won't unless you rise above the sandlot level."

"Well, we can get some money if we have the school parents hold a bake sale and car wash or bazaar," one lady offered.

"Yeah, that's right," a few other women backed her up.

Jake stood up and all eyes turned toward him. "I want your whole deck of cards, white girl. You're good at getting people revved up, but I want the name of the whole game and now."

"Jake, she's real," Adrienne said.

"Good, then let her prove it. Where's the money coming from? What level is she talking about and what does she mean by professional? Wake up, people. Nobody gives anything without something in return. There's a catch to this, it's got a price tag, and I want to know what it is. Why the hell do you even care, white girl? The neighborhood's on the south side. Our rats won't touch you."

"Shut up, Jake," several people spoke up, and the group began to talk together excitedly.

Jake stared at Jeneil then shook his head and walked toward the dining room. As he got to Peter and Steve, he stopped. "Someone said you were her man. I'd like to know what you think about her generosity and her interest in this," he asked, looking at Steve.

Steve smiled. "Ask her man," he answered, nodding to Peter.

Jake looked at Peter, surprised. "You're her man?"

"You have a problem with that?" Peter asked.

Jake smiled and rubbed his chin. "No. No not at all. I just don't believe in fairytales. Let's just say you being you makes her more real to me. Thank you very much," and he turned and walked back to the group. "Let's have the whole picture. I'd like to believe the pretty colors you're using."Jake sat down and folded his arms, staring at Jeneil. "Quiet people, we're about to hear the whole truth and nothing but the truth, right pretty lady?"

Jeneil looked at the floor then at the group, who was waiting and watching. "Okay," she said and sighed, "I've been listening to Adrienne and Charlie talk about this center you're trying to organize with deep interest. Why? Because I believe that's where the real change in our society will come from; smaller groups in troubled neighborhoods who really care, groups who are autonomous for the most part, groups who won't get big and political so they actually can have an effect on the lives of the youth they intend to help. Why am I putting in personal money? Because I can't get a foothold in the neighborhoods I'm interested in. You are my first real break. That's why tonight is special. In listening to you, I've learned a lot. I can't get you any help if you don't meet certain qualifications like supplying initial funds of which a portion is provided by the youth itself." She looked at Jake. "You asked what the hook is, there are several but they don't have to be painful if you keep your perspective. You're looking at an abandoned building for the center but that's a long way around. That building won't qualify because you'll use too much funding to maintain its present level of decay. You'll need a new building. The biggest qualification is that most of the money reaches the youth. That's why it needs to be a volunteer project."

The group laughed. Jake sat up straight and watched.

"Please listen carefully or you'll get discouraged and lose the purpose of what I'm trying to do."

"Lady, a new building?" One man laughed. "We're having problems getting an old one."

"If you'll just let yourselves work together more united, I can get you more funding." They looked at each other, shaking their heads. Jeneil pinched her lower lip and sighed. "You won't even get the old building unless you work together. You don't even have the same vision. Several of you see it one way and several see it another way. You'll work against yourselves doing that. You can only hope to achieve your goal by staying small and by reaching the needs of the youth without a highly visible specialized image. You have to be incredibly organized and project a very laid back image in order to be appealing or you won't reach the people you want to. There are other hooks. One is that parents in the neighborhood must be educated. The organization feels you won't help kids if the parents don't have at least an idea of what you'll be giving their kids, so there's a promotional clause. Another clause is education. The organization won't allow funding if their films aren't allowed to be shown in the building. There's a wealth of help available if you'll accept the work needed to make it run. You'll need a director, a board of directors, and a strong desire to see the center succeed."

Jake raised his hand. "You said films. What kind of films?"

"They lean heavily on the history of the ethnic or racial group starting the center and progress toward achieving equality through peaceful means. There's also a very heavy emphasis on personal education and development in order to improve mankind and the world. Any hint at a militant attitude and the funding is pulled. They're very adamant about that. A communication skills program is required."

"That sounds very professional. How can we look laid back with that kind of stuff around?"

"It's soft sell. Mostly it's done through learning centers which would be equivalent to a library. There are professionals who will help from behind the scenes, but all that's really needed are the people who will make the magic work, people who really care."

"We all care but we don't agree on how to do this with each other. That's our biggest problem."

Jeneil smiled and nodded. "I understand and I'd like to read something to you. It has to deal with groups and people coming together and trying to agree. It's from a speech."

Jeneil picked up a paper and began to read. *"I doubt that any other group we get together can do any better because when you gather a group of people you also gather their prejudices, their passions, their errors in opinion, their self interests, and their selfish views. When you gather all that together can they produce anything perfect? That's why I'm so surprised to find this system as close to working well as it does. It will surprise our enemies and that's why I agree to our adopting this constitution with all its faults, because I think a general government is better than no government at all."*

Jeneil smiled, setting the paper down. "That was said by Benjamin Franklin before the Continental Congress as they decided on the Constitution of the United States in 1787. What you are trying to do is just as important if not more so. You are trying to fight the general unrest in our cities and replace it with purpose and meaning. If you don't succeed then law will become lawlessness and order will be disorder. No constitution can protect people from that. We need to do that for ourselves in order to remain free and civilized. The funding organization strongly believes that and it's prepared to help in any way it can if its rules are accepted. History has proven that there is more freedom in a group that conforms itself to high ideals and laws. The foundation can provide a constitution for your youth center, and the organization is non-racial and non-sectarian."

Jake smiled. "That's almost unheard of. Why was the organization founded?"

"In order to promote an understanding of acceptance of differences amongst all people and to eliminate barriers which prevent that goal such as poverty and ignorance."

"Who started it?" Jake asked.

Jeneil smiled. "A white woman who fell in love with a black man in an era when that was unacceptable. The hatred encountered by both families prevented the relationship. She never married and decided the money she accumulated would go toward promoting her beliefs in equality and peace. I can tell you agree on one thing, a desire to help your neighborhoods and the organization can help you achieve that. There's enough flexibility in the rules to allow you autonomy in the areas you seem interested in. They're only interested in direction and achievement of its goals of peace, understanding, and education. Talk about it together. I can provide as much background material as you need. Why am I into this? I believe in the goals, too. The woman was a close personal friend of mine and I don't want to see her money wasted or her life and suffering will be, too." Jeneil held back her emotion and cleared her throat. "I'm interested in seeing your youth center succeed. Now let me see if I can get the other five hundred dollars for you."

Jeneil went to the telephone and dialed. "Hi. Is Mr. Reynolds in? This is Jeneil. No, don't interrupt him." Jeneil paused. "Bill, I didn't want to interrupt you. Oh good. I'm trying to rustle up some funding. Would you happen to have any extra money lying around you could write-off on your taxes? Our goal is five hundred more. No not five hundred thousand, just five hundred. Oh, stop laughing. You know I deal in grass roots. What? You'll send it to me? Bill, thank you very much and I mean that sincerely. Before you go to Barbados? Why are you going there? Listen to yourself. Is that pretentious or isn't it? You'd better be careful or the jet will be called the capitalist pig, not me." She laughed.

"I'm still the simple and humble country girl who left Loma. Don't call me a liar, fool. No, it isn't. It's Corinthians 12:4. Yes, it is. Ooo, listen to the smut that proceedeth from thy tongue. Hellfire and damnation's an inch to your left, boy." She laughed again. "You want to bet on that? You're asking me to gamble? Me? What are the stakes?" She chuckled. Peter and Steve stood nearby listening. "That's small stuff. You're not too sure you're right, are you? Yes, I know exactly what I want if I'm right, round trip passage to China on your next flight." Peter stared at her dumbfounded. Steve smiled. "Yes, I am serious. What are the stakes if I'm wrong? I don't like the sound of that laugh. What is it? Ooo, I hope your office is empty. That's all we need to be overheard. Yes, of course I'm taking the bet. I'll get back to you, and thanks again for your contribution. Love to you. Bye."

"Charlie," she signaled to him, "you have one thousand dollars whether you sign with the foundation or not."

Charlie shook his head in disbelief. "You work miracles, my girl."

"I need to look something up. If you'll handle things here, I'll be right back."

Peter and Steve followed her to the bedroom. She took a bible from a drawer and went through the pages with deliberate direction. Stopping, she read a verse quickly then smiled broadly. "I won!" she said excitedly. "I won, I was right!" She hugged Peter.

"You won what?" Peter asked.

"The trip to China from Bill! I quoted the exact chapter and verse." She kissed his cheek.

"Why are you going to China?" Peter asked, stunned.

"Not me, your grandfather. Bill flies to China quarterly. I was planning to ask if your grandfather could go, but this is even better. Now I can tell him I won the trip and he can go in my place. That'll be a terrific birthday gift, don't you think?"

Peter stared, still a bit numb. "Jeneil, what was Bill's reward if he was right?"

Jeneil looked at him. "I had to spend a cozy weekend with him."

Steve choked on a laugh. Peter turned and stared at him. Steve shrugged. "Well, she won!" He tried to stop laughing, but Peter's expression of shock was too much for him and he laughed harder.

"Jeneil." Peter rubbed his forehead. "Jeneil, I can't believe you'd make a bet like that."

Jeneil smiled. "Peter, Bill knew he was wrong. I was better at scripture search in Sunday school than he was. He knows that. The only question was whether I was right in my guess. He probably chose the weekend idea to shake my confidence. There was no danger in his guess being right. You're not really upset, are you?"

Steve laughed harder not believing she would even ask such a question. Jeneil and Peter looked at him. "Ummm, I think I'll get some coffee. You two are a comedy team." He turned and walked out of the room, laughing to himself and shaking his head.

"Do you think your grandfather will accept this?"

Peter shook his head. "I guess so, once the shock wears off, and what's happening in this group?"

"Oh gosh! The group!"

Adrienne had served coffee and everything was quiet and friendly. Several people smiled as Jeneil joined them, including Jake. "Thank you, Jeneil. Thank you very much."

"Why are you thanking me?"

"For coffee and pastries." Jake grinned and winked.

"No matter what decision your group makes, I care. I know what good the organization can do for you. I hope you'll look into it carefully and check every hook." Jake smiled and extended his hand to her. She took it and returned his smile.

Adrienne hugged Jeneil as the last of the group left. "Thank you, baby. This is the most united I've seen them for awhile." She shook her head. "Do you really believe in peace? People can't get along when we're alike, let alone different."

"I believe," Jeneil smiled, "and I know it'll take slow, hard work and a lot of money, but there's magic in the youth center. I can feel it."

Charlie kissed Jeneil's cheek. "We've got to get home. The alarm rings real early in the morning."

Jeneil leaned her back against the door after they left, taking a few seconds to think. Steve walked over to her. "This peace thing is really important to you, isn't it?"

She smiled. "It is, I know another triad that would've been overjoyed to have the foundation in on this. Why are some people destined to be misfits in history?" She sighed. "Poor Mandra. Today a racially mixed marriage isn't so shocking. Darn those short straws anyway." She looked at Steve then grinned. "And look who I complain to, the man who hears the full orchestra at the prom and sees every balloon and streamer." She laughed. "To you I'm speaking TAI, right?"

Steve shrugged. "Sort of, but I like that you care. I heard the hopes these people had that the youth center would work. You gave them that hope." He looked at her then leaned forward and kissed her cheek gently.

Jeneil laughed from embarrassment. "I think I'm finding out what keeps Mother Theresa going," she said, taking the glass of juice from Peter who was looking from one to the other. "Does anyone mind the nine-fifteen feature of Trufever's, *The Lawless*?"

Steve smiled. "Well it ain't bumming out, but I'll sign up."

"Me, too," Peter answered quietly, and sipped his coffee.

Jeneil snuggled into Peter's free arm. "I'm high right now. Please stop brooding about my bet." She kissed his cheek and hugged him. "I'll clean up in here and then we can go to the movies." She went to the kitchen.

Peter looked at Steve. "You two are making real progress. I never expected to see you kiss her."

Steve smiled. "Me neither, but she got to me. The way she is, her fire, she's real. The life I saw in that group after she touched them, I don't know, it all got to me. It's nice to be around her. It was the moment, the feeling, the fire."

"Yeah," Peter answered quietly and finished his coffee.

Steve watched him. "Hey, Pete, are you upset about the kiss?" Peter shook his head. "That's good because nobody knows that she's yours more than I do, man. She belongs to you. She's the kid sister I never had."

Peter nodded. "Yeah, I know that. I guess we'd better help collect coffee cups," he said as he began gathering the few empty cups and napkins. He remembered how things had developed with Dennis and Robert from the same kind of beginning. He pushed the thought to the back of his mind and sighed. Peter told Chang they couldn't keep her chained, that she needed to fly free. After all, Steve was his best friend. He pushed the thought to the far corner of his mind, but the uneasiness in Chang stayed. Peter felt it just beneath the surface where he kept Chang controlled. It was completely against Chang's nature to share his woman. With Robert, Chang only suspected his deeper interest. Dennis had been a total shock that left Chang insecure about Peter's judgment. Jeneil's words, 'If I didn't belong to you, I'd probably be closer to Dennis,' passed through him. It had been a shock to see Steve kiss her. He was used to Jeneil kissing people, but Steve's kiss had feeling behind it. They were very close, Peter knew that. Peter understood that, but Chang's uneasiness churned within him.

"You're going to ruin the birthday gift if you don't stop brooding about that bet," Jeneil whispered in his ear. Peter returned from his thoughts. She put her arms around him. "Chang, come on. So your woman sold herself in a bet. Is that any reason to sulk?" she jokingly asked, then lovingly touched his face. "I'm sorry, Chang. It is reason enough to you but please trust my judgment. There was never any danger of Bill collecting on the bet and he never intended to." She looked deep into his eyes. "Chang, I would never do that to you, never."

Peter heard the difference in the tone of her voice. She had been doing that a lot lately. This looking deeply into the eyes thing, she practiced it regularly now. She insisted it was her path to his soul. He found it comical, but there was always a difference in what happened. He rarely turned away now whenever she did it. He even liked it. At times, it stirred something deep within him and he enjoyed the experience. It wasn't sexual. It reminded him of the experience on the balcony in Vermont except he didn't become disconnected. It also wasn't as intense. Peter watched her and realized she was interpreting his silence as concern over the bet. She wasn't giving Steve's kiss any significance. Peter felt Chang relax.

"You belong to Chang," Peter answered in a hoarse whisper.

Jeneil looked at him steadily. "I know that. Tell Chang to remember it, Peter."

Steve walked into the living room from the kitchen. He stopped and watched them with their arms around each other, the way they looked at each other, and an ache passed briefly through his core. He cleared his throat to let them know he was there. "I think we should skip the movie."

"No." Peter smiled. "Let's go."

Jeneil nodded in agreement with Peter. "We were just sharing a moment." She shrugged, embarrassed.

Thirty-Two

Peter and Steve stopped to pick up messages on their way in from the ER. Steve put his in the pocket of his lab coat. "These can wait for coffee. I'm beat."

Peter stared at one of his messages.

"Trouble?"

"The mother."

"So much for silence."

"I'd better call her. I'll meet you in the lounge." Steve nodded and walked on. Peter dialed the restaurant. It was Friday so she'd be too busy to have a lengthy conversation. "Can I speak to Mrs. Lee? It's her son returning her call." He waited.

"Peter, I expected you to call at home. It's very busy here right now."

"What did you want?"

"We're planning a birthday party for your grandfather next Wednesday night. Can you come?"

"I'm on days next week. I get out at seven. I can be there."

"Oh good. Come over when you can."

Peter noticed she didn't mention Jeneil. He hesitated. "Mom, what about Jeneil?"

There was a brief silence. "Oh, are you still together? I would have guessed that she'd be finished with you by now."

Peter's back stiffened. "I won't be there either then," Peter answered coldly.

"He's your grandfather!" his mother said, truly shocked.

"And she's my wife."

"No, she isn't," she snapped. "She lives with you, there's a big difference. This is for the family only."

Peter held his anger in check. "Look, if you don't want her then you don't get me. That was the deal, remember? Could you take Tom leaving you home from something like this?"

"I married Tom. I know honor and responsibility."

"Mom, she's my wife," he repeated deliberately.

"Then let her prove it by marrying you. You said you've asked her to marry you. Why is she waiting, Peter? Maybe she's not sure you're who she wants?"

He heard the taunt in her voice and his throat tightened. "Mom, I'm being paged. I've got to go," and he hung up quickly.

Peter took a deep breath and exhaled. It was the first time in an argument with his mother where he had no words for defense. He felt helpless. He knew his mother thought Jeneil wasn't sure because of Steve. His grandfather was right; she was out of proportion about Steve and Jeneil. He snapped open the booth door and headed for the lounge, concentrating on emptying his unspent anger.

Steve bought a cup of coffee for Peter. He waited at a table while Peter made the phone call. The lounge door swung open and Peter walked in. Steve sat up straight at the sight of him.

"Holy shit, man, she twisted you clear to the spine," he said as Peter sat down.

"She's warped," Peter answered sharply. "I swear the woman enjoys trying to destroy me." He broke the wooden coffee stirrer in his hand.

"But you've always handled it before. What is it?" Steve asked, genuinely concerned.

Peter thought before answering. "She doesn't want Jeneil at my grandfather's party next week."

Steve looked puzzled. "And that's what's got you all knotted?"

Peter spoke carefully. "No, she made some remarks about Jeneil and not being married."

Steve sighed. "Yeah, that would twist my spine, too." He shook his head. "And you're also left with having to tell Jeneil that she's not wanted there. Boy, that's a lousy spot to be in."

Peter drank his coffee quickly and crushed the cup. "Yeah, let's hope she takes it as well as last time," he said, standing up. "I've got to keep moving, Steve. I've got anger raging through me right now. I need to spend some energy. Maybe I'll help Turcell scrub walls or something, or go over to the exercise room and swing at the punching bag." He tried to laugh. "I'll catch up to you in the ER."

Steve watched him leave. He felt bad for Peter. "Steve, my man, maybe you are lucky. You have no parents to hassle you and no woman who turns you inside out. It sure doesn't look worth it." He drank his coffee and got up to leave. "No," he answered himself, "no, Jeneil's worth it. She's worth anything, any price at all." He sighed and tossed his cup away.

*****

Peter was edgy as he unlocked the apartment door. He was still off-center and he'd had to keep his bad mood in check through the rest of his shift. It left him worn out. He kept trying to psych himself into a mood change and now he was counting on Jeneil to help him through it. They had planned on this Friday night. Their lives had been filled with people and schedule problems the past week and this night was going to be theirs. He heard her in the kitchen. Stopping at the door, he smiled.

"Hi, baby."

She kissed him on her path to return the milk to the refrigerator. "Hi, love. Goodness, you look done in."

He liked her peach colored nightgown. It was his all time favorite. "Oh, woman, even your words heal me. Keep talking, I need the love of my woman right now." He slipped his arms around her waist.

She held his chin gently in her hand and studied his face. "No, you need pampering." She touched his forehead. "You're incubating something."

"Don't you dare put me in quarantine," he warned.

She smiled and reached for the vitamin C. "No argument, you will take these," she ordered, handing him some tablets.

"No quarantine, baby. I'll take the whole damn bottle if you want me to, but no quarantine."

She grinned cozily. "Why are you complaining? You've never experienced my quarantine. You might like it." She slithered to him with the vitamins and a glass of water. She was obviously feeling playful and he liked her like that, too.

Taking the tablets from her, he put them in his mouth and drank the water. "I feel fine, you know. I'm just playing your cute game because I like cute."

"That isn't what your symptoms are telling me."

"Oh, you've got to be careful that you read symptoms right, sexy lady." He grinned. "Don't mistake simple anticipation for a virus. That nightgown would give any guy a fever."

"Ooo, so you want to play doctor, Doctor. Get changed for bed then. I'll bring you some warm Ovaltine. These fall nights are getting cooler."

He grinned. "Yes, ma'am," and he left for the bedroom.

Peter propped up their pillows and sat back, waiting for her to come to bed. He smiled to himself; she was right, his throat was slightly scratchy. He was probably developing a cold. She spotted symptoms in him before he realized them himself most times. That knack of hers impressed him. She guarded health like some people guarded money. To her, health was something you watched over like you did teeth and decay. He had come to like that about her. It was a certainty that he'd pick up a cold during the late summer and be on an antibiotic by mid fall and that was about all he'd get. Since med school, the pattern was the same. This was the first season that he hadn't been sick. He knew it was her watchful eye over him. He enjoyed it and even drank the potions and took the vitamins she'd hand him. He'd tease her and tell her he was playing her cute game, but in actuality he had come to trust her judgment about his health. He grinned as he thought about a doctor allowing that.

"What are you grinning at?" Jeneil asked, walking in with two mugs.

"I just wondered how secure my medical license would be if the board knew I let you boss me around with your herbs and things." She handed him his drink and got under the covers, sitting close to him. He kissed her temple. "Hey, do you watch my health because you love me or because you don't want to catch something yourself?" She sipped her drink. "Uh-oh, you're not answering my question."

"I think Chang would answer that well. He'd probably get all huffy and say that's not a question, that's something that belongs in the chicken yard."

Peter chuckled. "No, lit major, he'd say that's shit."

She smiled. "Thank you, Chang, for answering Peter's question."

Peter laughed lightly. "Oh, baby, I love Friday nights with you." He sighed a relaxing sigh.

She looked at him and smiled. "Who would ever have guessed that Chang would enjoy quiet Friday nights just sitting in bed sipping Ovaltine. I told you that you'd like my quarantine."

Peter snickered. "You little tease," and he leaned over and kissed her neck gently.

"Say, speaking of Friday nights, next Friday is your grandfather's birthday." Peter sat back against his pillow quickly; Jeneil noticed. "Well, that struck a nerve. What is it? Are you embarrassed about my giving him the trip to China?"

Peter hated the subject of his grandfather's birthday. He didn't answer.

"I'll give him something else then. Maybe that is a little overpowering. I just love him so much. I'd like to see him visit his family. Bill doesn't mind at all."

Peter pulled himself together. "No, honey, give him the trip. I think I'd like to see his face when he hears about it."

"I've decided to make it into a certificate and wrap it in a box like a gift." Jeneil smiled excitedly.

Peter smiled. "Let's go over Monday night and give it to him."

"Monday? Is that when he's celebrating it?" Peter didn't answer. "Peter, why don't you tell me everything, it'll be easier on both of us. Every question I ask makes you uncomfortable. Now what is it?"

"His party is Wednesday night."

She looked at him, studying his face. "Oh," she said quietly, turning away. "I see. Well then you can take it on Wednesday night when you go. But, I'd give it to him privately if I were you. Don't spoil the atmosphere of the party. You should get him a gift, too." She turned the mug around in her hand then put it on the table near the bed.

Peter's heart sank. He felt her hurt. He knew she understood that she wasn't invited. "I'm not going."

She looked up quickly. "What? You have to, he's your grandfather."

"Yeah, and she's counting on that. Well, it won't work. No, I'm not going."

"Don't put your grandfather in the middle of this struggle with your mother."

"I'm not going, Jeneil. That's it," he said strongly. He heard a slight sniff and turned to look at her as she opened the drawer for a tissue. "Oh, baby, don't cry. Please. We'll go to visit my grandfather on Monday night. He'll understand."

She wiped the tears. "Oh, Peter, this is such a mess already."

"What mess?"

"She doesn't accept me so now you won't go to a family party. I hate this. I really hate it," she cried softly.

"Jeneil, I'm not going. If I back down she'll think she has me. No. No. No."

"I'm lost, Peter. I don't know how to reach her. There's no defense against silence and no cure. I can't deal with the problem if I don't know why she's resisting me."

Peter looked at her. "Jeneil, marry me."

She looked at him. "Is that her complaint? We're not married?"

"Honey, my family doesn't live this way." Jeneil sat thinking. "Where'd you go?"

She shook her head. "You won't go to the party so you don't give in to her pressure, but you want me to marry you so I give in to her pressure?"

"Wait a minute," Peter said. "That's not quite true."

"Yes, it is."

"No, it isn't," Peter defended. "I thought we were heading toward marriage anyway?"

"We are."

"Then how do you feel you'd be giving in to her?"

"Because we're not ready yet."

"Why?"

"Why?"

"Yes, Jeneil. Why? She wants to know why you won't marry me, but you'll live with me. Give me an answer I can take back to her."

"No," she answered cautiously. "There's something wrong here. You had accepted waiting for marriage. Now I hear something in your tone. No, I'm not playing he said, she said with her. If she wants an answer to that question let her ask me the question like your grandfather did."

Peter sat forward. "Well, we have an interesting twist here. You don't want my grandfather in the middle of a struggle with me and my mother, but isn't that where I am with the two of you?"

"You will be if we play he said, she said. No, if I don't answer then you're not in the middle."

"So we have silence from you and silence from her. Nice going, peace freak." Peter sat back against his pillow.

She looked at him. "Why are you calling me names? Why are you pressuring me? I don't understand your annoyance with me. This isn't making any sense, but then why am I surprised? Your mother rarely does make sense."

"Hey, kid, all she wants to know is why you won't marry me. I can understand her asking."

Jeneil moved to the edge of the bed and sat stiffly. "There are pieces missing to this, Peter. Something is not being said. I can feel it, but I can't figure it out."

"It's simple enough," he answered. "My living here embarrasses her, Jeneil. She doesn't want to flaunt us at the family. To her, life is simple; you fall in love and get married. You don't start with dessert then go the other way."

Jeneil stood up quickly and put on her robe. She kept her back to him. "Peter, you seem to understand her feelings very well. Is that because you have the same ones? Are you embarrassed, too?" Peter didn't answer. She turned to face him. "My question is as simple as your mother's."

"Yes," he answered softly.

"Then why did you compromise your standards and move in here?" she asked, choking up.

"Oh, Jeneil, really. This is getting silly, isn't it?"

"No, I don't think so. Why did you move in?"

"Because I fell in love with you. Jeneil, what are you doing? I don't follow your word game."

"Oh, this isn't a game, Peter. There is something very insidious happening here."

"What does insidious mean?"

"Deceitful and treacherous."

"Treacherous?" he questioned. "Who's being deceived?"

"Us," she answered. "Treachery Peter, it means a violation of allegiance, a betrayal of trust." She shivered as she put her hand to her throat.

Peter sat up. "Jeneil, you're freaking out."

"Oh no I'm not. I'm trying to see things clearly, and right now the water isn't very clear and I'm scared."

"Who violated any allegiance? Geez baby, don't go twilight zone on me now. This is crazy."

"You violated an allegiance, Peter...."

"Now wait a minute," he interrupted.

"Peter, you violated an allegiance to yourself. If living with someone was against your standards then you shouldn't have betrayed that standard. I didn't know this arrangement embarrassed you." She swallowed hard, fighting tears.

He put his robe on and went to her. "Hey, honey, this is enough." He took her arm; she moved away.

"No, no touching. We talk."

"I'll talk if we make sense," he said. "I'm not following any of this."

"Neither am I, Peter."

"Then let's not continue this if we're both confused."

"But where was the confusion, Peter, then or now?"

"Jeneil, I need an interpreter."

She paced a few times. "Peter, the only thing I can think of is if this arrangement embarrasses you then you should leave."

The words hit him hard. "Leave? You mean move out?"

"Yes." Her answer was barely audible.

"Is that what you want?"

"That isn't the issue here." She took a deep breath. "The issue is embarrassment, your mother's and yours. I'll accept a different arrangement. You live at the dorms and we'll…."

"We'll what?"

She rubbed her temples. "We'll sneak, I guess. Or do you want to stop the physical part of our relationship, too. I'll accept whatever morality you decide on."

"Are you listening to what you're saying?"

She stopped pacing. "Yes, of course I am. I'm trying to deal with your embarrassment. I don't want you embarrassed about us. I'm trying to be honest, but if living here is too embarrassing then we'll sneak around or whatever you can deal with. I can understand that. It was difficult facing Uncle Hollis's questions about us, but I worked it out. He finally got over his guilt thinking he had failed me. It wasn't easy; I had to admit a lot of personal things to him but it worked. He's okay with us now." She turned away. "Actually Peter, I'd like to see what your mother's next reason for not accepting me will be, and I feel very strongly that there will be a long list. So it might do well if you moved back to the dorm then we can see if race is behind this. There are pieces missing, Peter, and it frightens me. How can we be sure our decisions are sound if the facts aren't clear?"

Peter watched her with deep interest; her incredible sensitivity, her devotion to being honest with herself and others, her willingness to deal with his mother's complaints, and her struggle to live sensibly and fairly in a world where people had lost the definition to those words. She truly was misplaced in time. Embarrassment surfaced in him. She was right; pieces were missing and he was holding them like cards hidden up a sleeve at a poker game. She sensed it but couldn't understand or prove it. All she had was her keen instincts, her sensitivity, and her code of justice.

He felt embarrassed but he couldn't bring himself to supply her with the missing pieces, one being that his mother thought she was interested in Steve and the other, which was more embarrassing, that he was pushing for marriage to prove she wasn't interested in Steve. He thought it odd how his dishonesty had put him in allegiance with his mother, but for different reasons. He didn't like seeing that in himself. He had uncovered many feelings for Jeneil since their relationship began but at this moment one surfaced higher. And that was respect. He respected her for her honesty and courage. In many ways, she was like Ki. Peter looked at her now standing there completely innocent of his mother's charge against her and undeserving of the pressure he was putting on her. He saw his betrayal clearly. He had betrayed her trust in him and his allegiance to her to wait until she was ready for marriage.

"Why are you speechless?"

He looked at her, wishing he could be as honest with her as she was with him. She was right; they weren't ready to get married. He wasn't anyway. She was more ready than anyone he'd ever met. He realized that, besides trying to find Jeneil, she was helping him get ready for marriage. All he had was an overwhelming love for her that he had never explored or examined like she had.

"Baby, since starting college Chang has been embarrassed. He didn't feel like he belonged there. He didn't recognize himself at times. You once asked why I was burying him. It's because I had trouble fitting him into what Peter was after in life. I've always been at odds with what's around me. College was necessary if I wanted to be a doctor so Peter stifled Chang. Even now Chang wonders what the hell he's doing here with you. He's embarrassed." Peter looked down at the floor.

Jeneil came closer to him, her face showing deep concern. "Peter, you've got to get rid of that. It leaves you so vulnerable to mistakes in judgment. It puts you at odds with yourself."

He looked at her. "I don't want to leave, Jeneil. We'll get married whenever you give the word."

She looked at him steadily. "And so you'll stifle embarrassment in order to stay? Peter, how can you be true to yourself doing that?"

"Jeneil, I'm not embarrassed about us. The only uncomfortable moments are when I face my mother. My grandfather doesn't approve of us being together unmarried, but he's given us his trust that we'll change this arrangement."

Jeneil smiled. "The man understands dignity."

Peter fidgeted. "I wish I had inherited that from him."

"It's learned, Peter."

He felt like a school boy being admonished by the teachers and he gained a better understanding of dignity. It was something you gave up by causing yourself embarrassment. And an embarrassment was different from a mistake. There was dignity in making an honest mistake, but an embarrassment lacked honor. He marveled at how Jeneil had cut through the shame he was projecting on her simply by being honest. Her effort to spare him the supposed embarrassment had exposed his deceit anyway. She was still looking at him, taking him at his word. She still allowed him the trust he had betrayed with his dishonesty. And the closer he looked, the clearer he saw and he had to admit that he knew he was doing it. He had tried to manipulate her and with that incredibly mature and stable love of hers, she had trapped him in his own snare. He had learned his lesson; he discovered what caused embarrassment. He also knew how to get rid of the bad taste. He had seen Jeneil do this before, too. He stood tall before her.

"Jeneil, I was pushing you to get married deliberately. That's why I said I was embarrassed."

"Why?" she asked innocently, not hiding her surprise.

He resisted mentioning Steve. "To shut my mother up." He felt his embarrassment begin to leave and dignity began to fill him.

Jeneil shook her head. "I'm afraid it's going to take more than marriage to achieve that. Nothing as simple as a wedding ceremony will do it." She sighed.

"How do you know that?"

"From Jack London and Shakespeare." He looked at her puzzled. She smiled. "Literature, White Fang and Taming of the Shrew."

He smiled then looked down at the floor. "Jeneil, I'm sorry I pushed you and I'm sorry I ruined our Friday." He paused. "I don't want to leave. I don't want us separated ever." He looked up; she was wiping tears away as quickly as they fell. He opened his arms to her and held her close. "Jeneil, I love you."

"Oh, Peter, I love you so much." She clung to him. His arms felt strong and protective. She let the feeling fill and heal her. He kissed her. She blended into it, enjoying the feeling of his growing passion. They needed each other. She was finding that being physical was a great way to repair a slightly damaged relationship. It was a way of communicating when words confused or didn't quite achieve the desired results.

*****

Peter read the duty list for the following week. He smiled as he saw his name scheduled for a double on Wednesday. Somehow having to work took the fuel out of the fire over the party. Friday night had been good for them. Life could chisel away at a relationship, but the honesty and closeness they had shared heightened their excitement. They were more loving toward each other and their needs were more easily understood. She fussed over him more. He loved that. If ever Chang should uproot chauvinism from his nature, he knew that loving to be fussed over would never go with it. He was convinced that fussing over had nothing to do with possessiveness and chauvinism. It was basic. It was hormonal. He basked in it. Her kiss as she walked by, her hand rubbed across his back as he sat and read, and as much as being fussed over met his basic needs, his subtle, overt, sexual behavior made him walk on air. The long meaningful looks that were followed by a slight smile, the sensuous snuggling, they were the by-products of their Friday night together. The magic they shared Friday continued to stay alive through the fussing and overtures. Peter loved it all. Making a moment last was a highly developed skill with her. To Peter, it was the warmth of her fire and passion. She had taught him to be demonstrative by example more than anything else.

They drove to his mother's house sharing a strong closeness and an excitement to bring their gifts to his grandfather. Being shunned over the party was taken in stride and Peter was grateful as well as impressed that Jeneil was dealing with it all so nicely. Every kind remark she made added gleam and luster to their closeness, while it had the opposite effect on his mother's image, becoming more tarnished by comparison for her lack of basic kindness. Peter was more determined to stand by Jeneil because of it.

Peter's grandfather was deeply disappointed with his daughter. He was ashamed that Jeneil should have to experience that kind of insult. It was hard for him to not insist that Jeneil be invited, but his daughter's anger was rekindled by Peter's determination to forsake the family for Jeneil. It seemed wiser to not force the issue so early in the struggle since it was Jeneil who ended up receiving more anger with every defense of her. The old man found silence bitter to tolerate. He began to wonder more about his daughter's unyielding position toward Jeneil.

Peter held the car door for Jeneil. She handed him the gifts to hold and picked up the tiny cake she had made for the private birthday party. He put his arm around her shoulder. She looked fantastic. It was a special visit for her and she had treated it that way, from the choice of her outfit to the cake. He kissed her cheek. The back door slammed. They both stopped on their path to the greenhouse. A young Chinese woman stood on the back stairs, completely shocked at seeing Peter with a girl, a white girl. He had his arm around a white girl. She stared at them, speechless.

Peter smiled. "Karen, you're in college, you must know how to put words together to form sentences. Jeneil, this is Karen, Tom's daughter. Karen, this is Jeneil. We're visiting my grandfather." He squeezed Jeneil and kissed her cheek. "Bye, Karen."

"Nice to have met you, Karen," Jeneil said quietly.

"Uh, yeah, uh, hi," Karen stammered as they walked past her.

"I hope her major isn't English," Peter laughed as they reached the greenhouse.

"Don't pick on her. She was thunderstruck."

"She sure was. I like her better speechless."

Peter opened the door. His grandfather came to them. "Peter, you look good." He looked at Jeneil, torn by shame that she had to visit privately for his birthday. "Jeneil, you look wonderful." He smiled warmly. He surprised Jeneil and Peter by hugging her. Peter could see that it wasn't easy for his grandfather to accept the poor treatment Jeneil was receiving. It buoyed him up and softened the anger inside of him.

Jeneil handed him the cake. "Happy Birthday, Mr. Chang."

"Thank you, how nice," he said, taking it from her. "Come and sit down. Can you visit for a while?"

"We were planning to," Peter answered.

"Oh good," his grandfather said. Jeneil checked the cages. Seeing that they were empty, she scanned the trees and began chirping quietly, calling to them. Peter smiled. His grandfather looked at him. "How is she?"

"Dealing with it. She's disappointed that she's causing trouble in the family."

The grandfather shook his head. "She has more understanding of Chinese dignity than your mother, and that's my fault. If I had trained my daughter as well as Jeneil's father trained her, this might have gone better than this ugliness. I'm really sorry, Peter."

Peter shrugged. "Like you said, it's what happens when you step outside what's accepted. I'm angry. Jeneil understands that."

Jeneil found a dowel stick. Holding it in the air, she chirped. A parakeet flew close and fluttered then ascended to the trees again.

"Come on," she called for it in return.

Peter smiled as his grandfather went to her. "That's Chu Ling."

"That's pretty; it sounds like a bird call. Here, Chu Ling."

"Would you like to see him up close?"

"Oh, yes." She smiled, handing him the stick. He held it out before him and called. Both parakeets flew to the dowel. "Oh, how pretty. They really trust you, they're accepting my presence."

"The blue one is Chu Ling and the green one is Chun Su. Chu Ling is more trusting."

"I wonder why Chun Su isn't as trusting."

"I don't know."

Peter stood behind Jeneil. "That's easy," he said, "it's more intelligent. Would you be so trusting after having been captured, shipped to a strange country, and kept in a cage with a bunch of other birds?" His grandfather and Jeneil both laughed.

His grandfather smiled. He liked these two. Their combined life force was magnetic and pleasant to watch. He had watched his other grandchildren as they brought dates home to be introduced to him. He could sense when he was meeting the 'right one.' He watched the marriages as they weathered their different stages, the settling in of life's routine and children. He watched when in some cases the life force became dulled and in other cases ignored. That seemed to happen too routinely and too often, except with Janice, Liam's middle daughter. The zest she showed as a young girl was evident in her marriage. They were an odd couple compared to the others in the family. But they seemed the happiest.

He found Jeneil and Peter exciting, and he wished the younger children could see it. Theirs was a relationship that possessed all the qualities that made a marriage beautiful. It was a romance. He hoped his grandson, Ron, would have the chance to see them together. Ron was serious about Sue. They were engaged but the life force was very weak. It troubled him. Ron troubled him. He could be wrong, but Ron seemed to run his life with excessive efficiency and seemed to rule his emotions the same way. Perhaps being an accountant did that to a person. He had tried to talk to Ron, but Ron wasn't one to be talked to, he talked at you. Ron's life was too efficient; it couldn't be penetrated by conversation.

He watched Peter and Jeneil. Jeneil had taken the dowel and was trying to get to know the birds better. He watched Peter with pride. He had to admit of the three of his grandsons Peter was special to him and for many reasons, but mainly because only Peter carried the Chang name. Of the three, Peter had had a more difficult life. He was a ruffian, always in trouble and confused about how he got there. Ron by comparison was an ideal son, well behaved and a source of pride to his parents. The two hadn't gotten along as young boys. Ron had preached and Peter had hit. As a result, Lien and Risa had struggled in their relationship. Everyone blamed Peter's beginnings on the unfortunate circumstances surrounding his birth, but as the grandfather watched the two mothers, he understood the two sons. Risa was quiet and even when young had treated life gently. Lien had boundless energy and an insatiable curiosity, but she lacked the wisdom to control it. She had changed only after having Peter.

On the other hand, Malien was a combination of her older sisters, and her son, Rick, was a combination of his cousins, Ron and Peter. He was a rebel, dressing only in black, refusing to cut his hair until it looked shaggy. Everyone blamed Peter's influence on Rick's choice of clothes and rebelliousness, but the grandfather saw the difference. Rick was dressing a part, wearing costumes. With Peter, the black leather jacket had been part of him. Peter, at Rick's age, had been far more steady and predictable with strong convictions. Even Malien would complain to her father she wished her son had Peter's honesty. Peter had lied growing up in given situations, but he had an honesty that made him stronger and wiser than both his cousins. His endurance was stronger, too. His cousins had grown up in a less hostile environment while Peter had developed strengths and resources his cousins could never match. Peter lacked the gentility of a civilized boyhood, but it was a skill he was learning as a man and it seemed to be the leading edge between him and Ron now. He was a beginner, a novice, but his honesty and strength were pulling him through.

Watching the civilized girl Peter had chosen, the old man was curious about the bond between them. She possessed the same kind of inner honesty as if she had struggled, yet she wasn't from the streets and seemed very skilled in a civilized world. He could tell she was intelligent enough to know the difference between skilled and skillful, and he was impressed she understood morals and ethics and had chosen to be skilled instead of skillful. While Peter plodded along like a puppy examining a new environment, Jeneil walked through it, directing, controlling, guiding, and aware of her power to create her environment. Why had she taken Peter on? He had seen Karen stare in shock at them. It was understandable. Besides being white, Jeneil was not what one would expect Peter to be attracted to or expect Peter to be what Jeneil would want. Another odd couple.

The grandfather smiled as he watched Peter move in to look at the birds with Jeneil. He laughed as Chu Su bit Peter, his startled withdrawal causing both birds to flutter in panic and fly to safety in a flurry of squawks and feathers. Peter shook his hand and examined his finger.

Looking at the tree, Peter growled. "You've had it, you dirty…. Come near me again and I'll feed you to the cat!" Jeneil covered her mouth, hiding a laugh.

"Peter, you went near him. Chu Ling is more trusting. Why did you go near Chu Su?"

"Because I understand his distrust of people."

She laughed. "Did you tell him that?"

"He didn't bite you."

"I didn't intrude on him. You pushed him beyond the limit of his instincts."

"How did you know that?"

"I read White Fang. He didn't trust easily either. Chu Su and White Fang are like you." She smiled. "Strong raw instincts with deeper, kinder inner feelings."

The grandfather listened. Jeneil was carrying the relationship and he became troubled at the thought. He needed to talk to Peter. The songbird was too delicate to carry the master forever and for the first time he saw the vulnerability of their relationship. Was that what Lien saw? But how could Lien see more clearly than he? She didn't even know Jeneil. She hadn't seen Peter and Jeneil together like they were at that moment. He knew Lien to be sharp-sighted and instinctive, and he had feared that in her as she was growing up. It made her manipulative. It wasn't until having Peter that she toned down a few degrees, but she had lost objectivity toward their relationship and it was blinding her. Her lack of wisdom combined with sharp-sightedness and keen instincts was a volatile combination. He watched Peter and Jeneil, putting aside his worry and enjoying the wonder that existed between them. Whatever the bond was, it was obviously mutual. They were completely taken with each other. He smiled and wished his daughter could see that.

"Does your finger need to be treated?" the grandfather asked.

"No, it broke the skin but it's not bleeding. It'll be okay, but you should have told me Chu Su means dwarfed vulture in Chinese. Man, what a bite."

"Mr. Chang, how do you say crème puff in Chinese?" Jeneil asked, teasing Peter.

"Quiet you," he said, smiling, bumping her arm with his elbow.

"Grandfather, can you open your gifts now?" Peter asked. "Open Jeneil's last, it's special."

The grandfather smiled. "Oh, now I'm curious." He sat in his chair and opened the larger package. "A leather carryall and my name is monogrammed! Thank you, Peter." He gave a look of doubt.

"Jeneil and I paid for it," Peter answered, understanding the look.

"Two gifts from Jeneil?"

"No, one didn't cost…well, you'll see," Jeneil added.

The old man opened the slender box and read the note inside. *Dear Mr. Chang, I recently won a roundtrip to China. I would be thrilled if you'd accept it as a gift from me. Please go and search for more ancestors and bring back a box of pictures for me and Peter to enjoy. Much, much love, Jeneil.* He looked up, staring from one to the other. Peter smiled broadly, enjoying his reaction.

"This is real?" the grandfather questioned.

Jeneil nodded and went to him. Kneeling by his side, she smiled. "Will you go? You have the choice of staying for two weeks or two or three months or longer."

"How?" he asked, still at a loss for words.

"I have a good friend who has his own plane. He flies to China on business every three months or so. I won this trip, but he doesn't mind having a passenger."

"This is incredible." The old man smiled.

Jeneil squeezed his arm. "I've been hoping you'd go. The International Arts League has very little material on China. I was thinking what a help you'd be to them if you could go there and gather material for them. They have money available to cover costs and I'm associated with a foundation that could supply money through an educational fund if you'd gather material to use in exhibits."

The extra money was news to Peter and he watched as Jeneil spread her fire to his grandfather in her 'you'd be doing me a favor' style. She had expanded the trip from visiting family to a full-fledged tour of China. He'd probably see more of China now than if he had spent his life there. She was something else entirely. She wouldn't settle for less than superlative in life let alone birthday gifts. As he watched her, his heart expanded to fit the increase of love he was experiencing for her.

The grandfather shook his head. "Jeneil, I don't know what to say."

"Say you'll go," she pleaded.

"Yes, yes, I'll go. Thank you seems so little to say."

"No, thank you is enough. The pictures and material you'll gather are priceless to me, the foundation, and the International Arts League. Thank you is more than enough."

"I am really overwhelmed. I don't know what to say." The old man sat back in his chair, smiling.

"Say can we have some cake now?" Peter joked.

"Yes," the grandfather answered, "that's a good idea. It'll be good for me to move around so my heart will start beating again."

Jeneil laughed and Peter smiled. Jeneil and his grandfather were a natural combination and as they sat and talked while having their cake he hoped things would go as well with the rest of his family.

"Peter?" The door leading from the house opened and Peter stopped breathing as he heard his mother call him. The grandfather looked at him. Jeneil put her plate down quietly and clasped her hands together nervously. "Peter, I'd like to talk to you." His mother's voice grew louder as she stepped into the back of the greenhouse. She stopped short as she caught sight of Jeneil. No one spoke. Peter looked at Jeneil. She was staring at her hands. He put his arm around her shoulder. The silence was deafening.

Jeneil stood up. "If you'll excuse me, Mr. Chang, I'll leave now, Happy Birthday." She smiled, surprising Peter with her casualness. He stood up and Jeneil turned to him. "Peter, I'll wait in the car so you and your mother can talk. Don't rush on my account." She picked up her shawl and purse. Peter was shocked at how controlled she was, but she had to pass his mother to leave. He smiled as she held her head high and walked straight toward his mother. As she reached her, Jeneil nodded slightly at his mother as a goodbye and continued past her. Peter's chest all but burst with pride by how Jeneil dealt with the situation.

His grandfather stood. "Jeneil," he called then turned to Peter. "We've forgotten our manners here, Peter," he said with authority. "Your mother has never met Jeneil. They should be introduced." Peter saw Jeneil's shoulders slump then straighten. She turned and walked back slowly, still in control.

The old man looked at his daughter. "Lien, Jeneil and Peter brought some birthday presents for me." Peter saw his mother fidget, but she remained silent. He went to Jeneil and put his arm around her, feeling how rigid her shoulders were.

"Mom, I think you should meet Jeneil." His mother turned to face them, gaining her composure. She was the Mrs. Lee who greeted people at the restaurant.

"Jeneil, thank you for caring about my father's birthday."

Jeneil looked at her. "I care about Peter's grandfather because Peter is very special to me and much more special now that I've had a chance to meet his mother. My family isn't as large as yours and I'm impressed with the traditions you manage in such a large group. Peter's told me that you're at the center of it; that you run and plan the parties. I can't arrange large parties without getting overwhelmed so I admire that ability. I know the work that's involved. My mother had that talent, too."

"Thank you," his mother responded formally. Peter thought he glimpsed a crack in her armor.

Jeneil looked at Peter. "I'll wait in the car," then turning to his mother, she smiled. "I'm really glad I've had this chance to at least say hello." She looked at the grandfather. "Goodnight, Mr. Chang."

The grandfather smiled, impressed with how Jeneil had handled herself. "Jeneil, thank you very much," he said sincerely.

"Believe me, you're more than welcome and I'll be in touch with the details." She turned and walked out the door. Peter's heart felt three times its normal size and was beating rapidly, pride and fear shooting through him.

His mother looked at the floor for a few seconds. "She's well mannered and carries herself with dignity," she said, looking up at Peter. "Where is she from, I don't recognize the accent."

"Nebraska," Peter answered through a dry throat.

"What's her last name?"

"Alden-Connors."

She wrinkled her brow. "Two last names?"

"Her mother's maiden name was Alden, her father's was Connors. They combined them."

"They're modern types then? English and Irish, too. Do they know about you?"

"Mom, why didn't you ask her all these questions?"

The door opened and John, the normally cool eighteen-year-old, rushed in somewhat flustered. "Pete! Karen just introduced me to this classy chick out there. Karen said she's your girl. Is that just hype?"

"Classy chick, huh?" Peter laughed.

"Oh man, what a fox! Is she yours?"

"Yeah." Peter glanced at his mother. She looked down.

"Holy sh…umm. She's a total blast. She walks up to us and uppity Karen trips over her tongue like it's a stale board and your girl looks at me and says, 'you must be John, I met Karen earlier.' Then Karen picks her chin up off the pavement and tries to equal your girl's class by saying, 'John, this is Jeneil, she's here with Pete.'" John laughed. "Oh man, Karen always thinks she's so uppity and your girl walks through and aces the pins from under her without missing a beat. I'd have paid admission to have seen that and I got it for free."

Peter smiled, remembering the grief Karen had given him and John about their bad manners and slovenly ways. He enjoyed and understood John's appreciation. Peter's stepfather, Tom, came in. He looked at his wife then at Peter. "She's very nice, Pete."

John laughed. "Very nice? Dad, come on. She makes Lin Chi look like dog food."

Peter's mother stiffened and fixed her collar. "John, I'd like to talk to Peter. It would be rude to keep the girl much longer."

"Hey, I'll keep her company." John smiled. Peter grinned, noticing John never mentioned Jeneil being white.

"John, let Pete and his mother talk. Or is it Peter now? She calls you Peter," Tom said.

"So does my grandfather."

"I like her, Pete," Tom commented, and he noticed Lien look at him. "Let's go, John."

John turned as he left with his father. "Hey, Pete, leave me instructions on how to catch one like that and I'll owe you my life. That would fry Karen's socks." Peter grinned and shook his head as they disappeared into the house. His mother wrung her hands, obviously concerned.

"Mom, if this is about the party Wednesday I'm scheduled for a double so I can't be here."

"Oh," she said, almost in a sigh of relief. "Then that's what I'll tell the family, and I'll tell them you brought your gift for father today."

"You'll have to tell them about Jeneil since John and Karen met her."

"I'll handle that. You're dating a girl who's white and that's it."

Peter shrugged. "Whatever works for you, Mom. Was there anything else?"

"Yes, did you introduce her to Steve or did he know her already? You said they're good friends."

Peter wondered where she was going with this. "She works at the hospital so she knows both of us. I was friends with her first then Steve got to know her. Why?"

His mother slouched in disappointment. "Peter," she paused, choosing her words carefully, "she has surprised me. I expected the coarseness of Lin Chi only with better taste in clothes. She's, well, she handles herself nicely." She fidgeted. "Peter, be careful."

"What do you mean?"

"Whites end up going to white. Steve has style, polish, good manners, and good looks."

Peter stared at her. "And I'm from the gutter?"

"He's on her level. You could get hurt, that's all."

"Too late, Mom, if I lost her now to anybody, not just Steve, it would hurt. And you're wrong, Steve's not on her level, nobody is. Mom, she's different."

"She's white, Peter. Believe me; they go with their own kind."

He sighed. "I know you're worried about me but give her a chance."

His mother ignored him. "Maybe now that you know you can handle yourself around that level of girl you should try meeting Chinese girls. There are Chinese girls like her, too. Not only whites have style. Give Chinese girls a chance, too."

Peter shook his head. "You're not listening. I'm not in love with her level or her style or her color; I'm in love with her." He was surprised he and his mother were having a civilized conversation, they should have been yelling by now. He figured Jeneil had aced his mother as well as Karen. That was the only thing that could account for the change.

"Peter, can she be happy with all of us? She'll be different from everyone. She's only a girl. Women change as they get older and start looking at things differently. This might be something new to her, being outside her own kind. Is she rebelling against parents? The Midwest and its ways?"

"Mom, she wants to marry me. That means something, doesn't it?" Peter saw a look come over his mother's face that he had never seen before and that he couldn't identify. At best, he would have called it sadness.

"Peter, you don't know what you're saying, it's not that simple or that easy. She's white, you're Chinese; believe me, that's a strong force against you."

"Mom, people are different today. Races intermarry now."

"It's not that common."

"It's too late. I love her. Besides, I am half white."

"No, Peter. You're Chinese. You were raised Chinese, you look Chinese. Does she know you have white blood?"

"She knows." His mother fidgeted and sighed. "Mom, stop worrying. Get to know her. You'll see. Everything's okay. I really should go."

"Peter," she called, as he started to leave. "Steve cares for her. Jeneil's back was to me so I didn't see her face, but she likes him. She's comfortable with him. I could see that, but he cares for her."

"Mom, I know that. We joke that we're a triad. She sees him as my brother. To him, she's the kid sister he's never had."

"No, Peter. He really likes her, believe me, he does."

Peter sighed. "I guess I should be grateful you're not on Jeneil anymore, now it's Steve. Before we start to argue, I think I should leave." He opened the door then looked at her. "I understand that you're worried about me but trust me in this," and he closed the door behind him.

The grandfather had watched silently. He had watched his daughter and he had listened. Now he understood more clearly.

"He's not listening, Father." She sighed.

He looked at her with deep compassion. "Lien, that's all a parent can do at times is warn and caution. The child has to choose to listen and understand."

"Yes, that's certainly true." She stared out the window into the darkened night. "She's really nice. If only she was Chinese."

"Lien, it's his choice."

"No, it isn't, Father. It's only a matter of time before she makes the switch to Steve. Poor, poor Peter." She sighed again and shook her head.

*****

Peter walked to the car with his own words ringing in his ears. 'I understand that you're worried about me, but trust me in this.' Those were words he'd heard Jeneil say as he cautioned her from time to time; Robert and Dennis. In the back of his mind was the gnawing feeling that his mother was right. He had felt at times that Steve was attracted to Jeneil. He got in the car and sat quietly, mulling the thought over in his mind.

"What happened?" Jeneil asked.

He shook his head. "Nothing really, we talked more easily than we ever have."

"Well, that's certainly an improvement. I feel like I've been holding my breath for the last hour. Even the roots of my hair hurt." She massaged her temples and did some deep breathing.

He leaned back against the seat, staring straight ahead. "You impressed her, Jeneil."

She looked at him, not quite believing. "I did? She didn't call me names?"

"No, not one." He sat unemotional.

"I don't understand. Why are you down?"

"I'm not down. I'm thinking."

She studied him a few seconds. "What are you thinking?"

He sighed and pushed his hand against the roof of the car. "Baby, are you sure I'm what you want?"

Her heart stopped. "Peter, what exactly did she say to you?"

He paused. "She said that you're young. She wondered if you could deal with being around so many Chinese. She pointed out that you'd be different and asked if that would bother you after awhile."

"Oh, wow." She leaned back. "Now she's going to kill me with kindness. Boy, she takes odd angled turns, doesn't she?"

Peter sighed again. "I must be maturing or aging. She's beginning to make more sense to me than she used to."

Jeneil stared at him. "That's very reassuring."

He looked at her. "Well, at twenty-four I guess I'm long overdue, aren't I?"

"Peter, how can I answer her questions? They're the type of questions that only time answers. Think about it. I can reverse them. Am I what you want? Or are you settling for me because of your scars? Can you accept me being different than your family? Will that bother you after awhile?" He stared at her. "I'll bet your first instinct is to refute each one but can you? You can only prove it by commitment, the same as I have to. This tactic is worse than hostility. Those aren't questions, they're innuendos. Again, I'm without a defense. She's quite an opponent, and as far as me being young, I've thought about all those things. Mandra and I used to talk about the problems facing a mixed marriage, but that's the extent of my experience. It's all hypothetical." She touched his arm. "Oh, Peter, how can I defend myself? All I know is I love you. I belong to you."

He put his arm around her. "That's it, baby. You've said it." He kissed her deeply and she clung to him for security that seemed to be slipping from her too often lately. He kissed her cheek. "Let's go home, kid."

Thirty-Three

Peter found himself watching Steve more closely. One day as Peter and Steve walked toward the cafeteria, they had seen Jeneil coming toward them. Steve had pulled out a small pad from his pocket and scribbled a note then slipped it onto the stack of material she was carrying as she passed by. He had turned and walked backwards for a few steps then turned around and grinned. He had commented that she had great control and that she had totally ignored him. Peter's back had stiffened and he immediately felt guilty, but he still watched every move Steve made when they were all together, even going so far as to deliberately leave the room then return quietly so he could watch them. After a few days, he had gotten sick of it. He hated himself and he was having trouble facing Steve. He had come to the decision that Steve liked Jeneil a lot, he was quite taken with her but that was it. He was Peter's best friend and that was how he was going to see it. As for Jeneil, her schedule had gotten even busier and she and his grandfather were going to a planning meeting for the International Arts League that night. Peter chuckled as he leaned against the elevator wall thinking about it.

"Well, Chang, want to worry about him, too? There's a genuine love between those two," he said out loud to himself as the elevator stopped.

"Hi, Pete," Steve said quietly as Peter got on.

"Hey, Steve. How about a sandwich and a beer tonight? Jeneil's got a date with my grandfather, or we could go home and shove something from the freezer into the microwave."

Steve smiled. "Let's eat out. Things okay now?"

"What things?"

"I don't know. I asked you. This is the first time you've loosened up in days. I just figured you were going through some storm. You married guys get like that sometimes. I can tell when Jeff's wife has her period, he's in a silent scowl for three or four days then it passes."

Peter smiled. "You're a smart ass. You'll probably replace Sprague someday."

"Not me." Steve laughed. "I don't see myself as nursemaid to new surgeons."

Peter grinned. "Then get married and let me see how you deal with it."

"Pete, Jeff may scowl for a few days but the look on his face on that fifth day makes me jealous. I could tell yours was different."

"Why?"

Steve laughed. "Because it lasted too long, unless she was hemorrhaging."

Peter shook his head. "I can't wait until you get married. You're going to eat crow."

Steve laughed again. "It's good to have you back."

*****

The night out was good for Peter and Steve. It felt like the days before Jeneil had come into their lives, laughing easily and talking openly about whatever came up. It had been good for their friendship. Peter thought that as he took off his jacket and hung it up just as Jeneil opened the apartment door.

"Hi," she said, putting her briefcase down. "Have a nice evening?"

"Very nice, Steve and I went out for a sandwich and a beer."

"Oh, good." She smiled, folding her shawl. "I've been worried lately that I've interfered with your friendship."

"How?" He was surprised both she and Steve had noticed.

"I can't say for sure. It just seemed that Steve and I were talking more than the three of us were. It was just a feeling, so I'm glad you and Steve got a chance to be alone. You two have such a great friendship; I wouldn't want to change that." Her words removed the last few wrinkles he had about her and Steve. The evening had reassured him about Steve's loyalty and her admission now that she didn't want to change their friendship cemented his sense of security. "Why are you staring at me like that?"

"Because you're beautiful," he said, putting his arms around her and kissing her.

"Mmm, it's nice to be away from you for short periods of time. You always fuss over me when I get home. I love it."

"How did your meeting go?"

"Very well." She smiled. "Your grandfather will be in China for seven weeks. He'll be home a couple of days before Thanksgiving. He'll fly there with Bill and the foundation is flying him home."

Peter smiled. "Jeneil, if you only knew how many years I've listened to him talk about a trip to China." He shook his head. "And now it's real. He'll be leaving in a couple of weeks then?"

She nodded. "He's really good with groups. I think the International Arts League wants him around permanently. China hasn't gotten very good representation with them and when you consider the large Chinese population here that really is a shame. They feel that what they have on China is too professional and too academic to be appealing to the general community so they're counting on this trip to gather material that will reach the general population. They're so enthusiastic I'm concerned about your grandfather having time to visit his family. I mentioned that to Bill. He said he'd be happy to take your grandfather to China whenever he goes, so I guess I'll relax."

Peter laughed. "My grandfather, a jetsetter."

Jeneil smiled. "He handles himself so well. You're a lot like him, you know."

"Oh, don't I wish."

"You are, Peter. He's worked harder at packaging himself than you have, and really you're only beginning, but you share the same type of character fiber."

"Hey, I'm encouraged. You're crazy about him so I guess that means if I'm like him when I'm his age, you'll still be interested in me."

She smiled warmly. "Always, Chang, always. You are an absolute fascination to me, totally superlative." He held her and all the worry seemed to drain from him.

"Baby, keep saying that, say it often and loud so we both remember it." He kissed her, the kiss warm and loving, and he could tell Chang was settled by her words. She snuggled to him as she responded to his kiss and Chang welcomed her, comforted knowing she was his. She belonged to him and he was going to prove that ownership. He wanted her to know how he felt.

*****

Peter was pleased with how life was settling in and calming down. His mother had been impressed with Jeneil's gift to his grandfather and was letting bits and pieces about Jeneil trickle to the family. Pulling off his grandfather's trip to China was only the beginning. John had reported to Peter that Karen was rattled by all the praise and compliments Jeneil received from their grandfather, and Jeneil's connection to the International Arts League had Karen permanently gagged. Peter could see the smoke seethe from her every pore whenever Jeneil's name was mentioned. John loved it, too. He said anytime he wanted to ace out Karen, he'd bring up Jeneil and totally run her off the track, and Peter didn't worry because in the overall scheme of things Karen hardly mattered. His mother was easing up, that's what mattered. While she liked Jeneil, she was still cautious. She asked questions about Steve whenever Peter saw her, but at least she didn't yell.

Peter turned the light off on the viewer and replaced the x-rays in their envelope then sat down to fill in the medical report. The telephone rang. He reached for it.

"Dr. Chang? Dr. Chang, this is your mother."

He smiled. "Hi, Mom." He liked the way she acted toward him lately and he gave Jeneil the credit for that. He could tell his mother liked the package that Jeneil offered and was pleased with him for having chosen her.

"I won't keep you. I just wanted to let you know that a week from Saturday we're having a going away breakfast for your grandfather. It wasn't easy to get everyone together so we decided on a breakfast."

Peter laughed. "Boy, the Chang family stops at nothing for a party."

"Can you be here?"

"I can't be sure. I'm on days next week, but if I have Saturday morning off I'll be there. What time?"

"We decided on eight-thirty so everyone could get their errands done afterwards. Saturdays are busy so we thought everything could be over by eleven at the latest. We all want to say goodbye to Father properly."

"I'll see what I can do, Mom."

"Good, it'll be nice when you're finished with your residency and your hours are normal."

"I don't let myself think about that yet. There are a lot of double shifts between now and then." He wondered for a moment. "Mom, what about Jeneil?"

"She should come, Peter. This trip is her doing. Father's right. I have to tell you I'm nervous, not many people know you two are together. It sticks in my throat whenever I think of telling everybody."

"So what are you saying, yes or no?"

"You don't have to tell people you live with her do you?"

"No."

"Then I think she should come."

Peter sighed. "Thanks, Mom. Thanks a lot."

"I'm trying not to be difficult," she defended.

"I know. It's okay. I understand."

*****

Peter and Steve walked to the parking lot together. "You look happy."

"I am, Steve. My mother just okayed Jeneil going to a family party."

"Oh wow, that's a skull splitter that one," Steve said, shocked, then he chuckled. "So Sunshine did her thing and the mother is now a convert. That's great news." Peter could tell Steve was genuinely happy for them.

"It's not a whole parade of happiness but it's sure more than I ever expected with us living together, and she's not saying anything about Jeneil being white. That's the real shock. I never expected my mother to take that."

"You two have handled your relationship wisely, just the two of you until you were ready to handle more. That was smart thinking."

"Guess whose smart thinking it was?" Peter grinned.

Steve smiled. "Who cares, it worked. She is sharp though. Talking to her sometimes, I stare in amazement at some of the things she thinks about. I don't remember noticing a girl's brain before or being impressed by it. Boy, celibacy is doing wonders for me."

Peter laughed. "By February you'll have a good idea of what your ideal woman is like."

"February, hell," Steve laughed, "I know already. I'm going to find one who comes as close to Jeneil as possible." Peter smiled understandingly.

Peter rolled the thought on how to tell Jeneil she was invited through his brain several times as he drove home. He rehearsed several ways to tell her and each one felt great. As he put the key in the lock to the apartment door, the front door opened and Jeneil walked in behind him balancing a tripod and a leather case. He left the apartment door open and went to help her.

"What's all this?" he asked, taking the tripod.

She smiled excitedly as they walked up the stairs. "I'm making a short film."

Peter collected his thoughts as he helped her off with her jacket. "When did you get interested in film making?"

"I'm not really. There was an announcement about a film festival at Elios's. The morning celebration we went to sort of inspired me so I've been working on setting, timing, and graphics. I like film festivals but this is the first time I'm entering one. Robert is letting me use his equipment."

"Is that why you've been leaving the house early in the morning?"

"Yes, and this is my best weekend for the actual filming."

"Can I go with you?"

"You want to?"

"Yes, I'd like to see what you're doing," he answered, smiling.

She hugged him. "Peter, you're so great. You really are," and she hugged him again.

"Hey, baby, my family's having a farewell breakfast for my grandfather."

"Oh, that's very nice." She smiled and he kissed her forehead gently.

"My mom has invited you." He watched her as the statement penetrated her mind.

"What!" she gasped in a whisper. She swallowed hard as she held back tears. It helped, only one rolled down her cheek and he wiped it gently with his finger. She closed her eyes and sighed. "Oh, Peter, I can barely believe it. I can't believe it." She held onto him as he rubbed her back.

"I'll try to get next Saturday off."

She pulled away. "Next Saturday?"

"Yeah, why?"

"Peter, that's my weekend in Nebraska and I can't miss the meetings. With the holiday season coming, we don't meet in November or December. The meetings this month and next month are vital because we complete as much business as we can. Oh, this is terrible."

"Honey, relax! It's okay."

"But I don't want to offend anyone, especially your mother, and especially not now."

"I'll make sure I work. She never blinks when my excuse is work. But I have to admit, I was really going to enjoy introducing you to my cousin, Ron."

"Why?"

Peter looked embarrassed. "Because Ron has been Mr. Perfect; the right clothes, the right everything, a great son, never did anything wrong. I was the opposite; street kid, smart mouthed, always in trouble. When I went into medicine, I think it made life easier for my mother. That's why I became my son, the doctor. I was her son, the delinquent, for so many years. To bring you home would be the final step in Peter Chang getting civilized. You're a lady, that in itself will shock everybody."

Her smile was filled with understanding and compassion. She hugged him gently and kissed his cheek. "I'm sorry," she said softly.

"It's okay, baby, the Changs get together a lot. I'll have my chance."

She grinned. "I'm flattered you feel that way about me."

"Honey, I was so proud when you met my mother. I knew she'd like you once she stopped to listen."

She kissed him lightly and snuggled into his arms. "Peter, things are settling in for us and it feels so good."

"I know, baby. I'm feeling pretty good about it, too. Nothing can touch us now. The brass ring is just ahead of us."

*****

Peter pushed the elevator button for the sixth floor and leaned against the wall next to Steve. "Killer shift next week, two doubles," he said, yawning.

"Yeah, we both got lucky," Steve answered. "I'm looking forward to Sunday at your place to prepare for it."

Peter smiled. "Hey, how would you like to have some offbeat fun?"

Steve looked at him. "Doing what?"

"Let's go watch Jeneil make a short film she's been working on."

"A film for what?"

"Some amateur film festival she heard of."

"What's the film about?"

Peter shrugged. "I don't know. She just said that Elio's inspired her."

Steve laughed. "Elio's? Count me in. Shit, I'm just in the mood for TAI kicks. When?"

"Tomorrow morning."

"Great."

"I'll call her and let her know you're going, too."

*****

The lights were off in the apartment except for a small lamp in the living room. The sofa bed was prepared for Steve and there was a note on the small dining table. *Honey, left a snack in the kitchen. I suggest you go to bed early and sleep in your clothes. Everything is gathered and ready to go. See you in the morning. Love, Who Else. P.S. Goodnight Steve, see you in the A.M.*

Peter looked at Steve, who was smiling. "Some fun, early to bed?"

Steve chuckled. "Hey, it'll be different, you can count on that. Let's go find that snack."

There was a plate on the counter covered with a cloth napkin and the coffee server was hot. A note leaned against two mugs. *Hi again, made some Ovaltine. Was making sweet bread dough to freeze for holiday baking and decided to make a treat for you. Love again. P.S. You too, Steve.*

Peter looked at Steve. "Gee, this gets better and better. Hot Ovaltine and cinnamon rolls."

Steve grinned and took a bit. "Mmm, they're good."

Peter laughed softly. "Sorry, Steve, this isn't exactly TAI fun."

"TAI fun Sunshine style." He chuckled. "She's cute. Notes and treats, and she's all snuggled in your bed keeping it warm. That's okay too, Pete. That's okay, too."

"I'm not complaining," Peter said, biting into a roll. "I like her cute and cuddly, but you were expecting TAI."

"This is nice." Steve smiled. "I like this, too."

*****

The alarm clock sounded. Peter stirred and struggled to open his eyes. "Honey, what time is it? I feel like I just fell asleep."

"You probably did. It's three forty-five," Jeneil answered, tying her robe.

He propped himself up on one elbow. "That's almost midnight!"

She chuckled. "Go back to sleep. You don't have to come." He fell back on his pillow and Jeneil left the room.

Peter and Steve had taken her advice and slept in their clothes. Peter was glad because he was having trouble putting his shoes on the correct feet; he was sure he wouldn't have been up to dressing. It reminded him of his early intern days. Jeneil returned dressed in sweaters, warm-looking slacks, and leather boots.

"Where the hell are you filming, Alaska?" he asked, still groggy.

She smiled. "Are you sure you're up to this?"

"I got this far, just lead me to the door." He stood up, yawning.

They went to the living room. Steve stood up and rubbed his face. "Are we having fun yet?" he joked, still half asleep.

"Fun? You two thought you were going to have fun?" Jeneil laughed. "You'd better crawl back into bed then."

"No, I'm half awake now. Besides I want to know what the hell you can film, it's dark out there," Steve answered, as Peter put on his jacket then handed Steve his.

"Guys, you have to dress warmer than that. It's a fall morning out there. I'll get some sweatshirts to wear under your jackets."

"Where are we going, Alaska?"

Jeneil smiled. "You two are stereo brothers. That's what Peter asked me."

Jeneil had suggested they bring their pillows so they could sleep in the car. They had said they didn't want to, but Steve was asleep in the back seat and Peter was snuggled up against his pillow sleeping soundly in the front seat. Jeneil smiled as she drove in to the parking lot and parked the car. Peter stirred and lifted his head from the pillow.

"Where are we?" he asked, looking around, confused.

"East Beach," Jeneil answered. "And I can't wait for you to wake up. I have to set up the equipment, so follow if you can or keep sleeping, but I have to move out. Okay?"

"Okay, honey," Peter answered, snuggling against his pillow again, starting to doze. Jeneil closed the door gently and Peter felt the cool morning air hit his face. He could smell the ocean. He sat up quickly. "East Beach!"

Steve raised his head. "What?"

"Steve, she's filming on East Beach. Isn't that where the cops found the guy half dead in the water? Remember the case the emergency unit shipped to us because he was so far gone."

Steve sat up quickly. "Yes, it was. What's she doing?"

"I don't know, but if she comes across a dead body in the water she'll be sick for months. I'm going with her. Geez, she doesn't think. East Beach is where college kids maraud and the statistics on rapes here are high. Damn that girl! She has the worse survival instincts."

Peter got out of the car quickly. Steve followed. The sky was dark but not pitch black, and they stumbled along heading for the light from the two lanterns ahead that lit a small area on the beach. They could see Jeneil working with the equipment.

"Jeneil, are you crazy coming to East Beach in the middle of the night!" Peter scolded. "This place is a high crime area."

"I didn't have much choice, Peter. The sun rises in the east and it's matutinal."

"What's that?" Steve asked.

Jeneil giggled. "It means in the morning. Isn't that a funny sounding word? Matutinal. I like the sound of nocturnal better. I don't think matutinal has enough majesty to it to describe something from the morning." Steve looked at Peter and grinned.

"She didn't hear one word I said." Peter sighed as he zipped his jacket against the cold, damp breeze coming in off the ocean.

"I heard you, Peter, and I'll bet it's the sunrise that attracts people to East Beach. They just get out of hand celebrating and miss it. You really need to prepare for it. You can't be semi-conscious or hung over or you'll miss the magic, the glory. There's an energy about it that's absolutely fascinating. It's breathtaking actually," she said, working quickly.

"How do you know that?" Peter asked, beginning to wonder.

"I've been coming here for almost two and a half weeks to time the sunrise."

"Jeneil," Peter groaned, thinking of her here by herself.

Steve smiled. "Why are you working so hard to film a sunrise, kid?"

Jeneil positioned herself behind the camera and checked a reading compass. "That should be it," she said, snapping the compass case shut. She looked at Steve. "Why? Because ever since the morning celebration at Elio's I've wanted to express my feeling about mornings, nothing I saw there fit my interpretation. John Polsnak's poem got close, but he was preaching, calling to his audience to put aside their bawdy distractions and actually look at the morning. He was calling them from their night visions. 'Stumble on,' he said, 'pull yourself closer to the night. Distinguish the two personages of Nocturnal and Matutinal with clear sight. Free your memories from the Master of Silence and Cover. Reach for the gifts offered by his younger sister. However, guard your moment of audience with her. She is fleeting in her youth. Watch before she matures to fire and passion.'" Jeneil sighed. "That man has seen sunrises, he has felt them. Hey, Peter, I just realized that Nocturnal and Matutinal are Yen and Yang."

Steve looked at Peter. "Did she answer my question?"

Peter laughed. "Jeneil, you've left the 'n' in eccentric and you're climbing onto the 't.'"

"Tease, tease, if you please, they'll slip on past with velvet ease." She chuckled. "I apologize to poets everywhere for that, but that's the energy. It's starting. The horizon is getting lighter, see." She pointed. "Come on, when I found out that I'd have an audience I decided to do the full film for you, music and all. You guys are lucky. You get to see the actual brilliance, not a second best happening on celluloid. Sit." She motioned to chairs beside the tripod.

"You people want to tell us what you're doing here?" They turned around at the sound of the voice. Two leather jacketed policemen entered the inner circle of their camp.

"The theatre's getting crowded Jeneil." Steve looked at her, amused.

"I'm making a film of the sunrise," Jeneil answered.

"For school or an ad agency?" one policeman asked.

"Neither," Jeneil replied. "It's for an amateur film festival I heard about." The policemen looked at each other.

"Well, I'm glad you didn't try to snow us. The schools and agencies always notify us when they want to use the beach. It closes at eleven," the other policeman said.

"Oh that's right," Jeneil replied. "I keep forgetting that America isn't free."

Peter choked slightly. "Jeneil, watch your mouth."

"My mouth?" She turned to him confused then looked back at the policemen. "Oh my goodness," she said apologetically. "I wasn't being a smart-mouth. I was making an observation on the complications of life. They don't make the laws. I believe in law and order. I really do." The policemen grinned at her nervousness. "And these two guys are doctors. This is all my doing. They're only here to protect me. They had no idea I forgot to get a permit."

"That's a smart move." The other policeman grinned. "Are you from TAI?"

"No, I just like sunrises and sunsets."

"Let's have some I.D.'s."

Jeneil took the policeman's arm pleadingly. "Oh please, could you arrest me after this is over? You wouldn't believe the precision involved in this. It's about to start. I don't want this ruined. I've worked so hard. Oh please, I'll even work in handcuffs. Just let me do this, it's all set up."

The policemen looked at each other. The older one shrugged. "I guess."

Jeneil hugged him. "Oh thank you. You're a wonderful man." She went to the tripod and started the camera. The policeman straightened his jacket, flustered by her action. His partner covered his mouth, trying to hide a smile. Peter began to breathe again.

Steve held back a laugh and grinned as he watched her unpack foam cups and pour hot Ovaltine for everyone. Peter and Steve sat on the chairs. The policemen refused the offer since they'd been sitting most of their shift in the squad car. They accepted the Ovaltine and Jeneil's invitation to stand on the other side of the tripod and watch.

"Look, look," she stammered. "Look straight ahead. See how the curtain of night begins to separate at the horizon. It looks like the sun is lifting its head from under the quilt of cool ocean. Magnificent!" Peter and Steve looked at each other and smiled. The two policemen looked at each other and smiled, too. Bending down, Jeneil pushed the button on a tape player. The sound of trumpets pierced the air, rising above the pulsing ocean waves. A full orchestra blasted two notes and was followed by snare drums for a few rapid beats, then again the horns, the orchestra, and the drums again and again as the sun moved slowly above the horizon, beginning its daily journey across the sky, whether people took notice of it or not.

The music was bold, intense, dramatic. It called for one to wake up their senses and witness magnificence. The weather cooperated and nothing marred the performance of the sunrise as if it had been ordered because someone had worked hard to capture the magnificence of the moment, to record, to share, and to inspire. The sun liked an audience and worked its boldness and majesty on the small group gathered on the beach.

The sun called out, "Behold my power, you lesser inhabitants of the universe. My light has power to separate the blackness of night from its grip on the horizon of your small planet. I observe the lights you have created with your technology. They only illuminate the night, they don't erase it. Have you tried to duplicate me through your inventions? I'm flattered and pleased because I've not come to make you cower before me, but to give you hope as you strive for the superlative in your existence."

Only Jeneil heard the sun's words. Her level was closer to the sun than that of the others in the group. Their ears were untrained to its voice, but their eyes were being educated. Without exception, the other four witnesses were moved by the moment just as Jeneil suspected. All the morning needed was to be observed and witnessed. It would reach each witness on her own, touching each on their own level using the greatest of her gifts, the sun. Morning grinned, "I don't need inferior and artificial celebrations in my honor. I have the power to celebrate life itself. That is my superlative, mankind. Come and celebrate with me."

Peter swallowed past the lump in his throat. Steve cleared his. Hearing Jeneil sniff, they turned their heads to look at her as she wiped tears away and reached for another tissue from her jacket pocket. Peter went to her. She slipped her arms around his waist and clung to him. He held her, enjoying the feeling he recognized from their experience on the balcony in Vermont. She kissed him lightly and stepped back.

"That got to me, Jeneil. It really did. The work was worth it," Steve said, walking to her. She smiled at him, deeply touched by his words. She hugged him and he held her, surprised by the electrical impulse that shot through him with fury.

"Thank you for telling me that," she said, stepping back. He just nodded, waiting for his breathing to normalize before he tried to talk again.

Jeneil poured more Ovaltine for everyone. Holding her cup out in front of her, she smiled. "Gentlemen, let's toast today, we have just witnessed its beginning." They accepted her toast with unspoken understanding. Finishing her drink, she looked at the policemen. "You can arrest me now. My crime was worth it."

"No, we'll call this a warning," the older one said.

The younger one nodded. "Just notify us next time."

"I won't forget. I promise."

The policemen walked away, leaving the three on the beach which was getting brighter and warmer from the gift the morning had brought, and for their effort warmth radiated within each of them stirred by the superlative of magnificence, each feeling it at their own level of understanding. It was a positive warmth binding them to life's energy.

*****

Peter and Steve helped Jeneil carry the gear into the apartment. She insisted they change to sleep. She went about her Sunday routine, high from the experience of the sunrise. By the time the two woke up, she had dinner ready and was doing an interpretive dance routine to spend the energy that still flowed through her. Steve stood near the kitchen watching her when Peter joined him.

"She looks like she enjoys doing that," Steve commented.

"She does. She says it cleanses her, buoys her up and brings her down depending on the need."

Noticing them standing there, Jeneil stopped, turned off the music and walked over to them. Her cheeks were flushed and wisps of hair fell softly around her face. She smiled broadly. Peter was relieved that she was wearing the knee length, airy-looking skirt over her leotard. She looked too, too good in the leotard for the general audience and he considered anyone other than him a general audience; triads be damned in this case. Her sense of modesty seemed to have brought that to her attention because she rarely wore the skirt and he smiled with appreciation.

"I'm still high," she said, hugging Peter.

Steve watched, enjoying her glow. He wondered why he had never seen that as attractive in a woman before. He had been doing a lot of wondering about himself and what he'd been missing by being the White Stallion. Those days seemed far in the past now and as he watched Jeneil with Peter, he wasn't sorry they were gone. She was very, very easy to take and he realized he had missed her qualities as a woman because of his crazy theory of all things to all women. All women except Jeneil. She had resisted him and no matter what he did, he could never break through that cool exterior. She had caught his attention at work because she always ignored him. At first, she was a challenge, but the challenge wore thin with her cool attitude. Before her, he could melt even the coolest woman. He finally put her down as strange. Now that he knew her, and himself, he couldn't blame her for resisting him and he was glad Peter had found her. At least she was in his life as a good friend. In some ways, she reminded him of Marcia, and he thought back to six months of what he thought was real happiness.

"Earth calling Steve Bradley." Jeneil waved her hand in front of him.

"What?"

"Toast and coffee okay with you? Dinner is in another hour."

"Fine." He smiled, still distracted.

She looked at Peter. "Wherever he was, it was pleasant."

Peter hugged her gently. "Want some help?"

"No thanks. Get comfortable. I won't be long."

Dinner was soul satisfying and they went to the living room to enjoy the rest of their Sunday. Peter sat back in a chair with a recent issue of a medical magazine while Jeneil challenged Steve to backgammon. They sat at a small game table she had set up. Challenging the legality of a move, she reached for the instructions printed on the cover of the game. Putting his foot out quickly, Steve pushed the cover, sending it across the floor. Jeneil smiled and stood up, going to get it. Peter watched, amused, as Steve stood up to get to it before her. She got to it first and Steve grabbed her arm to stop her.

"Be careful," Peter called, "she knows…." He was too late. Jeneil executed a perfect hip throw placing Steve on the sofa in stunned surprise. Peter put his head back and laughed. He figured that must have been how stunned he looked the day she tossed him onto the beach.

Jeneil folded her arms. "Bad move, Bradley, bad."

Steve ran his hand over his hair wondering if his head had been tossed over the sofa. "You are one hell of a kick. I mean it." He chuckled. "You could get arrested for impersonating a lady."

Jeneil put her hand over her heart delicately and smiled sweetly. "What's a lady to do when there are no gentlemen around?" she drawled in a thick southern accent. Steve started to sit up. "Stay, you savage beast!" and she picked up the cover to check the rules.

"Savage beast?"

She hit his arm with the cover. "I was right, you big cheater, and you knew it. That's why you tried so hard to keep this out of my hands." She hit his arm several more times. "Apologize you bandit."

He laughed and stood up, knocking the cover to the floor, grabbing her wrists. "Apologize, hell wench. That karate move makes us even. You're lucky you're Pete's woman. He puts up with your antics. Personally, I'd take my belt to you and get you broken in right from the start, you little spitfire. Now get back to the table and I'll whip you the only way left to me, at the backgammon board." She wriggled to be free, her hair spilling over one eye. Steve grinned. "You through wrangling?"

She returned his grin. "Yes," she answered. "Let's get this whipping done with. Do you eat crow with ketchup."

"Don't threaten me. You have to win first."

"Fine," she replied, and he let go of her wrists. She picked up the cover and went back to the table. Pushing her sleeves to her elbows, she leaned on the table. "Come on, you barbaric…," she made a blipping sound. "Sit, let the game begin."

"You have a foul tongue, always cussing." They continued the game and Steve edged her out, winning narrowly. She put her head down on her arms and growled. "Poor sport." Steve chuckled. "Shall I get the ketchup for your crow, Jeneil?" Lifting her side of the board, she spilled the discs from the game into his lap. Steve shook his head. "Bad, bad move Jeneil, now you have to pick them all up."

"Then you don't know the rules of backgammon. The winner has to pick them up to keep him humble," she said, quickly grabbing the cover of the game from his reach.

"Show me that rule."

"Everyone knows that to the victor goes the spoils. I just gave the spoils to you." She grinned, holding the cover behind her back.

Steve stood up and Jeneil jumped up quickly. He walked toward her and she backed away. "Give me the cover." He held out his hand. She hit his hand from underneath with the cover and moved farther away. He quickly moved toward her and she ran into the bedroom, slammed the door behind her, and locked it. He knocked gently. "Open the door, Jeneil."

"Why should I? I may have lost the game but I haven't lost my mind. I'm not stupid," she sing-songed the words.

"No wonder you won't eat crow, you're a chicken."

"Go, pick up your spoils, victor." She laughed. He smacked the door lightly with his hand.

"Frustrating wench, you're so lucky you're Pete's." He walked back to the living room. Peter had been watching, enjoying Steve's reaction to her spoiled brat routine. Steve sat on the sofa. "Damned wildcat."

Peter smiled. "I think it makes life fun."

Steve laughed. "For you maybe, you have the key to the bedroom. Me, I'd like to strangle her."

Jeneil opened the bedroom door and walked into the living room, stopping near Steve. "Here's the cover and there's the rule," she said, looking pleased.

"What? That can't be," he answered, taking it from her, reading it. "You wrote this in!"

"But you didn't say that I couldn't. You just wanted the cover in order to read the rule. That's what you said, I heard you. That's my cover, my game, my rule." She smiled and pointed to the discs on the floor. "To the spoils, victor. Next time, be specific."

Steve smiled, sensing her need to be right. She was fun and he liked her spunk. He stood up, hit her head gently with the cover then went to pick up the backgammon game. "How come I feel like the loser when I won?"

"I don't know, ask a psychiatrist, but you can have two desserts. Does that help?"

"It's a start." Steve smiled and looked up as Jeneil stopped to give Peter a kiss on her way to the kitchen. "Hey, how come I get all the grief and he gets all the kisses? I'd like to review the rules of this triad," he said jokingly, picking up the discs. She looked at Peter and raised her eyebrows mischievously then turned and ran back to Steve. Putting her arms loosely around his neck, she frowned deliberately.

"Oh, our poor Stevie." She kissed his check lightly several times, completely surprising him. He turned a deep red and she looked at him. "Ooo, I want a dress that shade of red, it's beautiful."

"Get out of here." Steve threw the cover at her then turned an even deeper shade of red.

Peter stared at Steve, not believing the embarrassment written on his face. "Steve Bradley, I have never seen you blush! I don't believe it!"

"Oh shut up already. It's my blood pressure. That damned wench. Man, she's sure lucky she's yours. I'm telling you. Does she always have to get the last word in?"

"Yup." Peter chuckled.

"How the hell do you stand it? Don't answer that stupid question." Steve put the cover on the box and Peter smiled.

*****

Steve, Peter, and Dan Morietti met as they changed in the locker room after completing their shift. Dan stretched and yawned. "I think slow shifts are as tiring as hectic ones."

"Me, too," Peter answered, combing his hair. The shift had dragged by and he was anxious to get home. He had called Jeneil earlier and asked her to wait up for him. He liked her when she was a spitfire and they always had some real fun after a spitfire attack.

Steve buttoned his shirt slowly then noticed they were waiting for him. "Don't wait for me, guys. I think I'll go over to the exercise room. The hectic shift has me keyed up. The rowing will help me unwind."

"Is he okay?" Dan asked, as he and Peter left.

"Yes, why?"

"We had duty together, the shift wasn't hectic. He's been really quiet all night. I wondered if there was trouble with him and his girl. Man, he lives in the exercise room lately. What is she, a nothing-until-we're-married type?"

Peter grinned. "Actually, she is."

"Holy shit, that's a bummer. Who'd have guessed that Steve would fall for that kind?" Dan reached his parking spot. "Catch you tomorrow, Pete."

"Bye, Dan," Peter answered, heading for his car. The thought of Jeneil all soft and smoldering had him revved up.

Steve turned on the lights in the weight room. Changing into sweats, he walked to the rowing machine. He looked at himself in the mirror. "You are in big trouble, Dr. Bradley. Cure it now. You can't have her," he told himself. "She's Pete's."

Thirty-Four

Life increased in velocity as Jeneil became part of Dennis's existence again. They were working on a project that had reached a panicked pace. Peter didn't ask about it. Dennis was still a sore subject for him, but he had relaxed since Dennis had become involved with a woman named Karen. Jeneil had paired them up having promised to find Karen a man with five's qualities and had them to dinner a few times until they took her strong hints to get to know each other better. Jeneil was pleased with herself as their relationship blossomed and evolved, but Peter wasn't fooled. He could tell Dennis would switch to Jeneil on nothing more than a wink from her. Trusting Jeneil and having Dennis's loneliness satisfied, he felt he didn't have to worry too much.

Jeneil was high energy over the project. That's what kept Peter calm as he spent each night waiting for her to come home. One night she had even prepared his and Steve's favorite pot roast dinner and left it warming for them. Peter was surprised to find he was taking her absences better than Steve. They had almost had an argument over the dangers of letting her work too much and too closely with a guy who scooped her into his arms, tied ribbons around flowers, and threw kisses to her from the stage. Peter had told Steve what an insult that was to Jeneil and he had backed off, but Steve was still on edge and people were beginning to notice. Peter wondered if maybe celibacy was losing its strong hold on him and decided to cautiously address the subject.

"You look like an expectant father," Peter said, smiling as he watched Steve pace restlessly. "Sit down before you drag me into your mood."

"How does she find time for everything?" Steve asked, scanning the books on the shelves.

"Steve, have you ever thought about, well, maybe a real pro might be worth the money?"

Steve turned around, puzzled. "What pro?"

"Someone physical who knows how to take the edge off."

Steve laughed. "Pete, say prostitute. Jeneil's got you doing her word thing."

"No, not a prostitute, a more experienced type who is guaranteed disease-free."

"There's something odd happening here. You want me to break celibacy and Rita came up to me at work yesterday and very sincerely offered to help meet my needs. She promised me absolute secrecy so my girl wouldn't find out." He laughed and shook his head. "She said people had noticed how much time I spent in the exercise room. Word is my girl is a virgin who is determined to wait until marriage."

Peter stared at him, wondering if his comment to Dan Morietti had started the rumor. "That was nice of Rita. She must care about you."

"I guess. It sure shocked the hell out of me, but the gossip is vicious. It could get out and ruin my cover. Its better they think my girl is a don't touch, and as far as a pro, who has the money? No, I don't think so. Celibacy is easier if you stay celibate. For me, it's like liquor must be to an alcoholic. Stay away from it or you'll fall off the wagon. My career is too important to mess up now." He smiled. "But boy, Rita had me about convinced. I had to concentrate really hard on imagining Sprague kicking my ass if I messed up. Celibacy needs a strong motivation; Sprague's probation gives me that." He turned and finished looking over the books. "Hey, since when has Jeneil been interested in the occult?"

"Never."

"Then why are there books about it over here?" Peter got up and joined Steve at the bookshelves. "Look," Steve pointed, *"The Occult, Witches and Covens.* And this one looks great, *Ancient Secrets of the Spiritual and Ritualistic."* He stopped. "Holy shit, look at the cover on this one, *History of the Black Mass."* Reading the inside of the book jacket, he smiled. "Whoa, this covers the essentials and purpose of flesh sacrifice and the transference of spirits through human bodies."

"Oh shit." Peter sighed.

"Hi, guys." Jeneil walked in and smiled, putting her papers and carryall down.

"What's this?" Peter asked, waving the book.

"I'm doing some research for Dennis's play. Going into rehearsal, we saw a need to be more accurate in the occult. We're pressed for time so I just picked up what I thought would help." She studied Peter's face. "Why are you so upset?"

Steve laughed. "All your Halloween decorations in here are getting to him. That huge black spider has green eyes that follow you around."

"Laugh all you want to," Peter said, replacing the book, "but we had a kid in the Dragons who grabbed onto this occult stuff like it was air. He got weirder and weirder, and finally stopped coming around. Ki was sharp, he listened to the rumblings and overheard two of the younger kids talk about a meeting so he followed them. The kid was sacrificing animals in the basement of an abandoned building. He drank the warm blood, too." Peter held his stomach and grimaced. "How the hell he got the first swallow down and kept going is beyond me."

"What did Ki do?" Steve asked, interested.

"He spent days thinking about that one. He finally decided the kid needed help. The only way he'd get real attention was an arrest for the sacrifice."

"He turned the kid in?" Steve was shocked.

"It was handled quietly. The police captain sent two officers on a routine investigation of the building. The captain liked to keep his precinct clean."

"What happened to him?" Steve asked.

Peter sighed. "State Hospital. Ki was sick about the whole thing. That's when he added the spiritual stuff to our training."

"Where did Ki get trained?" Jeneil asked.

"Ki was into the whole martial arts thing. He never thought the kids would sit still for the spiritual aspect, but they ate it up. Ki had them swear to secrecy. He was scared word would reach the other gangs and our guys would be persecuted for it. He said that spiritual strength was too often mistaken for weakness, especially among warring gangs."

Jeneil smiled. "Ki was misplaced in history. He was definitely twelfth century."

"What's the big deal about the twelfth century?" Steve asked. Jeneil pointed to the print of The Lady and The Unicorn.

"The Lady and The Unicorn is twelfth century. It's a representation of the beliefs of the era. See all the little animals painted amongst the foliage. Nature and life were important then. The woman represents purity and we're told the unicorn holding her cape represents lust and the lion represents ferociousness, which is interpreted as meaning that the purity and reverence the people had for nature and life tamed lust and fierceness. Some spiritual giants came from that era."

"Why is it called The Lady and The Unicorn if the lion is holding the hem of her cape, too?" Steve asked.

"I'd like that question answered myself," Jeneil commented.

Steve chuckled. "Maybe they knew that the lady would eventual give in to lust."

Jeneil turned and stared at Steve. "Vile blasphemer! Forsooth! Be about the extermination of the debasement which defiles thee, savage beast."

"Oh shit, now I'm back to savage beast." Steve smiled.

She gasped dramatically. "My ears are pained by thy smut. Let me get a potion that will cleanse the filth and elevate thee to the warmth and sweetness of the twelfth century." She made a formal curtsy and walked away.

"What the hell did she just say? All I understood was savage beast."

Peter laughed. "I never understand her when she talks like that."

Jeneil turned around. "I said that I'd get us something to drink to wash the filth from your tongue, garbage mouth. Is that clear enough?" She grinned.

Steve smiled. "What's the drink?"

"Warm apple cider with doughnuts for a treat. It's Halloween time, it's what we celebrate fall with." She turned and went toward the kitchen then stopped. "By the way, today many people believe the unicorn represents the purity and magic of life, so there," and she continued on to the kitchen.

Steve chuckled. "You know, she's the only person I've ever met who makes English sound like a foreign language." Peter laughed, glad to see that Jeneil had cheered Steve up. "More celebrating, sunrises, mornings, fall, no wonder she has so much fun. I'm telling you, lit majors are a special breed. I'm going to get myself one and soon. They're out there, Pete. Librarians, English teachers, I'll date them all if I have to."

"But Jeneil isn't one either," Peter argued. "She's a clerk. She just likes to read."

"Well, I have to start somewhere." Steve grinned. "I think about the prim and proper librarians and English teachers who have passed through my life and I wonder if they were secretly wildcats."

Peter chuckled. "I don't know about that. Some of them acted like real ice cubes."

Steve nodded. "But Pete, that's what I thought about Jeneil remember?"

"What did you think about me?" Jeneil asked, returning with a plate of doughnuts and a pitcher of cider. She poured a drink and added a cinnamon stick.

"I don't want a twig in mine," Peter said.

She smiled. "Peter, it's a cinnamon stick not a twig. It adds flavor. Try it. Sip mine and decide." Steve watched her as she filled the other mugs. "What did you think of me?" she asked again.

Peter took a doughnut. "I'm glad these occult books are only for research. That stuff makes me nervous."

"What did you think about me?"

Steve drank his cider. "This is good."

"Will somebody tell me what Steve thought about me?"

"I thought you were an ice cube," he answered quietly, looking full of guilt.

She smiled. "I was." Steve looked surprised.

"You were not," Peter defended.

"Well, I was an ice cube who had struggled to get into the sun."

Peter grinned. "Jeneil, an ice cube is very different from cerebral. Trust me."

"What's cerebral?" Steve asked.

"Intelligent celibacy," Peter answered.

Steve looked at Jeneil. "Big difference, kid. Pete's right and I'm sorry, I read you all wrong."

"We're even." She smiled. "I had you all wrong, too."

Steve sighed. "Well, it's time for me to go. I have surgery in the morning." He stood up. "I'll see you two tomorrow. Jeneil, the triad misses you when you're busy." She smiled and helped him with his jacket sleeve. "And thank you for dinner." He kissed her cheek. "Bye, Pete," and he closed the door behind him.

She sighed. "Sometimes I wish he could live with us."

"Why?" Peter asked, startled by the remark.

"Because I hate him having no home and no one in it."

He hugged her and smiled. "You'd mother the world if you could, honey."

"Yeah, I'm a real yenta." She laughed lightly. "And we know that mother can turn into smother if we're not careful, right?"

"Steve's right, we do miss you in the triad." He kissed her gently and it felt good. He kissed her again warmly. She responded and snuggled to him.

*****

Jeneil became absorbed in her research for Dennis's play. Peter found her reading every night after he got in from work. Changing quickly, he slipped into bed and faced her. She smiled at him then continued reading.

"Hey, I'm home," he teased, hitting her arm gently.

"I know," she answered, not looking at him.

"What's that book got that I can't equal?" He grinned.

"Secrets to sorcery," she replied, not looking up.

"Put the book away."

"No."

"Woman, put the book away, now!"

"No." Taking the book, he tossed it to the floor. "You brute, I didn't put the bookmark in it and you can ruin the binding treating it that way," she lectured.

"Is it screaming with pain?" he teased.

"Yes, I can hear it."

"Then I think I'll distract you." He tugged at her arm for her to lie down.

"I'm going to a coven meeting in Saybrook Friday night," she said, turning off the lamp and slipping under the covers.

"What's that?" Peter asked, smoothing his chin gently over her shoulder.

"A meeting of witches and warlocks."

"Jeneil," he said, lying back on his pillow, "I don't see why that's necessary."

"I do. We want as much realism as possible in the play. I'd like to see a coven first hand."

"Shit." He sighed.

"I'll be fine. Mara sounded very civilized."

"And how the hell did you find a meeting of witches? In the yellow pages?"

"One of the crew members at The Rep has a witch living in his building."

"Wonderful." He sighed again, staring at the ceiling.

"Relax." She snuggled to him. "Maybe I can get them to mix up a love potion for us."

He looked at her. "You have some complaints?"

"No, just curious."

"Oh, curious are you?" He grinned. "Good, ask me anything. I can teach you whatever you're curious about."

"Do you know that you have an inordinate desire to suppress me? You want to be my only source of information about life." She smiled.

Peter laughed. "Holy shit, is this the same girl who tells me she doesn't like kinky? Believe me, you don't have a clue what kinky is."

"Knowing about it and trying it are two different things. I don't want to try it." Peter laughed and raised himself on his elbow and leaned down to kiss her. "You do, Peter. You want me to stay a little girl."

"That's crazy."

"I don't think so. To you, I'm a storybook princess."

"So what?"

"I'm a woman."

"Nobody knows that more than I do, honey."

"See, you're not taking me seriously now."

"Jeneil."

"What?"

"Shut up and I'll show you how much of a woman I think you are. Do you want to see inordinate desire?"

"Chang, sometimes your simplicity about our relationship strangles me." She ran her fingers through his hair. "But this is not one of those times." She kissed him passionately.

*****

Friday night Peter waited anxiously for Jeneil to get home. It wasn't like her to be this late and not call. As the time neared twelve-forty, he began wondering if he should call Dennis then heard a car door slam. Going to the window, he sighed with relief as he saw Jeneil headed for the building. She opened the door and walked in quickly. "Hi, honey, are you okay?"

"Isn't that my line?" Peter asked, helping her with her jacket.

"You must be worried, but there were no phones. I think Saybrook is the last holdout to technology. I've never seen a town so remote and removed from everything. People have said that it was a strange town, but I had never seen it before." She kissed him.

"I made some Ovaltine."

"Oh great, I can use it. I ate a pastry with the strangest taste to it. It's left a funny taste in my mouth." She followed him to the kitchen where he poured her a cup. She sipped it and sighed.

"How was the meeting?"

"I'm not sure. They didn't do anything that would help me with the play, but it took a turn for the strange at refreshment time. I had a conversation with a man named Gorsen. I don't even know if that's his first or last name. He kept telling me that I had a magnificent aura. Apparently my energy field was playing havoc with his." She shrugged.

Peter grinned. "Pick up?"

"No, really," Jeneil insisted, "because he dragged me to a woman he called Pickering and she agreed with him. They made me nervous. As we talked about some of the rituals I've been reading about, they'd pass meaningful looks to each other but they never elaborated when I asked why. They just smiled. Mara was more to my liking. She was easy to relate to. Even the long drive with her was pleasant. They've invited me back. Invited, goodness, they insisted. Pickering kept saying I couldn't get to know them in one meeting. She and Gorsen hovered over me." She shivered. "I wish I knew what was in that pastry, the sides of my head tingled after I ate it. Pickering kept insisting that I try it. Maybe it had some liquor in the filling and it's an allergic reaction." She shook her head. "What odd, pushy people she and Gorsen were. Between them and the pastry, I could barely breathe. It was a relief to get out of there." Peter put his mug down and went to her. He checked her eyes. "What's wrong?"

"Did you have any trouble functioning after you ate the pastry? Was reality difficult for you?"

"No, just tingling, why?"

"You're sure?"

"Yes, I'm sure. Why, do you think I was drugged? They wouldn't risk something like that, would they? What am I saying? Peter, these are nice people, just a little odd, that's all. They were very nice, even ordinary, except for Gorsen and Pickering, and they were just eccentric. I can understand eccentric. Mara had nothing but praise for them. She said they know their craft well. But I didn't see any craft."

Peter shook his head. "Learned your lesson yet?"

"Oh stop." She smiled. "They're harmless people."

"Do they know they're harmless? Why the hell study witchcraft if you want to be harmless."

Jeneil laughed lightly. "Peter, you're thinking of the Hollywood version of witches. It's another dimension of existence, that's all, another way of interpreting life's meaning, a religion. There's good and bad in everything. Hmm," she said, realizing a thought, "Yen and Yang. There needs to be a balance in both. Does that mean they would cancel themselves out if there wasn't a balance?"

Peter smiled. "It's time for bed. You're thinking at right angles."

She nodded. "I'm strangely tired." She put her cup down and walked to the bedroom, yawning.

He watched her and smiled to himself. "I don't know, Grandfather. Your songbirds bite and sense danger. Mine lives in a dream state. She trusts everybody too much."

Peter stirred and opened his eyes. He felt Jeneil move and sit up quickly. He turned to look at her. "What's wrong, honey?"

She put her head back. "A dream, it was only a dream." She sighed and slipped into his arms.

"Are you okay?"

She nodded and snuggled closer. "Just hold me."

"You had a nightmare? I thought you didn't have dreams."

"I don't usually but when I do they stay with me."

"What was it?" She didn't answer. "That bad?"

She nodded. "It was a ceremony of some kind. The people were all in hooded black robes. Their faces were almost all covered, but they had faces, all except one. She had red eyes staring out from inside the blackness of her hood."

"How do you know it was a she?"

Jeneil looked at him, surprised by the question. "I don't know. I just did. She spoke to my mind, calling me to them."

"That's not so scary."

"It isn't, is it?" she agreed. "But I was so frightened. I was being drawn to them and I felt like I didn't have a choice, like it was out of my control." She shivered. "I'm glad its morning and I'm glad you're here. I feel like I've been awake dealing with them all night." He kissed her forehead and held her closer as she relaxed in his arms.

*****

Peter became concerned after the weekend. Jeneil seemed more off-center than usual and seemed distant but when Steve was over she seemed more like her old self. By Monday night, he was finding papers with sketches of geometric designs. When he asked her about it, she shrugged and said she had done them for no reason she could think of. Eventually there was only one design; a circle with a large inverted triangle with its apex crossed forming a smaller triangle. A medium sized triangle rested on the upright base with a smaller triangle inside of that. The same design kept showing up on papers Jeneil sketched absentmindedly. They had had an argument over the telephone when she told him she was going to another meeting in Saybrook. Gorsen had called saying they were planning a ceremony she might be interested in seeing. With Halloween being so near, there were celebrations and feasts. Peter had forbid her to go. They argued and she ended it by hanging up on him.

He stormed into the viewing room with two cups of coffee and gave one to Steve. "Well, I hope this isn't as sour as your expression. What bit you?"

"Damn it! Sometimes she makes me so mad," and Peter took a drink of his coffee.

"Who, Turcell?"

"No, Jeneil."

Steve smiled. "Check the calendar."

"To hell with the calendar," Peter snapped. "She's gotten herself into some trouble. Something is wrong."

"What do you mean?"

"She's been acting very strange lately."

Steve chuckled. "How can you tell?"

Peter sat down. "Every morning she wakes up from a nightmare she's been having. She's been drawing this strange design and leaving them all over the place on everything. She's been absentminded ever since the meeting with the witches. She thought they were odd and pushy, but she's going back. Can you believe that?"

"Witches?"

"I'm serious, Steve. She's weird."

"She seemed fine when I saw her and she's okay here."

"Not when you look closely. Every night it's the same thing. Just before bed she gets spacey."

Steve grinned. "Leave it to her to not use the headache excuse. It's too common."

Peter continued, grateful to be sharing his worry. "Last night a candle with a cardboard with the same design that she's been drawing showed up. She doesn't know where it came from. Then I found her standing in front of it staring at the flame. She had lit the damn thing and got angry when I blew it out. I broke it and threw it away. She was furious. She wouldn't talk to me for an hour. Then she snaps out of it like it never happened. She's making me crazy." He shook his head and finished his coffee. "It had better be over this weekend or I'm taking her to a doctor. I probably should have already. I keep trusting her ability to deal with things. She's different and I can understand her not fitting the mold, but this is getting to be more than enough."

"Maybe it's something for the play," Steve replied, sensing his concern.

"No, she's into this deep." Peter sighed and stood up. "I've got to go check on a patient."

"Take it easy."

"Yeah." Peter nodded and left.

*****

Peter climbed the stairs quickly, anxious to see Jeneil. The apartment was empty. He sat and waited. He was beginning to doze when he heard the key in the lock. He sat up straight. Jeneil walked in slowly. Her hair was mussed, wisps fell here and there. He went to her then stopped. There was a faint smell to her clothes. He couldn't identify the sweet odor, but the faint smell of smoke was unmistakable. Her face was flushed.

"Hi, Peter," she said, beginning to remove her jacket.

"Jeneil, are you okay?" he asked, taking the jacket from her.

"I'm very tired," she said quietly. Her eyes were glassy. Peter held her shoulder.

"Jeneil, what happened at the meeting?"

"Happened?" she asked, seeming confused.

"You don't look right, honey."

"I don't feel right either," she answered slowly.

"What kind of ceremony was it?"

"I don't remember too well." She rubbed her left temple. "There were people in black robes, but I had a red one. I wonder why I had a red one. I didn't want the red one. I didn't want to be different. I remember that. Pickering insisted on it. And Gossen, Gossen said it was because I wasn't a member of the coven." She exhaled. "Why am I so tired?"

He put his arms around her. "Honey, let's go to the drug center. I want a blood test." She leaned against him in silence. "Honey?" He rubbed her back

"Ouch!"

"What's wrong?"

"You hurt my back."

He looked at her. "Honey, we're going in for a blood test."

"No. No, I want to take a shower. I feel funny and I smell funny. I want to get clean."

"Jeneil, no, I think you better get checked just the way you are."

"Why?" she asked sleepily.

"Damn it, honey. What the hell happened at that meeting? You can't remember, you're tired, way off-center, how do you know what else happened? Shit, why the hell can't you obey me? We're going in," he said, taking her arm.

"Are you worried about rape?"

"It was a ceremony. Anything could have happened."

Jeneil chuckled. "But they use virgins, don't they?"

"Very funny, you look like one, maybe they settled for naïve."

"No, I just need to sleep. I just want to shower and sleep. Please, Peter. I would know if I'd been hurt, wouldn't I?"

"You're not hurt then?"

"No."

He sighed and held her to him. "You're coherent, too. Shit, none of this makes sense. You have symptoms but not enough for a diagnosis. It's weird, baby, very weird." He looked at her. "You are not going back to Saybrook or another meeting with that bunch. Is that clear? I mean it, Jeneil. You're going to obey me on this."

She nodded. "Now can I take a shower?"

The Songbird / Volume Two

Peter paced as Jeneil showered then sat on the bed, laid back and turned on his side. Looking up at the bureau, he stood up quickly and walked over to it. There was a cardboard with the design drawn on it with two black candles at each corner of its base and a red one at its apex. Jeneil walked in.

"Where did this come from?" he snapped.

She stared at it. "I don't know. How come there are three candles now and one is red?"

"Why are you asking me? This stuff is your hobby. Damn it, Jeneil. I don't like this at all." He took the cardboard and candles and threw them in the trash. "Let's get to bed."

Jeneil could tell he was upset. "Will you hold me?" she asked, after they had been lying together in silence.

"Boy, I need to hold you. This place is strange lately."

"Are you going to move back to the dorms?"

"Not without you." He smiled at her and rubbed her back.

"Ouch!"

"Ouch? What's with you?"

"My back hurts, just to the left of my spine."

"Let me check it."

"You're off duty, Doctor." She chuckled.

"Turn over, Jeneil." Peter switched on the lamp. Pulling down the neck of her nightgown, he stared in disbelief. His heart stopped. "Oh shit."

"What is it?"

"Honey, does any other place hurt, even the slightest?"

"No. What's wrong? Peter, you're scaring me."

"Honey, your back has that triangle design on it. It looks like you leaned against a branding iron, but it's not burned, just imprinted in the skin."

"What?" She stood up and went to the mirror. She gasped. "Peter, what happened at that meeting? I'm scared!" He held her. "I'm going to call Mara," she said, pulling away.

"No, honey," he said, pulling her back to him, "forget it. Stay away from them. Make an appointment for a physical tomorrow."

*****

Peter ran into Steve as he headed to the OR. "Will you be free in a couple of hours?"

Steve looked at his watch. "I'll have rounds then."

"Shit." Peter sighed.

"Why?"

"I've got to talk to you."

"Ok, make it three hours in the lounge."

Peter nodded. "I've got to scrub. I'll catch you then."

As planned, Steve went to the lounge and bought some coffee. Peter rushed in. "Can you break right now for fifteen minutes?"

"I'll get Dan to cover for me. What's wrong?"

"I want you to check Jeneil. She came home from a witches' meeting last night with a brand on her back. She can't remember how it happened."

"What?"

"I've got her heading for the catacombs right now."

"Let's go," Steve said, heading for the door.

Peter paced as they waited for the elevator to reach the basement. They rushed off and ran to the records storage room. Peter knocked softly and Jeneil opened the door.

"What's wrong?" she asked, surprised to see Steve.

"I want Steve to check your back."

"What?" Jeneil gasped and held her throat. "No!"

"Jeneil, I'm a doctor," Steve assured her.

"I don't care. You're not my doctor, you're my friend. My doctor is a nice older man who doesn't come to my house for dinner."

"Right now I'm a doctor and I want to see your back."

"Peter!" she pleaded.

"Jeneil, the mark isn't that far down. Just undo the front buttons on your blouse and turn around."

"Peter!" she gasped.

"Jeneil, do it or I will," Steve said strongly.

"This is ridiculous!"

"Now, Jeneil."

She sighed and turned away then slowly unbuttoned her blouse. Peter pulled the collar down until the design was exposed.

"Holy shit!" Steve said, totally shocked.

"It's not as bad this morning," she insisted.

Steve touched the redness and felt the area around it. "No marks anywhere else?" Peter shook his head. "Okay, Jeneil, you can dress." Steve took a packet from his pocket.

"You two turn around," Jeneil ordered.

"Why?" Steve asked.

"I need to tuck my blouse inside my skirt." They turned their backs to her. "Okay. What now?" Jeneil asked, seeing the packet and backing away.

"I want a blood sample," Steve answered, opening the packet.

"No, come on you two, I don't want my name running around that lab."

"Steve worked in a lab, honey. He'll do the tests."

"No," she said. "I'm leaving."

"Jeneil, shut up," Steve snapped. "Pete should have dragged you in last night for routine tests. Now give me your arm." He worked quickly. "She should have a GYN exam."

"Oh no you don't," she flared.

"Relax, not by me."

"But she said she was fine," Peter said.

"And she can't account for part of the night." Steve paced. "Shit, Pete. How the hell could you let her get away without a physical? Boy, now I know why they don't let doctors work on their own families. I can do the urinalysis."

"That's it, I'm leaving," Jeneil said, going to the door.

Steve watched her. "Jeneil, you've got some strange friends. We're only trying to protect you."

"Fine," she answered, standing by the door. "I'll go to my doctor immediately. Goodbye, you two."

"Do you promise?" Steve asked.

"Yes."

He shook his head. "Kid, you and your curiosity are going to give me a heart attack. Are you okay otherwise?"

"I feel fine."

Steve sighed and stared at her for a second. "I'm just worried. The branding is strange."

"I know it is."

Peter kissed her. "He's right. I should have dragged you in here last night." He held her. "If something's wrong with you…."

"Go back to work. I feel fine. Both of you be home tonight for dinner." They left reluctantly and Jeneil locked the door, heaving a deep sigh.

Later, Steve met up with Peter as he was filing some paperwork at the nurse's station and they walked to the locker room together. "What did you find out from the blood tests?"

"She had enough ascorbic acid in her to be growing from a tree in Florida."

Peter laughed. "Vitamin C. That's it?"

"She's a healthy girl. If they did drop something on her, she's passed it now, but that brand on her back is so weird. That makes me damn nervous. What did they knock her out with and why? I wish she had let me do the urinalysis."

"Are you kidding, it was all we could do to look at her back."

*****

Steve waited for Peter by the front door. Going upstairs, they noticed the stairs had Jack-o-lanterns with painted faces on them greeting everyone who entered.

"Jack-o-lanterns, witches, boy you two aren't dull."

"Witches, shit," Peter said, "she's forbidden to deal with them again, and I think the branding scared her into submission."

"Good," Steve replied. "Howe Blake knows a guy who worked in Zambia. Boy, the oddities he's seen!" Peter unlocked the apartment door and blackness surrounded them.

"What's this?" Peter asked, walking inside and feeling for the light switch. He flipped it several times. Nothing happened. "Jeneil?"

"Why is it so black in here? How come we can't see the streetlights?"

"I don't know. Jeneil?" Peter called again. "Steve, stay here. I'll work my way to the kitchen." Steve heard the light switch flick several times. Nothing happened. Steve heard Peter edging his way back. "I don't understand. Was Jeneil's car here? I didn't notice."

Steve grabbed Peter's arm. "Stay cool, Pete. Somebody or something is to our right."

"What?" Peter turned. "Where?"

"You are, Peter?" The voice was distorted by vibrato.

"Jeneil?" Peter called.

"Jeneil is gone," the voice replied.

"Gone?" Peter chuckled, sensing a game being played. "Where?"

"Where she belongs, where she is needed, she's come home."

"And who are you?" Peter asked, holding back a laugh.

"I can see why you have been a problem. You are a disbeliever."

"I've been a problem?"

"We had no idea Medra was with a son of the Earth Ancients."

"Who's Medra?"

"The one you call Jeneil. You have been interrupting our signals. Your destruction of our fire calls has caused problems."

"If she's with you, why are you here?"

"To cancel the bond, to free Medra."

"To free her from what?"

"From you," the voice replied. "You interrupted our signals. She wasn't prepared because you broke the fire calls. We had no knowledge of you until we came here to do them. She would have returned easily had you not broken the calls. Medra would have been ours by now but instead she is still bound to you. Because of that we had to take her."

"You kidnapped her?" Peter leaned toward Steve and whispered, "This is a gotcha."

"No, she's ours. This dimension has kidnapped her," the voice corrected.

"But she wants to be with me."

"Medra's been lost. This isn't her world. We have her back now. She will respond to us once the ceremony is completed."

"Why can't she stay with me?"

"Medra belongs to a son of the Druidic Copos. She must have gravitated to you because you are the blood of the Earth Ancients. It was something familiar to her but she is assigned and thus must return. She is a being of life and we must separate her from these consciousness in time for his arrival by the fullest moon or we could damage her aura. We need to separate you from her energy force, then she will turn naturally to Roween, but we need to hurry. He travels here even as we speak. There's been a flurry of energy since we found her through energy from the sun. Roween has a command unit with him and expects Medra to be prepared for cosmic separation."

"Why should I cooperate?" Peter chuckled.

"Because I have chosen it," the voice grew stronger. "I'm saddened for you but you must understand you have no choice but to release her. She is Roween's by Paltic ceremony."

"Okay, Jeneil," Peter said. "I've had enough, I'm tired and hungry. It's over."

The voice spoke again. "I'm sorry, you have a companion. Both of you must understand the use of that earth name will double Medra's risk. If you but cooperate, we can be finished quickly. I need to help Gorsen and Pickering prepare Medra. It was I who lost her by a chance mistake when I was newly aviated. I'll stop at nothing to correct my error. For twelve of your moon cycles I've been scoping galaxies for her."

"Stop at nothing, huh? That's tough talk from a person who hides in the dark."

"Sit," the voice commanded. "If I damage you, Medra's energy field will be affected but I will have to chance that. Our cosmic has suffered because of my error and Roween is not pleased with Medra's drift into this dimension. She has been spoiled by this level of consciousness. If you care about her, you'll be agreeable. She could be destroyed if she resists Roween and she will resist without this ceremony."

Peter laughed. "Well, don't worry; when Roween meets Jeneil, he's in for a shock. She's not easily pushed. In fact, she's a downright pain in the ass at times. I hope he likes spitfires."

"Sit!" the voice raged, and two red eyes peered from what was only blackness.

"Hey, that's really good, Jeneil. Just like your dream. You've been setting me up, you little bitch. Wait until you see the marks I'm going to leave on your back for this gotcha."

"Come," the voice taunted, "I'm wasting energy on you. I find Medra's attraction to you strangely primitive. It would be a courtesy to her to vapor you but for the damage. Sit!"

Peter laughed. "You have pushed me all week, bitch. I'm not moving. Use your power if you're so damned anxious to play Halloween." The red eyes moved toward them accompanied by the sound of a low growl.

Steve hit Peter's arm. "Pete, I don't know if it's the total blackness in here, but I'd like more proof that's Jeneil. Let's play it her way. Remember, she's been playing with some strange books lately."

Peter laughed. "Okay by me. She's good though. Where'd she get the red eyes?"

"Yeah," Steve replied quietly, "that's a good question."

"Jeneil, we've decided to put you through your paces. Give us the whole spiel. We want to see the ceremony." The red eyes disappeared into the blackness followed by silence. "What's wrong, Jeneil? Didn't plan on a ceremony? Did you think we'd cave by now? Well, we want a ceremony." He laughed and hit Steve's arm. "We've got her now, the little bitch. Ooo, when this thing is over."

The voice broke the silence. "Be at the long chair."

"Long chair?" Steve questioned.

"The sofa, she's at the sofa," Peter explained, and inched his way through the blackness until he felt the arm of the sofa. He eased himself onto it with Steve following him.

"Jeneil, I hope you know that we're both going to bruise you bad for making us look stupid. You've signed your death warrant with this one, baby." There was silence and they could sense a shape opposite them. "She's stalling," Peter said to Steve. "She wasn't ready for a ceremony. I'm glad I listened to you. If I had kept it up, she'd have gotten us. This way, she's under pressure." He laughed. "I love it. We can make this backfire."

"This is extreme, Pete, even for her; the work, the details, a whole week of pretense, the brand on her back. Who would go that far?"

"Are you kidding? She'd arrange a direct cable to the moon for a gotcha. Just swing with it. The end is near. She's having trouble thinking up a ceremony." They waited. "Come on, Jeneil. Stop stalling. Start with the abracadabra."

"The vibrations need to be more peaceful," the voice answered.

Peter laughed and leaned forward. "Oh shit, that's slick. Clever bitch, isn't she?" He laughed again, enjoying her comeback, but Steve was silent. "Don't let her get to you, Steve."

"Pete, I can't believe she'd go this far."

"Oh shit." Peter laughed. "Who do you think this is then, a real witch with red eyes?" He laughed harder. "Because if this isn't Jeneil, that's what you're left with. She's crazy, trust me." Peter sighed from laughing. "This is good, Jeneil. I'll give you that much. You've got Steve doubting himself."

"How did she disguise her voice?" Steve asked.

"How do I know, she just did and we'll find out when she's good and ready. This is getting fun." He chuckled. "Okay, wise guy," he continued, "you've gotten to Steve, that leaves me, but you've got to be damn good because I'm wise to your tricks. He didn't know how eccentric you were."

The voice sighed. "Xanu palla il vetsu. Barahm visu dol crera."

"Damn it," Peter said. "See that, we gave her enough time to scramble up a language. Shit and we had her pinned down, too." He sat back, disappointed.

There was a low growl. "Silence you son of fragmented ancients."

Peter laughed. "That's Jeneil, Steve. That's her style of language."

The voice was silent then exhaled. "She is one of us, you barbarian. That's why you recognize the language of Varahana Il Pihoo. She hasn't been completely transformed. Roween will be pleased."

"How did you find her?" Peter asked, hoping to trap Jeneil by pushing for details.

"Medra is of the fire energy source, that's why she is assigned to a Druidic Copos. We heard her cosmic vibrations through elements here and she used the sun to communicate.

This world is foreign to her, she was lost and she sensed it. It is exceptional that she was not discovered sooner. As we approached to sensor her energy field, the vibrations became fewer. For seven of your moon cycles we have scoped, but the communications were interrupted and became less frequent. We scoped her south of here several times and once north at a place called Veermont."

Peter smiled. "Jeneil, that's really good. Honest, honey, I'm impressed, Veermont instead of Vermont."

"We scoped vibrations in this area and began ceremonies for her. We knew it wouldn't be long before she came to us. Once she went to the coven and was identified, we gave her sensor fluid and scoped her to this center. All that's left is transference to the Vedric dimension to Roween."

"I've always liked that about her," Peter whispered, "she's quick to think."

"I need time to prepare," the voice said. "Allow me silence for energy control and I will blend into the ceremony. After that, all will be completed."

"Okay with us. Right, Steve?"

Steve smiled. "Jeneil, sweetheart, if this is you, I'm having you fired from your hospital job. You're wasting yourself there."

Peter chuckled. "Better hurry, Jeneil; you're losing your hold on Steve."

There was silence then the voice spoke. "Xanu pall il vetsu. Basahm. Visu dol cedar. Xariu pall il vetsu. Basahm. Visa dol cedar." The chant was slow and rhythmic with a sense of peace. Peter smiled, impressed by Jeneil's dramatic flair. "Xanu pall il vetsu. Barahm. Visu dol cedar." There was a pause. "Xanu, xanu, xanu. Basahm votra, basahm, basahm." There was a soft hum and a triangle glowed red from the center of the being.

Peter clapped. "Now that's good."

"Hey, Pete," Steve said, "for not having a ceremony ready this is awfully good. You'd better be right about this or you've lost your girl. Blake's stories about Zambia were stranger than what's happening here and they were real." The red triangle disappeared and they could hear deep breathing.

"Please," the voice said, straining, "I need silence for energy flow. Please, for Medra. Once into the energy pulse, strict silence is necessary until completion."

"How will we know when that is?" Peter chuckled.

"I will be completed," the voice answered.

Peter laughed. "It's Jeneil. That's her kind of sense; completeness is after I'm completed."

"Do you mean finished?" Steve asked the voice.

"Come on, Steve. You're holding a conversation with her. That's risky. Next she'll have you believing."

"But she's good. I'm struggling with the language."

"Oh boy, she's swallowed you whole."

"Does completeness mean finished?" Steve asked again.

"No," the voice answered, "it is…," there was a pause, "…disappeared."

Peter burst into laughter. "You're going to disappear before us? That's pretty easy, we can't see you now."

"That's true," Steve said. "How will we know?"

"You will see it. There isn't much time. Please, silence for Medra. You can't keep her here. She will eventually be spent. Please help me help Medra."

The voice began chanting again. There was a hum and the triangle glowed red. The darkness pressed against their eyes like a blindfold then there was a soft light, a dull red glow from a bowl on the table before them, and for the first time the voice took shape as they watched black-gloved hands create a symbol of three triangles by entwining its fingers over the bowl.

The hands moved away from the glow and returned with long strands of hair. Peter stared and reached out to touch it. The gloved hands gave a slight start then handed it to him, but guarded the bowl. Peter touched the hair and smelled it. It was Jeneil's. His throat tightened. She had cut her hair off for this? It was further than she'd gone before for a gotcha. He gave the strands back, which were then placed in the bowl with both ends hanging over the rim.

The hands moved away and returned holding a white square of paper. "Xanu sahna vetra sol Earthnu. Basahm," the voice chanted. One hand held the paper while the other lifted the strands of hair from the bowl. Placing the paper on the hair, the hand turned the paper over. Peter jumped from shock as he saw the square of paper was the photograph of Chang; Jeneil never took it out of the frame on the bureau. The strands of hair were wrapped around the photograph and held over the bowl by one hand while the other moved out of view. "Xanu pasok sol Medra sol Earthnu. Basahm pasok voltra, pasok voltra, pasok voltra." The second hand returned holding a small metal blade.

Peter stared in disbelief. He wanted to stop her but he remained quiet. He closed his eyes as the blade cut through the strands of hair and the photograph. She wouldn't do this for a gotcha. What was this? His chest felt tight. The hair and photograph fell into the bowl. There was a quick flame then the red glow again. The hands moved away then returned. Positioning entwined fingers over the bowl, another chant began. "Xanu visnu Medra vos lastu sol Medra votol posak sol Roween du Vetrie. Basahm." There was silence as the hands stayed in position then, moving slowly, they turned palm up and a flame shot from them. Peter and Steve sat back quickly. Three small explosions sounded followed by a puff of smoke in rapid succession.

"Holy shit!" Steve said, waving his hand before his face and coughing. Peter was silent. "Are you okay, Pete?"

"Yeah," Peter answered quietly.

"Where did she go? Is she still there? Can you tell?" Steve asked, flustered.

"I don't know," Peter answered, still very quiet.

Steve sat forward reaching for the table. "Where the hell is the bowl? At least the red stuff gave some light. That flame damn near blinded me." He felt around in the darkness. "Pete, you've got to get some lights in here. My senses are all screwed up. This feels like a pair of gloves and a bunch of cloth, but no bowl. Say something now, mouth. What now, no joking, no laughing? Where the hell is a flashlight? I've had enough of this. Damn it, Pete, if this was real I'm going to beat the shit out of you, so help me. All we had to do was talk to stop it and we sat there and let it happen. Pete, move. Do something for crying out load. I want to check this out and I can't see. What if that was Jeneil and the brand has warped her. Pete, move."

The lamp on the shelf behind them came on, startling them. They covered their eyes then Steve looked up and chuckled. "Hey, Pete, check this out."

Peter looked up. Jeneil was standing before them dressed in a black sweater and black slacks. She smiled. "Gotcha." Peter sighed deeply, leaning forward and resting his head on his arms.

Steve stood up fast and grabbed Jeneil. "You little bitch," he said, hugging her. "I should beat you until your energy field is bright red."

She laughed. "You're not too hard to fool."

"Not hard, shit. This was damn good." He shook his head and smiled then kissed her cheek. "Where the hell did you get all this stuff?"

"From the theatre."

"You're crazy, you know, totally crazy and off the wall."

She smiled. "Happy Halloween."

"You even branded yourself?"

"Uh-huh."

"That's pretty sick, kid."

"How else would I be convincing? It was a necklace from the play. I wore it backward and leaned up against the wall for a while. It didn't hurt."

"I didn't think you'd go that far. It was the damn brand that got me." He kissed her again. "I'm glad it wasn't real."

Jeneil smiled at Steve then turned to look at Peter. He still had his head buried in his arms, quietly listening to the conversation. Slipping from Steve's arms, she went to Peter and knelt beside him. "Are you angry at me?" He shook his head but didn't look up. "Did I really gotcha?" He nodded, keeping his head down. "You were tough. When did I reach you?"

"The strands of hair started it, but cutting the photograph did it. I was in shock after that. That's something I didn't expect from you." She chuckled and kissed the side of his head.

"It was only a copy. You're used to me now. I knew I had to do something sensational."

"You tortured me for almost a week for this. You're a bitch and you know it. I've been a wreck worrying about you."

She stroked his hair, smiling. "But that's why I'm yours. So you'll be jolted away from the anesthesia." Steve smiled, watching her.

"Oh, I'm jolted. That damn ceremony left me speechless. I feel cut in two."

"No, you're probably more hungry than cut in two. Dinner's ready by the way."

"You're kidding," Peter said, looking up slowly. "In the middle of all this you made dinner?"

"It's only sandwiches, but you'll feel better after you've eaten." She kissed his shoulders then his temple. "Come on, I even bought beer." She held his arm and he kissed the hand she had resting on him.

"I didn't want to find out if this was real. I was afraid it was." Peter sighed and Steve could see how deeply Peter cared for Jeneil. His chest tightened.

Jeneil kissed Peter's lips lightly. "I love you." Steve turned away and took a deep breath. Jeneil hugged Peter. "You know, if it's any consolation, I was almost done in when you two stormed in wanting to examine me this afternoon. Gosh, I was going to confess if you kept at it, and all I could think of was all the work and preparation I'd be wasting." Peter and Steve laughed. "So you see we're pretty much even." She stood, taking Peter's hand. He stood up and put his arm around her shoulder. "If you guys will help me, we'll get to that beer." She smiled, slipping one hand around Peter's waist and holding Steve's hand with her other. "You guys deserve to bum out for being good sports."

Peter and Steve looked at each other and shook their heads. "I'd like Digitalis for dessert," Steve commented.

"Make mine Valium," Peter added.

"Jeneil, show us the bag of tricks?" Steve asked, as they walked to the kitchen. "The flame was great and the eyes were something else. How'd you change your voice?" As they walked, Peter squeezed her shoulder and kissed her temple, starting to relax now that he knew she wasn't really into sorcery.

Thirty-Five

Peter set the cups of coffee in front of Steve and Dan then sat down with his own. Dan yawned. "Saturday morning. Anyone for a bet against us having burns, smoke inhalation, and back problems today?"

Steve laughed. "Easy money, everybody's burning leaves and cleaning yards, and putting on storm windows." Steve noticed Dan yawn again. "You should sleep nights like normal people."

Dan smiled. "I haven't recovered from Wednesday night. I went to the play at The Rep. It was pretty good. There was a super witch in it; red glowing eyes, chanting, flames. My date said there's a lot of mystery surrounding her, and her name isn't on the program and she's not on stage for the final curtain. It's a small part, but it's so damn real people are noticing and the newspaper is hot to know her. That's why we went to see it. It's probably only a publicity stunt, and it's working." He laughed. "The theatre was packed."

Peter sat up in his chair and looked at Steve, who was already staring at him having begun to wonder the same thing. "Is that the play Dennis Blair wrote?" Steve asked Dan.

"I think that's his name. I never remember the writers. It's the same with movies. Who remembers writers?" Dan stretched in his chair. "Why, do you know him?"

"No," Steve answered, "but I've heard about the play."

"Go see it," Dan said, standing up. "It's terrific, and that witch is so good you feel like you're part of it."

"I'll just bet you do." Steve smiled at Peter. "What name did she use?"

"Nobody knows who she is," Dan said. "The cast won't talk. The word is she's a real witch and doesn't want the publicity. In the play, they call her Medra. Well, I'd better get going. I have to stop at the lab before going to the ER. I'll catch you later," and he backed out the door.

"Medra, huh? Sound familiar? Would she do it?"

Peter shrugged. "Dennis keeps telling her she belongs in theatre. Maybe he finally talked her onto the stage. She hasn't said a word to me." He grinned. "But I've got to know," and he stood up and went to the telephone.

The phone rang a few times and Jeneil answered. "Peter! You're supposed to be healing people."

"I'm not on duty. Jeneil, tell me about Medra in Dennis's play."

Jeneil paused. "What about her?" she asked cautiously.

"Do you know who it is?"

"We're all sworn to secrecy, Peter. Did you hear about it at work?"

"Yes. Come on, honey, is it you?"

"No."

"Jeneil?"

"Well, not anymore," she added sadly.

"How come?"

"Oh Peter, I was having so much fun. The part was supposed to be played by the female lead but the quick changes kept interrupting the tempo so I suggested that Dennis slip a person in for just a few minutes. The witch is totally disguised and the voice alteration device made it easy to give the bit part to someone. Dennis gave it to me. I didn't want to be listed on the program so we let everyone assume it was the female lead. But now for some crazy reason it's getting a lot of attention. The gossip is totally out of hand. I quit the part Wednesday night after a reporter jumped out at me as I went to my dressing room. I got so rattled." She sighed. "Peter, I ninja'd him." Peter burst into laughter.

"It isn't funny," Jeneil said. "You should see what he wrote about me in the paper. It really didn't help the situation, and now I've heard that I'm a real witch who doesn't want her identity revealed." She sighed again. "Why did this happen? It's a stupid bit part. Even the female lead was mad at me for stealing her thunder. I guess it's just as well that I quit."

"I think people noticed the fun you were having. Why didn't you just own up that it was you?"

"Are you serious? The frenzy would eat me alive. It actually scared me. The mystery was good for ticket sales, so the theatre loved it."

"The stage isn't for you, huh?"

"Oh, that's definite. I felt strangled by the attention."

Peter laughed. "Maybe Dennis should do the part."

"Why do you say that?"

"Because Dan Morietti couldn't remember the name of the writer but he wanted to know who was playing the witch. If Dennis wants his name known that's a great way to do it."

Jeneil laughed. "That's so true, isn't it? The poor writer has to clamor for his share of the applause and fight anonymity. What a strange game life plays."

"How come you never told me?"

"Because I was having so much fun setting you up that if I had told you about Medra I'd have ruined the trick I was playing on you." She giggled.

"Cute." He smiled. "I still owe you payback."

"Spoil sport," she teased. "That was a Halloween gift."

Peter smiled. "I've got to go, honey."

"Me, too, I have to get the props back to Dennis. He wanted me to tape the trick for him."

"Did he coach you?"

"No." She laughed. "He's not to blame. Get mad at me, not him. I did it all."

"You're lucky I love cute," he teased.

"Want some fun tonight? It's shift change."

"What do you have in mind?"

"Tonight is the film festival."

"Okay, it's a deal. I want to see you get your Oscar."

"Are you serious? I've been to film festivals. There's some good stuff. I'm only in it for the fun."

"Okay, count on me and Steve."

"Great. See you later, and I love you, Chang."

"Same here." Peter smiled as he put the receiver back.

"Well?" Steve asked, smiling.

"It was her."

"Was?"

"She quit, couldn't stand the attention. Where are the old newspapers that are always around here?"

"By the drink machine. Why?"

"A reporter jumped her Wednesday night trying to find out who she was and she ninja'd him. He wrote her up in his column."

"Oh shit." Steve laughed, heading for the newspapers. Peter opened the paper to the section for Arts and Cinema. "There it is," Steve said, pointing to a small section entitled, *Witch Casts Spell at The Rep*. Peter and Steve laughed, and read on.

A fascinating mystery surrounding the part of the witch, Medra, in Dennis Blair's play, "POSSESSED", has audiences spellbound and ticket sales soaring. The play is well written. Blair is a master of mystery and the cast is a precision instrument. The FX is super, but the real fire is the part of Medra which comes from the bit player herself. She plays the role like she's living it.

"She was living it, the little bitch." Steve laughed and Peter continued reading.

Nothing at all is known about the actress. Everyone connected with the play guards her identity as if severe punishment would result from exposure. This reporter can tell you firsthand the actress rivals The Great Garbo for wanting to be alone.

Peter and Steve chuckled as they read on.

Wanting my readers to meet this latest flash to the local art scene, I positioned myself behind the scenes for a personal interview with her. The lighting was low and my heart was pounding as her black-robed figure emerged from the wings. She stopped, shocked by my presence, and for a brief moment I felt like Obi-Wan Kenobi facing Darth Vader. She stood tall and rigid. She does not have the power to read minds, however, because she asked who I was and why I was in a restricted area. "No interviews," she replied, and headed past me. She was unimpressed my editor had insisted on one. It's possible she's related to real show biz people in Hollywood as she knows how to discourage the news media. When I put my arms around her hoping to hold her long enough to hear my plea, I found myself wrapped in her robes dancing through one of the slickest karate moves, leaving me sitting on the floor. "Stay if you know what's good for you," she commanded, and disappeared behind the FX of smoke she uses in the play.

Peter and Steve laughed hysterically and finished reading.

That was my close encounter with the mysterious witch, Medra. All I know for sure is that she's female. She's very definitely female and mystery lady. If ever you'd like to cast a real spell, just ring my bell, bring your book, and I'll provide the candles. I like your style on stage and off. The whole play is worth seeing. Don't miss it.

Peter chuckled, shaking his head.

"That's a riot." Steve laughed. "The kid has her problems staying down. Do you get the feeling that she's going to explode somewhere? Somewhere big?"

"What do you mean?"

"I'm not sure," Steve answered. "She desperately clings to a simple, private life, but life keeps telling her otherwise. She helps with a play and gets scooped up by the director. She has fancy cars she doesn't want. She gets into a small part in a play and becomes the main attraction. She wants a twenty-five watt life and gets neon. I don't think life wants her in the background she clings to so hard."

"Well, I sure hope you're wrong," Peter said, "because the only place I see her is married to me and the mother of my kids. That's twenty-five watt, not neon."

Steve shrugged. "Maybe I'm wrong. It just seems like things sizzle around her. She's fiery."

Peter smiled. "Speaking of sizzled, I'm going to get fried if I don't get on duty."

"Oh shit, me, too." They headed for the door. "She's fun though, odd and cute."

"Want more fun? The film festival's tonight. Are you game?"

"Oh, you bet. I'll catch up to you on lunch break." Steve went to the nurse's desk as Peter got on the elevator.

*****

Steve could feel the tightness in his neck. The day had been busy and he was tired. He joined Peter at the medical charts. "What are you planning for dinner?"

"Oh right. We have this film thing so we'll have to eat here. Is The Pit okay with you?"

"Anything," Steve answered, "just so I get to sit for a few minutes."

"Dr. Chang." A nurse walked over to him carrying a brown paper bag with a letter taped to it. "This was left for you. Do you have a relative in China? The letter's from China."

"My grandfather's visiting. This came in the mail?"

"No," she answered, "it was on the desk. Your mom must have left it. We just found it here."

"Thanks," Peter said, taking the bundle. He looked puzzled as he put the letter in his pocket and opened the bag, laughing.

"What is it?" Steve asked, as he went over to look.

"It's dinner." Peter laughed, holding up a cardboard Jack-o-lantern.

"That Sunshine is all right." Steve smiled and rubbed his hands together. "I really wasn't up to the noise and crowd at The Pit."

Peter chuckled. "Dr. Bradley, celibacy is taming you. Ho-hum is now your speed."

"Just getting ready to search for my spitfire librarian." Steve grinned, relaxing from the day's schedule, and they headed to the lounge for a quiet dinner together.

*****

Peter stopped the car to check the hand drawn map to the film festival. "This place is nestled in a forest. Does anybody else think that's odd for a film festival?"

Steve smiled. "If it's from TAI, that's normal."

"Don't blame TAI," Jeneil defended. "It was posted at Elio's and this is State's territory. I don't think it's committed to a college, but I do think it's strange that it's so far off the main streets. Maybe they were limited in the location that was available to them."

"Wasn't there a sponsor?" Steve asked.

"No, just a reference to a Gleeson Group for the entry fee."

Steve raised an eyebrow. "You paid to put your film in this?"

"You sound shocked."

Steve nudged her shoulder. "It shocks me, but for you it's fun. Forget I reacted."

Jeneil smiled. "Is that tolerance I hear developing in you?"

"Oh, it might be," he joked. "All sorts of new qualities are being revealed in me."

"They look nice on you."

Steve looked at her, surprised she had noticed. She turned away.

"Peter, what did your grandfather have to say in his letter?"

"Just that everything is so changed. He knew it was changing but seeing it, he's shocked. He can't get used to seeing modern appliances in the country. I guess he expected everything to be the way it was when he left. It was difficult to reunite with his family after such a long separation, even though they've been writing."

"In my letter, he said he's enjoying the work the Art's League has for him and that seeing China through their eyes is an education for him. I'm glad he went. It's too bad the personal part of the trip is a letdown, but I think reunions are difficult. Bridging a gap isn't easy. Separations can be damaging to a relationship and it takes time to renew and restore. Your grandfather will do it though. The Arts League and the foundation hired interpreters for him."

"What?" Both Peter and Steve were shocked. "That's crazy," Peter said, "he speaks Chinese."

"No, it isn't crazy. There are so many dialects that the people have trouble understanding each other. Their bond is their writing. That's the common denominator. Can you imagine that? Now I understand why calligraphy became so important to them."

"Why would that happen in a country?" Steve asked.

"Possibly for protection," Jeneil answered.

"Protection?" Peter asked, surprised.

"Don't forget that China was a large empire. All the rulers weren't peaceful like Han. If a portion of a group doesn't have complete freedom, a subculture can evolve with its own language. We have it here in our own country. A lot of our slang and phrases come from one subculture or another; the drug group, the gay movement, even yuppies. It isn't easy uniting groups with different interests. Not many people want to stray in and out of all of them, and who can really afford the time unless it's their field of interest. Specialization keeps us isolated and then comes the danger of the loss of understanding and acceptance of each other and our differences. I hope we don't forget united we stand, divided we fall. Freedom is so fragile."

Peter grinned. "Ben Franklin's a friend of hers."

Steve smiled. "I've been so busy with my career I haven't noticed too much else."

Jeneil sighed. "Some people would be shocked at how little freedom we actually have. People back home in Croft complained about the police in their town not settling disputes and arguments like the police chief in Loma, but my father was actually frightened that a police chief who stepped in and became judge and jury could be reelected time after time. Croft wasn't as quiet a town as Loma, but what price is Loma paying for peace? The police chief was the first person Bill bought off when he decided to buy Loma."

"Bill is that into it?" Peter asked.

"I'm afraid so." She sighed again. "It's shocking that Bill has joined the ranks of despot, but that's the game in town. And he's learned to play the game; he intends to win. Can anyone win traveling that route?" She shook her head. "But he's happy."

Steve smiled. "Power doesn't impress you, does it?"

"Oh, I'm very impressed. I'm impressed with nuclear weapons in the same way. Freedom is so fragile and power is gossamer. It's difficult to hold in check. Power in the wrong hands can become evil and cancel freedom. Freedom without fair rules can become lawless disorder. Benjamin Franklin made a prediction when he said a well administered form of government can be a blessing for a course of years, but can only end in despotism because the people will become so corrupt they need a despotic government being capable of any other. Can we avoid the prediction? Where would the people learn to not be corrupt? I think of church and yet look at the Christian religion alone. There are so many sects within the bounds called Christianity. If they can't get along amongst themselves, how can they teach their members peace? All religions have their struggles helping man achieve superlative." Jeneil sighed and became quiet then added, "Maybe as a civilization we lack a definition of superlative. How can man grow without a clear path and goals before him? Oh, who knows really?" She shrugged and leaned her head back.

Peter looked at Steve. "Now you know why she's so good at gotchas. It's her way of peacefully breaking out of intense, that and crying."

"I think you're right," Steve agreed. "She sure gets into it. I'm happy memorizing chemical equations. She romps through unanswerable questions."

"You two are talking about me like I'm not even here. You're even using 'she.' I'm right here. I'm awake. I'm not a cadaver waiting for a postmortem. Why are you studying me anyway?"

"She gets touchy when she's intense." Peter chuckled.

Steve jostled her. "Hey, it's our favorite hobby. Why, are you insulted?"

Jeneil sighed, rubbing her temples. "I don't know. I apologize."

"Pete, I'll write you a prescription for intense."

"I'll bet it's X-rated," Jeneil added dryly.

Steve grinned. "And just how do you know that, smart mouth?"

"Because every solution with you two is physical."

Peter laughed and Steve gasped dramatically. "Jeneil, you have a smart mind, even taking two aspirin is physical."

"Alright, Steve, one point for us guys," Peter cheered.

Jeneil laughed. "I love you two. I really do. I don't know why, buy I do. Isn't that a line from a song? Where is this place anyway? It's taking so long to get there."

"You're nervous," Peter observed. "That's why you're bitchy."

"No, I'm not," she argued. "Yes, I am. I don't like groups. Why have I done this to myself?" She sighed. "Submitting a film in a festival was too crazy, even for me."

Peter smiled. "Come on, lean against me."

"That won't help," she whined.

"Lean against me, Jeneil."

"But Peter...."

"Jeneil, shut up and do it," Peter said softly.

"Okay."

Steve smiled as he watched Jeneil calm down and snuggle against Peter. He loved the shape of her ears and the way strands of hair fell on her neck. He looked away and opened the window for cool air, and began reciting chemical equations in his mind to distract himself from thinking about her.

"There you are, baby," Peter said. "The sign says Welcome to Randall. We're only seconds away from your film debut according to this map."

Jeneil groaned. "I wish I had been more thorough about this whole thing. Every time I do something on a whim, it's usually the wrong thing. Even my gotchas and malfunctions have to be well planned. How did I get so neurotic?"

"Eccentric," Steve corrected her.

She smiled broadly, appreciating his support. "Thank you, I needed that."

He winked at her. "It's okay, kid."

Peter made a left turn onto a small unpaved road. Jeneil looked ahead. "This is really too strange, a film festival in an area so remote the road is unpaved."

Peter smiled. "This is the driveway, not a road."

"Are you serious?" she asked, surprised that it was so long.

"According to the map it is." The driveway opened to a large parking area with a walk up to a large house.

"It looks Victorian."

Peter pulled into a space next to a van and turned off the engine. "Well its zero hour, baby." Steve opened his door and got out, scanning the parking area. "What are you looking for?" Peter asked, locking the door.

"Just looking."

Peter took Jeneil's hand. "Come on, honey. It'll be fine."

"I hope so but if I don't like what I see, I'll just ask for my tape and leave."

He smiled and kissed her cheek. "They'll love you." They climbed the stairs and rang a bell since the door was locked. "What are you so quiet about Steve?"

"Just looking," Steve answered.

A young woman opened the paneled door and smiled through the screen. "Yes?"

"Is the Gleeson Film Festival being held here?" Jeneil asked.

The woman snickered. "Well, all those cars and vans don't mean we're having a Tupperware party. Are you an entrant?"

"Yes, and why is the door locked?"

"We're particular about who visits us. Are you...," the woman looked at the list, "...Jeneil?"

"Yes, how did you know?"

The woman grinned, trying not to laugh. "All the other entrants are here. You're the last to arrive."

"Oh, I'm sorry."

A man in baggy pants and a loose fitting, loud print shirt appeared from behind the woman. He smiled, his teeth under his moustache making his smile look like a sneer. "Is there a problem?"

"It's okay." The woman smiled. "This is Jeneil."

"You're sure?" he asked, his smile disappearing.

She nodded and bit her lower lip. "She's exactly like her film."

The man smiled and opened the screen door. "Come in, Jeneil. You didn't put your last name on your entry fee application. We like to be careful. The film business can attract all types. We didn't mean to be rude."

They stepped inside. The house had been converted into a business and looked like it might have been a restaurant at one time. Jeneil studied the house and its two hosts. "If the door is locked, does that mean I can't get out without permission?" she asked, unashamed of her lack of sophistication. The woman swallowed a laugh. Peter and Steve looked at each other, silently agreeing on a disapproving vote of her.

The man smiled warmly. "Good gosh no. Why would you think that?"

"Well, like you said, the film business attracts all types. We might not all be compatible. I like to know the rules before I play a game."

Peter and Steve grinned at each other. The man studied Jeneil's face, still smiling, and then looked her over slowly. Peter was glad Jeneil had worn a shirt over the outside of her jeans. Something about the guy spelled dirty old man, even though he didn't seem to be much older than them. His playmate had 'rough life' written across her face. The back of Peter's neck tingled. It was a feeling from the streets and it happened whenever a situation required him to be on guard. Looking at Steve, he could tell he was studying the situation closely, too.

"I like your name," the man said. "Did you make it up?" He continued studying her, still smiling.

"No, my parents did."

"It sounds Midwest."

"That's odd," Jeneil replied, "my mother's from New England and my father's from Ireland." Peter and Steve smiled. Jeneil was meeting the situation head on with a one-step dodge. They both relaxed and continued to watch their hosts. The woman looked at the man with growing annoyance as he looked at Jeneil.

"You have beautiful eyes and there's a serene expression to them. Clear conscience?" the man asked.

"Would no sense of guilt and a lack of conscience do the same thing?" Jeneil replied. The man laughed lightly and flashed his eyes at her. Peter felt another tingle pass through him. Steve straightened his shoulders and fidgeted.

"Is this your first film?" the man asked.

"Yes, and what did she mean that I'm just like my film?"

"Who, Sonnet?" The man shrugged. "Sometimes she says things that are as deep as morning dew. She can't even explain them." Jeneil looked from the man to the woman and back again.

"If your name is Prose, I'd like my film back and I'll leave now," Jeneil said rudely.

The man laughed. "Stay Jeneil, please stay. My name is Arthur." He extended his hand to her. Jeneil took it and he held her hand in both of his, rubbing his unclasped hand lightly across the back of hers.

"Arthur, you'd better get things started," Sonnet said, stepping closer to him as she glared at Jeneil.

"Yeah, I'd like that, Sonnet. I'd really like that," he answered wistfully, staring at Jeneil without smiling. The woman walked away mumbling. Jeneil withdrew her hand. "Jeneil, Sonnet's right, you are like your film." He touched her cheek gently. "It was called Hope, wasn't it?"

"How come you remember it?"

Arthur looked steadily at her. "It was different."

"Do you mean odd?"

"I mean different." He smiled at her sincerely. "It's not odd since seeing you. Defend it, Jeneil."

"Against what?"

Sonnet returned. "Move it now Arthur."

"Right," he answered. "Come in and find a seat."

Arthur walked from the large entry hall to a larger room with folding chairs facing one wall with an enormous TV screen against it. Peter and Steve followed Jeneil.

"I'd like to sit on the end near the exit," Steve said as they approached the chairs. Jeneil looked at him and wondered why. Peter nodded.

Arthur began the festival with a few words of welcome, smiling his personable smile for the audience. "The film festival was only posted at Elio's. We're pleased with the amount of aspiring filmmakers who responded. Some of our regulars have submitted entries too, so let's begin with our first entry called Fatigue." There was mild applause as the lights dimmed.

Jeneil leaned toward Peter. "I wish I had asked about his background in the business." Peter took her hand and Steve scanned the crowd.

Jeneil watched as the film began with footage from an Army recruiting center with a boy accepting his uniform then continued into newsreels of wars in different countries spliced together. The boy reappeared again badly wounded and suffering from shock. The film stayed with him as he suffered through the effects of his trauma. Jeneil was touched as she realized the boy wasn't acting and wondered how the filmmaker had gotten the material. Again there was mild applause and a man's voice could be heard agreeing with the film's title.

The next film dealt with poverty followed by one on nuclear weapons. As that film ended and the lights went up, some of the crowd called, "Defend it, defend it." The producer of the film appeared at the front of the room and stood in front of the screen. The audience shot cutting remarks at him and he struggled to defend his film.

Jeneil looked at Peter. "I think I'm in big trouble."

"Get your tape and let's go, baby. This group's not all it seems to be."

"I think you're right. My film doesn't belong here. Where's Steve?"

"He'll be right back." Jeneil's heart sank as she heard the title of the next film; Hope.

"Hope?" one man commented. "And I hope Hope's hopping around in it, hoping for some fun. I'm fatigued by serious already. Give us hope," he shouted, and several people laughed.

Jeneil sighed. "Oh my, I'm knee deep in trouble now." There was an unexpected silence and Jeneil held her breath as the film ended.

"Where the hell is the producer to that one? Oh, defend it," the same man said. "Defend it." The audience chimed in calling, "Defend it, defend it."

"Oh, Peter," Jeneil said, wringing her hands.

"Tell them to go to hell, baby. Get the film and we'll go." The lights went on.

"Come on, Jeneil," Sonnet called, smiling broadly, enjoying the moment.

Jeneil felt Peter start to stand up. She held his arm. "No, Peter. I'll take care of this. It's my own fault." She stood up. There was a whistle as she walked to the front.

"Hey, Jeneil, you should have showed your legs in the film," someone in the audience called out. Peter fidgeted anxiously in his seat.

"What's happening here?" Steve asked, sitting down.

"They're about to nail Jeneil to the wall." Peter sighed and rubbed his forehead.

"Oh great." Steve shook his head. "Pete, this place is reeking with drugs."

Peter stared in disbelief. "It's that open?"

"Are you kidding? There's so much free basing equipment here we could get rich just selling matches."

"Oh shit." Peter slouched.

"And I don't need to tell you how great a bust in this joint would look on our records. My probation needs this worse than Rita and Lucy. I'm so nervous, everybody's starting to look like an undercover cop. Let's get the hell out of here."

Jeneil stood up in front of the blank screen in silence. "So what made you do that piece of garbage anyway?" one man asked.

"It's her first film," Arthur commented.

"Well, let's hope it's her last," Sonnet commented, laughing, exaggerating 'hope.' There was more laughter. Jeneil stayed silent as she looked at the audience.

"Oh I disagree," one man added. "I'd like to see her star in a film, a remake of Lady Godiva. With her hair and those legs, she wouldn't even need to rent a horse. No one would notice it was missing. I'm available to co-star, Jeneil. You can use me instead of the horse." There was laughing again and Jeneil remained silent. Peter leaned forward and rubbed his face. His jaw hurt from being clenched.

"Well, defend yourself," one girl shouted.

"Yeah!" several others agreed. The crowd became hushed as Jeneil continued to stand silently before them.

"Defend yourself," a man called.

Jeneil shook her head disgustingly. "You don't want me to defend myself or my film. You just want to ridicule. So finish your pathetic game and return my film to me."

"All right, Sunshine," Steve whispered, and Peter sat up straight, both of them smiling.

"Cheeky slut, ain't you?" one woman called.

Peter started to stand up but Steve grabbed his arm. "Don't do it, Pete. Unless it's really spilling on her, she won't like it, even in this dump."

"What does that remark have to do with my film?" Jeneil asked. "How can I defend it? No one has given me an intelligent review yet. What are your credentials as critics anyway?" The audience looked at each other in surprise.

"It was naïve," one man answered.

"Thank you, at last an intelligent opinion. Do you mean the way I presented hope was naïve? Then my defense would be my definition of naïve means artless or lacking in sophistication. My opinion is that as people we're too sophisticated, too self involved that we need to be upstaged by a sunrise and a sunset or the moon and every other aspect of nature to bring us back to our proper place in the whole scheme of life. Our technology can't match any of nature's greatness. We're blinded by our achievements in science and yet our technology is dwarfed by nature."

"Oh good grief, I don't think she's from this century."

"I'm proud of that fact," Jeneil responded. "If you mean being hopeful is naïve then I'd like to ask what the psychotherapist will tell his patient in the film, Fatigue. What will the people running the food centers tell the people lined up for food in the film we saw here on poverty, and what do you tell the people who live under the threat of a nuclear war? Living without hope can cause a bigger problem and a greater holocaust to man and civilization than any of the plagues we've just seen on film. Without hope of changing the problems tomorrow, there's no reason to finish today. Actually it seems more naïve to just present the problem on film without a hint of a solution. Newsreels do that. I thought you people were artists and free thinkers. I was taught that artists, poets, composers, and writers are the hope of civilization and mankind because they are its conscience and its intellect. They are supposed to lead the masses to a solution. What can lead them to great achievements and ideals? What can artists as a group accomplish if they jump into the sewer with the rest of mankind and end up losing the path out? I'd like my film back now."

One man shouted an obscenity at her. "That's not her problem. She here with two guys." Several people laughed. Peter sat forward and clenched his hands.

"You seem to like to tear down and mock. I once heard a writer asked if she'd be willing to die for what she believed in her writings. She answered that she would but added that she'd rather live for it, which is far more difficult. I agree, create something, believe it, and live it, then I'll be impressed enough to listen to your criticism, and that's what the general public thinks about you and your art too or you wouldn't need to play this pathetic game. My film please."

There was an angry silence from the group. "Go to hell, Jeneil."

"Thanks, but I'm standing in it. I'm heading for some fresh air and hope."

Some mumbled. Sonnet walked over to Jeneil with the tape. "And screw you."

"Oh Sonnet, that's brilliant. That should improve life's problems."

"Beat it," Sonnet sneered.

"Gladly," Jeneil answered, and walked to a smiling Peter and Steve, who were waiting by the door.

"Jeneil," a voice called. Turning, she saw an emaciated young man walking toward her. The young man fidgeted. "Jeneil, if that's your reality then aim for the sun and keep running toward it. Ignore the screams, the clamor, and avoid the sewer, Jeneil. Run like hell until you have outdistanced all of us." A tear streamed down his cheek and disappeared into the scraggly growth of hair on his face.

Jeneil choked up. "Did you understand it really? This isn't just pity, is it?"

"No," he answered, "I felt it, Jeneil. It was a feeling I thought was long gone, cauterized by my neglect and anger. It felt good to hurt over the loss of hope. I didn't know I cared anymore. Run, sweetheart. Shout it all the way to the sun itself."

Tears filled Jeneil's eyes as she felt a connection with the young man. She went to him and put her arms around him in a hug, surprising him.

"Who's that?" Steve asked Peter.

"A fan, I think."

"What's with her? The guy could have lice. He looks like he's diseased."

Peter shrugged and smiled as the young man put his arms around Jeneil and hugged her tightly. "That's Jeneil."

"Pete," Steve cautioned, "go get her, please. He could be on something."

"It's okay Steve. I think he's impressed with her. It's like sitting in the warm sun after a cold rainy day."

"You're both crazy. I swear it." Steve paced, watching Jeneil carefully.

The young man released his hold and took her hands. "Don't stop caring even if it hurts. At least you'll know you're alive." She squeezed his hands. He nodded and returned to the group. Jeneil turned and joined Peter and Steve. She was quiet as they walked to the car and Peter unlocked the doors.

"I'd like to sit in the back seat for awhile." Jeneil sighed.

Peter looked at her. "Are you okay?"

"No," she said softly. "I don't like me very much right now. It was too easy to slip into the insulting attack I took. It was their game and I joined in. It doesn't feel too good. I feel pompous."

Peter kissed her and opened the back door. "They're shitheads, honey."

"I agree," Steve added.

Peter headed down the driveway, watching Jeneil in the rearview mirror. Steve looked back at her. She sat staring down at her hands. The road back to the city was ahead of them and Peter stopped to yield to traffic. Hearing a soft giggle, Peter and Steve turned to look at Jeneil. She sighed and leaned forward, resting her arms on the back of their seat.

"It's hopeless! Repentance won't come. My mind is displeased but my heart doesn't feel remorse. I wanted to hit Sonnet." She chuckled and put her head down on her arms. She sighed and looked up again. "It's too late for me. I've been ruined by the corporation. I tried to feel bad for what I said to those people but all I kept wondering was if I could sell the film to schools for their science programs. Please let me in the triad. I'm dangerous on my own. You two inspire the best in me. I want to sit in front with you." Peter stopped the car, and Steve got out and held the door for her as she switched seats. She looked from one to the other. "What do you say, pizza and beer at Lenny's?"

"Hey, triad survival food." Steve smiled and put his arm on the seat behind her. She kissed Peter's shoulder.

"Don't lose me, guys. This triad is home to me. It's where I live."

"That's a deal," Peter said, easing the car into traffic.

"The film is great, Jeneil. Don't let them get to you."

"They won't, Steve, because deep inside of me I know I created something that had a positive effect on the universal force. The reciprocal energy will sustain me and make me incredibly alive. The high will be intense."

"Cosmic?" Peter asked.

"Cosmic." Jeneil smiled.

Thirty-Six

The film festival became a passing thought for Jeneil as she went about her life. Peter still laughed when he thought of her standing before the audience defending herself. He had seen a change in her, she had become more confident, and he liked it. She was still practicing the business of soul and he was participating more easily now that he realized he needed to concentrate on something special about her and stare into her eyes. The thought couldn't be physical or soul didn't happen, passion did. While he enjoyed that too, he had developed a taste for soul. He had asked why she hadn't told him how to achieve it and she had simply smiled and told him it was part of his journey for self-discovery. He noticed sometimes soul didn't work or he felt awkward with it, usually finding the problem within himself, either being out of sorts with life, himself, or Jeneil. When that happened it took longer and required touching. Jeneil seemed to sense those times and helped him by touching his cheek, holding his hand or resting her hands on his shoulders.

Peter was impressed with Jeneil's ability to express love without words in so many ways, being totally comfortable with soul. He knew he was the student and soul was becoming one of the greatest stress relievers he'd ever used, and there were moments when everything was perfect and soul was incredible. It was those moments he was developing a strong taste for. The closeness they achieved was exhilarating; the awareness of their togetherness in those moments filled him with a sense of completeness and peace; a compatibility between them and life. It was never physical and only became so afterwards when he wanted to make the feeling last, but even that was different as a result and passion only began to describe the experience.

Peter laid in bed thinking about it; the night before had been one of those moments. He smiled and stretched knowing the hospital had given him a Sunday off.

Steve and Jeneil had gone to a warehouse she'd heard of to look at men's clothes. As Steve approached the end of his residency it was time to start looking the part of a professional, but it wasn't easily accomplished with little money. Jeneil had suggested having two suits made by a tailor then finish with things from the warehouse, which were good quality brand name items. Peter had smiled as he remembered Steve at work the day after. Steve had been impressed that Jeneil was so careful about shopping and spending money, looking for things in clothes he never knew existed. She knew quality and could substitute keenly, and he had come back from the trip with more clothes than he had expected.

Peter could tell Steve was anxious to begin private practice and was getting restless in the meantime. He had been assured he would be joining Sprague's group and Peter was happy things were beginning to fall into place. In a way, he envied Steve beginning a normal life with regular hours. It was something Peter felt ready for; a solid job, a home, a wife and kids. He smiled as the thought settled in his mind.

"Is that a Cheshire cat grin?" Jeneil asked, noticing his smile as she slipped into bed and rested on her elbows to face him.

"Cheshire cat?" he asked, puzzled.

"Are you up to something wicked?"

"What do you have in mind?"

She rested back on her pillow and laughed. "For two people who were so close last night, we sure missed each other by a mile in that conversation."

"Are we speaking the same language?"

"Not for the past few seconds. Ignore it." She smiled, touching his face lovingly. "I love you so much," she said, kissing him lightly.

"Marry me." He kissed her neck. "Let's go find a judge right now."

"What brought that on?"

He lay back on his pillow. "I was thinking about Steve ending his residency."

"Oh, well, that explains clearly why you want to marry me." She giggled.

He smiled and took her hand. "I want life to begin, too."

"What do you mean begin? We're in it now, aren't we?"

"Not a normal life. I want regular hours, a home, you as my wife and a few kids."

She looked at him and smiled slowly. "Peter Chang, you're making square, normal noises. Aren't you frightened you'll be bored?"

"No." He smiled. "No, I don't think so. I'm ready." She kissed his cheek. "Are you afraid you'll be bored?" he asked, studying her closely.

"No, but I know I'm not ready."

"Why?"

"I don't know; I just don't feel ready. I want to be your wife and I want to have children with you, but I'm not ready right now."

"I don't understand that."

"Neither do I," she answered, sighing.

"If you don't understand it then how will you know when you're ready?"

She smiled at him. "I'll never win the discussion if you use logic. I can only promise that I will marry you."

"And I promised I wouldn't push but I'll hold you to your promise. Count on it." He pulled her close and kissed her cheek softly.

"You don't have to worry, Peter. I'll always belong to you. I know that much."

"How do you know that?"

She shrugged. "I don't know. I just do."

"Honey, you're getting spacier."

"It's the truth."

"Lopsided is normal for you now and you're more confident because of it."

"If that's how you see me then I don't understand why you want to marry me."

"Because for some unexplainable reason I find lopsided cute as hell, sexy, and exciting, it makes me crazy." He bit her shoulder playfully, and she grinned and snuggled to him.

Jeneil's telephone rang and she reached for it. "Sienna! Hi. Oh good, very good. Yes. See you then."

"Who's Sienna?" Peter asked, after Jeneil had replaced the receiver.

"A friend I ran into at the theatre. She was stopping for tickets. We used to work at the library."

"The library? When did you work at a library?"

"Before I worked at the hospital."

"I didn't know that."

"Well, it wasn't that long. I'm not a good librarian."

"That's odd, you love books."

"Too much." She grinned. "And I better get up. If I'm starting a salon, I've got to get things going."

"Whoa, whoa, whoa, get back here."

"What?"

"You've already got things going here, finish them." He grinned and kissed her.

She moved closer to him, smiling. "Peter, soul leaves us turned on for days."

"I've noticed," he said, getting even closer to her. "I think it's great."

"Me, too," she agreed, as his lips met hers.

*****

Peter watched as Jeneil rushed into the kitchen as he came from the bathroom, drying his hair with a towel. He walked to the door smiling. "Hey, why are you moving at high speed?"

She grinned. "Because I'm behind schedule and paying for my fun with you this morning. Steve is due here any minute and Sienna will be here in a half hour."

"Sienna's coming here? Jeneil, are you matchmaking again?"

"No, I'm starting a salon," she replied, putting something into the slow cooker.

"A what?"

"A salon, a gathering where literary people get together and exchange ideas or discuss whatever. I thought it would be fun."

"Jeneil, you can't do that to our Sundays," Peter said, disappointed.

"But wait until you meet Sienna. I liked her when we worked together. I didn't even recognize her at the theatre. It's a good thing she remembered me or I'd have passed right by her. She's gone through a whole transformation. She wore glasses and had a single braid a year ago. Now she's got it all together. Auburn hair and green eyes are a striking combination. Green eyes?" Jeneil paused, thinking. "She used to have blue eyes and she doesn't wear glasses anymore. She's even changed her name. It used to be Shawna."

Peter laughed as he headed for the bedroom. "Will my real friend please stand up?"

"Behave yourself, Chang. I mean it," Jeneil warned.

He stuck his head out of the bedroom door. "Hey, does she have a split personality to go with the real her and the store bought her."

"Peter, don't get started. If you and Steve get locked into a laugh session, the whole day could be ruined." The doorbell rang. "I'll get it," she said, putting a dish in the oven.

She opened the front door. "I'll have to give you a key."

"Yeah, I know you then you'll charge me rent, too," Steve said, smiling then kissing her cheek.

"Oh my goodness," she replied. "It's doomed."

"What is?"

"The day, you and Peter are into tease time."

"Not me," Steve said, pulling something green from his jacket. "For you." He handed her a yellow rose rolled in green tissue paper. "Thank you for helping me shop for clothes."

"Oh! Thank you." Jeneil took the flower, surprised by the gift. "You're going to make someone a great husband. You think of little touches. That's really nice. What did you decide about your suits?" she asked, heading up the stairs.

"Steel grey and dark blue."

"Oh good choices, that steel grey material looked great with your eyes."

"What's with all the compliments?" Steve asked, stopping at the apartment door.

"Nothing," she replied, shrugging. He looked at her suspiciously as she smelled the rose.

"Jeneil, I know you. What's up?"

"I have a friend coming over. Be nice." She tugged nervously at the tissue paper.

"I think I'm insulted." He grinned.

"I'm sorry, but Peter's begun teasing and you're all kind of bubbly. When you two get started...," the front doorbell rang. "Oh gosh, she's early. Will you put this in the kitchen while I get the door?" She pushed the flower into his hand and ran down the stairs, and Steve went into the apartment.

Peter smiled when he saw Steve. "Well gosh, what a thrill. I love flowers, sweetie."

Steve laughed. "It's a rose, you brute. Can't you ever be sensitive?" Steve lisped, and they both laughed. "The kid wants it in the kitchen."

"Okay," Peter said, standing at the kitchen door. "Pass it to me, big boy."

"Oh now really," Steve continued in a sensitive tone, "that's no way to deal with a yellow rose. It should be coddled."

Peter growled jokingly, going at Steve like a football player. "Give me the flower."

"Oh, you brute," Steve hit Peter's arm as Peter grabbed the rose.

Jeneil cleared her throat and they both turned quickly to look at her. A slender girl stood by Jeneil studying them.

"Uh, we, uh, we were going to put your flower in the kitchen," Peter stammered, looking embarrassed.

"So I gathered. Sienna, these two clowns are very good friends. This is Peter Chang and Steve Bradley. Sienna Parker and I once worked together."

"Hi," Steve said.

"Hi, Sienna." Peter smiled.

"Are you botanists?" Sienna asked in a smooth-toned, well-controlled voice, looking from one to the other.

"Hey, we ain't even married," Steve joked.

"That's bigamist, dummy," Peter said, laughing. Jeneil closed her eyes, knowing the day was doomed. Sienna looked puzzled.

"We're joking," Steve apologized. "No, we're not botanists."

"They're doctors, Sienna," Jeneil added.

"Oh," Sienna smiled, "how interesting."

"Why?" Steve asked.

"Why what?" Jeneil questioned.

"Why does Sienna think being a doctor is interesting?"

"I wouldn't have guessed you were doctors, that's all," Sienna said, smiling as she looked Steve over.

"What did you think we were?" Peter asked.

Sienna shrugged. "Just not doctors, that's all." She smiled showing off a row of perfectly straight white teeth.

"Are you a model?" Steve asked.

Sienna gave a throaty, sensuous laugh. "Not even a close guess but I'm flattered."

"You seem so posed," Steve said. Jeneil raised her eyebrows, giving Steve a warning.

Sienna laughed again. "I think you mean poised."

"No, I meant posed." Steve smiled.

"Sienna, let's get comfortable." Jeneil walked to the living room, glaring back at Steve. "I'll take your coat."

"Thank you, Jeneil. Your apartment is charming. It's from another era. The owner has put some care into it, but why do you live here? My building has some vacancies you might like to see. Security is great and the rent is quite reasonable."

"Well, actually I enjoy this neighborhood."

"Oh really, how interesting. Is it safe?" Sienna asked, as Peter and Steve looked at each other disapprovingly as they walked to the living room.

"Yes, it is. I promise your car will be in one piece when you leave."

Sienna laughed. "You've changed, Jeneil. You look different, too." Peter wondered if she was begging a compliment for herself.

"That's what I noticed about you." Jeneil smiled.

Sienna leaned back against the sofa and crossed her legs, crossing her hands at the wrists and resting them to one side of her. "I decided that Shawna needed a do-over, poor girl, so I turned myself over to a stylist and closed my eyes until he was finished, and now I'm Sienna."

"You really let him decide what image you were going to have? Did he offer you some choices?" Jeneil asked, shocked.

Sienna laughed sensually again. "No, I honestly threw caution to the wind."

Jeneil stared. "Shawna, I mean Sienna, that boggles my mind. It's incredibly daring."

"But it was the best thing I've ever done. The whole thing turned into a scene from a movie. Gilbert had just opened a new beauty spa and took a personal interest in me, and that began my journey to Sienna."

"It was that easy? I mean you caught up to Sienna with no trouble? It was as easy as changing your hairstyle?"

Sienna smiled. "You seem stunned."

"Well, honestly I really am. I think we all go through a transformation. I know I am, but mine is so slow. You really seem comfortable with your image and it's so different from the you I remember."

Sienna nodded. "It certainly is and it transformed me inside, too. I applied for a day manager's job in Weller's Bookstore at Highland Mall. Can you imagine Shawna being that assertive? I wasn't wasting this image. I needed to be free to taste life. Now I get to meet some interesting people who enjoy reading."

Jeneil smiled. "I love it. I absolutely love the fact you did that and that it worked well."

"What are you doing now?" Sienna asked.

"Mostly trying to find myself, which sounds adolescent, but it's true."

"Where are you working?"

"The records department at a hospital."

Sienna frowned. "Oh Jeneil, your job is an important choice. It's where you meet people. Maybe I can arrange a job for you at one of Weller's other branches. I could introduce you to Gilbert." Steve looked at Peter and raised his eyebrows.

Jeneil shook her head. "I don't think so, Sienna. I'd get the bends emerging so quickly into another me. I'm impressed that you accomplished it so easily. That's wonderful." Peter and Steve grinned at each other.

Sienna nodded. "I can understand your caution. I was ready to step into life, I wanted to taste it, but do something about your job. Who can you meet at a hospital? Everyone there is sick."

Jeneil smiled then laughed. "Well, I know they act sick, but I met Peter and Steve there." Peter and Steve chuckled.

Sienna laughed her throaty laugh. "Oh excuse me, you two. That was really rude of me."

"It's okay," Steve assured her. "You can't remember everything."

"What kind of doctors are you?"

"Good ones," Steve answered quickly, and Peter chuckled.

"No, I meant what is your particular field?"

"Oh, we're surgeons," Steve answered, and noticed Sienna make a face. "Don't like the thought of cutting people open, huh?" Peter put his head down to keep from laughing.

"Well, I guess somebody has to do it."

"Yeah, that and garbage collecting," Steve commented, smiling. Peter couldn't hold back his laugh.

"Would you like juice or coffee?" Jeneil asked, standing up quickly.

"I'll take juice." Sienna straightened her jacket. "Coffee is really not good for your health."

Steve grinned. "I'll take coffee, strong and black."

"You usually don't drink black coffee," Jeneil said.

"I'm feeling daring. I think I'm ready to taste it."

Peter cleared his throat and bit his lip. Jeneil shook her head and went to the kitchen.

Sienna smiled. "Well, they say that doctors make the worst patients."

"Oh yeah," Steve commented, smiling, "who's they who say that."

Sienna wrinkled her brow. "Are doctors always so literal? I've only dealt with them professionally."

Steve shrugged. "I don't know. I'm too busy during surgery to take surveys. Hey, Pete, are you always literal?"

"I'm not sure," Peter replied, going along with the conversation.

"There you go, Sienna." Steve grinned. "Two I'm not sures. Glad to help out with your survey." Peter covered his mouth.

Sienna looked puzzled. "I'm not taking a survey. You're being too literal again."

"They're teasing you, Sienna," Jeneil said, returning with drinks. "It's a form of comic relief brought on by standing too close to the anesthesia. Breathe deeply you two, in with the good, out with the bad." Peter and Steve chuckled.

"That's curious." Sienna smiled.

"Now how come that wasn't interesting but it was curious?" Steve asked, and Sienna was a bit startled by the question. Jeneil put a cup onto a saucer with a loud clinking noise and Peter sensed her annoyance.

"Because interesting denotes intelligence, curious embraces odd; right now curious is very applicable. Here's your black coffee, Steve," Jeneil said, staring at him as she handed him the cup and saucer, forcing a smile. Steve grinned.

"Jeneil, I love the way you use words," Sienna said, as she sipped her juice. "I've noticed your wall grouping." Sienna pointed casually toward it. "It's African, isn't it?"

"Yes, it is."

"Where did you get your pieces?"

"A friend gave them to me."

"Well, it must be a good friend. They're not inexpensive."

"Actually she picked them up herself. She traveled a lot. They're not from a museum."

"How interesting." Sienna fidgeted after having said it, aware that Steve noticed her use of the phrase.

"Yes, I find it interesting, too." Jeneil looked directly at Steve.

Steve shrugged. "So do I."

Sienna smiled and relaxed. "Have you traveled much?"

"Not recently," Jeneil answered.

"I love to travel. I'd love to go to Barbados."

"Why?" Steve asked.

"Because it's very chic right now."

"What makes it so chic?" Steve asked, and Jeneil looked cautiously at him. "Well, why is it so chic? What's in Barbados, and what's chic?"

Sienna shrugged. "Sand and sea. It's a very 'in' place to go. Why does one place become 'in.' I don't know."

"I think it's a cycle," Jeneil explained. "The rich and famous try desperately to find secluded places for getaways, but because they're so newsworthy they're always spotted.

Wherever they go becomes the new travel destination. The Virgin Islands, Aruba, Cancun. I guess it's a status thing."

Steve smiled. "That's interesting, I didn't know that."

"Too busy in surgery, Doctor." Sienna smiled.

"Must be. That's what I like about Jeneil. I learn a lot from her."

Jeneil raised her eyebrows. "And you'll go far with the trivia I collect. Sienna, you said you love to travel. Have you done much?"

"Not on the salary I used to make. I'm still paying for a trip to California. I'd love to go to the Caribbean too, but it'll have to wait until California is paid for. What about you Peter or is it Pete?"

"Either one's okay. What about me?"

"Do you like to travel?"

"I don't think so. Sounds like a lot of work for nothing but long lines."

Jeneil smiled. "Peter is in his first year of residency. His concentration is on education right now, but he gets away on a Harley Davidson. That's his getaway tour."

"Now that's a trip." Peter smiled at Jeneil.

"Peter's a man of simple tastes." Jeneil smiled back at him.

"What about you, Steve?" Sienna asked.

"I'm a student too, and when I finish I'm facing student loans. I haven't thought about traveling but I think having to keep paying for something after I've had the fun would get to me."

"It does," Sienna agreed, "but I try to think of it as an educational expense."

Steve shrugged. "Whatever works for you."

Jeneil put her glass down. "The weather is gorgeous today. I'd like to walk the nature trail in the park and gather some dried grasses and flowers. Is anyone else interested in getting some fresh air?"

"Yeah." Steve stood up.

"Me, too." Peter joined him. "Bring the basketball."

"Basketball?" Sienna looked surprised. "I've just had my nails done."

"Are those fake?" Steve asked.

"Yes, and expensive. You don't think they get this long naturally, do you?"

"Jeneil's do," Peter replied.

"Let me see." Sienna went to Jeneil. Jeneil looked uncomfortable but held out her hands. "They do! How?"

"I have to protect them like you do, I'm sure."

"But mine split. They never get that long. What do you do?"

Jeneil shrugged. "What you do I guess; keep an emery board in my hip pocket, rub oil in them, and cover them when I use a scouring pad."

"Scouring pad!" Sienna laughed. "I don't dare put my hands in dishwater. What kind of oil? Maybe that's the secret. There's a boutique in the mall but it's expensive. Is that where you get it?"

"No." Jeneil looked uncomfortable. "I use cooking oil."

Sienna was stunned. "Cooking oil! You're kidding!" Peter and Steve smiled at each other.

"Well, it's not very glamorous, but it's cheap."

Sienna laughed. "Jeneil, you're still odd."

"And I've added eccentric to that, too. What can I say? Let's go for a walk." Jeneil looked at Peter. "Would you get the coats?" Peter left the room and Steve followed him. Sienna watched them walk away.

"Jeneil, I'm not clear about something here. Which one did you have in mind for me? Peter is nice but I've never thought of dating an Asian."

It was Jeneil's turn to be surprised. "Well, I wasn't matchmaking at all. This was just supposed to be a casual gathering."

"Oh, so you've got your eye on Steve, huh?"

Jeneil's mouth dropped open. "Why do you think that?"

"Whenever I'm told we're not paired off it's usually because the other girl is scanning both men."

"Sienna, I honestly hadn't given it any thought but I think you should know that Peter and I live together."

"What?" Sienna smiled broadly. "Jeneil, how ultra, ultra 'in.' You are a shock. You were frightened of men a year ago and you've gone from that to this. And Asian, too. You've really broken loose, and here I thought you were still huddled in that awful shell you were trapped in." She hugged Jeneil. "That's wonderful. He really is very nice."

"I'm surprised you didn't see that," Jeneil answered, a bit piqued by the whole thing.

"Well, I wasn't really looking Jeneil. And they both like you, I can see that. In fact, you all seem very close."

"Well we are, I guess. We're close friends with Steve."

"So Steve is mine?" Sienna asked, smiling. "He's so incredibly good looking."

Jeneil looked at her and smiled. "Steve is free Sienna, very, very free. I hadn't thought about it, but go for it. Yes indeed, go for it by all means."

"Is the competition tough? Oh gosh, it must be, he's so good looking."

"It's non-existent. There is no woman in his life right now. The entire field is clear."

"What a stroke of luck," Sienna whispered, as the men returned with the coats.

"My feelings exactly, very interesting." Jeneil grinned then noticed Peter was holding Sienna's coat and she reached for it. "Oh, this is Sienna's, and Steve that's mine. Thank you." She had both coats and deliberately fumbled them. "I'm in the way here. Here," and she handed Sienna's coat to Steve, "I'll just put on another sweater. I hate being cold. Be right back." Looking back, she saw Steve hold Sienna's coat while Sienna put it on. She smiled and went to the bedroom giggling to herself; very interesting indeed.

*****

Peter and Steve played basketball while Jeneil collected dried grasses and empty milkweed pods. Sienna became a basketball fan, offering to hold their jackets while she watched them play.

The nature trail had been full of giggling teenagers on the make so they passed on the nature walk and made a stop at the Museum of Natural History instead. Peter got to see the geodes that fascinated Jeneil so much. He had to admit he was impressed with the ordinary looking rock that had a hollowed center and light blue crystals clustered within it. Jeneil stood in front of the glass case with Peter to her left. Steve joined them, standing to her right.

"Hey, Pete, we should bring her some kidney stones," Steve teased, bumping her arm.

"I'm thinking of having one put on a chain as a necklace for her." Peter squeezed the back of her neck and kissed her temple.

"I'm not listening." She grinned.

"What causes kidney stones?" Sienna asked, taking Steve's arm and walking away with him. Jeneil noticed and smiled.

Peter grinned. "Looks like Steve's got a nibble."

"Looks like it."

"You're matchmaking, aren't you?" Peter put his arm around her shoulder.

"That happened on its own, I didn't plan it." She walked to the next area while Peter stayed to look at a quartz display.

"Peter Chang!" Jeneil heard the voice and looked up. She recognized a nurse from the hospital standing near Peter with two children and a man. Panicking, Jeneil stooped to the floor, opened her purse and spilled out a few items, gathering them slowly, hoping to hide herself. "Steve Bradley, too! I should have guessed." Jeneil didn't dare look up. "And you must be his fiancée." Jeneil held her head, hoping everything would settle down quickly. She giggled at how lucky for Steve to finally have been seen with a girl. The gossip line was getting suspicious since he didn't have pictures and little details were missing. "Where's your girl, Pete?" There was silence.

"She was just here a minute ago," Jeneil heard Sienna answer, and she slipped behind a display base for cover.

"Mommy, I'm hungry," one of the children whined.

"Okay, honey. Well, I'm sorry I won't meet your girlfriend, Pete, but it was great seeing all of you. It really was."

Jeneil smiled. She just bet it was. The nurse was going to be the only one who'd seen Steve's girl and almost met Peter's. That was the scoop of the year and the hospital wouldn't lie still for a month. Jeneil heard the goodbyes and peeked around the base carefully. She caught sight of the family leaving through the front door.

"Here she is guys." Jeneil looked up at a smiling Sienna. She stooped down to help Jeneil gather the spilled items. "That lady thought I was Steve's fiancée, Jeneil, and he didn't deny it. I like him. I really do."

Peter and Steve joined them. "What happened?" Peter asked, looking at the spilled purse.

"Clumsy," Jeneil offered limply.

"Jeneil, that woman wanted to meet you. If you all work together, how come she didn't know who Peter's girl was?" Sienna questioned.

Jeneil looked at her and decided to be honest. "Because I'm afraid of the gossip there so Peter and I have kept us a secret."

"I understand." Sienna smiled. "Gosh, I'm glad I didn't ruin it by looking for you then. I'm glad I know better now."

Jeneil liked Sienna. She had at the library, too. Once a person got to know her, she was easy to take.

Steve stooped down. "Jeneil, what's wrong with your knee? You're bleeding."

"What?" She looked at her knee that had been hurting. "Oh, when I was gathering grasses I stepped into a hole and lost my balance."

"But you're cut."

"There was a broken bottle. It isn't serious."

"Let me look at it." Steve reached out his hand.

"No." Jeneil stopped him with hers. "It's not serious. My jeans aren't torn. I'll treat it at home."

"Have you had a tetanus shot?" Peter asked.

"Yes, I'm fine, really guys."

Sienna laughed. "Doctors are great to have around. They get so concerned over things."

Jeneil smiled. "Too much sometimes."

Peter picked up her hair brush and makeup case from the floor and put them in her purse. "Come on, honey, let's go home. We should at least look at that cut."

"I'm okay, Peter, just hungry. Everybody for home?" she asked, and Steve and Sienna nodded.

Peter unlocked the front door and scooped Jeneil into his arms, shocking her. "Peter, really. I like this though." She smiled, putting her arms around his neck, halfway up the stairwell. He smiled at her and kissed her lightly.

Sienna followed next to Steve. "They're a great couple, aren't they, romantic and caring," she said, watching as Peter kissed Jeneil.

"Yeah, they are," Steve answered quietly, putting his head down.

Jeneil changed quickly to a long dress and headed to the bathroom to patch her knee. Peter followed and Steve stood at the door. Sienna peered over his shoulder. "Sit down, baby," Peter said, bringing a wicker stool to her. He wet a clean washcloth in hot water then knelt down and smiled at her. "I can't see the cut if you won't show me the knee."

"I can do it," she insisted.

"I'm the doctor." Peter smiled, and she sighed and lifted the hem of her dress to expose her knee. A trickle of blood had ran down her leg and he cleaned the area around the cut.

"Just put a bandage on it for now so I can get lunch," Jeneil ordered.

"That's open, Pete," Steve commented.

"I know," Peter answered. He poured peroxide on a gauze pad then pressed it on the cut.

"Ow." Jeneil jumped.

Peter looked at Steve. "There's a piece of glass in it."

Steve walked over and knelt down. "Is it big?"

"No, but I felt it just before she jumped."

"Get the magnifier and tweezers then," Jeneil suggested. "Treat it like a sliver."

Steve smiled at her. "How long did you spend in medical school?"

"Well, it's hardly surgery," she said, as Peter returned with a first aid kit.

Steve chuckled. "Jeneil, this kit is ready for surgery; flashlight, fine point and flat tweezers, two Exacto knives. Who's probing and who's assisting?"

"I'll try the probe." Peter sterilized the equipment while Steve kept the blood from trickling. Jeneil covered her mouth and laughed.

Steve looked up at her. "What's so funny?"

"You two." She laughed. "It's like a bypass to you. Who'll probe, who'll assist?" Steve grinned and wiped away the blood.

"Hold her leg. I'm worried that she'll jump," Peter instructed, checking the cut through the magnifier, holding the flashlight.

"See it?" Steve asked.

Peter shook his head. "The damn blood keeps seeping around it."

"How about a tourniquet," Jeneil suggested, laughing.

"Smart mouth." Steve grinned. "Now I know why we knock patients out."

"I can try it blind."

"Go ahead."

"Hold her," Peter said, and Steve positioned his hand on her leg. Peter looked at Jeneil. "Honey, try not to jump."

"Okay," she answered, watching them. Sienna covered her mouth and grimaced.

"Steve, swab it fast and I'll probe."

"I will," Jeneil offered, "and Sienna, inside that closet is a plastic bag with herbal packets that look like teabags, and a plastic beaker. Would you put two inches of hot water in the beaker and let the packets steep in that."

"Sure." Sienna went to work.

"Honey, brace yourself," Peter warned, and began to probe for the glass.

"Ouch, that's enough," Jeneil said, as the pressure turned into pain.

"I'm sorry, honey."

"Want me to try it?" Steve asked.

"I can't," Peter said. "I'm afraid I'll hurt her. Boy, it's different when you know the patient.

"Okay, Jeneil, hang tough," Steve said, positioning himself and checking the wound, approaching the cut with the tweezers.

Jeneil closed her eyes until she felt the pain. "Ouch, that's it for me."

Steve looked at her. "I'm sorry, kid."

Jeneil covered her face and sighed. "I know you are. Give me a minute to think." She sat quietly. "I have an idea," she said, brightening. "Give me the eyedropper that's in the kit." Steve sterilized it then watched as she squeezed the cut gently with her fingers.

"What are you doing?"

"If blood is in the way, let it do the work. I'm hoping squeezing it will loosen the glass enough for the blood to push it. The blood's coming out anyway; maybe it'll bring the glass with it." Peter and Steve looked at each other. Jeneil took the eyedropper. "This one's too small. The one with the light blue syringe is…," she stopped. "The ear syringe has stronger suction." Peter got it for her while she kept squeezing around the cut.

"Honey, we need to be able to see what you're drawing out so we can look for the glass," Peter said, as she suctioned the wound.

Jeneil sighed. "Okay, there's a Petri dish in the closet, put water in it and I'll use the glass eyedropper." She worked, totally absorbed in what she was doing. Peter checked the eyedropper after each suction. "There it is." Jeneil smiled, taking the magnifier glass.

"Where?" Steve leaned forward. "It is. Hey, great work."

Peter pulled out the piece of glass with the tweezers. "Is that all of it?"

"I'll check." Steve got up and sterilized his fingers then returned to press on the cut.

"It's fine." Jeneil smiled. "I can feel the difference. Now, I'll just bathe it with the herbal solution and we're done."

Peter shook his head. "I'm embarrassed."

Jeneil smiled and patted his arm. "You guys are trained in bone grafts and bypasses. I'm a splinter person. Ooo," Jeneil winced, dabbing the solution on her leg then chuckled as she finished. "Hey everyone," she laughed, "so much for a refined salon. We spent our time in the bathroom."

Steve smiled. "You've got a knack for healing, sweetheart."

"You do," Peter agreed. "You seem to understand health and the body."

"Just mine, I know me well." She stood up and tested the knee. "I'm fine, let's do lunch."

Peter and Steve left the bathroom. Sienna watched Jeneil. "They hover over you, Jeneil. They actually guard you."

"I know, they think I'm mentally incompetent sometimes because I'm odd but I'll show them someday when I grow up." They both laughed and followed the guys.

Peter, Steve, and Sienna sat at the dining table. Steve avoided Sienna's smiles, dodging the vibrations she was sending his way. Peter was glad when Jeneil brought in the food.

"Jeneil, hot dogs!" Sienna blurted out.

"Coney Island style wieners," Jeneil replied. "Why?"

"If you had told me, I would have brought a gourmet lunch. I'm into gourmet cooking."

"My mother was, too," Jeneil said, sitting down.

"I love wieners," Steve said, looking at Sienna.

"There's a place for them, I suppose," Sienna said, putting a wiener on her plate.

"There's a place for a few of them in my stomach." Peter smiled. "I love them, too."

Sienna watched as the guys ate. "You're smart, Jeneil. Cook for your man."

Jeneil smiled and stood up. "I'll get dessert." She returned with a plate of fudge.

"Oh, you make fudge. I didn't think you liked to cook," Sienna said, and Steve glared at her. Peter noticed; she was getting to him, too.

"This isn't cooked. It's fast fudge. I just melt the chocolate, take it off the heat and add the other things. It's smooth, that's all that matters, isn't it?"

Sienna laughed. "Jeneil, that's cheating. Real fudge has to be cooked just so to avoid a hard sugary consistency."

Jeneil shrugged and sat down. "Oh well, anyone for faked fudge?" Peter and Steve laughed as they reached for some.

"I'll try it." Sienna took a piece and bit it daintily. "It isn't bad. But really Jeneil, you should learn to cook. Didn't your mother teach you?"

"Hey," Steve snapped, "she's a great cook. What difference does gourmet make anyway?" Jeneil saw the look on Sienna's face; Steve's remark had hurt her.

Jeneil smiled. "Sienna, the guys know I'm defensive about my cooking. I never could cook like my mother. I don't have the patience." She looked at Steve. "You don't understand gourmet dining, Steve. It's an art. There's cafeteria, plain, and gourmet cooking." She looked at Sienna. "I can't cook gourmet, but my mother's food was great. I loved it. I'd like to have you prepare a meal for us then these two will see the difference." Sienna smiled, and Peter and Steve looked at each other.

"What's your favorite dish?" Sienna asked Peter.

"A cheeseburger with the works," he replied dryly. Steve laughed.

"I would've thought it was Chinese." Sienna struggled with a smile. Jeneil felt for her.

"Peter," Jeneil interrupted, "Chinese food properly done is a real experience." Peter shrugged. "I wouldn't mind learning, Sienna." Hoping to ease the tension, she stood up. "I'm in the mood for some music. Why don't we get comfortable in the living room?"

"Jeneil, I have to get going," Sienna said, looking at her watch.

Jeneil looked at her, disappointed. "Do you really?"

"Yes, I do. Thanks for inviting me. It's been interesting."

"Please visit again," Jeneil said. "I'd like you to."

"Maybe we can have lunch sometime." Sienna smiled and Jeneil nodded, going to get Sienna's coat. Sienna avoided talking to Peter and Steve while she waited. "It was nice meeting you," she said coolly, putting on her coat and opening the door, not waiting for a reply. Jeneil went into the hallway with her, closing the door behind her.

"Don't give up on us, Sienna. We're plain folk."

Sienna smiled. "You haven't changed since the library. You still have a bleeding heart. They don't like me, Jeneil. Don't push it."

"I don't believe that's it at all," Jeneil fumbled. "They just get into these teasing jags. I lashed at Steve when I first got to know him but he has a finer side, even sensitive, that he doesn't show too easily, but he's worth getting to know."

Sienna looked at her keys. "I think I made my position clear to him. Anything more is beyond me, even as Sienna. Thank you, Jeneil. You always were easy to talk to. Really, let's have lunch."

Jeneil smiled and nodded. "Take care." Sienna smiled and walked down the stairs.

Jeneil went back to the apartment disappointed and annoyed. She closed the door loudly. Peter and Steve looked up from the newspapers they were reading. "What you two did to her was awful. It was rude. How could you be so mean?"

"She asked for it," Peter said.

"That's right," Steve agreed.

"How did she ask for it?" Jeneil's voice rose.

"For crying out loud Jeneil, she was putting you down," Steve replied. "Why aren't you mad at her for being rude?"

"She wasn't being rude. At least she didn't realize it. She was new to our group. It takes a while to fit in. You and I went through that, Steve. Besides, if I wasn't angry, why did you two get angry?"

"Jeneil, you're not a pimp. I'll find my own women." Steve got up and walked away.

Jeneil was shocked. "That's terrible, that's awful! You apologize. I didn't invite her for you! She happened to like you. Right now I think she's crazy to think you were nice." She headed out of the room, shouting, "Why does everything end up being physical?"

Steve paced then sat down on the sofa again. "I'm sorry, Pete."

Peter laughed. "You weren't fighting with me. She's the one mad at you, but why did you call her a pimp?"

"I didn't."

"You might as well have."

Steve put his head back. "I thought she was matchmaking."

"And what if she was? Is that so wrong? Look how far she's come about you and it hardly makes her a pimp."

Steve sighed. "Yeah, you're right."

"Boy, you sure got tipped off at Sienna."

"She was putting Jeneil down."

"I thought so, too," Peter agreed, "but Jeneil is slow to anger."

"Well, she's angry now." Steve laughed. "I'm afraid to apologize to her."

"Let her cool off a little. She'll be okay."

Jeneil came back, walked over to the plants, watered them, and then went back to the kitchen, all without talking to them.

"She's cute when she's mad. Her cheeks get red."

Peter laughed. "Why is everything physical? That question drives her crazy."

"Can't answer it, huh?" Steve grinned.

"No, she can't figure it out."

Jeneil made another silent trip to the plants and went back to the kitchen. On her third trip, she walked in as they were laughing hysterically. Steve caught his breath. "Hey, Jeneil," he called, trying not to laugh, "Pete figured out why everything is physical."

"Why?" she asked quietly.

"Not me," Peter said, laughing.

"Oh, I can imagine the explanation," Jeneil said, and started to walk away.

"It's intelligent, Jeneil. It makes sense."

"What is it?" she asked, stopping.

"It's a matter of economics," Steve answered, trying not to smile.

"Economics?"

"Sure," Steve continued. "It's like war, there's a lot of money in it."

"I don't understand."

"Well, if everything stopped being physical then obstetricians would be out of work, lingerie stores would be out of business, and chemical companies couldn't push pills." Peter and Steve's silliness had gone too far and they both began to laugh again.

Jeneil looked at them. "You're both crazy. And you pick on me," and she walked away.

"No sense of humor, Jeneil," Steve called after her, still laughing. She returned to water the plants on the shelf behind them. "Okay, Jeneil," Steve said, calming down. "We're going to be straight with you. We have the answer to the physical question."

"Sure you do," she said, cleaning a spot off a leaf.

"It's basic and simple. Man has certain biological needs and it's a woman's place to meet them."

"Oh, you're a brave man." Peter laughed.

"Why?" Steve asked, laughing. He looked up as Jeneil spilled a pitcher of water over both of them. "Hey!" Steve yelled. "Stop, that's cold!"

Peter stood up, sputtering. "You little bitch." He stared at her, wiping his face with his shirt sleeve.

"Oh, I'm sorry," she answered, feigning innocence. "I was watering the plants and when I heard Steve say that, I figured anyone at that level was vegetation and needed water, too." Then she stuck out her tongue.

"Oh, you're brave when you're on that side of the sofa. Wait until I get hold of you," and Peter started after her.

"It was an accident," she defended, giggling as she ran behind the dining table.

"Like hell it was," Peter said, grabbing for her. She backed away and slipped through a space near the sofa and into the living room.

"Grab her, Steve," Peter called to him as he came into the living room.

"No, Steve. Don't, please," Jeneil pleaded, taking his arm. "He's really angry at me now. I'm afraid of him when he's this angry. Protect me."

"Jeneil, you liar, wait until I get you," and he moved closer.

"Please, Steve. He gets violent," she said, getting behind him. "Please."

"Jeneil, you damn liar!" Peter said, and Steve looked at him. Jeneil looked out from behind Steve and seeing Peter, she stuck out her tongue then hid behind Steve again. "See that!" Peter shouted. "She's setting us up. You're catching it for this, Jeneil, I mean it."

"Maybe you should calm down, Pete," Steve said.

"What!" Peter was shocked. "You believe her! She's using you for a rug. Wake up, she's lying through her teeth, you lying little bitch." Peter moved closer to Steve.

"No, Peter. Don't, please," Jeneil pleaded, near tears.

"Pete, wait," Steve said.

"Get out of the way, man. I'll prove she's lying," Peter shouted. "Jeneil, you're bad. You need to be taught a lesson about getting people wet and lying. Get out of the way, Steve."

"Let's talk about this," Steve said calmly.

Peter shook his head and laughed. "Holy shit, she suckered you even after the witch thing. You're a wet rag, Bradley. Let me have her." Peter moved to Steve's side and Jeneil slipped out from the other. "Slippery snake," Peter called, charging for her and grabbing her around the waist. Steve watched, totally amazed at the craziness. Jeneil tried to ninja Peter but couldn't budge him. "It's over now, bitch." He held her, out of breath. "I know karate, too." She wiggled wildly causing him to lose balance, sending him to the floor. He held on to her tightly, bringing her down. "Give it up, bitch. You're mine now." He held her legs in a scissor hold and moved her to the bottom. Steve watched, staring in disbelief. Peter leaned over her, holding her arms down as she struggled. "Help me with payback, Steve. Go get a tall glass of very cold water. I'll keep the snake still."

Steve looked at Jeneil. "You were lying," he said, realizing her game.

"Sure she was." Peter grinned. "Go get the water."

"Gladly," Steve answered, heading for the kitchen. Jeneil struggled wildly to be free but Peter held her down.

"Oh, Peter," she gasped, "you're hurting me. I can't breathe. Get up! Get up!" she said, breathless. Steve knelt next to them, holding the water as she gasped for air.

"Pete, she can't breathe," Steve said, concerned.

"She's faking again, Steve. Don't listen to her. Hit her with the water. Come on!" Peter said, and Jeneil went limp. "Steve, move it! Come on!"

"Pete, she's hurt," Steve said, watching her face.

"No, she's not, Steve. She's messing with your sympathy again."

"Pete, she's limp. Get off her!"

"Steve, I'd know if I was hurting her, wouldn't I? Use your head, she's faking it."

"Pete, get off her damn it!" Steve pushed him.

"Oh shit, you'll never learn. Okay, I'll get off." Peter raised his body, moving but holding her legs. Jeneil opened her eyes quickly and seeing the glass of water, she pushed it, spilling it over Steve. Struggling to be free, Peter grabbed her arms and eased his body back over hers, pinning her down again. He looked at Steve. "Need more proof?"

"You bitchin' spitfire," Steve said, pulling at his wet shirt. "I'll get more water Pete, with ice cubes this time. Hold her, but good. I don't care if she turns blue now. She's had it." He got up and went to the kitchen.

Jeneil looked at Peter. "You won't put ice cubes on me, will you? I don't like being cold. Please, I deserve the water, even two glasses, but no ice cubes. I'm sorry, honey. It started out as fun," she purred.

Peter looked at her. "You little sneak, there's no end to your tricks." He grinned. "But I like this. Purr some more, sweetheart."

She kissed his ear gently. "I love you, Chang." She smoothed her mouth over his face seductively. "Kiss me, Peter," she whispered. He held her arms tightly and turned his head to kiss her. She responded passionately.

He moved his head to be free of her lips. He smiled, looking at her. "You're dangerous."

"I love the way you kiss." She grinned, and Peter felt her move gently beneath him.

He stared into her eyes and smiled. "You have absolutely no conscience at all."

"Not when it comes to you. I love you." She kissed his neck, snuggling to him as best she could. "Kiss me again," she whispered, and he smiled and slowly put his lips to hers. She responded powerfully with what he had come to call her killer kiss. It always did him in. He let go of her arms. She wrapped them around him and rubbed his back, continuing to kiss him. Steve returned and stopped short as he saw them kissing. He cleared his throat.

Peter looked up. "I think we'll cancel the ice cubes, Steve."

"Why not, they'd probably turn to steam anyway." He started backing away. "I'll just put the glass back and leave quietly."

"Don't go," Jeneil called. "We're just sharing a moment. I put dinner on earlier."

"Yeah," Peter agreed, "stay."

"I'll just put this back then." Steve pointed to the glass of water, turned and walked into the kitchen. Staring at the kitchen sink, he sipped the water absentmindedly. A moment, he thought, what the hell was the real thing like then? He sighed. "Sweetheart, you are total wildfire." Pouring the water and ice cubes into the sink, he put his head back. "Oh Jeneil, I didn't find you because of the damned White Stallion." He sighed again. "You need the triad. Get rid of it, Bradley. We need the triad."

Thirty-Seven

Jeneil was right about the gossip at the hospital; the nurse they had run into at the museum was savoring her gossip about Steve and Peter. Word was their girlfriends got along together and that they were into cultural things because they had been at a museum. Jeneil giggled when she heard that, finding it funny that a love of geodes constituted culture. The women at the hospital were surprised by Steve's choice; a girl who was styled to the teeth yet he had always seemed interested in down to earth types. It made them wonder what type Peter's girlfriend was. But the gossip that interested Jeneil the most was that Steve's birthday was coming up.

Peter joined Steve at a table in the cafeteria and watched as Steve swirled his fork around in his mashed potatoes. Peter noted Steve had been quiet every time he had run into him lately. Opening his lunch, Peter tossed a bag of grapes to Steve.

"Hey, real food." Steve sighed and broke one off, holding it in his hand.

Peter looked at Steve. "Tell me about it."

"What?" Steve asked.

"What's eating you?"

"It's party time."

"I don't know what that means." Peter took a bite of his sandwich.

"Sprague and his associates want to look me over socially."

"So." Peter shrugged.

"Everybody's two by two. Damn that Morgan Rand. He and Sondra set their wedding date, and George Tashe is married. Geez is he married, his wife is a baby machine."

"And you're the lone wolf, huh."

Steve nodded "How many excuses can I make for my missing girl?"

"Bring your girl." Peter handed Steve two cookies. "The one the hospital thinks is yours."

"Sienna!" Steve put his head back. "Aw Pete, she's not my type."

"I didn't tell you to marry her, just bring her to the parties."

"Besides, I don't think I'm on her list of favorites after what I did to her."

"So apologize. Who else can you get, Steve?"

"Nobody." Steve sighed. "I was thinking of a dating service until the gossip hit on Sienna. I don't want to break up with my girl story until I have the key to the practice in the palm of my hand."

"Well, you said that you'd start dating librarians. Sienna was a librarian."

"She was?"

Peter nodded. "She and Jeneil worked in a library together"

Steve shook his head, looking doubtful. "But she can't be wildfire. Don't mess the hair, be careful of her fake nails, and those green eyes can't be real."

"What do you want; to take her to a party or to bed?"

Steve pushed at some mushy carrots. "It's the twentieth century. I think both are expected."

Peter chuckled. "I would never have guessed that the Steve Bradley I ran into at med school would ever be dealing with this problem."

Steve grinned. "Well let me tell you it shits and as soon as the key is securely in my hand, I start living. Watch me. I'll do it my way."

"My way?"

"Yeah, super secret."

Peter laughed. "I happen to think the secrecy shits. I want a normal life. I'm ready for it. Or I think I am until I compare myself to Jeneil."

Steve chuckled. "Normal? Then you're marrying the wrong girl. She can't even spell it."

Peter smiled and nodded. "She may not be normal but she's getting fierier."

"Then screw normal, Pete."

"Hey, aren't you the one trying to fit into your own medical group, Dr. Bradley," Peter teased.

Steve laughed. "I'd tell Morgan Rand and his normal to go to hell if I could have Jeneil." Steve choked as he heard himself say it. "I mean somebody like her," he clarified.

Peter smiled. "I know what you meant, and I don't want Jeneil to change. I want our life to change. Call Sienna, Steve."

Steve exhaled. "Get the number from Jeneil," he said, with resignation.

"She's at the Waller Bookstore in Highland Mall. Go overwhelm her with your good looks. Take her to lunch. Warm up to the idea at least."

Steve sighed. "I know you're right, but I'll need time to warm up to the whole thing. Are you scheduled for ER?"

"No, I'm on Five."

"Okay, I'll run into you somewhere then."

*****

Peter walked in carefully carrying a white paper bag. He had stopped to pick up two sundaes. He had known he was in trouble when he approached the apartment door and heard the voices. The only face familiar to him was Dennis. The two other men were strangers. Jeneil came to Peter, smiling. "What's in the bag?" she whispered.

"Strawberry sundaes," he whispered in return. She made a face of disappointment then smiled broadly.

"Take them to the bedroom in a minute and I'll meet you there." She winked, put the bag on the small table, and took him over to the group of men.

"Hi, Peter." Dennis smiled.

Peter nodded. "Dennis, how's it going?"

"Fairly well really."

Jeneil slipped her arm through Peter's. "Peter, I'd like you to meet Phil Rokowski and Marty Fienberg. They're from The Rep."

"Hi." Peter smiled. The blonde haired Phil smiled back.

"Hey, Peter. Good to meet you. Jeneil's been telling me about her man. I'm disappointed," Phil commented to which Peter wrinkled his brow. "I expected a beard, white robes, and a staff. Do you really walk on water?"

Marty was standing near Peter and extended his hand. "Nice meeting you, Peter, hope you don't mind the intrusion."

"No problem," Peter assured him.

Jeneil smiled at Peter and squeezed his arm. "If you men will excuse him though, I think he's earned some relaxation. He had early surgery today."

Phil smiled. "You're a hero, Peter. I'd need therapy if I attempted a career as a surgeon. Go take your rest."

"Thanks for letting me borrow Jeneil," Dennis said, smiling.

"It's okay," Peter replied. "Why don't you get back to work?" He kissed Jeneil's cheek and left, taking the bag with him to the bedroom. He sprawled across the bed and stretched, hearing his spine snap. Jeneil joined him a few minutes later.

"Are they all mushy yet?" She smiled broadly as she opened the bag. He put his arms around her, bringing her to the bed.

"How'd you explain being in here?"

"I gave them coffee and sandwich fixings then told them I'd take my break with you." She grinned as he kissed her warmly. "Well then, that was a special kiss."

"For a special girl." He smiled. "Phil's coming onto you, huh?"

She looked surprised as she stared at him. "How'd you know?"

Peter smiled and touched her check gently. "Why else would you be singing my praises?"

"You're clever, my precious love, very clever."

"Can you handle it, honey?"

"Piece of cake," and she snapped her fingers.

He smiled. "Learning all the ropes, huh?"

"It's easy when I say I belong to you." She smiled as he kissed her cheek then handed him a sundae. "Mmmm, good," she said, sitting back on the bed. "But I'm awfully suspicious of ice cream that doesn't melt."

"Don't look, just eat. Life's easier that way," he said, and she smiled and kissed his cheek.

"Ooo, do I have some news for you," she squealed with delight. "Sienna called me. Steve stopped by the bookstore. There's gonna be some datin' going on. How 'bout them apples, Jaspa."

Peter was surprised. He had asked, but Steve hadn't stopped to see her yet so Peter figured the idea was a zero. "Very interesting."

"Isn't it though? And you're trying to make me believe that you didn't know." Jeneil nuzzled his shoulder.

"I didn't know he'd gone there. I knew he was thinking about it."

"And you didn't tell me. Some lover you are."

Peter choked on a laugh. "What the hell does not telling you have to do with us in bed?"

"Well, I'm not good enough to get you to tell me everything when we're in bed."

Peter chuckled. "When we're in bed, honey, I'm not thinking about Sienna and Steve. Trust me." She kissed his shoulder. "When did she call you?"

"Today."

"Geez, did she let him get out the door before she told you."

"Well, she was shocked. I can understand that. He went from ice cold to dating."

"Honey, don't coach her. Don't even get involved with it, okay?"

She studied his face, curious about the remark. "What aren't you telling me?"

"Nothing, just let them live through it. It's not fair to Steve if you drop all the inside info you know about him in her lap."

"Speaking of which," Jeneil put the plastic ice cream cup on the floor, "the scuttlebutt at work is that Sienna is more high-styled than Steve usually goes for, but wasn't he totally bonkers over someone with high style? The girl he fell in love with. Marcia, wasn't it?"

Peter nodded. "I think that's why he avoids the type."

"Uh-uh, past tense now, looks like Sienna broke through the barrier. Good for her. She likes him a lot."

Peter sighed. "Honey, he's not looking to settle down yet. Be careful. I mean it. There are parties the medical group is holding for their new associates."

"Oh my gosh! He's not using her, is he?"

"Jeneil, he needs a date for the parties. Is it insulting that he asked her?"

She sighed. "No. No, not really. Besides, who knows what Sienna can achieve with even the flimsiest of opportunities. I'm not discouraged yet."

Peter shook his head. "I think you were Cupid in another life."

"I love romance." She put her arms around his neck.

"Just confine yourself to ours. Leave theirs alone, okay?"

"Okay, you're right. I'm out of it. I promise."

He smiled. "Thanks."

"And now I'd better get back to work. When I knew the guys were coming here tonight, I got a spy versus spy versus spy video for you."

"You're okay, kid, even lopsided."

She smiled. "Love ya, Chang"

"Keep telling Phil that."

Jeneil grinned and went to the door, threw him a kiss and left.

*****

Peter saw Steve at the medical charts as he got off the elevator.

"Well, what's new?" Peter asked, grinning.

"Not much." Steve read the first sheet on a chart, checked it against a previous one then returned it to its slot.

"Not much? What's the story on Sienna?"

"Why do I get the feeling you already know I stopped at the bookstore?"

Peter grinned. "I was only asking."

"Sure you were. What did she do, call Jeneil?"

"Why didn't you tell me?"

Steve chuckled. "Because I wanted to see if she'd call Jeneil."

"What if she did?"

"Would you like it, Peter?"

"Jeneil's staying out of it, and she thinks Sienna only called because she was shocked."

"Oh, she was that all right." Steve grinned.

"When are you going out?"

"We went to lunch."

"That's it?"

"She reminds me of Marcia."

"Is that good or bad?"

"It's not good. I keep wishing the real her would introduce herself."

Peter laughed. "Well, date her long enough and maybe you'll find Shawna."

"Who's Shawna?"

"Sienna before finding a stylist."

Steve stared blankly. "You mean even her name is fake? What else is fake? Oh shit, I sure hope her name wasn't Shawn before it was Shawna." He laughed. "Because damn, that's been my kind of luck lately."

Peter laughed, leaning against the chart bin. He sighed from laughing. "Give her a chance. Jeneil likes her. Maybe she'll grow on you."

"Yeah, so could warts," Steve mumbled.

"Eh, you're never satisfied. The girl isn't bad looking. She's got style."

Steve looked up. "Do you hand out bibles with your preachin', Reverend Chang?"

Peter laughed, realizing Steve was not going to budge from his bad mood. "Bye, Steve. Catch you for lunch. The kid sent one for you."

Steve smiled. "Love that kid."

Peter punched Steve's arm lightly, smiled, and headed toward the East Wing.

*****

The youth center project had been approved by both the people Jeneil had gathered through Charlie and Adrienne, and the foundation board. Jeneil was happier than Peter had ever seen her about any project and had actually cried when Adrienne and Charlie brought her the results of the vote. After that they had people over for dinner often. Two representatives flew in from Nebraska and Jeneil provided a dinner meeting at a restaurant for them and all the people who had been at the first meeting at her apartment.

Peter admired Jeneil's skill with diplomacy, being careful to avoid insult or injury. He had been invited to the dinner and went only to be with Jeneil. They had spent little time together since the youth center project and her volunteer work at the playhouse were moving full throttle. He was glad the dinner was over; it marked the end of a hectic schedule for that area of her life now that the foundation would be monitoring the center. He had visited his family so often while Jeneil was involved in business that his mother was suspicious. He could tell by her questions; where's Jeneil, more business meetings, volunteer work for the play, have you seen her at all lately. He was anxious for his grandfather to return home. His mother had honored their agreement of not calling names but an iciness had developed. Peter visited as often as he could hoping to thaw the chill, but he had more confidence in his grandfather's ability. As Peter and Jeneil arrived home, he was surprised neither of them had spoken, both involved in their own thoughts.

Peter got under the covers, the sheets cold against his skin. The weather felt like snow even though Thanksgiving was a little more than a week away. He watched Jeneil brush her hair at the bureau. She shivered and rubbed her arms, feeling the chill in the air, too.

"I'll go turn the thermostat up," she said, walking out of the room.

Peter's phone rang and he answered. He replaced the receiver, sighing. The iciness in his mother's voice was still present even as she invited Jeneil to join the family for Thanksgiving. Peter was sure her icy demeanor had to do with Steve, especially after she snapped a clear 'no' to inviting him to Thanksgiving, too. Peter hadn't pushed it. Without his grandfather there to put out any flames an argument might start, he thought it best to ignore her hostile attitude. Peter was tired of it anyway. Her groundless accusations about Steve and Jeneil were becoming insulting. He knew her questions of Jeneil's absences had been her way of getting him to notice. Clearly she wondered if Jeneil was actually with Steve. Jeneil ran into the room and jumped into bed.

"I'm freezing." She snuggled against him. Peter groaned as the cool air followed her under the covers and cooled the body heat he had generated while waiting for her. "Warm me up quickly, please." She shivered. "I hate being cold. Who was on the phone? If it was the hospital, you call and tell them you have to deal with a frostbite victim first and then you'll be in." She pressed against him, hugging him to absorb any heat available.

He smiled and held her. "Winter's here."

"Not until December twenty-first," Jeneil chattered. "This is just a pre-arrival notice. We'll have a cold snap and then a few warm days just before Thanksgiving. Always the way it's been since I can remember."

Peter squeezed her gently. "The call was my mother inviting us to Thanksgiving dinner."

Jeneil lifted her head quickly. "Fantastic!" She was thrilled; Peter saw it. She hugged him, squealing softly with delight. "A real Thanksgiving with a house full of people. I can't wait! What do you have for dinner?"

"Turkey."

"With all the traditional dishes?" she asked, smiling.

"Well, did you expect bamboo shoots and bean sprouts?"

She kissed him. "That would be fine, too. Ooo, this is going to be great, really great."

"Will your uncle mind if you don't go home?"

"I haven't gone home for Thanksgiving since Mandra died."

Peter was surprised. "Then what did you do?"

"I usually went to the center that prepares food for the needy and elderly who are alone."

"You ate with the homeless?"

"There was no time to eat. I worked in the kitchen. We usually had tuna or egg salad sandwiches that we ate while we worked. We wanted the feast to go as far as possible."

He stared at her. "But why? I'm sure Hollis invited you."

"Sure he did, and don't you ever tell him that I spent my holidays at a food kitchen. Thanksgiving is special to me. It gets me ready for Christmas. Working in the kitchen and serving those people was more like home to me. I had something in common with them. I was alone, too. Being there, I felt like part of a family."

"And really needy too, right?" Peter teased.

She thought for a second. "Yes, I really was. I was in need of giving so I wouldn't feel sorry for myself." He kissed her forehead gently, sorry for teasing her after hearing her answer. "I'd get home so tired that I'd eat my dinner quickly, go to bed and sleep soundly. But I outright lied to Uncle Hollis and told him that friends invited me." She chuckled. "Well they did in a sense, they asked if I could help cook."

"Does that mean you won't go to my mother's?"

"Of course I'll go to your mother's. Are you serious? I can't wait to meet your family." She squealed with delight again. Peter relaxed not knowing how he would have explained to his mother if Jeneil hadn't shown up. Her excitement gave him hope. "But I think I'll send some vegetables to the center. I can prepare them here and take them over in the morning. It might even be better to have three cooked turkeys delivered ready for serving. That could be my contribution. Last year food started to get scarce because so many people showed up. We suspected not all of them were needy but for whatever reason they wanted to be with the group. I think that's enough to justify being there. Don't you?"

He smiled and kissed her lips, and held her close. "Sure."

She was silent for a few minutes. "Peter, what about Steve? Did your mother invite him, too? She does sometimes, doesn't she?"

Peter felt his throat tighten. "We'll see what the hospital schedule is first. I asked for the day off hoping I'd be bringing you to meet my family." She lifted her head and looked at him with a pleased expression.

"What am I worried about." She rested her head back down with a laugh. "He's been seeing so much of Sienna lately that he's probably going to her house for the holiday, too. Mmm, mmm, I think Stevie's making a nest for himself. His birthday's this Sunday, what are we going to do for him? We've seen so little of him lately since he's been with Sienna. I bought some gifts for him from us."

"How do you know that?" Peter interrupted.

"Know what?"

"How do you know that he's been with Sienna?"

"She told me."

"Jeneil, I thought you were staying out of that."

"Peter, that's all she told me when she invited me to lunch this week. We never talked about him. She apologized for not calling me sooner about lunch and said that she and Steve were having lunch together often since he was on second shift last week. Is there something wrong with that?" She noticed he was silent. "Peter, what's wrong."

"Nothing."

"I can't accept that answer." She looked at him with a fixed stare.

Peter sighed. "Honey, he's not serious about her. You're talking about nesting. He's not. Now lay off him."

Jeneil leaned on her elbow. "Wait just a minute here. I'm hearing a double standard in that answer. And I want you to know that I am not laying on him. I have never mentioned Sienna to Steve. I barely see him lately, but obviously you and he have discussed Sienna. Why are you allowed and I'm not?"

"We don't discuss her. I just asked about her once."

"And?"

"And nothing."

"What does nothing mean?"

"Nothing means I don't know. Once he said that she reminds him of Marcia." Jeneil smiled, encouraged. "Honey, that's not good news. Marcia hurt him, remember?"

"But Sienna isn't Marcia."

"Baby, lay off it, okay?"

Jeneil stared at him. "Good grief. It can't be that bad for him to be with her or he wouldn't see her so often, don't you think?"

"Jeneil."

"What?"

"Shut up," Peter said tenderly then smiled.

"Make me shut up."

"Should I introduce myself first?"

"Ooo, was that a remark about my schedule lately and how little time we've had together?"

"Well, at least you noticed." He grinned.

She touched his face lovingly. "Peter."

"What?"

"Shut up." She smiled.

He pulled her closer to him and kissed her, enjoying the warmth of her body.

*****

Jeneil pushed the elevator button marked down and waited. A woman joined her, wiping away tears with a handkerchief. Jeneil turned away to allow some privacy. She hated the sadness of hospitals. It was good that she worked with records; the tragedies of the hospital would be too much for her. She knew that about herself. The elevator door opened and she was surprised to see Steve inside. The woman got in ahead of her. Standing near the woman, Jeneil held her purse to her not speaking to Steve, which was their understanding. When others were around, they never spoke to each other as friends. She wished she could talk to him; she wanted to ask about his birthday. Peter was so preoccupied lately and kept forgetting to ask.

Steve leaned against the back of the elevator, watching Jeneil. She seemed more dressed up than usual and he loved her in that suit. Her hair looked soft and small wisps fell gently behind her ear. At the hospital, she was known for legs and long hair that interns wanted to get wrapped up in. Steve looked at both and smiled understandingly. But it was her ears that drove him crazy, which was a total shock to him. He had never noticed her ears before. He looked at the gold earring clipped on each lobe. He missed her. He missed her more than he knew he should. Closing his eyes, he put his head down and took a deep breath, exhaling slowly. The elevator stopped and the woman stepped off, leaving Steve and Jeneil alone. As the door closed, Jeneil turned to Steve and was surprised by his expression. He looked sad. Her smile faded.

"Steve, is something wrong?"

"No, why?" he asked with almost no inflection.

Jeneil shrugged, not knowing how to answer. "You seem a little down."

He shook his head. "Just a little tired." His lack of enthusiasm confused her.

"Do you remember me? We used to be friends two weeks ago. The name's Jeneil."

He smiled. He really missed her and her crazy humor. "Oh yeah, now I remember you. Where are you heading all decked up?"

"Lunch with a friend," she answered, and wondered why she didn't tell him it was Sienna. She was annoyed with herself. Peter had her touchy. "We have some birthday gifts for you. Can you come to dinner with us? We'd like to celebrate with you. There's a very good French restaurant in Boston called Jeaneau's. We'd like to treat you to a special dinner. We miss you."

He looked at her. "I talk to Peter every day."

"Okay, I miss you. Gosh, picky, picky, aren't we?"

He smiled. Her words felt good and her enthusiasm began to fill him. "I'd like that. I've missed you guys, too. But your pot roast dinner would be just fine with me."

"No," she insisted, "we're doing this up big. You'll even need to wear one of your new suits. Champagne, candles. All of it." She smiled. "I'm in the mood for a fancy night out at a splashy restaurant, so don't ruin my fun."

He watched her as she made her sales pitch. He loved the way she twisted everything to make it sound like you were doing her a favor. He could tell she was excited about her plans. Her eyes danced with excitement. He felt his heart pound and a surge of electricity filled his chest and spread through him. Noticing her coat over her arm, he reached for it. "Here, put your coat on. It isn't summer anymore."

"Don't remind me." She sighed and turned to allow him to help her with it. He could smell her perfume lightly scenting her coat as he fixed the back of her collar. She was so incredibly soft and warm. His heart skipped. She turned to face him as she did the buttons. "You can invite Sienna or anyone you'd like."

"Jeneil, could it be just the three of us? It'd be nice to be the triad for an evening." She studied his eyes, hoping to understand. She didn't dare ask why; Peter would be angry.

"Well, okay. It is your birthday so it's your choice, I guess."

"Thanks." He smiled and kissed her cheek gently. "You're a shot in the arm, kid. I wish you were twins."

"Why? Double trouble?" She laughed. The doors opened and she stepped off. He didn't answer her question and followed her off the elevator.

Peter was waiting and was surprised to see Jeneil and Steve step off the elevator. Jeneil looked around. The corridors were empty. "Peter, look what I found in the elevator, the missing piece to the triad. Birthday dinner Saturday night at Jeaneau's okay?"

Peter smiled, watching her back away. "You look great."

She bowed regally then stood up quickly remembering where she was. She scanned the corridors again, then looking at Peter, she pointed to her lips then to her cheek. He grinned as she turned away, walking quickly toward the exit.

"What did she just do?" Steve asked.

Peter smiled. "She said pretend I've kissed your cheek because I want to."

Steve smiled. "She's cute as hell."

"Yeah, she is." Peter handed Steve a lunch bag as they walked toward the cafeteria. "And I don't know what I'd do to anybody who tried to mess with her now."

Steve looked at him. "Whoa, she brings out the streets in you."

"Damn right," Peter admitted. "She's the force that keeps me breathing. Chang has claimed ownership. She belongs to him."

"Any man who's ever had a woman purring for him like she does would acquit you of murder."

Peter looked at him and smiled. "I'm glad she got to you about your birthday. I was supposed to ask you. Sorry about that."

"It's okay. It sounds great. She's got me looking forward to it," Steve answered, and Peter held the door to the cafeteria as they walked in.

*****

Jeneil poured French dressing on her salad. Sienna watched. Jeneil looked up and smiled. "Someday I'm going to be able to eat and not worry about a diet. I think it's due me. This is my hungry week." She chuckled, and Sienna grinned and watched her steadily. "Well what's new in your life? Is business picking up for Christmas yet?" Jeneil continued, cutting some lettuce leaves and wondering about Sienna's silence.

Sienna sipped her water. "Jeneil, I asked you to lunch to talk about Steve."

The half of a cherry tomato slipped down Jeneil's throat having been chewed only once. She cleared her throat. "Sienna, please don't put me in the middle," Jeneil answered quickly. Sienna studied Jeneil's face intently, making Jeneil uncomfortable. "Sienna, did I hurt you by saying that?"

"No." Sienna shook her head. "I'm just very puzzled, that's all."

Jeneil rested her forehead on her hand and sighed. "I hope I don't live to regret this but here goes. What's wrong?"

Sienna fidgeted. "You did say there was no one in Steve's life now. Is that still true?"

"Yes," Jeneil answered, curious. Sienna sighed and put her head down, disappointed. Jeneil couldn't stand it. "What's the matter?" Sienna looked up. Jeneil was stunned by the look of anger in Sienna's eyes. "What's the matter?"

The look of anger disappeared as Sienna composed herself. "Jeneil, there is someone in Steve's life."

"There can't be."

Sienna looked at Jeneil steadily then smiled slowly. "You don't know about it then?"

"Sienna, there is no one else in Steve's life. I would know about it. Are you working through a jealousy thing? That won't help you at all, especially if you imagine it. That's very damaging."

"Jeneil, all the signs are there. He doesn't touch me."

"Touch you?" Jeneil was becoming uncomfortable; she hadn't counted on getting this deeply involved. The thought of Peter's anger if he knew surfaced in her mind, and she really didn't want to talk about Steve's sex life with anyone.

"Sometimes I kiss him," Sienna continued. Jeneil fidgeted.

"Sienna, I'm not the best one to ask about this. I don't understand relationships at all. I don't know what you mean when you say you kiss him. Doesn't he respond?" Jeneil gasped silently, shocked she had asked.

"Casually, Jeneil. He's holding back, I know it."

"Well, I know he isn't ready to settle."

Sienna wrinkled her eyebrows then smiled broadly. "Jeneil, I'm not talking marriage. I'm talking about being intimate."

"Well, have you asked him about all this?" Jeneil felt very uncomfortable.

"He dodges, Jeneil. He's so slick. He's one of the shrewdest guys I've ever dated, and the most frustrating. I've tried everything I know of. Don't you think it's odd that we've seen each other so much and we're not even kissing seriously?"

"Sienna, honestly I don't know. I'm sorry to be so dense about all this, but I don't know."

"Well I do, Jeneil. There's another woman in his life." Sienna stared straight at Jeneil. "Someone he can't have."

Jeneil stared as the words struck her. "Oh my gosh."

Sienna settled back. "Light bulb turn on?"

Jeneil nodded. "Yes, poor Steve. If you're right, Sienna, then he's been hurt worse than I thought."

"What do you mean?" Sienna sat forward. "Hurt how?"

"He was totally in love with a girl once awhile back. For whatever reasons, she ended the relationship. You're closer to her type than he's dated in years. Is it possible that you're competing with her memory? I know he was crushed. Maybe he's holding back because he's working through mixed feelings about you and a relationship because of her."

Sienna sighed and covered her mouth then put her head back and laughed. Jeneil saw Shawna for an instant then Sienna returned. "Thank you, Jeneil. Thank you. I'm so glad I was wrong."

"About what?"

"Jeneil, when I added everything up in my mind, it totaled up to you."

Jeneil sat back like she had been slapped in the face. "Why? How? What made you even think that?"

"The questions he's asked about you?"

"Questions?"

"Yes, about us working together."

"But I'm the common bond with you two. Isn't it natural he'd start there? Does he still ask questions about me?"

"Well, no."

Jeneil sighed. "Sienna that is pretty flimsy evidence."

"But not having any other avenues and his hovering and defending you. It's understandable, isn't it?"

"I told you the day you met him about our friendship."

"It looked like more to me, Jeneil. I'm sorry."

Jeneil laughed. "Poor Steve, I think he's destined to be misinterpreted. He's forever getting done in on how things look."

"I don't understand."

"It's too long a story." Jeneil laughed again. "Tell me, Sienna, what would you have done if I hadn't known about the other girl? Beat me with a breadstick thinking I was in your way?"

Sienna laughed. "I'm sorry, Jeneil. This is embarrassing but I'm so confused and frustrated. I was planning to ask you to step out of the picture. After all, Peter and Steve both? That's hardly fair to be granted to one girl."

Jeneil smiled. "No need to worry about me. I belong to Peter and I'm not Steve's type. We could barely stand each other a few months ago."

"Jeneil thank you for taking this so well. Please don't tell Steve or Peter. I'd die, I think. It's so dumb but I feel better that I asked. I guess I just need to be more patient with him."

Jeneil shook her head. "I'm hardly the one to be giving advice on relationships, but I think I agree with you. And knowing Steve, you'll have to wait for him to make the move. He's pretty traditional in his attitude toward woman."

"What do you mean?"

"I am man, you are woman. That's as complicated as he gets."

"Gosh, how sexy." Sienna wriggled in her seat. Jeneil looked at her and smiled.

"Is that what it is? Sexy is knowing you're a man or a woman. I mean really knowing it and you function from that point. Well, that would make why everything is physical more understandable."

Sienna shook her head, puzzled. "What are you talking about?"

"My eccentricities." Jeneil smiled. "We'd better finish lunch. Our jobs are looking over our shoulders."

"Thanks again, Jeneil. I mean that."

"It's okay. I really want to see Steve happily married. He deserves it, and if you and he can be happily married together then that's doubly great."

Thirty-Eight

Peter sat staring at the sandwich he had made for dinner. He hated when Jeneil was gone. She had flown to Nebraska after a problem arose with paperwork on the youth center. The community had been discouraged and suspicious so in a show of good faith, and in an effort to assure them it was an honest mistake, she had invited Jake to go with her. Charlie had stopped by to let Peter know how well the idea had worked. Jeneil was working hard for the youth center and Peter had come to realize her devotion to the project was tied to her love for Mandra. He sat thinking about that as he ate. Jeneil worked hard as if she had to report to Mandra herself. He understood even though he missed her a lot. This was supposed to be their Friday night together. She had warned him all week to prepare for a soul session but then the call came about the oversight. She had dropped everything and focused her attention on that. Now he was worried about the weather and their plans. Since she had left, weather reports from across the country had caught his attention. His telephone rang, surprising him from his thoughts.

"Grandfather?"

"Peter, I'm back and I need a ride."

"I thought you were coming in tomorrow?"

"We finished sooner than expected. We were all homesick and decided to leave early. So here I am."

Peter laughed. "You're homesick? Grandfather, you were born in China."

His grandfather chuckled. "I'm an American, Peter. I knew that when I stepped off the plane in Boston today. It's more than a certificate that tells me I'm a citizen."

Peter was surprised. "That's good, Grandfather. I've never thought about my feelings for my country."

"It was given to you. I had to choose for myself. Can you pick me up at the bus station downtown?"

"Sure. I'll be right there."

"Boy, I'm glad you were home. I guess with everyone expecting me tomorrow, no one's home today. I'll wait out front."

"No, wait inside. It's cold. I'll come inside for you."

Peter made record time to the bus station. He was surprised he had missed his grandfather so much. Pushing the glass door open, he scanned the benches. He caught sight of his grandfather sitting on a chair reading. "Taxi's here, sir."

His grandfather looked up. Standing, he put his arms around Peter and held him. The show of emotion shocked Peter but he joined in on the moment and returned the hug. "Peter, I'm very proud of you. I thought of you often in China. With the memories of our ancestors, I couldn't help but think of the future. You are the future, Peter, the future of the Chang family. You're going to be a fine patriarch."

"Patriarch? I'm still struggling with surgeon." Peter smiled, embarrassed but very deeply touched, knowing the honor his grandfather attached to that title.

"Where's Jeneil? I've missed her, too," the grandfather said, looking around.

"She's in Nebraska until tomorrow." Peter smiled, enjoying his grandfather's words.

Peter made tea while his grandfather unpacked some of his things, and then they went to the greenhouse to sit and visit. "Tell me what's happening?" his grandfather asked, settling back in his chair and stirring the steaming tea to cool it.

Peter leaned against the arm of the bench and rested his ankle on his knee. "Well, Rick has added more color to his wardrobe. He wears white once a week."

The old man smiled. "Does he say why?"

Peter grinned. "I think he's doing it for affect. It's called making a statement, I think."

The grandfather sipped his tea. "Someday he'll concentrate less on the affect and more on the statement."

"Ugh, he's okay, just young." Peter slouched, changing ankles. "Ron and Sue set their wedding date for mid January." The grandfather sighed. "What are you worried about?"

"Ron and Sue," the old man answered quietly.

"What's wrong with them?"

"I'd like to see more life between them that's all. I'd be happier if they had more of what you and Jeneil have."

"At least they're getting married," Peter said, leaning forward, staring at the floor.

"Are you worried?" his grandfather asked, noticing the tone in Peter's voice.

"Not worried really. But something deep inside of me wants to marry Jeneil now."

"Does she know that?"

Peter shook his head. "I promised not to push. She's not ready, but she doesn't know why. It's a feeling with her. She has a clock she goes by and the timing has to be right or she won't budge. I should have her see a doctor; she gets more lopsided every day."

"What do you mean lopsided?"

"Off-center; different from when I met her."

"And you think it's medical?"

"I don't know. In a lot of ways, she's like Rick."

"But Rick's trying to find himself."

Peter looked up. "So is Jeneil. That's why she wants to wait a while longer."

"Isn't that strange for her age?"

Peter smiled. "She knows it's adolescent. That's the frustrating part. She sees it all. It's like she's teaching herself to grow up, like she's the mother and the child. She's working through something."

"Would marriage get in the way?"

"She thinks so and in a way I know what she means. I had a hard time shaking off Chang when I went into med school but having gotten this far I can see that becoming a doctor has changed Chang. In some ways, it dictated what I've become. Jeneil doesn't want that. She's trying to work out who she is without more titles and claims on her."

The grandfather smiled. "You're gentle with her, like she's a wounded bird."

"She is, Grandfather. She's very fragile, sensitive, and struggling to know Jeneil."

"I like that in you, Peter. I thought she was carrying the relationship but you have your strengths, too. That's good because eventually you've got to take full control; the songbird will need it."

"I'm not in a position to take full control. You're right; she's carrying me in this relationship. I just wish she was mine."

"Whose is she?" the grandfather asked, surprised.

Peter thought for a minute. "Hers, she belongs to her. That's exactly what's happening." He savored the revelation. "When I met her, she was fragile like an injured bird. She clung to me like I was life itself. Now she's emerging into another stage and she needs me less. She clings less. My songbird is independent, Grandfather. She's flying farther and farther from our cage."

"All the more reason to watch her more carefully."

"You said that you can't close the cage on a songbird."

"No, you can't, but you can take control. She'll need you to be responsible. It's a survival thing with songbirds. You've got to learn fast. She's moving quickly."

"Learn what?"

"About yourself, your songbird, and survival. She's loyal, Peter. A true songbird is."

"I'm lost." Peter shook his head. "I just want us to get married. I like life simple."

"That's not the whole answer. Do you know there are birds that will survive their owners and when you buy one you have to provide for it in a will? It needs the protection. The songbird is like that. It needs looking after because it will extend itself in a very wide circle. You'll see. What does the family think of her?"

"They'll meet her on Thanksgiving." Peter rubbed his forehead. "Grandfather, I'm glad you're home. My mother is slipping backwards about Jeneil." He paused. "About Jeneil and Steve."

"How did that happen?"

"I don't know. I just noticed it when I visited a few times."

The grandfather sighed. "Karen and John."

"What about them?"

"John pushes Karen to get even any way he can. For some reason, Karen isn't fond of Jeneil. John knows it and praises Jeneil to annoy Karen. She in turn tears down Jeneil. She's got a temper."

"What would that have to do with my mother?"

"Nothing unless she was looking for reasons to dislike Jeneil and Karen was providing those reasons."

"You mean more than just Steve?" Peter asked. The old man nodded and Peter sighed. "Great and I thought my mother had accepted Jeneil."

"Don't get discouraged. Let's see what Jeneil can work out from all of it."

Peter exhaled. "Well, I hope it's good because my mother is tossing the whites stay with their own kind theory everywhere lately. And the name Steve brings fire into her eyes."

"It's that bad?"

Peter nodded. "She was furious when I asked if he could come to Thanksgiving dinner, too. She does a slow burn when I mention the three of us doing things together. I'm just glad you're home. You seem to keep her thinking clear, and Karen's just a snippy brat. She should get married and face reality. I just can't think of anyone I hate enough to see that happen to."

"She's difficult. That's certainly true. Losing her mother wasn't easy on her. Between you and Karen, I don't know how Tom and your mother's marriage lasted."

Peter stood up, annoyed. "Karen's a nothing. She doesn't scare me. My mother does. Jeneil is really excited about the holiday and meeting the family."

The grandfather smiled. "I'm anxious to see her, too. My trip to China was all from her. And I've been asked to stay with the International Arts League. I think I'd like that. They speak highly of her, Peter. She's well thought of. Her friend, Bill, loves her deeply."

Peter looked up quickly. "As a friend?"

"It's more than friendship, she's special to him. The respect he has for her when he talks about her impresses me. You've been given a woman who turns heads."

"Tell me about it," Peter mumbled.

"But that's a songbird, Peter. Their music is very pleasing."

*****

Peter pulled down the covers of the bed and smiled. Attached to his pillow was a cartoon drawing of a girl with a sad face holding drooping flowers. There was a note written beside her. *I'm sorry about all of this. You're too wonderful to be real. Thank you for understanding so often about so many things. I love you. Miss like crazy, Chang. I miss you already.* She had signed it with a lipstick-impression kiss.

"Oh he does, baby, he does," Peter said half aloud, tracing the kiss with his finger.

The telephone rang. "Peter, have I called at a bad time?"

"No, Mom, not at all."

"Oh good, I want to thank you for getting your grandfather tonight. What a surprise it was to see him."

"He looks great, doesn't he?"

"Yes, he does. We're having an open house tomorrow night, just coffee and dessert. Will you be able to be there?"

Peter closed his eyes. "Jeneil and I are taking Steve to dinner. It's his birthday."

Her silence rang through his head. "Where are you taking him?"

"Some place called Jeaneau's in Boston."

"Some place? Peter, that's a very nice French restaurant. You'll be spending a good amount of money or at least Jeneil will. You don't have a good amount of money to spend."

"Mom, please. She wants to."

"Of course, he's a good friend, very good I'd say to rate Jeaneau's."

Peter sighed. "Mother, I'm tired."

"Where's Jeneil?"

"In Nebraska on business."

"Peter, what kind of life does she lead? Meetings at night, flying to Nebraska, she seems so quiet and shy but she isn't. Can you stand that kind of marriage? You're always waiting for her."

"It's not always. Just these past two weeks. It's a special project."

"Well, I hope you know what you're doing."

"I do, Mom. I do."

"Where's Steve?"

Peter's neck tingled. "Let's see, it's Friday night. Oh, I remember. He's at a dinner party hosted by the medical group he's joining in February. That's right, he's there with Sienna. She's Jeneil's good friend. Jeneil introduced them a couple of weeks ago and go figure, Steve stops in at the girl's place of business and invites her to lunch. They've been seeing a lot of each other lately from what Jeneil's hearing from Sienna. We've barely seen Steve since they met." Peter rubbed his forehead to relieve the tension.

His mother was silent for a few seconds. "Are you sure?"

"It looks promising, Mom. I think you should stop worrying now," he said, hearing the shock in her voice.

"Well, I don't know what to say."

Peter grinned. "Nothing; say nothing at all."

"That's good to hear, Peter, really it is," she said, and he could sense her relief.

"I won't be able to stop by tomorrow, but I'll be by Sunday to see Grandfather."

"That's fine. Bring Jeneil, too. I haven't really seen her enough to talk to her. I'd like to before Thanksgiving."

Peter smiled. "I will, Mom."

"And thank you again for getting your grandfather, Peter. I'll see you Sunday."

Peter listened as the dial tone buzzed. He grinned and replaced the receiver. He could feel himself relaxing and he expected to sleep well. Looking at the note from Jeneil, he smiled. "I think I just killed a dragon for you, baby."

*****

Jeneil hurried from the shower, shaking her hair loose. The clock was winning the race. She sighed as she quickly browsed through the closet for an outfit. Deciding on her basic black, she undid the garment bag. The apartment door opened and Peter called for her.

"I'll be right out." She snapped the dress and headed for her brush. Peter opened the bedroom door.

"Hi, honey." He stopped and stared. "I love that dress on you. It's a killer." She smiled and went to him, letting her hair fall again. He welcomed her into his arms and held her close. "I missed you."

"I did, too." She kissed him several times and snuggled against him.

"Steve's changing into his suit in the bathroom. I'll get dressed."

Jeneil nodded then went back to the mirror and tying her hair. She double-checked the clasp on her bracelet, added a handkerchief to her purse then snapped it shut. Turning to Peter, she sighed. "I'm ready, I think. Here's the money," she added, handing him an envelope, "and don't worry, I can back it up with a credit card if we have to."

He looked at her. "Honey, should we?"

"Yes," she answered emphatically. "This is probably the first and last celebration as a triad for his birthday. Next year, he'll probably be married and his wife will want to handle it." She straightened his collar.

Peter smiled. "You're beautiful."

She touched his face lovingly. "Peter, I love you so much." Giving him a hug, she then turned and headed for the door.

Taking her hand, he kissed the palm of it. "Me, too."

Steve stood looking out the living room window. Jeneil noticed the cut of his new gray suit and it looked very nice on him. Hearing her footsteps, he turned and was stunned by her outfit. He'd never seen her in black. She looked less like a kid and very much like a woman, a sophisticated woman. He grinned. "Wow."

She smiled. "I think you look wow, too. The suit fits you nicely, and the tie and handkerchief. My goodness, Dr. Bradley, you do look like a successful professional."

"I still prefer jeans."

"And I prefer long casual dresses, but sometimes we need to get ourselves into high gear just to know that we're capable." She put her hands on his shoulders. "Happy Birthday," she said, touching her cheek to his. "I don't want to get lipstick on you. I thought we could come back here for cake and presents after dinner. By then my lipstick will have worn off and I can kiss your cheek." She hugged him again. "Gosh, I'm excited for you starting your career. I wish I was graduating into something instead of drifting. I feel ready."

"Maybe you're supposed to be a fairytale."

"What?" She laughed.

"Nice to listen to and not quite real, but the message is logical. It's a nice change of pace. You're cute." He looked at her. "No, you're beautiful, incredibly beautiful."

"Well, that makes my drifting easier. Thanks for the compliment."

"Thank you for this birthday."

Peter walked out of the bedroom, fixing his tie. "Oh geez, you two look natural all spruced up."

"Now Peter, don't complain. I love the blazer on you. It suits you, too."

"I miss my jeans."

Steve chuckled. "Me, too."

Jeneil held the blazer while Peter slipped it on. "Oh, you two are in for a culture shock when you begin practice."

"Do you feel any different, Steve?" Peter asked.

"Do you mean because I'm twenty-seven or almost into practice."

"Both."

Steve shrugged. "You know me; I take it one day at a time until it's all in my hands for a while."

Jeneil smiled. "Come on you two, I think we're ready to deal with escargot."

"What's that?" Peter asked.

"Snails," Jeneil answered.

He groaned. "Oh shit, honey. I'm ordering whatever comes closest to looking like a cheeseburger. To hell with snails, I mean it."

Steve laughed. "I've always liked that about you, Pete. Who cares what Rome is doing? You like life simple. Me, I feel compelled to swallow whatever we're supposed to. Stand your ground, Pete. Stand your ground."

"Don't encourage him, Steve." Jeneil laughed.

"He's an original, Jeneil, a rare breed."

The whole atmosphere of the restaurant spelled money, and the staff was trained to pamper and fuss unobtrusively. From the moment Steve walked in, he knew Jeneil had meant the night to be special and he was deeply touched. It was the most special thing anyone had ever done for his birthday. And that included the one where a girlfriend had wrapped herself in layers of gift wrap as a present. That was more of a joke, but in this he sensed Jeneil's sincere caring. She had made his probation easier with her fussing and he felt she cared about who he was and what he was doing.

Casually taking in the flowers, the candles, the good linen, the napkins and the real silverware, which only indicated to him her kind of caring, he knew she wanted him to feel special. He looked at her sitting across the table and the feelings he had been fighting accumulated within him and became one strong and solid word – love. He knew he was genuinely in love with her. He had known but had not wanted to admit it. It surpassed what he had ever felt for Marcia, and it confused him that he should be in love with her since their relationship wasn't physical at all, and it scared him to think how easily it could be for him. He looked down at his plate, glad to be nearing the end of his probation and residency. He had to leave the triad and get his own life going. He knew that and being in private practice would give him that chance. Jeneil looked at Steve and saw his sadness, which puzzled and concerned her.

Peter noticed Jeneil watching Steve and turned to look at him, too. "Steve, are you okay?" he asked, seeing his expression. Steve looked up quickly, emerging from his thoughts.

"Yes." He laughed lightly. "Just day dreaming. Comes with age I hear. I apologize."

Jeneil smiled. "I'm glad it's age and not the company."

He looked at her, embarrassed. "I'm sorry, really."

She wrinkled her nose at him. "It's okay. We know you're worried about leaving the carefree days of double shifts and emergency room duty for the hectic life of private practice."

"Oh, I envy you," Peter groaned.

Steve smiled. "You know, it's just suddenly here. In high school, I can remember the look my guidance counselor gave me when I told him I had decided to become a doctor. I thought of that look a lot while I was in college. It was a you'll-never-make-it expression and it's just what I needed to keep me going. Every time I wanted to dump it all, I remembered his smugness and I bit in harder."

Jeneil smiled warmly. "You're really fierce, aren't you?"

"Yeah, especially when somebody dumps on me but I can't really blame him. My grades were lousy. I was a sophomore. It wasn't the best time to decide to become a doctor. Boy, I walked into his office with my letter of acceptance to Downes and enjoyed watching his chin hit the desk."

Peter laughed. "Way to go, Steve."

Steve chuckled. "I put my head down my sophomore year in high school and I feel like I'm just looking up for the first time since I started the race. The end is here and it's real."

Jeneil shook her head and sighed. "We three are such oddities."

"We love you, too." Peter laughed.

"No, really," she added. "I was a straight A student in high school and my teachers loved me, my entrance exam score was impressive and I'm a college dropout. You both came from the weakest of beginnings to where you are. It's absolutely maddening. None of our high school counselors would believe where we are today. We three do not fit the bell-shaped pattern. We're not normal."

Peter and Steve looked at each other then back at her. "What do you mean we, paleface," they answered simultaneously and laughed.

She smiled at them. "If you two say that enough, I'm going to believe that I'm not eccentric." Peter squeezed her hand.

Steve smiled at her. "You're okay, kid. In a lot of ways, you've got guts. It isn't easy to be different and follow your own path when everybody is saying otherwise. I should know. I've spent my life working hard to blend in."

"You didn't at the hospital. You made headlines there," Jeneil commented.

"That was crazy. You know, Jeneil, I really have to thank you for rescuing me from all that."

"Are you rescued?" she asked. The waiter poured the champagne and quietly left.

"What do you mean?"

"I've wondered how you and Sienna are doing at the parties. With everyone thinking she's your fiancée except Sienna, doesn't it get tight? Don't you wonder who'll trip over the truth?"

Peter laughed. "Steve knows how to live on the edge and not panic."

Steve laughed, too. "Most people are too polite, except for my buddy, Morgan P. Rand. The guy has made a career of nosing around my life. He never did believe that story of my girlfriend and a spy. He's been trying to uncover it ever since you started it."

Jeneil shook her head. "I had one of those, too. Mine was called Amy Farber."

Steve leaned one arm on the table. "What about you, Pete? Who noses into your life?"

"My mother."

Steve laughed. "Why did I ask?"

Jeneil pursed her lips. "Peter, that's not fair. She's been pretty decent lately." Peter looked at her and was glad she had been spared the ugliness of his mother's thoughts about her and Steve.

"Yeah, I guess she's been okay," he lied.

Jeneil patted his hand and lifted her champagne glass. "Let's drink a toast to Steve, a happy birthday wish that you get whatever your heart desires."

Steve smiled and sipped his champagne. That can never be, sweetheart, he thought, I can't have you.

*****

The drive home from the restaurant seemed shorter than the ride to it. Peter helped Jeneil with her coat and went to hang it for her. Jeneil slipped her arm through Steve's and led him to the sofa. "Sit and get comfortable while I get a few things done."

"Then let me take my jacket and tie off so I can get comfortable."

"Oh, but you look so pretty."

He looked at her and smiled. "Crazy kid." He took his jacket off and started on his tie. Peter returned and noticed Steve undoing the top button on his shirt.

"Oh great, we get to relax." Peter undid his tie and pulled off his blazer.

Jeneil sighed. "Well, at least I saw you guys pretty for a short while. I think I'll be brave and stay dressed."

"Hell, you're no fun," Steve teased. Peter laughed as Jeneil raised an eyebrow.

"Coffee and dessert will be right out."

"Good, I'm starved," Peter said.

Jeneil chuckled. "Don't start again on how small the portions were. You're tough, Chang."

Peter grinned and slipped his arm around her waist. "Want some help?"

"Yes, I could use some." She took his arm, dragging him to the kitchen.

Steve sat thinking about the evening. It had been both special and enjoyable. He was comfortable with them and they seemed like family to him. He sat back, smiling.

Peter opened the refrigerator and took a slice of cold cut. "You are hungry," Jeneil said, pouring coffee into a serving set and putting it on a tray.

"I learned one thing, I'm not meant to be rich."

Jeneil, thinking of Mandra's estate, looked up quickly. "Why do you say that?"

"Those restaurants are not my speed. They're too stuffy and too skimpy."

"You can be rich and go to less expensive restaurants."

"Honey, I don't think Chang will ever be civilized."

"I sure hope not." She smiled. "I like him as a Neanderthal."

He bumped her hip with his. "You always did understand him."

She kissed his lips lightly. "The candles are on the cake, so if you'll strike the match, we can take it to him."

Slipping his arm around her, he kissed her warmly. "Thank you for all of this, baby, you're terrific."

She smiled. "I enjoyed all of it, Peter. It was fun getting it together."

Steve blew at the candles sending up a puff of smoke. He waved it away. "That could set off a smoke detector."

Jeneil smiled. "Who cares? You'll get your wish. You blew them all out with one breath."

"Sure I will." He grinned, showing his disbelief.

Jeneil began removing the candles. "Uh-oh, sounds like the doctor needs some magic in his life. He's forgotten how to hope. Clap for Tinkerbelle boys and girls."

"You are spacey," Steve teased. "Good thing you're cute."

"Cut your cake while I get the gifts. I love this part of parties." Jeneil disappeared and Steve set about making precise incisions in the cake for the three of them. Jeneil returned with several packages of different sizes and put them on the serving table before him. She sat next to him on the sofa. "Okay, I'm ready," she said excitedly.

He looked at her and smiled. "You really get into it, don't you?"

"Yeah, I do. I had fun shopping. I love gifts."

"You've gone overboard, you know."

"Don't lecture and spoil it all for me. Come on, open them."

Peter smiled. "You'd better, Steve, or she will."

Steve took a blue package from the top of the stack. He smiled as he opened the box and saw the giant silver dollar sign decorating the money clip. Jeneil had put a note in it. *For the big bills you'll be making soon, ha-ha.* He shook his head. "Everybody must know something I don't. You gave me a money clip and Dr. and Mrs. Sprague gave me a wallet."

Peter laughed. "Hey Steve, he should know."

Steve nodded. "That wasn't a complaint, believe me."

Jeneil handed him the next gift. It was very small and he wondered what it was then smiled as he unwrapped it. "You're mean, Jeneil. Very mean," he said, holding the white die cast toy. He bumped her arm. "I've never thought as big as a Lamborghini. A nice SX7 is okay."

Peter leaned forward and smiled. "Gosh Jeneil, you've really been practical about his birthday."

Steve smiled. "I like them."

Jeneil smiled. "Keep going."

The next box was long and flat. "It looks like jewelry but the box is too long for a man's piece of jewelry." Steve opened it and laughed. "Oh geez, I like this." He held up the Sterling silver tongue depressor. Peter laughed. Jeneil had inserted a note, *Until it's time for platinum.* Steve looked at her and smiled then shook his head.

"Next," she said, wiggling with delight.

"Now this looks like jewelry," Steve said. He unwrapped it and flipped back the cover then raised his eyebrows. "Ooo, Jeneil, that's really nice. I mean really, really nice."

"Hey, I like that, too," Peter said, looking at the black onyx tie tack and diamond clip outlined in gold. He examined it while Steve opened the next box, a black onyx tie clasp with a diamond clip matching the tie tack.

"Oh, Jeneil, come on now," Steve said.

"Shh," she answered. "Now you're covered for whatever is in. Keep going."

"Jeneil," Steve said quietly.

"Shh."

"More jewelry," Peter commented, seeing the box Steve was unwrapping. Steve stared at the cuff links then looked at Jeneil.

"Now this I'm not sure of. I don't own a dress shirt with French cuffs."

"You'll need one for the dinner jackets you'll wear to those fund raising charity dinners that come up."

Steve sighed. "I have one in early December. Fifty dollars a plate. They don't let you ease into the fast lane in medicine. Plus renting the clothes. I'm going stag, I can tell you that much."

Peter smiled. "This career is getting complicated."

Steve nodded. "And I can't even have a dish for a tongue depressor yet." Jeneil and Peter laughed.

The next box was thin and rectangular. "What can this be?" Steve asked, smiling at Jeneil as he unwrapped it. "Hey, all right Jeneil, a black bow tie. Great, at least I won't have to rent that. Thanks."

"Don't lose the instructions on how to tie it," she warned.

Steve looked at the next box. "Finally, we've hit bottom. You're too much kid, really."

"Open it, please." She shrugged and smiled.

Steve opened it quickly. His mouth opened in surprise as he pulled back the tissue paper. He felt the white material. "Jeneil, a silk dress shirt!"

"I chose the pleats instead of ruffles."

"Oh, Jeneil, really." Steve shook his head.

Peter looked at it. "That's an odd looking label." Steve looked closer then stared at Jeneil.

"Custom made by the tailor who did my suits. Jeneil, I don't know what to say honestly." He sighed. "Thank you doesn't cover any of it."

She slipped her arm through his and squeezed it. "Steve, we're so excited about you beginning your career. We just wanted to be a part of it." She kissed his cheek. "Happy Birthday."

Peter laughed. "What do you mean, we, honey? I'll go get my gift."

Steve took the hand Jeneil had slipped through his arm. He looked at it in silence then looked up at her. "Jeneil, you're terrific. I mean it. Thank you isn't enough."

"Yes, it is," and she kissed his cheek. He felt her lips on his face. He wanted to hold her. She squeezed his hand and smiled. "I think you're pretty terrific too, you know." He patted her hand and smiled.

Peter returned carrying a thin box. "It looks like we had the same kind of idea, Steve."

Letting go of Jeneil's hand, Steve took the package and unwrapped it.

Jeneil smiled. "Peter, a leather stock portfolio, what a great idea."

Steve smiled. "Thanks, Pete. Thanks a lot for a lot of things. You've been a great friend."

"It's okay, Steve. You've been the best friend I've had here. I'm Dr. Chang because of you."

"Nah, it was in you, Pete. We just leaned on each other a few times to get through it all."

Jeneil wiped away her tears. "You two are so good at friendship. Don't ever let anything change that."

Thirty-Nine

Peter turned over and smiled to himself as he stretched. Shift change. He looked at Jeneil. She was facing away from him, her hair spilling across her pillow. He buried his hand in it and grinned when she stirred slightly. He wanted to wake her up but felt guilty about it since she had flown to Nebraska and back the next day in time for Steve's birthday and for them later that night. Separations made them both romantic. He smiled and decided to let her sleep. Turning gently so he wouldn't wake her, he started to get out of bed.

"Quitter," Jeneil said, turning onto her back, smiling. Peter got back into bed quickly, settling next to her.

"Hey, baby." He kissed her. "Good morning."

She stretched and snuggled closer to him. "Chang, I think you're wonderful." She kissed his chin lightly.

"I don't find you boring either sexy lady." Peter grinned as she began the soul thing and stared into his eyes. "It won't work, honey. Not with you looking like you do right now. It'll become passion, not soul."

"And who's complaining?" She smiled, fixing the strands on his forehead.

"Baby, what you've become is beyond belief." He kissed her passionately and she moved in seductive response.

Later she lay in his arms, enjoying him gently rubbing her back. "I like passion," she said quietly.

Peter smiled and kissed her forehead. "I think that's what makes you so darn sexy."

"Sexy is an interesting quality," Jeneil said. "I think it starts by knowing and liking yourself as a man or a woman. Hmm, I wonder if passion is the superlative then."

Peter laughed. "You study it. I'll just enjoy it, thanks." Jeneil smiled and snuggled to him. They lay together, enjoying the warmth and closeness. "I wonder what Steve's doing today," he said, breaking the silence.

"Something with Sienna probably," Jeneil answered.

"I wonder if something's wrong with him."

"I've wondered that, too."

"Why didn't she come with us last night?"

"He just wanted the triad."

"A couple of guys who know him real well have asked me if he's okay. He's been really quiet."

"It's a transition time in his life, Peter. I find him unsettled, maybe he's reacting to it quietly. And I'm wondering if he's struggling over his relationship with Sienna. Is it possible that she's bringing back memories?"

"I don't know, honey. He doesn't talk about any of it. He says everything's okay. What are we doing today?"

"I haven't thought past stopping to see your grandfather and a Sunday dinner."

"Then let's call Steve and ask him along. We'll bum around."

Jeneil smiled. "That's good. Have him bring Sienna."

"That's up to him, baby. Maybe he needs a break from her. That might be why he just wanted the triad."

"But I'd like to see them together since they've been dating."

"Jeneil, stay out of it. You promised," Peter warned.

She sighed. "But if it's memories of Marcia, he'd need somebody to talk it out with."

"Jeneil, stay out of it. I'm serious."

She sighed again. "So what do we all do, stand around and watch him be sad. We do that too much as a society anyway. I think life gets complicated when people don't talk openly. I like directness. Everything should be said and discussed openly. You can avoid big trouble that way. It may hurt at the time, but at least the truth can be exposed. And truth is concrete. It's healthy. It's healing."

He smiled at her. "Not everybody can take directness like you can. Who sees clearly enough to do that? Sometimes you nearly do me in with your directness."

"But you survive. We become stronger from truth. I thought you liked life simple."

"Jeneil, I don't think truth is simple."

The thought struck her. "Hmm, it isn't, is it? It makes life simple, but getting to it isn't easy or simple. I think you have waxed philosophical, Peter." She kissed his chest.

"Comes from loving an eccentric lit major." He kissed her and smiled then reached for the telephone. "I'm going to call him."

"He can come for breakfast if he wants to." Jeneil grabbed her robe and left the room.

Peter waited while Steve was located in the dorm. "Hey, Pete. What's going down?"

"Are you struggling over something?"

Steve fidgeted. "I don't know what you mean."

"You've got something bothering you."

"I'm just impatient that's all. My life isn't here or there right now. You know me, I like things moving."

Peter paused. "You sure that's all of it?"

"Yeah, Pete. I just want my own life, that's all, a real one."

"Want to join us today? Bummin' and Sunday dinner?"

"Yeah, that sounds good." Steve hesitated. "No, maybe I better not."

Peter laughed. "Boy, you are bad, first yes then no. Sounds like you need to bum. You're stressed." Steve leaned against the wall and ran his fingers through his hair. "Jeneil invited you for breakfast. She said you could bring Sienna, too."

"I don't want to bring Sienna," Steve snapped.

"Hey, ease up, Steve. I'm not pushing."

"I'm sorry, Pete. If there's stress in my life, it's from her."

"Why?"

Steve started to laugh. "Pete, you're not going to believe this, but I can understand the struggle a lot of women have saying no to sex in the dating game."

Peter laughed. "Shit, I don't believe it."

Steve groaned. "Damn it. I spend most of my time trying to head her off or dodge her. I don't want to sleep with her and I don't even recognize myself when I say that. I've always felt it was my duty to sleep with any girl who wanted to. This celibacy has played with my mind, I guess. I don't want to be a sex object anymore," Steve said, imitating a woman's voice.

Peter was quiet. "Steve, are you sure it's not more serious? After all, what you went through because of your probation notice was rough. Stress can do a lot of damage. I don't need to tell you. We both see it."

Steve chuckled. "Dr. Chang, are you diagnosing impotency?"

Peter laughed. "You tell me. Are you at least finding some women you'd be interested in?"

Steve pushed at a small piece of paper on the floor with his foot. "Oh, yes I am, Pete," he answered quietly. "And that's why I'm in the exercise room so much. I can't touch what I want."

Peter sighed. "I can see it. Your life is a mess right now, man; probation, celibacy, trying to cover up the lie at the hospital, trying to avoid Sienna, waiting for residency to end and life to begin. Spend the day with us, Steve. That's an order. It sounds like you need the simplicity of the triad. Come over for breakfast, too. Come on," Peter insisted.

"Okay, it sounds good. I'll be there." Steve hung up and leaned against the wall. "The simplicity of the triad." He sighed as he slowly walked back to his room. "Pete, it's your woman I want and can't have, but I need the triad. It's where I relax and unwind. You guys are my family. Her fire and warmth let me know I'm alive."

Steve enjoyed breakfast; he knew he would. He and Peter had a chance to sit and talk while Jeneil knitted. It was what Peter and Steve both liked about Sundays; the quietness, the peace, the friendship.

*****

"I haven't seen your grandfather in a month," Steve said, as they drove to Peter's mother's house. The day was warm, almost spring-like by comparison to the cold snap they had just experienced. It added to the feeling of contentment.

"What a great day," Jeneil said. "I don't like feeling cold. The only thing I miss in my apartment is a fireplace during winter."

Peter wondered how his mother would react to the three of them visiting. He hoped she'd see how groundless her fears were about Steve and Jeneil. There were two cars parked near the driveway; Karen was home. Peter's throat tightened. Parking on the street in front of the house, he held the car door open for Jeneil. He liked the way she looked. Her jeans and long rust-colored sweater with the brown turtleneck were vibrant. She was casually dressed, but looked styled and put together, and a little nervous.

"It's okay, honey. We've got us," he said, as she stepped out of the car. She smiled at him and nodded. They headed to the greenhouse. Peter walked in first. "Grandfather?"

"The birds, Peter!" Jeneil squeezed beside him. "Close the door."

"I'll see if he's in the house." Peter headed to the connecting door. Jeneil went to the back of the greenhouse to see the birds. Steve followed her. She surveyed the trees and chirped. Steve smiled, watching her. The birds chirped a response from their cages and she turned in surprise.

"Oh, how come you're at home today? Are you being punished?" The birds hopped around on their perches, chirping. "Don't look at me; I can't open the cage for you." Steve smiled broadly as she talked to them and they went mad chatting to her. "Tell me, why are you being punished, huh? What did you do? Who started it, Chu Ling?" Steve stood next to her, watching her fun as Peter and his grandfather appeared. Steve looked up and smiled. Peter grinned. Jeneil stood up and noticed everyone.

She smiled and went to Peter's grandfather excitedly. "Mr. Chang." She hugged him and kissed him on the cheek. "Oh, you look so great. Peter said you did. Are you settling back into your routine here?"

"Not quite. You look wonderful. You've been busy too, haven't you?"

"It's been a hectic two weeks for me. Oh, I missed you." She hugged him again, and he smiled and hugged her. Steve watched them then looked at Peter, who was totally overwhelmed. "Why are the birds in the cages?"

"Because I have to begin my training with them again. They've been in the cages since I left. There have been so many people stopping by that I want to wait until things quiet down before the birds and I settle into our old habits."

"That makes sense. I thought they were being punished."

"No, they're being protected."

"I understand it now."

The grandfather looked at Steve. "And Steve, I haven't seen you in a long, long time." He extended his hand.

"Mr. Chang, good to see you," Steve said, shaking the grandfather's hand.

"Almost finished training, aren't you?"

"Two months, one week, two days, five hours, thirty minutes, and two seconds to go."

The old man laughed. "My goodness, it must seem like an eternity to you, but to me it was only a few months ago that you and Peter met at med school."

Steve chuckled. "These last few months have been the toughest for me, but Peter and Jeneil keep me pointing in the right direction. I'll get there."

"Well, congratulations." The old man smiled. "What's next?"

"I'm joining Dr. Sprague and his associates."

"Dr. Sprague. That's not the minor leagues." The old man was impressed.

"Well, they're the major leagues, us new kids will still be rookies, but I'm looking forward to their exclusive training."

"Yes, I guess so," the grandfather said, and then looked at Peter. "Do you have any idea where you'll be going yet?"

"No," Peter answered.

"Don't be modest, Pete," Steve interrupted. "Dr. Maxwell is watching you like crazy. He's grinning over you with delight."

The old man smiled with pride. "I've heard Peter mention Dr. Maxwell. He respects him."

Steve nodded. "And Dr. Maxwell calls for Peter exclusively on emergency assists. That means he's testing him. It usually indicates the surgical group is interested in you."

"That's good to hear." The grandfather smiled at Peter. "And Jeneil, what about you?"

She shrugged. "I'm not even sure of what I'll decide on for breakfast let alone my life." Peter and Steve laughed.

The grandfather smiled. "No, I meant what are you doing? I hear you're involved with The Repertory Theater."

"Oh, yes, I'm a volunteer. It's a lot of fun for me."

"You work very hard at life. You're busier than most people I know."

"I guess that way I can convince myself that I'm not just drifting."

"Bill said that he's glad to see you just playing at working," the old man continued. "He said your father thought you were going to apply for sainthood while you were still alive because you took life so seriously. Bill's glad to see you relax."

Jeneil smiled and nodded. "My father used to tease me about that. He called me Saint Jeneil of the Perfected." The old man smiled at her with deep affection. "But I guess I've changed because I'm Lilly of the Lopsided to these two."

Peter and Steve laughed, and Peter put his arm around her shoulders. "You're okay, kid. We like to tease you, too." The grandfather looked at the three of them and could see the closeness between them.

The connecting door opened. "Father, is Peter here? Tom said he heard him call you, but I don't see his car."

"I have Jeneil's, Mom."

"Oh." She closed the door and walked to the back of the greenhouse. Peter hoped she'd take Steve being with them in stride. Peter's grandfather looked at him and they exchanged a meaningful glance. "Then I'll come in and say hello to her." Jeneil smiled and relaxed. The mother showed surprise at seeing Steve, but remained pleasant. "Are there only the three of you? Peter mentioned that you're dating Jeneil's friend."

Steve looked at Peter, surprised. Jeneil was shocked. "My mother thinks she's Jewish. Now that you're a doctor, you should get married and settle down. I told her you were working on it," Peter said, grinning at Steve.

His mother looked at Jeneil. "It's nice to see you again, Jeneil."

"Thank you." Jeneil smiled. "You've been very understanding of my crazy schedule lately. Thank you for that, too. Life seemed to put some special projects in my path and I'm sorry to have missed some visits here. I'm looking forward to meeting your family on Thanksgiving Day."

"They're looking forward to meeting you. And don't worry, none of us expect you to remember all our names in one day." Jeneil smiled, surprised and pleased by the woman's pleasantness toward her. She choked up with emotion and swallowed several times to keep from crying. Peter stared at his mother, near shock, and Steve looked from one to the other, surprised at the way things had settled in for Peter and Jeneil. The grandfather sat down and watched it all. "Where are you all going?"

"Nowhere, we're bumming around to relax. It's shift change for Steve and me," Peter said.

"You work the same shifts then?" she asked, and Peter nodded. "Jeneil, my father has been asked to work for the International Arts League. We feel that's your doing. Thank you for all you've done. The trip to China left us all stunned."

"It's nothing really. I just provided the opportunity. Mr. Chang was just what the league was looking for," Jeneil said, while Peter's mother studied her and smiled graciously.

"Would you like something hot to drink?" Peter's mother asked.

"Sounds good," Steve said, and Peter nodded.

"I wouldn't mind some tea," Jeneil added quietly, still surprised.

"Then come with me." Peter and his grandfather followed everyone to the kitchen, and Peter raised his eyebrows at him questioningly. The grandfather shrugged, indicating his surprise. Peter's mother went to the cupboard for cups. Everyone stood along the kitchen wall. "Please sit and be comfortable." She smiled at them, and Jeneil and Steve started to sit on the same chair.

"It's mine, I was here first," Jeneil teased, pushing him.

"Oh yeah, prove it, brat." Steve smiled and nudged her gently with his arm. Peter watched as he held his breath. His mother watched then turned quickly to pour hot water into the teapot. Steve squeezed Jeneil's neck. "You're lucky I'm in a good mood." He grinned, moving to an available chair on the other side of the table.

Taking a chair, Peter put it beside Jeneil and sat down, resting his arm on the back of her chair, and she smiled as he softly rubbed her arm. His grandfather smiled and his mother watched them closely as she put the cups and saucers on the table then sat across from them. Jeneil noticed and started to move away from Peter, thinking his mother disapproved of the open display of affection. Peter stopped her by taking her hand. She squeezed it and leaned against him. Keeping his arm around her, he sipped his coffee.

"I thought I smelled coffee." Tom came in, fixing his tie.

"I'll get you a cup. Take my seat." His wife got up.

Steve stood. "No, take mine. I'll bring another over," and he took the chair from the telephone table and sat beside Jeneil.

Peter's mother sat down. "We had a cancellation on a birthday party last night. There are chicken wings and ribs piled in our refrigerator. Is anyone hungry?"

"We just finished eating," Peter answered.

"Can I take some home?" Jeneil asked. "I love the ribs and wings at China Bay." Tom smiled, pleased by her compliment. "I rarely eat Chinese food anymore since Peter doesn't like it."

His mother smiled. "I'll make up a package for you. Steve would you like to take some home?"

"That sounds great. I wouldn't mind either."

"How do you control your profit margin when a large party cancels?" Jeneil asked, curious about the variables in the restaurant business. "I would think the waste could be catastrophic." Peter's mother was obviously impressed by the question.

"We require a deposit when the reservation is made," Tom answered. "But the restaurant business is like a sick child, you have to watch for every symptom. You can't take your attention from it for too long."

"I can understand that." Jeneil nodded. "It's a lot of work. You must enjoy it."

"We get tired of it now and then. But it's here and it's what we do. Lien has a good head for the business." Tom smiled at his wife and she looked down at her cup of tea.

"Is John showing an interest in the business yet?"

"He's heading to college. He's not sure what he's interested in studying yet. I don't think he'll have the stamina for restaurant work. It's too dull. Kids today want glamorous jobs."

Jeneil nodded. "What they'll learn is even glamorous jobs have a dull, routine side to them. Life is a maze of detail work."

"It is." Tom liked her; she was easy to talk to.

"Do you have a young employee with promise?"

Tom looked at Lien. "Suik?" he asked, and Lien nodded. "He seems to be a real restaurant person. He's a whiz with meat. We've had less waste since he's been around."

"He's a natural," Lien agreed.

Jeneil stirred her tea. "I find it effective to have a great management team. They run the ship and I deal with the headaches. They like the freedom of running a business without the worries and I deal with the details without being tied to the business. They have their kind of freedom and I have mine. I've been very lucky, my people are very good."

"You're in business?" Peter's mother asked, surprised.

"My father left me a small company of a few investments. I dabble in it," Jeneil answered, and Peter looked at Steve and they both grinned.

"How do you manage a business in Nebraska from here?" Peter's mother asked.

"With a lot of help." Jeneil smiled. "But that's good for the country's economy, isn't it? That's my business, I guess, I provide jobs for America."

"That's a good deal," Tom said, smiling at his wife. "That would make retirement bearable for us. Neither one of us can sit and do nothing, but we know we can't keep up this pace forever."

"Good, are we selling the restaurant?" Karen asked, walking into the kitchen dressed in her waitress uniform.

"What would you do for money?" Tom asked.

"Who knows, but anything's better than balancing plates of hot food."

Tom chuckled. "Siuk is looking better and better."

"Suik." Karen rolled her eyes. "He should be a surgeon. The guy has a fetish about cutting meat." Peter and Steve looked at each other and shrugged.

"Is he still in love with you Karen?" Peter teased.

"He's only been in America since he was ten. Can you see me with him? All that politeness makes me nervous."

"And what does Greg do, toss you around?" Peter grinned.

"You know what I mean, Pete. Don't be dense."

"No, I don't know what you mean. What's Greg got going for him that Siuk doesn't? They're both Chinese."

"But Greg is with it. He's now. He's in college."

Peter kept on pushing. "But your father just said that Siuk is tomorrow. He's got a real future in the restaurant business."

"Well, if you think cutting meat is so great why aren't you doing it?"

Steve looked at Peter and winked. "Well Karen, Pete tried Siuk's job but he wasn't good enough so he decided to become a surgeon." Everyone laughed except Karen.

"You and Peter are so alike; it must come from the sadistic kind of work you do."

Peter's mother stepped in. "Do you want to have lunch here?"

"As long as it's not wings or ribs."

"Hey, there are a lot of people in China who are starving," Tom added, laughing.

"No, that's not true anymore," the grandfather added.

"Well Africa then," Tom corrected.

"Try America," Jeneil said.

"That's true, too." Tom nodded.

Karen sighed. "You people don't take life seriously. That's your problem." She went to the refrigerator.

Peter smiled. "You're right, Karen, and after my two double shifts this week and early surgery, I'm going to buckle down and seriously learn to boogie as well as Greg does." Steve put his head down, smiling.

Karen turned around holding a container of milk. "And you, Pete, I don't know how you are where you are. You must be bribing people."

"You got it, Karen. That's why Steve is so rich. I paid him to take all my tests for me."

"I don't doubt it," Karen answered, pouring milk into a glass.

"Where are you three off to?" Tom interrupted.

"Nowhere special," Peter answered. "It's shift change today. We like to loaf around."

Steve finished his coffee. "Can we use the basketball hoop outside? The warm weather makes me want to move around a little."

"Hey, I like that," Peter agreed. "John won't mind, he's a good kid, the only one in his family."

Karen sneered. "You don't bother me anymore, Pete. I've matured and grown past you." She headed toward the living room.

"You'll need a certificate of proof, Karen, sorry." Peter smiled, standing. "Let's get the basketball."

"That sounds great to me," Jeneil said, standing.

Steve looked at her. "And how can we have a game with three people?"

Jeneil thought a minute then smiled. "The boys against the girl."

Peter laughed. "Are you serious?"

Steve put his arm around her. "Let's do it, Pete. Come on let's cream the little show off."

"You're on." Peter headed to the door.

Steve pushed Jeneil gently ahead of him, holding her shoulder. "Come on, smart mouth. Hit the court. This is going to be real fun."

Peter's mother watched them as they went outside. "Peter doesn't seem to mind Steve touching her."

"They're all close," the grandfather answered.

She went to the kitchen window to watch. "They're too close."

"Lien." The old man sighed.

"They are, Father." She watched as Peter got two basketballs from the garage. Jeneil went to her car and changed into a blue sweatshirt then returned carrying a basketball. They all practiced shooting as a warm up. "Father, she's a real puzzle. She's in business but doesn't work at it and spends her time playing around cultural things but works at the hospital. She can't seem to settle on one thing. Let's hope it isn't the same with men."

"Lien, really."

"But Father, even that man Bill who flew you to China was disappointed she wasn't at the airport."

"They're good friends, Lien. He hadn't seen her in a while."

"He lives in Nebraska, doesn't he? She flies there a lot."

"That's enough, Lien." The grandfather poured more tea for himself, wanting to change the subject.

"She's odd, very odd." She watched as the three stood talking to each other.

"How are we going to handle this?" Peter asked Jeneil.

"Well, it's obvious that I can't go a full game against the two of you so how about the game being over when I reach six points and win."

"Okay." Peter laughed at her confidence.

Steve listened carefully. "Wait a minute, Pete. Don't trust her. We could have twelve points and when she reaches six, she'll yell that she won because that's what she said."

Jeneil grinned. "You're getting tougher, Bradley."

Steve smiled. "An eccentric lit major taught me."

"Okay, first team to reach six points wins."

"Who starts on offense?" Peter asked.

"I do of course." Jeneil smiled. "Can't you even compensate a little for my handicap of one against two?"

"Sounds fair," Peter agreed.

Steve looked at her. "I smell a rat."

Jeneil bounced the ball. "You're too suspicious, Steve. I'll come up the court, that's the boundary." She pointed to the first section of the driveway cement.

"Okay, let's get to it," Peter said, standing back and facing her. "I can't see how you'll get past our defense."

"She'll cry a lot." Steve laughed.

Jeneil left the boundary line dribbling. Peter and Steve stood side by side waiting for her to go to one side or the other. She held the ball as they stood facing her.

"Well, give me a slight advantage and at least separate a little. Be fair," she said, and Peter and Steve looked at each other then moved apart a couple of feet. She ran between them straight to the basket and laid up the ball, hitting the backboard, dropping it through the net. "Two points," she cheered.

"Hey," Peter and Steve both yelled.

"We were on time out," Peter argued.

"That's right," Steve backed him up.

"No one called time out. I never heard the words." She shook her head.

Tom was standing at the kitchen window and laughed. Peter's mother looked up from the sandwich she was making for Karen.

"What is it?" she asked.

"Jeneil just tricked them and scored. She's funny. She walked all over them but they've got her number now. Well, at least she got two points. They've tightened against her for that." His wife joined him at the window and the grandfather stood up to watch, too.

Jeneil bounced the ball while Peter and Steve continued to argue with her. "What poor sports." She sighed. "One girl against two guys and they can't even give her a two point lead because of a dumb technicality. What are you afraid of, do I look that threatening?"

Steve broke into laughter. "Oh, she's good. Give her the damn points," he said, moving back into position. Peter looked at her. She shot the ball. It hit the rim and bounced back.

"Ouch!" she said, catching the ball then shaking her hand. "I hurt my finger."

Steve laughed. "Serves you right. You'd probably call two more points if it had gone in."

"I'm not that bad," Jeneil defended, going to the boundary line, looking at her finger. She dribbled the ball out of bounds a few times as they surrounded her. She stopped, holding the ball in one arm. "Ow," she said, looking at her hand, "what does a broken finger look like?" They both rushed to her. She broke away, dribbling straight to the basket and laying up the ball. "Four to nothing," she screamed, dribbling the ball.

Peter and Steve looked at each other. "She did it to us, again. Twice, Pete, twice." Steve gritted his teeth and folded his arms, looking at Jeneil, squinting. "I'm going to kill her," he said, and headed after her.

"No," she screamed, and turned her back to him waiting for her punishment. He grabbed her around the neck from behind with one arm.

"Play fair, cheater." He laughed.

"Okay, okay." She laughed. "I will. Let go. Can I keep the two points?"

"Beat her up," Peter called, smiling.

"Can I? Really?" Steve asked. "I'd love to." He felt Jeneil move a little to the left then move into him with her hip.

"Steve! Watch it!" Peter called.

Steve let go, stepping away from her. "She was going to ninja me," he said, staring at her in disbelief. "On cement. You're cold blooded. You're dangerous."

She smiled, pushing her sleeves up to her elbows. "Don't mess with us Dragon groupies."

Peter laughed. "Groupie, hell, you're tough enough to have been a member."

"I still have four points."

"Ugh." Steve rested his arms across his head in frustration and paced in a circle.

Tom laughed and held onto the sink. "Oh, she's too much. She snookered them twice." The grandfather smiled, seeing the fire in her and realizing Peter's attraction. He smiled and nodded gently in approval. The mother watched as Steve stopped pacing and grabbed Jeneil's arms, pushing her against the garage. Her stomach knotted as she watched Peter shoot baskets while Steve held Jeneil and lectured. She closed her eyes.

Tom rested his arms on the counter. "I've got to get ready for work soon, but I want to see who wins. There's no way she can catch them asleep again."

Steve finished lecturing Jeneil and released her arms. "Were you listening, wench?"

"Oh, I thought you were just kidding." She grinned. "I should have placed a money bet on this game. I feel lucky."

Peter looked at Steve and laughed. "I could have told you it was a waste of time. She has no conscience."

"Get to the boundary," Steve ordered. "I'm ready for you." Jeneil took the ball to the line and practiced dribbling while Peter and Steve got into position and discussed strategy. She watched as they nodded to each other and stood waiting for her. She dribbled slowly to where they waited a few feet from the basket. She stopped and held the ball again.

"No more chances?" she asked. They shook their heads. "No more broken fingers?" They shook their heads. "I have to do this on my own?" They nodded. "Okay," she said, shrugging, and then shot the ball into the air toward the basket. Peter and Steve spun around to see where it would go. It hit the backboard, dropped to the rim, and fell through the net. "I did it!" she screamed, shocked. "I did it. I really did it. I won! I won!"

Peter stared at her. "I don't believe it."

Steve draped his arm on Peter's shoulder. "She did it, Peter. She beat us. She actually beat us, and I can't stand it anymore. I'm going to put her through the hoop." He rushed at her and lifted her off the ground into his arms.

"What's happening?" she asked, surprised, holding onto his neck. Peter watched, smiling.

"You're going to get your reward for winning." Steve smiled and headed for the hoop.

"What reward?" she asked suspiciously. "What reward, Peter?" she asked again, as they went past him.

"You'll see." Peter smiled and waved at her.

"Put me down, Steve. I don't trust this." She wiggled to be free. He held her tighter. She wiggled more and her hair spilled out of its pins. "Put me down you spoil sport. I won."

"You cheat," Steve said.

"I didn't. I took advantage a little." She grinned. "You're a big baby. There were two of you."

"Pete's right, you don't have a conscience." Steve smiled as Peter joined them.

"Put her through the hoop, Steve," Peter said, grinning at her.

"The hoop? I won't fit." She laughed.

"That's the idea." Peter smiled. "You'll be stuck there upside down. Do it, Steve. I can't wait." Jeneil took one hand from around Steve's neck and pretended to punch Peter's face. Steve lowered one arm, causing her other arm to slip from around his neck, sending her toward the ground. She screamed and caught herself, balancing with one hand on the ground while Steve held her.

"Put me down," she sputtered to get her hair out of her mouth.

Peter nodded. "Let's play a game without her. It'll show her what happens to cheats."

"That's not what I meant to do to her, but okay." Steve lowered her body to the ground. She lay on the cement, covered by her hair. Steve smiled. "It'll take her a week to get all the knots out of her hair. Let's play basketball, Pete."

Jeneil sat up, throwing her hair back as they walked away together. "You guys are soreheads, poor losers. I think I'll burn your dinner for this," she called, pretending to be angry. They ignored her and began a game. Holding her hair to one side, she started looking for hairpins on the cement.

Tom laughed, shaking his head. "This girl is wild. She actually beat the two of them. I can't believe she won." The grandfather laughed too and nodded his head in agreement. Peter's mother watched, unsmiling.

Jeneil opened her purse for her hairbrush. She brushed and unknotted her hair as she watched Peter and Steve play. A grin curled her lips as she watched Steve dribble away from Peter and toward her. Watching for her chance, she bent down and moved her leg, sending him sprawling backwards over her onto the grass.

"Hey," he yelled, as he hit the ground.

"Oh, sorry," she said, grinning. "I was looking for a hairpin."

"You're a little liar." He smiled, sitting up. "You're getting even with me."

"Goodness, Stevie, you're so suspicious," she baby talked, kneeling on the ground beside him. "I think you're out of bounds." He shook his head slowly and smiled. He liked her spunk. Peter laughed as he stood next to them, resting his left foot on the ball.

"Peter, he thinks I knocked him down deliberately. He doesn't realize that if it was deliberate I would have done it this way," and she elbowed the back of Peter's right knee causing him to lose balance and then, leaning into him, she sent him onto the grass. "See Steve, that's deliberate." Steve lay back on the grass and laughed.

Peter sat up. "Finished getting even?"

"I think so." She continued brushing her hair and pinning it up. Steve and Peter sat watching her. Putting her brush away, she smiled. "Okay, I'm ready."

Steve grinned slyly. "Oh yeah? There are three of us, sweetheart."

"What?" she asked, looking at him, not understanding his remark.

Peter caught on and smiled. "Hey, that's pretty kinky, Nebraska."

"Smut," she said, getting it. She shook her head prudishly and headed for the car.

"Hey, don't go away mad," Steve called.

"She's not," Peter assured him.

Jeneil opened the trunk of the car and changed back to her sweater then walked back to them. "What are we doing now?" she asked, as they tucked in and rearranged their shirts.

"Sunday dinner, honey?" Peter looked at his watch. "I'll go get our jackets."

"How'd you get so tough?" Steve asked, smiling at her, taking a leaf off her shoulder.

"My best friend growing up was a boy." She laughed. "I'm a tomboy." A gust of wind loosened a strand of her hair and blew it across her face. Steve reached out and placed it gently back under its pin. "Thank you."

"It's okay." He smiled. "You're a lot of fun. Let's wait in the car before the wind undoes your hair." He put his arm around her shoulder and they walked to the car.

Karen had joined Peter's mother, who was the last one standing at the window. "What's she doing, dangling bait for the two of them?"

Peter's mother looked at Karen. "Dangling bait?"

"Yeah, is she trying to catch them both? Whose is she?" Karen asked, wanting to be sure. "I saw them from my bedroom window. Steve can't keep his hands off her. Boy, has she got Pete snowed. Everybody thinks she's Miss Goody Two Shoes. Let me tell you, that is one clever lady. She's got them both running a race for her. And Pete puts up with it. Boy, has he changed. What a shock." Karen turned to leave. "I'm taking that fruit to work for my break. Don't put it away or I'll forget it."

Peter came in as Karen left the kitchen. "Is my jacket here?"

"Yes, it's on that chair." His mother pointed. "Here are the packages for Steve and Jeneil." She pushed two aluminum foil packages across the table to him.

"Thanks." He smiled, picking them up. He paused. "Mom, thanks for the way you treated them today." She nodded but stayed silent. "I'll see you Thanksgiving Day."

Peter went to the greenhouse. His grandfather was standing at a window having watched the rest of their fun. "We're leaving, Grandfather. It was good to see you." The old man turned and studied his grandson's face, wondering if he should say something.

"Peter, you three are earth, wind, and fire, all strong energies. Be careful of fire."

Peter looked puzzled. "Is something wrong?"

"Protect the songbird, Peter. Learn to protect the songbird."

Peter smiled, a little embarrassed. "I know. We do rough her up sometimes, don't we? I'll watch it. Don't worry. I'll see you Thursday," he said, and headed out the door.

The grandfather sighed as he watched Peter run to the car. "I'm failing him. He lacks so much. He doesn't see it. He doesn't understand."

"Father, are you worried, too?" Peter's mother asked, coming into the greenhouse.

"Worried?"

"About the three of them?"

The old man thought carefully. His answer could cause an explosion. "They're all very close to each other, Lien. Very, very close. They're like a family, more really."

"Well, I think it's dangerous." She sighed.

"It could be. It makes all three vulnerable."

She watched the car pull away. "Well, Peter's mine. I'm more concerned about him."

Peter stropped for the traffic light at the end of the street. "My grandfather just said that we were strong energies. He called us earth, wind, and fire."

"We're lucky that's all he called us the way we behaved out there," Steve said. "I can't believe I'm twenty-seven and acted like that."

Jeneil laughed. "We do get bad, really."

Steve nudged her. "It's your fault. You're the kid in the group. Grow up," he teased, smiling.

She nudged him back then leaned against Peter. "Did he say which one was which?"

"No, I didn't think to ask. He just said to be careful of fire."

Steve leaned forward and looked at Peter. "Who should be careful of fire? You?"

"No, I thought he meant that the group should."

"Did he say why?" Jeneil asked.

"No, that's all he said."

"Because somebody could get burned?" Steve asked.

"I don't know." Peter shrugged. "Why is this getting complicated?"

Steve laughed. "It's not. I just wondered why he thinks someone could get burned, that's all."

"That's not necessarily true," Jeneil commented. "He might have been worried about fire. Earth and wind can damage fire. You put out campfires by smothering it with earth and you put out a match by blowing on it."

"I never thought of that," Steve said, resting his arm behind Jeneil.

"That's interesting," Jeneil mused. "It's actually fire that needs to be protected." That caught Peter's attention and he remembered his grandfather's reminder to protect the songbird.

He looked at Jeneil and back at the road. He signaled and moved into the left lane as Jeneil listened to Steve. He took her hand and squeezed it, wondering what his grandfather meant. Was Jeneil fire, and why did she need to be protected in the group? What was so dangerous?

Forty

By Tuesday, Jeneil was showing signs of anxiety. She didn't have words for it, just a concern that she would make a good impression on Peter's family. Peter would find her awake when he got in from second shift, and he wondered what he would find as he unlocked the apartment door Wednesday when he arrived home from work. All the lights were on and the apartment smelled good. Peter smiled as he saw Jeneil at the dining table wrapping something. She looked up and smiled then went to him, blending into his arms. She felt warm to him after being in the cold air.

"Honey, it's almost midnight. What are you doing? The lights are all on and you look busy enough for it to be eight."

"I'm glad you're home." She sighed and snuggled closer to him. "I got nervous and started baking. There are cookies all over the place and the pumpkin pie in the oven is nearly done. I've scraped pounds and pounds of carrots for the center's dinner tomorrow. Now I'm wrapping a small basket of fruit I thought I'd take to your mother. I was running out of things to do! So I'm glad you're home. Hold onto me."

"Relax, honey. You'll ruin yourself over this."

She looked at him. "I even roasted a small turkey because I like holiday leftovers. I always do one for myself. Turkey sandwiches are part of my childhood memories."

Peter shook his head. "With all your Thanksgiving decorations around here, who can forget the holiday? Pilgrims, turkeys, pumpkins all over the place."

"I guess I go overboard." She sighed again.

"No, baby, it's you. It's even kind of nice really. You've had the decorations up since early November. The holiday lasts longer that way. I like it." He held her to him. "Let's get to bed though. My mother wants us there at one so you better get some rest."

She nodded. "Would you like to help me gather the cookies?"

Peter held a plastic container and added another layer of cookies to it. "Hey, these turkey ones are pretty good." He bit into another one.

Jeneil smiled as she gathered chocolate chip cookies. "Those are butter cookies. I started with those because they take more time to make but the evening was longer than two batches of butter cookies." She placed the container on the table. "I'll just leave the cover resting on top for tonight. They'll finish cooling that way." The oven timer buzzed.

Peter followed her to the kitchen. A fully cooked turkey sat on the counter covered in clear plastic wrap. He watched her take the pie from the oven. "Jeneil, you've made a whole dinner." She shook her head as she looked around.

"I did, didn't I?" she snickered. "I guess I'm really nervous."

"What are you nervous about? My mother likes you. That's the whole war right there. You've got it made. My grandfather thinks the sun rises and sets on you. What more do you want? And I think you've got Tom completely charmed. John would marry you if he was older. You're home free."

"You didn't mention Karen."

Peter grimaced. "Karen's an idiot."

"She doesn't like me, Peter. I can tell."

"You outclass her, honey. It makes her crazy."

"Are you sure it isn't because we're living together?"

Peter was shocked. "What? Honey, you're going over the edge. Karen doesn't even know. My mother hasn't told anyone in the family. She doesn't want them to know."

Jeneil's heart stopped. "Oh, Peter, I don't like the sound of that. I wish you had told me before this."

"Why?"

"We embarrass her." Jeneil wrung her hands.

"Jeneil, come on."

"We do, Peter, we do." Jeneil's voice cracked with emotion.

"Honey, that's enough. She simply asked that we not mention we're living together, that's all. We do that at the hospital, so what's the difference?"

Jeneil rubbed her temples. "The people at the hospital are strangers. Your family is important to me." She sighed. "Why didn't you tell me all this before?"

"Jeneil, really, you're making too much of it."

"No. No, I'm not. It's how I am. I need to know what's around me so I can protect myself."

"From what?" Peter shrugged, confused about her reaction.

"I don't know." She sighed again. "I thought your family knew about us. I don't like lying to them. It isn't good." She paused. "I feel, I don't know, it's dangerous. I feel vulnerable.

I'd feel better if they knew. And now that I know your mother couldn't tell them or doesn't want to, I mean, I'm not seeing her clearly either. I don't like it at all." She closed her eyes and breathed deeply.

"Jeneil, you're tired. Let's get to bed. Come on." He took her hand and turned out the kitchen light.

"Wait, I'll put the food in the fridge while you get the other lights."

Peter waited in bed, noting a big change in her mood as she slipped quietly under the covers. "Jeneil, let it go, okay? You're working yourself up over nothing," he said, getting annoyed. "You make trouble for yourself doing that."

"Peter, you and I have been on different paths since your mother found out about us."

"What do you mean?"

She thought for a minute, hoping her feelings would clear. "You keep things from me."

"How?" he asked cautiously, stunned by her remark.

"I'm not sure. It's just a feeling. A glimpse here, a remark there, and now hearing this, I get the feeling that what I think I'm seeing and feeling isn't true or real. I don't like it. I don't like it when I sense it in business and I especially don't like it here. It's dangerous."

Peter marveled at her sensitivity. "You keep saying it's dangerous. How the hell can it be dangerous?"

"I feel like pieces are missing, like I'm making decisions and feeling things based on incomplete information. Are you keeping things from me?"

Peter held his breath, struggling whether he should tell her about his mother's accusation about Steve and her. "No," he answered, "you're imagining things. You're tired."

She looked at him. "Peter, don't hide things from me, ever. It's dangerous."

"Again with it's dangerous. Come over here." He pulled her into his arms and held her. "Honey, forget it. It's just us that matter anyway."

"That's what I'm concerned about, us. If you hide things from me it means there's a weakness in our relationship that could cause trouble. That would undo us more than those around us. I can deal with anything, Peter. I may shake through it, but I do get through it. Promise me you'll never hide things from me."

Peter hesitated at hearing promise. "Baby, I tell you everything I think is worth talking about. Let's drop this now, okay?"

She sighed. "Okay, Peter. I'm going to trust you, but I feel like I'm on the Titanic and the fog is beginning to roll in."

"Well, that sounds safe. Really, honey, life isn't like a novel where every detail matters."

She looked up quickly and shook her head. "Don't kid yourself. You live in fiction, Peter. I live in reality. I need details."

He chuckled. "I don't know how you can stand all that worrying. Stick to fairy tales, honey, it's a good distraction." He squeezed her gently.

"Someday you'll take me seriously, Peter, and you'll know that I see more clearly than you ever thought. But I can't see clearly and make wise decisions when pieces are missing. You may not think they're important, but I know there are pieces missing. Everything in me is screaming it."

Peter was silent. Her instincts and sensitivity impressed him. He kissed her forehead tenderly. "I love you, Jeneil. That's all that matters."

She smiled. "That's what I'm trying to protect, Peter. It's part of my quest. You're as important to me as breathing, as important as finding my pieces in life. I need both. I need to know that I'm complete and I need you in my life in order to be complete."

She kissed him, and sensing her intensity, he kissed her more passionately.

*****

The bed was empty when Peter opened his eyes. It was still dark so he knew it was early. He turned over and thought about taking Jeneil to meet his family and it felt great. He thought about all those other Thanksgiving holidays where he stayed against the wall, waiting for the day to end. He had never seemed to fit in and had never liked being there. Today was different; he was going to have Jeneil with him. He pictured them at the table and it felt right. He wanted that. He wanted to be normal. "Normal?" he asked himself. "Not Chinese. I think they'll notice." He held Jeneil's pillow to his chest. He felt normal. He had a girl who was terrific and they were going to get married. That was more normal than his family probably ever expected of him. Laughing, he reached for his robe. He could wait but the excitement was building.

"What are you doing?" he asked, finding Jeneil in the kitchen packing sandwiches in a small cardboard box.

She continued working without looking up. "I'm taking all this to the center. The carrots are cooling. There's some banana bread for breakfast if you're hungry. I won't be gone very long."

"Honey, it's seven."

"I know. The group gets there at five. I've got to move fast." She kissed him as she walked by. "Happy Thanksgiving," she called over her shoulder. He looked around the kitchen and shook his head. Seeing the banana bread, he cut a slice and ate it. She returned with her jacket on. "I'll be right back."

"Can I go with you?"

"If you want to," she said, smiling as she picked up the sandwich box.

"I want to. I'll dress fast." He took another slice of banana bread and walked out.

The center was in a poorer neighborhood. Jeneil pointed to an area designated for parking.

Opening the door to the back seat, Peter lifted a large pot of carrots. "I'll have to come back for the other."

"I'll stay with the car and wait."

Leaving the pot just inside the door, Peter ran back for the rest.

"I can carry that bag of frozen peas and this box of sandwiches, Peter. We can lock the car."

"This is how you spend Thanksgiving?" he asked, setting the pot on the pavement.

She nodded and smiled. "Does it seem strange to you?"

"Yeah, it does. It really does. My family got all dressed up, had a big meal and sat around talking."

"This might be depressing for you then."

He laughed. "Honey, I'm a doctor. Tragedy is a part of my life. Let's take this in before that other pot of carrots gets ripped off."

Jeneil knocked on the glass door and shook it. A man stepped into the inner doorway and, seeing who it was, waved and smiled as he let them in.

"Hi, Jeneil, you have some help this year, do you?" The man had merry blue eyes and a warm smile. He extended his hand to her and she shook it.

"Reverend Petersen, I'm sorry I can't stay this year. Peter's mother has invited me to spend Thanksgiving with them and I'm meeting the rest of his family for the first time today. We're planning to get married." The man looked surprised then smiled his warm smile.

"Well, that's wonderful news. Put the pot down so I can congratulate you, young fella." He held his hand out to Peter.

"This is Peter Chang." Jeneil smiled. "Peter, Reverend Petersen is pastor of the church next door."

"Nice to meet you," Peter said, shaking the pastor's hand.

"Same here." The pastor shook Peter's hand vigorously and patted his shoulder. "You have chosen one terrific girl, Peter. In fact, my wife will weep when she hears the good news." Jeneil looked puzzled and the pastor grinned. "We've been sent a young pastor in training. He's single. My wife thought of you immediately, Jeneil. She's been thinking up all sorts of ways to get you two to meet. Can you take a minute to say hi to them? They're in the kitchen."

"Sure." She smiled and looked around. "Where is everyone? Shouldn't the tables be set by now?"

The pastor laughed. "You know, I think if you were involved one more year, you and my wife could organize this on your own. The Bladins are sick this year and some of the others couldn't come until closer to noon."

Peter held his breath wondering what Jeneil would do. The pastor picked up the other pot and carried it to the kitchen. Several people were bustling about preparing food. A thin woman with a serene smile came over to them and hugged Jeneil. "How are you? We got the turkeys this morning at seven-thirty. Thank you so much. And the carrots, you really are a wonder."

Peter could see Jeneil was embarrassed. "Here are some frozen peas to add to your pot, and some sandwiches and cookies for the helpers."

The woman smiled warmly. "We'll miss you here."

The pastor interrupted. "Millie, she's meeting her fiancé's family this year."

"Fiancé?" the woman asked disappointedly.

Her husband laughed. "Yes, she found someone without your help. Imagine that. This is the man, Peter Chang."

Peter smiled. "Hi." The woman smiled at him and hugged Jeneil again.

"Gosh you've changed, too. Look at you. You're absolutely radiant. Love agrees with you."

A young minister joined them. "I've finished potato duty. Shall I start on the tables?"

"Yes," Mrs. Petersen answered. "And this is Jeneil."

"Oh." The young minister smiled broadly. "Jeneil, I expected you to be older from everything I've heard about you. You've got quite a command of the scriptures I hear." Peter noticed the young man seemed pleased with Jeneil.

Jeneil smiled. "It's not a command at all, but I did win a few ribbons in scripture search, and for whatever reason some have stayed with me."

"Where did you get your knowledge of religious history?" he asked, studying her eyes. Peter laughed to himself. The guy was a goner; he'd never get past her eyes alive.

"At our dinner table. My father was good friends with a protestant minister and a catholic priest. He'd really put them through their paces."

"This is her fiancé, Peter Chang," Reverend Petersen interrupted. Peter saw the disappointment in the young minister's face as he turned to meet him.

"Congratulations." He smiled and shook Peter's hand. "When are you getting married?" He looked from one to the other.

"That's Jeneil's decision," Peter answered, not knowing what to say.

"How long have you been engaged?"

"We're not formally engaged yet either. We're planning to get married," Jeneil added.

"Oh, that's nice. Marriage isn't too popular with some today. It's nice to meet people who are committed to each other in an old fashioned way. I wish you both a lot of happiness." The young minister looked at the pastor and his wife then smiled at Jeneil and Peter. "I'd better start on the tables. It was nice meeting you both."

Jeneil looked at Peter. "Peter, I'd like to help set up for an hour. It's a lot of work and they're shorthanded. If you'll come back for me then, that should give us enough time to get ready for your mother's dinner."

"I'll help, too," Peter replied. "I'm here now anyway."

"Thank you both." Mrs. Petersen squeezed their arms. "Reverend Scott will show you where everything is."

"Call me Ted." The young minister smiled as they went to the main hall. "At least the tables are set up. That's what takes a lot of time."

The three worked quickly and had one section completed in a half hour. Peter couldn't believe the number of people being planned for. It was so different from his family's holiday. Things were hectic and crowded at home with everybody trying to be seated at once, but this felt cold to him, more like a restaurant.

"It warms up when people fill it." The young minister smiled at Peter, reading his expression.

"I'm sorry," Peter said, as he continued putting napkins in place.

"It's okay. When you don't work with the needy and lonely this can seem cold. But believe me, the laughter and spirit that will fill this room later will actually sound like a big happy family. I've served in soup kitchens where the food was meager but the warmth that filled the dining hall was always strong. People have a common bond. They're alone and need a place to spend the holiday. They become family because they genuinely care. For the day at least, but it's genuine. That's what makes it warm. Jeneil can tell you that."

Peter looked at Jeneil, who smiled and nodded. He couldn't believe this was how she had spent her last two Thanksgivings and it choked him up. The thought of her sharing his family's holiday warmed him. She was going to enjoy it for sure, and he was beginning to understand her feelings about families and closeness. It had never meant much to him before but bringing her home this year made it special for him, too. In fact, he was looking forward to it.

Peter looked at his watch as he put the last napkin in place. "We've got to leave, honey. I still have to shower and change."

The young minister studied them. "Thank you both for helping today. Jeneil, those turkeys shocked the Petersens. They really think you're something special and I agree with them. It's too easy for people to send money. It's nice to see some who offer their time as well. Thanks again for all you've done here."

"It's nothing." She smiled. "We're all family, aren't we?"

The minister smiled at her. "Yeah, we are, and you'd better leave if Peter has to drive home to get ready and get back to pick you up."

Jeneil looked at him. "We live together."

"Oh," the young minister replied quietly. Peter felt uncomfortable.

"I'm sorry," Jeneil said. "I know that's not in keeping with your beliefs, but with all the compliments being showered on me I wanted to make sure my image was accurate. My beliefs are different from yours, but my care about the work here isn't."

The young minister smiled at her warmly. "Jeneil, you're all right. I'd like to see more of your kind of caring in the churches I've been serving. I didn't come from a dairy farm to theology school and then here. I was a runaway who lived on the streets. I stumbled into a shelter like this one holiday. I felt the warmth and wondered what I was doing with my life. I volunteered in the kitchen for the next holiday and so on and so on. I hope they keep me in inner city parishes. I'd die from over-piousness in a small town church where everyone is perfect."

Jeneil laughed. "Serve in a small church somewhere in a small town. It'll round out your education about people."

The young minister laughed. "You speak with conviction."

Jeneil shrugged and smiled. "People are people, small town or inner city. Piety isn't geographical. Sin is sin and the devil wants us all so we're told."

The young minister laughed again and extended his hand. "Jeneil, you're okay. Thanks again for your help." She shook it and nodded. "And Peter, thank you, too."

"It wasn't much," Peter answered uncomfortably. "This is Jeneil's doing, really."

The young minister smiled. "The best of everything in your life together. Enjoy your Thanksgiving day."

Jeneil said her goodbyes and gathered her pots. Peter watched her and was filled with pride. He had always liked her caring nature, but had never realized how far it went.

They arrived home and bustled about, excitement growing inside of him. He watched her pin up her hair as he buttoned his shirt. "You look sensational, honey. You really do. Is that a new dress?" She nodded and added her earrings while he did his tie. "I'm going to look strange. I've never gotten this dressed up for a holiday before. I really didn't need another sports jacket."

She went to him and put her arms around him. "Kiss me before I put on my lipstick. Tell me everything will be fine."

"Honey, it is." He kissed her warmly. "It's fine. You look great. Stop worrying." She nodded and returned to her mirror. He slipped his sports jacket on. "Honey, why do you have me looking like a yuppie?"

"So you can relate. You need to learn about customs."

He laughed. "You and Rick will get along well."

"Who's Rick?"

"My cousin."

"There's a Ron and a Rick?"

"Yeah."

"Are they brothers?"

"No."

She sighed. "And how many girls are there?"

"Let's see, three, six, seven, yeah seven, eight if Rick brings his girlfriend."

"Do they all have husbands?"

"Four do."

"Oh wow." She smiled. "I'm usually pretty good with names, but I'm not usually this nervous."

"Time to go, honey. We're going to be a few minutes late as it is."

She sighed again. "Okay. I'm about as ready as I can get."

He smiled. "They're going to love you."

*****

The cars were parked tightly in every available space. Children played. Adults talked and laughed. John kept looking out the window. "They're late."

The grandfather smiled. "Peter called a few moments ago. Jeneil took some food to a center that feeds the needy. She and Peter stayed to help set up so they're a little late."

Peter's Aunt Malien smiled. "The girl never sits still. I can't wait to meet her. Peter looks so happy." Karen shook her head in disgust.

"Wait until you see her. She's gorgeous," John said, smiling.

Karen couldn't take it. "Oh, John, really, she has style but she's hardly gorgeous."

John grinned. "How would you know what gorgeous is? You've never seen it in your mirror."

Tom stepped in. "Don't start, please."

Ron sipped his drink. "I can't believe Pete's dating a white girl. He was always so careful."

"She's very nice," the grandfather said. "Don't call her white, it annoys Peter."

Peter's Aunt Risa smiled. "I'm happy for him. It sounds like he has changed. Imagine him getting up early enough to go get her and work at a center for the needy, too. She sounds like a wonderful girl."

John went to the window. "Here they come." He whistled. "Man, she looks great. That outfit is money all the way."

Karen seethed. "I don't know how she can afford it. She's only a clerk at the hospital, and he didn't have to go far to pick her up, he lives with her." Everyone stared at her in shock and then at Peter's mother, the color draining from her face.

Peter's grandfather stood up nervously, wondering what would happen and what to do. "Please, everyone make her feel welcomed."

Karen headed past John, sticking her tongue out at him. "You vicious bitch," he mumbled, as she passed by. "You couldn't stand her getting the attention."

Risa was shocked. "Is that true? They live together?"

Ron laughed. "Pete will never change. I've got to meet her. He's never been wild enough to live with anyone before. She must be something else."

Peter's mother left the room quickly. The grandfather felt bad that the two of them should have this type of beginning in the family. He sighed.

Peter stood with Jeneil at the front door. "We'll never get through the kitchen." He smiled and kissed her. "I love you."

"Me, too." She smiled. "It's zero hour, Peter."

"Yes, it is, honey." He opened the door and walked in. Taking Jeneil's coat, he hung it in the hall closet then took her hand and headed to the living room, wondering why it was so quiet. Usually you couldn't hear yourself think. They stood at the entrance to the room. Everyone stared. Even the young children had stopped playing and were staring at the new lady. Jeneil fidgeted and looked down at the floor. She couldn't blame them. She looked different from everyone there, reminding herself it was natural to stare as Peter put his arm around her shoulder.

Peter's grandfather went to them quickly. "Jeneil, you look beautiful."

"Thank you," she managed to say. Her throat was tight and dry. She handed him the basket of fruit. "I brought this for Mrs. Lee as a thank you."

The grandfather felt sick inside as he saw the effect everyone staring was having on her. "That was nice of you, Jeneil."

Malien came to them. "Peter." She kissed his cheek. "You look so terrific. I've heard so many nice things about your girl." She smiled at Jeneil. "John's right, you're gorgeous."

Peter noticed the tenseness in Jeneil's smile. "Honey, this is my Aunt Malien."

Malien smiled warmly. "Jeneil, it's nice to meet you at last." She hugged Jeneil.

"It's nice to meet you, too. I'm a little overwhelmed and very nervous, so you'll have to excuse me."

"I think you're fine. Don't be nervous. We're harmless, really."

Jeneil laughed lightly. Peter slipped his arm around her waist and squeezed her gently. His mother came into the room and walked to them slowly, unsmiling.

"Peter, you look well," she said formally. He stared at her, confused by her attitude as his grandfather handed her Jeneil's basket. "Thank you. I'll put it in the kitchen," she answered, still unsmiling. "Malien, I can use your help."

"Of course," Malien replied. "I'll be right there." Peter's mother, not looking at Jeneil, turned and walked away. Jeneil was shocked by the obvious shun and her stomach started to hurt. Malien sighed and went to the kitchen.

The grandfather brought Jeneil a chair. "Jeneil, sit down please."

"Something feels very wrong here Peter," she whispered, feeling numb from being nervous and confused.

The grandfather overheard and his heart felt sick for her. "Jeneil, if you'll sit here a minute, I'd like to talk to Peter."

"I'll be right back, honey." Peter kissed her cheek then followed his grandfather. Jeneil looked around the room at people who avoided looking at her. When she met their stare, it felt very familiar to her from a time long ago in her childhood.

The grandfather closed the door to the greenhouse. "Peter."

"Grandfather, what's happening out there?"

"Peter." He sighed. "Just seconds before you walked in Karen told everybody that you and Jeneil are living together. I don't know how she found out. She must have overheard it. Everyone is still dealing with the shock."

Peter closed his eyes. "The bitch, the little bitch." He sighed. "Shit!" He rubbed his forehead. "That sure explains my mother's treatment of Jeneil. At least she didn't yell. Oh gosh, poor Jeneil. I've got to get back to her, Grandfather."

"Peter, do whatever you have to."

"Grandfather, I'm sorry. You must be embarrassed about this."

"Peter, worry about Jeneil. She looks sick."

The room was silent as Peter walked in. Jeneil sat staring at her hands and he felt sick for her. Kneeling beside her, he took her hand.

"Peter, where's the bathroom? I don't feel well." He stood up, still holding her hand, and took her from the room. He paced as he waited for her then went to the hall telephone and dialed the hospital.

"Dr. Steve Bradley in ER. Dr. Chang calling."

Steve picked up. "Hey, Pete. Can't you stay away from here even on your day off?"

"Steve, I need a favor."

Steve heard the panic in Peter's voice. "What is it, Pete?"

"Have me called at my mother's house from the hospital after I hang up, okay?"

"Pete, what is it? Trouble?"

"Steve, I can't talk right now."

"Okay, Pete."

"Thanks, Steve. Thanks a lot." Peter hung up as Jeneil came out of the bathroom. She looked pale. Peter heard the telephone ring and he went to Jeneil. Taking her hand, he kissed it gently. "I love you, honey."

"Peter, I don't understand what's happening," she said, near tears.

"Peter, telephone, it's the hospital," Tom called.

"Wait here for me, honey." He kissed her cheek then went to pick up the receiver. "This is Dr. Chang," he said, so everyone could hear

"Pete, can you talk yet?"

"No, we haven't had dinner. Why?"

"What are you talking about?" Steve asked, bewildered.

"Well, that's okay. I understand. I can be there in a half hour. Bye." He hung up, leaving Steve more confused.

Peter looked at Tom. "They're shorthanded. I have to go in. I'm sorry. Apologize to my mother for me." He made sure everyone heard him. Taking Jeneil's hand, he rushed through the room. He stopped long enough to help her with her coat then opened the door quickly and left.

"What a job. His time is never his own," Peter's Uncle Liam commented, and his grandfather struggled with anger.

Risa shook her head. "I can't believe they live together. She looks so decent, so nice."

"That was one neat lady." Ron smiled. "He's doing okay. What that girl will teach him about living in polite society is invaluable to his career. She's an education to him."

The grandfather glared. "They're planning to be married."

"Married?" Ron couldn't believe it.

"We never got to meet her," Peter's cousin, Sarah, commented. "With Aunt Lien treating her like the plague, I didn't know what to do. Why didn't we know before this? I just found out a few days ago that she was white. I was at a complete loss. We must seem rude to her."

Ron poured another drink. "Don't worry about it, Grandfather. They may be talking marriage, but Pete's still got another year of training to go. He'll understand better by that time and she'll go the same path as Lin Chi. He's not stupid." The grandfather remained silent, displeased with the family surrounding him this holiday. He thought about Jeneil and his heart went out to her.

*****

Peter pulled away from the curb slowly, resisting the anger inside of him so he could drive.

Jeneil was silent for a moment then spoke quietly. "Peter, I'll just drop you off at your car and go to the ocean. I need to clear my head."

"I'll take you to the ocean, honey."

She looked surprised. "But what about the hospital?"

"The call was a fake."

Jeneil stared, trying to absorb everything. Tears rolled down her cheeks as her confusion worsened and mixed with her disappointment. "I don't understand any of what's happening, Peter. I must be tired."

Peter choked up and he took her hand. "Honey, it's not you. Just before we walked into the house, Karen told everyone we were living together. That's why my grandfather wanted to talk to me. Everyone was shocked, that's why things felt strange. I'm sorry, baby. I'm really sorry."

She thought for a few seconds. "Did your grandfather want us to leave, or maybe your mother? She couldn't look at me. Is that why you faked the call?"

It was Peter's turn to be surprised. "Honey, nobody asked us to leave. I didn't want you to have to deal with what was happening so I had Steve call and say I had to go to work."

Jeneil shook her head and sighed. "What an absolute mess. How thoroughly ridiculous."

Peter was puzzled. "Who are you annoyed at?"

"You, Peter. That was not the way to handle the situation. That was stupid," she said, her annoyance building. She turned her head and stared out the window.

"Jeneil, you saw my mother. I was afraid she'd explode. Believe me, honey. She's nasty when she goes over the top." Jeneil didn't answer and kept her head turned away from him for the entire drive. Peter didn't try to make conversation either. He needed to calm down himself. His own thoughts raced through his mind and unsettled his emotions.

The ocean stretched before them sending white capped waves crashing onto shore. Gulls flew about their business, screeching their songs. The sky was blue grey and cold; a winter sky designed to send people inside to get warm.

Jeneil took in the view. "I never liked the winter ocean scene. It's not very comforting. It's too preoccupied mourning its loss of summer, and fall's bloom and radiance. So it will sit and mourn with you, but it never comforts." She sighed and put on her gloves.

"Then why are you going out there?"

"I need the wind," she said, and opened the car door and got out.

Peter got out too and felt the cold wind hit him like a wall of ice. He turned his head away from it so he could breathe. Turning around, he faced Jeneil as she walked toward his side of the car and into the wind.

"Peter, I'd like to walk alone." He nodded and watched her slowly walk away.

He got into the car and started the engine to get warm. He watched the wind tear at her and wondered how she could stand it. It whipped at her hair savagely like a hungry animal, swirling it in different directions, yet she continued walking steadily into it. He turned the car's heater to high while he watched her. It surprised him how comfortable she looked out there, almost peaceful, except for her hair. She had stopped and faced the ocean, standing on the firm surface of the parking area. He guessed it was because her shoes weren't made for walking in sand.

He wondered where things would go for them now with his family. He disagreed with Jeneil about faking the call. It had been the safest way to not insult anyone yet Jeneil had been insulted. Except for his grandfather and Malien, his family had shunned her. Had they been putting her down or just in shock from the news? No one in his family had ever lived common law with anyone. They must have been shocked. He sighed and wondered what had happened just before he and Jeneil arrived. He could tell his mother had been very upset and it had been her way of telling Malien to leave Jeneil alone when she asked for help. He'd seen her do that hundreds of times with Lin Chi; his mother was an expert at shunning people. Lin Chi had been bold and put herself before his mother, forcing her to talk, deliberately ignoring the shun. His mother would end up exploding with embarrassing remarks and Lin Chi would behave even more pleasantly, saying sweet goodbyes to everyone then asking Peter if they could leave. Peter had obliged, knowing it was best to leave.

Peter turned his head to look at Jeneil. She was playing with the wind now like he had seen her do when he first met her on the beach. He smiled as she held her head at an angle so the wind pushed at her hair in one direction like it was being brushed. Undoing her coat, she tucked her hair inside and buttoned it up again. She walked slowly back toward the car. She knew the wind. Peter could see that and it fascinated him. He remembered his grandfather telling him to protect fire. Jeneil was fire. He thought about the triad and wondered who was earth and who was wind. She loved wind, he mused. He smiled as he waited for her to get in the car. Her cheeks were bright with color from the cold air and wisps of hair framed her face. She pulled her hair out of her coat and pinned it up haphazardly. He could tell her mood was improved.

"What did your wind tell you?" he asked, smiling.

She looked directly at him. "There are pieces missing in this. I can't control it. It's out of my hands."

Peter's face got serious. "The wind told you that?"

"Have you ever heard of a strong prairie wind, Peter?" He shook his head. "It actually sounds like a human moan. The Indians call it Mariah."

"Come on." He laughed lightly. "You really believe the wind has substance, human qualities?"

She stared into his eyes. "One day it'll tell me what you're not."

"You're a crazy kid, off the wall." He started the car engine and backed away. "I'm starved. I've been surrounded by food everywhere I've been today and all I've eaten are two slices of banana bread. The hungry and lonely have it made. This is their day to be fussed over. Hell, I may go to the center myself. I feel like I qualify for both categories."

Jeneil stifled a laugh and choked slightly. "Peter, on you, self pity looks very funny." He smiled and pulled the car off the road. Putting it in park, he turned and kissed her.

"I love you, Jeneil."

Surprised, she stared at him, tears filling her eyes. "I feel very insecure, Peter. Very vulnerable, but I love you, too." She kissed him tenderly.

"It'll be okay, honey. We've got each other." She nodded as he touched her cheek gently. "There, that takes care of the lonely category, now I'm only down to one."

She smiled. "There's all kind of food for you at home." He kissed her cheek and smiled then pulled away from the curb and headed home.

*****

Jeneil sat brushing her hair at the bureau mirror. Peter lay across the bed watching her. She looked better, he thought, and she had cheered up. He only caught her looking sad occasionally. She had pampered him by giving him a small snack and was determined to make them a Thanksgiving dinner so had the turkey warming in the oven. She had changed into a long dress and things felt pretty good between them. Peter smiled, enjoying the moment. Jeneil's telephone rang and they looked at each other.

"Marlene! Happy Thanksgiving. How are Uncle Hollis and the children? You must have a house full of people. Wow, from both sides. Do you think being able to cook for a large group is taught somewhere before we come to Earth? I feel like I came to Earth unprepared. I must have missed that lesson." Peter smiled. "Uh yes, we went to Peter's family's for dinner. Just fine. Really, fine. They're very nice people. Yes." Peter sighed. "His grandfather is a really social person. I love him. A large family, very large. Yes, it was different from my childhood. Okay, that was nice of you and thanks for calling."

"Hi, Uncle Hollis. Things went fine at Peter's family's. Why?" Peter watched as tears filled her eyes and he wished the telephone had never been invented. "No, they don't like our arrangement any more than you do, but they were okay with me." She wiped her tears. "Bill's right, Peter's grandfather is a very nice man. Not too much, just resting from all the excitement. No, he's an only child but he has a few cousins. Oh, the usual, they're a traditional American family, turkey and all the trimmings. Yes, it feels really good to be in a family." Peter closed his eyes as Jeneil wiped more tears. "No, no. His dad is gone. Yes, his mother married a very nice man. No, I was the only one who wasn't Chinese. It was fine, I felt very comfortable. They're nice people." More tears fell. "Thank you for being concerned. Yes, I know you worry about me, but I'm doing just fine." She reached for a tissue. "I will, Uncle Hollis, thanks for calling. Bye."

Peter went to her and held her in his arms as she cried softly. Would this damn day ever stop, he thought, kissing her temple gently.

"I'm all right, Peter, really." She took a deep breath and smiled. He kissed her forehead right as his telephone rang.

"Shit," he mumbled, "now what?" He lifted the receiver reluctantly. "Grandfather." He put his arm around Jeneil and she snuggled to him. "No, we took a drive. We just got back. She's coping. I'm sorry about what happened. The family must have been shocked." Jeneil watched Peter's face as she listened. "I can understand that. What's mother like now? Good, it'll keep her busy. I don't know what to think. It's really up to my mother from here on. I know you do. Well, let's wait and see." Peter swallowed hard. "I will,

Grandfather. Thanks." He hung up and held Jeneil tightly. "My grandfather told me to tell you that he loves you." Jeneil tried to hold back her tears but couldn't. Peter sighed. "Honey, let's let the damn phones ring from now on." The front door bell rang. "More?" Peter snapped. "I can't believe all this."

Jeneil wiped her eyes. "I'm really not in the mood for company."

"Too late," Peter said, as the apartment door buzzer sounded. "I'll get it."

Steve stood at the door looking very serious. "I came in with the tenants from upstairs. I saw both your cars so I stopped."

"Come on in." Peter stepped aside.

"Why didn't you call me back? Geez, I spent the afternoon imagining all kinds of stuff. Is everything okay? Where's the kid?"

"In the bedroom," Peter answered. "Karen decided to tell the family we live together just as we were getting there."

Steve took a deep breath. "What happened to Jeneil?"

"Everybody was in shock. Nobody talked to her but there was lots of staring. It was a mess. Mother pretended Jeneil wasn't there. I was afraid she'd blow up at Jeneil eventually so I called you to get us out of there without a big scene."

"Smart move," Steve said, nodding understandably.

"She was starting to settle down then her uncle from Nebraska called asking her how the day went and all kinds of questions. She's in there crying."

Steve looked toward the bedroom. "Can I talk to her?"

"She said she wasn't in the mood for company."

"I'm not company," Steve said, walking to the bedroom. The room was getting darker as dusk approached. He called to her from the bedroom door.

"Don't come in, I look a mess," Jeneil called, sitting on the edge of the bed.

"Too late, I'm already in and I can barely see you." Steve sat next to her and Peter sat on the other side.

"I'm not very good company right now," she said quietly, putting her head down. "I'm wallowing in self pity. Really both of you go. I'm a sight."

"Ooo, you are," Steve said. "Worse than the burn victim I had this morning, and the woman whose oven door exploded and cut her arm. Or the kid who got two fingers slammed in a door. There was a heart attack victim admitted, not expected to make it; and a bunch of little kids in Pediatrics who missed dinner with their families."

She looked at him. "You're right. There are people with bigger problems."

Steve put his arm around her. "Don't listen to the squeaky wheels. They're just making a lot of noise. Trust the ones who really know you. We know what you're really like."

Jeneil began to cry again. "No one has looked at me like that since years ago in my home town." Steve pulled her to him and she leaned against him. Peter watched them, totally surprised. "Only it wasn't true," she sobbed. "I didn't deserve it. It's different this time."

Steve rubbed her arm and held her closely. "What's this nonsense about deserving it? What exactly do you deserve for loving a guy and making him happy? So you're not playing the game the way they think it should be. So you've got different rules. Isn't it the end result that matters? He's never been this happy. You took him off the most-likely-to-die-tomorrow list."

Peter smiled but wished Steve would let her go. He wanted to hold her. He took her hand. "Honey, listen to him, he's right. Come on, baby, pull it together. Get rid of it for good, okay."

Steve squeezed her. "Yeah, kid. I'm starved. I bought a sandwich that was in a pile marked chicken salad. Who the hell knows what it really was. They let us out at four so we could have a holiday meal. Whatever's in your oven smells good. Is there enough for three? I need pampering, too." Jeneil laughed lightly and nodded. Steve kissed her forehead. "Oh great, I'm glad I came over."

"I'm glad you did, too." She sniffed. "Give me a few minutes to pull myself together."

"Two, not a few, or Pete and I attack what's in the oven without your help."

She smiled. "Two minutes then."

"Great," he said, standing up. "I'll wait on the sofa. The time starts now, 120-119-118-117," he counted down, walking out the door.

She shook her head. "He's so bossy."

Peter smiled and kissed her cheek. "I love you, Jeneil."

"I love you, too." She put her arms around his neck and kissed him.

"86-85-84-83," Steve called from the living room.

Jeneil laughed. "I love that guy."

"I'll try to slow down his counting, but you'd better hurry," Peter said, and she nodded and gave him a quick kiss. He left the room smiling.

Jeneil put vegetables into the microwave and set the table with china, crystal, and silverware. The table looked festive as she lit the candles. "Let's have dinner."

Peter smiled. "Honey, this looks great!"

"It does, now this feels like a holiday," Steve said, and kissed her cheek. "Thanks."

They ate slowly, enjoying being together. They lingered over coffee, talking and laughing about small things.

"We weren't a religious family, but we had our traditions. My father always started our Thanksgiving meal with a toast so I think I'd like to end ours by quoting him. 'May we never take ourselves so seriously that we become more important than the rest of life around us, but we always listen so we can learn and love so we can share.' I'm really grateful for both of you," Jeneil said. Steve smiled at her and Peter squeezed her hand. She sighed. "The only thing missing is the big stone fireplace and the warm fire crackling in it. I'd lie in front of it and we'd all spend the day talking and reading."

"Let's go sit in the living room and pretend," Steve suggested.

Jeneil grinned. "Would you guys clear the table for me?" They nodded and she disappeared.

Peter and Steve finished in the kitchen and headed to the living room. Steve sat on the sofa, sighing. "This has been one of the nicest Thanksgivings for me. I really relax with the two of you."

Peter smiled. "In spite of the trouble, I've enjoyed this part, too." Jeneil appeared carrying a dining chair and placed it several feet from the sofa. "What's that for?"

"Pretending." She laughed as she disappeared again. Steve and Peter looked at each other.

"You did it, Steve." Peter grinned. "I heard you say it to her."

Jeneil returned and taped a section of paper in a red brick design along the back of the chair to the floor. She added flames made from construction paper at the base. "My fireplace."

"I like it." Steve smiled, sitting forward as Jeneil spread a large quilt on the floor in front of the fake fire and sat down.

"Come on, guys."

"Why not." Peter laughed.

"Why not is right." Steve smiled. They each got beside her and all three lay on their backs.

"We can't see the fire." Jeneil chuckled.

"I can feel it." Steve laughed. Jeneil looked at him and smiled then the three lay silently for a few minutes.

"My bones are hurting," Jeneil groaned, and got up to get the sofa cushions and brought pillows for Peter and Steve to rest their heads. Sitting on the cushions, she sighed. "Much, much better." There was silence as they entertained their own thoughts. Jeneil turned to Peter. "What affect do you think my being in your family will have on the little children who were playing there today? I noticed they were shocked to see me. They noticed I was different."

Peter shrugged. "I haven't thought about it. Did it bother you?"

"Being different?" Jeneil asked, and Peter nodded. "No, I've lived with prejudice all my life. I grew up different." Peter began to laugh. Steve did, too. "Okay, okay, so it wasn't like what Peter had to face, but you guys need to live in a small town to understand the life there. My parents were older. They were the age of the grandparents of all the other kids. My father was Catholic in a Protestant town; that was second class. My mother was an artist and didn't like ladies' church groups; that was second class. I went to church and I was different in a Catholic or a Protestant church from all the others. I saw it when people looked at me. I think that's why I was so good at scriptures and tried hard to earn my white choir robe. I wanted to prove I belonged there. That's what hurt so much when the gossip started." She looked at Steve. "And what are you laughing at, WASP. With blonde hair and blue eyes, you don't even know what I'm talking about."

"Oh no? Jeneil, I know exactly what you're talking about. The looks from people, the way they deal with you. Hey, I was one of those other kids from 'the home.' At school that was worse than being black. Our own parents didn't want us. Especially if you were older and still not adopted. Then that meant nobody wanted you."

Jeneil stared at him with a lump in her throat. "What happened to your parents?"

Steve laughed. "I don't know. Believe it or not, I was left on the doorstep of the home in a box."

Peter laughed. "Are you serious?"

Steve laughed. "So help me, it's the honest truth. I know it's a classic tale, but it's true."

The lump pained Jeneil and she swallowed hard. "But you're so pretty. I can't understand why you didn't get adopted immediately."

Steve looked at her and smiled. "Pretty, huh? That didn't impress anybody. They were afraid of what might be lacking in my chromosomes. With no history, I may have had blue eyes, but who knew what my kids would look like."

"Oh my gosh. I think I've just come across the ultimate prejudice. I'll bet your mother was very young when she had you."

"Why do you say that?" Steve asked, surprised.

"Because anyone older would have realized the damage to your future a totally anonymous beginning would do. The poor girl, she has to live with the fact that somewhere in the world lives a beautiful blonde-haired, blue-eyed son."

Steve chuckled. "You're good, Jeneil. I've never given any serious thought to my parents. My beginning is blackness to me, a void. You've just given it a human form with its own problems."

Peter laughed. "Yeah, she is good, Steve. You should see what she's done for my father."

"Hey, Pete, who knows, he might have been my father, too. Maybe we're half brothers," and they both laughed.

Jeneil looked from one to the other. "You guys are something else. I love your lack of anger."

Steve leaned on his elbow and looked at her. "Who's to get angry at a faceless woman? What good does it do? Where'd you get such a bleeding heart?"

She shrugged. "I don't know that it's a bleeding heart really. It's just in how we perceive things, isn't it? How we understand and what we accept. I don't know. Peter, did your people know you were half white?"

Peter nodded. "Are you kidding? The Chinese know how many teeth you have filled."

Steve laughed. "Hey, Pete, that doesn't sound like the phrase you guys used to say on the streets."

Peter laughed. "No, but I thought the phrase we used was impossible until I became a doctor and realized it wasn't. The nurses mark the information on charts after they empty the bedpans."

Jeneil looked at Peter. "Did you face any prejudice from Chinese because of being half white?"

"Damn right I did, especially because of my father. Ki was one of the few who didn't. I would've never been made a guard in the Dragons if it hadn't been for him."

"That's really tough." Jeneil sighed.

Peter laughed. "Hey, being a half-breed had its advantages, too."

Jeneil was surprised. "Oh, like what?"

Peter chuckled. "Forget it."

"What?" Jeneil asked, becoming more curious.

Steve began to laugh. "I had the same advantage coming from the home."

"Oh yeah? Not too bad was it? Once you got older."

"Damn right. And at a time in your life when it's important to have confidence," and they both laughed.

"What?" Jeneil asked. "What, tell me?"

Peter and Steve looked at each other and shook their heads, and then Peter spoke, "She won't be able to take it."

"What?" Jeneil insisted. "I can take it. It must be about sex. I can tell by the way you're laughing."

"You're too shrewd, baby." Peter chuckled.

Steve smiled. "Jeneil, stay in front of your stone fireplace in your white house with the white picket fence."

"Oh, you guys are so smug. Do you really think small town country life is so easy and safe? You came across sex early in the country. Every time you turned around, the bull and the cows were doing it. The horses were never apart. And the dogs, gosh they were real pigs."

Peter and Steve laughed hysterically. Steve sighed from laughing so hard. "Oh geez, Jeneil, you're so cute. That was real pressure to put up with."

Peter kissed her arm. "You're funny."

She sat up on the cushions and turned to face them. "So tell me what was so different where you grew up."

Peter and Steve looked at each other then Steve looked at her. "Jeneil, how old were you when you first had sex?"

She fidgeted and fixed a hairpin, gathering her composure. "I was twenty-two."

"What?" Steve was shocked and he looked at Peter. Peter smiled. "Whew," Steve whistled. "I spotted you as a beginner but not a trainee."

"Don't be insulting." Jeneil frowned.

"I'm not." Steve chuckled. "You're not ready to hear what we're laughing about then."

"Why? How old were you guys? Fourteen?" Peter and Steve laughed hysterically. "Stop laughing at me."

Steve bit his lip to keep from laughing. "Jeneil, I was six. Eight held more detailed stuff for me."

"I was nine," Peter answered.

Jeneil was shocked and looked it. "No wonder you're so good," she blurted out. Peter choked. Steve laughed. Jeneil turned red. "You guys are exaggerating, aren't you? At eight and nine, sex is more an exploration of innocent curiosity."

Steve shook his head. "Jeneil, I hope you never wake up."

"But, but." She shook her head in disbelief. Peter smiled and took her hand. "Two little kids, what could you and little girls even understand at that age?"

Steve looked at Peter. "Doesn't know kinky, huh?" Peter shook his head. "Wow." Steve smiled at Jeneil and held her other hand.

"Kinky?" She looked from one to the other.

"Skip it," Steve said.

"Forget it, honey," Peter added.

She stared at them as she began to understand. "It wasn't little girls, was it?" She sighed. "Adults." She closed her eyes and shook her head slowly, biting her lower lip.

Steve sat up and grabbed her shoulders. "Jeneil, look at us. We're here. We're okay; reasonably sane and healthy. It's the end result that matters, isn't it? Not everybody is a tragic statistic. You survive as best you can. What matters is that you survive, the end result, Jeneil, the end result. Isn't it?"

"Yes. Yes, it is," she whispered, swallowing to relieve the pain in her throat, but she didn't cry. She put her arms around Steve's neck and hugged him. "You guys are both superlatives. Incredible superlatives," she said, her voice shaking. Peter sat up, watching the two of them, surprised by how comfortable they had become with each other.

Steve rubbed her back gently. He sensed how fragile she was and he was becoming aware of her as a woman. He pushed her away and smiled. "Hey, you've got to toughen up kid or life will swallow you whole."

She nodded and smiled. "I know, I haven't found my balance yet but I'm working on it."

She turned to Peter and kissed him. She nestled herself into a sitting position in front of him and leaned her back against him. She took his one free arm and wrapped it around her. He smiled and kissed her cheek. She wanted comfort and security and turned to him. He kissed her temple and squeezed her. He smiled to himself. Songbird, he thought as he gently kissed her shoulder

The Thanksgiving decorations were exchanged for Christmas ones as life moved on. Peter's mother was back to total silence. Word from his grandfather was she was silent about them at home, too. Jeneil had suggested she call and apologize, but Peter panicked and forbid her to even try. He felt it would do more harm than good and she had promised she wouldn't. Frustrated and confused about the whole family matter, she busied herself with Christmas. Peter smiled as every day a Christmas tree showed up in a different room of the apartment; a small plastic one glittered on the bedroom bureau, a ceramic one on the small dining table, a two foot artificial one on the buffet in the dining area, plus the large real tree in the living room. She had invited Steve for dinner one night and they had spent the evening decorating it. Peter had openly laughed when he found the one on the bathroom vanity. Sprays of real green decorated the front hall banister and large red bows hung merrily on every one. She obviously loved Christmas.

There were parties they were invited to; Robert's, Dennis's, and a charity party Jeneil had gone to alone. Steve had been invited to the same one through the medical group he was joining. Steve had warned Peter about Morgan Rand; Sondra had the flu and he had gone to the party alone. It annoyed Steve that Morgan got to dance with Jeneil several times while he wasn't allowed to; they pretended they didn't know each other. Two other residents had danced with her and even Dr. Sprague, but of them all Steve insisted that Morgan had shown far too much interest. "Watch him," Steve had told Peter. "You shouldn't let her look that good when she's alone." Peter chuckled at Steve's hovering.

A few inches of snow had fallen and Jeneil had brought out sleds. They went to the park during a full moon and acted like kids. Steve had gotten to see Jeneil touch the moon for the first time. Peter was used to her standing to the full moon and connecting her hand to it. She had invited them to try it so they could feel the energy. They laughingly tried but insisted that all they felt was stupid. She had told them they were too earthbound.

Peter's family always had a Christmas party and he was waiting to see what would happen. He picked up the call in the viewing room. His mother sounded formal. "We're having our Christmas party, Peter. I wanted you to know you're welcomed to come."

"Just me?" he asked, knowing the answer by the tone in her voice.

"Just you, Peter. I'm sorry, but the embarrassment from Thanksgiving was too much for me. This is your family, we would like you to be with us, but the embarrassment in your life is something I don't feel I should have to sit with," she said calmly. It wasn't open for discussion, and oddly enough, Peter understood. "You should also know that it'll be the same for Christmas and any other party we have here so we don't have to discuss this again."

"I understand, Mom," he answered quietly. "Thank you for not yelling. It's your house."

"Then what will you do?"

"I told you before, Mom. You don't take Jeneil, you don't take me." Peter heard her sigh.

"Has she decided when you'll get married?"

Peter braced himself. "No, she hasn't."

"Then that's it, Peter. I want you to know that you're welcomed. This is your family."

"Okay, I understand."

"Bye, Peter."

"Bye, Mom." He sighed and rubbed his forehead. It wasn't as easy as he thought it would be, especially when his mother was so calm about it. He took a deep breath, picked up the medical charts and went back to work, but there was a sadness in him.

His mother replaced the receiver and wiped away the tears that rolled down her cheeks. Karen watched. "He won't come without her?" Karen asked, feeling compassion for her.

His mother shook her head and sighed.

"What is it with that girl?" Karen stood up angrily. "I hope she makes up her mind soon, and I hope its Steve."

"Karen, Peter's going to be badly hurt in this. He's prepared to give up his family for her and she can't even decide if she wants him. I wish he'd find someone else and leave her before she hurts him." She began to cry again.

Karen patted her arm sympathetically, and then a thought came to her. Karen sat down next to her. "Lien, if Pete's taste is the sweet innocent type then I have someone who might interest him."

The mother looked up. "Who?"

"Uette Wong."

"Wong? The importers?"

"Yes, the youngest daughter."

The mother shook her head. "Karen, the Wongs are the elite of the Chinese. They'd never stand for their daughter with Peter. Their girls wouldn't look twice at him."

"Uette is different from the whole family. She's not a snob. She's a drama major. She wants to be an actress and she deals with all types. The kids say they think she's doing character studies on them. She's not too popular; people think she's not real. She reminds me of Jeneil in a lot of ways. Why don't I see what happens? She might not have heard about Pete's wild life."

The mother shook her head. "Everybody's heard of Pete's wild life. Her father especially with four daughters. He knows about everybody."

"But it can't hurt to try, can it? She's beautiful. She makes Jeneil look plain by comparison."

"Karen, you can try, but her father will have a fit, I know it."

"But Pete's a doctor now."

"Peter can't erase his birth." The mother broke down in tears.

"But that's just it. Uette isn't into the family stuff. I don't know why, but she's not. She's got all their class, but not the attitude. Pete should flip over her. I'm going to see if I can introduce them."

The mother gathered herself. "Believe me, Karen, there's nothing I'd rather have for Peter than a good Chinese marriage to a good girl in a good family."

"That's Uette then," Karen said. "Leave it to me. As soon as the holiday recess is over, I'll approach her."

*****

Peter pressed the elevator button. He was worn out and his mother's call had drained him. The thought of having to tell Jeneil weighted him down even more. He sighed and hit the button again, anxious to get to his car.

"Hey, Pete, it's the season to be jolly," Steve said, joining him. Peter smiled wearily. "What is it, Pete?" Steve asked seriously. The elevator doors opened and they stepped inside.

"The mother made her final judgment on the Thanksgiving Day mess."

Steve looked at him, dreading to ask. "What is it?"

"As long as we're not married, don't bring Jeneil to the house. We embarrass her."

Steve shook his head. "And when you get married, it'll be something else, Pete. The kid can't win in your family. You'd better face it."

"I don't know, Steve. The mother has never complained that she's not Chinese. She just wants us married. That's not hard to understand. Nobody in my family has lived common law before this."

"So what does that make Jeneil, a sinner, a tramp, white trash?" Steve was annoyed.

"What are you mad at?"

"Oh damn it, Pete. You go home and tell her that and she'll feel like a zero again. Every time she turns around somebody shovels dirt on her. She doesn't deserve it, that's all. For as long as I've known you, your mother has been taking you apart in chunks. Now it's Jeneil. She's sensitive and she's caught in the crossfire. It stinks. Like I'm telling you, you'd better face it because Jeneil will never be part of your family. She'll never be good enough for them."

"My mother is just complaining about my not being married." The elevator stopped at the doctor's indoor parking area and the doors opened.

"Yeah, I know and you understand her," Steve snapped and got off. "I'll see you tomorrow," he said, heading to his car. Peter watched him for a second then headed to his own car.

Jeneil was asleep when he got home. He slipped into bed and lay on his back. Turning, he saw her hair spread across the pillow. He moved his head slightly and kissed a strand lying near him. Why was this so complicated? He loved her. He wanted to marry her. It was so simple in his mind. He had liked it better when nobody knew about them. Life was easy then. He sighed. It was still simple. He loved her. He wanted to marry her. He promised he wouldn't push. He promised he'd give up the family for her. He turned on his side and smelled her hair. Smiling, he began to relax and drifted to sleep.

*****

Peter decided not to tell Jeneil about his mother's call. She was in high gear over Christmas and he was enjoying her excitement. It was too close to Christmas anyway and he didn't want to ruin things. When he got home, Jeneil was sitting at the dining table decorating gingerbread men. He took off his jacket and hung it in the closet.

"What are those for?"

"To wrap in plastic and hang on the tree."

"Who gets to eat all the stuff on it now?" he asked, smiling.

"We do," she answered, adding eyes to a half dozen boys. "One year, Billie and I decided to see if we could save one until Easter Sunday." She giggled. "We had to hit it with a hammer to break it. We let it sit in milk all day to get soft then threw it away because we were too full of chocolate eggs and jelly beans to eat it."

Peter smiled. "Our kids are in for a lot of fun with you as their mother."

She looked at him and smiled. "Will you color some shirts and pants while you sit there?"

"Why not?" He picked up a knife and scooped it into the blue frosting.

"I'll probably let Mrs. Rezendes's children raid the tree New Year's Day. She has the most peaceful and loving children I've ever seen. For a large family, they are well behaved and really nice kids. I'm going to visit her a lot and find out her secrets. I'd like ours to be as nice as hers"

Peter looked at her and smiled. "Soon?"

"Soon what? To visit her?"

"No, to get married and have children."

"You still have a year of training yet."

"Is that why we're waiting?"

"When did your mother call?"

He grinned. "Smart ass kid, aren't you?"

"Have you heard from her? It's only days until Christmas. Is she still angry at me?" She stopped breathing when Peter didn't answer. "You might as well tell me. I've been expecting something since Christmas is so close." Peter continued frosting cookies without answering. "Let me guess, we're back to you're invited, I'm not." She watched him then snapped her fingers. "Yo, Chang, nod if I'm getting close."

He looked up. "She wants us married before we go to anymore parties with the family."

"You mean before I can go there, don't you?"

He sighed. "Jeneil, can you blame her?"

She stopped abruptly and slammed her knife down. "What's her concern, that I have the morals of an alley cat and can't be trusted around righteous people? Yes, I can blame her, Peter. I'm tired of her passing judgment on me. I'm sick of it. I could roll out a few scriptures that would shake her eligibility as a Christian starting with, 'Judge not, lest ye be judged.' She got up from her chair. "Listen to me!" She rubbed her temples. "I am becoming an alley cat." She took a deep breath, folded her arms and began to pace. "I refuse to do this to me." She went to the stereo and inserted a tape of Christmas carols. Pulling her hairpins out, she paced in the living room. Peter sighed and leaned back in his chair. Jeneil returned to the table and began cleaning up. "I have gifts for your family. We can take my name off your mother's, Tom's, John's, and Karen's. I knitted your grandfather a sweater. I don't think he'll mind. You can deliver them anytime. They're all wrapped. I'll be in Nebraska this weekend."

"I thought you didn't have a meeting this month."

"I usually go home for Christmas Day. I didn't expect to be free this year so I told them I'd fly in this weekend. Marlene would like to meet you."

"What about your uncle?"

"Marlene said it."

"Jeneil, aren't you a little tired of the pressure from both sides?"

"My people are in Nebraska. Hollis seldom mentions anything. You're the one under pressure. It's your people who are embarrassed. I've said it before, Peter. If it's too much for you then leave." She picked up the tray of dishes and went to the kitchen. He closed his eyes trying hard not to get angry then went to the kitchen ready for a fight.

"You know, I'm finding it interesting that your solution is always for me to move out. It's never okay, let's get married."

She threw the sponge into the dishwater. "And exactly what are you making out of that."

"You tell me. Are you really not ready to get married or maybe you don't want to marry me. Am I just some kind of game for you, Jeneil?"

Jeneil shook her head. "Boy, she's really got you thinking clearly hasn't she?"

"Leave my mother out of this," he snapped.

Jeneil turned quickly and angrily. "She's in it, Peter. She's in it up to my neck. She's at my jugular. Stop quoting her if you want her to stay out of this." She picked up the tray and returned to the dining room.

Peter stood there amazed he had taken his mother's side and asked himself where the hell this was going. He could feel it; this was going to be one of those arguments that didn't get resolved, the kind that was never over and just ate away at you from under your skin. Jeneil returned and began washing dishes. She didn't talk, anger pulsating through her. He could see he wasn't going to reach her and decided the best thing to do was get out of her way, so he went to the bedroom and turned on the TV.

Peter awoke feeling cold. TV programming was over and snowy static filled the screen. He had fallen asleep on top of the bedding. He sat up and checked his watch; it was two-thirty. He ran his fingers through his hair. Getting up, he opened the bedroom door. The apartment was dark. He walked to the living room and found Jeneil asleep on the sofa bed. "Go ahead, Jeneil. When you grow up, let me know and we'll talk about it," he yelled at her in his mind. He turned angrily and went back to the bedroom. They avoided each other that morning. His lunch was ready and breakfast was waiting, but she never stayed more than a few seconds in a room with him. It made him angrier and he left for work without saying goodbye.

*****

Christmas was everywhere and it was misery since he wasn't in the mood for the merriment. Peter saw Steve get off the elevator smiling, putting something in his mouth. Steve signed a paper a nurse held for him. She broke off a piece of what he had hanging from his mouth and ate it, wishing him a merry Christmas. Steve walked over to Peter.

"Boy, this place is crawling with department Christmas parties." Steve took a bite of the cookie. Peter recognized the gingerbread man.

"Where'd you get that?"

"From Jeneil. Her office is partying. I went in on business and she gave it to me."

For some reason that annoyed Peter. He went to the medical charts. He sighed. This was getting out of hand and he decided to talk to her. He headed to Records. Mrs. Sousa was on duty. Peter looked at her surprised.

"She won't be back until Tuesday."

"Oh, that's pretty close to Christmas."

"Yes, it is. I hope the traffic won't cause a problem for her." Mrs. Sousa shrugged. "It was sudden; I know because she called the airlines to change her flight schedule from here. I don't envy her. The airport will be jammed with people traveling for Christmas."

Peter nodded. "Well, I'll wait until she gets back, I guess."

"Are you sure?"

"Yes, it can keep. Thanks anyway." He left quickly. Stopping at a phone, he dialed the apartment. There was no answer. His chest felt empty. He knew she was really angry; she hadn't even let him know. He was worried. They hadn't argued like this in a long time and he went back to the floor feeling really low.

"Hey, Pete, here, I got some candy from Accounting's party." Steve put several pieces of wrapped candy on the table in front of Peter.

"What are you doing for the weekend?"

Steve bit into a piece of candy. "Sienna's company Christmas party. I owe her big for all the dinner and cocktail parties she's gone to with me lately. And a party at Dr. Sprague's tomorrow night. She's been really different lately, really easy to take. No more pressing me. Why?"

"Jeneil's away." Peter had trouble saying it.

"Yeah, she's visiting Nebraska for Christmas, isn't she?"

Peter nodded. "How did you know?"

"She told me when she invited me for Christmas Eve and Christmas dinner."

"When was that?"

"Over the weekend. What's wrong Pete?"

"Uh, nothing."

"Life getting ahead of you?" Steve smiled. "It happens to me, too. Seems like I spend days catching up. The kid survived the mother's rejection, I guess?"

"What do you mean?"

Steve shrugged. "She seemed fine when she invited me for Christmas."

Peter was surprised. "She didn't know about my mother's call until yesterday. I guess she wasn't planning to go to my mother's even if she had been invited." Peter didn't like it at all. They were losing touch with each other.

"Well good for her. Why stand around and wait to have your teeth kicked in." Steve gathered up the paper pieces and got up. "I've got to meet with Dr. Sprague. I'll see you later."

*****

"Hey, Pete, it's been a long time. You look lost," Joe Artoli said, and continued shooting pool. Peter felt lost. He wandered around the room. He felt like a stranger there.

An intern stuck his head in. "Dr. Chang?" Peter turned quickly. "Telephone."

"Peter, what are you doing at the dorm?" his grandfather asked when Peter picked up the receiver.

"Jeneil's in Nebraska. I thought I'd stay here a few days."

"Your mother told me that you're not coming to the Christmas party. I'm sorry about her attitude toward Jeneil. Is she upset about it?"

"I don't think so, Grandfather. I don't think she would have gone if she had been invited."

"There's trouble isn't there, Peter? You two are having problems about this?"

"Jeneil's fed up, Grandfather. Really, how much put down can anyone take?"

"I know, I know." The grandfather sighed. "Are you two surviving all of it?"

"We're okay," Peter lied.

"Well, that's good. Learn to keep things constant between you when everything else starts changing."

Peter didn't understand and he didn't want to. He wanted to be alone. "What was it you called about?"

"Will you and Jeneil stop by before Christmas? I have some gifts."

"I doubt it, Grandfather. I don't think my mother would like it. We'd better stay away."

His grandfather sighed. "We seem to be moving backwards in this."

"Looks like it," Peter agreed.

"I'm sorry, Peter. I really am. It looked so promising for a while. You know the family has accepted your living with Jeneil."

"You mean it?" Peter asked, surprised.

"It's just your mother who's having trouble with it. And Karen."

"Karen," Peter spat out the name. "Just the sound of it irritates me."

"I can understand that," the grandfather sympathized. "I can't understand her and your mother. They're so close lately. Karen's been so very caring toward her."

"She should be. The mouth. Looks like everybody has a place in the family except Jeneil." Peter sighed. "Maybe Steve's right."

"About what?"

"He said she'd never be accepted by the family."

"What does he want you to do?"

"He didn't suggest anything except that I realize my mother will always be after Jeneil about something."

"We can hope it's not true, Peter."

"Sure," Peter said, but he had trouble hoping tonight.

"Are you and Steve spending the weekend together?"

"No, Steve's with Jeneil's girlfriend."

"Oh, then he is interested in someone."

"They're friends."

"Well Peter, I should let you go. Will you stop by for the gifts?"

"Okay, and thanks a lot. Your caring about us keeps us going, Grandfather. You'll never know how much."

The grandfather smiled. "I really love Jeneil. She feels like she's part of my family. She's more Chinese than you are, Peter."

Peter laughed and it felt good. "I think I'll tell her that. Thanks for calling, Grandfather."

"Keep your relationship constant, Peter."

"I'll try, Grandfather." Peter hung up. The call made him miss Jeneil. He went back to his room and fell asleep.

*****

Steve was asked to work a double Saturday night and Peter took it for him. The thought of facing the family with the damage between him and Jeneil was more than he wanted to deal with. Plus, the thought of facing Karen seemed like torture. He couldn't trust himself around her yet. Steve smiled as Peter woke up Sunday morning.

"Well, I thought you were going to be in bed all day."

"The shift was hectic. I was exhausted. What are you doing today?" Peter yawned.

"I'm yours, buddy. How about some breakfast?"

"Oh good, I'm starved."

"Hey, Pete, the paperwork is going through on the medical associates deal."

Peter smiled broadly. "Congratulations."

Steve sighed and held his chest. "Yeah, I feel like my life is just beginning. It's beginning to be real to me. Come on, get up; let's celebrate with a huge breakfast."

"You're on." Peter got out of bed quickly.

The day stretched before Peter. With shift change, it almost felt like a day off. "What are you doing today, Steve?" he asked, finishing breakfast.

"Sienna's making a Sunday dinner." Steve drank his coffee slowly.

"Then why did you eat like this for breakfast this late?"

Steve put his head down. "She can't cook, Pete."

"I thought she was a gourmet cook?"

Steve smiled. "Then I don't like gourmet. I went there for dinner last week. She said we were having steak. That sounded great, I was starved. The damn thing had all this stuffing in it." He shook his head. "It looked like she rolled it through the parking lot before she put it on my plate. All these bits and pieces of stuff. Oh geez, it made my stomach sick." He sighed and ordered more coffee. "And we can't drink coffee; it has to be espresso or café au lait or some European blend. You know, she's really okay if she'd drop the whole Sienna thing. Underneath I think she's a nice kid."

"Have you told her that?"

Steve shook his head. "She likes Sienna and she spent a fortune in the role. I think I could really like the person I see underneath, she's a little like Jeneil. Soft, caring, real."

"How do you know that?"

"I had to tell her about the lie at the hospital. Rand was really leaning on her at the last party. That guy is on my ass like he's getting a reward if he uncovers something. He's got to be weird, at least warped. I held my breath and told her the whole thing."

"What happened?"

Steve shrugged and smiled. "She was shocked and turned into this Jeneil kind of person, all warm and sympathetic. It felt really good to be talking to her for a change. I liked her at that moment. I mean, I really liked her. She hasn't been pushing so much for a physical relationship, and being all soft and sympathetic. It's been nice."

"What happened?" Peter asked, noticing Steve's grin.

Steve sighed. "I kissed her for the first time. She started to get to me and then she turned into Sienna in the middle of the kiss. Damn, I wanted to strangle her. It made me mad. You start out kissing a Jeneil and you end up with a Marcia."

"Can't you tell her that?"

Steve shook his head. "It won't work between us, Pete. At her party last night I got the feeling I was important to Sienna because I'm a doctor and...."

"And what?"

"My looks," Steve said quietly.

Peter smiled. "Turn off?"

Steve nodded. "Damn, where can I find a girl who crawls into your head and your gut, sees the real you and accepts it, even thinks you're okay and special."

"She's in Nebraska."

Steve looked at Peter and laughed. "And she's yours."

Peter pushed a piece of sausage on his plate with his fork and remembered her note. At that moment he wondered if she was his. He missed her and the feeling of missing her was getting worse. It brought an emptiness with it. He thought of Steve's words about crawling into your head and your gut. He smiled to himself. And when she lives in your soul, it's over for you, he thought, remembering Jeneil's words.

*****

Peter unlocked the apartment door and looked at his watch; eleven in the morning. It was two hours earlier in Nebraska. He went to Jeneil's telephone directory, looked up Hollis and began to dial. He hung up as the thought of talking to Hollis surfaced. He picked up the phone and dialed again, holding his breath. A kid answered.

"Is Jeneil there?"

"Mommy, a man wants Aunt Jeneil."

"I'm sorry, Jeneil isn't here. Can I take a message?" a woman asked.

"This is Peter Chang."

"Oh Peter!" The woman was pleasant and cheerful. Peter was encouraged. "This is Marlene. Jeneil's been in Loma with Bill Reynolds since Thursday. She's expected here for dinner. I can have her call you."

"Thanks, I'd appreciate that," he said, surprised by Marlene's news.

"Well, it's good to meet you by telephone at least. You know, if it's urgent I'll call Bill's house. I know Jeneil's staying on the estate and there's no telephone there, but Bill can drive over. His house is only a meadow away. He bought Hadley's Bluff, the rascal, and built a gorgeous house on it. Those two are the funniest. Loma can't believe the two of them. With Jeneil in the estate and Bill on the Bluff, it has put the townspeople in their place. And it couldn't happen to two nicer kids. They deserve it."

"What do you mean, Jeneil's in the estate?"

"Mandra's estate, the one she left to Jeneil. It's where Jeneil grew up. I don't think she'll ever get used to the big house. She always stays at the guest cottage where she lived as a child. I've never seen a girl so reluctant about being rich. But Mandra trained her and prepared her for it. Do you want me to call Bill for you?"

"No." Peter was stunned. "It'll be fine if Jeneil calls when she gets there."

"Okay, then I'll tell her, and it's been nice talking to you. Maybe one day we'll meet in person."

"Yes. Thank you, Mrs. Wells."

"Merry Christmas, Peter."

Peter sat on the edge of the bed, completely stunned by the news. Mandra's estate belonged to Jeneil. No wonder she lectured him about money and being rich. He stood up. She had been lying to him. He thought they were past that. He thought Mandra left her cars when she'd really left her the whole estate. What the hell would she want with a doctor here in the east if her money was in Nebraska? He had pictured them in a normal house where he would be practicing and all the while she had a palace somewhere in the Midwest. No wonder she wouldn't marry him. No wonder Hollis was upset. They really didn't belong together at all!

Peter paced. What the hell was he supposed to do now? He ran his fingers through his hair. He sat down and slammed his fist against the pillow. What the hell was she doing to him? Had she been messing with his head? Was it all a big gotcha? She must realize a street kid could never make it in a palace. He didn't even want to. He sighed heavily from anger and frustration. This was a big fairy tale to her. She wasn't real, this wasn't real, they weren't real. He remembered her words, "If it's too much for you, then leave." He stood up. His stomach was beginning to pain. "It's that easy for you, isn't it?"

He remembered the time at the beach house; she had told him there were people who expected her to accept her responsibility. Now it made sense. He remembered she didn't go away with Jack because of her responsibilities. She came out here and decided to do some slumming; a country western singer, a street kid. That was it, wasn't it? That was the big attraction to Chang. She had gotten bored in the palace and came here for some fun. His mother was right! Jeneil was rebelling against what she was, and he had walked right into it thinking it was all real. He sighed. His chest felt knotted. Shit Jeneil, another gotcha? His mother's words came to him, "They'll go to their own kind." Peter laughed. And his mother thought it was Steve. Hell, she was good. The Chinese Stud and the White Stallion both thought she was real. It wasn't Steve. Hell no, her kind was Bill Reynolds. Diamonds, private jets, that was her kind. Son of a bitch, he had walked right into it and the whole fairy tale she made for herself. Peter paced as he waited for her call. At two-thirty his whole body was knotted. He couldn't wait anymore. He got his clothes and headed to the gym at the hospital. Steve broke into laughter as Peter walked in.

"Join me on the rowing machine, Pete."

"Why are you here, Steve? I thought you had a dinner to go to."

"Oh, Pete, that would have been some Sunday dinner. Sienna came out of the kitchen in this apron that looked like a sundress in the front and tied in the back." Steve laughed. "She had nothing else on."

Peter stared, realizing the shock it must have been to Steve. "Oh great."

"No, it's not great, Pete. That's what I mean about her. I think I'm getting dinner and all the while she's setting me up. Shit, I hate that! I hate it when a woman sets me up for sex. It makes me crazy. I hate it when women think I'm that much of a pushover."

Peter put on boxing gloves. "I know exactly how you feel about being set up." He swung at the bag with his fist, and Peter and Steve spent an hour working hard. They were both tense and very discouraged. They went to work unwound physically, but were still tense emotionally.

*****

No call came from Jeneil at the hospital. Peter went to the apartment after work to see if there was a message on the answering machine. There wasn't. He looked at the time; eleven forty-five, it was only nine forty-five out west. He waited. Maybe she'd call knowing he was out of work. He lay on the bed and soon fell asleep covered by the bedspread.

He opened his eyes as he heard the key in the lock. The room was light. He sat up. Nine o'clock! He heard Jeneil set her luggage in the apartment. He stood up and straightened his clothes. He felt pretty rested for having slept in his clothes. He began to get annoyed as he realized she never returned his call. He sat on the bed and waited. She appeared at the bedroom door, surprised to find him awake. She hung the garment bag on the clothes tree. Peter could tell she was uneasy. She headed toward the door again.

"Hey, we've got to talk."

She clasped her hands and stared at them. "I know we do, I just need some juice. I left at five this morning. I'm starved." She walked out. He wanted to follow her but decided against it. It surprised him that he even cared. She looked really good. He was hurt and angry, and he didn't want to get caught up in her looks, or her eyes, or her perfume. He wanted truth. He sat on the edge of the bed and sighed. She returned with a glass of juice for both of them. Handing one to him, she then sat in the soft chair near the bed. She sipped her juice and avoided looking at him. She crossed her legs gracefully. Peter looked down at his glass to avoid looking at her legs. He forced himself to remember the situation. Anger began to stir again.

"Why didn't you return my call?" he asked, surprising himself with the calmness of his voice.

"Because when Marlene told me about the conversation, I figured I better deal with it in person. I flew in with Bill on his plane. He's heading for New York. Why did you call?"

"That isn't important anymore. Marlene's news is. So you're a rich bitch, aren't you? No wonder the role came so easy to you in Vermont."

Jeneil sighed. "I am not rich. Mandra left her estate to me. I was named sole heir to her fortune." She never looked up. "As far as I'm concerned, the money is still hers."

Peter was surprised fortune meant more than rich to him. "Jeneil, don't you think that was a major oversight on your part? Don't you think you should have told me?"

"Peter, when I found out about the inheritance, I had Uncle Hollis intervene. It hasn't gone through probate yet. I asked for a stay of four years to have blood relatives traced with the hopes that enough of them would come forward and contest the will. I don't want the money!" Her voice cracked and she sipped her juice. Peter felt himself becoming calmer. She was closer to the Jeneil he knew to be real than the one he had imaged since talking to Marlene.

"Have they found her family?"

She shook her head. "But I still have two years left."

"What happens if nobody is found?"

She looked up. "That's impossible! Mandra must have people somewhere!"

"Jeneil, what happens if nobody is found?" he asked again. "You're in business; I can't believe you haven't thought about it."

"I have," she answered quietly. "If it happens then I've got major problems. I refuse to live on the estate. I will not live in Loma. That is definite. Bill has offered to buy it."

"Are you going to sell it to him?"

She shook her head. "I can't for a lot of reasons. The first is Mandra. Loma is named after one of her grandmothers. The estate is in the heart of town, something like Buckingham

Palace would be to the British. Secondly, if I sold it then its value would make me incredibly cash rich. I can't imagine Bill being able to buy it. So it seems the place would cost me money to hold onto. That way, Mandra's ancestors are happy, the town is happy, and the white elephant costs me Mandra's money and that makes me happy." She stared at her juice glass.

Peter smiled. She really was reluctant to be rich.

"My plan is to treat the place like a historical monument. In two years, if I'm still sole heir, I plan to ask Bill's parents to be the curators. That's why Bill wants it. It gripes him that his mother has had to watch where she shopped and what she bought. If she spent too much, donations to the church stopped. I remember her telling my mother that. She had to be very careful. I've put all of Mandra's furs in storage with the plan to let Mrs. Reynolds choose from them. With the salaries they'd earn as curators, they could travel, which is something they could never do as a minister. Bill is very bitter toward the town. He's working hard at getting his father to agree to my offer so they can live on the estate and enjoy the feel of snobbing it. They won't, they're not the type, but they care about history and they loved Mandra. That might convince them to accept my offer. Bill is contributing a huge amount of money to the church so they'll get used to it. When his father retires, he plans to stop so the church will feel the loss." She sighed. "I can't believe how deep his scars are, that's why I won't live in Loma. I feel the anger if I stay too long. My hope is to restore the old farm buildings that spread across the estate and make it a historical working farm using old fashioned methods, the cost should really eat into the fortune."

"How large is the fortune?"

Jeneil shrugged. "It's still earning money. I don't want to know and I've closed my mind to it for now. I think it made Mandra a prisoner. Hollis was worried about my neglect. He had me named something or other of the estate so the buildings, grounds, and assets wouldn't deteriorate while we're searching for heirs. So, at the moment, I'm not actually rich. I'm more powerful than rich. In a sense, I haven't lied. And I don't want anyone to know about the money, Peter. I saw how people dealt with Mandra. They'd smile to her face then rip her apart behind her back. I wondered how she could even trust anything. Was anything real or sincere? I've wondered if that's why she never married, too. People treat you differently when you're rich. I want a real life. I don't want Mandra's prison. It's not my family or my money. That's not true really. I love Mandra deeply."

Peter noticed Jeneil spoke about Mandra like she was still alive. Peter felt for her. He had never thought about the problems that came with being rich. She looked fragile sitting there overwhelmed by money, fighting to be Jeneil, the Jeneil she was trying to find and protect from other people's ideas for her. He understood her a little better now. She sat there looking helpless and conscience stricken about her lies regarding Mandra's estate. And he liked catching her being wrong in an argument; she got all weak and apologetic. She was apologetic now. He could see it in her face and hear it in the tone of voice. It was in those moments that she'd reach out for him and cling to him like the girl he first met back on the beach. It was when she needed him most. Finding out she wasn't what he was imagining lifted a great weight from his mind. She was real. She knew she had deliberately withheld information about Mandra's money and she was sorry.

Peter smiled a relaxed smile as he watched her stare at the glass in her hand. The truth wasn't as tough to take as he thought it would be. The problem with his mother seemed senseless right now. He looked at Jeneil's legs, enjoying what they did to him. She looked great. He had missed her. He got up and stood in front of her with his hands in his pockets. She looked up. He smiled and touched her cheek gently.

"You're not angry with me?" she whispered, surprised by his tenderness. "It's okay with you? The money, the whole thing?"

"I don't like the money, but I like your attitude about it," he answered, giving a slight smile.

"Oh, Peter," she whispered, leaning against him, slipping her arms around his waist. "I thought this was the end for sure, the problems with your family and now the money. I thought Chang would never accept the whole money issue and the social thing with it."

Jeneil sighed. She was clinging. She needed him. Peter smiled and held her. He moved his lips along her cheek to her mouth and braced himself for the jolt of electricity he knew would result from her kiss. She felt incredibility great to him and she responded passionately to his kiss. They were good together. Chang had missed her. Peter had missed her. The problems of the past few days were forgotten as they concentrated on their love for each other. The feeling of oneness returned and the unity was as strong as he remembered.

Forty-Two

Tuesday was Christmas Eve. Even in a hospital the season brought good cheer and there was good natured, lighthearted fun amongst the staff. Peter and Steve were sitting in the medical room. Peter was working on a report while a group of interns and residents were standing around a nurse's deck enjoying a short break. Steve turned and saw Morgan Rand staring at something. Steve looked in the direction of his stare. Jeneil was standing by the elevators leafing through manila envelopes. She looked radiant. Steve noticed the grin on Morgan Rand's face. He turned to Peter. "Look at Morgan Rand's expression."

Peter looked up and smiled. "What's he looking at?"

"Jeneil." Steve went to the door.

"Dr. Rand, it's unprofessional and unethical to look at women like that. I think I'll tell Sondra."

"What?" Rand spun around and sneered. "Don't be ridiculous, Bradley. You see everything from the gutter. I find the girl charming and interesting. She has an old fashioned quality about her. It's a pleasant change from the barbed wire bracelets of the liberated female. That's hardly enough to cause Sondra to lose sleep. We're getting married in a week."

Steve smiled. "Get in line behind the interns at the counter."

Rand raised an eyebrow of learned tolerance. "Oh, those boys wouldn't know how to deal with her even if they got the chance. She fascinates me. She has a gentility that she tries to hide. If this was Europe, I'd say she was from nobility that had come upon economic difficulties. She has breeding and it shows. Must be from the Alden in her name."

"You're a snob, Rand," Steve said flatly.

"I am not, Bradley, because I think she got the fire in her eyes from the Connors, and gentility and breeding with a mixture of fire looks delicious. She's come alive lately which makes me curious about the man in her life."

Steve smiled. "Rand for the first time since I've known you, I almost like you. You're human. That's good to know."

Jerry Tollman, an intern, rushed into the medical room past Steve. Removing the cap from a small container of breath spray, he squirted it into his open mouth. Peter and Steve watched amused by the one intern who really had Jeneil-fever badly. Jerry had assumed Jeneil wouldn't be into sex, but the change in her lately told him differently and he was annoyed at himself for passing her up. He now felt she was serious dating, marriage, and fun material. Jerry combed his hair quickly. "I've been waiting all day to nail her."

"Who?" Peter asked.

"Jeneil." Jerry smiled and showed a cluster of white berries and green leaves he had hidden in his pocket. "Bless the guy who invented mistletoe. I can't have her, but I can have a Christmas kiss and keep hoping her boyfriend croaks. Wish me luck." He hit Steve's arm as he went by. Peter stared in disbelief and Steve began to laugh.

"Notice any headaches lately, Pete? The interns might have a voodoo doll of you. Jerry's got Jeneil-fever and I think he's infected the others. I've got to see this. She'll probably ninja him."

They watched Jerry join three other interns who obviously knew his game plan. Peter could see Jeneil was self-conscious as she approached the group. The interns made her nervous. She had told him that. They had adolescent grins and she found it unnerving.

"What are the boys up to?" Rand asked, joining Peter and Steve.

"Who knows with interns?" Steve smiled at Peter.

"Barbara, here's the eggnog," Jeneil said, walking to the desk and putting a brown bag on the counter. Peter noticed she was aware of the interns and they had her nervous. She looked fragile. He suddenly realized it was that fragility that drove him crazy.

Rand smiled. "Good gosh, look at those interns. It's like the rape of innocence. See what I mean about her. She's defenseless."

"Defenseless, ha," Steve whispered to Peter.

Barbara opened the bag. "Thanks, Jeneil. My husband hates store-bought eggnog. It sounds easy to make. I think I'll try some now."

"Can we have some, too?" the interns pleaded.

"Is the recipe in the bag, too?" Barbara asked. Jeneil nodded.

Jerry moved to her side. "Jeneil, eggnog is a Christmas tradition. Do you like Christmas traditions?"

"Yes, I do."

Jerry moved his arm behind her, slowly bringing up the mistletoe. "All of them?"

"The ones I know about," she answered cautiously, turning her head, aware of his arm behind her. As she did, she caught sight of his moving arm. Looking up, she reacted quickly, hitting Jerry's hand, sending the mistletoe flying, causing it to land on Morgan Rand's chest. Steve and Peter broke up laughing. Jeneil was more shocked than anyone and she took his hand, apologizing profusely. "I'm sorry, Dr. Tollman. You scared me. I didn't know what you were doing. Did I hurt you?" She was bright red from the situation and the people laughing.

"Can I have a Christmas kiss as compensation, even though I lost the mistletoe?" he asked, letting her hold his hand and apologize.

"Mistletoe, is that what this was all about? I thought it was an insect or something that had been removed during surgery." Everyone laughed. Steve and Peter were hysterical.

Morgan Rand smiled and went to her. He looked at the intern. "Really Tollman, improve your approach. Are you all right, Jeneil?" He placed his hand on her shoulder.

"Be careful of Rand. He's sneaky," Steve warned Peter, no longer laughing.

"You need finesse when approaching a lady of refinement and sensitivity like Jeneil. You don't pounce or lunge at her." Rand looked at Jeneil. "With your permission lovely lady, would you help me educate this yearling?" Rand noticed Jeneil's hesitation. "I understand your concern, but it would be a service to your gender. Imagine the young women you'll be sparing the fright you just experienced because he's so inept." His voice was velvety smooth.

"Ooo, Jeneil, do it," Barbara swooned. "What can happen right here?"

Morgan Rand looked at Jeneil and smiled. "Please."

"All right," she said quietly. "What do I have to do?"

Rand grinned. "Just stand there and be yourself. Just keep looking like that."

Steve jammed his fists into his lab coat pockets. "Peter, do something."

"Do what? My hands are tied, remember." Peter watched, curious about Rand.

"Now Tollman, watch carefully," Rand continued, taking Jeneil's hand gently. "Jeneil, you are lovely. Your beauty overwhelms me. This sprig of mistletoe is only a second rate frame for your loveliness. The sparkle and brilliance of the holiday is paled by the radiance of your presence. To frame your loveliness." He reached up and put the mistletoe in her hair. Everyone watched in awe, surprised by the smoothness of the normally stodgy Morgan Rand. Leaning forward, a couple of inches from her lips, he whispered, "Merry Christmas." Steve gritted his teeth. Peter was annoyed. Jeneil started to step back but Rand slipped his arms around her and touched his lips to hers in a genuine kiss. Everyone ooooed.

Jeneil pushed herself away gently and stared at him. "Merry Christmas."

"Ooo, lucky Sondra," Barbara swooned. "That's quite a technique, Dr. Rand."

"Just so you know Bradley doesn't have all the talent." Rand smiled and kept an arm around Jeneil's shoulder. "Jeneil, you're a good sport." He rubbed her arm gently. "You are beautiful and you look much too fragile for your own good."

Steve leaned to Peter. "Tell me he's not attracted to her."

"He's getting married next week. Who cares?" Peter replied.

"Yeah, I know. Sondra's tough as nails," Steve continued. "But he's definitely got an attraction to Jeneil, her fire and her gentility. He studies her too much if you ask me. That kiss was real. He meant it."

Jerry Tollman looked at Rand. "What do I look like, a beginner? I know seduction when I see it." Jeneil looked from one to the other, studying the situation.

Steve smiled. "There you are, Pete. A rookie intern spotted it."

"I'm not blind," Peter answered.

Jerry smiled at Jeneil. "I'm not suave, I'm just honest." The interns applauded. "I really would like a Christmas kiss from you."

"Ooo, Jeneil, you're on a roll here." Barbara smiled.

"What did the cafeteria serve for lunch today?" Jeneil asked, and everyone laughed.

"You're wearing my mistletoe," Jerry argued.

"Oh." Jeneil went to take it from her hair.

Jerry stopped her. "Uh-uh, my kiss first." He smiled, holding her wrist. He leaned into her and she let him kiss her lips. He smiled at her and kissed her cheek, too. "Thanks, you've made my day."

She looked a bit puzzled and smiled uncomfortably. "Merry Christmas."

"Would you consider dumping your boyfriend and making it a Happy New Year for me?" Everyone laughed, including Peter and Steve. Jeneil was done in, aware of Peter standing there. The laughter had her blushing.

"I've got to get back to work before I'm in trouble with my boss. Here are the envelopes for your floor." She left them on the counter and turned to leave.

Steve had become aware of whispers among the interns who were grinning and looking at her. "Jeneil," Steve called, going to her, realizing what the interns were up to. He took the mistletoe from her hair and handed it to her. "Here, before you get into real trouble."

"Killjoy," the interns yelled at him. "We were going to ride down the elevator with her and put the mistletoe to good use."

Jeneil put the mistletoe on the counter. "What is in those berries?" She shook her head and walked away.

Jerry watched her and sighed. "What does her boyfriend have that I don't?"

Steve laughed. "Her."

*****

Peter and Steve drove to the apartment together after leaving Steve's car at the dorm. "Do you realize that the dorms won't be home in another month or so?"

"You're getting closer to real," Peter said, as he turned down the street.

They passed the front of the apartment building. "Wow." Steve stared. "Who drives the Porsche, and who would drive a red one?"

"Nobody on this street," Peter answered. They walked to the front sidewalk, looking casually at the shiny red automobile parked in front of the building. The front door opened and Peter and Steve turned.

"Hey, Peter. Merry Christmas." Robert Danzieg came toward them.

"New car, Robert?"

Robert smiled. "Yes, a Christmas present from my parents."

"Nice," Peter replied.

"I picked it up yesterday. Jeneil and I went to Boston for dinner tonight. It was a dream to drive. I wanted to show it to her." Peter noticed Robert held Jeneil's Christmas gift to him in his arms. "Well, I better get moving. Hey, Pete, she's a sweetheart. Marry her soon or I will." He smiled and got in the car, sitting behind the tinted windshield.

"What a shithead," Steve mumbled, barely moving his lips. "Likes to apply the thumb screws, doesn't he?"

"That's my Morgan Rand, Robert Danzieg, Mr. Sensitivity."

"Poor guy," Steve chuckled as they climbed the stairs, "can't get a tie for Christmas like the rest of us." Peter laughed, opening the apartment door.

Jeneil was lighting red candles clustered around the room in several places, nestled in sprays of evergreen branches. The room had a mellow glow from them and the Christmas tree lights. The atmosphere spelled holiday. Jeneil smiled as they came in and Steve whistled at her.

"Jeneil, you look fantastic."

"You wore that to dinner with Robert?" Peter asked, looking her over. The dark green dress looked soft and she was wearing the diamond jewelry Bill had given her. She looked outstanding and the dress was definitely lower cut at the neckline than her usual. "No wonder he wants to marry you."

Jeneil laughed. "He likes to tease you."

"Where did you go in Boston to eat?" Peter asked, getting irritated.

"Pacifica. It's a Polynesian restaurant. The booths look like grass huts, and there were dancers doing flaming sword acts and Hawaiian dancers. It was really pleasantly spectacular," Jeneil said, picking up a jacket.

Peter didn't recognize it. "What's that?"

"Robert's Christmas gift." She put on the grey fur jacket, a gardenia corsage pinned to it.

"What the hell! Jeneil, fur! What's he pulling?" Peter asked, showing his annoyance.

"Peter, it's fake fur."

"Oh, well that makes it just fine then. Damn it, Jeneil, that's not right."

"Peter, he's chairman of the Animal Preservation Group. They got a special rate and they're giving them as gifts this year to promote an alternative to animal sacrifice. I think they've got something here." She ran her hand over the sleeve. "It looks and feels great."

Peter growled. "A corsage, too? Just a last minute dinner? He's such a phony."

"That's enough, Peter. You're going to have yourself in a real mood if you don't stop." She kissed him lightly. "I'll hang the jacket and be right back."

Steve looked her over as she went by. "Pete, she looks more and more like a sophisticated woman every day. That outfit screams sophistication."

"I know, I know," he snapped.

Steve looked at him. "The guy really gets to you, huh?"

Peter sighed heavily. "He's not kidding. Believe me; he wants to show her off more than the Porsche. For all his family's money, he's the best street kid I've met in her civilized life."

Steve laughed. "Chuck it, Pete. She's yours. That's what makes him crazy."

Peter grinned. "Yeah, he went home alone with a cold sculpture from her in his arms."

Jeneil returned and put on some Christmas music. "What would you like, eggnog or Irish coffee to put the hospital in the past? Let's celebrate a little."

"What's Irish coffee?" Steve asked.

"It's a Neil Connors thunderbolt, strong coffee mixed with thick cream and Irish whiskey. Mine's tamer than his was. His caused memory lapses.

Steve laughed. "I'll try an Irish coffee."

"What about you, grumpy?" She smiled at Peter and put her arm around his waist.

"Why didn't you wear the dark blue dress with the white collar tonight?"

She sighed. "Because I didn't want to sing in a choir. I wanted to wear green for the holiday. Aw, Chang, don't spoil Christmas for me." He put his arms around her shoulder and smiled then leaned down and kissed her. "Thanks."

Steve watched. "Hey, by New Years you'll be a real pro with all your kissing experience at the hospital."

"That was strange today. Must be a new virus going around." She laughed and went to the kitchen.

"She doesn't really grasp that it's her, does she?"

Peter shook his head. "Her mind doesn't work that way. Sex is something two people share when they know each other well. She grew up surrounded by nasty gossip about her, and the interns and their teasing remind her of that. They genuinely like her, but she doesn't understand. Their attention makes her nervous. She backs away from what she doesn't trust, and Jerry gets more crazed about her when she does that." Peter smiled. "I think that's what's attracting Morgan Rand, too. He senses her fear of the intentions of men. To some guys, that's a turn on. She doesn't understand them. It's also not a high priority for study with her either. It's all clear in her mind; you love one man and the others are friends. She hates it when the two get mixed up. She likes life simple."

Steve smiled. "Damn, at least you can sleep with a woman like that purring for you. Then why the hell lean on her like you do, Pete?"

"Because I don't trust Danzieg. I can't control him so I try to control her." He shook his head. "I have a blind spot about him, I know."

"I can understand that, Pete. I'm the same way with Morgan Rand."

"Morgan Rand," Jeneil said, returning and putting a tray on the serving table. "Should he be kissing other women like that when he's getting married next week? Or am I being a prude?" Peter and Steve looked at each other and smiled. She handed them their cups and held up her glass of eggnog in a toast. "Merry Christmas and may the season's merriment last all year, along with the message of peace and love." She smiled and sipped her drink. "And here's an official Christmas kiss." She kissed Peter's lips warmly. "You too, Steve," and she kissed his lips lightly. He felt electricity spread through his chest. He drank his Irish coffee and sat down.

They talked for a while and nibbled on Christmas cookies. Jeneil set up the fake fireplace again and using three S hooks hung three stockings from the back of the chair. They were already filled with small gifts and treats. Peter and Steve were fascinated and went to look more closely.

"No, in the morning guys," Jeneil said, stopping them.

"What's in it?" Steve asked. "I've never had a Christmas stocking."

Jeneil stared in disbelief. "Have you, Peter?"

"Yeah, my Aunt Risa used to bring one for me. They had more money than the rest of the family. More than my mother and me, that's for sure. She used to put candy and fruit in it, and toy cars and soldiers. I wanted a switch blade."

Steve and Jeneil laughed, and Jeneil hugged Peter. "You showed signs of being a surgeon even then." Peter chuckled and kissed her cheek.

Steve looked inside his stocking. He smiled as he saw fruit, candies, nuts, and Christmas cookies. There were a few wrapped gifts, too. Jeneil watched him. He looked up at her and shook his head. "You're something else."

Jeneil hugged him to erase the thought of his other Christmases from her mind. Steve felt her caring for him and held her. He liked her as a person; it was separate and apart from what he felt for her as a woman. Together the feelings were love. He held her, knowing it and feeling it strongly. He didn't care. It all felt good to him; the atmosphere, the moment, his feelings, and her.

"Merry Christmas Steve, I love you."

He nodded. "I know. Thanks, kid." He kissed her cheek and released her reluctantly.

"Hey you two, I'm feeling left out." Peter smiled.

Jeneil put her arms around them. "You two have made this Christmas special. I love fussing and the two of you are so wonderful to me that the fussing exhilarates me." She squeezed them, leaning her head on Peter's arm. Peter and Steve smiled at each other.

*****

Peter watched as Jeneil brushed her hair before getting into bed. He was in love with her and the feeling filled him at the moment. The evening, her care for him and Steve, made her look even more special as she stood there doing her hair. Taking the gift from his robe pocket, he went to her. "Jeneil, I want to give this to you now while we're alone. It's a surprise. I want to see your reaction."

"Okay." Curious, she smiled and took the small gift wrapped box, untying the ribbon carefully. Lifting the lid, she looked at Peter, completely surprised. "The ring! Guinevere's crown ring from the secondhand store in the Sutton market! Peter! You were the one who bought it!" She hugged him, filled with love by the sentiment as he held her tightly. "No wonder the salesman was grinning at me when he said it was sold."

Peter kissed her. "Jeneil, wear it so you'll be mine while we're waiting to get married."

"Peter, I am yours, all yours." She smiled and touched his face lovingly. "I wanted the ring for our soul wedding ceremony."

He smiled and pulled her to him. His whole body tingled from the love he felt for her at that moment. He kissed her. Passion began to stir and she pulled away, whispering, "Peter, we can't. The bed makes too much noise."

"Do you want to?" he asked, and she nodded. "Then trust me." She gave in to her feelings and him.

Jeneil lifted the blanket to get out of bed. Peter stirred and opened his eyes. "Hey, where's my kiss?"

She smiled and snuggled to him. "I love you." She kissed him warmly. "Chang, I adore you." She kissed him again.

"Where were you heading?"

"To get Christmas breakfast going. It's more like a brunch. You and Steve have to go in at four today. I have to work our Christmas around that."

"Okay, I'll have my shower after you then."

"Fine, it's still early, you can sleep a while longer."

"One more kiss."

She kissed him and smiled, fixing his hair. "Merry Christmas. This one is special. It's our first Christmas together."

He smiled. "In a long line of them, honey."

She kissed him once more and got up quickly. "I'd better get moving. You and the bed feel too warm and comforting."

Peter opened his eyes as Jeneil stepped from behind the dressing screen. The long red dress she wore was well fitted. "Honey, you look sensational. You look special."

"I love dressing up for the holidays." She put on pearl earrings and a matching necklace.

Peter rested on his elbow. "I can't believe you're mine."

She smiled. "I am. The shower is, too."

Peter got up and Jeneil went to the kitchen. Steve was still sleeping. Putting her apron on, she put the small breakfast ham in the oven. Peter's telephone rang and Jeneil panicked. Hearing the shower running, she went to Steve and woke him. "Peter's telephone is ringing. It might be the hospital. Will you get it?"

"Sure," he said groggily, and got up, answering the phone sleepily.

"Peter?"

"No, he's in the shower. Can he call you back?"

There was a pause. "Steve?"

"Yes," Steve replied. "Who's this?"

"Peter's mother."

"Oh. He'll be out of the shower soon. I'll have him call you."

"You sound sleepy."

"I just woke up."

"You slept there?"

"Yes." Steve covered a yawn.

"Have Peter call me." Her voice sounded tight.

"Okay," Steve said, "Merry Christmas."

"Yes, same to you."

Steve heard the click and replaced the receiver, shaking his head. "Woman's on the warpath. I can hear it even half awake."

"Who?" Jeneil asked.

"Pete's mother."

Jeneil sighed with relief. "Oh, I thought he was being called into work." Steve fixed his robe and stared at Jeneil. "What are you staring at?"

"Uh, you look really nice." The apron she wore was the same kind Sienna had worn with nothing underneath. Seeing Jeneil in it startled him, but he smiled. He noticed the red dress and the jewelry. "You like holidays don't you?"

She nodded. "I really do."

"What happened?" Peter asked, walking in the room.

"Your phone rang. It was your mother. Call her back," Jeneil said, and then went to the kitchen.

Steve patted his shoulder. "Get the bandages ready. I answered the phone."

"Oh shit." Peter sighed. "Bad luck."

"She wasn't singing Christmas carols," and Steve left the room.

Peter shook his head as he dialed. "What did I do now?"

"I just found out that you stopped by the other day and dropped off gifts for all of us. Grandfather said you won't bring Jeneil here anymore and that you didn't stay to visit either. You didn't even call me to wish me a Merry Christmas. What are you giving up for that girl? Have you even asked yourself that?"

"Mom, I'm playing by your rules."

"I said not to bring her to parties," she said, getting louder. "I didn't say to drop us. You're trying to be nasty to teach me a lesson, that's all."

Peter sat down. "Mom, listen, I've been busy at work. I don't sit around thinking up ways to get even with anybody."

She wasn't listening. "This is all since she's been in your life, Peter. You've always called me. You've always visited. She's behind all of this and you listen to her. That really hurts." She began to cry.

Peter exhaled and leaned forward. "Mom, Jeneil has nothing to do with anything. Gosh, the kid is just trying to stay out of your way."

"Oh please, stay out of my way. This is just what she wanted, isn't it? You chose her over the family. She's delighted."

"That's not true."

"Oh, yes it is. We're not even going to see you for Christmas and she's got the two of you there to parade around for. Oh, she's having a very Merry Christmas all right."

"Parade around?"

"Oh, Peter, will you please wake up. What decent girl would have two men sleep in her apartment and not be married to either one?"

Peter stood up fast. "That's enough!" he said, trying to control himself.

"Where did Steve sleep?"

Peter rubbed his forehead. "Mom, you're getting out of line. Steve slept on the sofa bed."

"Can you watch them every moment?"

"That's it, Mom. I've heard enough. I warned you about picking on her, didn't I?"

"She's playing you for a fool, Peter. Why should she get married? She's having too much fun with both of you."

"Mom, I swear. You're pushing me."

"She's trash, Peter."

He slammed the receiver down and began to pace. He looked up and his heart stopped. Jeneil was standing at the door. "What did you hear?"

"Enough," she said angrily, and walked out.

"Jeneil," he called after her, "Jeneil, wait." He followed her to the kitchen. Steve turned, surprised by the outburst, and followed them. Jeneil was shaking, trying not to cry.

"Baby, wait a minute."

"No, Peter. No, I'm not even going to discuss this. Do you hear me? We will not talk about it. It's Christmas. She will not ruin my Christmas. I won't let her." She got a glass of water and drank it slowly, breathing carefully between sips. "The woman is sick."

"What happened?" Steve asked, concerned.

"Nothing." Peter sighed.

Jeneil looked at Peter. "Nothing?"

"Jeneil," Peter pleaded, "understand."

"Oh, I do now, Peter. I most certainly do." She really broke down.

"What?" Steve asked. "What happened?"

Jeneil looked at Steve. "His mother thinks I'm a lowlife. She thinks we're playing the three bears in Goldilocks' bed." She took a deep breath and put her head back.

Steve stared at Peter, speechless. Peter put his head down, completely embarrassed. Peter's telephone rang. "Let it ring," Peter snapped angrily.

"We can't, Pete. It might be the hospital. I left this number for them to reach me, too."

"Then you answer it. If it's her, hang up."

Steve went to the telephone. It was Peter's grandfather. "Steve, I would like to talk to Peter."

Steve sighed. "Mr. Chang, he's upset."

"I'm sure he must be. I can't believe what I heard."

"Neither can Jeneil," Steve said quietly, and heard the shock in the grandfather's silence.

"Oh my heavens, Steve, I'd better talk to Peter. Please!"

"Okay." Steve put the receiver down and went to Peter. "It's your grandfather."

Peter sighed, rubbed his forehead, and went to the bedroom. "Grandfather, I don't want to talk right now. I mean it. I've reached my limit."

"Peter, I can understand that. I'm sorry. Steve said Jeneil heard?"

"Some of it." Peter sighed again.

"Are you both all right? Is she angry at you?"

"I don't know yet. She's getting herself under control."

"Then go to her, Peter. I'll let you go. Call me."

Peter held his breath. "Grandfather, I want to be left alone," he paused, "by all of you."

"Peter, I can't do that. I'm upset for both you and Jeneil. You won't turn your back on me. I won't let you. Go to Jeneil. I'll call again another time." He hung up and Peter put the receiver on its base.

Jeneil was pacing in the living room. Peter went to her and put his arms around her, and Steve went to the bedroom and closed the door to allow them privacy.

"Honey, look at me."

Jeneil resisted. "No, Peter. Please, I'll cry. I just want to put this past me. This is going to be a nice Christmas. I insist on it. I'm seeing more clearly now. Your mother will never accept me. She's unreasonable. She's completely turned around about me and nothing I do will help, even if you didn't live here. There's nothing I can do, nothing. I'm sorry."

He held her close. "Why are you apologizing, baby."

She shrugged. "Because you're in the middle, I guess."

"I love you, Jeneil. Don't let this ruin us or last night or today."

She looked at him. "She can't take you from me, Peter. You're my whole life. I love you." It's what he wanted to hear and he kissed her, letting her know how much her words meant to him. "Let's get Christmas going here."

Peter knocked on the bedroom door. "Steve, it's safe to come out."

Steve opened the door. "What happens now?"

"Breakfast," Jeneil said, smiling.

Steve looked at her. "You're okay kid, really okay?"

"I will be if you help me have a great Christmas."

Steve went to her and put his arms around her. "Kid, you're tougher than you look." He kissed her temple. "I was wondering if I should leave. I don't want to be the cause of anything weird for you."

Jeneil smiled. "Mandra used to tell me to step back, look and listen at the shouting. If I deserved it then rectify it. If not, walk past it or it will swallow you. I don't deserve what she's shouting. Neither do you."

Steve smiled. "I like your family. They know how to grow great kids."

Jeneil stepped back. "Let's have breakfast. I want my gifts." Peter and Steve laughed. "Bring your coffee to the living room so we can open our presents."

Jeneil brought the gifts from under the tree and placed them in piles for each of them. Peter looked at her pile. "Where did you get all those gifts? Steve and I couldn't afford many."

She shrugged. "Uncle Hollis, Marlene, the kids, Tony, The James Gang, Adrienne and Charlie, Adrienne's mother, Bill, his parents, Dennis and Karen, Robert, Franklin, the Breiostes who run the motel, the people who run the farm, Mrs. Rezendes, your grandfather." Peter and Steve looked at each other and smiled.

"Steve and I expected to be embarrassed. We knew you wouldn't stop at just one for us."

"That doesn't matter. We're together and this is really becoming a special Christmas for me. I'm glad you guys are in my life."

They each opened their gifts and enjoyed showing them to each other. Jeneil had concentrated on Steve's new career. She had gotten him an expensive pen set with his name engraved on it, a black marble desk set including a letter opener with a black marble handle and a leather desk blotter. He liked the Danzieg sculpture even though the artist didn't impress him much. Then she added clothes to that. He was overwhelmed as he got to the last box. He turned as he heard Peter laugh.

"Jeneil, the painting of the seaport town that you did, I love it," Peter commented.

"I didn't know you painted," Steve said, looking at the painting.

"It's a well kept secret and any art critic will tell you that it should be," Jeneil replied. "Peter said he liked it and I believed him."

Steve laughed. "I like it, too. Who cares what critics think?"

"You went crazy on Chang." Peter laughed, looking at all his gifts. "The denim jacket, the black sports shirt, the ID bracelet with Chang engraved on it. I'll never run out of clothes, but why the book, White Fang?"

"Because Chang reminds me of him." She smiled, and he smiled and chucked her chin gently.

Steve smiled at them. "How are you doing with your pile, Jeneil?"

"I have yours and Peter's to open and this big box from Uncle Hollis. I can't imagine what it is. It isn't a Christmas gift." She struggled with the reinforced cardboard. Peter snapped it open for her and pulling out the crushed newspapers that filled the top, she stared at the contents. Lifting a note, she opened it and read it out loud. "Jeneil, I came across this amongst some of your father's papers. After wondering how to handle it all, I decided that it belonged to you. This was his life, his pride. So are you. That's why they seemed to be naturally connected in my opinion." Jeneil choked up but continued reading. "Brilliant children don't grow up to become unsettled. Take the material he left and find a market for it or create one. Love, Hollis."

Jeneil shook her head and laughed. "Uncle Hollis never gives up on me." She looked in the box and lifted some of the papers. "My gosh, look at this! Research material, notes, videos. What a treasure! I'm glad Uncle Hollis thought of me. This is great. Boy, I feel like a slug when I think of the hours this took. My father was never still. There was never enough work for him and never enough hours in the day. He loved his work." She sighed. "That must be a nice feeling." She looked at the videos. Raising her eyebrows, she smiled. "He made historical travel films. I never saw these. How exciting! You guys can see and hear him. That Irish brogue of his was a killer. My mom must have recorded these while they traveled. What a nice surprise!" Peter and Steve watched her, both completely caught up in her excitement. She looked up at them. "I'm sorry, nostalgia is setting in. I'll open your gifts and get back to the present. Hey." She frowned. "You're not done. You're both missing my handmade gifts. Where did they go?" She looked around, moving some boxes. "Here they are."

Steve smiled as he opened his. "Hey, I like this." He lifted the light blue knitted sweater.

Peter pulled out a grey one. "Oh, honey, this is nice. I like it."

She smiled with pride as they both put them on. "Oh, they fit. They look good on you."

"How did you know my size?" Steve asked.

"You and Peter share clothes, I just measured his shirts."

Steve smiled. "This is another first. No girl ever made a sweater for me. Thanks."

Jeneil smiled. "You really are welcome."

Peter leaned toward her and gave her a kiss. "No girl ever made one for me either. It feels good."

"Let's see what you guys chose for me." She opened the smaller one from Steve and raised her eyebrows. "Steve, a cloisonné bracelet! It's gorgeous!" She slipped it on, admiring it. "Oh, you really went overboard."

Steve shrugged. "I figured I'd be working for real money soon so why not. I owe you big. I wanted it for you."

Jeneil moved it around on her wrist. "It's really beautiful. Thank you very much!" She threw him a kiss.

Peter looked at Steve. "Thanks a lot, Steve. Wait until you see mine by comparison."

Jeneil interrupted. "Aw, Peter, that's not what matters. You wanted the gift for me. Don't lessen its value or compare it."

"There you go," Steve said. "Listen to the kid."

Jeneil lifted the box. "It's so heavy. Is it a bowling ball?" Peter laughed as Jeneil unwrapped it. The cardboard box read, *twenty cartons of filter tipped cigarettes*. She looked puzzled.

"I couldn't get a box that would fit. I told you it would look bad," Peter said, shaking his head.

Jeneil laughed. "Now I'm really curious." She undid the tape and pulled out the crushed newspapers. She looked at Peter. "Oh, a pet rock." And then her expression changed to disbelief as she looked at it again. "Peter! A geode! A geode! Oh my gosh! Where did you get it?" She lifted out one half. "It's beautiful. You stinker, where did you find it?"

"I went to a professor I had at Downes. He got it for me." He smiled, knowing she was pleased.

"That is such a simple solution." She giggled and shook her head. "Oh, I love it!" She touched the crystals gently. "I'm going to have an acrylic case made to protect it. Thank you." She put the geode down and sat in Peter's lap. She took Steve's hand. "Both of you are so good to me." She kissed Peter's cheek. "I never would have guessed the sensitivity lying underneath your hospital images. You're entirely different people up close."

Steve laughed. "Yeah, I think the same about you."

"Well, I better get this debris cleared away and put the roast on." She smiled and went to the kitchen.

"Pete, you're a lucky guy," Steve said quietly. "She's really terrific."

Peter looked at him and smiled. "I know. Believe me, I know."

Jeneil returned wearing her apron and carrying a plastic garbage bag. "Will you clear away the wrapping paper?" The front doorbell rang and they looked at each other. "I'll get it," and Jeneil went to the apartment door.

Adrienne and Charlie were heading out. "We'll let them in for you, Jeneil," Adrienne called.

"Oh, thanks. Say hello to your mom." Jeneil waved and closed the door. She rushed to help pick up. "Look at this place. It's not ready for guests. We sure made a mess, guys." The apartment door buzzer sounded. "Well, they'll have to take us with our shoes off, whoever it is." She went to answer it. "Sienna! Come in."

"Oh shit!" Steve whispered to Peter.

"Hi, Jeneil, I'm sorry I didn't call."

"It's really okay." Jeneil stepped aside as Sienna walked in carrying a gift. Sienna stopped abruptly when she saw Steve. Jeneil looked from one to the other, wondering why things felt tense.

"Hi, Sienna," Peter greeted her.

"Peter, how are you?" Sienna smiled uncomfortably. "Hi, Steve."

"Sienna," Steve said, without inflection. Jeneil again looked from one to the other.

"Sienna, I'll take your coat. Stay and visit."

"No, really, I just brought a gift for you." Sienna kept looking nervously at Steve.

Jeneil studied her. "What is it?"

"What?"

"Something's wrong here." Jeneil looked at Sienna and Steve. Steve stared at the floor.

"Honey," Peter said, "don't be so curious."

"Why?" Jeneil asked. "Have they argued?"

"Jeneil!" Peter warned.

Sienna held back tears.

"You have argued. Sienna's upset, Steve."

Peter went to her. "Jeneil."

"But, Peter, fate has brought them here. They should talk." She took Sienna's arm and led her to the sofa, and Steve. "There's nothing that can't be settled by discussing things openly."

Peter grabbed Jeneil. "I want to see you alone," he said, dragging her away.

"Good idea. We'll leave so Steve and Sienna can talk it out, or I'll be furious," she called, as Peter pushed her gently ahead of him to the bedroom.

"Stay out of it," he said, taking her wrist.

"But they need help, just until the tension eases."

"No," he said emphatically.

She looked at him steadily. "You know why there's tension, don't you? Why won't you help them?"

He walked to the bed and lay across it, sighing. "You are so stubborn."

She went to him. "What happened, Peter? You know. I can see it." She sat next to him. "What happened to Steve and Sienna?"

He looked at her. "No, drop it."

"Then I'll go out there and ask them." She started to get up.

He grabbed her. "Get back here! Damn it, you don't listen."

"What happened, Peter?"

"Oh shit, Jeneil, she invited him to dinner and came out of the kitchen wearing nothing but an apron."

Jeneil tried not to laugh but couldn't help it. "Sienna did that? Well, isn't she a minx! Then what's the problem?" she asked, puzzled. "Guys like that, don't they?"

"Well, it depends on the relationship. Steve isn't interested in a physical relationship with her."

Jeneil stared, not believing what she heard. "Steve Bradley?" Peter grinned. "Is there someone else?" Jeneil asked, wondering if Sienna might be right about another woman.

"Honey, he just wants to get his career going."

"So he ignores his life while he's waiting?"

Peter scowled. "Why do men have to say yes because women want it?" he asked sharply.

"It seems to me that's been the struggle women face. We're not allowed to say no."

"He can't win with you, can he? You picked on him because he slept around too much and now you criticize because he's not."

"It's not a criticism. I feel bad for her. She must feel pretty bad. That's serious rejection. How did it end? How did Steve tell her no?" She sighed. "What a miserable situation. She's out there with not much more than a smile on and he tells her no. Neither one could win." She shook her head. "I'm glad you dragged me away. What a mess." She snuggled and kissed his shoulder. "I'll never understand relationships between men and women."

"We're okay," Peter reminded her.

"I don't understand us sometimes."

He took her hand. "Well, I think you're really easy to live with."

She smiled. "Steve has changed a lot. His probation has been good for him in some ways."

Peter nodded. "Even he likes some of the changes."

"Yen and Yang," she mused. "Bad to good and good to bad creating a balance. What about your mother, Peter?"

"What about her?"

"She's your mother. You're an only child, Peter. It doesn't seem right."

"Baby, she's out of line."

Jeneil sighed. "I know."

Peter smiled at her. "Can't ignore it, can you?"

"No, she's your mother, a tough one, but your mother." There was a knock at the bedroom door. "Come in."

Steve put his head in. "Sienna's gone."

"What do you mean gone?" Jeneil asked.

"Baby, stay out of it," Peter reminded her.

"Peter, please. Steve, join us on the analysis couch." She patted the bed.

Steve laughed. "Are we doing group therapy?" He got beside Jeneil and faced her.

"That's us all right." Jeneil laughed and then looked at Steve seriously. "Sienna's gone sounded final to me."

"Jeneil," Peter groaned.

"It is," Steve answered. "We couldn't agree on the kind of relationship for us so we decided on no relationship at all."

"I'm sorry." She patted his arm.

Steve sighed. "It's good that we got things settled. I'm glad we're not mad at each other since she's your friend."

"Me, too. She liked you, Steve.

"Not really, Jeneil. She didn't even know me. I'm a doctor. I was an arm ornament for her."

"But she wanted to sleep with you."

"Jeneil!" Peter was shocked she felt comfortable enough to say that.

Jeneil looked at Peter. "Well, it's true. That means something, doesn't it?"

"Geez, baby, sometimes you're too damn direct."

She giggled. "But this is an analysis couch, we're supposed to be."

Steve laughed. "Who's the analyst?"

"Whoever's most sane at the moment, it's the blind leading the blind. We can't tell the staff from the inmates." She began to laugh. "Trust me guys, you'll love lopsided." She laughed harder. Peter and Steve looked at her then smiled at each other.

Peter kissed her cheek. "Are you finished?"

Jeneil sighed from laughing. "Yes, yes I am, for the moment. What will you do now for a date to parties, Steve?"

Steve shrugged. "There aren't any more left. I'll lie." He lay on his back and stared at the ceiling.

Jeneil watched him. "Why can't life be simple so the simple can get through life?" she asked rhetorically.

Peter chuckled. "Why is grass green?"

"What is air?" Steve added.

She looked at them. "You two are lousy psych patients. You're too mentally sound."

They laughed then quietness settled in as they lay on their backs staring at the ceiling. No one spoke and the mood became peaceful. Jeneil took her hairpins out, letting her hair fall free. The atmosphere was warm and comfortable, and each drifted to sleep.

The telephone rang. Jeneil opened her eyes and Peter stirred. Seeing her snuggled against his arm, he kissed her forehead then lifted his head. Steve, nestled in Jeneil's hair, opened his eyes and sat up quickly.

"The phone behind you," Peter said, laughing at Steve's disorientation. "It's Jeneil's, we can relax." Steve lifted the receiver, handed it to Jeneil, lying back down.

"Uncle Hollis, Merry Christmas. I'm just fine. What am I doing?" She looked from Steve to Peter then raised her eyebrows. "Uh, I was taking a nap. No, no, it's all right. I should get up." She looked at her watch. "Or my roast will be a burnt offering. Yes, I did open the box. Thank you for sending it. I can tell I'm going to enjoy browsing through it. It does belong to me, Uncle Hollis. I felt that when I opened the box and saw the work. I don't know. Those travel films must be pretty dated. I'll bet my father still had the same hairstyle and tweed jacket." She laughed. "He didn't care what was in style. He had his own. Yes, you're right, that did make him what he was. Fine, I'll do that. Thank you, Uncle Hollis. You too, bye." She handed the receiver to Steve and he replaced it. Jeneil yawned and looked at them. "I think I like growing up. The teddy bears are warmer."

Peter and Steve laughed as she got up. "Gentlemen, it's been fun," and she curtsied and left the room.

Steve smiled. "Hey, Pete, this triad is getting kinky. Three in a bed, no wonder your mother's worried."

Peter laughed. "We are weird. Jeneil's right."

*****

Jeneil finished drying the last dish and went to the living room. The apartment was quiet. She turned the lights to the tree on and stood back to admire the array of colors. She squinted so the bulbs distorted to look like pointed stars, a trick she'd discovered as a child. She smelled the tree, enjoying the unmistakable Christmas tree smell. She checked the root ball; it was moist.

"We'll plant you along the property in the spring," she talked to the tree. "I think you're just what I need to keep those foul balls from hitting the windows. Maybe we'll buy a friend for you so your job will be more pleasant, but I'll leave a piece of yarn on your branch as a reminder of your badge of courage and honor for standing tall and straight in an overheated house decorated by ornaments and tinsel just for me." She smiled and shook a branch lightly. "You know it's not an insult, don't you? Why you rascal, I'll bet you even like the decorations. Yes, the Beau Brummel of fir trees."

She straightened an ornament and stood up, lighting the red Christmas candles. She sat on the sofa absorbing the peace and serenity of the room, locking it into a vivid memory to be enjoyed long after the decorations were put away and the room felt dismal from the absence of the holiday gayety. She picked up half of the geode, smiling at the effort Peter had made to please her with the gifts he had given. Chang was a softy, and she smiled. His heart was so gentle. She ran her hand over the dark grey-brown rock lovingly as she thought about him.

Her eye caught sight of the bracelet on her wrist and she touched it with her finger. Her feelings for Steve surprised her. Had it been less than a year that she'd known them? Peter sharing her life and planning a future together, and Steve, growing from such strong feelings of resistance and fear to one of the closest friends she'd ever made. Steve stirred deep feelings in her and she was puzzled by that. He was a strong energy, forceful and strong, qualities that drew her to him for security and comfort just as Peter's gentle steadiness did. She shook her head and smiled. If those two were what the year had brought her then the next year was going to be one of the happiest New Years ever. Peter's telephone rang. Jeneil looked toward the bedroom. It couldn't be the hospital; that's where he was. She got up to answer it.

"Is Peter there?" The voice was ice cold and Jeneil recognized it as Peter's mother.

"He's at the hospital. He's on second shift." Jeneil held her hand to her throat. "Mrs. Lee?"

"Yes?"

Jeneil swallowed hard. "I'm sorry things have gotten so out of hand between us. I'd like you to know that."

"I'll call Peter again sometime. Thank you."

The click as she hung up passed through Jeneil's body. It felt final. She sighed as she replaced the receiver. "What is it, Mrs. Lee? My race? Me? Do you even know? What am I fighting?" Jeneil felt herself choking up and took a deep breath. "Oh no you don't Mrs. Lee, you will not ruin this Christmas for me. Uh-uh. Sorry." She left the room quietly to warm herself with the atmosphere of her Christmas and its exciting new memories. "This year has given me a special love and a special friend. I'm expecting a very Happy New Year, too."

Forty-Three

Christmas eventually passed and the electricity and activity of New Year's Eve plans replaced it. Peter and Steve headed to the cafeteria. The doctor's lounge was getting too full and the cafeteria became more private when that happened. Opening his lunch bag and seeing Christmas cookies, Steve smiled. "Christmas was really a lot of fun for me this year," he said, biting into a thick roast beef and rye sandwich.

Peter nodded. "Me, too."

"What does she do with New Year's?"

Peter shrugged. "All I know is she has Sienna, Franklin Pierce, and Robert Danzieg coming to dinner tonight. She asked if you could take me to dinner."

Steve looked up, shocked. "It's a foursome?"

Peter shook his head. "No, she can't stay out of things. She's matchmaking. She's afraid I'll inhibit Sienna with memories of you." Peter chuckled. "I hope Sienna chooses Danzieg."

"Somehow inhibition and Sienna don't match."

Peter stifled a laugh. "Prude."

Steve raised an eyebrow. "I'm finding that I really like a woman who leaves a little mystery. It's a turn-on for me. I knew I wasn't completely liberated, but I'm surprised I want a woman who needs me. Really needs me, like Jeneil with you."

"I like it, too. Let's keep it to ourselves though. The ninth floor shrinks might tell us it's from feelings of denial in childhood. We never had pets." They both laughed.

*****

Peter got in at eleven after spending the evening with Steve.

Jeneil smiled. "Well teddy bear, I was beginning to feel abandoned." She went to him and snuggled. "Did you miss me?"

He kissed her temple. "Sure did. And what happened here? Anything?"

Jeneil grinned, loving her news. "Peter, it was instant chemistry! Franklin and Sienna were totally taken with each other. I even got the feeling that Shawna may have more to say about Sienna's style from now on. They were great together. I love romance," she crooned. "Seeing them made me miss you."

"That's what I like to hear," he said, as he held her. "Now, who can you get for Robert?"

"He's tough," she answered. "He has women throwing themselves at him. Who can compete with that?" Peter grinned to himself. He knew who but eat your heart out Danzieg, she was all his. Jeneil looked up. "Speaking of Robert, he's having a party at his place New Year's Eve. He's invited us."

"Us?" Peter asked, doubtful.

She nodded. "It sounds like real fun. Like Elio's at night. It's a costume party and he's asking people who can contribute talent to come."

Peter looked at her. "That leaves me out. All I can play is the radio."

Jeneil smiled. "Twit. I'm paying for us. He asked me to help make decorations and set up. He's going to put up huge nets filled with balloons to drop at midnight. It's a dry party. He wants to control the drinks so he's asking people to bring the food. He knows how to have some fun. Let's go."

Peter sighed, looking for an excuse. "What about Steve?"

Jeneil thought for a minute. "He can come with us. I'll get the costumes. I just hired a receptionist at the office. She's beautiful. I can ask if she's free that night for Steve. Those two shouldn't wear costumes. Their faces are true works of art. They're both strikingly beautiful. I'd like to see what happens to pretty people who date each other."

Peter laughed. "Jeneil, you're becoming a chronic matchmaker." He hugged her. "But you'd better forget Steve in your matchmaking plans."

"Why?" she asked, disappointed.

"Honey, he's a different Steve when it comes to women. About himself, too. He has a definite idea of what he's looking for. Leave the job to him."

She shrugged. "Maybe Charlene is for Robert then. Her beauty should be captured on canvas or somewhere. She completely disarms men who come into the office. Between Adrienne's great looks and style and Charlene's beauty, I feel like a troll around them."

Peter laughed. "Hey, ugly, it's past our bedtime."

Jeneil smiled at him. "I'm glad you're not a push over for a pretty face. At least I can sleep nights."

"Shut up," he whispered, and took out her hairpins.

"Okay," she said, and melted into his kiss.

*****

The excitement of the party had Jeneil buzzing. Peter hadn't realized that Robert meant to go to his place two nights to help with decorations. He and Steve sat watching TV and pouting about it the second night as they waited for her. They were both surprised when she whisked in early.

"Hi!" She was breathless as she rushed into the bedroom. "Steve, I'm glad you're still here."

"Why?"

She took a bite of the cookie Peter was eating. "I need to fit the costumes. My hat won't fit with all my hair so I came home early to work on that, too. Tomorrow's the party."

"Honey, you're not going to wear that outfit you wore to Elio's are you?"

Steve laughed. "You're a chicken, Pete."

"No, I'm going as Peter Pan. He didn't want to grow up either," she said, as she brought out her sewing basket. Steve tried not to laugh. "What's so funny?" Jeneil asked, as she pulled some clothes from a box.

Peter chuckled, catching the joke. "Get out of that one, Steve."

"Tell me," Jeneil threatened, holding a hat pin.

Steve smiled. "You'll never pass as a boy, Jeneil."

She smiled at him. "I don't have to. I'm using artistic license."

"Good." Peter laughed. "Go as a boy. As long as you don't wear the outfit from Elio's. I don't want to spend the night protecting you. I'd have to go dressed as Chang."

Jeneil laughed. "Hey, why didn't I think of that?"

"No, Jeneil," Peter insisted.

"Then you have a choice, a pirate or a magician. Decide between the two of you. The pirate wears a scarf on his head. The magician wears a top hat."

Peter sat up. "No top hat for me."

"Okay, I'm the magician then," Steve said, picking up a gingerbread man.

"Then I'll need to try this red cummerbund on you. Stand here." Steve stood up and Jeneil put the cummerbund on him inside out for fitting. Being that close to her made him fidgety. She smiled. "We're getting in each other's way. Lift your arms until I finish fitting you."

Steve held the gingerbread man with his mouth and rested his arms on Jeneil's shoulders. She stood up straight checking the fit and he was very aware of her touch. Then, noticing the cookie in his mouth, she bit off one foot and went to get a black cape. It took his breath away for a second. He watched her then closed his eyes. She didn't have a clue what she was doing to him. No wonder Peter worried about her; she was dense. He started to recite chemical formulas in his mind to distract himself.

"You can relax and put your arms down," she said, as she touched his arm. He opened his eyes. She put the cape around his shoulders. "Now the red bow tie and you are done." She stepped back. "Good, you're not much work at all. If you have black pants, they'll be fine, but you can wear jeans if you have to. The idea is to have fun."

He took the cookie from his mouth. "Thanks."

She nodded. "You can take the costume off but be careful of the pins. Peter's all set, I guess." She took inventory of the clothes. "No fitting problems except the belt and we can punch a hole in it if we need to. Good, I can work on my hairstyle then."

Steve joined Peter on the bed to watch TV while Jeneil went to the bureau. He became distracted as he watched her separate strands of hair and knot them behind her head. Her hair had fascinated him ever since he woke up nestled in it on Christmas Day. It was beautiful. She took a dark green hat with a yellow feather on the side and pinned it in place at an angle.

Steve smiled. "She'll never make it as a boy," he whispered to Peter. "Even her face gives her away." Peter watched as she pulled out wisps of hair then turned to face them.

"Tell me it looks okay. Lie to me if you have to. I've made three hats trying to fit my hair inside. This is it, ready or not."

Steve smiled. "You look great, kid."

"You do, honey, but Steve's right, you're not the boy type."

"Doesn't matter." She turned and looked in the mirror.

"How about some coffee?" Peter asked Steve.

"Yeah, I'd like some. Let's sit out there and drink it." He knew he wasn't up to seeing the long strands of hair being undone again.

*****

Their work schedule cooperated and they left after their twelve hour shift ended. Jeneil was pleased as she wrapped packages of food in aluminum foil. Peter joined her in the kitchen minus the head scarf. "Ooo, you look so nice." She smiled.

"I feel dumb."

"Ignore it." She took ribs and placed them on foil.

Steve came in, sniffing the air. "Are we eating here?"

"No, it's food for the party." She handed him a rib and he took it hungrily. She went to the refrigerator and brought out a bowl of grapes. "Maybe you guys need nibbles." She sliced some cheese while both Peter and Steve ate.

"Where'd you get the wings and ribs?" Peter asked, watching her.

"The China Bay."

Steve and Peter looked at her. Peter took a deep breath. "I know my mother was there, she never let's anyone else handle New Year's Eve. What happened?"

"Nothing, nothing at all, she walked away when I got there and Tom handled the order. He was very nice. I picked up orders for Franklin and Sienna, and Dennis and Karen for the party, so it was a fair amount of business for them. Tom thanked me. He asked me to remind you of him and whispered that visits would ease the ugliness."

"Well, tough shit," Peter snapped.

Jeneil stopped wrapping. She stared at him, trying to decide if she should pursue it. She smiled, deciding not to. "Happy New Year."

He grinned, went to her and kissed her lightly. "I'm sorry."

"We'll get through it, Peter. But tonight, let's party." She finished wrapping the food, leaving some out for them. "I'm going to change into my costume then we can leave."

Peter and Steve sat at the small table, sharing a short bottle of beer they had divided into glasses. Jeneil came from the bedroom. Steve was facing her and his mouth dropped open. Peter turned to look at her.

"Oh damn," Peter sighed, taking in the green leotard and the dark green belted tunic that stopped at the top of her thighs, her legs on display. Peter stood up slowly. Steve smiled as Peter looked her over. "No, Jeneil. I don't think so."

She looked up from doing the belt. "What?"

"No, honey, put jeans on."

"Jeans! I'll look like a mutated Peter Pan. What's wrong with this?"

Steve raised his eyebrows not believing she had to ask. He had never seen her legs so revealed. He had only suspected they were terrific, but the outfit proved it.

"It's too short," Peter replied.

She folded her arms. "I'm not arguing with you over this. I'm covered. I even have matching shorts under the tunic. There's nothing immodest about this. It was worn on stage in a play. I'm not changing."

Peter walked around her. "I'll make a deal, honey. Wear the dress you wore to Elio's."

She sighed. "Peter, I'd have to redo my hair. We'll be late. My hair wouldn't look right anyway after being knotted like this. Why do you always do this to me?" she pouted. "You know I was planning to go as the Ace of Spades, a playing card, but the costume was shorter than this. I knew you'd complain so I chose Peter Pan. No, I'm not changing." She went to get her coat.

Peter watched her walk away. "Shit, Steve, I'm going to need a real sword instead of this wooden one." Steve chuckled. "Jeneil, how about going as a ghost? A nice long sheet, two holes for eyes, your hair won't even show." Steve broke into laughter.

"I'm ready to leave," she said, putting on her coat.

Peter got his jacket. "If you're supposed to be a boy then you should look like one."

"Will you carry the bags of food?" She ignored his remark.

"Jeneil, it's cold outside. You'll freeze."

"Lock the door behind you, Peter." She walked past him.

Steve followed her. "Give it up, Pete. Besides, I like it a lot. She looks great." He raised an eyebrow and grinned, teasing Peter.

Peter hit his arm. "I'm going to make you disappear, magician. Stuff you right into that hat of yours." Steve laughed as Peter locked the door.

Peter was surprised by the number of cars in the lot. "Honey, this is a pretty big crowd."

"He lives in a warehouse?" Steve was equally surprised.

"Lives and works," she explained. "The party is on the first floor. The room is huge and painted orange. This is going to be fun."

There was an anteroom as they walked in where a man and two women were checking coats and invitations. A man headed toward them as they entered the main room. Peter knew it was Danzieg despite the black half mask. He wore a loose fitting white shirt with very full sleeves. It was opened to the waist and tucked into tight fitting pants that were designed to cling.

"Who's he supposed to be?" Peter asked, annoyed by the sex appeal of the outfit.

"Casanova," Jeneil replied.

"Who's that?" Peter asked.

"A notorious womanizer."

Peter looked at Steve. "I'd say appropriate."

Robert took off his mask and smiled. He extended his hand to Peter. "Happy New Year." He looked at Steve. "Have we met?"

"Steve Bradley, a friend of ours," Peter answered.

"Good to have you here, Steve." Robert shook his hand. He turned to Jeneil and cleared his throat as he looked her over slowly. "Jeneil, sweetheart, if Peter Pan had looked like this, those boys he led would have raped him and Wendy would have scratched his eyes out from jealousy. Damnation, why did I paint you in a long dress?"

Jeneil fidgeted, tugging at the tunic. Robert stared into her eyes and grinned.

"I'd like you to see my Wind Cruiser. Maybe a trip to the vineyard one weekend. You must look terrific in a bathing suit. You too, Peter, if you're not working." Robert never took his eyes off Jeneil. "Happy New Year, sweetheart." She smiled and held out her hand. "Hey, we're good friends. From you, I get a hug." Robert frowned and put his arms around her, holding her close and rubbing her back

Jeneil pushed away gently, smiling. "Where shall I put the food? Franklin's and Dennis's are in these bags, too."

"I'll show you." Robert slipped his arm around her shoulder, and reached for the bags Peter and Steve were holding. "I'll bring her back, soon." He smiled at Peter, rubbing Jeneil's upper arm gently. "There's a pictorial history in that corner and a trunk section."

Peter stared at Robert, unsmiling, as he walked away with Jeneil. Peter exhaled loudly. "And me with a wooden pirate's sword. I should have come as Chang. I need my switchblades."

Steve scowled. "Ooo, Jeneil, see my great chest. He probably lives on steroids, nobody's that solid naturally. Lots of chest hair too, not too far up the evolutionary chart. I like him less than Morgan Rand."

"Thank you, Steve. I thought I was prejudiced because of Jeneil. It's good to have a more objective opinion of him."

Jeneil returned to find Steve and Peter milling about the historical display. "The party's beginning to move now," she said, as the band warmed up. "We're gonna rock," and she did a dance step.

Steve watched her. She looked cute and he had come to like cute a lot since knowing her. "Do you like to dance?"

She nodded. "Love it. I've always used it as exercise. It's up tempo. You blend to the beat. It's fun." Steve smiled, enjoying her enthusiasm.

Robert came over to Jeneil. "Sweetheart, it's time for the toast and official kickoff dance. Be my partner for it." He put his arm around her, not waiting for her answer or approval from Peter, and walked to the microphone.

Steve shook his head. "You should have brought a date, Pete, or one for him."

"Surgeons," Peter said, "we should have come as surgeons. I can think of a few ways to use my scalpel here." Steve laughed.

Robert held onto Jeneil as he spoke into the microphone. "Friends, thank you for coming and helping me welcome the New Year. It's going to be a great one, right?"

"Right!" the crowd shouted and applauded.

"You bet." Robert smiled. "Let's do our earthling tradition and start this celebration with an official toast. Think carefully now because you may get what you wish for. Help me out. What do we want next year to bring us?" He squeezed Jeneil. "What do you want, sweetheart. I'll personally get it for you."

"Happiness," Jeneil answered.

"Yeah!" the crowd agreed.

"Okay," Robert said. "And what else, people? Let's hear it." The audience began suggesting peace, fun, love, sex, money, global freedom, end to world hunger, health. "Okay then, that's it. Grab a glass and hold it high." The crowd obeyed. "A toast to the New Year and may our desires be granted because we deserve it, right?"

"Right!" the crowd roared.

Robert smiled and held up his glass. "Then drink to the New Year and let's party people!" The band broke into a rock number. Robert took Jeneil and headed to the dance floor. Steve and Peter watched Jeneil dance, slightly self-conscious until the dance floor filled and then she loosened up and enjoyed it. Robert hugged her when it ended.

"He has charisma. He can charm the masses." She smiled as she returned to Peter. "He could easily be a politician."

"He also has a lot of nerve," Peter added, and Steve laughed.

"Do you want to dance with me?" she asked Peter.

"I don't dance, remember?"

"Just wondered." She snuggled to his arm. "I love you, anyway."

A man dressed as a mime tapped Jeneil's shoulder, pointed to him then her and whirled his finger around, asking her to dance. Jeneil let go of Peter's arm, fascinated.

"Are you really a mime?" she asked, watching him. He nodded and took her arm, leading her to the dance floor.

Steve shook his head and chuckled. "Like a kid, she wanders off fascinated. She's too much."

Peter sighed. "She's a nightmare where people are concerned. That's the only area her parents screwed up with her. She's not afraid to talk to strangers. To her, the whole world is related. There are no strangers."

Steve laughed. "But that's what makes her magical, Peter. She really cares. She's open, she's sunshine. I like it."

The music ended and they watched as Jeneil and the mime returned. They were having a conversation with no words. The mime smiled warmly at her as he returned her to Peter. He pointed to himself, covered his heart with his hand and pointed to her. Jeneil smiled and without embarrassment put her finger to her lips, kissed it, and touched it to his lips. He smiled and nodded, pleased she had gotten into mime so well. He waved to her. She waved back and he disappeared into the crowd again.

Jeneil smiled broadly. "What an odd experience. We never used words, but we stopped dancing to talk. You get away from the unnecessary when you mime. You have to have a simple thought then you struggle to make the other person understand you. He's good. That was fun." She looked around. "This is like a street festival. It's a good party. I like it." She looked at Peter and Steve. "Let's get something to drink. All that miming made me thirsty." They laughed and headed to the bar. "Oh, Robert, I love you. He has fruit juice, too." She scanned the list of choices. "Papaya with a bit of ice, please," she said to the waiting bartender.

"Hi, Jeneil."

"Franklin, Sienna! Happy New Year!"

Franklin kissed her cheek. "Jeneil, you make a lovely boy." He laughed as Jeneil gently punched his nose then hugged him.

"Well, I think you look natural as Charlie Chaplin."

Sienna hugged her. "Jeneil, you look great."

"So do you." Jeneil smiled. "A fairy, I like that. I wanted to come as a butterfly, but I was afraid I'd be bumping people all night with my wings."

Sienna laughed. "You were right. I'm having trouble with even these small ones. They're already bent."

Jeneil looked her over. "I like the wings made from silver lame, they shimmer more. You did a great job stitching a design in the wings. You really look gossamer."

"Thank you, Jeneil. Thank you for a lot of things." Sienna grinned.

Jeneil smiled at her knowingly, appreciating her excitement.

Sienna turned to Peter and Steve. "How are you two guys?"

"Fine," they answered simultaneously.

"Where's your date, Steve?" Sienna asked.

"I'm here with Pete and Jeneil."

"I see," Sienna said, nodding. She stared at him. "Hmm, I think you two got your costumes mixed up. Peter should be the magician because he's going to need a few tricks to protect himself from pirates."

"What?" Franklin questioned, as Peter and Jeneil laughed. Sienna continued staring at an unsmiling Steve. Franklin chuckled. "Sienna, that doesn't make sense."

Sienna smiled. "It's New Year's Eve. It doesn't have to make sense to everybody." She continued to stare at Steve and he turned away, annoyed. "Happy New Year to all of you," Sienna said lightly, and hugged Jeneil again. "Thank you again for getting the food for us. That was awfully nice of you."

"It was nothing. I had to get some for me anyway."

Sienna looked at Jeneil with a serious look. "Don't stay too long in the Land of Make Believe, Peter Pan, or Captain Hook might cause serious trouble."

Jeneil raised her eyebrows while Steve fidgeted. "Captain Hook! Oh, Peter, you could have come as Captain Hook. I never thought of that! We could have been a matching couple."

Sienna looked at her and sighed. "Jeneil, it's too late. You've been too long in the Land of Make Believe already. Remember you heard it from Tinkerbelle." She glared at Steve.

A girl dressed as Little Red Riding Hood came over to Steve. "I can't dance with wolves, but I can dance with nice magicians. Are you a nice magician?"

Steve smiled broadly. "That's me. I don't do nasty tricks." He looked at Sienna then took the girl to the dance floor.

"Happy New Year you two," Franklin said, and led Sienna away.

Peter watched Steve. "Sienna's still mad at Steve. I wonder why he let it bother him."

Jeneil shrugged. "Sienna did sound strange," then she smiled, "but like she said, it's New Year's Eve. Who needs to make sense tonight? We have 364 days to do that." She took Peter's arm. "Come on, this is a slow dance. You can dance with me now. Peter Pan and a pirate, I never even saw that. Sienna's really good."

Peter put his arm around Jeneil and she leaned against him as they danced. "Imagine Chang dancing in public with a stupid scarf on his head," he whispered. "I barely recognize him anymore. What have you done to this guy? He's completely changed." He kissed her forehead and she smiled and reached up, taking the scarf off.

Running her fingers through his hair, she shook her head. "I'd never do anything to make Chang different. He's great as he is." She brought strands of hair onto his forehead, which was her way of relating to Chang. She kissed him warmly, and he smiled and held her closer.

"The guy's crazy about you too, Irish."

"Hey, all that kissing stuff is supposed to happen at midnight." Jeneil and Peter turned their heads.

"Dennis! Karen!" Jeneil smiled. "I hadn't seen you two. I thought you might not have made it."

"It was tough getting into this armor but I'm here." Dennis laughed. "Karen had to be a matching couple."

"Who are you?" Jeneil asked.

"Guinevere and Lancelot," Karen replied.

Peter frowned. "I thought she was married to Arthur?"

Karen and Dennis looked at each other. "Geez, that's right," Dennis said.

Karen shrugged. "Isn't that odd. When I think of the romance, I think of her with Lancelot. Meet us at the eats table after the dance."

Peter shook his head as they moved away. "I hate that story. Damn it. She's married to Arthur. Lancelot was a lousy knight and a worse friend."

Jeneil laughed. "Arthur needed to be more like Chang. Mess with my woman and I'll dent your armor."

Peter laughed and squeezed her. "Make fun, but at least Chang's way they'd be here as Guinevere and Arthur."

"That's very true. Get your feelings out in the open and there's no confusion. It makes life simple. I like Chang."

Steve was talking to Red Riding Hood and Bo Peep as Jeneil and Peter joined Dennis and Karen at a small table to eat. Jeneil waved seeing Steve walk by alone. He came over to them and sat down next to her.

"Are you three together?" Karen asked. They nodded.

"Then why didn't you three come as Arthur, Guinevere, and Lancelot?" Dennis asked, chuckling as he looked at them. "That would have really been a great twist."

Jeneil smiled. "Because that's not our story. We really should have come as The Three Musketeers." Peter laughed, and Jeneil gave Steve some of her food.

Dennis shook his head, disagreeing. "Uh-uh Jeneil, you really make a lousy boy." Peter and Steve laughed as Jeneil kicked Dennis under the table. "I'm glad I'm wearing armor. She's really into the part of being a delinquent. Tough kid." He smiled warmly at her and touched her cheek gently to show he was teasing.

Robert walked by and stopped as he saw them. Standing behind Jeneil, he massaged her shoulders. "The ribs and wings are a big hit. Thanks." He kissed her cheek. "I've got to get a case of Perrier. I'll catch all of you again." He squeezed Jeneil's neck as he left.

Karen smiled. "I think the role of Peter Pan fits Jeneil. Peter Pan was surrounded by boys who admired him, too."

"Meow," Dennis whined.

"That wasn't catty." Karen hit him, making a pinging sound against the metal sleeve. "My mistake, I should have come as a welder." They all laughed.

The group ate and talked for awhile. Dennis mentioned a professional juggler was there dressed as a clown. Robert had hired several people to mingle amongst the guests; a fortune teller, a magician, a balloon artist, and a clinical psychologist who was asked to bring tests to see if you were sane or fit into the norm. Several of the guests were invited to share their talents. The evening had an even, easy flow to it with interesting things happening so the party never lagged. The band returned from a break and played a slow song. Steve asked Jeneil to dance. He was enjoying the party; it was sane fun and he had a chance to see Jeneil with her friends. They were sensitive and caring people, like Jeneil.

"This has been a great party."

"It has," Jeneil agreed. "Robert is good at planning. He says he's a big kid. I guess he's right, it's part of his charm."

Robert joined them on the dance floor. "Jeneil, honey, it's getting close to midnight and I haven't danced with you since the party began. I'd like an old year dance before the New Year arrives. Would you mind?" he asked Steve. Steve wanted to say yes, but he shook his head. "Thanks," Robert said, patting Steve's shoulder. "I'm the only one who hasn't had time for fun at my party. I appreciate this." He took Jeneil and danced off with her.

"Where's Jeneil?" Peter asked, as Steve joined him at a table near the bar.

"Robert wanted an old year dance," Steve replied. "Some things you just can't fight."

Peter shook his head. "I guess." Peter slouched in his chair and stretched his legs.

People were gathering around the band. The big clock behind them was almost at one minute to midnight and the lead singer got on the microphone. "Ready for countdown everyone? One minute to New Year. Robert," the singer called, "Robert, what are you doing? He's kissing that girl and it's not even midnight." Everyone whistled. "Play fair, Robert," the singer teased. Steve and Peter looked at each other. They couldn't see Robert or the girl but they had the same guess. Some people laughed as they heard Robert talking. The singer at the microphone laughed. "Robert just said he had to kiss her now because she was going to be with her boyfriend for midnight countdown." Peter and Steve looked at each other. The singer laughed again. "Robert, kissing another man's girl like that you might not see midnight." Everyone laughed, except Steve and Peter.

Jeneil joined them, excited. "It's countdown time. Let's get on the dance floor so we're under the balloons when they fall."

Peter and Steve got up and followed her. The crowd counted with the band backwards from ten seconds. Jeneil put her arm around Peter's waist and he wrapped his arm around her shoulder. Steve stood next to them with his arms folded so Jeneil slipped her arm through his. He smiled at her and held her hand. At midnight, the masses of balloons dropped from the ceiling. The horns, shouting, and whistling of the midnight madness went off like a bomb. Everyone was kissing, hugging, and smiling.

"Happy New Year, Peter." Jeneil leaned toward him and kissed him, smiling. "I'm crazy in love with you, Chang."

"I love you, too, Irish." He squeezed her. "I'll get us some drinks. Meet me at the table."

She turned to Steve, who was standing quietly next to her. "Hey, you." She hit his arm. "Get with the jive, fella. It's a new year, a big exciting one for you. Whoop it up. Show some enthusiasm." She put her arms around him and smiled. "Is it okay to kiss you?"

"I won't complain." He smiled and put his arms around her.

"Happy New Year, Steve, I hope it's the best. Better than you could ever imagine. I really mean that."

"I know you do. Thank you for everything. Being a great friend, caring, fussing. I love it. You are terrific." The frenzy of the moment got to him and he leaned forward and kissed her lips lightly. They felt soft and warm. She felt good to him. He pulled her closer and kissed her more strongly. The kiss spun through him and he pulled away. "I'm sorry, Jeneil. I shouldn't have done that." She looked at him, puzzled.

"It's okay. New Years' kisses are allowed. You should have seen Robert's." She smiled. "Steve Bradley, at the beginning of last year did you ever think you'd be kissing me at midnight one year later?"

"No." He laughed. "No, that never crossed my mind. Believe me, we sure didn't get along."

She looked at him steadily. "You have become very special to me. You are one of the closest friends I've ever had in my life. It's so odd. I trust you and Peter like I've known you both my whole life." She hugged him. "People say this is a magic moment in the year. I guess it is. I'm standing here dripping sentimentality all over Steve Bradley. That's not magic, that's miraculous." He laughed, holding her and kissed her cheek.

"Where's Pete?"

"He's waiting at the table with drinks for us. He wanted to avoid the crowd at the bar."

Steve nodded. "Smart move."

Jeneil took his hand. "Let's join him and keep the celebration moving." Peter waited at a table where Jeneil and Steve sat down. "What should our toast be?"

Steve stared at her. "To friendship." Peter nodded.

Jeneil held up her glass. "Friendship it is. To a long lasting, close friendship that will see many new years."

They all touched glasses and drank a toast filled with the excitement and hope of a brand new year.

Thank you for taking the time to read
"The Songbird / Volume Two - Author's Limited Edition."

In The Songbird/Volume One we introduced the main characters of the story. Jeneil and Peter were able to keep their relationship private and a secret and as such were able to establish a firm foundation with promises for a bright future together.

In The Songbird/Volume Two outside forces have loomed it's ugly head. Protecting the Songbird is not easy for Peter as Jeneil continues to expand her search for superlative in her life. Is Peter up to the task? And what about Steve? Is he really Peter's best friend? Will Peter and Jeneil survive?

Stay tuned...

"The Songbird / Volume Three" will be available in the April of 2011.

Please if you haven't read The Songbird / Volume One it is recommended that you do. It will add so much background and understanding to Peter and Jeneil and the direction of the path that brought these two of society's misfits together.

"The Songbird"

by

Beverly Louise Oliver-Farrell

Author's Limited Edition / Five Volume Series

This unedited version of "The Songbird/Volume Two" is as the author intended it to be read. Only a limited numbers of copies will be available for the family and her friends. (A more condensed offering of "The Songbird Story" with be made available for the public at a later time along with a screenplay version.

We invite you to visit "The Songbird Story"website at:

http://www.TheSongbirdStory.com

Register your Email address to receive information on upcoming Volumes. (The Songbird /Volume Three will be available in April of 2011.)

For Further Information and Inquiries Contact:

Brian B. Farrell
4844 Keith Lane
Colorado Springs, CO 80916

Tel: (719)380-8174 / Fax: (719)380-8365

Email: farrell_family@usa.net

BUY DIRECT FROM THE FAMILY AND SAVE
Volume One & Volume Two are now available at Discount

Made in the USA
Charleston, SC
04 October 2013